John Grisham

THE FIRM

THE PELICAN
BRIEF

D0928799

ARROW

This edition published by Arrow in 1999
an imprint of the Random House Group
20 Vauxhall Bridge Road, London SW1V 2SA

Copyright © John Grisham 1999

The right of John Grisham to be identified as the
author of this work has been asserted by him in
accordance with the Copyright Designs and
Patents Act, 1988

The Firm copyright © John Grisham 1991
The Pelican Brief copyright © John Grisham 1992

Papers used by Random House UK Ltd are natural,
recyclable products made from wood grown in sustainable
forests. The manufacturing processes conform to
the environmental regulations of the country of origin

A catalogue record for this book is available
from the British Library

Printed and bound in Germany by
Elsnerdruck, Berlin

ISBN 0 09 187007 0

THE FIRM

ONE

The senior partner studied the résumé for the hundredth time and again found nothing he disliked about Mitchell Y. McDeere, at least not on paper. He had the brains, the ambition, the good looks. And he was hungry; with his background, he had to be. He was married, and that was mandatory. The firm had never hired an unmarried lawyer, and it frowned heavily on divorce, as well as womanizing and drinking. Drug testing was in the contract. He had a degree in accounting, passed the CPA exam the first time he took it and wanted to be a tax lawyer, which of course was a requirement with a tax firm. He was white, and the firm had never hired a black. They managed this by being secretive and clubbish and never soliciting job applications. Other firms solicited, and hired blacks. This firm recruited, and remained lily white. Plus, the firm was in Memphis, of all places, and the top blacks wanted New York or Washington or Chicago. McDeere was a male, and there were no women in the firm. That mistake had been made in the mid-seventies when they recruited the number one grad from Harvard, who happened to be a she and a wizard at taxation. She lasted four turbulent years and was killed in a car wreck.

He looked good, on paper. He was their top choice.

1

In fact, for this year there were no other prospects. The list was very short. It was McDeere or no one.

The managing partner, Royce McKnight, studied a dossier labeled 'Mitchell Y. McDeere – Harvard.' An inch thick with small print and a few photographs, it had been prepared by some ex-CIA agents in a private intelligence outfit in Bethesda. They were clients of the firm and each year did the investigating for no fee. It was easy work, they said, checking out unsuspecting law students. They learned, for instance, that he preferred to leave the Northeast, that he was holding three job offers, two in New York and one in Chicago, and that the highest offer was $76,000 and the lowest was $68,000. He was in demand. He had been given the opportunity to cheat on a securities exam during his second year. He declined, and made the highest grade in the class. Two months ago he had been offered cocaine at a law school party. He said no and left when everyone began snorting. He drank an occasional beer, but drinking was expensive and he had no money. He owed close to $23,000 in student loans. He was hungry.

Royce McKnight flipped through the dossier and smiled. McDeere was their man.

Lamar Quin was thirty-two and not yet a partner. He had been brought along to look young and act young and project a youthful image for Bendini, Lambert & Locke, which in fact was a young firm, since most of the partners retired in their late forties or early fifties with money to burn. He would make partner in this firm. With a six-figure income guaranteed for the rest of his life, Lamar could enjoy the twelve-hundred-dollar tailored suits that hung so comfortably from his tall, athletic frame. He strolled nonchalantly across the thousand-dollar-a-day suite and poured another cup of decaf. He checked his watch. He glanced at the two partners sitting at the small conference table near the windows.

Precisely at two-thirty someone knocked on the door. Lamar looked at the partners, who slid the résumé and dossier into an open briefcase. All three reached for their jackets. Lamar buttoned his top button and opened the door.

'Mitchell McDeere?' he asked with a huge smile and a hand thrust forward.

'Yes.' They shook hands violently.

'Nice to meet you, Mitchell. I'm Lamar Quin.'

'My pleasure. Please call me Mitch.' He stepped inside and quickly surveyed the spacious room.

'Sure, Mitch.' Lamar grabbed his shoulder and led him across the suite, where the partners introduced themselves. They were exceedingly warm and cordial. They offered him coffee, then water. They sat around a shiny mahogany conference table and exchanged pleasantries. McDeere unbuttoned his coat and crossed his legs. He was now a seasoned veteran in the search for employment, and he knew they wanted him. He relaxed. With three job offers from three of the most prestigious firms in the country, he did not need this interview, this firm. He could afford to be a little overconfident now. He was there out of curiosity. And he longed for warmer weather.

Oliver Lambert, the senior partner, leaned forward on his elbows and took control of the preliminary chitchat. He was glib and engaging with a mellow, almost professional baritone. At sixty-one, he was the grandfather of the firm and spent most of his time administering and balancing the enormous egos of some of the richest lawyers in the country. He was the counselor, the one the younger associates went to with their troubles. Mr. Lambert also handled the recruiting, and it was his mission to sign Mitchell Y. McDeere.

'Are you tired of interviewing?' asked Oliver Lambert.

'Not really. It's part of it.'

Yes, yes, they all agreed. Seemed like yesterday they were interviewing and submitting résumés and scared to death they wouldn't find a job and three years of sweat and torture would be down the drain. They knew what he was going through, all right.

'May I ask a question?' Mitch asked.

'Certainly.'

'Sure.'

'Anything.'

'Why are we interviewing in this hotel room? The other firms interview on campus through the placement office.'

'Good question.' They all nodded and looked at each other and agreed it was a good question.

'Perhaps I can answer that, Mitch,' said Royce McKnight, the managing partner. 'You must understand our firm. We are different, and we take pride in that. We have forty-one lawyers, so we are small compared with other firms. We don't hire too many people; about one every other year. We offer the highest salary and fringes in the country, and I'm not exaggerating. So we are very selective. We selected you. The letter you received last month was sent after we screened over two thousand third year law students at the best schools. Only one letter was sent. We don't advertise openings and we don't solicit applications. We keep a low profile, and we do things differently. That's our explanation.'

'Fair enough. What kind of firm is it?'

'Tax. Some securities, real estate and banking, but eighty percent is tax work. That's why we wanted to meet you, Mitch. You have an incredibly strong tax background.'

4

'Why'd you go to Western Kentucky?' asked Oliver Lambert.

'Simple. They offered me a full scholarship to play football. Had it not been for that, college would've been impossible.'

'Tell us about your family.'

'Why is that important?'

'It's very important to us, Mitch,' Royce McKnight said warmly.

They all say that, thought McDeere. 'Okay, my father was killed in the coal mines when I was seven years old. My mother remarried and lives in Florida. I had two brothers. Rusty was killed in Vietnam. I have a brother named Ray McDeere.'

'Where is he?'

'I'm afraid that's none of your business.' He stared at Royce McKnight and exposed a mammoth chip on his shoulder. The dossier, oddly, was silent on Ray.

'I'm sorry,' the managing partner said softly.

'Mitch, our firm is in Memphis,' Lamar said. 'Does that bother you?'

'Not at all. I'm not fond of cold weather.'

'Have you ever been to Memphis?'

'No.'

'We'll have you down soon. You'll love it.'

Mitch smiled and nodded and played along. Were these guys serious? How could he consider such a small firm in such a small town when Wall Street was waiting?

'How are you ranked in your class?' Mr. Lambert asked.

'Top five.' Not top five percent, but top five. That was enough of an answer for all of them. Top five out of three hundred. He could have said number three, a fraction away from number two, and within striking distance of number one. But he didn't. They came from inferior schools – Chicago, Columbia and Vanderbilt, as he recalled from a cursory examination of Martindale-Hubbell's Legal Directory. He knew they would not dwell on academics.

'Why did you select Harvard?'

'Actually, Harvard selected me. I applied at several schools and was accepted everywhere. Harvard offered more financial assistance. I thought it was the best school. Still do.'

'You've done quite well here, Mitch,' Mr. Lambert said, admiring the résumé. The dossier was in the briefcase, under the table.

'Thank you. I've worked hard.'

'You made extremely high grades in your tax and securities courses.'

'That's where my interest lies.'

'We've reviewed your writing sample, and it's quite impressive.'

'Thank you. I enjoy research.'

They nodded and acknowledged this obvious lie. It was part of the ritual. No law student or lawyer in his right mind enjoyed research, yet, without fail, every prospective associate professed a deep love for the library.

'Tell us about your wife,' Royce McKnight said, almost meekly. They braced for another reprimand. But it was a standard, nonsacred area explored by every firm.

'Her name is Abby. She has a degree in elementary education from Western Kentucky. We graduated one week and got married the next. For the past three years she's taught at a private kindergarten near Boston College.'

'And is the marriage –'

'We're very happy. We've known each other since high school.'

'What position did you play?' asked Lamar, in the direction of less sensitive matters.

'Quarterback. I was heavily recruited until I messed up a knee in my last high school game. Everyone disappeared except Western Kentucky. I played off and on for four years, even started some as a junior, but the knee would never hold up.'

'How'd you make straight A's and play football?'

'I put the books first.'

'I don't imagine Western Kentucky is much of an academic school,' Lamar blurted with a stupid grin, and immediately wished he could take it back. Lambert and McKnight frowned and acknowledged the mistake.

'Sort of like Kansas State,' Mitch replied. They froze, all of them froze, and for a few seconds stared incredulously at each other. This guy McDeere knew Lamar Quin went to Kansas State. He had never met Lamar Quin and had no idea who would appear on behalf of the firm and conduct the interview. Yet, he knew. He had gone to Martindale-Hubbell's and checked them out. He had read the biographical sketches of all of the forty-one lawyers in the firm, and in a split second he had recalled that Lamar Quin, just one of the forty-one, had gone to Kansas State. Damn, they were impressed.

'I guess that came out wrong,' Lamar apologized.

'No problem.' Mitch smiled warmly. It was forgotten.

Oliver Lambert cleared his throat and decided to get personal again. 'Mitch, our firm frowns on drinking and chasing women. We're not a bunch of Holy Rollers, but we put business ahead of everything. We keep low profiles and we work very hard. And we make plenty of money.'

'I can live with all that.'

'We reserve the right to test any member of the firm for drug use.'

'I don't use drugs.'

'Good. What's your religious affiliation?'

'Methodist.'

'Good. You'll find a wide variety in our firm. Catholics, Baptists, Episcopalians. It's really none of our business, but we like to know. We want stable families. Happy lawyers are productive lawyers. That's why we ask these questions.'

Mitch smiled and nodded. He'd heard this before.

The three looked at each other, then at Mitch. This meant they had reached the point in the interview where the interviewee was supposed to ask one or two intelligent questions. Mitch recrossed his legs. Money, that was the big question, particularly how it compared to his other offers. If it isn't enough, thought Mitch, then it was nice to meet you fellas. If the pay is attractive, *then* we can discuss families and marriages and football and churches. But, he knew, like all the other firms they had to shadowbox around the issue until things got awkward and it was apparent they had discussed everything in the world but money. So, hit them with a soft question first.

'What type of work will I do initially?'

They nodded and approved of the question. Lambert and McKnight looked at Lamar. This answer was his.

'We have something similar to a two-year apprenticeship, although we don't call it that. We'll send you all over the country to tax seminars. Your education is far from over. You'll spend two weeks next winter in Washington at the American Tax Institute. We take great pride in our technical expertise, and the training is continual, for all of us. If you want to pursue a master's in taxation, we'll pay for it. As far as practicing law, it won't be very exciting for the first

8

two years. You'll do a lot of research and generally boring stuff. But you'll be paid handsomely.'

'How much?'

Lamar looked at Royce McKnight, who eyed Mitch and said, 'We'll discuss the compensation and other benefits when you come to Memphis.'

'I want a ballpark figure or I may not come to Memphis.' He smiled, arrogant but cordial. He spoke like a man with three job offers.

The partners smiled at each other, and Mr. Lambert spoke first. 'Okay. A base salary of eighty thousand the first year, plus bonuses. Eighty-five the second year, plus bonuses. A low-interest mortgage so you can buy a home. Two country club memberships. And a new BMW. You pick the color, of course.'

They focused on his lips, and waited for the wrinkles to form on his cheeks and the teeth to break through. He tried to conceal a smile, but it was impossible. He chuckled.

'That's incredible,' he mumbled. Eighty thousand in Memphis equaled a hundred and twenty thousand in New York. Did the man say BMW! His Mazda hatchback had a million miles on it and for the moment had to be jump-started while he saved for a rebuilt starter.

'Plus a few more fringes we'll be glad to discuss in Memphis.'

Suddenly he had a strong desire to visit Memphis. Wasn't it by the river?

The smile vanished and he regained his composure. He looked sternly, importantly at Oliver Lambert and said, as if he'd forgotten about the money and the home and the BMW, 'Tell me about your firm.'

'Forty-one lawyers. Last year we earned more per lawyer than any firm our size or larger. That includes every big firm in the country. We take only rich clients – corporations, banks and wealthy people who pay our healthy fees and never complain. We've developed a specialty in international taxation, and it's both exciting and very profitable. We deal only with people who can pay.'

'How long does it take to make partner?'

'On the average, ten years, and it's a hard ten years. It's not unusual for our partners to earn half a million a year, and most retire before they're fifty. You've got to pay your dues, put in eighty-hour weeks, but it's worth it when you make partner.'

Lamar leaned forward. 'You don't have to be a partner to earn six figures. I've been with the firm seven years, and went over a hundred thousand four years ago.'

Mitch thought about this for a second and figured by the time he was thirty he could be well over a hundred thousand, maybe close to two hundred thousand. At the age of thirty!

They watched him carefully and knew exactly what he was calculating.

'What's an international tax firm doing in Memphis?' he asked.

That brought smiles. Mr. Lambert removed his reading glasses and twirled them. 'Now that's a good question. Mr. Bendini founded the firm in 1944. He had been a tax lawyer in Philadelphia and had picked up some wealthy clients in the South. He got a wild hair and landed in Memphis. For twenty-five years he hired nothing but tax lawyers, and the firm prospered nicely down there. None of us are from Memphis, but we have grown to love it. It's a very pleasant old Southern town. By the way, Mr. Bendini died in 1970.'

'How many partners in the firm?'

'Twenty, active. We try to keep a ratio of one partner for each associate. That's high for the industry, but we like it. Again, we do things differently.'

'All of our partners are multi-millionaires by the age of forty-five,' Royce McKnight said.

'All of them?'

'Yes, sir. We don't guarantee it, but if you join our firm, put in ten hard years, make partner and put in ten more years, and you're not a millionaire at the age of forty-five, you'll be the first in twenty years.'

'That's an impressive statistic.'

'It's an impressive firm, Mitch,' Oliver Lambert said, 'and we're very proud of it. We're a close knit fraternity. We're small and we take care of each other. We don't have the cutthroat competition the big firms are famous for. We're very careful whom we hire, and our goal is for each new associate to become a partner as soon as possible. Toward that end we invest an enormous amount of time and money in ourselves, especially our new people. It is a rare, extremely rare occasion when a lawyer leaves our firm. It is simply unheard of. We go the extra mile to keep careers on track. We want our people happy. We think it is the most profitable way to operate.'

'I have another impressive statistic,' Mr. McKnight added. 'Last year, for firms our size or larger, the average turnover rate among associates was twenty-eight percent. At Bendini, Lambert & Locke, it was zero. Year before, zero. It's been a long time since a lawyer left our firm.'

They watched him carefully to make sure all of this sank in. Each term and each condition of the employment was important, but the permanence, the finality of his acceptance overshadowed all other items on the checklist. They explained as best they could, for now. Further explanation would come later.

Of course, they knew much more than they could talk about. For instance, his mother lived in a cheap trailer park in Panama City Beach, remarried to a retired truck driver with a violent drinking problem.

11

They knew she had received $41,000 from the mine explosion, squandered most of it, then went crazy after her oldest son was killed in Vietnam. They knew he had been neglected, raised in poverty by his brother Ray (whom they could not find) and some sympathetic relatives. The poverty hurt, and they assumed, correctly, it had bred the intense desire to succeed. He had worked thirty hours a week at an all night convenience store while playing football and making perfect grades. They knew he seldom slept. They knew he was hungry. He was their man.

'Would you like to come visit us?' asked Oliver Lambert.

'When?' asked Mitch, dreaming of a black 318i with a sunroof.

The ancient Mazda hatchback with three hubcaps and a badly cracked windshield hung in the gutter with its front wheels sideways, aiming at the curb, preventing a roll down the hill. Abby grabbed the door handle on the inside, yanked twice and opened the door. She inserted the key, pressed the clutch and turned the wheel. The Mazda began a slow roll. As it gained speed, she held her breath, released the clutch and bit her lip until the unmuffled rotary engine began whining.

With three job offers on the table, a new car was four months away. She could last. For three years they had endured poverty in a two room student apartment on a campus covered with Porsches and little Mercedes convertibles. For the most part they had ignored the snubs from the classmates and coworkers in this bastion of East Coast snobbery. They were hillbillies from Kentucky, with few friends. But they had endured and succeeded quite nicely all to themselves.

She preferred Chicago to New York, even for a lower salary, largely because it was further from

12

Boston and closer to Kentucky. But Mitch remained noncommittal, characteristically weighing it all carefully and keeping most of it to himself. She had not been invited to visit New York and Chicago with her husband. And she was tired of guessing. She wanted an answer.

She parked illegally on the hill nearest the apartment and walked two blocks. Their unit was one of thirty in a two-story red-brick rectangle. Abby stood outside her door and fumbled through the purse looking for keys. Suddenly, the door jerked open. He grabbed her, yanked her inside the tiny apartment, threw her on the sofa and attacked her neck with his lips. She yelled and giggled as arms and legs thrashed about. They kissed, one of those long, wet, ten minute embraces with groping and fondling and moaning, the kind they had enjoyed as teenagers when kissing was fun and mysterious and the ultimate.

'My goodness,' she said when they finished. 'What's the occasion?'

'Do you smell anything?' Mitch asked.

She looked away and sniffed. 'Well, yes. What is it?'

'Chicken chow mein and egg foo yung. From Wong Boys.'

'Okay, what's the occasion?'

'Plus an expensive bottle of Chablis. It's even got a cork.'

'What have you done, Mitch?'

'Follow me.' On the small, painted kitchen table, among the legal pads and casebooks, sat a large bottle of wine and a sack of Chinese food. They shoved the law school paraphernalia aside and spread the food. Mitch opened the wine and filled two plastic wineglasses.

'I had a great interview today,' he said.

'Who?'

'Remember that firm in Memphis I received a letter from last month?'

'Yes. You weren't too impressed.'

'That's the one. I'm very impressed. It's all tax work and the money looks good.'

'How good?'

He ceremoniously dipped chow mein from the container onto both plates, then ripped open the tiny packages of soy sauce. She waited for an answer. He opened another container and began dividing the egg foo yung. He sipped his wine and smacked his lips.

'How much?' she repeated.

'More than Chicago. More than Wall Street.'

She took a long, deliberate drink of wine and eyed him suspiciously. Her brown eyes narrowed and glowed. The eyebrows lowered and the forehead wrinkled. She waited.

'How much?'

'Eighty thousand, first year, plus bonuses. Eighty-five, second year, plus bonuses.' He said this nonchalantly while studying the celery bits in the chow mein.

'Eighty thousand,' she repeated.

'Eighty thousand, babe. Eighty thousand bucks in Memphis, Tennessee, is about the same as a hundred and twenty thousand bucks in New York.'

'Who wants New York?' she asked.

'Plus a low-interest mortgage loan.'

That word – mortgage – had not been uttered in the apartment in a long time. In fact, she could not, at the moment, recall the last discussion about a home or anything related to one. For months now it had been accepted that they would *rent* some place until some distant, unimaginable point in the future when they achieved affluence and would then qualify for a large mortgage.

She sat her glass of wine on the table and said matter-of-factly, 'I didn't hear that.'

'A low-interest mortgage loan. The firm loans enough money to buy a house. It's very important to these guys that their associates look prosperous, so they give us the money at a much lower rate.'

'You mean as in a *home*, with grass around it and shrubs?'

'Yep. Not some overpriced apartment in Manhattan, but a three bedroom house in the suburbs with a driveway and a two car garage where we can park the BMW.'

The reaction was delayed by a second or two, but she finally said, 'BMW? Whose BMW?'

'Ours, babe. Our BMW. The firm leases a new one and gives us the keys. It's sort of like a signing bonus for a first-round draft pick. It's worth another five thousand a year. We pick the color, of course. I think black would be nice. What do you think?'

'No more clunkers. No more leftovers. No more hand-me-downs,' she said as she slowly shook her head.

He crunched on a mouthful of noodles and smiled at her. She was dreaming, he could tell, probably of furniture, and wallpaper, and perhaps a pool before too long. And babies, little dark eyed children with light brown hair.

'And there are some other benefits to be discussed later.'

'I don't understand, Mitch. Why are they so generous?'

'I asked that question. They're very selective, and they take a lot of pride in paying top dollar. They go for the best and don't mind shelling out the bucks. Their turnover rate is zero. Plus, I think it costs more to entice the top people to Memphis.'

'It would be closer to home,' she said without looking at him.

'I don't have a home. It would be closer to your parents, and that worries me.'

She deflected this, as she did most of his comments about her family. 'You'd be closer to Ray.'

He nodded, bit into an egg roll and imagined her parents' first visit, that sweet moment when they pulled into the driveway in their well-used Cadillac and stared in shock at the new French colonial with two new cars in the garage. They would burn with envy and wonder how the poor kid with no family and no status could afford all this at twenty-five and fresh out of law school. They would force painful smiles and comment on how nice everything was, and before long Mr. Sutherland would break down and ask how much the house cost and Mitch would tell him to mind his own business and it would drive the old man crazy. They'd leave after a short visit and return to Kentucky, where all their friends would hear how great the daughter and the son-in-law were doing down in Memphis. Abby would be sorry they couldn't get along but wouldn't say much. From the start they had treated him like a leper. He was so unworthy they had boycotted the small wedding.

'Have you ever been to Memphis?' he asked.

'Once when I was a little girl. Some kind of convention for the church. All I remember is the river.'

'They want us to visit.'

'Us! You mean I'm invited?'

'Yes. They insist on you coming.'

'When?'

'Couple of weeks. They'll fly us down Thursday afternoon for the weekend.'

'I like this firm already.'

TWO

The five-story building had been built a hundred years earlier by a cotton merchant and his sons after the Reconstruction, during the revival of cotton trading in Memphis. It sat in the middle of Cotton Row on Front Street near the river. Through its halls and doors and across its desks, millions of bales of cotton had been purchased from the Mississippi and Arkansas deltas and sold around the world. Deserted, neglected, then renovated time and again since the first war, it had been purchased for good in 1951 by an aggressive tax lawyer named Anthony Bendini. He renovated it yet again and began filling it with lawyers. He renamed it the Bendini Building.

He pampered the building, indulged it, coddled it, each year adding another layer of luxury to his landmark. He fortified it, sealing doors and windows and hiring armed guards to protect it and its occupants. He added elevators, electronic surveillance, security codes, closed-circuit television, a weight room, a steam room, locker rooms and a partners' dining room on the fifth floor with a captivating view of the river.

In twenty years he built the richest law firm in Memphis, and, indisputably, the quietest. Secrecy was his passion. Every associate hired by the firm was indoctrinated in the evils of the loose tongue. Everything was confidential. Salaries, perks, advancement and, most especially, clients. Divulging firm business, the young associates were warned, could delay the awarding of the holy grail – a partnership. Nothing left the fortress on Front Street. Wives were told not to ask, or were lied to. The associates were expected to work hard, keep quiet and spend their healthy paychecks. They did, without exception.

With forty-one lawyers, the firm was the fourth largest in Memphis. Its members did not advertise or seek publicity. They were clannish and did not fraternize with other lawyers. Their wives played tennis and bridge and shopped among themselves. Bendini, Lambert & Locke was a big family, of sorts. A rather rich family.

At 10 A.M. on a Friday, the firm limo stopped on Front Street and Mr. Mitchell Y. McDeere emerged. He politely thanked the driver, and admired the vehicle as it drove away. His first limo ride. He stood on the sidewalk next to a streetlight and admired the quaint, picturesque, yet somehow imposing home of the quiet Bendini firm. It was a far cry from the gargantuan steel-and-glass erections inhabited by New York's finest or the enormous cylinder he had visited in Chicago. But he instantly knew he would like it. It was less pretentious. It was more like himself.

Lamar Quin walked through the front door and down the steps. He yelled at Mitch and waved him over. He had met them at the airport the night before and checked them into the Peabody – 'the South's Grand Hotel.'

'Good morning, Mitch! How was your night?' They shook hands like lost friends.

'Very nice. It's a great hotel.'

'We knew you'd like it. Everybody likes the Peabody.'

They stepped into the front foyer, where a small billboard greeted Mr. Mitchell Y. McDeere, the guest of the day. A well-dressed, but unattractive receptionist smiled warmly and said her name was Sylvia and if he needed anything while he was in Memphis just let her know. He thanked her. Lamar led him to a long hallway where he began the guided tour. He explained the layout of the building and introduced Mitch to various secretaries and paralegals as they walked. In the main library on the second floor a crowd of lawyers circled the mammoth conference table and consumed pastries and coffee. They became silent when the guest entered.

Oliver Lambert greeted Mitch and introduced him to the gang. There were about twenty in all, most of the associates in the firm, and most barely older than the guest. The partners were too busy, Lamar had explained, and would meet him later at a private lunch. He stood at the end of the table as Mr. Lambert called for quiet.

'Gentlemen, this is Mitchell McDeere. You've all heard about him, and here he is. He is our number one choice this year, our number one draft pick, so to speak. He is being romanced by the big boys in New York and Chicago and who knows where else, so we have to sell him on our little firm here in Memphis.' They smiled and nodded their approval. The guest was embarrassed.

'He will finish at Harvard in two months and will graduate with honors. He's an associate editor of the *Harvard Law Review*.' This made an impression, Mitch could tell. 'He did his undergraduate work at Western Kentucky, where he graduated summa cum laude.' This was not quite as impressive. 'He also played football for four years, starting as quarterback his junior year.' Now they were really impressed. A few appeared to be in awe, as if staring at Joe Namath.

The senior partner continued his monologue while Mitch stood awkwardly beside him. He droned on about how selective they had always been and how well Mitch would fit in. Mitch stuffed his hands in his pockets and quit listening. He studied the group. They were young, successful and affluent. The dress code appeared to be strict, but no different than New York or Chicago. Dark gray or navy wool suits, white or blue cotton button downs, medium starch, and silk ties. Nothing bold or nonconforming. Maybe a couple of bow ties, but nothing more daring. Neatness was mandatory. No beards, mustaches or hair over the ears. There were a couple of wimps, but good looks dominated.

Mr. Lambert was winding down. 'Lamar will give Mitch a tour of our offices, so you'll have a chance to chat with him later. Let's make him welcome. Tonight he and his lovely, and I do mean lovely, wife, Abby, will eat ribs at the Rendezvous, and of course tomorrow night is the firm dinner at my place. I'll ask you to be on your best behavior.' He smiled and looked at the guest. 'Mitch, if you get tired of Lamar, let me know and we'll get someone more qualified.'

He shook hands with each one of them again as they left, and tried to remember as many names as possible.

'Let's start the tour,' Lamar said when the room cleared. 'This, of course, is a library, and we have identical ones on each of the first four floors. We also use them for large meetings. The books vary from floor to floor, so you never know where your research will lead you. We have two full-time librarians, and we use microfilm and microfiche extensively. As a rule, we don't do any research outside the building. There are over a hundred thousand volumes, including every conceivable tax reporting service. That's more than some law schools. If you need a book we don't have, just tell a librarian.'

They walked past the lengthy conference table and between dozens of rows of books. 'A hundred thousand volumes,' Mitch mumbled.

'Yeah, we spend almost half a million a year on upkeep, supplements and new books. The partners are always griping about it, but they wouldn't think of cutting back. It's one of the largest private law libraries in the country, and we're proud of it.'

'It's pretty impressive.'

'We try to make research as painless as possible. You know what a bore it is and how much time can be wasted looking for the right materials. You'll spend a lot of time here the first two years, so we try to make it pleasant.'

Behind a cluttered workbench in a rear corner, one of the librarians introduced himself and gave a brief tour of the computer room, where a dozen terminals stood ready to assist with the latest computerized research. He offered to demonstrate the latest, truly incredible software, but Lamar said they might stop by later.

'He's a nice guy,' Lamar said as they left the library. 'We pay him forty thousand a year just to keep up with the books. It's amazing.'

Truly amazing, thought Mitch.

The second floor was virtually identical to the first, third and fourth. The center of each floor was filled with secretaries, their desks, file cabinets, copiers and the other necessary machines. On one side of the open area was the library, and on the other was a configuration of smaller conference rooms and offices.

'You won't see any pretty secretaries,' Lamar said softly as they watched them work. 'It seems to be an unwritten firm rule. Oliver Lambert goes out of his way to hire the oldest and homeliest ones he can find.

21

Of course, some have been here for twenty years and have forgotten more law than we learned in law school.'

'They seem kind of plump,' Mitch observed, almost to himself.

'Yeah, it's part of the overall strategy to encourage us to keep our hands in our pockets. Philandering is strictly forbidden, and to my knowledge has never happened.'

'And if it does?'

'Who knows. The secretary would be fired, of course. And I suppose the lawyer would be severely punished. It might cost a partnership. No one wants to find out, especially with this bunch of cows.'

'They dress nice.'

'Don't get me wrong. We hire only the best legal secretaries and we pay more than any other firm in town. You're looking at the best, not necessarily the prettiest. We require experience and maturity. Lambert won't hire anyone under thirty.'

'One per lawyer?'

'Yes, until you're a partner. Then you'll get another, and by then you'll need one. Nathan Locke has three, all with twenty years' experience, and he keeps them jumping.'

'Where's his office?'

'Fourth floor. It's off limits.'

Mitch started to ask, but didn't.

The corner offices were twenty-five by twenty-five, Lamar explained, and occupied by the most senior partners. Power offices, he called them, with great admiration. They were decorated to each individual's taste with no expense spared and vacated only at retirement or death, then fought over by the younger partners.

Lamar flipped a switch in one and they stepped inside, closing the door behind them. 'Nice view, huh,' he said as Mitch walked to the windows and looked at the river moving ever so slowly beyond Riverside Drive.

'How do you get this office?' Mitch asked as he admired a barge inching under the bridge leading to Arkansas.

'Takes time, and when you get here you'll be very wealthy, and very busy, and you won't have time to enjoy the view.'

'Whose is it?'

'Victor Milligan. He's head of tax, and a very nice man. Originally from New England, he's been here for twenty-five years and calls Memphis home.' Lamar stuck his hands in his pockets and walked around the room. 'The hardwood floors and ceilings came with the building, over a hundred years ago. Most of the building is carpeted, but in a few spots the wood was not damaged. You'll have the option of rugs and carpet when you get here.'

'I like the wood. What about the rug?'

'Some kind of antique Persian. I don't know its history. The desk was used by his great-grandfather, who was a judge of some sort in Rhode Island, or so he says. He's full of crap, and you never know when he's blowing smoke.'

'Where is he?'

'Vacation, I think. Did they tell you about vacations?'

'No.'

'You get two weeks a year for the first five years. Paid, of course. Then three weeks until you become a partner, then you take whatever you want. The firm has a chalet in Vail, a cabin on a lake in Manitoba and two condos on Seven Mile Beach on Grand Cayman Island. They're free, but you need to book early. Partners get priority. After that it's first come. The Caymans are extremely popular in the firm. It's an international tax haven and a lot of our trips are written off. I think Milligan's there now, probably scuba diving and calling it business.'

Through one of his tax courses, Mitch had heard of the Cayman Islands and knew they were somewhere in the Caribbean. He started to ask exactly where, but decided to check it himself.

'Only two weeks?' he asked.

'Uh, yeah. Is that a problem?'

'No, not really. The firms in New York are offering at least three.' He spoke like a discriminating critic of expensive vacations. He wasn't. Except for the three day weekend they referred to as a honeymoon, and an occasional drive through New England, he had never participated in a vacation and had never left the country.

'You can get an additional week, unpaid.'

Mitch nodded as though this was acceptable. They left Milligan's office and continued the tour. The hallway ran in a long rectangle with the attorneys' offices to the outside, all with windows, sunlight, views. Those with views of the river were more prestigious, Lamar explained, and usually occupied by partners. There were waiting lists.

The conference rooms, libraries and secretarial desks were on the inside of the hallway, away from the windows and distractions.

The associates' offices were smaller – fifteen by fifteen – but richly decorated and much more imposing than any associates' offices he had seen in New York or Chicago. The firm spent a small fortune on design consultants, Lamar said. Money, it seemed, grew on trees. The younger lawyers were friendly and talkative and seemed to welcome the interruption. Most gave brief testimonials to the greatness of the firm and of Memphis. The old town kind of grows on you, they kept telling him, but it takes time. They, too, had been recruited by the big boys in Washington and on Wall Street, and they had no regrets.

The partners were busier, but just as nice. He had been carefully selected, he was told again and again, and he would fit in. It was his kind of firm. They promised to talk more during lunch.

An hour earlier, Kay Quin had left the kids with the baby nurse and the maid and met Abby for brunch at the Peabody. She was a smalltown girl, much like Abby. She had married Lamar after college and lived in Nashville for three years while he studied law at Vanderbilt. Lamar made so much money she quit work and had two babies in fourteen months. Now that she had retired and finished her childbearing, she spent most of her time with the garden club and the heart fund and the country club and the PTA and the church. Despite the money and the affluence, she was modest and unpretentious, and apparently determined to stay that way regardless of her husband's success. Abby found a friend.

After croissants and eggs Benedict, they sat in the lobby of the hotel, drinking coffee and watching the ducks swim in circles around the fountain. Kay had suggested a quick tour of Memphis with a late lunch near her home. Maybe some shopping.

'Have they mentioned the low-interest loan?' she asked.

'Yes, at the first interview.'

'They'll want you to buy a house when you move here. Most people can't afford a house when they leave law school, so the firm loans you the money at a lower rate and holds the mortgage.'

'How low?'

'I don't know. It's been seven years since we moved here, and we've bought another house since then. It'll be a bargain, believe me. The firm will see to it that you own a home. It's sort of an unwritten rule.'

'Why is it so important?'

'Several reasons. First of all, they want you down here. This firm is very selective, and they usually get who they want. But Memphis is not exactly in the spotlight, so they have to offer more. Also, the firm is very demanding, especially on the associates. There's pressure, overwork, eighty-hour weeks and time away from home. It won't be easy on either of you, and the firm knows it. The theory is that a strong marriage means a happy lawyer, and a happy lawyer is a productive lawyer, so the bottom line is profits. Always profits.

'And there's another reason. These guys – all guys, no women – take a lot of pride in their wealth, and everyone is expected to look and act affluent. It would be an insult to the firm if an associate was forced to live in an apartment. They want you in a house, and after five years in a bigger house. If we have some time this afternoon, I'll show you some of the partners' homes. When you see them, you won't mind the eighty-hour weeks.'

'I'm used to them now.'

'That's good, but law school doesn't compare with this. Sometimes they'll work a hundred hours a week during tax season.'

Abby smiled and shook her head as if this impressed her a great deal. 'Do you work?'

'No. Most of us don't work. The money is there, so we're not forced to, and we get little help with the kids from our husbands. Of course, working is not forbidden.'

'Forbidden by whom?'

'The firm.'

'I would hope not.' Abby repeated the word 'forbidden' to herself, but let it pass.

Kay sipped her coffee and watched the ducks. A small boy wandered away from his mother and stood near the fountain. 'Do you plan to start a family?' Kay asked.

'Maybe in a couple of years.'

'Babies are encouraged.'

'By whom?'

'The firm.'

'Why should the firm care if we have children?'

'Again, stable families. A new baby is a big deal around the office. They send flowers and gifts to the hospital. You're treated like a queen. Your husband gets a week off, but he'll be too busy to take it. They put a thousand dollars in a trust fund for college. It's a lot of fun.'

'Sounds like a big fraternity.'

'It's more like a big family. Our social life revolves around the firm, and that's important because none of us are from Memphis. We're all transplants.'

'That's nice, but I don't want anyone telling me when to work and when to quit and when to have children.'

'Don't worry. They're very protective of each other, but the firm does not meddle.'

'I'm beginning to wonder.'

'Relax, Abby. The firm is like a family. They're great people, and Memphis is a wonderful old town to live in and raise kids. The cost of living is much lower and life moves at a slower pace. You're probably considering the bigger towns. So did we, but I'll take Memphis any day over the big cities.'

'Do I get the grand tour?'

'That's why I'm here. I thought we'd start downtown, then head out east and look at the nicer neighborhoods, maybe look at some houses and eat lunch at my favorite restaurant.'

'Sounds like fun.'

Kay paid for the coffee, as she had the brunch, and they left the Peabody in the Quin family's new Mercedes.

The dining room, as it was simply called, covered the west end of the fifth floor above Riverside Drive and high above the river in the distance. A row of eight-foot windows lined the wall and provided a fascinating view of the tugboats, paddle-wheelers, barges, docks and bridges.

The room was protected turf, a sanctuary for those lawyers talented and ambitious enough to be called partners in the quiet Bendini firm. They gathered each day for lunches prepared by Jessie Frances, a huge, temperamental old black woman, and served by her husband, Roosevelt, who wore white gloves and an odd-fitting, faded, wrinkled hand-me-down tux given to him by Mr. Bendini himself shortly before his death. They also gathered for coffee and doughnuts some mornings to discuss firm business and, occasionally, for a glass of wine in the late afternoon to celebrate a good month or an exceptionally large fee. It was for partners only, and maybe an occasional guest such as a blue chip client or prospective recruit. The associates could dine there twice a year, only twice – and records were kept – and then only at the invitation of a partner.

Adjacent to the dining room was a small kitchen where Jessie Frances performed, and where she had cooked the first meal for Mr. Bendini and a few others twenty-six years earlier. For twenty-six years she had cooked Southern food and ignored requests to experiment and try dishes she had trouble pronouncing. 'Don't eat it if you don't like it,' was her standard reply. Judging from the scraps Roosevelt collected from the tables, the food was eaten and enjoyed immensely. She posted the week's menu on Monday,

28

asked that reservations be made by ten each day and held grudges for years if someone canceled or didn't show. She and Roosevelt worked four hours each day and were paid a thousand each month.

Mitch sat at a table with Lamar Quin, Oliver Lambert and Royce McKnight. The entrée was prime ribs, served with fried okra and boiled squash.

'She laid off the grease today,' Mr. Lambert observed.

'It's delicious,' Mitch said.

'Is your system accustomed to grease?'

'Yes. They cook this way in Kentucky.'

'I joined this firm in 1955,' Mr. McKnight said, 'and I come from New Jersey, right? Out of suspicion, I avoided most Southern dishes as much as possible. Everything is battered and fried in animal fat, right? Then Mr. Bendini decides to open up this little café. He hires Jessie Frances, and I've had heartburn for the past twenty years. Fried ripe tomatoes, fried green tomatoes, fried eggplant, fried okra, fried squash, fried anything and everything. One day Victor Milligan said too much. He's from Connecticut, right? And Jessie Frances had whipped up a batch of fried dill pickles. Can you imagine? Fried dill pickles! Milligan said something ugly to Roosevelt and he reported it to Jessie Frances. She walked out the back door and quit. Stayed gone for a week. Roosevelt wanted to work, but she kept him at home. Finally, Mr. Bendini smoothed things over and she agreed to return if there were no complaints. But she also cut back on the grease. I think we'll all live ten years longer.'

'It's delicious,' said Lamar as he buttered another roll.

'It's always delicious,' added Mr. Lambert as Roosevelt walked by. 'Her food is rich and fattening, but we seldom miss lunch.'

Mitch ate cautiously, engaged in nervous chitchat

and tried to appear completely at ease. It was difficult. Surrounded by eminently successful lawyers, all millionaires, in their exclusive, lavishly ornamented dining suite, he felt as if he was on hallowed ground. Lamar's presence was comforting, as was Roosevelt's.

When it was apparent Mitch had finished eating, Oliver Lambert wiped his mouth, rose slowly and tapped his tea glass with his spoon. 'Gentlemen, could I have your attention.'

The room became silent as the twenty or so partners turned to the head table. They laid their napkins down and stared at the guest. Somewhere on each of their desks was a copy of the dossier. Two months earlier they had voted unanimously to make him their number one pick. They knew he ran four miles a day, did not smoke, was allergic to sulfites, had no tonsils, had a blue Mazda, had a crazy mother and once threw three interceptions in one quarter. They knew he took nothing stronger than aspirin even when he was sick, and that he was hungry enough to work a hundred hours a week if they asked. They liked him. He was good-looking, athletic-looking, a man's man with a brilliant mind and a lean body.

'As you know, we have a very special guest today, Mitch McDeere. He will soon graduate with honors from Harvard –'

'Hear! Hear!' said a couple of Harvard alumni.

'Yes, thank you. He and his wife, Abby, are staying at the Peabody this weekend as our guests. Mitch will finish in the top five out of three hundred and has been heavily recruited. We want him here, and I know you will speak to him before he leaves. Tonight he will have dinner with Lamar and Kay Quin, and then tomorrow night is the dinner at my place. You are all expected to attend.' Mitch smiled awkwardly at the partners as Mr. Lambert rambled on about the greatness of the firm. When he finished, they continued eating as Roosevelt served bread pudding and coffee.

Kay's favorite restaurant was a chic East Memphis hangout for the young affluent. A thousand ferns hung from everywhere and the jukebox played nothing but early sixties. The daiquiris were served in tall souvenir glasses.

'One is enough,' Kay warned.

'I'm not much of a drinker.'

They ordered the quiche of the day and sipped daiquiris.

'Does Mitch drink?'

'Very little. He's an athlete and very particular about his body. An occasional beer or glass of wine, nothing stronger. How about Lamar?'

'About the same. He really discovered beer in law school, but he has trouble with his weight. The firm frowns on drinking.'

'That's admirable, but why is it their business?'

'Because alcohol and lawyers go together like blood and vampires. Most lawyers drink like fish, and the profession is plagued with alcoholism. I think it starts in law school. At Vanderbilt, someone was always tapping a keg of beer. Probably the same at Harvard. The job has a lot of pressure, and that usually means a lot of booze. These guys aren't a bunch of teetotalers, mind you, but they keep it under control. A healthy lawyer is a productive lawyer.'

'I guess that makes sense. Mitch says there's no turnover.'

'It's rather permanent. I can't recall anyone leaving in the seven years we've been here. The money's great and they're careful about whom they hire. They don't want anyone with family money.'

'I'm not sure I follow.'

31

'They won't hire a lawyer with other sources of income. They want them young and hungry. It's a question of loyalty. If all your money comes from one source, then you tend to be very loyal to that source. The firm demands extreme loyalty. Lamar says there's never talk of leaving. They're all happy, and either rich or getting that way. And if one wanted to leave, he couldn't find as much money with another firm. They'll offer Mitch whatever it takes to get you down here. They take great pride in paying more.'

'Why no female lawyers?'

'They tried it once. She was a real bitch and kept the place in an uproar. Most women lawyers walk around with chips on their shoulders looking for fights. They're hard to deal with. Lamar says they're afraid to hire one because they couldn't fire her if she didn't work out, with affirmative action and all.'

The quiche arrived and they declined another round of daiquiris. Hundreds of young professionals crowded under the clouds of ferns, and the restaurant grew festive. Smokey Robinson sang softly from the juke-box.

'I've got a great idea,' Kay said. 'I know a realtor. Let's call her and go look at some houses.'

'What kind of houses?'

'For you and Mitch. For the newest associate at Bendini, Lambert & Locke. She can show you several in your price range.'

'I don't know our price range.'

'I'd say a hundred to a hundred and fifty thousand. The last associate bought in Oakgrove, and I'm sure he paid something like that.'

Abby leaned forward and almost whispered, 'How much would the notes be?'

'I don't know. But you'll be able to afford it. Around a thousand a month, maybe a little more.'

Abby stared at her and swallowed hard. The small

apartments in Manhattan were renting for twice that. 'Let's give her a call.'

As expected, Royce McKnight's office was a power one with a great view. It was in one of the prized corners on the fourth floor, down the hall from Nathan Locke. Lamar excused himself, and the managing partner asked Mitch to have a seat at a small conference table next to the sofa. A secretary was sent for coffee.

McKnight asked him about his visit so far, and Mitch said he was quite impressed.

'Mitch, I want to nail down the specifics of our offer.'

'Certainly.'

'The base salary is eighty thousand for the first year. When you pass the bar exam you receive a five thousand dollar raise. Not a bonus, but a raise. The exam is given sometime in August and you'll spend most of your summer reviewing for it. We have our own bar study courses and you'll receive extensive tutoring from some of the partners. This is done primarily on firm time. As you know, most firms put you to work and expect you to study on your own time. Not us. No associate of this firm has ever flunked the bar exam, and we're not worried about you breaking with tradition. Eighty thousand initially, up to eighty-five in six months. Once you've been here a year, you'll be raised to ninety thousand, plus you'll get a bonus each December based on the profits and performance during the prior twelve months. Last year the average bonus for associates was nine thousand. As you know, profit sharing with associates is extremely rare for law firms. Any questions about the salary?'

'What happens after the second year?'

'Your base salary is raised about ten percent a year

until you become a partner. Neither the raises nor the bonuses are guaranteed. They are based on performance.'

'Fair enough.'

'As you know, it is very important to us that you buy a home. It adds stability and prestige and we're very concerned about these things, especially with our associates. The firm provides a low-interest mortgage loan, thirty years, fixed rate, nonassumable should you decide to sell in a few years. It's a one shot deal, available only for your first home. After that you're on your own.'

'What kind of rate?'

'As low as possible without running afoul with the IRS. Current market rate is around ten, ten and a half. We should be able to get you a rate of seven to eight percent. We represent some banks, and they assist us. With this salary, you'll have no trouble qualifying. In fact, the firm will sign on as a guarantor if necessary.'

'That's very generous, Mr. McKnight.'

'It's important to us. And we don't lose any money on the deal. Once you find a house, our real estate section handles everything. All you have to do is move in.'

'What about the BMW?'

Mr. McKnight chuckled. 'We started that about ten years ago and it's proved to be quite an inducement. It's very simple. You pick out a BMW, one of the smaller ones, we lease it for three years and give you the keys. We pay for tags, insurance, maintenance. At the end of three years you can buy it from the leasing company for the fair market value. It's also a one shot deal.'

'That's very tempting.'

'We know.'

Mr. McKnight looked at his legal pad. 'We provide complete medical and dental coverage for the entire family. Pregnancies, checkups, braces, everything. Paid entirely by the firm.'

Mitch nodded, but was not impressed. This was standard.

'We have a retirement plan second to none. For every dollar you invest, the firm matches it with two, provided, however, you invest at least ten percent of your base pay. Let's say you start at eighty, and the first year you set aside eight thousand. The firm kicks in sixteen, so you've got twenty-four after the first year. A money pro in New York handles it and last year our retirement earned nineteen percent. Not bad. Invest for twenty years and you're a millionaire at forty-five, just off retirement. One stipulation: If you bail out before twenty years, you lose everything but the money you put in, with no income earned on that money.'

'Sounds rather harsh.'

'No, actually it's rather generous. Find me another firm or company matching two to one. There are none, to my knowledge. It's our way of taking care of ourselves. Many of our partners retire at fifty, some at forty-five. We have no mandatory retirement, and some work into their sixties and seventies. To each his own. Our goal is simply to ensure a generous pension and make early retirement an option.'

'How many retired partners do you have?'

'Twenty or so. You'll see them around here from time to time. They like to come in and have lunch and a few keep office space. Did Lamar cover vacations?'

'Yes.'

'Good. Book early, especially for Vail and the Caymans. You buy the air fare, but the condos are free. We do a lot of business in the Caymans and from time to time we'll send you down for two or three days and write the whole thing off. Those trips are not counted as vacation, and you'll get one every year or

35

so. We work hard, Mitch, and we recognize the value of leisure.'

Mitch nodded his approval and dreamed of lying on a sundrenched beach in the Caribbean, sipping on a pina colada and watching string bikinis.

'Did Lamar mention the signing bonus?'

'No, but it sounds interesting.'

'If you join our firm we hand you a check for five thousand. We prefer that you spend the bulk of it on a new wardrobe. After seven years of jeans and flannel shirts, your inventory of suits is probably low, and we realize it. Appearance is very important to us. We expect our attorneys to dress sharp and conservative. There's no dress code, but you'll get the picture.'

Did he say five thousand dollars? For clothes? Mitch currently owned two suits, and he was wearing one of them. He kept a straight face and did not smile.

'Any questions?'

'Yes. The large firms are infamous for being sweatshops where the associates are flooded with tedious research and locked away in some library for the first three years. I want no part of that. I don't mind doing my share of research and I realize I will be the low man on the pole. But I don't want to research and write briefs for the entire firm. I'd like to work with real clients and their real problems.'

Mr. McKnight listened intently and waited with his rehearsed answer. 'I understand, Mitch. You're right, it is a real problem in the big firms. But not here. For the first six weeks you'll do little but study for the bar exam. When that's over, you begin practicing law. You'll be assigned to a partner, and his clients will become your clients. You'll do most of his research and, of course, your own, and occasionally you'll be asked to assist someone else with the preparation of a brief or some research. We want you happy. We take pride in our zero turnover rate, and we go the extra mile to keep careers on track. If you can't get along with your partner, we'll find another one. If you discover you don't like tax, we'll let you try securities or banking. It's your decision. The firm will soon invest a lot of money in Mitch McDeere, and we want him to be productive.'

Mitch sipped his coffee and searched for another question. Mr. McKnight glanced at his checklist.

'We pay all moving expenses to Memphis.'

'That won't be much. Just a small rental truck.'

'Anything else, Mitch?'

'No, sir. I can't think of anything.'

The checklist was folded and placed in the file. The partner rested both elbows on the table and leaned forward. 'Mitch, we're not pushing, but we need an answer as soon as possible. If you go elsewhere, we must then continue to interview. It's a lengthy process, and we'd like our new man to start by July 1.'

'Ten days soon enough?'

'That's fine. Say by March 30?'

'Sure, but I'll contact you before then.' Mitch excused himself, and found Lamar waiting in the hall outside McKnight's office. They agreed on seven for dinner.

THREE

There were no law offices on the fifth floor of the Bendini Building. The partners' dining room and kitchen occupied the west end, some unused and unpainted storage rooms sat locked and empty in the center, then a thick concrete wall sealed off the remaining third of the floor. A small metal door with a button beside it and a camera over it hung in the center of the wall and opened into a small room where an armed guard watched the door and monitored a wall of closed circuit screens. A hallway zigzagged through a maze of cramped offices and workrooms where an assortment of characters went secretly about their business of watching and gathering information. The windows to the outside were sealed with paint and covered with blinds. The sunlight stood no chance of penetrating the fortress.

DeVasher, head of security, occupied the largest of the small, plain offices. The lone certificate on his bare walls recognized him for thirty years of dedicated service as a detective with the New Orleans Police Department. He was of medium build with a slight belly, thick shoulders and chest and a huge, perfectly round head that smiled with great reluctance. His wrinkled shirt was mercifully unbuttoned at the collar, allowing his bulging neck to sag unrestricted. A thick polyester tie hung on the coatrack with a badly worn blazer.

Monday morning after the McDeere visit, Oliver Lambert stood before the small metal door and stared at the camera over it. He pushed the button twice, waited and was finally cleared through security. He walked quickly through the cramped hallway and entered the cluttered office. DeVasher blew smoke from a Dutch Masters into a smokeless ashtray and shoved papers in all directions until wood was visible on his desk.

'Mornin', Ollie. I guess you want to talk about McDeere.'

DeVasher was the only person in the Bendini Building who called him Ollie to his face.

'Yes, among other things.'

'Well, he had a good time, was impressed with the firm, liked Memphis okay and will probably sign on.'

'Where were your people?'

'We had the rooms on both sides at the hotel. His room was wired, of course, as was the limo and the phone and everything else. The usual, Ollie.'

'Let's get specific.'

'Okay. Thursday night they checked in late and went to bed. Little discussion. Friday night he told her all about the firm, the offices, the people, said you were a real nice man. I thought you'd like that.'

'Get on with it.'

'Told her about the fancy dining room and his little lunch with the partners. Gave her the specifics on the offer and they were ecstatic. Much better than his other offers. She wants a home with a driveway and a sidewalk and trees and a backyard. He said she could have one.'

'Any problems with the firm?'

'Not really. He commented on the absence of blacks and women, but it didn't seem to bother him.'

'What about his wife?'

'She had a ball. She likes the town, and she and Quin's wife hit it off. They looked at houses Friday afternoon, and she saw a couple she liked.'

'You get any addresses?'

'Of course, Ollie. Saturday morning they called the limo and rode all over town. Very impressed with the limo. Our driver stayed away from the bad sections, and they looked at more houses. I think they decided on one, 1231 East Meadowbrook. It's empty. Realtor by the name of Betsy Bell walked them through it. Asking one-forty, but will take less. Need to move it.'

'That's a nice part of town. How old is the house?'

'Ten, fifteen years. Three thousand square feet. Sort of a colonial-looking job. It's nice enough for one of your boys, Ollie.'

'Are you sure that's the one they want?'

'For now anyway. They discussed maybe coming back in a month or so to look at some more. You might want to fly them back as soon as they accept. That's normal procedure, ain't it?'

'Yes. We'll handle that. What about the salary?'

'Most impressed. Highest one so far. They talked and talked about the money. Salary, retirement, mortgage, BMW, bonus, everything. They couldn't believe it. Kids must really be broke.'

'They are. You think we got him, huh?'

'I'd bet on it. He said once that the firm may not be as prestigious as the ones on Wall Street, but the lawyers were just as qualified and a lot nicer. I think he'll sign on, yeah.'

'Any suspicions?'

'Not really. Quin evidently told him to stay away from Locke's office. He told his wife that no one ever went in there but some secretaries and a handful of partners. But he said Quin said Locke was eccentric and not that friendly. I don't think he's suspicious, though. She said the firm seemed concerned about some things that were none of its business.'

'Such as?'

'Personal matters. Children, working wives, etc. She seemed a bit irritated, but I think it was more of an observation. She told Mitch Saturday morning that she would be damned if any bunch of lawyers would tell her when to work and when to have babies. But I don't think it's a problem.'

'Does he realize how permanent this place is?'

'I think so. There was no mention of putting in a few years and moving on. I think he got the message. He wants to be a partner, like all of them. He's broke and wants the money.'

'What about the dinner at my place?'

'They were nervous, but had a good time. Very impressed with your place. Really liked your wife.'

'Sex?'

'Every night. Sounded like a honeymoon in there.'

'What'd they do?'

'We couldn't see, remember. Sounded normal. Nothing kinky. I thought of you and how much you like pictures, and I kept telling myself we should've rigged up some cameras for old Ollie.'

'Shut up, DeVasher.'

'Maybe next time.'

They were silent as DeVasher looked at a notepad. He stubbed his cigar in the ashtray and smiled to himself.

'All in all,' he said, 'it's a strong marriage. They seemed to be very intimate. Your driver said they held hands all weekend. Not a cross word for three days. That's pretty good, ain't it? But who am I? I've been married three times myself.'

'That's understandable. What about children?'

'Couple of years. She wants to work some, then get pregnant.'

'What's your opinion of this guy?'

'Very good, very decent young man. Also very ambitious. I think he's driven and he won't quit until he's at the top. He'll take some chances, bend some rules if necessary.'

Ollie smiled. 'That's what I wanted to hear.'

'Two phone calls. Both to her mother in Kentucky. Nothing remarkable.'

'What about his family?'

'Never mentioned.'

'No word on Ray?'

'We're still looking, Ollie. Give us some time.'

DeVasher closed the McDeere file and opened another, much thicker one. Lambert rubbed his temples and stared at the floor. 'What's the latest?' he asked softly.

'It's not good, Ollie. I'm convinced Hodge and Kozinski are working together now. Last week the FBI got a warrant and checked Kozinski's house. Found our wiretaps. They told him his house was bugged, but of course they don't know who did it. Kozinski tells Hodge last Friday while they're hiding in the third-floor library. We got a bug nearby, and we pick up bits and pieces. Not much, but we know they talked about the wiretaps. They're convinced everything is bugged, and they suspect us. They're very careful where they talk.'

'Why would the FBI bother with a search warrant?'

'Good question. Probably for our benefit. To make things look real legal and proper. They respect us.'

'Which agent?'

'Tarrance. He's in charge, evidently.'

'Is he good?'

'He's okay. Young, green, overzealous, but competent. He's no match for our men.'

'How often has he talked to Kozinski?'

'There's no way to know. They figure we're listening, so everybody's real careful. We know of four meetings in the last month, but I suspect more.'

'How much has he spilled?'

'Not much, I hope. They're still shadowboxing. The last conversation we got was a week ago and he didn't say much. He's bad scared. They're coaxing a lot, but not getting much. He hasn't yet made the decision to cooperate. They approached him, remember. At least we think they approached him. They shook him up pretty bad and he was ready to cut a deal. Now he's having second thoughts. But he's still in contact with them, and that's what worries me.'

'Does his wife know?'

'I don't think so. She knows he's acting strange, and he tells her it's office pressure.'

'What about Hodge?'

'Still ain't talked to the Fibbies, as far as we know. He and Kozinski talk a lot, or whisper I should say. Hodge keeps saying he's scared to death of the FBI, that they don't play fair and they cheat and play dirty. He won't move without Kozinski.'

'What if Kozinski is eliminated?'

'Hodge will be a new man. But I don't think we've reached that point. Dammit, Ollie, he ain't some hotshot thug who gets in the way. He's a very nice young man, with kids and all that.'

'Your compassion is overwhelming. I guess you think I enjoy this. Hell, I practically raised these boys.'

'We'll get them back in line, then, before this thing goes too far. New York's getting suspicious, Ollie. They're asking a lot of questions.'

'Who?'

'Lazarov.'

'What have you told them, DeVasher?'

'Everything. That's my job. They want you in New York day after tomorrow, for a full briefing.'

'What do they want?'

'Answers. And plans.'

'Plans for what?'

'Preliminary plans to eliminate Kozinski, Hodge and Tarrance, should it become necessary.'

'Tarrance! Are you crazy, DeVasher? We can't eliminate a cop. They'll send in the troops.'

'Lazarov is stupid, Ollie. You know that. He's an idiot, but I don't think we should tell him.'

'I think I will. I think I'll go to New York and tell Lazarov he's a complete fool.'

'You do that, Ollie. You do that.'

Oliver Lambert jumped from his seat and headed for the door. 'Watch McDeere for another month.'

'Sure, Ollie. You betcha. He'll sign. Don't worry.'

FOUR

The Mazda was sold for two hundred dollars, and most of the money was immediately invested in a twelve foot U-Haul rental truck. He would be reimbursed in Memphis. Half of the odd assortment of furniture was given or thrown away, and when loaded the truck held a refrigerator, a bed, a dresser and chest of drawers, a small color television, boxes of dishes, clothes and junk and an old sofa which was taken out of sentiment and would not last long in the new location.

Abby held Hearsay, the mutt, as Mitch worked his way through Boston and headed south, far south toward the promise of better things. For three days they drove the back roads, enjoyed the countryside, sang along with the radio, slept in cheap motels and talked of the house, the BMW, new furniture, children, affluence. They rolled down the windows and let the wind blow as the truck approached top speeds of almost forty-five miles per hour. At one point, somewhere in Pennsylvania, Abby mentioned that perhaps they could stop in Kentucky for a brief visit. Mitch said nothing, but chose a route through the Carolinas and Georgia, never venturing within two hundred miles of any point on the Kentucky border. Abby let it pass.

They arrived in Memphis on a Thursday morning, and, as promised, the black 318i sat under the carport as though it belonged there. He stared at the car. She stared at the house. The lawn was thick, green and neatly trimmed. The hedges had been manicured. The marigolds were in bloom.

The keys were found under a bucket in the utility room, as promised.

After the first test drive, they quickly unloaded the truck before the neighbors could inspect the sparse belongings. The U-Haul was returned to the nearest dealer. Another test drive.

An interior designer, the same one who would do his office, arrived after noon and brought with her samples of carpet, paint, floor coverings, curtains, drapes, wallpaper. Abby found the idea of a designer a bit hilarious after their apartment in Cambridge, but played along. Mitch was immediately bored, and excused himself for another test drive. He toured the tree lined, quiet, shady streets of this handsome neighborhood of which he was now a member. He smiled as boys on bicycles stopped and whistled at his new car. He waved at the postman walking down the sidewalk sweating profusely. Here he was, Mitchell Y. McDeere, twenty-five years old and one week out of law school, and he had arrived.

At three, they followed the designer to an upscale furniture store where the manager politely informed them that Mr. Oliver Lambert had already made arrangements for their credit, if they so chose, and there was in fact no limit on what they could buy and finance. They bought a houseful. Mitch frowned from time to time, and twice vetoed items as too expensive, but Abby ruled the day. The designer complimented her time and again on her marvelous taste, and said she would see Mitch on Monday, to do his office. Marvelous, he said.

With a map of the city, they set out for the Quin residence. Abby had seen the house during the first visit, but did not remember how to find it. It was in a section of town called Chickasaw Gardens, and she remembered the wooded lots, huge houses and professionally landscaped front yards. They parked in the driveway behind the new Mercedes and the old Mercedes.

The maid nodded politely, but did not smile. She led them to the living room, and left them. The house was dark and quiet – no children, no voices, no one. They admired the furniture and waited. They mumbled quietly, then grew impatient. Yes, they agreed, they had in fact been invited to dinner on this night, Thursday, June 25, at 6 P.M. Mitch checked his watch again and said something about it being rude. They waited.

From the hallway, Kay emerged and attempted to smile. Her eyes were puffy and glazed, with mascara leaking from the corners. Tears flowed freely down her cheeks, and she held a handkerchief over her mouth. She hugged Abby and sat next to her on the sofa. She bit the handkerchief and cried louder.

Mitch knelt before her. 'Kay, what's happened?'

She bit harder and shook her head. Abby squeezed her knee, and Mitch patted the other one. They watched her fearfully, expecting the worst. Was it Lamar or one of the kids?

'There's been a tragedy,' she said through the quiet sobbing.

'Who is it?' Mitch asked.

She wiped her eyes and breathed deeply. 'Two members of the firm, Marty Kozinski and Joe Hodge, were killed today. We were very close to them.'

Mitch sat on the coffee table. He remembered Marty Kozinski from the second visit in April. He had joined Lamar and Mitch for lunch at a deli on Front Street. He was next in line for a partnership, but had seemed less than enthused. Mitch could not place Joe Hodge.

'What happened?' he asked.

She had stopped crying, but the tears continued. She wiped her face again and looked at him. 'We're not sure. They were on Grand Cayman, scuba diving. There was some kind of an explosion on a boat, and we think they drowned. Lamar said details were sketchy. There was a firm meeting a few hours ago, and they were all told about it. Lamar barely made it home.'

'Where is he?'

'By the pool. He's waiting for you.'

He sat in a white metal lawn chair next to a small table with a small umbrella, a few feet from the edge of the pool. Near a flower bed, a circular lawn sprinkler rattled and hissed and spewed forth water in a perfect arc which included the table, umbrella, chair and Lamar Quin. He was soaked. Water dripped from his nose, ears and hair. The blue cotton shirt and wool pants were saturated. He wore no socks or shoes.

He sat motionless, never flinching with each additional dousing. He had lost touch. Some distant object on the side fence attracted and held his attention. An unopened bottle of Heineken sat in a puddle on the concrete beside his chair.

Mitch surveyed the back lawn, in part to make sure the neighbors could not see. They could not. An eight-foot cypress fence ensured complete privacy. He walked around the pool and stopped at the edge of the dry area. Lamar noticed him, nodded, attempted a weak smile and motioned to a wet chair. Mitch pulled it a few feet away and sat down, just as the next barrage of water landed.

His stare returned to the fence, or whatever it was in the distance. For an eternity they sat and listened to the thrashing sound of the sprinkler. Lamar would sometimes shake his head and attempt to mumble. Mitch smiled awkwardly, unsure of what, if anything, needed to be said.

'Lamar, I'm very sorry,' he finally offered.

He acknowledged this and looked at Mitch. 'Me too.'

'I wish I could say something.'

His eyes left the fence, and he cocked his head sideways in Mitch's direction. His dark hair was soaked and hung in his eyes. The eyes were red and pained. He stared, and waited until the next round of water passed over.

'I know. But there's nothing to say. I'm sorry it had to happen now, today. We didn't feel like cooking.'

'That should be the least of your concern. I lost my appetite a moment ago.'

'Do you remember them?' he asked, blowing water from his lips.

'I remember Kozinski, but not Hodge.'

'Marty Kozinski was one of my best friends. From Chicago. He joined the firm three years ahead of me and was next in line for a partnership. A great lawyer, one we all admired and turned to. Probably the best negotiator in the firm. Very cool and dry under pressure.'

He wiped his eyebrows and stared at the ground. When he talked the water dripped from his nose and interfered with his enunciation. 'Three kids. His twin girls are a month older than our son, and they've always played together.' He closed his eyes, bit his lip and started crying.

Mitch wanted to leave. He tried not to look at his friend. 'I'm very sorry, Lamar. Very sorry.'

After a few minutes, the crying stopped, but the water continued. Mitch surveyed the spacious lawn in search of the outside faucet. Twice he summoned the courage to ask if he could turn off the sprinkler, and twice he decided he could last if Lamar could. Maybe it helped. He checked his watch. Darkness was an hour and a half away.

'What about the accident?' Mitch finally asked.

'We weren't told much. They were scuba diving and

49

there was an explosion on the boat. The dive captain was also killed. A native of the islands. They're trying to get the bodies home now.'

'Where were their wives?'

'At home, thankfully. It was a business trip.'

'I can't picture Hodge.'

'Joe was a tall blond-headed guy who didn't say much. The kind you meet but don't remember. He was a Harvard man like yourself.'

'How old was he?'

'He and Marty were both thirty-four. He would've made partner after Marty. They were very close. I guess we're all close, especially now.'

With all ten fingernails he combed his hair straight back. He stood and walked to dry ground. Water poured from his shirttail and the cuffs of his pants. He stopped near Mitch and looked blankly at the treetops next door. 'How's the BMW?'

'It's great. A fine car. Thanks for delivering it.'

'When did you arrive?'

'This morning. I've already put a thousand miles on it.'

'Did the interior woman show up?'

'Yeah. She and Abby spent next year's salary.'

'That's nice. Nice house. We're glad you're here, Mitch. I'm just sorry about the circumstances. You'll like it here.'

'You don't have to apologize.'

'I still don't believe it. I'm numb, paralyzed. I shudder at the thought of seeing Marty's wife and the kids. I'd rather be lashed with a bullwhip than go over there.'

The women appeared, walked across the wooden patio deck and down the steps to the pool. Kay found the faucet and the sprinkler was silenced.

They left Chickasaw Gardens and drove west with the traffic toward downtown, into the fading sun. They held hands, but said little. Mitch opened the sunroof and rolled down the windows. Abby picked through a box of old cassettes and found Springsteen. The stereo worked fine. 'Hungry Heart' blew from the windows as the little shiny roadster made its way toward the river. The warm, sticky, humid Memphis summer air settled in with the dark. Softball fields came to life as teams of fat men with tight polyester pants and lime-green and fluorescent-yellow shirts laid chalk lines and prepared to do battle. Cars full of teenagers crowded into fast-food joints to drink beer and gossip and check out the opposite sex. Mitch began to smile. He tried to forget about Lamar, and Kozinski and Hodge. Why should he be sad? They were not his friends. He was sorry for their families, but he did not really know these people. And he, Mitchell Y. McDeere, a poor kid with no family, had much to be happy about. Beautiful wife, new house, new car, new job, new Harvard degree. A brilliant mind and a solid body that did not gain weight and needed little sleep. Eighty thousand a year, for now. In two years he could be in six figures, and all he had to do was work ninety hours a week. Piece of cake.

He pulled into a self-serve and pumped fifteen gallons. He paid inside and bought a six-pack of Michelob. Abby opened two, and they darted back into the traffic. He was smiling now.

'Let's eat,' he said.

'We're not exactly dressed,' she said.

He stared at her long, brown legs. She wore a white cotton skirt, above the knees, with a white cotton button-down. He had shorts, deck shoes and a faded black polo. 'With legs like that, you could get us into any restaurant in New York.'

'How about the Rendezvous? The dress seemed casual.'

'Great idea.'

They paid to park in a lot downtown and walked two blocks to a narrow alley. The smell of barbecue mixed with the summer air and hung like a fog close to the pavement. The aroma filtered gently through the nose, mouth and eyes and caused a rippling sensation deep in the stomach. Smoke poured into the alley from vents running underground into the massive ovens where the best pork ribs were barbecued in the best barbecue restaurant in a city known for world-class barbecue. The Rendezvous was downstairs, beneath the alley, beneath an ancient red-brick building that would have been demolished decades earlier had it not been for the famous tenant in the basement.

There was always a crowd and a waiting list, but Thursdays were slow, it seemed. They were led through the cavernous, sprawling, noisy restaurant and shown a small table with a red checked tablecloth. There were stares along the way. Always stares. Men stopped eating, froze with ribs hanging from their teeth, as Abby McDeere glided by like a model on a runway. She had stopped traffic from a sidewalk in Boston. Whistles and catcalls were a way of life. And her husband was used to it. He took great pride in his beautiful wife.

An angry black man with a red apron stood before them. 'Okay, sir,' he demanded.

The menus were mats on the tables, and completely unnecessary. Ribs, ribs and ribs.

'Two whole orders, cheese plate, pitcher of beer,' Mitch shot back at him. The waiter wrote nothing, but turned and screamed in the direction of the entrance: 'Gimme two whole, cheese, pitcher!'

When he left, Mitch grabbed her leg under the table. She slapped his hand.

'You're beautiful,' he said. 'When was the last time I told you that you are beautiful?'

'About two hours ago.'

52

'Two hours! How thoughtless of me!'

'Don't let it happen again.'

He grabbed her leg again and rubbed the knee. She allowed it. She smiled seductively at him, dimples forming perfectly, teeth shining in the dim light, soft pale brown eyes glowing. Her dark brunet hair was straight and fell perfectly a few inches below her shoulders.

The beer arrived and the waiter filled two mugs without saying a word. Abby took a small drink and stopped smiling.

'Do you think Lamar's okay?' she asked.

'I don't know. I thought at first he was drunk. I felt like an idiot sitting there watching him get soaked.'

'Poor guy. Kay said the funerals will probably be Monday, if they can get the bodies back in time.'

'Let's talk about something else. I don't like funerals, any funeral, even when I'm there out of respect and don't know the deceased. I've had some bad experiences with funerals.'

The ribs arrived. They were served on paper plates with aluminum foil to catch the grease. A small dish of slaw and one of baked beans sat around a foot long slab of dry ribs sprinkled heavily with the secret sauce. They dug in with fingers.

'What would you like to talk about?' she asked.

'Getting pregnant.'

'I thought we were going to wait a few years.'

'We are. But I think we should practice diligently until then.'

'We've practiced in every roadside motel between here and Boston.'

'I know, but not in our new home.' Mitch ripped two ribs apart, slinging sauce into his eyebrows.

'We just moved in this morning.'

'I know. What're we waiting for?'

'Mitch, you act as though you've been neglected.'

'I have, since this morning. I suggest we do it tonight, as soon as we get home, to sort of christen our new house.'

'We'll see.'

'Is it a date? Look, did you see that guy over there? He's about to break his neck trying to see some leg. I oughta go over and whip his ass.'

'Yes. It's a date. Don't worry about those guys. They're staring at you. They think you're cute.'

'Very funny.'

Mitch stripped his ribs clean and ate half of hers. When the beer was gone, he paid the check and they climbed into the alley. He drove carefully across town and found the name of a street he recognized from one of his many road trips of the day. After two wrong turns, he found Meadowbrook, and then the home of Mr. and Mrs. Mitchell Y. McDeere.

The mattress and box springs were stacked on the floor of the master bedroom, surrounded by boxes. Hearsay hid under a lamp on the floor and watched as they practiced.

Four days later, on what should have been his first day behind his new desk, Mitch and his lovely wife joined the remaining thirty-nine members of the firm, and their lovely wives, as they paid their last respects to Martin S. Kozinski. The cathedral was full. Oliver Lambert offered a eulogy so eloquent and touching not even Mitchell McDeere, who had buried a father and a brother, could resist chill bumps. Abby's eyes watered at the sight of the widow and the children.

That afternoon, they met again in the Presbyterian church in East Memphis to say farewell to Joseph M. Hodge.

FIVE

The small lobby outside Royce McKnight's office was empty when Mitch arrived precisely at eight-thirty, on schedule. He hummed and coughed and began to wait anxiously. From behind two file cabinets an ancient blue-haired secretary appeared and scowled in his general direction. When it was apparent he was not welcome, he introduced himself and explained he was to meet Mr. McKnight at this appointed hour. She smiled and introduced herself as Louise, Mr. McKnight's personal secretary, for thirty-one years now. Coffee? Yes, he said, black. She disappeared and returned with a cup and saucer. She notified her boss through the intercom and instructed Mitch to have a seat. She recognized him now. One of the other secretaries had pointed him out during the funerals yesterday.

She apologized for the somber atmosphere around the place. No one felt like working, she explained, and it would be days before things were normal. They were such nice young men. The phone rang and she explained that Mr. McKnight was in an important meeting and could not be disturbed. It rang again, she listened, and escorted him into the managing partner's office.

Oliver Lambert and Royce McKnight greeted Mitch and introduced him to two other partners,

Victor Milligan and Avery Tolleson. They sat around a small conference table. Louise was sent for more coffee. Milligan was head of tax, and Tolleson, at forty-one, was one of the younger partners.

'Mitch, we apologize for such a depressing beginning,' McKnight said. 'We appreciate your presence at the funerals yesterday, and we're sorry your first day as a member of our firm was one of such sadness.'

'I felt I belonged at the funerals,' Mitch said.

'We're very proud of you, and we have great plans for you. We've just lost two of our finest lawyers, both of whom did nothing but tax, so we'll be asking more of you. All of us will have to work a little harder.'

Louise arrived with a tray of coffee. Silver coffee server, fine china.

'We are quite saddened,' said Oliver Lambert. 'So please bear with us.'

They all nodded and frowned at the table. Royce McKnight looked at some notes on a legal pad.

'Mitch, I think we've covered this before. At this firm, we assign each associate to a partner, who acts as a supervisor and mentor. These relationships are very important. We try to match you with a partner with whom you will be compatible and able to work closely, and we're usually right. We have made mistakes. Wrong chemistry, or whatever, but when that happens we simply reassign the associate. Avery Tolleson will be your partner.'

Mitch smiled awkwardly at his new partner.

'You will be under his direction, and the cases and files you work on will be his. Virtually all of it will be tax work.'

'That's fine.'

'Before I forget it, I'd like to have lunch today,' Tolleson said.

'Certainly,' Mitch said.

'Take my limo,' Mr. Lambert said.

'I had planned to,' said Tolleson.

'When do I get a limo?' Mitch asked.

They smiled, and seemed to appreciate the relief. 'In about twenty years,' said Mr. Lambert.

'I can wait.'

'How's the BMW?' asked Victor Milligan.

'Great. It's ready for the five-thousand-mile service.'

'Did you get moved in okay?'

'Yes, everything's fine. I appreciate the firm's assistance in everything. You've made us feel very welcome, and Abby and I are extremely grateful.'

McKnight quit smiling and returned to the legal pad. 'As I've told you, Mitch, the bar exam has priority. You've got six weeks to study for it and we assist in every way possible. We have our own review courses directed by our members. All areas of the exam will be covered and your progress will be closely watched by all of us, especially Avery. At least half of each day will be spent on bar review, and most of your spare time as well. No associate in this firm has ever failed the exam.'

'I won't be the first.'

'If you flunk it, we take away the BMW,' Tolleson said with a slight grin.

'Your secretary will be a lady named Nina Huff. She's been with the firm more than eight years. Sort of temperamental, not much to look at, but very capable. She knows a lot of law and has a tendency to give advice, especially to the newer attorneys. It'll be up to you to keep her in place. If you can't get along with her, we'll move her.'

'Where's my office?'

'Second floor, down the hall from Avery. The interior woman will be here this afternoon to pick out the desk and furnishings. As much as possible, follow her advice.'

Lamar was also on the second floor, and at the

moment that thought was comforting. He thought of him sitting by the pool, soaking wet, crying and mumbling incoherently.

McKnight spoke. 'Mitch, I'm afraid I neglected to cover something that should've been discussed during the first visit here.'

He waited, and finally said, 'Okay, what is it?'

The partners watched McKnight intently. 'We've never allowed an associate to begin his career burdened with student loans. We prefer that you find other things to worry about, and other ways to spend your money. How much do you owe?'

Mitch sipped his coffee and thought rapidly. 'Almost twenty-three thousand.'

'Have the documents on Louise's desk first thing in the morning.'

'You, uh, mean the firm satisfies the loans?'

'That's our policy. Unless you object.'

'No objection. I don't quite know what to say.'

'You don't have to say anything. We've done it for every associate for the past fifteen years. Just get the paperwork to Louise.'

'That's very generous, Mr. McKnight.'

'Yes, it is.'

Avery Tolleson talked incessantly as the limo moved slowly through the noontime traffic. Mitch reminded him of himself, he said. A poor kid from a broken home, raised by foster families throughout southwest Texas, then put on the streets after high school. He worked the night shift in a shoe factory to finance junior college. An academic scholarship to UTEP opened the door. He graduated with honors, applied to eleven law schools and chose Stanford. He finished number two in his class and turned down offers from every big firm on the West Coast. He wanted to do tax work, nothing but tax work. Oliver Lambert had recruited him sixteen years ago, back when the firm had fewer than thirty lawyers.

He had a wife and two kids, but said little about the family. He talked about money. His passion, he called it. The first million was in the bank. The second was two years away. At four hundred thousand a year gross, it wouldn't take long. His specialty was forming partnerships to purchase supertankers. He was the premier specialist in his field and worked at three hundred an hour, sixty, sometimes seventy hours a week.

Mitch would start at a hundred bucks an hour, at least five hours a day until he passed the bar and got his license. Then eight hours a day would be expected, at one-fifty an hour. Billing was the lifeblood of the firm. Everything revolved around it. Promotions, raises, bonuses, survival, success, everything revolved around how well one was billing. Especially the new guys. The quickest route to a reprimand was to neglect the daily billing records. Avery could not remember such a reprimand. It was simply unheard of for a member of the firm to ignore his billing.

The average for associates was one-seventy-five per hour. For partners, three hundred. Milligan got four hundred an hour from a couple of his clients, and Nathan Locke once got five hundred an hour for some tax work that involved swapping assets in several foreign countries. Five hundred bucks an hour! Avery relished the thought, and computed five hundred per hour by fifty hours per week at fifty weeks per year. One million two hundred fifty thousand a year! That's how you make money in this business. You get a bunch of lawyers working by the hour and you build a dynasty. The more lawyers you get, the more money the partners make.

Don't ignore the billing, he warned. That's the first rule of survival. If there were no files to bill on, immediately report to his office. He had plenty. On the tenth day of each month the partners review the prior month's billing during one of their exclusive luncheons. It's a big ceremony. Royce McKnight reads out each lawyer's name, then the total of his monthly billing. The competition among the partners is intense, but good-spirited. They're all getting rich, right? It's very motivational. As for the associates, nothing is said to the low man unless it's his second straight month. Oliver Lambert will say something in passing. No one has ever finished low for three straight months. Bonuses can be earned by associates for exorbitant billing. Partnerships are based on one's track record for generating fees. So don't ignore it, he warned again. It must always have priority – after the bar exam, of course.

The bar exam was a nuisance, an ordeal that must be endured, a rite of passage, and nothing any Harvard man should fear. Just concentrate on the review courses, he said, and try to remember everything he had just learned in law school.

The limo wheeled into a side street between two tall buildings and stopped in front of a small canopy that extended from the curb to a black metal door. Avery looked at his watch and said to the driver, 'Be back at two.'

Two hours for lunch, thought Mitch. That's over six hundred dollars in billable time. What a waste.

The Manhattan Club occupied the top floor of a ten story office building which had last been fully occupied in the early fifties. Avery referred to the structure as a dump, but was quick to point out that the club was the most exclusive lunch and dinner refuge in the city. It offered excellent food in an all-white rich-male, plush environment. Powerful lunches for powerful people. Bankers, lawyers, executives, entrepreneurs, a few politicians and a few aristocrats. A gold-plated elevator ran nonstop past the deserted offices and stopped on the elegant tenth floor. The maître d' called Mr. Tolleson by name and asked about his good friends Oliver Lambert and Nathan Locke. He expressed sympathies for the loss of Mr. Kozinski and Mr. Hodge. Avery thanked him and introduced the newest member of the firm. The favorite table was waiting in the corner. A courtly black man named Ellis delivered the menus.

'The firm does not allow drinking at lunch,' Avery said as he opened his menu.

'I don't drink during lunch.'

'That's good. What'll you have?'

'Tea, with ice.'

'Iced tea, for him,' Avery said to the waiter. 'Bring me a Bombay martini on the rocks with three olives.'

Mitch bit his tongue and grinned behind the menu.

'We have too many rules,' Avery mumbled.

The first martini led to a second, but he quit after two. He ordered for both of them. Broiled fish of some sort. The special of the day. He watched his weight carefully, he said. He also worked out daily at a health club, his own health club. He invited Mitch to come sweat with him. Maybe after the bar exam. There were the usual questions about football in college and the standard denials of any greatness.

Mitch asked about the children. He said they lived with their mother.

The fish was raw and the baked potato was hard. Mitch picked at his plate, ate his salad slowly and listened as his partner talked about most of the other people present for lunch. The mayor was seated at a large table with some Japanese. One of the firm's bankers was at the next table. There were some other big-shot lawyers and corporate types, all eating furiously and importantly, powerfully. The atmosphere was stuffy. According to Avery, every member of the club was a compelling figure, a potent force both in his field and in the city. Avery was at home.

They both declined dessert and ordered coffee. He would be expected to be in the office by nine each morning, Avery explained as he lit a Montesino. The secretaries would be there at eight-thirty. Nine to five, but no one worked eight hours a day. Personally, he was in the office by eight, and seldom left before six. He could bill twelve hours each day, every day, regardless of how many hours he actually worked. Twelve a day, five days a week, at three hundred an hour, for fifty weeks. Nine hundred thousand dollars! In billable time! That was his goal. Last year he had billed seven hundred thousand, but there had been some personal problems. The firm didn't care if Mitch came in at 6 A.M. or 9 A.M., as long as the work was done.

'What time are the doors unlocked?' Mitch asked.

Everyone has a key, he explained, so he could come and go as he pleased. Security was tight, but the guards were accustomed to workaholics. Some of the work habits were legendary. Victor Milligan, in his younger days, worked sixteen hours a day, seven days a week, until he made partner. Then he quit working on Sundays. He had a heart attack and gave up Saturdays. His doctor put him on ten hour days, five days a week, and he hasn't been happy since. Marty Kozinski knew all the janitors by first name. He was a 9 A.M. man who wanted to have breakfast with the kids. He would come in at nine and leave at midnight. Nathan Locke claims he can't work well after the secretaries arrive, so he comes in at six. It would be a disgrace to start later. Here's a man sixty-one years old, worth ten million, and works from six in the morning until eight at night five days a week and then a half day on Saturday. If he retired, he'd die.

Nobody punched a clock, the partner explained. Come and go as you please. Just get the work done.

Mitch said he got the message. Sixteen hours a day would be nothing new.

Avery complimented him on the new suit. There was an unwritten dress code, and it was apparent Mitch had caught on. Avery had a tailor, an old Korean in South Memphis, he would recommend when Mitch could afford it. Fifteen hundred a suit. Mitch said he would wait a year or two.

An attorney from one of the bigger firms interrupted and spoke to Avery. He offered his sympathies and asked about the families. He and Joe Hodge had worked together on a case last year, and he couldn't believe it. Avery introduced him to Mitch. He was at the funeral, he said. They waited for him to leave, but he rambled on and on about how sorry he was. It was obvious he wanted details. Avery offered none, and he finally left.

By two, the power lunches were losing steam, and the crowd thinned. Avery signed the check, and the maître d' led them to the door. The chauffeur stood patiently by the rear of the limo. Mitch crawled into the back and sank into the heavy leather seat. He watched the buildings and the traffic. He looked at the pedestrians scurrying along the hot sidewalks and wondered how many of them had seen the inside of a limo or the inside of the Manhattan Club. How many of them would be rich in ten years? He smiled, and felt good. Harvard was a million miles away. Harvard with no student loans. Kentucky was in another world. His past was forgotten. He had arrived.

The decorator was waiting in his office. Avery excused himself and asked Mitch to be in his office in an hour to begin work. She had books full of office furniture and samples of everything. He asked for suggestions, listened with as much interest as he could muster, then told her he trusted her judgment and she could pick out whatever she felt was appropriate. She liked the solid cherry work desk, no drawers, burgundy leather wing chairs and a very expensive oriental rug. Mitch said it was marvelous.

She left and he sat behind the old desk, one that looked fine and would have suited him except that it was considered used and therefore not good enough for a new lawyer at Bendini, Lambert & Locke. The office was fifteen by fifteen, with two six-foot windows facing north and staring directly into the second floor of the old building next door. Not much of a view. With a strain, he could see a glimpse of the river to the north-west. The walls were sheet-rock and bare. She had picked out some artwork. He determined that the Ego Wall would face the desk, behind the wing chairs. The diplomas, etc., would have to be mounted and framed. The office was big, for an associate. Much larger than the cubbyholes where the rookies were placed in New York and Chicago. It would do for a couple of years. Then on to one with a better view. Then a corner office, one of those power ones.

Miss Nina Huff knocked on the door and introduced herself as the secretary. She was a heavyset woman of forty-five, and with one glance it was not difficult to understand why she was still single. With no family to support, it was evident she spent her money on clothes and makeup – all to no avail. Mitch wondered why she did not invest in a fitness counselor. She informed him forthrightly that she had been with the firm eight and a half years now and knew all there was to know about office procedure. If he had a question, just ask her. He thanked her for that. She had been in the typing pool and was grateful for the return to general secretarial duties. He nodded as though he understood completely. She asked if he knew how to operate the dictating equipment. Yes, he said. In fact, the year before he had worked for a three-hundred-man firm on Wall Street and that firm owned the very latest in office technology. But if he had a problem he would ask her, he promised.

'What's your wife's name?' she asked.

'Why is that important?' he asked.

'Because when she calls, I would like to know her name so that I can be real sweet and friendly to her on the phone.'

'Abby.'

'How do you like your coffee?'

'Black, but I'll fix it myself.'

'I don't mind fixing your coffee for you. It's part of the job.'

'I'll fix it myself.'

'All the secretaries do it.'

'If you ever touch my coffee, I'll see to it that you're sent to the mail room to lick stamps.'

'We have an automated licker. Do they lick stamps on Wall Street?'

'It was a figure of speech.'

'Well, I've memorized your wife's name and we've settled the issue of coffee, so I guess I'm ready to start.'

'In the morning. Be here at eight-thirty.'

'Yes, boss.' She left and Mitch smiled to himself. She was a real smart-ass, but she would be fun.

Lamar was next. He was late for a meeting with Nathan Locke, but he wanted to stop by and check on his friend. He was pleased their offices were close. He apologized again for last Thursday's dinner. Yes, he and Kay and the kids would be there at seven to inspect the new house and the furniture.

Hunter Quin was five. His sister Holly was seven. They both ate the spaghetti with perfect manners from the brand-new dining table and dutifully ignored the grown-up talk circulating around them. Abby watched the two and dreamed of babies. Mitch thought they were cute, but was not inspired. He was busy recalling the events of the day.

The women ate quickly, then left to look at the furniture and talk about the remodeling. The children took Hearsay to the backyard.

'I'm a little surprised they put you with Tolleson,' Lamar said, wiping his mouth.

'Why is that?'

'I don't think he's ever supervised an associate.'

'Any particular reason?'

'Not really. He's a great guy, but not much of a team player. Sort of a loner. Prefers to work by himself. He and his wife are having some problems, and there's talk that they've separated. But he keeps it to himself.'

Mitch pushed his plate away and sipped the iced tea. 'Is he a good lawyer?'

'Yes, very good. They're all good if they make partner. A lot of his clients are rich people with millions to put in tax shelters. He sets up limited partnerships. Many of his shelters are risky, and he's known for his willingness to take chances and fight with the IRS later. Most of his clients are big-time risk takers. You'll do a lot of research looking for ways to bend the tax laws. It'll be fun.'

'He spent half of lunch lecturing on billing.'

'It's vital. There's always the pressure to bill more and more. All we have to sell is our time. Once you pass the bar your billing will be monitored weekly by Tolleson and Royce McKnight. It's all computerized and they can tell down to the dime how productive you are. You'll be expected to bill thirty to forty hours a week for the first six months. Then fifty for a couple of years. Before they'll consider you for partner, you've got to hit sixty hours a week consistently over a period of years. No active partner bills less than sixty a week – most of it at the maximum rate.'

'That's a lot of hours.'

'Sounds that way, but it's deceptive. Most good lawyers can work eight or nine hours a day and bill twelve. It's called padding. It's not exactly fair to the client, but it's something everybody does. The great firms have been built by padding files. It's the name of the game.'

'Sounds unethical.'

'So is ambulance chasing by plaintiff's lawyers. It's unethical for a dope lawyer to take his fee in cash if he has a reason to believe the money is dirty. A lot of things are unethical. What about the doctor who sees a hundred Medicare patients a day? Or the one who performs unnecessary surgery? Some of the most unethical people I've met have been my own clients. It's easy to pad a file when your client is a multimillionaire who wants to screw the government and wants you to do it legally. We all do it.'

'Do they teach it?'

'No. You just sort of learn it. You'll start off working long, crazy hours, but you can't do it forever. So you start taking shortcuts. Believe me, Mitch, after you've been with us a year you'll know how to work ten hours and bill twice that much. It's sort of a sixth sense lawyers acquire.'

'What else will I acquire?'

Lamar rattled his ice cubes and thought for a moment. 'A certain amount of cynicism. This business works on you. When you were in law school you had some noble idea of what a lawyer should be. A champion of individual rights; a defender of the Constitution; a guardian of the oppressed; an advocate for your client's principles. Then after you practice for six months you realize we're nothing but hired guns.

Mouthpieces for sale to the highest bidder, available to any body, any crook, any sleazebag with enough money to pay our outrageous fees. Nothing shocks you. It's supposed to be an honorable profession, but you'll meet so many crooked lawyers you'll want to quit and find an honest job. Yeah, Mitch, you'll get cynical. And it's sad, really.'

'You shouldn't be telling me this at this stage of my career.'

'The money makes up for it. It's amazing how much drudgery you can endure at two hundred thousand a year.'

'Drudgery? You make it sound terrible.'

'I'm sorry. It's not that bad. My perspective on life changed radically last Thursday.'

'You want to look at the house? It's marvelous.'

'Maybe some other time. Let's just talk.'

SIX

At five A.M. the alarm clock exploded on the new bed table under the new lamp, and was immediately silenced. Mitch staggered through the dark house and found Hearsay waiting at the back door. He released him into the backyard and headed for the shower. Twenty minutes later he found his wife under the covers and kissed her goodbye. She did not respond.

With no traffic to fight, the office was ten minutes away. He had decided his day would start at five-thirty, unless someone could top that, then he would be there at five, or four-thirty, or whenever it took to be first. Sleep was a nuisance. He would be the first lawyer to arrive at the Bendini Building on this day, and every day until he became a partner. If it took the others ten years, he could do it in seven. He would become the youngest partner in the history of the firm, he had decided.

The vacant lot next to the Bendini Building had a ten-foot chain link fence around it and a guard by the gate. There was a parking place inside with his name spraypainted between the yellow lines. He stopped by the gate and waited. The uniformed guard emerged from the darkness and approached the driver's door. Mitch pushed a button, lowered the window and produced a plastic card with his picture on it.

'You must be the new man,' the guard said as he held the card.

'Yes. Mitch McDeere.'

'I can read. I should've known by the car.'

'What's your name?' Mitch asked.

'Dutch Hendrix. Worked for the Memphis Police Department for thirty-three years.'

'Nice to meet you, Dutch.'

'Yeah. Same to you. You start early, don't you?'

Mitch smiled and took the ID card. 'No, I thought everyone would be here.'

Dutch managed a smile. 'You're the first. Mr. Locke will be along shortly.'

The gate opened and Dutch ordered him through. He found his name in white on the asphalt and parked the spotless BMW all by itself on the third row from the building. He grabbed his empty burgundy eel-skin attaché case from the rear seat and gently closed the door. Another guard waited by the rear entrance. Mitch introduced himself and watched as the door was unlocked. He checked his watch. Exactly five-thirty. He was relieved that this hour was early enough. The rest of the firm was still asleep.

He flipped on the light switch in his office, and laid the attaché case on the temporary desk. He headed for the coffee room down the hall, turning on lights as he went. The coffee-pot was one of those industrial sizes with multi-levels, multi-burners, multi-pots and no apparent instructions on how to operate any of it. He studied this machine for a moment as he emptied a pack of coffee into the filter. He poured water through one of the holes in the top and smiled when it began dripping in the right place.

In one corner of his office were three cardboard boxes full of books, files, legal pads and class notes he had accumulated in the previous three years. He sat the first one on his desk and began removing its contents. The materials were categorized and placed in neat little piles around the desk.

After two cups of coffee, he found the bar review materials in box number three. He walked to the window and opened the blinds. It was still dark. He did not notice the figure suddenly appear in the doorway.

'Good morning!'

Mitch spun from the window and gawked at the man. 'You scared me,' he said, and breathed deeply.

'I'm sorry. I'm Nathan Locke. I don't believe we've met.'

'I'm Mitch McDeere. The new man.' They shook hands.

'Yes, I know. I apologize for not meeting you earlier. I was busy during your earlier visits. I think I saw you at the funerals Monday.'

Mitch nodded and knew for certain he had never been within a hundred yards of Nathan Locke. He would have remembered. It was the eyes, the cold black eyes with layers of black wrinkles around them. Great eyes. Unforgettable eyes. His hair was white and thin on top with thickets around the ears, and the whiteness contrasted sharply with the rest of his face. When he spoke, the eyes narrowed and the black pupils glowed fiercely. Sinister eyes. Knowing eyes.

'Maybe so,' Mitch said, captivated by the most evil face he had ever encountered. 'Maybe so.'

'I see you're an early riser.'

'Yes, sir.'

'Well, good to have you.'

Nathan Locke withdrew from the doorway and disappeared. Mitch checked the hall, then closed the door. No wonder they keep him on the fourth floor away from everyone, he thought. Now he understood why he didn't meet Nathan Locke before he signed on. He might have had second thoughts. Probably hid him from all the prospective recruits. He had, without a doubt, the most ominous, evil presence Mitch had ever felt. It was the eyes, he said to himself again, as he propped his feet on the desk and sipped coffee. The eyes.

As Mitch expected, Nina brought food when she reported at eight-thirty. She offered Mitch a dough-nut, and he took two. She inquired as to whether she should bring enough food every morning, and Mitch said he thought it would be nice of her.

'What's that?' she asked, pointing at the stacks of files and notes on the desk.

'That's our project for the day. We need to get this stuff organized.'

'No dictating?'

'Not yet. I meet with Avery in a few minutes. I need this mess filed away in some order.'

'How exciting,' she said as she headed for the coffee room.

Avery Tolleson was waiting with a thick, expandable file, which he handed to Mitch. 'This is the Capps file. Part of it. Our client's name is Sonny Capps. He lives in Houston now, but grew up in Arkansas. Worth about thirty million and keeps his thumb on every penny of it. His father gave him an old barge line just before he died, and he turned it into the largest towing service on the Mississippi River. Now he has ships, or boats, as he calls them, all over the world. We do eighty percent of his legal work, everything but the litigation. He wants to set up another limited partner-ship to purchase another fleet of tankers, this one from the family of some dead Chink in Hong Kong. Capps is usually the general partner, and he'll bring in as many as twenty-five limited partners to spread the risk and pool their resources. This deal is worth about sixty-five million. I've done several limited partnerships for him and they're all different, all complicated. And he is extremely difficult to deal with. He's a perfectionist and thinks he knows more than I do. You will not be talking to him. In fact, no one here talks to him but me. That file is a portion of the last partnership I did for him. It contains, among other things, a prospectus, an agreement to form a partnership, letters of intent, disclosure statements and the limited partnership agreement itself. Read every word of it. Then I want you to prepare a rough draft of the partnership agreement for this venture.'

The file suddenly grew heavier. Perhaps five-thirty was not early enough.

The partner continued. 'We have about forty days, according to Capps, so we're already behind. Marty Kozinski was helping with this one, and as soon as I review his file I'll give it to you. Any questions?'

'What about the research?'

'Most of it is current, but you'll need to update it. Capps earned over nine million last year and paid a pittance in taxes. He doesn't believe in paying taxes, and holds me personally responsible for every dime that's sent in. It's all legal, of course, but my point is that this is high-pressure work. Millions of dollars in investment and tax savings are at stake. The venture will be scrutinized by the governments of at least three countries. So be careful.'

Mitch flipped through the documents. 'How many hours a day do I work on this?'

'As many as possible. I know the bar exam is important, but so is Sonny Capps. He paid us almost a half a million last year in legal fees.'

'I'll get it done.'

'I know you will. As I told you, your rate is one hundred an hour. Nina will go over the time records with you today. Remember, don't ignore the billing.'

'How could I forget?'

Oliver Lambert and Nathan Locke stood before the metal door on the fifth floor and stared at the camera above. Something clicked loudly and the door opened. A guard nodded. DeVasher waited in his office.

'Good morning, Ollie,' he said quietly while ignoring the other partner.

'What's the latest?' Locke snapped in DeVasher's direction without looking at him.

'From where?' DeVasher asked calmly.

'Chicago.'

'They're very anxious up there, Nat. Regardless of what you believe, they don't like to get their hands dirty. And, frankly, they just don't understand why they have to.'

'What do you mean?'

'They're asking some tough questions, like why can't we keep our people in line?'

'And what're you telling them?'

'That everything's okay. Wonderful. The great Bendini firm is solid. The leaks have been plugged. Business as usual. No problems.'

'How much damage did they do?' asked Oliver Lambert.

'We're not sure. We'll never be sure, but I don't think they ever talked. They had decided to, no doubt about that, but I don't think they did. We've got it from a pretty good source there were FBI agents en route to the island the day of the accident, so we think they planned to rendezvous to spill their guts.'

'How do you know this?' asked Locke.

'Come on, Nat. We've got our sources. Plus, we had people all over the island. We do good work, you know.'

'Evidently.'

'Was it messy?'

'No, no. Very professional.'

'How'd the native get in the way?'

'We had to make it look good, Ollie.'

'What about the authorities down there?'

'What authorities? It's a tiny, peaceful island, Ollie. Last year they had one murder and four diving accidents. As far as they're concerned, it's just another accident. Three accidental drownings.'

'What about the FBI?' asked Locke.

'Don't know.'

'I thought you had a source.'

'We do. But we can't find him. We've heard nothing as of yesterday. Our people are still on the island and they've noticed nothing unusual.'

'How long will you stay there?'

'Couple of weeks.'

'What happens if the FBI shows up?' asked Locke.

'We watch them real close. We'll see them when they get off the plane. We'll follow them to their hotel rooms. We may even bug their phones. We'll know what they eat for breakfast and what they talk about. We'll assign three of our guys for every one of theirs, and when they go to the toilet we'll know it. There ain't nothing for them to find, Nat. I told you it was a clean job, very professional. No evidence. Relax.'

'This makes me sick, DeVasher,' Lambert said.

'You think I like it, Ollie? What do you want us to do? Sit back and let them talk? Come on, Ollie, we're all human. I didn't want to do it, but Lazarov said do it. You wanna argue with Lazarov, go ahead. They'll find you floating somewhere. Those boys were up to no good. They should've kept quiet, driven their little fancy cars and played big-shot lawyers. No, they gotta get sanctimonious.'

Nathan Locke lit a cigarette and blew a heavy cloud of smoke in the general direction of DeVasher. The three sat in silence for a moment as the smoke settled across his desk. He glared at Black Eyes but said nothing.

Oliver Lambert stood and stared at the blank wall next to the door. 'Why did you want to see us?' he asked.

DeVasher took a deep breath. 'Chicago wants to bug the home phones of all nonpartners.'

'I told you,' Lambert said to Locke.

'It wasn't my idea, but they insist on it. They're very nervous up there, and they wanna take some extra precautions. You can't blame them.'

'Don't you think it's going a bit too far?' asked Lambert.

'Yeah, it's totally unnecessary. But Chicago doesn't think so.'

'When?' asked Locke.

'Next week or so. It'll take a few days.'

'All of them?'

'Yes. That's what they said.'

'Even McDeere?'

'Yes. Even McDeere. I think Tarrance will try again, and he might start at the bottom this time.'

'I met McDeere this morning,' said Locke. 'He was here before me.'

'Five thirty-two,' answered DeVasher.

The law school memorabilia were removed to the floor and the Capps file spread across the desk. Nina brought a chicken salad sandwich back from lunch, and he ate it as he read and as she filed away the junk on the floor. Shortly after one, Wally Hudson, or J. Walter Hudson as the firm letterhead declared him, arrived to begin the study for the bar exam. Contracts were his specialty. He was a five-year member of the firm and the only Virginia man, which he found odd because Virginia had the best law school in the country, in his opinion. He had spent the last two years developing a new review course for the contracts section of the exam. He was quite anxious to try it on someone, and McDeere happened to be the man. He handed Mitch a heavy three-ring notebook that was at least four inches thick and weighed as much as the Capps file.

The exam would last for four days and consist of three parts, Wally explained. The first day would be a four-hour multiple-choice exam on ethics. Gill Vaughn, one of the partners, was the resident expert on ethics and would supervise that portion of the review. The second day would be an eight-hour exam known simply as multi-state. It covered most areas of the law common to all states. It, too, was multiple choice and the questions were very deceptive. Then the heavy action. Days three and four would be eight hours each and cover fifteen areas of substantive law. Contracts, Uniform Commercial Code, real estate, torts, domestic relations, wills, estates, taxation, workmen's compensation, constitutional law, federal trial procedure, criminal procedure, corporations, partnerships, insurance and debtor-creditor relations. All answers would be in essay form, and the questions would emphasize Tennessee law. The firm had a review plan for each of the fifteen sections.

'You mean fifteen of these?' Mitch asked as he lifted the notebook.

Wally smiled. 'Yes. We're very thorough. No one in this firm has ever flunked –'

'I know. I know. I won't be the first.'

'You and I will meet at least once a week for the next six weeks to go through the materials. Each session will last about two hours, so you can plan accordingly. I would suggest each Wednesday at three.'

'Morning or afternoon?'

'Afternoon.'

'That's fine.'

'As you know, contracts and the Uniform Commercial Code go hand in hand, so I've incorporated the UCC into those materials. We'll cover both, but it'll take more time. A typical bar exam is loaded with commercial transactions. Those problems make great essay questions, so that notebook will be very important. I've included actual questions from old exams, along with the model answers. It's fascinating reading.'

'I can't wait.'

'Take the first eighty pages for next week. You'll find some essay questions you'll need to answer.'

'You mean homework?'

'Absolutely. I'll grade it next week. It's very important to practice these questions each week.'

'This could be worse than law school.'

'It's much more important than law school. We take it very seriously. We have a committee to monitor your progress from now until you sit for the exam. We'll be watching very closely.'

'Who's on the committee?'

'Myself, Avery Tolleson, Royce McKnight, Randall Dunbar and Kendall Mahan. We'll meet each Friday to assess your progress.'

Wally produced a smaller, letter-sized notebook and laid it on the desk. 'This is your daily log. You are to record the hours spent studying for the exam and the subjects studied. I'll pick it up every Friday morning before the committee meets. Any questions?'

'I can't think of any,' Mitch said as he laid the notebook on top of the Capps file.

'Good. See you next Wednesday at three.'

Less than ten seconds after he left, Randall Dunbar walked in with a thick notebook remarkably similar to the one left behind by Wally. In fact, it was identical, but not quite as thick. Dunbar was head of real estate and had handled the purchase and sale of the McDeere home in May. He handed Mitch the notebook, labeled *Real Estate Law*, and explained how his specialty was the most critical part of the exam. Everything goes back to property, he said. He had carefully prepared the materials himself over the past ten years and confessed that he had often thought of publishing them as an authoritative work on property rights and land financing. He would need at least one hour a week, preferably on Tuesday afternoon. He talked for an hour about how different the exam was thirty years ago when he took it.

Kendall Mahan added a new twist. He wanted to meet on Saturday mornings. Early, say seven-thirty.

'No problem,' Mitch said as he took the notebook and placed it next to the others. This one was for constitutional law, a favorite of Kendall's, although he seldom got to use it, he said. It was the most important section of the exam, or at least it had been when he took it five years ago. He had published an article on First Amendment rights in the *Columbia Law Review* in his senior year there. A copy of it was in the notebook, in case Mitch wanted to read it. He promised to do so almost immediately.

The procession continued throughout the afternoon until half of the firm had stopped by with notebooks, assignments of homework and requests for weekly meetings. No fewer than six reminded him that no member of the firm had ever failed the bar exam.

When his secretary said goodbye at five, the small desk was covered with enough bar review materials to choke a ten man firm. Unable to speak, he simply smiled at her and returned to Wally's version of contract law. Food crossed his mind an hour later. Then, for the first time in twelve hours, he thought of Abby. He called her.

'I won't be home for a while,' he said.

'But I'm cooking dinner.'

'Leave it on the stove,' he said, somewhat shortly.

There was a pause. 'When will you be home?' she asked with slow, precise words.

'In a few hours.'

'A few hours. You've already been there half the day.'

'That's right, and I've got much more to do.'

'But it's your first day.'

'You wouldn't believe it if I told you.'

'Are you all right?'

'I'm fine. I'll be home later.'

The starting engine awakened Dutch Hendrix, and he jumped to his feet. The gate opened and he waited by it as the last car left the lot. It stopped next to him.

'Evenin', Dutch,' Mitch said.

'You just now leaving?'

'Yeah, busy day.'

Dutch flashed his light at his wrist and checked the time. Eleven-thirty.

'Well, be careful,' Dutch said.

'Yeah. See you in a few hours.'

The BMW turned onto Front Street and raced away into the night. A few hours, thought Dutch. The rookies were indeed amazing. Eighteen, twenty hours a day, six days a week. Sometimes seven. They all planned to be the world's greatest lawyer and make a million dollars overnight. Sometimes they worked around the clock, slept at their desks. He had seen it all. But they couldn't last. The human body was not meant for such abuse. After about six months they lost steam. They would cut back to fifteen hours a day, six days a week. Then five and a half. Then twelve hours a day.

No one could work a hundred hours a week for more than six months.

SEVEN

One secretary dug through a file cabinet in search of something Avery needed immediately. The other secretary stood in front of his desk with a steno pad, occasionally writing down the instructions he gave when he stopped yelling into the receiver of his phone and listened to whoever was on the other end. Three red lights were blinking on the phone. When he spoke into the receiver the secretaries spoke sharply to each other. Mitch walked slowly into the office and stood by the door.

'Quiet!' Avery yelled to the secretaries.

The one in the file cabinet slammed the drawer and went to the next file cabinet, where she bent over and pulled the bottom drawer. Avery snapped his fingers at the other one and pointed at his desk calendar. He hung up without saying goodbye.

'What's my schedule for today?' he asked while pulling a file from his credenza.

'Ten A.M. meeting with the IRS downtown. One P.M. meeting with Nathan Locke on the Spinosa file. Three-thirty, partners' meeting. Tomorrow you're in tax court all day, and you're supposed to prepare all day today.'

'Great. Cancel everything. Check the flights to Houston Saturday afternoon and the return flights Monday, early Monday.'

'Yes, sir.'

'Mitch! Where's the Capps file?'

'On my desk.'

'How much have you done?'

'I've read through most of it.'

'We need to get in high gear. That was Sonny Capps on the phone. He wants to meet Saturday morning in Houston, and he wants a rough draft of the limited partnership agreement.'

Mitch felt a nervous pain in his empty stomach. If he recalled correctly, the agreement was a hundred and forty some pages long.

'Just a rough draft,' Avery said as he pointed to a secretary.

'No problem,' Mitch said with as much confidence as he could muster. 'It may not be perfect, but I'll have a rough draft.'

'I need it by noon Saturday, as perfect as possible. I'll get one of my secretaries to show Nina where the form agreements are in the memory bank. That will save some dictation and typing. I know this is unfair, but there's nothing fair about Sonny Capps. He's very demanding. He told me the deal must close in twenty days or it's dead. Everything is waiting on us.'

'I'll get it done.'

'Good. Let's meet at eight in the morning to see where we are.'

Avery punched one of the blinking lights and began arguing into the receiver. Mitch walked to his office and looked for the Capps file under the fifteen notebooks. Nina stuck her head in the door.

'Oliver Lambert wants to see you.'

'When?' Mitch asked.

'As soon as you can get there.'

Mitch looked at his watch. Three hours at the office and he was ready to call it a day. 'Can it wait?'

'I don't think so. Mr. Lambert doesn't usually wait for anybody.'

'I see.'

'You'd better go.'

'What does he want?'

'His secretary didn't say.'

He put on his coat, straightened his tie and raced upstairs to the fourth floor, where Mr. Lambert's secretary was waiting. She introduced herself and informed him she had been with the firm for thirty-one years. In fact, she was the second secretary hired by Mr. Anthony Bendini after he moved to Memphis. Ida Renfroe was her name, but everyone called her Mrs. Ida. She showed him into the big office and closed the door.

Oliver Lambert stood behind his desk and removed his reading glasses. He smiled warmly and laid his pipe in the brass holder. 'Good morning, Mitch,' he said softly, as if time meant nothing. 'Let's sit over there.' He waved to the sofa.

'Would you like coffee?' Mr. Lambert asked.

'No, thanks.'

Mitch sank into the couch and the partner sat in a stiff wing chair, two feet away and three feet higher. Mitch unbuttoned his coat and tried to relax. He crossed his legs and glanced at his new pair of Cole-Haans. Two hundred bucks. That was an hour's work for an associate at this money-printing factory. He tried to relax. But he could feel the panic in Avery's voice and see the desperation in his eyes when he held the phone and listened to this Capps fellow on the other end. This, his second full day on the job, and his head was pounding and his stomach hurting.

Mr. Lambert smiled downward with his best sincere grandfatherly smile. It was time for a lecture of some sort. He wore a brilliant white shirt, button-down, all-cotton, pinpoint, with a small, dark silk bow tie which bestowed upon him a look of extreme intelligence and wisdom. As always, he was tanned beyond the usual midsummer Memphis scorched bronzeness. His teeth sparkled like diamonds. A sixty-year-old model.

'Just a couple of things, Mitch,' he said. 'I understand you've become quite busy.'

'Yes, sir, quite.'

'Panic is a way of life in a major law firm, and clients like Sonny Capps can cause ulcers. Our clients are our only assets, so we kill ourselves for them.'

Mitch smiled and frowned at the same time.

'Two things, Mitch. First, my wife and I want you and Abby to have dinner with us Saturday. We dine out quite often, and we enjoy having our friends with us. I am somewhat of a chef myself, and I appreciate fine food and drink. We usually reserve a large table at one of our favorite restaurants in town, invite our friends and spend the evening with a nine-course meal and the rarest of wines. Will you and Abby be free on Saturday?'

'Of course.'

'Kendall Mahan, Wally Hudson, Lamar Quin and their wives will also be there.'

'We'd be delighted.'

'Good. My favorite place in Memphis is Justine's. It's an old French restaurant with exquisite cuisine and an impressive wine list. Say seven Saturday?'

'We'll be there.'

'Second, there's something we need to discuss. I'm sure you're aware of it, but it's worth mentioning. It's very important to us. I know they taught you at Harvard that there exists a confidential relationship between yourself, as a lawyer, and your client. It's a privileged relationship and you can never be forced to divulge anything a client tells you. It's strictly confidential. It's a violation of our ethics if we discuss our client's business. Now, this applies to every lawyer,

84

but at this firm we take this professional relationship very seriously. We don't discuss a client's business with anyone. Not other lawyers. Not spouses. Sometimes, not even each other. As a rule, we don't talk at home, and our wives have learned not to ask. The less you say, the better off you are. Mr. Bendini was a great believer in secrecy, and he taught us well. You will never hear a member of this firm mention even so much as a client's name outside this building. That's how serious we are.'

Where's he going with this? Mitch asked himself. Any second year law student could give this speech. 'I understand that, Mr. Lambert, and you don't have to worry about me.'

'"Loose tongues lose lawsuits." That was Mr. Bendini's motto, and he applied it to everything. We simply do not discuss our clients' business with anyone, and that includes our wives. We're very quiet, very secretive, and we like it that way. You'll meet other lawyers around town and sooner or later they'll ask something about our firm, or about a client. We don't talk, understand?'

'Of course, Mr. Lambert.'

'Good. We're very proud of you, Mitch. You'll make a great lawyer. And a very rich lawyer. See you Saturday.'

Mrs. Ida had a message for Mitch. Mr. Tolleson needed him at once. He thanked her and raced down the stairs, down the hallway, past his office, to the big one in the corner. There were now three secretaries digging and whispering to each other while the boss yelled into the telephone. Mitch found a safe spot in a chair by the door and watched the circus. The women pulled files and notebooks and mumbled in strange tongues among themselves. Occasionally Avery would snap his fingers and point here and there and they would jump like scared rabbits.

After a few minutes he slammed the phone down, again without saying goodbye. He glared at Mitch.

'Sonny Capps again. The Chinese want seventy-five million and he's agreed to pay it. There will be forty-one limited partners instead of twenty-five. We have twenty days, or the deal is off.'

Two of the secretaries walked over to Mitch and handed him thick expandable files.

'Can you handle it?' Avery asked, almost with a sneer. The secretaries looked at him.

Mitch grabbed the files and headed for the door. 'Of course I can handle it. Is that all?'

'It's enough. I don't want you to work on anything but that file between now and Saturday, understand?'

'Yes, boss.'

In his office he removed the bar review materials, all fifteen notebooks, and piled them in a corner. The Capps file was arranged neatly across the desk. He breathed deeply and began reading. There was a knock at the door.

'Who is it?'

Nina stuck her head through. 'I hate to tell you this, but your new furniture is here.'

He rubbed his temples and mumbled incoherently.

'Perhaps you could work in the library for a couple of hours.'

'Perhaps.'

They repacked the Capps file and moved the fifteen notebooks into the hall, where two large black men waited with a row of bulky cardboard boxes and an oriental rug.

Nina followed him to the second floor library.

'I'm supposed to meet with Lamar Quin at two to study for the bar exam. Call him and cancel. Tell him I'll explain later.'

'You have a two o'clock meeting with Gill Vaughn,' she said.

'Cancel that one too.'

'He's a partner.'

'Cancel it. I'll make it up later.'

'It's not wise.'

'Just do as I say.'

'You're the boss.'

'Thank you.'

The paperhanger was a short muscle-bound woman advanced in years but conditioned to hard work and superbly trained. For almost forty years now, she explained to Abby, she had hung expensive paper in the finest homes in Memphis. She talked constantly, but wasted no motion. She cut precisely, like a surgeon, then applied glue like an artist. While it dried, she removed her tape measure from her leather work belt and analyzed the remaining corner of the dining room. She mumbled numbers which Abby could not decipher. She gauged the length and height in four different places, then committed it all to memory. She ascended the stepladder and instructed Abby to hand her a roll of paper. It fit perfectly. She pressed it firmly to the wall and commented for the hundredth time on how nice the paper was, how expensive, how long it would look good and last. She liked the color too. It blended wonderfully with the curtains and the rug. Abby had long since grown tired of saying thanks. She nodded and looked at her watch. It was time to start dinner.

When the wall was finished, Abby announced it was quitting time and asked her to return at nine the next morning. The lady said certainly, and began cleaning up her mess. She was being paid twelve dollars an hour, cash, and was agreeable to almost anything. Abby admired the room. They would finish it tomorrow, and the wallpapering would be complete except for two bathrooms and the den. The painting was scheduled to begin next week. The glue from the paper and the wet lacquer from the mantel and the newness of the furniture combined for a wonderful fresh aroma. Just like a new house.

Abby said goodbye to the paperhanger and went to the bedroom where she undressed and lay across her bed. She called her husband, spoke briefly to Nina and was told he was in a meeting and would be a while. Nina said he would call. Abby stretched her long, sore legs and rubbed her shoulders. The ceiling fan spun slowly above her. Mitch would be home, eventually. He would work a hundred hours a week for a while, then cut back to eighty. She could wait.

She awoke an hour later and jumped from the bed. It was almost six. Veal piccata. Veal piccata. She stepped into a pair of khaki walking shorts and slipped on a white polo. She ran to the kitchen, which was finished except for some paint and a set of curtains due in next week. She found the recipe in a pasta cookbook and arranged the ingredients neatly on the countertop. There had been little red meat in law school, maybe an occasional hamburger steak. When she cooked, it had been chicken this or chicken that. There had been a lot of sandwiches and hot dogs.

But now, with all this sudden affluence, it was time to learn to cook. In the first week she prepared something new every night, and they ate whenever he got home. She planned the meals, studied the cookbooks, experimented with the sauces. For no apparent reason, Mitch liked Italian food, and with spaghetti and pork capellini tried and perfected, it was time for veal piccata. She pounded the veal scallops with a mallet until they were thin enough, then laid them in flour seasoned with salt and pepper. She put a pan of water on the burner for the linguine. She poured a glass of Chablis and turned on the radio. She had called the office twice since lunch, and he had not found time to return the calls. She thought of calling again, but said no. It was his turn. Dinner would be fixed, and they would eat whenever he got home.

The scallops were sautéed in hot oil for three minutes until the veal was tender; then removed. She poured the oil from the pan and added wine and lemon juice until it was boiling. She scraped and stirred the pan to thicken the sauce. She returned the veal to the pan, and added mushrooms and artichokes and butter. She covered the pan and let it simmer.

She fried bacon, sliced tomatoes, cooked linguine and poured another glass of wine. By seven, dinner was ready; bacon and tomato salad with tubettini, veal piccate, and garlic bread in the oven. He had not called. She took her wine to the patio and looked around the backyard. Hearsay ran from under the shrubs. Together they walked the length of the yard, surveying the Bermuda and stopping under the two large oaks. The remains of a long-abandoned tree house were scattered among the middle branches of the largest oak. Initials were carved on its trunk. A piece of rope hung from the other. She found a rubber ball, threw it and watched as the dog chased it. She listened for the phone through the kitchen window. It did not ring.

Hearsay froze, then growled at something next door. Mr. Rice emerged from a row of perfectly trimmed box hedges around his patio. Sweat dripped from his nose and his cotton undershirt was soaked. He removed his green gloves, and noticed Abby across the chain-link fence, under her tree. He smiled. He looked at her brown legs and smiled. He wiped his forehead with a sweaty forearm and headed for the fence.

'How are you?' he asked, breathing heavy. His thick gray hair dripped and clung to his scalp.

'Just fine, Mr. Rice. How are you?'

'Hot. Must be a hundred degrees.'

Abby slowly walked to the fence to chat. She had caught his stares for a week now, but did not mind. He was at least seventy and probably harmless. Let him look. Plus, he was a living, breathing, sweating human who could talk and maintain a conversation to some degree. The paperhanger had been her only source of dialogue since Mitch left before dawn.

'Your lawn looks great,' she said.

He wiped again and spat on the ground. 'Great? You call this great? This belongs in a magazine. I've never seen a puttin' green look this good. I deserve garden of the month, but they won't give it to me. Where's your husband?'

'At the office. He's working late.'

'It's almost eight. He must've left before sunup this morning. I take my walk at six-thirty, and he's already gone. What's with him?'

'He likes to work.'

'If I had a wife like you, I'd stay at home. Couldn't make me leave.'

Abby smiled at the compliment. 'How is Mrs. Rice?'

He frowned, then yanked a weed out of the fence. 'Not too good, I'm afraid. Not too good.' He looked away and bit his lip. Mrs. Rice was almost dead with cancer. There were no children. She had a year, the doctors said. A year at the most. They had removed most of her stomach, and the tumors were now in the lungs. She weighed ninety pounds and seldom left the bed. During their first visit across the fence his eyes watered when he talked of her and of how he would be alone after fifty-one years.

'Naw, they won't give me garden of the month. Wrong part of town. It always goes to those rich folks who hire yard boys to do all the work while they sit by the pool and sip daiquiris. It does look good, doesn't it?'

'It's incredible. How many times a week do you mow?'

'Three or four. Depends on the rain. You want me to mow yours?'

'No. I want Mitch to mow it.'

'He ain't got time, seems like. I'll watch it, and if it needs a little trim, I'll come over.'

Abby turned and looked at the kitchen window. 'Do you hear the phone?' she asked, walking away. Mr. Rice pointed to his hearing aid.

She said goodbye and ran to the house. The phone stopped when she lifted the receiver. It was eight-thirty, almost dark. She called the office, but no one answered. Maybe he was driving home.

An hour before midnight, the phone rang. Except for it and the light snoring, the second floor office was without a sound. His feet were on the new desk, crossed at the ankles and numb from lack of circulation. The rest of the body slouched comfortably in the thick leather executive chair. He slumped to one side and intermittently exhaled the sounds of a deep sleep. The Capps file was strewn over the desk and one formidable looking document was held firmly against his stomach. His shoes were on the floor, next to the desk, next to a pile of documents from the Capps file. An empty potato chip bag was between the shoes.

After a dozen rings he moved, then jumped at the phone. It was his wife.

'Why haven't you called?' she asked, coolly, yet with a slight touch of concern.

'I'm sorry. I fell asleep. What time is it?' He rubbed his eyes and focused on his watch.

'Eleven. I wish you would call.'

'I did call. No one answered.'

'When?'

'Between eight and nine. Where were you?'

She did not answer. She waited. 'Are you coming home?'

'No. I need to work all night.'

'All night? You can't work all night, Mitch.'

'Of course I can work all night. Happens all the time around here. It's expected.'

'I expected you home, Mitch. And the least you could've done was call. Dinner is still on the stove.'

'I'm sorry. I'm up to my ears in deadlines and I lost track of time. I apologize.'

There was silence for a moment as she considered the apology. 'Will this become a habit, Mitch?'

'It might.'

'I see. When do you think you might be home?'

'Are you scared?'

'No, I'm not scared. I'm going to bed.'

'I'll come in around seven for a shower.'

'That's nice. If I'm asleep, don't wake me.'

She hung up. He looked at the receiver, then put it in place. On the fifth floor a security agent chuckled to himself. '"Don't wake me." That's good,' he said as he pushed a button on the computerized recorder. He punched three buttons and spoke into a small mike. 'Hey, Dutch, wake up down there.'

Dutch woke up and leaned to the intercom. 'Yeah, what is it?'

'This is Marcus upstairs, I think our boy plans to stay all night.'

'What's his problem?'

'Right now it's his wife. He forgot to call her and she fixed a real nice supper.'

'Aw, that's too bad. We've heard that before, ain't we?'

'Yeah, every rookie does it the first week. Anyway, he told her he ain't coming home till in the morning. So go back to sleep.'

Marcus pushed some more buttons and returned to his magazine.

Abby was waiting when the sun peeked between the oak trees. She sipped coffee and held the dog and listened to the quiet sounds of her neighborhood stirring to life. Sleep had been fitful. A hot shower had not eased the fatigue. She wore a white terry-cloth bathrobe, one of his, and nothing else. Her hair was wet and pulled straight back.

A car door slammed and the dog pointed inside the house. She heard him unlock the kitchen door, and moments later the sliding door to the patio opened. He laid his coat on a bench near the door and walked over to her.

'Good morning,' he said, then sat down across the wicker table.

She gave him a fake smile. 'Good morning to you.'

'You're up early,' he said in an effort at friendliness. It did not work. She smiled again and sipped her coffee.

He breathed deeply and gazed across the yard. 'Still mad about last night, I see.'

'Not really. I don't carry a grudge.'

'I said I was sorry, and I meant it. I tried to call once.'

'You could've called again.'

'Please don't divorce me, Abby. I swear it will never happen again. Just don't leave me.'

She managed a genuine grin. 'You look terrible,' she said.

'What's under the robe?'

'Nothing.'

'Let's see.'

'Why don't you take a nap? You look haggard.'

'Thanks. But I've got a nine o'clock meeting with Avery. And a ten o'clock meeting with Avery.'

'Are they trying to kill you the first week?'

'Yes, but they can't do it. I'm too much of a man. Let's go take a shower.'

'I've taken one.'

'Naked?'

'Yes.'

'Tell me about it. Tell me every detail.'

'If you'd come home at a decent hour you wouldn't feel depraved.'

'I'm sure it'll happen again, dear. There will be plenty of all-nighters. You didn't complain in law school when I studied around the clock.'

'It was different. I endured law school because I knew it would soon end. But now you're a lawyer and you will be for a long time. Is this part of it? Will you always work a thousand hours a week?'

'Abby, this is my first week.'

'That's what worries me. It will only get worse.'

'Sure it will. That's part of it, Abby. It's a cutthroat business where the weak are eaten and the strong get rich. It's a marathon. He who endures wins the gold.'

'And dies at the finish line.'

'I don't believe this. We moved here a week ago, and you're already worried about my health.'

She sipped the coffee and rubbed the dog. She was beautiful. With tired eyes, no makeup, and wet hair, she was beautiful. He stood, walked behind her and kissed her on the cheek. 'I love you,' he whispered.

She clutched his hand on her shoulder. 'Go take a shower. I'll fix breakfast.'

The table was arranged to perfection. Her grandmother's china was taken from the cabinet and used for the first time in the new home. Candles were lit in silver candlesticks. Grapefruit juice was poured in the crystal tea glasses. Linen napkins that matched the tablecloth were folded on the plates. When he finished his shower and changed into a new Burberry glen plaid, he walked to the dining room and whistled.

'What's the occasion?'

'It's a special breakfast, for a special husband.'

He sat and admired the china. The food was warming in a covered silver dish. 'What'd you cook?' he asked, smacking his lips. She pointed and he removed the lid. He stared at it.

'What's this?' he asked without looking at her.

'Veal piccata.'

'Veal what?'

'Veal piccata.'

He glanced at his watch. 'I thought it was breakfast time.'

'I cooked it for dinner last night, and I suggest you eat it.'

'Veal piccata for breakfast?'

She grinned firmly and shook her head slightly. He looked again at the dish, and for a second or two analyzed the situation.

Finally, he said, 'Smells good.'

EIGHT

Saturday morning. He slept in and didn't get to the office until seven. He didn't shave, wore jeans, an old button-down, no socks and Bass loafers. Law school attire.

The Capps agreement had been printed and reprinted late Friday. He made some further revisions, and Nina ran it again at eight Friday night. He assumed she had little or no social life, so he didn't hesitate to ask her to work late. She said she didn't mind overtime, so he asked her to work Saturday morning.

She arrived at nine, wearing a pair of jeans that would fit a nose guard. He handed her the agreement, all two hundred and six pages, with his latest changes, and asked her to run it for the fourth time. He was to meet with Avery at ten.

The office changed on Saturday. All of the associates were there, as well as most of the partners and a few of the secretaries. There were no clients, thus no dress code. There was enough denim to launch a cattle drive. No ties. Some of the preppier ones wore their finest starched Duckheads with heavily starched button-downs and seemed to crackle when they walked.

But the pressure was there, at least for Mitchell Y. McDeere, the newest associate. He had canceled his bar review meetings on Thursday, Friday and Saturday, and the fifteen notebooks sat on the shelf, gathering dust and reminding him that he would indeed become the first member to flunk the bar exam.

At ten the fourth revision was complete, and Nina ceremoniously laid it on Mitch's desk and left for the coffee room. It had grown to two hundred and nineteen pages. He had read every word four times and researched the tax code provisions until they were memorized. He marched down the hall to his partner's office and laid it on the desk. A secretary was packing a mammoth briefcase while the boss talked on the phone.

'How many pages?' Avery asked when he hung up.

'Over two hundred.'

'This is quite impressive. How rough is it?'

'Not very. That's the fourth revision since yesterday morning. It's almost perfect.'

'We'll see. I'll read it on the plane, then Capps will read it with a magnifying glass. If he finds one mistake he'll raise hell for an hour and threaten not to pay. How many hours are in this?'

'Fifty-four and a half, since Wednesday.'

'I know I've pushed, and I apologize. You've had a tough first week. But our clients sometimes push hard, and this won't be the last time we break our necks for someone who pays us two hundred dollars an hour. It's part of the business.'

'I don't mind it. I'm behind on the bar review, but I can catch up.'

'Is that little Hudson twerp giving you a hard time?'

'No.'

'If he does, let me know. He's only a five year man, and he enjoys playing professor. Thinks he's a real academic. I don't particularly like him.'

'He's no problem.'

Avery placed the agreement in the briefcase. 'Where are the prospectus and other documents?'

'I've done a very rough draft of each. You said we had twenty days.'

'We do, but let's get it done. Capps starts demanding things long before their deadlines. Are you working tomorrow?'

'I hadn't planned on it. In fact, my wife has sort of insisted we go to church.'

Avery shook his head. 'Wives can really get in the way, can't they?' He said this without expecting a reply.

Mitch did not respond.

'Let's have Capps finished by next Saturday.'

'Fine. No problem,' Mitch said.

'Have we discussed Koker-Hanks?' Avery asked while rummaging through a file.

'No.'

'Here it is. Koker-Hanks is a big general contractor out of Kansas City. Keeps about a hundred million under contract, all over the country. An outfit out of Denver called Holloway Brothers has offered to buy Koker-Hanks. They want to swap some stock, some assets, some contracts, and throw in some cash. Pretty complicated deal. Familiarize yourself with the file, and we'll discuss it Tuesday morning when I get back.'

'How much time do we have?'

'Thirty days.'

It was not quite as thick as the Capps file, but just as imposing. 'Thirty days,' Mitch mumbled.

'The deal is worth eighty million, and we'll rake off two hundred grand in fees. Not a bad deal. Every time you look at that file, charge it for an hour. Work on it whenever you can. In fact, if the name Koker-Hanks crosses your mind while you're driving to work, stick it for an hour. The sky's the limit on this one.'

Avery relished the thought of a client who would pay regardless of the charges. Mitch said goodbye and returned to his office.

About the time the cocktails were finished, while they studied the wine list and listened to Oliver Lambert's comparison of the nuances, the subtleties, the distinctions of each of the French wines, about the time Mitch and Abby realized they would much rather be home eating a pizza and watching TV, two men with the correct key entered the shiny black BMW in the parking lot of Justine's. They wore coats and ties and looked inconspicuous. They sped away innocently and drove across midtown to the new home of Mr. and Mrs. McDeere. They parked the BMW where it belonged, in the carport. The driver produced another key, and the two entered the house. Hearsay was locked in a closet in the washroom.

In the dark, a small leather attaché case was placed on the dining table. Thin disposable rubber gloves were pulled and stretched over the hands, and each took a small flashlight.

'Do the phones first,' one said.

They worked quickly, in the dark. The receiver from the kitchen phone was unplugged and laid on the table. The microphone was unscrewed and examined. A tiny drop-in transmitter, the size of a raisin, was glued in the cavity of the receiver and held firmly in place for ten seconds. When the glue became firm, the microphone was replaced and the receiver was plugged into the phone and hung on the kitchen wall. The voices, or signals, would be transmitted to a small receiver to be installed in the attic. A larger transmitter next to the receiver would send the signals across town to an antenna on top of the Bendini Building. Using the AC lines as a power source, the small bugs in the phones would transmit indefinitely.

'Get the one in the den.'

The attaché case was moved to a sofa. Above the recliner they drove a small nail into a ridge in the paneling, then removed it. A thin black cylinder, one

99

twentieth of an inch by one inch, was carefully placed in the hole. It was cemented in place with a dab of black epoxy. The microphone was invisible. A wire, the thickness of a human hair, was gently fitted into the seam of the paneling and run to the ceiling. It would be connected to a receiver in the attic.

Identical mikes were hidden in the walls of each bedroom. The men found the retractable stairs in the main hallway and climbed into the attic. One removed the receiver and transmitter from the case while the other painstakingly pulled the tiny wires from the walls. When he gathered them, he wrapped them together and laid them under the insulation and ran them to a corner where his partner was placing the transmitter in an old cardboard box. An AC line was spliced and wired to the unit to provide power and transmission. A small antenna was raised to within an inch of the roof decking.

Their breathing became heavier in the sweltering heat of the dark attic. The small plastic casing of an old radio was fitted around the transmitter, and they scattered insulation and old clothing around it. It was in a remote corner and not likely to be noticed for months, maybe years. And if it was noticed, it would appear to be only worthless junk. It could be picked up and thrown away without suspicion. They admired their handiwork for a second, then descended the stairs.

They meticulously covered their tracks and were finished in ten minutes.

Hearsay was released from the closet, and the men crept into the carport. They backed quickly out the driveway and sped into the night.

As the baked pompano was served, the BMW parked quietly next to the restaurant. The driver fished through his pockets and found the key to a maroon Jaguar, property of Mr. Kendall Mahan, attorney-at-law. The two technicians locked the BMW

100

and slid into the Jag. The Mahans lived much closer than the McDeeres, and judging from the floor plans, the job would be quicker.

On the fifth floor of the Bendini Building, Marcus stared at a panel of blinking lights and waited for some signal from 1231 East Meadowbrook. The dinner party had broken up thirty minutes earlier, and it was time to listen. A tiny yellow light flashed weakly, and he draped a headset over his ears. He pushed a button to record. He waited. A green light beside the code McD6 began flashing. It was the bedroom wall. The signals grew clearer, voices, at first faint, then very clear. He increased the volume. And listened.

'Jill Mahan is a bitch,' the female, Mrs. McDeere, was saying. 'The more she drank, the bitchier she got.'

'I think she's a blue blood of some sort,' Mr. McDeere replied.

'Her husband is okay, but she's a real snot,' Mrs. McDeere said.

'Are you drunk?' asked Mr. McDeere.

'Almost. I'm ready for passionate sex.'

Marcus increased the volume and leaned toward the blinking lights.

'Take your clothes off,' demanded Mrs. McDeere.

'We haven't done this in a while,' said Mr. McDeere.

Marcus stood and hovered above the switches and lights.

'And whose fault is that?' she asked.

'I haven't forgotten how. You're beautiful.'

'Get in the bed,' she said.

Marcus turned the dial marked VOLUME until it would go no further. He smiled at the lights and breathed heavily. He loved these associates, fresh from law school and full of energy. He smiled at the sounds of their lovemaking. He closed his eyes and watched them.

NINE

The Capps crisis passed in two weeks without disaster, thanks largely to a string of eighteen hour days by the newest member of the firm, a member who had not yet passed the bar exam and who was too busy practicing law to worry about it. In July he billed an average of fifty-nine hours a week, a firm record for a nonlawyer. Avery proudly informed the partners at the monthly meeting that McDeere's work was remarkable for a rookie. The Capps deal was closed three days ahead of schedule, thanks to McDeere. The documents totaled four hundred pages, all perfect, all meticulously researched, drafted and redrafted by McDeere. Koker-Hanks would close within a month, thanks to McDeere, and the firm would earn close to a quarter of a mill. He was a machine.

Oliver Lambert expressed concern over his study habits. The bar exam was less than three weeks away, and it was obvious to all that McDeere was not ready. He had canceled half his review sessions in July and had logged less than twenty hours. Avery said not to worry, his boy would be ready.

Fifteen days before the exam, Mitch finally complained. He was about to flunk it, he explained to Avery over lunch at the Manhattan Club, and he needed time to study. Lots of time. He could cram it in for the next two weeks and pass by the hair of his ass. But he had to be left alone. No deadlines. No emergencies. No all-nighters. He pleaded. Avery listened carefully, and apologized. He promised to ignore him for the next two weeks. Mitch said thanks.

On the first Monday in August, a firm meeting was called in the main library on the first floor. It was the meeting room, the largest of the four libraries, the showplace. Half the lawyers sat around the antique cherry conference table with twenty chairs under it. The rest stood next to the shelves of thick leather law books which had not been opened in decades. Every member was present, even Nathan Locke. He arrived late and stood next to the door by himself. He spoke to no one, and no one looked at him. Mitch stole a glance at Black Eyes when possible.

The mood was somber. No smiles. Beth Kozinski and Laura Hodge were escorted through the door by Oliver Lambert. They were seated at the front of the room facing a wall where two veiled portraits hung. They held hands and tried to smile. Mr. Lambert stood with his back to the wall and faced the small audience.

He spoke softly, his rich baritone exuding sympathy and compassion. He almost whispered at first, but the power of his voice made every sound and every syllable clear throughout the room. He looked at the two widows and told of the deep sadness the firm felt, how they would always be taken care of as long as there was a firm. He talked of Marty and Joe, of their first few years with the firm, of their importance to the firm, of the vast voids their deaths created. He spoke of their love for their families, their dedication to their homes.

The man was eloquent. He spoke in prose, with no forethought as to what the next sentence would be. The widows cried softly and wiped their eyes. And then some of the closer ones, Lamar Quin and Doug Turney, began to sniffle.

When he had said enough, he unveiled the portrait of Martin Kozinski. It was an emotional moment. There were more tears. There would be a scholarship established at the Chicago Law School in his name. The firm would set up trusts for his children's education. The family would be taken care of. Beth bit her lip, but cried louder. The seasoned, hardened, tough-as-nails negotiators of the great Bendini firm swallowed rapidly and avoided looking at each other. Only Nathan Locke was unmoved. He glared at the wall with his penetrating lasers and ignored the ceremony.

Then the portrait of Joe Hodge, and a similar biography, similar scholarship and trust funds. Mitch had heard a rumor that Hodge purchased a two-million-dollar life insurance policy four months before his death

When the eulogies were complete, Nathan Locke disappeared through the door. The lawyers surrounded the widows and offered quiet words and embraces. Mitch did not know them and had nothing to say. He walked to the front wall and examined the paintings. Next to those of Kozinski and Hodge were three slightly smaller, but equally dignified portraits. The one of the woman caught his attention. The brass plate read: 'Alice Knauss 1948–1977.'

'She was a mistake,' Avery said under his breath as he stepped next to his associate.

'What do you mean?' Mitch asked.

'Typical female lawyer. Came here from Harvard, number one in her class and carrying a chip because she was a female. Thought every man alive was a sexist and it was her mission in life to eliminate discrimination. Super-bitch. After six months we all hated her but couldn't get rid of her. She forced two partners into early retirement. Milligan still blames her for his heart attack. He was her partner.'

'Was she a good lawyer?'

'Very good, but it was impossible to appreciate her talents. She was so contentious about everything.'

'What happened to her?'

'Car wreck. Killed by a drunk driver. It was really tragic.'

'Was she the first woman?'

'Yes, and the last, unless we get sued.'

Mitch nodded to the next portrait. 'Who was he?'

'Robert Lamm. He was a good friend of mine. Emory Law School in Atlanta. He was about three years ahead of me.'

'What happened?'

'No one knows. He was an avid hunter. We hunted moose in Wyoming one winter. In 1970 he was deer hunting in Arkansas and turned up missing. They found him a month later in a ravine with a hole through his head. Autopsy said the bullet entered through the rear of his skull and blew away most of his face. They speculate the shot was fired from a high-powered rifle at long range. It was probably an accident, but we'll never know. I could never imagine anyone wanting to kill Bobby Lamm.'

The last portrait was of John Mickel, 1940–1984. 'What happened to him?' Mitch whispered.

'Probably the most tragic of all. He was not a strong man, and the pressure got to him. He drank a lot, and started drugs. Then his wife left him and they had a bitter divorce. The firm was embarrassed. After he had been here ten years, he began to fear he would not become a partner. The drinking got worse. We spent a small fortune on treatment, shrinks, everything. But nothing worked. He became depressed, then suicidal. He wrote a seven-page suicide note and blew his brains out.'

'That's terrible.'

'Sure was.'

'Where'd they find him?'

Avery cleared his throat and glanced around the room. 'In your office.'

'What!'

'Yeah, but they cleaned it up.'

'You're kidding!'

'No, I'm serious. It was years ago, and the office has been used since then. It's okay.'

Mitch was speechless.

'You're not superstitious, are you?' Avery asked with a nasty grin.

'Of course not.'

'I guess I should've told you, but it's not something we talk about.'

'Can I change offices?'

'Sure. Just flunk the bar exam and we'll give you one of those paralegal offices in the basement.'

'If I flunk it, it'll be because of you.'

'Yes, but you won't flunk it, will you?'

'If you can pass it, so can I.'

From 5 A.M. to 7 A.M. the Bendini building was empty and quiet. Nathan Locke arrived around six, but went straight to his office and locked the door. At seven, the associates began appearing and voices could be heard. By seven-thirty the firm had a quorum, and a handful of secretaries punched in. By eight the halls were full and it was chaos as usual. Concentration became difficult. Interruptions were routine. Phones beeped incessantly. By nine, all lawyers, paralegals, clerks and secretaries were either present or accounted for.

Mitch treasured the solitude of the early hours. He moved his clock up thirty minutes and began waking Dutch at five, instead of five-thirty. After making two pots of coffee, he roamed the dark halls flipping light switches and inspecting the building. Occasionally, on a clear morning, he would stand before the window in Lamar's office and watch the dawn break over the mighty Mississippi below. He would count the barges lined neatly before their tugboats plowing slowly upriver. He watched the trucks inch across the bridge in the distance. But he wasted little time. He dictated letters, briefs, summaries, memorandums and a hundred other documents for Nina to type and Avery to review. He crammed for the bar exam.

The morning after the ceremony for the dead lawyers, he found himself in the library on the first floor looking for a treatise when he again noticed the five portraits. He walked to the wall and stared at them, remembering the brief obituaries given by Avery. Five dead lawyers in fifteen years. It was a dangerous place to work. On a legal pad he scribbled their names and the years they died. It was five-thirty.

Something moved in the hallway, and he jerked to his right. In the darkness he saw Black Eyes watching. He stepped forward to the door and glared at Mitch. 'What are you doing?' he demanded.

Mitch faced him and attempted a smile. 'Good morning to you. It happens I am studying for the bar exam.'

Locke glanced at the portraits and then stared at Mitch. 'I see. Why are you so interested in them?'

'Just curious. This firm has had its share of tragedy.'

'They're all dead. A real tragedy will occur if you don't pass the bar exam.'

'I intend to pass it.'

'I've heard otherwise. Your study habits are causing concern among the partners.'

'Are the partners concerned about my excessive billing?'

'Don't get smart. You were told the bar exam has

TEN

The Saturday after the bar exam Mitch avoided his office and his house and spent the morning digging in the flower beds and waiting. With the remodeling complete, the house was now presentable, and of course the first guests had to be her parents. Abby had cleaned and polished for a week, and it was now time. She promised they wouldn't stay long, no more than a few hours. He promised to be as nice as possible.

Mitch had washed and waxed both new cars and they looked as if they had just left the showroom. The lawn had been manicured by a kid down the street. Mr. Rice had applied fertilizer for a month and it looked like a puttin' green, as he liked to say.

At noon they arrived, and he reluctantly left the flower beds. He smiled and greeted them and excused himself to go clean up. He could tell they were uncomfortable, and he wanted it that way. He took a long shower as Abby showed them every piece of furniture and every inch of wallpaper. These things impressed the Sutherlands. Small things always did. They dwelt on the things others did or did not have. He was the president of a small county bank that had been on the verge of collapse for ten years. She was too good to work and had spent all of her adult life seeking social advancement in a town where there was none to be had. She had traced her ancestry to royalty in one of the old countries, and this had always impressed the coal miners in Danesboro, Kentucky. With so much blue blood in her veins, it had fallen her duty to do nothing but drink hot tea, play bridge, talk of her husband's money, condemn the less fortunate and work tirelessly in the Garden Club. He was a stuffed shirt who jumped when she barked and lived in eternal fear of making her mad. As a team they had relentlessly pushed their daughter from birth to be the best, achieve the best, but most importantly, marry the best. Their daughter had rebelled and married a poor kid with no family except a crazy mother and a criminal brother.

'Nice place you've got here, Mitch,' Mr. Sutherland said in an effort to break the ice. They sat for lunch and began passing dishes.

'Thanks.' Nothing else, just thanks. He concentrated on the food. There would be no smiles from him at lunch. The less he said, the more uncomfortable they would be. He wanted them to feel awkward, guilty, wrong. He wanted them to sweat, to bleed. It had been their decision to boycott the wedding. It had been their stones cast, not his.

'Everything is so lovely,' her mother gushed in his direction.

'Thanks.'

'We're so proud of it, Mother,' Abby said.

The conversation immediately went to the remodeling. The men ate in silence as the women chattered on and on about what the decorator did to this room and that one. At times, Abby was almost desperate to fill in the gaps with words about whatever came to mind. Mitch almost felt sorry for her, but he kept his eyes on the table. The butter knife could have cut the tension.

'So you've found a job?' Mrs. Sutherland asked.

'Yes. I start a week from Monday. I'll be teaching third-graders at St. Andrew's Episcopal School.'

'Teaching doesn't pay much,' her father blurted.

He's relentless, thought Mitch.

'I'm not concerned with money, Dad. I'm a teacher. To me, it's the most important profession in the world. If I wanted money, I would've gone to medical school.'

'Third-graders,' her mother said. 'That's such a cute age. You'll be wanting children before long.'

Mitch had already decided that if anything would attract these people to Memphis on a regular basis, it was grandchildren. And he had decided he could wait a long time. He had never been around children. There were no nieces or nephews, except for maybe a few unknown ones Ray had scattered around the country. And he had developed no affinity for children.

'Maybe in a few years, Mother.'

Maybe after they're both dead, thought Mitch.

'You want children, don't you, Mitch?' asked the mother-in-law.

'Maybe in a few years.'

Mr. Sutherland pushed his plate away and lit a cigarette. The issue of smoking had been repeatedly discussed in the days before the visit. Mitch wanted it banned completely from his house, especially by these people. They had argued vehemently, and Abby won.

'How was the bar exam?' the father-in-law asked.

This could be interesting, Mitch thought. 'Grueling.' Abby chewed her food nervously.

'Do you think you passed?'

'I hope so.'

'When will you know?'

'Four to six weeks.'

'How long did it last?'

'Four days.'

'He's done nothing but study and work since we

moved here. I haven't seen much of him this summer,' Abby said.

Mitch smiled at his wife. The time away from home was already a sore subject, and it was amusing to hear her condone it.

'What happens if you don't pass it?' her father asked.

'I don't know. I haven't thought about it.'

'Do they give you a raise when you pass?'

Mitch decided to be nice, as he had promised. But it was difficult. 'Yes, a nice raise and a nice bonus.'

'How many lawyers are in the firm?'

'Forty.'

'My goodness,' said Mrs. Sutherland. She lit up one of hers. 'There's not that many in Dane County.'

'Where's your office?' he asked.

'Downtown.'

'Can we see it?' she asked.

'Maybe some other time. It's closed to visitors on Saturdays.' Mitch amused himself with his answer. Closed to visitors, as if it was a museum.

Abby sensed disaster and began talking about the church they had joined. It had four thousand members, a gymnasium and bowling alley. She sang in the choir and taught eight-year-olds in Sunday school. Mitch went when he was not working, but he'd been working most Sundays.

'I'm happy to see you've found a church home, Abby,' her father said piously. For years he had led the prayer each Sunday at the First Methodist Church in Danesboro, and the other six days he had tirelessly practiced greed and manipulation. According to Ray, he had also steadily but discreetly pursued whiskey and women.

An awkward silence followed as the conversation came to a halt. He lit another one. Keep smoking, old boy, Mitch thought. Keep smoking.

'Let's have dessert on the patio,' Abby said. She began clearing the table.

They bragged about his gardening skills, and he accepted the credit. The same kid down the street had pruned the trees, pulled the weeds, trimmed the hedges and edged the patio. Mitch was proficient only in pulling weeds and scooping dog crap. He could also operate the lawn sprinkler, but usually let Mr. Rice do it.

Abby served strawberry shortcake and coffee. She looked helplessly at her husband, but he was noncommittal.

'This is a real nice place you've got here,' her father said for the third time as he surveyed the backyard. Mitch could see his mind working. He had taken the measure of the house and neighborhood, and the curiosity was becoming unbearable. How much did the place cost, dammit? That's what he wanted to know. How much down? How much a month? Everything. He would keep pecking away until he could work in the questions somewhere.

'This is a lovely place,' her mother said for the tenth time.

'When was it built?' her father asked.

Mitch laid his plate on the table and cleared his throat. He could sense it coming. 'It's about fifteen years old,' he answered.

'How many square feet?'

'About twenty-two hundred,' Abby answered nervously. Mitch glared at her. His composure was vanishing.

'It's a lovely neighborhood,' her mother added helpfully.

'New loan, or did you assume one?' her father asked, as if he were interviewing a loan applicant with weak collateral.

'It's a new loan,' Mitch said, then waited. Abby waited and prayed.

He didn't wait, couldn't wait. 'What'd you pay for it?'

Mitch breathed deeply and was about to say, 'Too much.' Abby was quicker. 'We didn't pay too much, Daddy,' she said firmly with a frown. 'We're quite capable of managing our money.'

Mitch managed a smile while biting his tongue.

Mrs. Sutherland was on her feet. 'Let's go for a drive, shall we? I want to see the river and that new pyramid they've built beside it. Shall we? Come on, Harold.'

Harold wanted more information about the house, but his wife was now tugging on his arm.

'Great idea,' Abby said.

They loaded into the shiny new BMW and went to see the river. Abby asked them not to smoke in the new car. Mitch drove in silence and tried to be nice.

ELEVEN

Nina entered the office in a rush with a stack of paperwork and laid it before her boss. 'I need signatures,' she demanded, and handed him his pen.

'What is all this?' Mitch asked as he dutifully scribbled his name.

'Don't ask. Just trust me.'

'I found a misspelled word in the Landmark Partners agreement.'

'It's the computer.'

'Okay. Get the computer fixed.'

'How late are you working tonight?'

Mitch scanned the documents and signed off on each. 'I don't know. Why?'

'You look tired. Why don't you go home early, say around ten or ten-thirty, and get some rest. Your eyes are beginning to look like Nathan Locke's.'

'Very funny.'

'Your wife called.'

'I'll call her in a minute.'

When he finished she restacked the letters and documents. 'It's five o'clock. I'm leaving. Oliver Lambert is waiting on you in the first-floor library.'

'Oliver Lambert! Waiting on me?'

'That's what I said. He called not more than five minutes ago. Said it was very important.'

Mitch straightened his tie and ran down the hall,

down the stairs, and walked casually into the library. Lambert, Avery and what appeared to be most of the partners sat around the conference table. All of the associates were present, standing behind the partners. The seat at the head of the table was empty, and waiting. The room was quiet, almost solemn. There were no smiles. Lamar was close by and refused to look at him. Avery was sheepish, sort of embarrassed. Wally Hudson twirled the end of his bow tie and slowly shook his head.

'Sit down, Mitch,' Mr. Lambert said gravely. 'We have something to discuss with you.' Doug Turney closed the door.

He sat and searched for any small sign of reassurance. None. The partners rolled their chairs in his direction, squeezing together in the process. The associates surrounded him and glared downward.

'What is it?' he asked meekly, looking helplessly at Avery. Small beads of sweat surfaced above his eyebrows. His heart pounded like a jackhammer. His breathing was labored.

Oliver Lambert leaned across the edge of the table and removed his reading glasses. He frowned sincerely, as if this would be painful. 'We've just received a call from Nashville, Mitch, and we wanted to talk with you about it.'

The bar exam. The bar exam. The bar exam. History had been made. An associate of the great Bendini firm had finally flunked the bar exam. He glared at Avery, and wanted to scream, 'It's all your fault!' Avery pinched his eyebrows as if a migraine had hit and avoided eye contact. Lambert eyed the other partners suspiciously and returned to McDeere.

'We were afraid this would happen, Mitch.'

He wanted to speak, to explain that he deserved just one more chance, that the exam would be given again

116

in six months and he would ace it, that he would not embarrass them again. A thick pain hit below the belt.

'Yes, sir,' he said humbly, in defeat.

Lambert moved in for the kill. 'The folks in Nashville told us that you made the highest score on the bar exam. Congratulations, Counselor.'

The room exploded with laughter and cheers. They gathered around and shook his hand, patted his back and laughed at him. Avery rushed forward with a handkerchief and wiped his forehead. Kendall Mahan slammed three bottles of champagne on the table and began popping corks. A round was poured into plastic wineglasses. He finally breathed and broke into a smile. He slugged the champagne, and they poured him another glass.

Oliver Lambert placed his arm gently around Mitch's neck and spoke. 'Mitch, we are very proud of you. You're the third member of our firm to win the gold medal, and we think that calls for a little bonus. I have here a firm check in the amount of two thousand dollars, which I am presenting to you as a small reward for this achievement.'

There were whistles and catcalls.

'This is, of course, in addition to the substantial raise you have just earned.'

More whistles and catcalls. Mitch took the check but did not look at it.

Mr. Lambert raised his hand and asked for quiet. 'On behalf of the firm, I would like to present you with this.' Lamar handed him a package wrapped in brown paper. Mr. Lambert peeled it off and threw it on the table.

'It's a plaque which we prepared in anticipation of this day. As you can also see, it is a bronzed replica of a piece of firm stationery, complete with every name. As you can see, the name of Mitchell Y. McDeere has been added to the letterhead.'

Mitch stood and awkwardly received the award. The color had returned to his face, and the champagne was beginning to feel good. 'Thank you,' he said softly.

Three days later the Memphis paper published the names of the attorneys who passed the bar exam. Abby clipped the article for the scrapbook and sent copies to her parents and Ray.

Mitch had discovered a deli three blocks from the Bendini Building between Front Street and Riverside Drive, near the river. It was a dark hole in the wall with few customers and greasy chili dogs. He liked it because he could sneak away and proofread a document while he ate. Now that he was a full-blown associate, he could eat a hot dog for lunch and bill a hundred and fifty an hour.

A week after his name was in the paper, he sat by himself at a table in the rear of the deli and ate a chili dog with a fork. The place was empty. He read a prospectus an inch thick. The Greek who ran the place was asleep behind the cash register.

A stranger approached his table and stopped a few feet away. He unraveled a piece of Juicy Fruit, making as much noise as possible. When it was apparent he was not being seen, he walked to the table and sat down. Mitch looked across the red-checkered tablecloth and laid the document next to the iced tea.

'Can I help you?' he asked.

The stranger glanced at the counter, glanced at the empty tables and glanced behind him. 'You're McDeere, aren't you?'

It was a rich brogue, undoubtedly Brooklyn. Mitch studied him carefully. He was about forty, with a short military haircut on the sides and a wisp of gray hair hanging almost to his eyebrows. The suit was a three-piece, navy in color, made of at least ninety percent polyester. The tie was cheap imitation silk. He wasn't much of a dresser, but there was a certain neatness about him. And an air of cockiness.

'Yeah. Who are you?' Mitch asked.

He grabbed his pocket and whipped out a badge. 'Tarrance, Wayne Tarrance, special agent, FBI.' He raised his eyebrows and waited for a response.

'Have a seat,' Mitch said.

'Don't mind if I do.'

'Do you want to frisk me?'

'Not till later. I just wanted to meet you. Saw your name in the paper and heard you were the new man at Bendini, Lambert & Locke.'

'Why should that interest the FBI?'

'We watch that firm pretty close.'

Mitch lost interest in the chili dog and slid the plate to the center of the table. He added more sweetener to his tea in a large styrofoam cup.

'Would you like something to drink?' Mitch asked.

'No, thanks.'

'Why do you watch the Bendini firm?'

Tarrance smiled and looked toward the Greek. 'I can't really say at this point. We got our reasons, but I didn't come here to talk about that. I came here to meet you, and to warn you.'

'To warn me?'

'Yes, to warn you about the firm.'

'I'm listening.'

'Three things. Number one, don't trust anyone. There's not a single person in that firm you can confide in. Remember that. It will become important later on. Number two, every word you utter, whether at home, at the office or anywhere in the building, is likely to be recorded. They might even listen to you in your car.'

Mitch watched and listened intently. Tarrance was enjoying this.

119

'And number three?' Mitch asked.

'Number three, money don't grow on trees.'

'Would you care to elaborate?'

'I can't right now. I think you and I will become very close. I want you to trust me, and I know I'll have to earn your trust. So I don't want to move too fast. We can't meet at your office, or my office, and we can't talk on the phone. So from time to time I'll come find you. In the meantime, just remember those three things, and be careful.'

Tarrance stood and reached for his wallet. 'Here's my card. My home number is on the back. Use it only from a pay phone.'

Mitch studied the card. 'Why should I be calling you?'

'You won't need to for a while. But keep the card.'

Mitch placed it in his shirt pocket.

'There's one other thing,' Tarrance said. 'We saw you at the funerals of Hodge and Kozinski. Sad, really sad. Their deaths were not accidental.'

He looked down at Mitch with both hands in his pockets and smiled.

'I don't understand.'

Tarrance started for the door. 'Gimme a call sometime, but be careful. Remember, they're listening.'

A few minutes after four a horn honked and Dutch bolted to his feet. He cursed and walked in front of the headlights.

'Dammit, Mitch. It's four o'clock. What're you doing here?'

'Sorry, Dutch. Couldn't sleep. Rough night.' The gate opened.

By seven-thirty he had dictated enough work to keep Nina busy for two days. She bitched less when her nose was glued to the monitor. His immediate goal was to become the first associate to justify a second secretary.

At eight o'clock he parked himself in Lamar's office and waited. He proofed a contract and drank coffee, and told Lamar's secretary to mind her own business. He arrived at eight-fifteen.

'We need to talk,' Mitch said as he closed the door. If he believed Tarrance, the office was bugged and the conversation would be recorded. He was not sure whom to believe.

'You sound serious,' Lamar said.

'Ever hear of a guy named Tarrance, Wayne Tarrance?'

'No.'

'FBI.'

Lamar closed his eyes. 'FBI,' he mumbled.

'That's right. He had a badge and everything.'

'Where did you meet him?'

'He found me at Lansky's Deli on Union. He knew who I was, knew I'd just been admitted. Says he knows all about the firm. They watch us real close.'

'Have you told Avery?'

'No. No one but you. I'm not sure what to do.'

Lamar picked up the phone. 'We need to tell Avery. I think this has happened before.'

'What's going on, Lamar?'

Lamar talked to Avery's secretary and said it was an emergency. In a few seconds he was on the other end. 'We've got a small problem, Avery. An FBI agent contacted Mitch yesterday. He's in my office.'

Lamar listened, then said to Mitch, 'He's got me on hold. Said he was calling Lambert.'

'I take it this is pretty serious,' Mitch said.

'Yes, but don't worry. There's an explanation. It's happened before.'

Lamar held the receiver closer and listened to the

instructions. He hung up. 'They want us in Lambert's office in ten minutes.'

Avery, Royce McKnight, Oliver Lambert, Harold O'Kane and Nathan Locke were waiting. They stood nervously around the small conference table and tried to appear calm when Mitch entered the office.

'Have a seat,' Nathan Locke said with a short, plastic smile. 'We want you to tell us everything.'

'What's that?' Mitch pointed to a tape recorder in the center of the table.

'We don't want to miss anything,' Locke said, and pointed to an empty chair. Mitch sat and stared across the table at Black Eyes. Avery sat between them. No one made a sound.

'Okay. I was eating lunch yesterday at Lansky's Deli on Union. This guy walks up and sits across my table. He knows my name. Shows me a badge and says his name is Wayne Tarrance, special agent, FBI. I look at the badge, and it's real. He tells me he wants to meet because we'll get to know each other. They watch this firm real close and he warns me not to trust anyone. I ask him why, and he said he doesn't have time to explain, but he will later. I don't know what to say, so I just listen. He says he will contact me later. He gets up to leave and tells me they saw me at the funerals. Then he says the deaths of Kozinski and Hodge were not accidents. And he leaves. The entire conversation lasted less than five minutes.'

Black Eyes glared at Mitch and absorbed every word. 'Have you ever seen this man before?'

'Never.'

'Whom did you tell?'

'Only Lamar. I told him first thing this morning.'

'Your wife?'

'No.'

'Did he leave you a phone number to call?'

'No.'

'I want to know every word that was said,' Locke demanded.

'I've told you what I remember. I can't recall it verbatim.'

'Are you certain?'

'Let me think a minute.' A few things he would keep to himself. He stared at Black Eyes, and knew that Locke suspected more.

'Let's see. He said he saw my name in the paper and knew I was the new man here. That's it. I've covered everything. It was a very brief conversation.'

'Try to remember everything,' Locke persisted.

'I asked him if he wanted some of my tea. He declined.'

The tape recorder was turned off, and the partners seemed to relax a little. Locke walked to the window. 'Mitch, we've had trouble with the FBI, as well as the IRS. It's been going on for a number of years. Some of our clients are high rollers – wealthy individuals who make millions, spend millions and expect to pay little or no taxes. They pay us thousands of dollars to legally avoid taxes. We have a reputation for being very aggressive, and we don't mind taking chances if our clients instruct us to. We're talking about very sophisticated businessmen who understand risks. They pay dearly for our creativeness. Some of the shelters and write-offs we set up have been challenged by the IRS. We've slugged it out with them in tax litigation for the past twenty years. They don't like us, we don't like them. Some of our clients have not always possessed the highest degree of ethics, and they have been investigated and harassed by the FBI. For the past three years, we, too, have been harassed.

'Tarrance is a rookie looking for a big name. He's been here less than a year and has become a thorn. You are not to speak to him again. Your brief conversation yesterday was probably recorded. He is dangerous, extremely dangerous. He does not play fair, and you'll learn soon enough that most of the feds don't play fair.'

'How many of these clients have been convicted?'

'Not a single one. And we've won our share of litigation with the IRS.'

'What about Kozinski and Hodge?'

'Good question,' answered Oliver Lambert. 'We don't know what happened. It first appeared to be an accident, but now we're not sure. There was a native of the islands on board with Marty and Joe. He was the captain and divemaster. The authorities down there now tell us they suspect he was a key link in a drug ring based in Jamaica and perhaps the explosion was aimed at him. He died, of course.'

'I don't think we'll ever know,' Royce McKnight added. 'The police down there are not that sophisticated. We've chosen to protect the families, and as far as we're concerned, it was an accident. Frankly, we're not sure how to handle it.'

'Don't breathe a word of this to anyone,' Locke instructed. 'Stay away from Tarrance, and if he contacts you again, let us know immediately. Understand?'

'Yes, sir.'

'Don't even tell your wife,' Avery said.

Mitch nodded.

The grandfather's warmth returned to Oliver Lambert's face. He smiled and twirled his reading glasses. 'Mitch, we know this is frightening, but we've grown accustomed to it. Let us handle it, and trust us. We are not afraid of Mr. Tarrance, the FBI, the IRS or anybody else because we've done nothing wrong. Anthony Bendini built this firm by hard work, talent and uncompromising ethics. It has been drilled into all of us. Some of our clients have not been saints, but no lawyer can dictate morals to his client. We don't want you worrying about this. Stay away from this guy – he is very, very dangerous. If you feed him, he'll get bolder and become a nuisance.'

Locke pointed a crooked finger at Mitch. 'Further contact with Tarrance will jeopardize your future with this firm.'

'I understand,' Mitch said.

'He understands,' Avery said defensively. Locke glared at Tolleson.

'That's all we have, Mitch,' Mr. Lambert said. 'Be cautious.'

Mitch and Lamar hit the door and found the nearest stairway.

'Get DeVasher,' Locke said to Lambert, who was on the phone. Within two minutes the two senior partners had been cleared and were sitting before DeVasher's cluttered desk.

'Did you listen?' Locke asked.

'Of course I listened to it, Nat. We heard every word the boy said. You handled it real well. I think he's scared and will run from Tarrance.'

'What about Lazarov?'

'I gotta tell him. He's the boss. We can't pretend it didn't happen.'

'What will they do?'

'Nothing serious. We'll watch the boy around the clock and check all his phone calls. And wait. He's not gonna move. It's up to Tarrance. He'll find him again, and the next time we'll be there. Try to keep him in the building as much as possible. When he leaves, let us know, if you can. I don't think it's that bad, really.'

'Why would they pick McDeere?' asked Locke.

'New strategy, I guess. Kozinski and Hodge went to them, remember. Maybe they talked more than we thought. I don't know. Maybe they figure McDeere is the most vulnerable because he's fresh out of school and full of rookie idealism. And ethics – like our

125

ethical friend Ollie here. That was good, Ollie, real good.'

'Shut up, DeVasher.'

DeVasher quit smiling and bit his bottom lip. He let it pass. He looked at Locke. 'You know what the next step is, don't you? If Tarrance keeps pushing, that idiot Lazarov will call me one day and tell me to remove him. Silence him. Put him in a barrel and drop him in the Gulf. And when that happens, all of you honorable esquires will take your early retirement and leave the country.'

'Lazarov wouldn't order a hit on an agent.'

'Oh, it would be a foolish move, but then Lazarov is a fool. He's very anxious about the situation down here. He calls a lot and asks all sorts of questions. I give him all sorts of answers. Sometimes he listens, sometimes he cusses. Sometimes he says he's gotta talk to the board. But if he tells me to take out Tarrance, then we'll take out Tarrance.'

'This makes me sick at my stomach,' Lambert said.

'You wanna get sick, Ollie. You let one of your little Gucci-loafered counselors get chummy with Tarrance and start talking, you'll get a helluva lot worse than sick. Now, I suggest you boys keep McDeere so busy he won't have time to think about Tarrance.'

'My God, DeVasher, he works twenty hours a day. He started like fire and he hasn't slowed down.'

'Just watch him close. Tell Lamar Quin to get real tight with him so if he's got something on his mind, maybe he'll unload.'

'Good idea,' said Locke. He looked at Ollie. 'Let's have a long talk with Quin. He's closest to McDeere, and maybe he can get closer.'

'Look, boys,' DeVasher said, 'McDeere is scared right now. He won't make a move. If Tarrance contacts him again, he'll do what he did today. He'll run straight to Lamar Quin. He showed us who he confides in.'

'Did he tell his wife last night?' asked Locke.

'We're checking the tapes now. It'll take about an hour. We've got so damned many bugs in this city it takes six computers to find anything.'

Mitch stared through the window in Lamar's office and selected his words carefully. He said little. Suppose Tarrance was correct. Suppose everything was being recorded.

'Do you feel better?' Lamar asked.

'Yeah, I guess. It makes sense.'

'It's happened before, just like Locke said.'

'Who? Who was approached before?'

'I don't remember. Seems like it was three or four years ago.'

'But you don't remember who it was?'

'No. Why is that important?'

'I'd just like to know. I don't understand why they would pick me, the new man, the one lawyer out of forty who knows the least about this firm and its clients. Why would they pick me?'

'I don't know, Mitch. Look, why don't you do as Locke suggested? Try to forget about it and run from this guy Tarrance. You don't have to talk to him unless he's got a warrant. Tell him to get lost if he shows up again. He's dangerous.'

'Yeah, I guess you're right.' Mitch forced a smile and headed for the door. 'We're still on for dinner tomorrow night?'

'Sure. Kay wants to grill steaks and eat by the pool. Make it late, say around seven-thirty.'

'See you then.'

TWELVE

The guard called his name, frisked him and led him to a large room where a row of small booths was occupied with visitors talking and whispering through thick metal screens.

'Number fourteen,' the guard said, and pointed. Mitch walked to his booth and sat down. A minute later Ray appeared and sat between his dividers on the other side of the screen. Were it not for a scar on Ray's forehead and a few wrinkles around the eyes, they could pass for twins. Both were six-two, weighed about one-eighty, with light brown hair, small blue eyes, high cheekbones and large chins. They had always been told there was Indian blood in the family, but the dark skin had been lost through years in the coal mines.

Mitch had not been to Brushy Mountain in three years. Three years and three months. They'd exchanged letters twice a month, every month, for eight years now.

'How's your French?' Mitch finally asked. Ray's Army test scores had revealed an amazing aptitude for languages. He had served two years as a Vietnamese interpreter. He had mastered German in six months while stationed there. Spanish had taken four years, but he was forced to learn it from a dictionary in the prison library. French was his latest project.

'I'm fluent, I guess,' Ray answered. 'It's kinda hard to tell in here. I don't get much practice. Evidently they don't teach French in the projects, so most of these brothers here are unilingual. It's undoubtedly the most beautiful language.'

'Is it easy?'

'Not as easy as German. Of course, it was easier to learn German since I was living there and everybody spoke it. Did you know that fifty percent of our language comes from German through Old English?'

'No, I didn't know that.'

'It's true. English and German are first cousins.'

'What's next?'

'Probably Italian. It's a Romance language like French and Spanish and Portuguese. Maybe Russian. Maybe Greek. I've been reading about the Greek isles. I plan to go there soon.'

Mitch smiled. Ray was at least seven years away from parole.

'You think I'm kidding, don't you?' Ray asked. 'I'm checking out of here, Mitchell, and it won't be long.'

'What are your plans?'

'I can't talk. But I'm working on it.'

'Don't do it, Ray.'

'I'll need some help on the outside, and enough money to get me out of the country. A thousand should do it. You can handle that, can't you? You won't be implicated.'

'Aren't they listening to us?'

'Sometimes.'

'Let's talk about something else.'

'Sure. How's Abby?'

'She's fine.'

'Where is she?'

'Right now she's in church. She wanted to come, but I told her she wouldn't get to see you.'

'I'd like to see her. Your letters sound like y'all are

doing real well. New house, cars, country club. I'm very proud of you. You're the first McDeere in two generations to amount to a damned thing.'

'Our parents were good people, Ray. They had no opportunities and a lot of bad luck. They did the best they could.'

Ray smiled and looked away. 'Yeah, I guess so. Have you talked to Mom?'

'It's been a while.'

'Is she still in Florida?'

'I think so.'

They paused and studied their fingers. They thought of their mother. Painful thoughts for the most part. There had been happier times, when they were small and their father was alive. She never recovered from his death, and after Rusty was killed the aunts and uncles put her in an institution.

Ray took his finger and followed the small metal rods in the screen. He watched his finger. 'Let's talk about something else.'

Mitch nodded in agreement. There was so much to talk about, but it was all in the past. They had nothing in common but the past, and it was best to leave it alone.

'You mentioned in a letter that one of your ex-cellmates is a private investigator in Memphis.'

'Eddie Lomax. He was a Memphis cop for nine years, until he got sent up for rape.'

'Rape?'

'Yeah. He had a tough time here. Rapists are not well regarded around this place. Cops are hated. They almost killed him until I stepped in. He's been out about three years now. He writes me all the time. Does mainly divorce investigations.'

'Is he in the phone book?'

'969-3838. Why do you need him?'

'I've got a lawyer buddy whose wife is fooling around, but he can't catch her. Is this guy good?'

'Very good, so he says. He's made some money.'

'Can I trust him?'

'Are you kidding? Tell him you're my brother and he'll kill for you. He's gonna help me get out of here, he just doesn't know it. You might mention it to him.'

'I wish you'd stop that.'

A guard walked behind Mitch. 'Three minutes,' he said.

'What can I send you?' Mitch asked.

'I'd like a real favor, if you don't mind.'

'Anything.'

'Go to a bookstore and look for one of those cassette courses on how to speak Greek in twenty-four hours. That plus a Greek-to-English dictionary would be nice.'

'I'll send it next week.'

'How about Italian too?'

'No problem.'

'I'm undecided about whether to go to Sicily or the Greek isles. It's really got me tore up. I asked the prison minister about it, and he was of no help. I've thought of going to the warden. What do you think?'

Mitch chuckled and shook his head. 'Why don't you go to Australia?'

'Great idea. Send me some tapes in Australian and a dictionary.'

They both smiled, then stopped. They watched each other carefully and waited for the guard to call time. Mitch looked at the scar on Ray's forehead and thought of the countless bars and countless fights that led to the inevitable killing. Self-defense, Ray called it. For years he had wanted to cuss Ray for being so stupid, but the anger had passed. Now he wanted to embrace him and take him home and help him find a job.

'Don't feel sorry for me,' Ray said.

'Abby wants to write you.'

'I'd like that. I barely remember her as a small girl in

131

Danesboro, hanging around her daddy's bank on Main Street. Tell her to send me a picture. And I'd like a picture of your house. You're the first McDeere in a hundred years to own real estate.'

'I gotta go.'

'Do me a favor. I think you need to find Mom, just to make sure she's alive. Now that you're out of school, it would be nice to reach out to her.'

'I've thought about that.'

'Think about it some more, okay?'

'Sure. I'll see you in a month or so.'

DeVasher sucked on a Roi-Tan and blew a lungful of smoke into his air purifier. 'We found Ray McDeere,' he announced proudly.

'Where?' asked Ollie.

'Brushy Mountain State Prison. Convicted of second-degree murder in Nashville eight years ago and sentenced to fifteen years with no parole. Real name is Raymond McDeere. Thirty-one years old. No family. Served three years in the Army. Dishonorable discharge. A real loser.'

'How'd you find him?'

'He was visited yesterday by his kid brother. We happened to be following. Twenty-four-hour surveillance, remember.'

'His conviction is public record. You should've found this earlier.'

'We would have, Ollie, if it was important. But it's not important. We do our job.'

'Fifteen years, huh? Who'd he kill?'

'The usual. A buncha drunks in a bar fighting over a woman. No weapon, though. Police and autopsy reports say he hit the victim twice with his fists and cracked his skull.'

'Why the dishonorable discharge?'

'Gross insubordination. Plus, he assaulted an officer. I don't know how he avoided a court-martial. Looks like a nasty character.'

'You're right, it's not important. What else do you know?'

'Not much. We've got the house wired, right? He has not mentioned Tarrance to his wife. In fact, we listen to this kid around the clock, and he ain't mentioned Tarrance to anyone.'

Ollie smiled and nodded his approval. He was proud of McDeere. What a lawyer.

'What about sex?'

'All we can do is listen, Ollie. But we listen real close, and I don't think they've had any in two weeks. Of course, he's here sixteen hours a day going through the workaholic rookie counselor routine that you guys instill. It sounds like she's getting tired of it. Could be the usual rookie's wife syndrome. She calls her mother a lot – collect, so he won't know. She told her mom that he's changing and all that crap. She thinks he'll kill himself working so hard. That's what we're hearing. So I don't have any pictures, Ollie, and I'm sorry because I know how much you enjoy them. First chance we get, we'll have you some pictures.'

Ollie glared at the wall but said nothing.

'Listen, Ollie, I think we need to send the kid with Avery to Grand Cayman on business. See if you can arrange it.'

'That's no problem. May I ask why?'

'Not right now. You'll know later.'

The building was in the low-rent section of downtown, a couple of blocks from the shadows of the modern steel-and-glass towers which were packed together as if land was scarce in Memphis. A sign on a door directed one's attention upstairs, where Eddie Lomax, private investigator, maintained an office. Hours by appointment only.

The door upstairs advertised investigations of all types – divorces, accidents, missing relatives, surveillance. The ad in the phone book mentioned the police expertise, but not the ending of that career. It listed eavesdropping, countermeasures, child custody, photographs, courtroom evidence, voice-stress analysis, location of assets, insurance claims and premarital background review. Bonded, insured, licensed and available twenty-four hours a day. Ethical, reliable, confidential, peace of mind.

Mitch was impressed with the abundance of confidence. The appointment was for 5 P.M., and he arrived a few minutes early. A shapely platinum blond with a constricting leather skirt and matching black boots asked for his name and pointed to an orange vinyl chair next to a window. Eddie would be a minute. He inspected the chair, and noticing a fine layer of dust and several spots of what appeared to be grease, he declined and said his back was sore. Tammy shrugged and returned to her gum chewing and typing of some document; Mitch speculated whether it was a premarital report, or maybe a surveillance summary, or perhaps a countermeasure attack plan. The ashtray on her desk was filled with butts smeared with pink lipstick. While typing with her left hand, the right one instantly and precisely picked another cigarette from the pack and thrust it between her sticky lips. With remarkable coordination, she flicked something with her left hand and a flame shot to the tip of a very skinny and incredibly long liberated cigarette. When the flame disappeared, the lips instinctively compacted and hardened around the tiny protrusion, and the entire body began to inhale. Letters became words, words became sentences, sentences became paragraphs as she tried desperately to fill her lungs. Finally, with an inch of the cigarette hanging as ashes, she swallowed, picked it from her lips with two brilliant red fingernails and exhaled mightily. The smoke billowed toward the stained plaster ceiling, where it upset an existing cloud and swirled around a hanging fluorescent light. She coughed, a hacking, irritating cough which reddened her face and gyrated her huge breasts until they bounced dangerously close to the typewriter keys. She grabbed a nearby cup and lapped up something, then reinserted the filter-tip 1000 and pecked away.

After two minutes, Mitch began to fear carbon monoxide. He spotted a small hole in the window, in a pane that for some reason the spiders had not draped with cobwebs. He walked to within inches of the shredded, dust-laden curtains and tried to inhale in the direction of the opening. He felt sick. There was more hacking and wheezing behind him. He tried to open the window, but layers of cracked paint had long since welded it shut.

Just when he began to feel dizzy the typing and smoking stopped.

'You a lawyer?'

Mitch turned from the window and looked at the secretary. She was now sitting on the edge of her desk, legs crossed, with the black leather skirt well above her knees. She sipped a Diet Pepsi.

'Yes.'

'In a big firm?'

'Yes.'

'I thought so. I could tell by your suit and your cute little preppie button-down with the silk paisley tie. I can always spot the big-firm lawyers, as opposed to the ham-and-eggers who hang around City Court.'

The smoke was clearing and Mitch was breathing easier. He admired her legs, which for the moment were positioned just so and demanded to be admired. She was now looking at his shoes.

'You like the suit, huh?' he said.

'It's expensive, I can tell. So's the tie. I'm not so sure about the shirt and shoes.'

Mitch studied the leather boots, the legs, the skirt and the tight sweater around the large breasts and tried to think of something cute to say. She enjoyed this gazing back and forth, and again sipped on her Diet Pepsi.

When she'd had enough, she nodded at Eddie's door and said, 'You can go in now. Eddie's waiting.'

The detective was on the phone, trying to convince some poor old man that his son was in fact a homosexual. A very active homosexual. He pointed to a wooden chair, and Mitch sat down. He saw two windows, both wide open, and breathed easier.

Eddie looked disgusted and covered the receiver. 'He's crying,' he whispered to Mitch, who smiled obligingly, as if he was amused.

He wore blue lizard-skin boots with pointed toes, Levi's, a well-starched peach button-down, which was unbuttoned well into the dark chest hair and exposed two heavy gold chains and one which appeared to be turquoise. He favored Tom Jones or Humperdinck or one of those bushy-headed, dark-eyed singers with thick sideburns and solid chins.

'I've got photographs,' he said, and yanked the receiver from his ear when the old man screamed. He pulled five glossy eight-by-tens from a file and slid them across the desk into Mitch's lap. Yes, indeed, they were homosexuals, whoever they were. Eddie smiled at him proudly. The bodies were somewhere on a stage in what appeared to be a queer club. He laid them on the desk and looked at the window. They were of high quality, in color. Whoever took them had to have been in the club. Mitch thought of the rape conviction. A cop sent up for rape.

He slammed the phone down. 'So you're Mitchell McDeere! Nice to meet.'

They shook hands across the desk. 'My pleasure,' Mitch said. 'I saw Ray Sunday.'

'I feel like I've known you for years. You look just like Ray. He told me you did. Told me all about you. I guess he told you about me. The police background. The conviction. The rape. Did he explain to you it was statutory rape, and that the girl was seventeen years old, looked twenty-five, and that I got framed?'

'He mentioned it. Ray doesn't say much. You know that.'

'He's a helluva guy. I owe him my life, literally. They almost killed me in prison when they found out I was a cop. He stepped in and even the blacks backed down. He can hurt people when he wants to.'

'He's all the family I have.'

'Yeah, I know. You bunk with a guy for years in an eight-by-twelve cell and you learn all about him. He's talked about you for hours. When I was paroled you were thinking about law school.'

'I finished in June of this year and went to work for Bendini, Lambert & Locke.'

'Never heard of them.'

'It's a tax and corporate firm on Front Street.'

'I do a lot of sleazy divorce work for lawyers. Surveillance, taking pictures, like those, and gathering filth for court.' He spoke quickly, with short, clipped words and sentences. The cowboy boots were placed gingerly on the desk for display. 'Plus, I've got some lawyers I run cases for. If I dig up a good car wreck or personal-injury suit, I'll shop around to see who'll give me the best cut. That's how I bought this building. That's where the money is – personal injury. These lawyers take forty percent of the recovery. Forty percent!' He shook his head in disgust as if he couldn't believe greedy lawyers actually lived and breathed in this city.

'You work by the hour?' Mitch asked.

'Thirty bucks, plus expenses. Last night I spent six hours in my van outside a Holiday Inn waiting for my client's husband to leave his room with his whore so I could take more pictures. Six hours. That's a hundred eighty bucks for sitting on my ass looking at dirty magazines and waiting. I also charged her for dinner.'

Mitch listened intently, as if he wished he could do it.

Tammy stuck her head in the door and said she was leaving. A stale cloud followed her and Mitch looked at the windows. She slammed the door.

'She's a great gal,' Eddie said. 'She's got trouble with her husband. He's a truck driver who thinks he's Elvis. Got the jet-black hair, ducktail, lamb-chop sideburns. Wears those thick gold sunglasses Elvis wore. When he's not on the road he sits around the trailer listening to Elvis albums and watching those terrible movies. They moved here from Ohio just so this clown can be near the King's grave. Guess what his name is.'

'I have no idea.'

'Elvis. Elvis Aaron Hemphill. Had his name legally changed after the King died. He does an impersonation routine in dark nightclubs around the city. I saw him one night. He wore a white skintight jumpsuit unbuttoned to his navel, which would've been okay except he's got this gut that hangs out and looks like a bleached watermelon. It was pretty sad. His voice is hilarious, sounds like one of those old Indian chiefs chanting around the campfire.'

'So what's the problem?'

'Women. You would not believe the Elvis nuts who visit this city. They flock to watch this buffoon act like the King. They throw panties at him, big panties, panties made for heavy, wide lardasses, and he wipes his forehead and throws them back. They give him

138

their room numbers, and we suspect he sneaks around and tries to play the big stud, just like Elvis. I haven't caught him yet.'

Mitch could not think of any response to all this. He grinned like an idiot, like this was truly an incredible story. Lomax read him well.

'You got trouble with your wife?'

'No. Nothing like that. I need some information about four people. Three are dead, one is alive.'

'Sounds interesting. I'm listening.'

Mitch pulled the notes from a pocket. 'I assume this is strictly confidential.'

'Of course it is. As confidential as you are with your client.'

Mitch nodded in agreement, but thought of Tammy and Elvis and wondered why Lomax told him that story.

'It must be confidential.'

'I said it would be. You can trust me.'

'Thirty bucks an hour?'

'Twenty for you. Ray sent you, remember?'

'I appreciate that.'

'Who are these people?'

'The three dead ones were once lawyers in our firm. Robert Lamm was killed in 1970 in a hunting accident somewhere in Arkansas. Somewhere in the mountains. He was missing for about two weeks and they found him with a bullet in the head. There was an autopsy. That's all I know. Alice Knauss died in 1977 in a car wreck here in Memphis. Supposedly a drunk driver hit her. John Mickel committed suicide in 1984. His body was found in his office. There was a gun and a note.'

'That's all you know?'

'That's it.'

'What're you looking for?'

'I want to know as much as I can about how these

139

people died. What were the circumstances surrounding each death? Who investigated each death? Any unanswered questions or suspicions.'

'What do you suspect?'

'At this point, nothing. I'm just curious.'

'You're more than curious.'

'Okay, I'm more than curious. But for now, let's leave it at that.'

'Fair enough. Who's the fourth guy?'

'A man named Wayne Tarrance. He's an FBI agent here in Memphis.'

'FBI!'

'Does that bother you?'

'Yes, it bothers me. I get forty an hour for cops.'

'No problem.'

'What do you want to know?'

'Check him out. How long has he been here? How long has he been an agent? What's his reputation?'

'That's easy enough.'

Mitch folded the paper and stuck it in his pocket. 'How long will this take?'

'About a month.'

'That's fine.'

'Say, what was the name of your firm?'

'Bendini, Lambert & Locke.'

'Those two guys who got killed last summer –'

'They were members.'

'Any suspicions?'

'No.'

'Just thought I'd ask.'

'Listen, Eddie. You must be very careful with this. Don't call me at home or the office. I'll call you in about a month. I suspect I'm being watched very closely.'

'By whom?'

'I wish I knew.'

THIRTEEN

Avery smiled at the computer printout. 'For the month of October you billed an average of sixty-one hours per week.'

'I thought it was sixty-four,' Mitch said.

'Sixty-one is good enough. In fact, we've never had a first-year man average so high in one month. Is it legitimate?'

'No padding. In fact, I could've pushed it higher.'

'How many hours are you working a week?'

'Between eighty-five and ninety. I could bill seventy-five if I wanted to.'

'I wouldn't suggest it, at least not now. It could cause a little jealousy around here. The younger associates are watching you very closely.'

'You want me to slow down?'

'Of course not. You and I are a month behind right now. I'm just worried about the long hours. A little worried, that's all. Most associates start like wildfire – eighty- and ninety-hour weeks – but they burn out after a couple of months. Sixty-five to seventy is about average. But you seem to have unusual stamina.'

'I don't require much sleep.'

'What does your wife think about it?'

'Why is that important?'

'Does she mind the long hours?'

Mitch glared at Avery, and for a second thought of

141

the argument the previous night when he arrived home for dinner at three minutes before midnight. It was a controlled fight, but the worst one yet, and it promised to be followed by others. No ground was surrendered. Abby said she felt closer to Mr. Rice next door than to her husband.

'She understands. I told her I would make partner in two years and retire before I was thirty.'

'Looks like you're trying.'

'You're not complaining, are you? Every hour I billed last month was on one of your files, and you didn't seem too concerned about overworking me.'

Avery laid the printout on his credenza and frowned at Mitch. 'I just don't want you to burn out or neglect things at home.'

It seemed odd receiving marital advice from a man who had left his wife. He looked at Avery with as much contempt as he could generate. 'You don't need to worry about what happens at my house. As long as I produce around here you should be happy.'

Avery leaned across the desk. 'Look, Mitch, I'm not very good at this sort of thing. This is coming from higher up. Lambert and McKnight are worried that maybe you're pushing a bit too hard. I mean, five o'clock in the morning, every morning, even some Sundays. That's pretty intense, Mitch.'

'What did they say?'

'Nothing much. Believe it or not, Mitch, those guys really care about you and your family. They want happy lawyers with happy wives. If everything is lovely, then the lawyers are productive. Lambert is especially paternalistic. He's planning to retire in a couple of years, and he's trying to relive his glory years through you and the other young guys. If he asks too many questions or gives a few lectures, take it in stride. He's earned the right to be the grandfather around here.'

'Tell them I'm fine, Abby's fine, we're all happy and I'm very productive.'

'Fine, now that that's out of the way, you and I leave for Grand Cayman a week from tomorrow. I've got to meet with some Caymanian bankers on behalf of Sonny Capps and three other clients. Mainly business, but we always manage to work in a little scuba diving and snorkeling. I told Royce McKnight you were needed, and he approved the trip. He said you probably needed the R and R. Do you want to go?'

'Of course. I'm just a little surprised.'

'It's business, so our wives won't be going. Lambert was a little concerned that it may cause a problem at home.'

'I think Mr. Lambert worries too much about what happens at my home. Tell him I'm in control. No problems.'

'So you're going?'

'Sure, I'm going. How long will we be there?'

'Couple of days. We'll stay in one of the firm's condos. Sonny Capps may stay in the other one. I'm trying to get the firm plane, but we may have to fly commercial.'

'No problem with me.'

Only two of the passengers on board the Cayman Airways 727 in Miami wore ties, and after the first round of complimentary rum punch Avery removed his and stuffed it in his coat pocket. The punch was served by beautiful brown Caymanian stewardesses with blue eyes and comely smiles. The women were great down there, Avery said more than once.

Mitch sat by the window and tried to conceal the excitement of his first trip out of the country. He had found a book on the Cayman Islands in a library. There were three islands, Grand Cayman, Little

Cayman and Cayman Brac. The two smaller ones were sparsely populated and seldom visited. Grand Cayman had eighteen thousand people, twelve thousand registered corporations and three hundred banks. The population was twenty percent white, twenty percent black, and the other sixty percent wasn't sure and didn't care. Georgetown, the capital, in recent years had become an international tax haven with bankers as secretive as the Swiss. There were no income taxes, corporate taxes, capital-gains taxes, estate or gift taxes. Certain companies and investments were given guarantees against taxation for fifty years. The islands were a dependent British territory with an unusually stable government. Revenue from import duties and tourism funded whatever government was necessary. There was no crime or unemployment.

Grand Cayman was twenty-three miles long and eight miles wide in places, but from the air it looked much smaller. It was a small rock surrounded by clear, sapphire water.

The landing almost occurred in a lagoon, but at the last second a small asphalt strip came forth and caught the plane. They disembarked and sang their way through customs. A black boy grabbed Mitch's bags and threw them with Avery's into the trunk of a 1972 Ford LTD. Mitch tipped him generously.

'Seven Mile Beach!' Avery commanded as he turned up the remnants of his last rum punch.

'Okay, mon,' the driver drawled. He gunned the taxi and laid rubber in the direction of Georgetown. The radio blared reggae. The driver shook and gyrated and kept a steady beat with his fingers on the steering wheel. He was on the wrong side of the road, but so was everybody else. Mitch sank into the worn seat and crossed his legs. The car had no air conditioning

144

except for the open windows. The muggy tropical air rushed across his face and blew his hair. This was nice.

The island was flat, and the road into Georgetown was busy with small, dusty European cars, scooters and bicycles. The homes were small one-stories with tin roofs and neat, colorful paint jobs. The lawns were tiny with little grass, but the dirt was neatly swept. As they neared the town the houses became shops, two- and three-story white frame buildings where tourists stood under the canopies and took refuge from the sun. The driver made a sharp turn and suddenly they were in the midst of a downtown crowded with modern bank buildings.

Avery assumed the role of tour guide. 'There are banks here from everywhere. Germany, France, Great Britain, Canada, Spain, Japan, Denmark. Even Saudi Arabia and Israel. Over three hundred, at last count. It's become quite a tax haven. The bankers here are extremely quiet. They make the Swiss look like blabbermouths.'

The taxi slowed in heavy traffic, and the breeze stopped. 'I see a lot of Canadian banks,' Mitch said.

'That building right there is the Royal Bank of Montreal. We'll be there at ten in the morning. Most of our business will be with Canadian banks.'

'Any particular reason?'

'They're very safe, and very quiet.'

The crowded street turned and dead-ended into another one. Beyond the intersection the glittering blue of the Caribbean rose to the horizon. A cruise ship was anchored in the bay.

'That's Hogsty Bay,' Avery said. 'That's where the pirates docked their ships three hundred years ago. Blackbeard himself roamed these islands and buried his loot. They found some of it a few years ago in a cave east of here near Bodden Town.'

145

Mitch nodded as if he believed this tale. The driver smiled in the rearview mirror.

Avery wiped the sweat from his forehead. 'This place has always attracted pirates. Once it was Blackbeard, now it's modern-day pirates who form corporations and hide their money here. Right, mon?'

'Right, mon,' the driver replied.

'That's Seven Mile Beach,' Avery said. 'One of the most beautiful and most famous in the world. Right, mon?'

'Right, mon.'

'Sand as white as sugar. Warm, clear water. Warm, beautiful women. Right, mon?'

'Right, mon.'

'Will they have the cookout tonight at the Palms?'

'Yes, mon. Six o'clock.'

'That's next door to our condo. The Palms is a popular hotel with the hottest action on the beach.'

Mitch smiled and watched the hotels pass. He recalled the interview at Harvard when Oliver Lambert preached about how the firm frowned on divorce and chasing women. And drinking. Perhaps Avery had missed those sermons. Perhaps he hadn't.

The condos were in the center of Seven Mile Beach, next door to another complex and the Palms. As expected, the units owned by the firm were spacious and richly decorated. Avery said they would sell for at least half a million each, but they weren't for sale. They were not for rent. They were sanctuaries for the weary lawyers of Bendini, Lambert & Locke. And a few very favored clients.

From the balcony off the second-floor bedroom, Mitch watched the small boats drift aimlessly over the sparkling sea. The sun was beginning its descent and the small waves reflected its rays in a million directions. The cruise ship moved slowly away from the island. Dozens of people walked the beach, kicking sand, splashing in the water, chasing sand crabs and drinking rum punch and Jamaican Red Stripe beer. The rhythmic beat of Caribbean music drifted from the Palms, where a large open-air thatched-roof bar attracted the beachcombers like a magnet. From a grass hut nearby they rented snorkeling gear, catamarans and volleyballs.

Avery walked to the balcony in a pair of brilliant orange-and-yellow flowered shorts. His body was lean and hard, with no flab. He owned part interest in a health club in Memphis and worked out every day. Evidently there were some tanning beds in the club. Mitch was impressed.

'How do you like my outfit?' Avery asked.

'Very nice. You'll fit right in.'

'I've got another pair if you'd like.'

'No, thanks. I'll stick to my Western Kentucky gym shorts.'

Avery sipped on a drink and took in the scenery. 'I've been here a dozen times, and I still get excited. I've thought about retiring down here.'

'That would be nice. You could walk the beach and chase sand crabs.'

'And play dominoes and drink Red Stripe. Have you ever had a Red Stripe?'

'Not that I recall.'

'Let's go get one.'

The open-air bar was called Rumheads. It was packed with thirsty tourists and a few locals who sat together around a wooden table and played dominoes. Avery fought through the crowd and returned with two bottles. They found a seat next to the domino game.

'I think this is what I'll do when I retire. I'll come down here and play dominoes for a living. And drink Red Stripe.'

'It's good beer.'

'And when I get tired of dominoes, I'll throw some darts.' He nodded to a corner where a group of drunk Englishmen were tossing darts at a board and cursing each other. 'And when I get tired of darts, well, who knows what I'll do. Excuse me.' He headed for a table on the patio where two string bikinis had just sat down. He introduced himself, and they asked him to have a seat. Mitch ordered another Red Stripe and went to the beach. In the distance he could see the bank buildings of Georgetown. He walked in that direction.

The food was placed on folding tables around the pool. Grilled grouper, barbecued shark, pompano, fried shrimp, turtle and oysters, lobster and red snapper. It was all from the sea, and all fresh. The guests crowded around the tables and served themselves while waiters scurried back and forth with gallons of rum punch. They ate on small tables in the courtyard overlooking Rumheads and the sea. A reggae band tuned up. The sun dipped behind a cloud, then over the horizon.

Mitch followed Avery through the buffet and, as expected, to a table where the two women were waiting. They were sisters, both in their late twenties, both divorced, both half drunk. The one named Carrie had fallen in heat with Avery, and the other one, Julia, immediately began making eyes at Mitch. He wondered what Avery had told them.

'I see you're married,' Julia whispered as she moved next to him.

'Yes, happily.'

She smiled as if to accept the challenge. Avery and his woman winked at each other. Mitch grabbed a glass of punch and gulped it down.

He picked at his food and could think of nothing but Abby. This would be hard to explain, if an explanation became necessary. Having dinner with two attractive women who were barely dressed. It would be impossible to explain. The conversation became awkward at the table, and Mitch added nothing. A waiter set a large pitcher on the table, and it quickly was emptied. Avery became obnoxious. He told the women Mitch had played for the New York Giants, had two Super Bowl rings. Made a million bucks a year before a knee injury ruined his career. Mitch shook his head and drank some more. Julia drooled at him and moved closer.

The band turned up the volume, and it was time to dance. Half the crowd moved to a wooden dance floor under two trees, between the pool and the beach. 'Let's dance!' Avery yelled, and grabbed his woman. They ran through the tables and were soon lost in the crowd of jerking and lunging tourists.

He felt her move closer, then her hand was on his leg. 'Do you wanna dance?' she asked.

'No.'

'Good. Neither do I. What would you like to do?' She rubbed her breasts on his biceps and gave her best seductive smile, only inches away.

'I don't plan to do anything.' He removed her hand.

'Aw, come on. Let's have some fun. Your wife will never know.'

'Look, you're a very lovely lady, but you're wasting your time with me. It's still early. You've got plenty of time to pick up a real stud.'

'You're cute.'

The hand was back, and Mitch breathed deeply. 'Why don't you get lost.'

'I beg your pardon.' The hand was gone.

'I said, "Get lost."'

She backed away. 'What's wrong with you?'

'I have an aversion to communicable diseases. Get lost.'

'Why don't you get lost.'

'That's a wonderful idea. I think I will get lost. Enjoyed dinner.'

Mitch grabbed a glass of rum punch and made his way through the dancers to the bar. He ordered a Red Stripe and sat by himself in a dark corner of the patio. The beach in front of him was deserted. The lights of a dozen boats moved slowly across the water. Behind him were the sounds of the Barefoot Boys and the laughter of the Caribbean night. Nice, he thought, but it would be nicer with Abby. Maybe they would vacation here next summer. They needed time together, away from home and the office. There was a distance between them – distance he could not define. Distance they could not discuss but both felt. Distance he was afraid of.

'What are you watching?' The voice startled him. She walked to the table and sat next to him. She was a native, dark skin with blue or hazel eyes. It was impossible to tell in the dark. But they were beautiful eyes, warm and uninhibited. Her dark curly hair was pulled back and hung almost to her waist. She was an exotic mixture of black, white and probably Latin. And probably more. She wore a white bikini top cut very low and barely covering her large breasts and a long, brightly colored skirt with a slit to the waist that exposed almost everything when she sat and crossed her legs. No shoes.

'Nothing, really,' Mitch said.

She was young, with a childish smile that revealed perfect teeth. 'Where are you from?' she asked.

'The States.'

She smiled and chuckled. 'Of course you are. Where in the States?' It was the soft, gentle, precise, confident English of the Caribbean.

'Memphis.'

'A lot of people come here from Memphis. A lot of divers.'

'Do you live here?' he asked.

'Yes. All my life. My mother is a native. My father is from England. He's gone now, back to where he came from.'

'Would you like a drink?' he asked.

'Yes. Rum and soda.'

He stood at the bar and waited for the drinks. A dull, nervous something throbbed in his stomach. He could slide into the darkness, disappear into the crowd and find his way to the safety of the condo. He could lock the door and read a book on international tax havens. Pretty boring. Plus, Avery was there by now with his hot little number. The girl was harmless, the rum and Red Stripe told him. They would have a couple of drinks and say good night.

He returned with the drinks and sat across from the girl, as far away as possible. They were alone on the patio.

'Are you a diver?' she asked.

'No. Believe it or not, I'm here on business. I'm a lawyer, and I have meetings with some bankers in the morning.'

'How long will you be here?'

'Couple of days.' He was polite, but short. The less he said, the safer he would be. She recrossed her legs and smiled innocently. He felt weak.

'How old are you?' he asked.

'I'm twenty, and my name is Eilene. I'm old enough.'

'I'm Mitch.' His stomach flipped and he felt light-headed. He sipped rapidly on his beer. He glanced at his watch.

She watched with that same seductive smile. 'You're very handsome.'

This was unraveling in a hurry. Keep cool, he told himself, just keep cool.

'Thank you.'

'Are you an athlete?'

'Sort of. Why do you ask?'

'You look like an athlete. You're very muscular and firm.' It was the way she emphasized 'firm' that made his stomach flip again. He admired her body and tried to think of some compliment that would not be suggestive. Forget it.

'Where do you work?' he asked, aiming for less sensual areas.

'I'm a clerk in a jewelry store in town.'

'Where do you live?'

'In Georgetown. Where are you staying?'

'A condo next door.' He nodded in the direction, and she looked to her left. She wanted to see the condo, he could tell. She sipped on her drink.

'Why aren't you at the party?' she asked.

'I'm not much on parties.'

'Do you like the beach?'

'It's beautiful.'

'It's prettier in the moonlight.' That smile, again.

He could say nothing to this.

'There's a better bar about a mile down the beach,' she said. 'Let's go for a walk.'

'I don't know, I should get back. I've got some work to do before morning.'

She laughed and stood. 'No one goes in this early in the Caymans. Come on. I owe you a drink.'

'No. I'd better not.'

She grabbed his hand, and he followed her off the patio onto the beach. They walked in silence until the Palms was out of sight and the music was growing dimmer. The moon was overhead and brighter now, and the beach was deserted. She unsnapped something and removed her skirt, leaving nothing but a

152

string around her waist and a string running between her legs. She rolled up the skirt and placed it around his neck. She took his hand.

Something said run. Throw the beer bottle in the ocean. Throw the skirt in the sand. And run like hell. Run to the condo. Lock the door. Lock the windows. Run. Run. Run.

And something said to relax. It's harmless fun. Have a few more drinks. If something happens, enjoy it. No one will ever know. Memphis is a thousand miles away. Avery won't know. And what about Avery? What could he say? Everybody does it. It had happened once before when he was in college, before he was married but after he was engaged. He had blamed it on too much beer, and had survived with no major scars. Time took care of it. Abby would never know.

Run. Run. Run.

They walked for a mile and there was no bar in sight. The beach was darker. A cloud conveniently hid the moon. They had seen no one since Rumheads. She pulled his hand toward two plastic beach chairs next to the water. 'Let's rest,' she said. He finished his beer.

'You're not saying much,' she said.

'What would you like for me to say?'

'Do you think I'm beautiful?'

'You are very beautiful. And you have a beautiful body.'

She sat on the edge of her chair and splashed her feet in the water. 'Let's go for a swim.'

'I, uh, I'm not really in the mood.'

'Come on, Mitch. I love the water.'

'Go ahead. I'll watch.'

She knelt beside him in the sand and faced him, inches away. In slow motion, she reached behind her neck. She unhooked her bikini top, and it fell off, very slowly. Her breasts, much larger now, lay on his left forearm. She handed the top to him. 'Hold this for me.' It was soft and white and weighed less than a millionth of an ounce. He was paralyzed and his breathing, heavy and labored only seconds ago, had now ceased altogether.

She walked slowly into the water. The white string covered nothing from the rear. Her long, dark, beautiful hair hung to her waist. She waded knee deep, then turned to the beach.

'Come on, Mitch. The water feels great.'

She flashed a brilliant smile and he could see it. He rubbed the bikini top and knew this would be his last chance to run. But he was dizzy and weak. Running would require more strength than he could possibly muster. He wanted to just sit and maybe she would go away. Maybe she would drown. Maybe the tide would suddenly materialize and sweep her out to sea.

'Come on, Mitch.'

He removed his shirt and waded into the water. She watched him with a smile, and when he reached her, she took his hand and led him to deeper water. She locked her hands around his neck, and they kissed. He found the strings. They kissed again.

She stopped abruptly and, without speaking, started for the beach. He watched her. She sat on the sand, between the two chairs, and removed the rest of her bikini. He ducked under the water and held his breath for an eternity. When he surfaced, she was reclining, resting on her elbows in the sand. He surveyed the beach and, of course, saw no one. At that precise instant, the moon ducked behind another cloud. There was not a boat or a catamaran or a dinghy or a swimmer or a snorkeler or anything or anybody moving on the water.

'I can't do this,' he muttered through clenched teeth.

'What did you say, Mitch?'

'I can't do this!' he yelled.

'But I want you.'

'I can't do it.'

'Come on, Mitch. No one will ever know.'

No one will ever know. No one will ever know. He walked slowly toward her. No one will ever know.

There was complete silence in the rear of the taxi as the lawyers rode into Georgetown. They were late. They had overslept and missed breakfast. Neither felt particularly well. Avery looked especially haggard. His eyes were bloodshot and his face was pale. He had not shaved.

The driver stopped in heavy traffic in front of the Royal Bank of Montreal. The heat and humidity were already stifling.

Randolph Osgood was the banker, a stuffy British type with a navy double-breasted suit, horn-rimmed glasses, a large shiny forehead and a pointed nose. He greeted Avery like an old friend and introduced himself to Mitch. They were led to a large office on the second floor with a view of Hogsty Bay. Two clerks were waiting.

'Exactly what do you need, Avery?' Osgood asked through his nose.

'Let's start off with some coffee. I need summaries of all the accounts of Sonny Capps, Al Coscia, Dolph Hemmba, Ratzlaff Partners and Greene Group.'

'Yes, and how far back would you like to go?'

'Six months. Every account.'

Osgood snapped his fingers at one of the clerks. She left and returned with a tray of coffee and pastries. The other clerk took notes.

'Of course, Avery, we'll need authorization and powers of attorney for each of these clients,' Osgood said.

'They're on file,' Avery said as he unpacked his briefcase.

'Yes, but they've expired. We'll need current ones. Every account.'

'Very well.' Avery slid a file across the table. 'They're in there. Everything's current.' He winked at Mitch.

A clerk took the file and spread the documents over the table. Each instrument was scrutinized by both clerks, then by Osgood himself. The lawyers drank coffee and waited.

Osgood smiled and said, 'It all appears to be in order. We'll get the records. What else do you need?'

'I need to establish three corporations. Two for Sonny Capps and one for Greene Group. We'll follow the usual procedure. The bank will serve as registered agent, etc.'

'I'll procure the necessary documents,' Osgood said, and looked at a clerk. 'What else?'

'That's all for now.'

'Very well. We should have these records within thirty minutes. Will you be joining me for lunch?'

'I'm sorry, Randolph. I must decline. Mitch and I have a prior commitment. Maybe tomorrow.'

Mitch knew nothing of a prior commitment, at least none he was involved in.

'Perhaps,' replied Osgood. He left the room with the clerks.

Avery closed the door and removed his jacket. He walked to the window and sipped coffee. 'Look, Mitch. I'm sorry about last night. Very sorry. I got drunk and quit thinking. I was wrong to push that woman on you.'

'Apology accepted. Don't let it happen again.'

'It won't. I promise.'

'Was she good?'

'I think so. I don't remember too much. What did you do with her sister?'

'She told me to get lost. I hit the beach and took a walk.'

Avery bit into a pastry and wiped his mouth. 'You know I'm separated. We'll probably get a divorce in a year or so. I'm very discreet because the divorce could get nasty. There's an unwritten rule in the firm – what we do away from Memphis stays away from Memphis. Understand?'

'Come on, Avery. You know I wouldn't tell.'

'I know. I know.'

Mitch was glad to hear of the unwritten rule, although he awakened with the security that he had committed the perfect crime. He had thought of her in bed, the shower, the taxi, and now he had trouble concentrating on anything. He had caught himself looking at jewelry stores when they reached George-town.

'I've got a question,' Mitch said.

Avery nodded and ate the pastry.

'When I was recruited a few months ago by Oliver Lambert and McKnight and the gang, it was impressed upon me repeatedly that the firm frowned on divorce, women, booze, drugs, everything but hard work and money. That's why I took the job. I've seen the hard work and money, but now I'm seeing other things. Where did you go wrong? Or do all the guys do it?'

'I don't like your question.'

'I knew you wouldn't. But I'd like an answer. I deserve an answer. I feel like I was misled.'

'So what are you going to do? Leave because I got drunk and laid up with a whore?'

'I haven't thought about leaving.'

'Good. Don't.'

'But I'm entitled to an answer.'

'Okay. Fair enough. I'm the biggest rogue in the firm, and they'll come down hard when I mention the divorce. I chase women now and then, but no one knows it. Or at least they can't catch me. I'm sure it's done by other partners, but you'd never catch them. Not all of them, but a few. Most have very stable marriages and are forever faithful to their wives. I've always been the bad boy, but they've tolerated me because I'm so talented. They know I drink during lunch and sometimes in the office, and they know I violate some more of their sacred rules, but they made me a partner because they need me. And now that I'm a partner, they can't do much about it. I'm not that bad of a guy, Mitch.'

'I didn't say you were.'

'I'm not perfect. Some of them are, believe me. They're machines, robots. They live, eat and sleep for Bendini, Lambert & Locke. I like to have a little fun.'

'So you're the exception –'

'Rather than the rule, yes. And I don't apologize for it.'

'I didn't ask you for an apology. Just a clarification.'

'Clear enough?'

'Yes. I've always admired your bluntness.'

'And I admire your discipline. It's a strong man who can remain faithful to his wife with the temptations you had last night. I'm not that strong. Don't want to be.'

Temptations. He had thought of inspecting the downtown jewelry shops during lunch.

'Look, Avery, I'm not a Holy Roller, and I'm not shocked. I'm not one to judge – I've been judged all my life. I was just confused about the rules, that's all.'

'The rules never change. They're cast in concrete. Carved in granite. Etched in stone. Violate too many and you're out. Or violate as many as you want, but just don't get caught.'

'Fair enough.'

Osgood and a group of clerks entered the room with computer printouts and stacks of documents. They made neat piles on the table and alphabetized it all.

'This should keep you busy for a day or so,' Osgood said with a forced smile. He snapped his fingers and the clerks disappeared. 'I'll be in my office if you need something.'

'Yes, thanks,' Avery said as he hovered over the first set of documents. Mitch removed his coat and loosened his tie.

'Exactly what are we doing here?' he asked.

'Two things. First, we'll review the entries into all of these accounts. We're looking primarily for interest earned, what rate, how much, etc. We'll do a rough audit of each account to make sure the interest is going where it is supposed to go. For example, Dolph Hemmba sends his interest to nine different banks in the Bahamas. It's stupid, but it makes him happy. It's also impossible for anyone to follow, except me. He has about twelve million in this bank, so it's worth keeping up with. He could do this himself, but he feels better if I do it. At two-fifty an hour, I don't mind. We'll check the interest this bank is paying on each account. The rate varies depending on a number of factors. It's discretionary with the bank, and this is a good way to keep them honest.'

'I thought they were honest.'

'They are, but they're bankers, remember.'

'You're looking at close to thirty accounts here, and when we leave we'll know the exact balance, the interest earned and where the interest is going. Second, we have to incorporate three companies under Caymanian jurisdiction. It's fairly easy legal work and could be done in Memphis. But the clients think we must come here to do it. Remember, we're dealing with people who invest millions. A few thousand in legal fees doesn't bother them.'

Mitch flipped through a printout in the Hemmba stack. 'Who's this guy Hemmba? I haven't heard of him.'

'I've got a lot of clients you haven't heard of. Hemmba is a big farmer in Arkansas, one of the state's largest landowners.'

'Twelve million dollars?'

'That's just in this bank.'

'That's a lot of cotton and soybeans.'

'Let's just say he has other ventures.'

'Such as?'

'I really can't say.'

'Legal or illegal?'

'Let's just say he's hiding twenty million plus interest in various Caribbean banks from the IRS.'

'Are we helping him?'

Avery spread the documents on one end of the table and began checking entries. Mitch watched and waited for an answer. The silence grew heavier and it was obvious there would not be one. He could press, but he had asked enough questions for one day. He rolled up his sleeves and went to work.

At noon he learned about Avery's prior commitment. His woman was waiting at the condo for a little rendezvous. He suggested they break for a couple of hours and mentioned a café downtown Mitch could try.

Instead of a café, Mitch found the Georgetown Library four blocks from the bank. On the second floor he was directed to the periodicals, where he found a shelf full of old editions of *The Daily Caymanian*. He dug back six months and pulled the one dated June 27. He laid it on a small table by a window overlooking the street. He glanced out the window, then looked closer. There was a man he had seen only moments earlier on the street by the bank. He was behind the wheel of a battered yellow Chevette parked in a narrow drive across from the library. He was a stocky, dark-haired, foreign-looking type with a gaudy green-and-orange shirt and cheap touristy sunglasses.

The same Chevette with the same driver had been parked in front of the gift shop next to the bank, and now, moments later, it was parked four blocks away. A native on a bicycle stopped next to him and took a cigarette. The man in the car pointed at the library. The native left his bicycle and walked quickly across the street.

Mitch folded the newspaper and stuck it in his coat. He walked past the rows of shelves, found a *National Geographic* and sat down at a table. He studied the magazine and listened carefully as the native climbed the stairs, noticed him, walked behind him, seemed to pause as if to catch a glimpse of what he was reading, then disappeared down the stairs. Mitch waited for a moment, then returned to the window. The native was taking another cigarette and talking to the man in the Chevette. He lit the cigarette and rode away.

Mitch spread the newspaper on the table and scanned the headline story of the two American lawyers and their dive guide who had been killed in a mysterious accident the day before. He made mental notes and returned the paper.

The Chevette was still watching. He walked in front of it, made the block and headed in the direction of the bank. The shopping district was squeezed tightly between the bank buildings and Hogsty Bay. The streets were narrow and crowded with tourists on foot, tourists on scooters, tourists in rented compacts. He removed his coat and ducked into a T-shirt shop with a pub upstairs. He climbed the stairs, ordered a Coke, and sat on the balcony.

Within minutes the native with the bicycle was at the bar, drinking a Red Stripe and watching from behind a hand printed menu.

Mitch sipped on the Coke and scanned the congestion below. No sign of the Chevette, but he knew it was close by. He saw another man stare at him from the street, then disappear. Then a woman. Was he paranoid? Then the Chevette turned the corner two blocks away and moved slowly beneath him.

He went to the T-shirt store and bought a pair of sunglasses. He walked for a block, then darted into an alley. He ran through the dark shade to the next street, then into a gift shop. He left through the back door, into an alley. He saw a large clothing store for tourists and entered through a side door. He watched the street closely and saw nothing. The racks were full of shorts and shirts of all colors – clothes the natives would not buy but the Americans loved. He stayed conservative – white shorts with a red knit pullover. He found a pair of straw sandals that sort of matched the hat he liked. The clerk giggled and showed him to a dressing room. He checked the street again. Nothing. The clothes fit, and he asked her if he could leave his suit and shoes in the back for a couple of hours. 'No problem, mon,' she said. He paid in cash, slipped her a ten and asked her to call a cab. She said he was very handsome.

He watched the street nervously until the cab arrived. He darted across the sidewalk, into the back seat. 'Abanks Dive Lodge,' he said.

'That's a long way, mon.'

Mitch threw a twenty over the seat. 'Get moving. Watch your mirror. If someone is following, let me know.'

He grabbed the money. 'Okay, mon.'

Mitch sat low under his new hat in the back seat as his driver worked his way down Shedden Road, out of the shopping district, around Hogsty Bay, and headed east, past Red Bay, out of the city of Georgetown and onto the road to Bodden Town.

'Who are you running from, mon?'

Mitch smiled and rolled down his window. 'The Internal Revenue Service.' He thought that was cute, but the driver seemed confused. There were no taxes and no tax collectors in the islands, he remembered. The driver continued in silence.

According to the paper, the dive guide was Philip Abanks, son of Barry Abanks, the owner of the dive lodge. He was nineteen when he was killed. The three had drowned when an explosion of some sort hit their boat. A very mysterious explosion. The bodies had been found in eighty feet of water in full scuba gear. There were no witnesses to the explosion and no explanations as to why it occurred two miles offshore in an area not known for diving. The article said there were many unanswered questions.

Bodden Town was a small village twenty minutes from Georgetown. The dive lodge was south of town on an isolated stretch of beach.

'Did anyone follow us?' Mitch asked.

The driver shook his head.

'Good job. Here's forty bucks.' Mitch looked at his watch. 'It's almost one. Can you be here at exactly two-thirty?'

'No problem, mon.'

The road ended at the edge of the beach and became a white rock parking area shaded by dozens of royal palms. The front building of the lodge was a large, two-story home with a tin roof and an outer stairway leading to the center of the second floor. The Grand House, it was called. It was painted a light blue with neat white trim, and it was partially hidden by

163

bay vines and spider lilies. The handwrought fretwork was painted pink. The solid wooden shutters were olive. It was the office and eating room of Abanks Dive Lodge. To its right the palm trees thinned and a small driveway curved around the Grand House and sloped downward to a large open area of white rock. On each side was a group of a dozen or so thatched-roof huts where divers roomed. A maze of wooden sidewalks ran from the huts to the central point of the lodge, the open-air bar next to the water.

Mitch headed for the bar to the familiar sounds of reggae and laughter. It was similar to Rumheads, but without the crowd. After a few minutes, the bartender, Henry, delivered a Red Stripe to Mitch.

'Where's Barry Abanks?' Mitch asked.

He nodded to the ocean and returned to the bar. Half a mile out, a boat cut slowly through the still water and made its way toward the lodge. Mitch ate the cheeseburger and watched the dominoes.

The boat docked at a pier between the bar and a larger hut with the words DIVE SHOP hand painted over a window. The divers jumped from the boat with their equipment bags and, without exception, headed for the bar. A short, wiry man stood next to the boat and barked orders at the deckhands, who were unloading empty scuba tanks onto the pier. He wore a white baseball cap and not much else. A tiny black pouch covered his crotch and most of his rear end. From the looks of his brown leathery skin he hadn't worn much in the past fifty years. He checked in at the dive shop, yelled at the dive captains and deckhands and made his way to the bar. He ignored the crowd and went to the freezer, where he picked up a Heineken, removed the top and took a long drink.

The bartender said something to Abanks and nodded toward Mitch. He opened another Heineken and walked to Mitch's table.

He did not smile. 'Are you looking for me?' It was almost a sneer.

'Are you Mr. Abanks?'

'That's me. What do you want?'

'I'd like to talk to you for a few minutes.'

He gulped his beer and gazed at the ocean. 'I'm too busy. I have a dive boat leaving in forty minutes.'

'My name is Mitch McDeere. I'm a lawyer from Memphis.'

Abanks glared at him with tiny brown eyes. Mitch had his attention. 'So?'

'So, the two men who died with your son were friends of mine. It won't take but a few minutes.'

Abanks sat on a stool and rested on his elbows. 'That's not one of my favorite subjects.'

'I know. I'm sorry.'

'The police instructed me not to talk to anyone.'

'It's confidential. I swear.'

Abanks squinted and stared at the brilliant blue water. His face and arms bore the scars of a life at sea, a life spent sixty feet down guiding novices through and around coral reefs and wrecked ships.

'What do you want to know?' he asked softly.

'Can we talk somewhere else?'

'Sure. Let's take a walk.' He yelled at Henry and spoke to a table of divers as he left. They walked on the beach.

'I'd like to talk about the accident,' Mitch said.

'You can ask. I may not answer.'

'What caused the explosion?'

'I don't know. Perhaps an air compressor. Perhaps some fuel. We are not certain. The boat was badly damaged and most of the clues went up in flames.'

'Was it your boat?'

'Yes. One of my small ones. A thirty-footer. Your friends had chartered it for the morning.'

'Where were the bodies found?'

'In eighty feet of water. There was nothing suspicious about the bodies, except that there were no burns or other injuries that would indicate they had been in the explosion. So I guess that makes the bodies very suspicious.'

'The autopsies said they drowned.'

'Yes, they drowned. But your friends were in full scuba gear, which was later examined by one of my divemasters. It worked perfectly. They were good divers.'

'What about your son?'

'He was not in full gear. But he could swim like a fish.'

'Where was the explosion?'

'They had been scheduled to dive along a series of reef formations at Roger's Wreck Point. Are you familiar with the island?'

'No.'

'It's around the East Bay on Northeastern Point. Your friends had never dived there, and my son suggested they try it. We knew your friends well. They were experienced divers and took it seriously. They always wanted a boat by themselves and didn't mind paying for it. And they always wanted Philip as their dive captain. We don't know if they made any dives on the Point. The boat was found burning two miles at sea, far from any of our dive sites.'

'Could the boat have drifted?'

'Impossible. If there had been engine trouble, Philip would have used the radio. We have modern equipment, and our divemasters are always in touch with the dive shop. There's no way the explosion could have occurred at the Point. No one saw it or heard it, and there's always someone around. Secondly, a disabled boat could not drift two miles in that water. And, most importantly, the bodies were not on the boat, remember. Suppose the boat did drift, how do you explain the drifting of the bodies eighty feet below. They were found within twenty meters of the boat.'

'Who found them?'

'My men. We caught the bulletin over the radio, and I sent a crew. We knew it was our boat, and my men started diving. They found the bodies within minutes.'

'I know this is difficult to talk about.'

Abanks finished his beer and threw the bottle in a wooden garbage box. 'Yes, it is. But time takes away the pain. Why are you so interested?'

'The families have a lot of questions.'

'I am sorry for them. I met their wives last year. They spent a week with us. Such nice people.'

'Is it possible they were simply exploring new territory when it happened?'

'Possible, yes. But not likely. Our boats report their movements from one dive site to the next. That's standard procedure. No exceptions. I have fired a dive captain for not clearing a site before going to the next. My son was the best captain on the island. He grew up in these waters. He would never fail to report his movements at sea. It's that simple. The police believe that is what happened, but they have to believe something. It's the only explanation they have.'

'But how do they explain the condition of the bodies?'

'They can't. It's simply another diving accident as far as they're concerned.'

'Was it an accident?'

'I think not.'

The sandals had rubbed blisters by now, and Mitch removed them. They turned and started back to the lodge.

'If it wasn't an accident, what was it?'

Abanks walked and watched the ocean crawl along

167

the beach. He smiled for the first time. 'What are the other possibilities?'

'There's a rumor in Memphis that drugs could have been involved.'

'Tell me about this rumor.'

'We've heard that your son was active in a drug ring, that possibly he was using the boat that day to meet a supplier at sea, that there was a dispute and my friends got in the way.'

Abanks smiled again and shook his head. 'Not Philip. To my knowledge he never used drugs, and I know he didn't trade in them. He wasn't interested in money. Just women and diving.'

'Not a chance?'

'No, not a chance. I've never heard this rumor, and I doubt if they know more in Memphis. This is a small island, and I would have heard it by now. It's completely false.'

The conversation was over and they stopped near the bar. 'I'll ask you a favor,' Abanks said. 'Do not mention any of this to the families. I cannot prove what I know to be true, so it's best if no one knows. Especially the families.'

'I won't tell anyone. And I will ask you not to mention our conversation. Someone might follow me here and ask questions about my visit. Just say we talked about diving.'

'As you wish.'

'My wife and I will be here next spring for our vacation. I'll be sure to look you up.'

FOURTEEN

St. Andrew's Episcopal School was located behind the church of the same name on a densely wooded and perfectly manicured five-acre estate in the middle of midtown Memphis. The white and yellow brick was occasionally visible where the ivy had for some reason turned and pursued another course. Symmetrical rows of clipped boxwoods lined the sidewalks and the small playground. It was a one-story L-shaped building sitting quietly in the shadows of a dozen ancient oaks. Cherished for its exclusivity, St. Andrew's was the most expensive private school in Memphis for grades kindergarten through six. Affluent parents signed the waiting list shortly after birth.

Mitch stopped the BMW in the parking lot between the church and the school. Abby's burgundy Peugeot was three spaces down, sitting innocently. He was unexpected. The plane had landed an hour earlier, and he had stopped by the house to change into something lawyerly. He would see her, then back to his desk for a few hours at one hundred and fifty per.

He wanted to see her here, at the school, unannounced. A surprise attack. A countermove. He would say hello. He missed her. He couldn't wait to see her, so he stopped by the school. He would be brief, the first touch and feel and words after that incident on the beach. Could she tell just by looking at him?

Maybe she could read his eyes. Would she notice a slight strain in his voice? Not if she was surprised. Not if she was flattered by this visit.

He squeezed the steering wheel and stared at her car. What an idiot! A stupid fool! Why didn't he run? Just throw her skirt in the sand and run like hell. But, of course, he didn't. He said what the hell, no one will ever know. So now he was supposed to shrug it off and say what the hell, everybody does it.

On the plane he laid his plans. First, he would wait until late this night and tell her the truth. He would not lie, had no desire to live a lie. He would admit it and tell her exactly what happened. Maybe she would understand. Why, almost any man – hell, virtually every man would have taken the dive. His next move would depend on her reaction. If she was cool and showed a trace of compassion, he would tell her he was sorry, so very sorry, and that it would never happen again. If she fell all to pieces, he would beg, literally beg for forgiveness and swear on the Bible that it was a mistake and would never happen again. He would tell her how much he loved her and worshipped her, and please just give him one more chance. And if she started packing her bags, he would probably at that point realize he should not have told her.

Deny. Deny. Deny. His criminal-law professor at Harvard had been a radical named Moskowitz, who had made a name for himself defending terrorists and assassins and child fondlers. His theory of defense was simply: Deny! Deny! Deny! Never admit one fact or one piece of evidence that would indicate guilt.

He remembered Moskowitz as they landed in Miami, and began working on Plan B, which called for this surprise visit at the school and a late-night romantic dinner at her favorite place. And no mention of anything but hard work in the Caymans. He opened the car door, thought of her beautiful smiling, trusting

170

face and felt nauseous. A thick, dull pain hammered deep in his stomach. He walked slowly in the late autumn breeze to the front door.

The hallway was empty and quiet. To his right was the office of the headmaster. He waited for a moment in the hall, waited to be seen, but no one was there. He walked quietly ahead until, at the third classroom, he heard the wonderful voice of his wife. She was plowing through multiplication tables when he stuck his head in the door and smiled. She froze, then giggled. She excused herself, told them to stay in their seats and read the next page. She closed the door.

'What're you doing here?' she asked as he grabbed her and pinned her to the wall. She glanced nervously up and down the hall.

'I missed you,' he said with conviction. He bear-hugged her for a good minute. He kissed her neck and tasted the sweetness of her perfume. And then the girl returned. You piece of scum, why didn't you run?

'When did you get in?' she asked, straightening her hair and glancing down the hall.

'About an hour ago. You look wonderful.'

Her eyes were wet. Those wonderfully honest eyes. 'How was your trip?'

'Okay. I missed you. It's no fun when you're not around.'

Her smile widened and she looked away. 'I missed you too.'

They held hands and walked toward the front door. 'I'd like a date tonight,' he said.

'You're not working?'

'No. I'm not working. I'm going out with my wife to her favorite restaurant. We'll eat and drink expensive wine and stay out late, and then get naked when we get home.'

'You did miss me.' She kissed him again, on the

lips, then looked down the hall. 'But you better get out of here before someone sees you.'

They walked quickly to the front door without being seen.

He breathed deeply in the cool air and walked quickly to his car. He did it. He looked into those eyes, held her and kissed her like always. She suspected nothing. She was touched and even moved.

DeVasher paced anxiously behind his desk and sucked nervously on a Roi-Tan. He sat in his worn swivel chair and tried to concentrate on a memo, then he jumped to his feet and paced again. He checked his watch. He called his secretary. He called Oliver Lambert's secretary. He paced some more.

Finally, seventeen minutes after he was supposed to arrive, Ollie was cleared through security and walked into DeVasher's office.

DeVasher stood behind his desk and glared at Ollie. 'You're late!'

'I'm very busy,' Ollie answered as he sat in a worn Naugahyde chair. 'What's so important?'

DeVasher's face instantly changed into a sly, evil smile. He dramatically opened a desk drawer and proudly threw a large manila envelope across the desk into Ollie's lap. 'Some of the best work we've ever done.'

Lambert opened the envelope and gaped at the eight by ten black-and-white photographs. He stared at each one, holding them inches from his nose, memorizing each detail. DeVasher watched proudly.

Lambert reviewed them again and began breathing heavily. 'These are incredible.'

'Yep. We thought so.'

'Who's the girl?' Ollie asked, still staring.

'A local prostitute. Looks pretty good, doesn't she?

We've never used her before, but you can bet we'll use her again.'

'I want to meet her, and soon.'

'No problem. I kinda figured you would.'

'This is incredible. How'd she do it?'

'It looked difficult at first. He told the first girl to get lost. Avery had the other one, but your man wanted no part of her friend. He left and went to that little bar on the beach. That's when our girl there showed up. She's a pro.'

'Where were your people?'

'All over the place. Those were shot from behind a palm tree, about eighty feet away. Pretty good, aren't they?'

'Very good. Give the photographer a bonus. How long did they roll in the sand?'

'Long enough. They were very compatible.'

'I think he really enjoyed himself.'

'We were lucky. The beach was deserted and the timing was perfect.'

Lambert raised a photograph toward the ceiling, in front of his eyes. 'Did you make me a set?' he asked from behind it.

'Of course, Ollie. I know how much you enjoy these things.'

'I thought McDeere would be tougher than that.'

'He's tough, but he's human. He's no dummy either. We're not sure, but we think he knew we were watching him the next day during lunch. He seemed suspicious and began darting around the shopping district. Then he disappeared. He was an hour late for his meeting with Avery at the bank.'

'Where'd he go?'

'We don't know. We were just watching out of curiosity, nothing serious. Hell, he might've been in a bar downtown for all we know. But he just disappeared.'

173

'Watch him carefully. He worries me.'

DeVasher waved another manila envelope. 'Quit worrying, Ollie. We own him now! He would kill for us if he knew about these.'

'What about Tarrance?'

'Not a sign. McDeere ain't mentioned it to anybody, at least not to anybody we're listening to. Tarrance is hard to trail sometimes, but I think he's staying away.'

'Keep your eyes open.'

'Don't worry about my end, Ollie. You're the lawyer, the counselor, the esquire, and you get your eight-by-tens. You run the firm. I run the surveillance.'

'How are things at the McDeere house?'

'Not too good. She was very cool to the trip.'

'What'd she do when he was gone?'

'Well, she ain't one to sit around the house. Two nights she and Quin's wife went out to eat at a couple of those yuppie joints. Then to the movies. She was out one night with a schoolteacher friend. She shopped a little.

'She also called her mother a lot, collect. Evidently there's no love lost between our boy and her parents, and she wants to patch things up. She and her mom are tight and it really bothers her because they can't be a big happy family. She wants to go home to Kentucky for Christmas, and she's afraid he won't go for it. There's a lot of friction. A lot of undercurrents. She tells her mom he works too much, and her mom says it's because he wants to show them up. I don't like the sound of it, Ollie. Bad vibes.'

'Just keep listening. We've tried to slow him down, but he's a machine.'

'Yeah, at a hundred and fifty an hour I know you want him to slack off. Why don't you cut all your associates back to forty hours a week so they can spend more time with their families? You could cut your salary, sell a Jag or two, hock your old lady's diamonds, maybe sell your mansion and buy a smaller house by the country club.'

'Shut up, DeVasher.'

Oliver Lambert stormed out of the office. DeVasher turned red with his high-pitched laughter, then, when his office was empty, he locked the photos in a file cabinet. 'Mitchell McDeere,' he said to himself with an immense smile, 'now you are ours.'

FIFTEEN

On a Friday, at noon, two weeks before Christmas, Abby said goodbye to her students and left St. Andrew's for the holidays. At one, she parked in a lot full of Volvos and BMWs and Saabs and more Peugeots and walked hurriedly through the cold rain into the crowded terrarium where the young affluent gathered to eat quiche and *fajitas* and black bean soup among the plants. This was Kay Quin's current hot spot of the year, and this was the second lunch they'd had in a month. Kay was late, as usual.

It was a friendship still in the initial stages of development. Cautious by nature, Abby had never been one to rush into chumminess with a stranger. The three years at Harvard had been friendless, and she had learned a great deal of independence. In six months in Memphis she had met a handful of prospects at church and one at school, but she moved cautiously.

At first Kay Quin had pushed hard. She was at once a tour guide, shopping consultant and even a decorator. But Abby had moved slowly, learning a little with each visit and watching her new friend carefully. They had eaten several times in the Quin home. They had seen each other at firm dinners and functions, but always in a crowd. And they had enjoyed each other's company over four long lunches at whatever happened to be the hottest gathering place at that moment for the young and beautiful Gold MasterCard holders in Memphis. Kay noticed cars and homes and clothes, but pretended to ignore it all. Kay wanted to be a friend, a close friend, a confidante, an intimate. Abby kept the distance, slowly allowing her in.

The reproduction of a 1950s jukebox sat below Abby's table on the first level near the bar, where a standing-room crowd sipped and waited for tables. After ten minutes and two Roy Orbisons, Kay emerged from the crowd at the front door and looked upward to the third level. Abby smiled and waved.

They hugged and pecked each other properly on the cheeks, without transferring lipstick.

'Sorry I'm late,' Kay said.

'That's okay. I'm used to it.'

'This place is packed,' Kay said, looking around in amazement. It was always packed. 'So you're out of school?'

'Yes. As of an hour ago. I'm free until January 6.'

They admired each other's outfits and commented on how slim and in general how beautiful and young they were.

Christmas shopping at once became the topic, and they talked of stores and sales and children until the wine arrived. Abby ordered scampi in a skillet, but Kay stuck with the old fern bar standby of broccoli quiche.

'What're your plans for Christmas?' Kay asked.

'None yet. I'd like to go to Kentucky to see my folks, but I'm afraid Mitch won't go. I've dropped a couple of hints, both of which were ignored.'

'He still doesn't like your parents?'

'There's been no change. In fact, we don't discuss them. I don't know how to handle it.'

'With great caution, I would imagine.'

'Yeah, and great patience. My parents were wrong,

177

but I still need them. It's painful when the only man I've ever loved can't tolerate my parents. I pray every day for a small miracle.'

'Sounds like you need a rather large miracle. Is he working as hard as Lamar says?'

'I don't know how a person could work any harder. It's eighteen hours a day Monday through Friday, eight hours on Saturday, and since Sunday is a day of rest, he puts in only five or six hours. He reserves a little time for me on Sunday.'

'Do I hear a touch of frustration?'

'A lot of frustration, Kay. I've been patient, but it's getting worse. I'm beginning to feel like a widow. I'm tired of sleeping on the couch waiting for him to get home.'

'You're there for food and sex, huh?'

'I wish. He's too tired for sex. It's not a priority anymore. And this is a man who could never get enough. I mean, we almost killed each other in law school. Now, once a week if I'm lucky. He comes home, eats if he has the energy and goes to bed. If I'm really lucky, he might talk to me for a few minutes before he passes out. I'm starved for adult conversation, Kay. I spend seven hours a day with eight-year olds, and I crave words with more than three syllables. I try to explain this to him, and he's snoring. Did you go through this with Lamar?'

'Sort of. He worked seventy hours a week for the first year. I think they all do. It's kind of like initiation into the fraternity. A male ritual in which you have to prove your manliness. But most of them run out of gas after a year, and cut back to sixty or sixty-five hours. They still work hard, but not the kamikaze routine of the rookie year.'

'Does Lamar work every Saturday?'

'Most Saturdays, for a few hours. Never on Sunday. I've put my foot down. Of course, if there's a big deadline or it's tax season, then they all work around the clock. I think Mitch has them puzzled.'

'He's not slowing down any. In fact, he's possessed. Occasionally he won't come home until dawn. Then it's just a quick shower, and back to the office.'

'Lamar says he's already a legend around the office.'

Abby sipped her wine and looked over the rail at the bar. 'That's great. I'm married to a legend.'

'Have you thought about children?'

'It requires sex, remember?'

'Come on, Abby, it can't be that bad.'

'I'm not ready for children. I can't handle being a single parent. I love my husband, but at this point in his life, he would probably have a terribly important meeting and leave me alone in the labor room. Eight centimeters dilated. He thinks of nothing but that damned law firm.'

Kay reached across the table and gently took Abby's hand. 'It'll be okay,' she said with a firm smile and a wise look. 'The first year is the hardest. It gets better, I promise.'

Abby smiled. 'I'm sorry.'

The waiter arrived with their food, and they ordered more wine. The scampi simmered in the butter-and-garlic sauce and produced a delicious aroma. The cold quiche was all alone on a bed of lettuce with a sickly tomato wedge.

Kay picked a glob of broccoli and chewed on it. 'You know, Abby, the firm encourages children.'

'I don't care. Right now I don't like the firm. I'm competing with the firm, and I'm losing badly. So I couldn't care less what they want. They will not plan my family for me. I don't understand why they are so interested in things which are none of their business. That place is eerie, Kay. I can't put my finger on it, but those people make my skin crawl.'

'They want happy lawyers with stable families.'

'And I want my husband back. They're in the process of taking him away, so the family is not so stable. If they'd get off his back, perhaps we could be normal like everyone else and have a yard full of children. But not now.'

The wine arrived, and the scampi cooled. She ate it slowly and drank her wine. Kay searched for less sensitive areas.

'Lamar said Mitch went to the Caymans last month.'

'Yes. He and Avery were there for three days. Strictly business, or so he says. Have you been there?'

'Every year. It's a beautiful place with gorgeous beaches and warm water. We go in June of each year, when school is out. The firm owns two huge condos right on the beach.'

'Mitch wants to vacation there in March, during my spring break.'

'You need to. Before we had kids, we did nothing but lie on the beach, drink rum and have sex. That's one reason the firm furnishes the condos and, if you're lucky, the airplane. They work hard, but they appreciate the need for leisure.'

'Don't mention the firm to me, Kay. I don't want to hear about what they like or dislike, or what they do or don't do, or what they encourage or discourage.'

'It'll get better, Abby. I promise. You must understand that your husband and my husband are both very good lawyers, but they could not earn this kind of money anywhere else. And you and I would be driving new Buicks instead of new Peugeots and Mercedes-Benzes.'

Abby cut a shrimp in half and rolled it through the butter and garlic. She stabbed a portion with a fork, then pushed her plate away. The wineglass was empty. 'I know, Kay, I know. But there is a hell of a lot more to life than a big yard and a Peugeot. No one around here seems to be aware of that. I swear, I think we were happier living in a two-room student apartment in Cambridge.'

'You've only been here a few months. Mitch will slow down eventually, and you'll get into your routine. Before long there will be little McDeeres running around the backyard, and before you know it, Mitch will be a partner. Believe me, Abby, things will get much better. You're going through a period we've all been through, and we made it.'

'Thanks, Kay, I certainly hope you're right.'

The park was a small one, two or three acres on a bluff above the river. A row of cannons and two bronze statues memorialized those brave Confederates who had fought to save the river and the city. Under the monument to a general and his horse a wino tucked himself away. His cardboard box and ragged quilt provided little shelter from the bitter cold and the tiny pellets of frozen rain. Fifty yards below, the evening traffic rushed along Riverside Drive. It was dark.

Mitch walked to the row of cannons and stood gazing at the river and the bridges leading to Arkansas. He zipped his raincoat and flipped the collar around his ears. He looked at his watch. He waited.

The Bendini Building was almost visible six blocks away. He had parked in a garage in midtown and taken a taxi back to the river. He was sure he had not been followed. He waited.

The icy wind blowing up from the river reddened his face and reminded him of the winters in Kentucky after his parents were gone. Cold, bitter winters. Lonely, desolate winters. He had worn someone else's coats, passed down from a cousin or a friend, and they had never been heavy enough. Secondhand clothes. He dismissed those thoughts.

The frozen rain turned to sleet and the tiny pieces of

ice stuck in his hair and bounced on the sidewalk around him. He looked at his watch.

There were footsteps and a figure in a hurry walking toward the cannons. Whoever it was stopped, then approached slowly.

'Mitch?' It was Eddie Lomax, dressed in jeans and a full-length rabbit coat. With his thick mustache and white cowboy hat he looked like an ad for a cigarette. The Marlboro Man.

'Yeah, it's me.'

Lomax walked closer, to the other side of the cannon. They stood like Confederate sentries watching the river.

'Have you been followed?' Mitch asked.

'No, I don't think so. You?'

'No.'

Mitch stared at the traffic on Riverside Drive, and beyond, to the river. Lomax thrust his hands deep into his pockets. 'You talked to Ray, lately?' Lomax asked.

'No.' The answer was short, as if to say, 'I'm not standing here in the sleet to chitchat.'

'What'd you find?' Mitch asked, without looking.

Lomax lit a cigarette, and now he *was* the Marlboro Man. 'On the three lawyers, I found a little info. Alice Knauss was killed in a car wreck in 1977. Police report said she was hit by a drunk driver, but oddly enough, no such driver was ever found. The wreck happened around midnight on a Wednesday. She had worked late down at the office and was driving home. She lived out east, in Sycamore View, and about a mile from her condo she gets hit head-on by a one-ton pickup. Happened on New London Road. She was driving a fancy little Fiat and it was blown to pieces. No witnesses. When the cops got there, the truck was empty. No sign of a driver. They ran the plates and found that the truck had been stolen in St. Louis three days earlier. No fingerprints or nothing.'

'They dusted for prints?'

'Yeah. I know the investigator who handled it. They were suspicious but had zero to go on. There was a broken bottle of whiskey on the floorboard, so they blamed it on a drunk driver and closed the file.'

'Autopsy?'

'No. It was pretty obvious how she died.'

'Sounds suspicious.'

'Very much so. All three of them are suspicious. Robert Lamm was the deer hunter in Arkansas. He and some friends had a deer camp in Izard County in the Ozarks. They went over two or three times a year during the season. After a morning in the woods, everyone returned to the cabin but Lamm. They searched for two weeks and found him in a ravine, partially covered with leaves. He had been shot once through the head, and that's about all they know. They ruled out suicide, but there was simply no evidence to begin an investigation.'

'So he was murdered?'

'Apparently so. Autopsy showed an entry at the base of the skull and an exit wound that removed most of his face. Suicide would have been impossible.'

'It could have been an accident.'

'Possibly. He could have caught a bullet intended for a deer, but it's unlikely. He was found a good distance from the camp, in an area seldom used by hunters. His friends said they neither heard nor saw other hunters the morning he disappeared. I talked to the sheriff, who is now the ex-sheriff, and he's convinced it was murder. He claims there was evidence that the body had been covered intentionally.'

'Is that all?'

'Yeah, on Lamm.'

'What about Mickel?'

'Pretty sad. He committed suicide in 1984 at the age of thirty-four. Shot himself in the right temple with a Smith & Wesson .357. He left a lengthy farewell letter in which he told his ex-wife he hoped she would forgive him and all that crap. Said goodbye to the kids and his mother. Real touching.'

'Was it in his handwriting?'

'Not exactly. It was typed, which was not unusual, because he typed a good bit. He had an IBM Selectric in his office, and the letter came from it. He had a terrible handwriting.'

'So what's suspicious?'

'The gun. He never bought a gun in his life. No one knows where it came from. No registration, no serial number, nothing. One of his friends in the firm allegedly said something to the effect that Mickel had told him he had bought a gun for protection. Evidently he was having some emotional problems.'

'What do you think?'

Lomax threw his cigarette butt in the frozen rain on the sidewalk. He cupped his hands over his mouth and blew in them. 'I don't know. I can't believe a tax lawyer with no knowledge of guns could obtain one without registration or serial number. If a guy like that wanted a gun, he would simply go to a gun shop, fill out the papers and buy a nice, shiny new piece. This gun was at least ten years old and had been sanitized by professionals.'

'Did the cops investigate?'

'Not really. It was open and shut.'

'Did he sign the letter?'

'Yeah, but I don't know who verified the signature. He and his wife had been divorced for a year, and she had moved back to Baltimore.'

Mitch buttoned the top button of his overcoat and shook the ice from his collar. The sleet was heavier, and the sidewalk was covered. Tiny icicles were beginning to form under the barrel of the cannon. The traffic slowed on Riverside as wheels began to slide and spin.

'So what do you think of our little firm?' Mitch asked as he stared at the river in the distance.

'It's a dangerous place to work. They've lost five lawyers in the past fifteen years. That's not a very good safety record.'

'Five?'

'If you include Hodge and Kozinski. I've got a source telling me there are some unanswered questions.'

'I didn't hire you to investigate those two.'

'And I'm not charging you for it. I got curious, that's all.'

'How much do I owe you?'

'Six-twenty.'

'I'll pay cash. No records, okay?'

'Suits me. I prefer cash.'

Mitch turned from the river and gazed at the tall buildings three blocks from the park. He was cold now, but in no hurry to leave. Lomax watched him from the corner of his eye.

'You've got problems, don't you, pal?'

'Wouldn't you say so?' Mitch answered.

'I wouldn't work there. I mean, I don't know all that you do, and I suspect you know a lot you're not telling. But we're standing here in the sleet because we don't want to be seen. We can't talk on the phone. We can't meet in your office. Now you don't want to meet in my office. You think you're being followed all the time. You tell me to be careful and watch my rear because they, whoever they are, may be following me. You've got five lawyers in that firm who've died under very suspicious circumstances, and you act like you may be next. Yeah, I'd say you got problems. Big problems.'

'What about Tarrance?'

'One of their best agents; transferred in here about two years ago.'

'From where?'

'New York.'

The wino rolled from under the bronze horse and fell to the sidewalk. He grunted, staggered to his feet, retrieved his cardboard box and quilt and left in the direction of downtown. Lomax jerked around and watched anxiously. 'It's just a tramp,' Mitch said. They both relaxed.

'Who are we hiding from?' Lomax asked.

'I wish I knew.'

Lomax studied his face carefully. 'I think you know.'

Mitch said nothing.

'Look, Mitch, you're not paying me to get involved. I realize that. But my instincts tell me you're in trouble, and I think you need a friend, someone to trust. I can help, if you need me. I don't know who the bad guys are, but I'm convinced they're very dangerous.'

'Thanks,' Mitch said softly without looking, as if it was time for Lomax to leave and let him stand there in the sleet for a while.

'I would jump in that river for Ray McDeere, and I can certainly help his little brother.'

Mitch nodded slightly, but said nothing. Lomax lit another cigarette and kicked the ice from his lizard-skins. 'Just call me anytime. And be careful. They're out there, and they play for keeps.'

SIXTEEN

At the intersection of Madison and Cooper in mid-town, the old two-story buildings had been renovated into singles bars and watering holes and gift shops and a handful of good restaurants. The intersection was known as Overton Square, and it provided Memphis with its best nightlife. A playhouse and a bookstore added a touch of culture. Trees lined the narrow median on Madison. The weekends were rowdy with college students and sailors from the Navy base, but on weeknights the restaurants were full but quiet and uncrowded. Paulette's, a quaint French place in a white stucco building, was noted for its wine list and desserts and the gentle voice of the man at the Steinway. With sudden affluence came a collection of credit cards, and the McDeeres had used theirs in a quest for the best restaurants in town. Paulette's was the favorite, so far.

Mitch sat in the corner of the bar, drinking coffee and watching the front door. He was early, and had planned it that way. He had called her three hours earlier and asked if he could have a date for seven. She asked why, and he said he would explain later. Since the Caymans he had known someone was following, watching, listening. For the past month he had spoken carefully on the phone, had caught himself watching the rearview mirror, had even chosen his words around the house. Someone was watching and listening, he was sure.

Abby rushed in from the cold and glanced around the parlor for her husband. He met her in the front of the bar and pecked her on the cheek. She removed her coat, and they followed the maître d' to a small table in a row of small tables which were all full with people within earshot. Mitch glanced around for another table, but there were none. He thanked him and sat across from his wife.

'What's the occasion?' she asked suspiciously.

'Do I need a reason to have dinner with my wife?'

'Yes. It's seven o'clock on Monday night, and you're not at the office. This is indeed a special occasion.'

A waiter squeezed between their table and the next, and asked if they wanted a drink. Two white wines, please. Mitch glanced around the dining room again and caught a glimpse of a gentleman sitting alone five tables away. The face looked familiar. When Mitch looked again, the face slid behind a menu.

'What's the matter, Mitch?'

He laid his hand on hers and frowned. 'Abby, we gotta talk.'

Her hand flinched slightly and she stopped smiling. 'About what?'

He lowered his voice. 'About something very serious.'

She exhaled deeply and said, 'Can we wait for the wine? I might need it.'

Mitch looked again at the face behind the menu. 'We can't talk here.'

'Then why are we here?'

'Look, Abby, you know where the rest rooms are? Down the hall over there, to your right?'

'Yes, I know.'

'There's a rear entrance at the end of the hall. It

goes out to the side street behind the restaurant. I want you to go to the rest room, then out the door. I'll be waiting next to the street.'

She said nothing. Her eyebrows lowered and the eyes narrowed. Her head leaned slightly to the right.

'Trust me, Abby. I can explain later. I'll meet you outside and we'll find another place to eat. I can't talk in here.'

'You're scaring me.'

'Please,' he said firmly, squeezing her hand. 'Everything is fine. I'll bring your coat.'

She stood with her purse and left the room. Mitch looked over his shoulder at the man with the familiar face, who suddenly stood and welcomed an elderly lady to his table. He did not notice Abby's exit.

In the street behind Paulette's, Mitch draped the coat over Abby's shoulders and pointed eastward. 'I can explain,' he said more than once. A hundred feet down the street, they walked between two buildings and came to the front entrance of the Bombay Bicycle Club, a singles bar with good food and live blues. Mitch looked at the headwaiter, then surveyed the two dining rooms, then pointed to a table in the rear corner. 'That one,' he said.

Mitch sat with his back to the wall and his face toward the dining room and the front door. The corner was dark. Candles lit the table. They ordered more wine.

Abby sat motionless, staring at him, watching every move and waiting.

'Do you remember a guy named Rick Acklin from Western Kentucky?'

'No,' she said without moving her lips.

'He played baseball, lived in the dorm. I think you may have met him once. A very nice guy, real clean-cut, good student. I think he was from Bowling Green. We weren't good friends, but we knew each other.'

She shook her head and waited.

'Well, he finished a year before we did and went to law school at Wake Forest. Now he's with the FBI. And he's working here in Memphis.' He watched her closely to see if 'FBI' would have an impact. It did not. 'And today I'm eating lunch at Obloe's hot-dog place on Main Street, when Rick walks up out of nowhere and says hello. Just like it was a real coincidence. We chat for a few minutes, and another agent, guy by the name of Tarrance, walks up and has a seat. It's the second time Tarrance has chased me down since I passed the bar.'

'The second . . . ?'

'Yes. Since August.'

'And these are . . . FBI agents?'

'Yes, with badges and everything. Tarrance is a veteran agent from New York. Been here about two years. Acklin is a rookie they brought in three months ago.'

'What do they want?'

The wine arrived and Mitch looked around the club. A band was tuning up on a small stage in a far corner. The bar was crowded with well-dressed professional types chitting and chatting relentlessly. The waiter pointed to the unopened menus. 'Later,' Mitch said rudely.

'Abby, I don't know what they want. The first visit was in August, right after my name was printed in the paper for passing the bar.' He sipped his wine and detailed play by play the first Tarrance visit at Lansky's Deli on Union, the warnings about whom not to trust and where not to talk, the meeting with Locke and Lambert and the other partners. He explained their version of why the FBI was so interested in the firm and said that he discussed it with Lamar and believed every word Locke and Lambert had said.

190

Abby hung on every word, but waited to start asking.

'And now, today, while I'm minding my own business, eating a foot-long with onions, this guy I went to college with walks up and tells me that they, the FBI, know for a fact that my phones are bugged, my home is wired and somebody down at Bendini, Lambert & Locke knows when I sneeze and take a crap. Think of it, Abby, Rick Acklin was transferred here after I passed the bar exam. Nice coincidence, huh?'

'But what do they want?'

'They won't say. They can't tell me, yet. They want me to trust them, and all that routine. I don't know, Abby. I have no idea what they're after. But they've chosen me for some reason.'

'Did you tell Lamar about this visit?'

'No. I haven't told anyone. Except you. And I don't plan to tell anyone.'

She gulped the wine. 'Our phones are tapped?'

'According to the FBI. But how do they know?'

'They're not stupid, Mitch. If the FBI told me my phones were tapped, I'd believe them. You don't?'

'I don't know whom to believe. Locke and Lambert were so smooth and believable when they explained how the firm fights with the IRS and the FBI. I want to believe them, but so much of it doesn't add up. Look at it this way – if the firm had a rich client who was shady and worthy of FBI scrutiny, why would the FBI pick me, the rookie, the one who knows the least, and begin following me? What do I know? I work on files someone else hands me. I have no clients of my own. I do as I'm told. Why not go after one of the partners?'

'Maybe they want you to squeal on the clients.'

'No way. I'm a lawyer and sworn to secrecy about the affairs of clients. Everything I know about a client

191

is strictly confidential. The feds know that. No one expects a lawyer to talk about his clients.'

'Have you seen any illegal deals?'

He cracked his knuckles and gazed around the dining room. He smiled at her. The wine had settled and was taking effect. 'I'm not supposed to answer that question, even from you, Abby. But the answer is no. I've worked on files for twenty of Avery's clients and a few other ones here and there, and I've seen nothing suspicious. Maybe a couple of risky tax shelters, but nothing illegal. I've got a few questions about the bank accounts I saw in the Caymans, but nothing serious.' Caymans! His stomach dropped as he thought of the girl on the beach. He felt sick.

The waiter loitered nearby and stared at the menus. 'More wine,' Mitch said, pointing at the glasses.

Abby leaned forward, near the candles, and looked bewildered. 'Okay, who tapped our phones?'

'Assuming they're tapped, I have no idea. At the first meeting in August, Tarrance implied it was someone from the firm. I mean, that's the way I took it. He said not to trust anyone at the firm, and that everything I said was subject to being heard and recorded. I assumed he meant they were doing it.'

'And what did Mr. Locke say about that?'

'Nothing. I didn't tell him. I kept a few things to myself.'

'Someone has tapped our phones and wired our house?'

'And maybe our cars. Rick Acklin made a big deal of it today. He kept telling me not to say anything I didn't want recorded.'

'Mitch, this is incredible. Why would a law firm do that?'

He shook his head slowly and looked into the empty wineglass. 'I have no idea, babe. No idea.'

The waiter set two new wineglasses on the table and

stood with his hands behind him. 'Will you be ordering?' he asked.

'In a few minutes,' Abby said.

'We'll call you when we're ready,' Mitch added.

'Do you believe it, Mitch?'

'I think something's up. There's more to the story.'

She slowly folded her hands on the table and stared at him with a look of utter fear. He told the story of Hodge and Kozinski, starting with Tarrance at the deli, then to the Caymans and being followed and the meeting with Abanks. He told her everything Abanks had said. Then Eddie Lomax and the deaths of Alice Knauss, Robert Lamm and John Mickel.

'I've lost my appetite,' she said when he finished.

'So have I. But I feel better now that you know.'

'Why didn't you tell me sooner?'

'I hoped it would go away. I hoped Tarrance would leave me alone and find someone else to torment. But he's here to stay. That's why Rick Acklin was transferred to Memphis. To work on me. I have been selected by the FBI for a mission I know nothing about.'

'I feel weak.'

'We have to be careful, Abby. We must continue to live as if we suspect nothing.'

'I don't believe this. I'm sitting here listening to you, but I don't believe what you're telling me. This is not real, Mitch. You expect me to live in a house that's wired and the phones are tapped and someone, somewhere is listening to everything we say.'

'Do you have a better idea?'

'Yeah. Let's hire this Lomax guy to inspect our house.'

'I've thought of that. But what if he finds something? Think about it. What if we know for sure that the house is wired? What then? What if he breaks a device that's been planted? They, whoever in hell they are, will know that we know. It's too dangerous, for now anyway. Maybe later.'

'This is crazy, Mitch. I guess we're supposed to run out in the backyard to have a conversation.'

'Of course not. We could use the front yard.'

'At this moment, I don't appreciate your sense of humor.'

'Sorry. Look, Abby, let's be normal and patient for a while. Tarrance has convinced me he's serious and he's not going to forget about me. I can't stop him. He finds me, remember. I think they follow me and wait in ambush. For the time being, it's important that we carry on as usual.'

'Usual? Come to think of it, there's not much conversation around our house these days. I sort of feel sorry for them if they're waiting to hear meaningful dialogue. I talk to Hearsay a lot.'

SEVENTEEN

The snow cleared long before Christmas, leaving the ground wet and making way for the traditional Southern holiday weather of gray skies and cold rain. Memphis had seen two white Christmases in the past ninety years, and the experts predicted no more in the century.

There was snow in Kentucky, but the roads were clear. Abby called her parents early Christmas morning after she packed. She was coming, she said, but she would be alone. They were disappointed, they said, and suggested that perhaps she should stay if it was causing trouble. She insisted. It was a ten-hour drive. Traffic would be light, and she would be there by dark.

Mitch said very little. He spread the morning paper on the floor next to the tree and pretended to concentrate as she loaded her car. The dog hid nearby under a chair, as if waiting for an explosion. Their gifts had been opened and arranged neatly on the couch. Clothes and perfume and albums, and for her, a full-length fox coat. For the first time in the young marriage, there was money to spend at Christmas.

She draped the coat over her arm and walked to the paper. 'I'm leaving now,' she said softly, but firmly.

He stood slowly and looked at her.

'I wish you would come with me,' she said.

'Maybe next year.' It was a lie, and they knew it. But it sounded good. It was promising.

'Please be careful.'

'Take care of my dog.'

'We'll be fine.'

He took her shoulders and kissed her on the cheek. He looked at her and smiled. She was beautiful, much more so than when they married. At twenty-four, she looked her age, but the years were becoming very generous.

They walked to the carport, and he helped her into the car. They kissed again, and she backed down the driveway.

Merry Christmas, he said to himself. Merry Christmas, he said to the dog.

After an hour of watching the walls, he threw two changes of clothes in the BMW, placed Hearsay in the front seat and left town. He drove south on Interstate 55, out of Memphis, into Mississippi. The road was deserted, but he kept an eye on the rearview mirror. The dog whimpered precisely every sixty minutes, and Mitch would stop on the shoulder – if possible, just over a hill. He would find a cluster of trees where he could hide and watch the traffic while Hearsay did his business. He noticed nothing. After five stops, he was sure he was not being followed. They evidently took off Christmas Day.

In six hours he was in Mobile, and two hours later he crossed the bay at Pensacola and headed for the Emerald Coast of Florida. Highway 98 ran through the coastal towns of Navarre, Fort Walton Beach, Destin and Sandestin. It encountered clusters of condominiums and motels, miles of shopping centers, then strings of run-down amusement parks and low rent T-shirt shops, most of which had been locked and neglected since Labor Day. Then it went for miles with no congestion, no sprawl, just an awesome view of the snowy-white beaches and brilliant emerald waters of the Gulf. East of Sandestin, the highway narrowed and left the coast, and for an hour he drove alone on the two-lane with nothing to look at but the woods and an occasional self-serve gas station or quick-shop convenience store.

At dusk, he passed a high rise, and a sign said Panama City Beach was eight miles ahead. The highway found the coast again at a point where it forked and offered a choice between the bypass to the north and the scenic route straight ahead on what was called the Miracle Strip. He chose the scenic route next to the beach – the strip that ran for fifteen miles by the water and was lined on both sides with condos, cheap motels, trailer parks, vacation cottages, fast-food joints and T-shirt shops. This was Panama City Beach.

Most of the ten zillion condos were empty, but there were a few cars parked about and he assumed that some families vacationed on the beach for Christmas. A hot-weather Christmas. At least they're together, he said to himself. The dog barked, and they stopped by a pier where men from Pennsylvania and Ohio and Canada fished and watched the dark waters.

They cruised the Miracle Strip by themselves. Hearsay stood on the door and took in the sights, barking at the occasional flashing neon of a cinder-block motel advertising its openness and cheap rates. Christmas on the Miracle Strip closed everything but a handful of diehard coffee shops and motels.

He stopped for gas at an all-night Texaco with a clerk who seemed uncommonly friendly.

'San Luis Street?' Mitch asked.

'Yes, yes,' the clerk said with an accent and pointed to the west. 'Second traffic light to the right. First left. That's San Luis.'

The neighborhood was a disorganized suburb of antique mobile homes. Mobile, yes, but it was apparent they had not moved in decades. The trailers were packed tightly together like rows of dominoes. The short, narrow driveways seemed inches apart and were filled with old pickups and rusted lawn furniture. The streets were crowded with parked cars, junk cars, abandoned cars. Motorcycles and bicycles leaned on the trailer hitches and lawn-mower handles protruded from beneath each home. A sign called the place a retirement village – 'San Pedro Estates – A Half Mile from the Emerald Coast.' It was more like a slum on wheels, or a project with a trailer hitch.

He found San Luis Street and suddenly felt nervous. It was winding and narrow with smaller trailers in worse shape than the other 'retirement homes.' He drove slowly, anxiously watching street numbers and observing the multitude of out-of-state license plates. The street was empty except for the parked and abandoned cars.

The home at 486 San Luis was one of the oldest and smallest. It was scarcely bigger than a camper. The original paint job looked to be silver, but the paint was cracked and peeling, and a dark green layer of mold covered the top and inched downward to a point just above the windows. The screens were missing. One window above the trailer hitch was badly cracked and held together with gray electrical tape. A small covered porch surrounded the only entrance. The storm door was open, and through the screen Mitch could see a small color television and the silhouette of a man walking by.

This was not what he wanted. By choice, he had never met his mother's second husband, and now was not the time. He drove on, wishing he had not come.

He found on the Strip the familiar marquee of a Holiday Inn. It was empty, but open. He hid the

BMW away from the highway, and registered under the name of Eddie Lomax of Danesboro, Kentucky. He paid cash for a single room with an ocean view.

The Panama City Beach phone book listed three Waffle Huts on the Strip. He lay across the motel bed and dialed the first number. No luck. He dialed the second number, and again asked for Ida Ainsworth. Just a minute, he was told. He hung up. It was 11 P.M. He had slept for two hours.

The taxi took twenty minutes to arrive at the Holiday Inn, and the driver began by explaining that he had been home enjoying leftover turkey with his wife and kids and kinfolks when the dispatcher called, and how it was Christmas and he hoped to be with his family all day and not worry about work for one day of the year. Mitch threw a twenty over the seat and asked him to be quiet.

'What's at the Waffle Hut, man?' the driver asked.

'Just drive.'

'Waffles, right?' He laughed and mumbled to himself. He adjusted the radio volume and found his favorite soul station. He glanced in the mirror, looked out the windows, whistled a bit, then said, 'What brings you down here on Christmas?'

'Looking for someone.'

'Who?'

'A woman.'

'Ain't we all. Anyone in particular?'

'An old friend.'

'She at the Waffle Hut?'

'I think so.'

'You some kinda private eye or something?'

'No.'

'Seems mighty suspicious to me.'

'Why don't you just drive.'

The Waffle Hut was a small, rectangular, boxlike

199

building with a dozen tables and a long counter facing the grill, where everything was cooked in the open. Large plate-glass windows lined one side next to the tables so the customers could take in the Strip and the condos in the distance while they enjoyed their pecan waffles and bacon. The small parking lot was almost full, and Mitch directed the driver to an empty slot near the building.

'Ain't you getting out?' the driver asked.

'No. Keep the meter running.'

'Man, this is strange.'

'You'll get paid.'

'You got that right.'

Mitch leaned forward and rested his arms on the front seat. The meter clicked softly as he studied the customers inside. The driver shook his head, slumped in the seat, but watched out of curiosity.

In the corner next to the cigarette machine a table of fat tourists with long shirts, white legs and black socks drank coffee, and all talked at the same time while glancing at the menus. The leader, the one with an unbuttoned shirt, a heavy gold chain draped upon his chest hair, thick gray sideburns and a Phillies baseball cap, looked repeatedly toward the grill, in search of a waitress.

'You see her?' asked the driver.

Mitch said nothing, then leaned forward and frowned. She appeared from nowhere and stood at the table with her pen and order book. The leader said something funny, and the fat people laughed. She never smiled, just kept writing. She was frail and much thinner. Almost too thin. The black-and-white uniform fit snugly and squeezed her tiny waist. Her gray hair was pulled tightly and hidden under the Waffle Hut bonnet. She was fifty-one, and from the distance she looked her age. Nothing worse. She seemed sharp. When she finished scribbling she snatched the menus from their hands, said something polite, almost smiled, then disappeared. She moved quickly among the tables, pouring coffee, handing ketchup bottles and giving orders to the cook.

Mitch relaxed. The meter ticked slowly.

'Is that her?' asked the driver.

'Yes.'

'What now?'

'I don't know.'

'Well, we found her, didn't we?'

Mitch followed her movements and said nothing. She poured coffee for a man sitting alone. He said something, and she smiled. A wonderful, gracious smile. A smile he had seen a thousand times in the darkness staring at the ceiling. His mother's smile.

A light mist began to fall and the intermittent wipers cleaned the windshield every ten seconds. It was almost midnight, Christmas Day.

The driver tapped the wheel nervously and fidgeted. He sank lower in the seat, then changed stations. 'How long we gonna sit here?'

'Not long.'

'Man, this is weird.'

'You'll be paid.'

'Man, money ain't everything. It's Christmas. I got kids at home, kinfolks visiting, turkey and wine to finish off, and here I am sitting at the Waffle Hut so you can look at some old woman through the window.'

'It's my mother.'

'Your what!'

'You heard me.'

'Man, oh man. I get all kinds.'

'Just shut up, okay?'

'Okay. Ain't you gonna talk to her? I mean it's Christmas, and you found your momma. You gotta go see her, don't you?'

'No. Not now.'

Mitch sat back in the seat and looked at the dark beach across the highway. 'Let's go.'

At daybreak, he dressed in jeans and a sweatshirt, no socks or shoes, and took Hearsay for a walk on the beach. They walked east, toward the first glow of orange peeking above the horizon. The waves broke gently thirty yards out and rolled quietly onto shore. The sand was cool and wet. The sky was clear and full of sea gulls talking incessantly among themselves. Hearsay ran boldly into the sea, then retreated furiously when the next wave of white foam approached. For a house dog, the endless stretch of sand and water demanded exploration. He ran a hundred yards ahead of Mitch.

After two miles they approached a pier, a large concrete structure running two hundred feet from the beach into the ocean. Hearsay, fearless now, darted onto it and ran to a bucket of bait next to two men standing motionless and staring down at the water. Mitch walked behind them, to the end of the pier, where a dozen fishermen talked occasionally to each other and waited for their lines to jump. The dog rubbed himself on Mitch's leg and grew still. A brilliant return of the sun was in progress, and for miles the water glistened and turned from black to green.

Mitch leaned on the railing and shivered in the cool wind. His bare feet were frozen and gritty. For miles along the beach in both directions, the hotels and condos sat quietly and waited for the day. There was no one on the beach. Another pier jutted into the water miles away.

The fishermen spoke with the sharp, precise words of those from the North. Mitch listened long enough to learn the fish were not biting. He studied the sea.

Looking southeast, he thought of the Caymans, and Abanks. And the girl for a moment, then she was gone. He would return to the islands in March, for a vacation with his wife. Damn the girl. Surely he would not see her. He would dive with Abanks and cultivate a friendship. They would drink Heineken and Red Stripe at his bar and talk of Hodge and Kozinski. He would follow whoever was following him. Now that Abby was an accomplice, she would assist him.

The man waited in the dark beside the Lincoln Town Car. He nervously checked his watch and glanced at the dimly lit sidewalk that disappeared in front of the building. On the second floor a light was turned off. A minute later, the private eye walked from the building toward the car. The man walked up to him.

'Are you Eddie Lomax?' he asked anxiously.

Lomax slowed, then stopped. They were face to face. 'Yeah. Who are you?'

The man kept his hands in his pockets. It was cold and damp, and he was shaking. 'Al Kilbury. I need some help, Mr. Lomax. Real bad. I'll pay you right now in cash, whatever you want. Just help me.'

'It's late, pal.'

'Please. I've got the money. Name the price. You gotta help, Mr. Lomax.' He pulled a roll of cash from his left pants pocket and stood ready to count.

Lomax looked at the money, then glanced over his shoulder. 'What's the problem?'

'My wife. In an hour she's supposed to meet a man at a motel in South Memphis. I've got the room number and all. I just need you to go with me and take pictures of them coming and going.'

'How do you know this?'

'Phone taps. She works with the man, and I've been suspicious. I'm a wealthy man, Mr. Lomax, and it's imperative I win the divorce. I'll pay you a thousand in cash now.' He quickly peeled off ten bills and offered them.

Lomax took the money. 'Okay. Let me get my camera.'

'Please hurry. Everything's in cash, okay? No records.'

'Suits me,' said Lomax as he walked toward the building.

Twenty minutes later, the Lincoln rolled slowly through the crowded parking lot of a Days Inn. Kilbury pointed to a second-floor room on the back side of the motel, then to a parking space next to a brown Chevy van. Lomax backed carefully alongside the van and parked his Town Car. Kilbury again pointed to the room, again checked his watch and again told Lomax how much he appreciated his services. Lomax thought of the money. A thousand bucks for two hours' work. Not bad. He unpacked a camera, loaded the film and gauged the light. Kilbury watched nervously, his eyes darting from the camera to the room across the parking lot. He looked hurt. He talked of his wife and their wonderful years together, and why, oh why was she doing this?

Lomax listened and watched the rows of parked cars in front of him. He held his camera.

He did not notice the door of the brown van. It quietly and slowly slid open, just three feet behind him. A man in a black turtleneck wearing black gloves crouched low in the van and waited. When the parking lot was still, he jumped from the van, yanked open the left rear door of the Lincoln and fired three times into the back of Eddie's head. The shots, muffled with a silencer, could not be heard outside the car.

Eddie slumped against the wheel, already dead. Kilbury bolted from the Lincoln, ran to the van and sped away with the assassin.

EIGHTEEN

After three days of unbillable time, of no production, of exile from their sanctuaries, of turkey and ham and cranberry sauce and new toys that came unassembled, the rested and rejuvenated lawyers of Bendini, Lambert & Locke returned to the fortress on Front Street with a vengeance. The parking lot was full by seven-thirty. They sat fixed and comfortable behind their heavy desks, drank coffee by the gallons, meditated over mail and correspondence and documents and mumbled incoherently and furiously into their Dictaphones. They barked orders at secretaries and clerks and paralegals, and at each other. There were a few 'How was your Christmas?' greetings in the halls and around the coffee-pots, but small talk was cheap and unbillable. The sounds of typewriters, intercoms and secretaries all harmonized into one glorious hum as the mint recovered from the nuisance of Christmas. Oliver Lambert walked the halls, smiling with satisfaction and listening, just listening to the sounds of wealth being made by the hour.

At noon, Lamar walked into the office and leaned across the desk. Mitch was deep into an oil and gas deal in Indonesia.

'Lunch?' Lamar asked.

'No, thanks. I'm behind.'

'Aren't we all. I thought we could run down to the Front Street Deli for a bowl of chili.'

'I'll pass. Thanks.'

Lamar glanced over his shoulder at the door and leaned closer as if he had extraordinary news to share. 'You know what today is, don't you?'

Mitch glanced at his watch. 'The twenty-eighth.'

'Right. And do you know what happens on the twenty-eighth of December of every year?'

'You have a bowel movement.'

'Yes. And what else?'

'Okay. I give up. What happens?'

'At this very moment, in the dining room on the fifth floor, all the partners are gathered for a lunch of roast duck and French wine.'

'Wine, for lunch?'

'Yes. It's a very special occasion.'

'Okay?'

'After they eat for an hour, Roosevelt and Jessie Frances will leave and Lambert will lock the door. Then it's all the partners, you see. Only the partners. And Lambert will hand out a financial summary for the year. It's got all the partners listed, and beside each name is a number that represents their total billing for the year. Then on the next page is a summary of the net profits after expenses. Then, based on production, they divide the pie!'

Mitch hung on every word. 'And?'

'And, last year the average piece of pie was three hundred and thirty thousand. And, of course, it's expected to be even higher this year. Goes up every year.'

'Three hundred and thirty thousand,' Mitch repeated slowly.

'Yep. And that's just the average. Locke will get close to a million. Victor Milligan will run a close second.'

'And what about us?'

'We get a piece too. A very small piece. Last year it was around nine thousand, on the average. Depends on how long you've been here and production.'

'Can we go watch?'

'They wouldn't sell a ticket to the President. It's supposed to be a secret meeting, but we all know about it. Word will begin drifting down late this afternoon.'

'When do they vote on who to make the next partner?'

'Normally, it would be done today. But, according to rumor, there may not be a new partner this year because of Marty and Joe. I think Marty was next in line, then Joe. Now, they might wait a year or two.'

'So who's next in line?'

Lamar stood straight and smiled proudly. 'One year from today, my friend, I will become a partner in Bendini, Lambert & Locke. I'm next in line, so don't get in my way this year.'

'I heard it was Massengill – a Harvard man, I might add.'

'Massengill doesn't have a prayer. I intend to bill a hundred and forty hours a week for the next fifty-two weeks, and those birds will beg me to become a partner. I'll go to the fourth floor, and Massengill will go to the basement with the paralegals.'

'I'm putting my money on Massengill.'

'He's a wimp. I'll run him into the ground. Let's go eat a bowl of chili, and I'll reveal my strategy.'

'Thanks, but I need to work.'

Lamar strutted from the office and passed Nina, who was carrying a stack of papers. She laid them on a cluttered corner of the desk. 'I'm going to lunch. Need anything?'

'No. Thanks. Yes, a Diet Coke.'

The halls quietened during lunch as the secretaries

escaped the building and walked toward downtown to a dozen small cafés and delicatessens nearby. With half the lawyers on the fifth floor counting their money, the gentle roar of commerce took an intermission.

Mitch found an apple on Nina's desk and rubbed it clean. He opened a manual on IRS regulations, laid it on the copier behind her desk and touched the green PRINT button. A red warning lit up and flashed the message: INSERT FILE NUMBER. He backed away and looked at the copier. Yes, it was a new one. Next to the PRINT button was another that read BYPASS. He stuck his thumb on it. A shrill siren erupted from within the machine, and the entire panel of buttons turned bright red. He looked around helplessly, saw no one and frantically grabbed the instruction manual.

'What's going on here?' someone demanded over the wailing of the copier.

'I don't know!' Mitch yelled, waving the manual.

Lela Pointer, a secretary too old to walk from the building for lunch, reached behind the machine and flipped a switch. The siren died.

'What the hell?' Mitch said, panting.

'Didn't they tell you?' she demanded, grabbing the manual and placing it back in its place. She drilled a hole in him with her tiny fierce eyes, as if she had caught him in her purse.

'Obviously not. What's the deal?'

'We have a new copying system,' she lectured downward through her nose. 'It was installed the day after Christmas. You must code in the file number before the machine will copy. Your secretary was supposed to tell you.'

'You mean this thing will not copy unless I punch in a ten digit number?'

'That's correct.'

'What about copies in general, with no particular file?'

'Can't be done. Mr. Lambert says we lose too much money on unbilled copies. So, from now on, every copy is automatically billed to a file. You punch in the number first. The machine records the number of copies and sends it to the main terminal, where it goes on the client's billing account.'

'What about personal copies?'

Lela shook her head in total frustration. 'I can't believe your secretary didn't tell you all this.'

'Well, she didn't, so why don't you help me out.'

'You have a four-digit access number for yourself. At the end of each month you'll be billed for your personal copies.'

Mitch stared at the machine and shook his head. 'Why the damned alarm system?'

'Mr. Lambert says that after thirty days they will cut off the alarms. Right now, they're needed for people like you. He's very serious about this. Says we've been losing thousands on unbilled copies.'

'Right. And I suppose every copier in the building has been replaced.'

She smiled with satisfaction. 'Yes, all seventeen.'

'Thanks.' Mitch returned to his office in search of a file number.

At three that afternoon, the celebration on the fifth floor came to a joyous conclusion, and the partners, now much wealthier and slightly drunker, filed out of the dining room and descended to their offices below. Avery, Oliver Lambert and Nathan Locke walked the short hallway to the security wall and pushed the button. DeVasher was waiting.

He waved at the chairs in his office and told them to sit down: Lambert passed around hand wrapped Hondurans, and everyone lit up.

'Well, I see we're all in a festive mood,' DeVasher said with a sneer. 'How much was it? Three hundred and ninety thousand, average?'

'That's correct, DeVasher,' Lambert said. 'It was a very good year.' He puffed slowly and blew smoke rings at the ceiling.

'Did we all have a wonderful Christmas?' DeVasher asked.

'What's on your mind?' Locke demanded.

'Merry Christmas to you too, Nat. Just a few things. I met with Lazarov two days ago in New Orleans. He does not celebrate the birth of Christ, you know. I brought him up to date on the situation down here, with emphasis on McDeere and the FBI. I assured him there had been no further contact since the initial meeting. He did not quite believe this and said he would check with their sources within the Bureau. I don't know what that means, but who am I to ask questions? He instructed me to trail McDeere twenty-four hours a day for the next six months. I told him we were already doing so, sort of. He does not want another Hodge-Kozinski situation. He's very distressed about that. McDeere is not to leave the city on firm business unless at least two of us go with him.'

'He's going to Washington in two weeks,' Avery said.

'What for?'

'American Tax Institute. It's a four-day seminar that we require of all new associates. It's been promised to him, and he'll be very suspicious if it's canceled.'

'We made his reservations in September,' Ollie added.

'I'll see if I can clear it with Lazarov,' DeVasher said. 'Give me the dates, flights and hotel reservations. He won't like this.'

'What happened Christmas?' Locke asked.

'Not much. His wife went to her home in Kentucky. She's still there. McDeere took the dog and drove to Panama City Beach, Florida. We think he went to see his mom, but we're not sure. Spent one night at a Holiday Inn on the beach. Just he and the dog. Pretty boring. Then he drove to Birmingham, stayed in another Holiday Inn, then early yesterday morning he drove to Brushy Mountain to visit his brother. Harmless trip.'

'What's he said to his wife?' asked Avery.

'Nothing, as far as we can tell. It's hard to hear everything.'

'Who else are you watching?' asked Avery.

'We're listening to all of them, sort of sporadically. We have no real suspects, other than McDeere, and that's just because of Tarrance. Right now all's quiet.'

'He's got to go to Washington, DeVasher,' Avery insisted.

'Okay, okay. I'll get it cleared with Lazarov. He'll make us send five men for surveillance. What an idiot.'

Ernie's Airport Lounge was indeed near the airport. Mitch found it after three attempts and parked between two four-wheel-drive swampmobiles with real mud caked on the tires and headlights. The parking lot was full of such vehicles. He looked around and instinctively removed his tie. It was almost eleven. The lounge was deep and long and dark with colorful beer signs flashing in the painted windows.

He looked at the note again, just to be sure. 'Dear Mr. McDeere: Please meet me at Ernie's Lounge on Winchester tonight – late. It's about Eddie Lomax. Very important. Tammy Hemphill, his secretary.'

The note had been tacked on the door to the kitchen when he arrived home. He remembered her from the one visit to Eddie's office, back in November. He remembered the tight leather skirt, huge breasts, bleached hair, red sticky lips and smoke billowing from her nose. And he remembered the story about her husband, Elvis.

The door opened without incident, and he slid inside. A row of pool tables covered the left half of the room. Through the darkness and black smoke, he could make out a small dance floor in the rear. To the right was a long saloon-type bar crowded with cowboys and cowgirls, all drinking Bud longnecks. No one seemed to notice him. He walked quickly to the end of the bar and slid onto the stool. 'Bud longneck,' he told the bartender.

Tammy arrived before the beer. She was sitting and waiting on a crowded bench by the pool tables. She wore tight washed jeans, faded denim shirt and kinky red high-heels. The hair had just received a fresh bleaching.

'Thanks for coming,' she said into his face. 'I've been waiting for four hours. I knew of no other way to find you.'

Mitch nodded and smiled as if to say, 'It's okay. You did the right thing.'

'What's up?' he said.

She looked around. 'We need to talk, but not here.'

'Where do you suggest?'

'Could we maybe drive around?'

'Sure, but not in my car. It, uh, it may not be a good idea.'

'I've got a car. It's old, but it'll do.'

Mitch paid for the beer and followed her to the door. A cowpoke sitting near the door said, 'Getta loada this. Guy shows up with a suit and picks her up in thirty seconds.' Mitch smiled at him and hurried out the door. Dwarfed in a row of massive mud-eating machinery was a well-worn Volkswagen Rabbit. She unlocked it, and Mitch doubled over and squeezed into the cluttered seat. She pumped the accelerator

212

five times and turned the key. Mitch held his breath until it started.

'Where would you like to go?' she asked.

Where we can't be seen, Mitch thought. 'You're driving.'

'You're married, aren't you?' she asked.

'Yes. You?'

'Yes, and my husband would not understand this situation right here. That's why I chose that dump back there. We never go there.'

She said this as if she and her husband were discriminating critics of dark redneck dives.

'I don't think my wife would understand either. She's out of town, though.'

Tammy drove in the direction of the airport. 'I've got an idea,' she said. She clutched the steering wheel tightly and spoke nervously.

'What's on your mind?' Mitch asked.

'Well, you heard about Eddie.'

'Yes.'

'When did you last see him?'

'We met ten days or so before Christmas. It was sort of a secret meeting.'

'That's what I thought. He kept no records of the work he was doing for you. Said you wanted it that way. He didn't tell me much. But me and Eddie, well, we, uh, we were . . . close.'

Mitch could think of no response.

'I mean, we were very close. Know what I mean?'

Mitch grunted and sipped the longneck.

'And he told me things I guess he wasn't supposed to tell me. Said you had a real strange case, that some lawyers in your firm had died under suspicious circumstances. And that you always thought somebody was following and listening. That's pretty weird for a law firm.'

213

So much for the confidentiality, thought Mitch. 'That it is.'

She turned, made the exit to the airport and headed for the acres of parked cars.

'And after he finished his work for you, he told me once, just once, in bed, that he thought he was being followed. This was three days before Christmas. And I asked him who it was. He said he didn't know, but mentioned your case and something about it was probably related to the same people who were following you. He didn't say much.'

She parked in the short-term section near the terminal.

'Who else would follow him?' Mitch asked.

'No one. He was a good investigator who left no trail. I mean, he was an ex-cop and an ex-con. He was very streetsmart. He got paid to follow people and collect dirt. No one followed him. Never.'

'So who killed him?'

'Whoever was following him. The paper made like he got caught snooping on some rich guy and was wasted. It's not true.'

Suddenly, from out of nowhere, she produced a filter-tip 1000 and shot a flame at the end. Mitch rolled down the window.

'Mind if I smoke?' she asked.

'No, just blow it that way,' he said, pointing to her window.

'Anyway, I'm scared. Eddie was convinced the people following you are extremely dangerous and extremely smart. Very sophisticated, was what he said. And if they killed him, what about me? Maybe they think I know something. I haven't been to the office since the day he was killed. Don't plan to go back.'

'I wouldn't if I were you.'

'I'm not stupid. I worked for him for two years and

learned a lot. There's a lot of nuts out there. We saw all kinds.'

'How did they shoot him?'

'He's got a friend in Homicide. Guy told me confidentially that Eddie got hit three times in the back of the head, point blank range, with a .22 pistol. And they don't have a clue. He told me it was a very clean, professional job.'

Mitch finished the longneck and laid the bottle on the floorboard with a half dozen empty beer cans. A very clean, professional job.

'It doesn't make sense,' she repeated. 'I mean, how could anyone sneak up behind Eddie, somehow get in the back seat and shoot him three times in the back of the head? And he wasn't even supposed to be there.'

'Maybe he fell asleep and they ambushed him.'

'No. He took all kinds of speed when he worked late at night. Stayed wired.'

'Are there any records at the office?'

'You mean about you?'

'Yeah, about me.'

'I doubt it. I never saw nothing in writing. He said you wanted it that way.'

'That's right,' Mitch said with relief.

They watched a 727 lift off to the north. The parking lot vibrated.

'I'm really scared, Mitch. Can I call you Mitch?'

'Sure. Why not?'

'I think he got killed because of the work he did for you. That's all it could be. And if they'd kill him because he knew something, they probably assume I know it too. What do you think?'

'I wouldn't take any chances.'

'I might disappear for a while. My husband does a little nightclub work, and we can get mobile if we have to. I haven't told him all this, but I guess I have to. What do you think?'

'Where would you go?'

'Little Rock, St. Louis, Nashville. He's laid off, so we can move around, I guess.' Her words trailed off. She lit another one.

A very clean, professional job, Mitch repeated to himself. He glanced at her and noticed a small tear on her cheek. She was not ugly, but the years in lounges and nightclubs were taking their toll. Her features were strong, and minus the bleach and heavy makeup she would be somewhat attractive for her age. About forty, he guessed.

She took a mighty drag and sent a cloud of smoke surging from the Rabbit. 'I guess we're in the same boat, aren't we? I mean, they're after both of us. They've killed all those lawyers, now Eddie, and I guess we're next.'

Don't hold back, baby, just blurt it out. 'Look, let's do this. We need to keep in touch. You can't call me on the phone, and we can't be seen together. My wife knows everything, and I'll tell her about this little meeting. Don't worry about her. Once a week, write me a note and tell me where you are. What's your mother's name?'

'Doris.'

'Good. That's your code name. Sign the name Doris on anything you send me.'

'Do they read your mail too?'

'Probably so, Doris, probably so.'

NINETEEN

At five P.M., Mitch turned off the light in his office, grabbed both briefcases and stopped at Nina's desk. Her phone was glued to one shoulder while she typed on the IBM. She saw him and reached in a drawer for an envelope. 'This is your confirmation at the Capital Hilton,' she said into the receiver.

'The dictation is on my desk,' he said. 'See you Monday.' He took the stairs to the fourth floor, to Avery's office in the corner, where a small riot was in progress. One secretary stuffed files into a massive briefcase. Another one spoke sharply to Avery, who was yelling on the phone to someone else. A paralegal shot orders to the first secretary.

Avery slammed the phone down. 'Are you ready?' he demanded at Mitch.

'Waiting for you,' Mitch replied.

'I can't find the Greenmark file,' a secretary snarled at the paralegal.

'It was with the Rocconi file,' said the paralegal.

'I don't need the Greenmark file!' Avery shouted. 'How many times do I have to tell you? Are you deaf?'

The secretary glared at Avery. 'No, I can hear very well. And I distinctly heard you say, "Pack the Greenmark file."'

'The limousine is waiting,' said the other secretary.

'I don't need the damned Greenmark file!' Avery shouted.

'How about Rocconi?' asked the paralegal.

'Yes! Yes! For the tenth time. I need the Rocconi file!'

'The airplane is waiting too,' said the other secretary.

One briefcase was slammed shut and locked. Avery dug through a pile of documents on his desk. 'Where's the Fender file? Where are any of my files? Why can't I ever find a file?'

'Here's Fender,' said the first secretary as she stuffed it into another briefcase.

Avery stared at a piece of notepaper. 'All right. Do I have Fender, Rocconi, Cambridge Partners, Greene Group, Sonny Capps to Otaki, Burton Brothers, Galveston Freight and McQuade?'

'Yes, yes, yes,' said the first secretary.

'That's all of them,' said the paralegal.

'I don't believe it,' Avery said as he grabbed his jacket. 'Let's go.' He strode through the door with the secretaries, paralegal and Mitch in pursuit. Mitch carried two briefcases, the paralegal had two, and a secretary had one. The other secretary scribbled notes as Avery barked the orders and demands he wanted carried out while he was away. The entourage crowded onto the small elevator for the ride to the first floor. Outside, the chauffeur sprang into action, opening doors and loading it all in the trunk.

Mitch and Avery fell into the back seat.

'Relax, Avery,' Mitch said. 'You're going to the Caymans for three days. Just relax.'

'Right, right. I'm taking with me enough work for a month. I've got clients screaming for my hide, threatening suits for legal malpractice. I'm two months behind, and now you're leaving for four days of boredom at a tax seminar in Washington. You're timing is great, McDeere. Just great.'

Avery opened a cabinet and mixed a drink. Mitch declined. The limo moved around Riverside Drive in the rush-hour traffic. After three swallows of gin, the partner breathed deeply.

'Continuing education. What a joke,' Avery said.

'You did it when you were a rookie. And if I'm not mistaken, you spent a week not long ago at that international tax seminar in Honolulu. Or did you forget?'

'It was work. All work. Are you taking your files with you?'

'Of course, Avery. I'm expected to attend the tax seminar eight hours a day, learn the latest tax revisions Congress has bestowed upon us and in my spare time bill five hours a day.'

'Six, if you can. We're behind, Mitch.'

'We're always behind, Avery. Fix another drink. You need to unwind.'

'I plan to unwind at Rumheads.'

Mitch thought of the bar with its Red Stripe, dominoes, darts and, yes, string bikinis. And the girl.

'Is this your first flight on the Lear?' Avery asked, more relaxed now.

'Yes. I've been here seven months, and I'm just now seeing the plane. If I had known this last March, I'd have gone to work with a Wall Street firm.'

'You're not Wall Street material. You know what those guys do? They've got three hundred lawyers in a firm, right? And each year they hire thirty new associates, maybe more. Everybody wants a job because it's Wall Street, right? And after about a month they get all thirty of them together in one big room and inform them they're expected to work ninety hours a week for five years, and at the end of five years, half of them will be gone. The turnover is incredible. They try to kill the rookies, bill them out at a hundred, hundred-fifty an hour, make a bundle off

219

them, then run them off. That's Wall Street. And the little boys never get to see the firm plane. Or the firm limo. You are truly lucky, Mitch. You should thank God every day that we chose to accept you here at good old Bendini, Lambert & Locke.'

'Ninety hours sounds like fun. I could use the rest.'

'It'll pay off. Did you hear what my bonus was last year?'

'No.'

'Four-eight-five. Not bad, huh? And that's just the bonus.'

'I got six thousand,' Mitch said.

'Stick with me and you'll be in the big leagues soon enough.'

'Yeah, but first I gotta get my continuing legal education.'

Ten minutes later the limo turned into a drive that led to a row of hangars. Memphis Aero, the sign said. A sleek silver Lear 55 taxied slowly toward the terminal. 'That's it,' Avery said.

The briefcases and luggage were loaded quickly onto the plane, and within minutes they were cleared for takeoff. Mitch fastened his seat belt and admired the leather-and-brass cabin. It was lavish and luxurious, and he had expected nothing less. Avery mixed another drink and buckled himself in.

An hour and fifteen minutes later, the Lear began its descent into Baltimore-Washington International Airport. After it taxied to a stop, Avery and Mitch descended to the tarmac and opened the baggage door. Avery pointed to a man in a uniform standing near a gate. 'That's your chauffeur. The limo is in front. Just follow him. You're about forty minutes from the Capital Hilton.'

'Another limo?' Mitch asked.

'Yeah. They wouldn't do this for you on Wall Street.'

They shook hands, and Avery climbed back on the plane. The refueling took thirty minutes, and when the Lear took off and turned south, he was asleep again.

Three hours later, it landed in Georgetown, Grand Cayman. It taxied past the terminal to a very small hangar where it would spend the night. A security guard waited on Avery and his luggage and escorted him to the terminal and through customs. The pilot and copilot ran through the post flight ritual. They too were escorted through the terminal.

After midnight, the lights in the hangar were extinguished and the half dozen planes sat in the darkness. A side door opened, and three men, one of them Avery, entered and walked quickly to the Lear 55. Avery opened the baggage compartment, and the three hurriedly unloaded twenty-five heavy cardboard boxes. In the muggy tropical heat, the hangar was like an oven. They sweated profusely but said nothing until all boxes were out of the plane.

'There should be twenty-five. Count them,' Avery said to a muscle-bound native with a tank top and a pistol on his hip. The other man held a clipboard and watched intently as if he was a receiving clerk in a warehouse. The native counted quickly, sweat dripping onto the boxes.

'Yes. Twenty-five.'

'How much?' asked the man with the clipboard.

'Six and a half million.'

'All cash?'

'All cash. U.S. dollars. Hundreds and twenties. Let's get it loaded.'

'Where's it going?'

'QuebecBank. They're waiting for us.'

They each grabbed a box and walked through the dark to the side door, where a comrade was waiting with an Uzi. The boxes were loaded into a dilapidated van with CAYMAN PRODUCE stenciled badly on the side. The armed natives sat with guns drawn as the receiving clerk drove away from the hangar in the direction of downtown Georgetown.

Registration began at eight outside the Century Room on the mezzanine. Mitch arrived early, signed in, picked up the heavy notebook of materials with his name printed neatly on the cover and went inside. He took a seat near the center of the large room. Registration was limited to two hundred, the brochure said. A porter served coffee, and Mitch spread the *Washington Post* before him. The news was dominated by a dozen stories of the beloved Redskins, who were in the Super Bowl again.

The room filled slowly as tax lawyers from around the country gathered to hear the latest developments in tax laws that changed daily. A few minutes before nine, a clean cut, boyish attorney sat to Mitch's left and said nothing. Mitch glanced at him and returned to the paper. When the room was packed, the moderator welcomed everyone and introduced the first speaker. Congressman something or other from Oregon, chairman of a House Ways and Means subcommittee. As he took the podium for what was supposed to be a one hour presentation, the attorney to Mitch's left leaned over and offered his hand.

'Hi, Mitch,' he whispered. 'I'm Grant Harbison, FBI.' He handed Mitch a card.

The congressman started with a joke that Mitch did not hear. He studied the card, holding it near his chest. There were five people seated within three feet of him. He didn't know anyone in the room, but it would be embarrassing if anyone knew he was holding an FBI card. After five minutes, Mitch shot a blank stare at Harbison.

Harbison whispered, 'I need to see you for a few minutes.'

'What if I'm busy?' Mitch asked.

The agent slid a plain white envelope from his seminar notebook and handed it to Mitch. He opened it near his chest. It was handwritten. Across the top, in small but imposing letters, the words read simply: 'Office of the Director – FBI.'

The note read:

Dear Mr. McDeere:
I would like to speak with you for a few moments during lunch. Please follow the instructions of Agent Harbison. It won't take long. We appreciate your cooperation.

Thanks.
F. Denton Voyles
Director

Mitch folded the letter in the envelope and slowly placed it in his notebook. We appreciate your cooperation. From the Director of the FBI. He realized the importance at this moment of maintaining his composure, of keeping a straight, calm face as if it was simply routine. But he rubbed his temples with both hands and stared at the floor in front of him. He closed his eyes and felt dizzy. The FBI. Sitting next to him! Waiting on him. The Director and hell knows who else. Tarrance would be close at hand.

Suddenly, the room exploded in laughter at the congressman's punch line. Harbison leaned quickly toward Mitch and whispered, 'Meet me in the men's room around the corner in ten minutes.' The agent left his notebooks on the table and exited among the laughter.

Mitch flipped to the first section of the notebook and pretended to study the materials. The congressman was detailing his courageous battle to protect tax

223

shelters for the wealthy while at the same time easing the burden on the working class. Under his fearless guidance, the subcommittee had refused to report legislation limiting deductions for oil and gas exploration. He was a one-man army on the Hill.

Mitch waited fifteen minutes, then another five, then began coughing. He needed water, and with hand over mouth he slid between the chairs to the back of the room and out the rear door. Harbison was in the men's room washing his hands for the tenth time.

Mitch walked to the basin next to him and turned on the cold water. 'What are you boys up to?' Mitch asked.

Harbison looked at Mitch in the mirror. 'I'm just following orders. Director Voyles wants to personally meet you, and I was sent to get you.'

'And what might he want?'

'I wouldn't want to steal his thunder, but I'm sure it's rather important.'

Mitch cautiously glanced around the rest room. It was empty. 'And what if I'm too busy to meet with him?'

Harbison turned off the water and shook his hands into the basin. 'The meeting is inevitable, Mitch. Let's not play games. When your little seminar breaks for lunch, you'll find a cab, number 8667, outside to the left of the main entrance. It will take you to the Vietnam Veterans Memorial, and we'll be there. You must be careful. Two of them followed you here from Memphis.'

'Two of whom?'

'The boys from Memphis. Just do as we say and they'll never know.'

The moderator thanked the second speaker, a tax professor from New York University, and dismissed them for lunch.

Mitch said nothing to the taxi driver. He sped away

like a maniac, and they were soon lost in traffic.
Fifteen minutes later, they parked near the Memorial.

'Don't get out yet,' the driver said with authority.
Mitch did not move. For ten minutes, he did not
move or speak. Finally, a white Ford Escort pulled
alongside the cab and honked. It then drove away.

The driver stared ahead and said, 'Okay. Go to the
Wall. They'll find you after about five minutes.'

Mitch stepped to the sidewalk, and the cab left. He
stuck his hands deep in the pockets of his wool
overcoat and walked slowly to the Memorial. Bitter
wind gusts from the north scattered leaves in all
directions. He shivered and flipped the collar of his
coat around his ears.

A solitary pilgrim sat rigidly in a wheelchair and
stared at the Wall. He was covered with a heavy quilt.
Under his oversized camouflage beret, a pair of
aviator's sunglasses covered his eyes. He sat near the
end of the wall, near the names of those killed in 1972.
Mitch followed the years down the sidewalk until he
stopped near the wheelchair. He searched the names,
suddenly oblivious to the man.

He breathed deeply and was aware of a numbness in
his legs and stomach. He looked slowly downward,
and then, near the bottom, there it was. Engraved
neatly, matter-of-factly, just like all the others, was the
name Rusty McDeere.

A basket of frozen and wilted flowers sat on its side
next to the monument, inches under his name. Mitch
gently laid them to one side and knelt before the Wall.
He touched the engraved letters of Rusty's name.
Rusty McDeere. Age eighteen, forever. Seven weeks in
Vietnam when he stepped on a land mine. Death was
instantaneous, they said. They always said that,
according to Ray. Mitch wiped a small tear and stood
staring at the length of the Wall. He thought of the
fifty-eight thousand families who had been told that

death was instantaneous and no one suffered over there.

'Mitch, they're waiting.'

He turned and looked at the man in the wheelchair, the only human in sight. The aviator's glasses stared at the Wall and did not look up. Mitch glanced around in all directions.

'Relax, Mitch. We've got the place sealed off. They're not watching.'

'And who are you?' Mitch asked.

'Just one of the gang. You need to trust us, Mitch. The Director has important words, words that could save your life.'

'Where is he?'

The man in the wheelchair turned his head and looked down the sidewalk. 'Start walking that way. They'll find you.'

Mitch stared for a moment longer at his brother's name and walked behind the wheelchair. He walked past the statue of the three soldiers. He walked slowly, waiting, with hands deep in his pockets. Fifty yards past the monument, Wayne Tarrance stepped from behind a tree and walked beside him. 'Keep walking,' he said.

'Why am I not surprised to see you here?' Mitch said.

'Just keep walking. We know of at least two goons from Memphis who were flown in ahead of you. They're at the same hotel, next door to you. They did not follow you here. I think we lost them.'

'What the hell's going on, Tarrance?'

'You're about to find out. Keep walking. But relax, no one is watching you, except for about twenty of our agents.'

'Twenty?'

'Yeah. We've got this place sealed off. We want to

make sure those bastards from Memphis don't show up here. I don't expect them.'

'Who are they?'

'The Director will explain.'

'Why is the Director involved?'

'You ask a lot of questions, Mitch.'

'And you don't have enough answers.'

Tarrance pointed to the right. They left the sidewalk and headed for a heavy concrete bench near a footbridge leading to a small forest. The water on the pond below was frozen white.

'Have a seat,' Tarrance instructed. They sat down. Two men walked across the footbridge. Mitch immediately recognized the shorter one as Voyles. F. Denton Voyles, Director of the FBI under three Presidents. A tough-talking, heavy-handed crime buster with a reputation for ruthlessness.

Mitch stood out of respect when they stopped at the bench. Voyles stuck out a cold hand and stared at Mitch with the same large, round face that was famous around the world. They shook hands and exchanged names. Voyles pointed to the bench. Tarrance and the other agent walked to the footbridge and studied the horizon. Mitch glanced across the pond and saw two men, undoubtedly agents with their identical black trench coats and close haircuts, standing against a tree a hundred yards away.

Voyles sat close to Mitch, their legs touching. A brown fedora rested to one side of his large, bald head. He was at least seventy, but the dark green eyes danced with intensity and missed nothing. Both men sat still on the cold bench with their hands stuck deep in their overcoats.

'I appreciate you coming,' Voyles started.

'I didn't feel as though I had a choice. You folks have been relentless.'

'Yes. It's very important to us.'

Mitch breathed deeply. 'Do you have any idea how confused and scared I am? I'm totally bewildered. I would like an explanation, sir.'

'Mr. McDeere, can I call you Mitch?'

'Sure. Why not.'

'Fine. Mitch, I am a man of very few words. And what I'm about to tell you will certainly shock you. You will be horrified. You may not believe me. But I assure you it's all true, and with your help we can save your life.'

Mitch braced himself and waited.

'Mitch, no lawyer has ever left your law firm alive. Three have tried, and they were killed. Two were about to leave, and they died last summer. Once a lawyer joins Bendini, Lambert & Locke, he never leaves, unless he retires and keeps his mouth shut. And by the time they retire, they are a part of the conspiracy and cannot talk. The firm has an extensive surveillance operation on the fifth floor. Your house and car are bugged. Your phones are tapped. Your desk and office are wired. Virtually every word you utter is heard and recorded on the fifth floor. They follow you, and sometimes your wife. They are here in Washington as we speak. You see, Mitch, the firm is more than a firm. It is a division of a very large business, a very profitable business. A very illegal business. The firm is not owned by the partners.'

Mitch turned and watched him closely. The Director looked at the frozen pond as he spoke.

'You see, Mitch, the law firm of Bendini, Lambert & Locke is owned by the Morolto crime family in Chicago. The Mafia. The Mob. They call the shots from up there. And that's why we're here.' He touched Mitch firmly on the knee and stared at him from six inches away. 'It's Mafia, Mitch, and illegal as hell.'

'I don't believe it,' he said, frozen with fear. His voice was weak and shrill.

The Director smiled. 'Yes you do, Mitch. Yes you do. You've been suspicious for some time now. That's why you talked to Abanks in the Caymans. That's why you hired that sleazy investigator and got him killed by those boys on the fifth floor. You know the firm stinks, Mitch.'

Mitch leaned forward and rested his elbows on his knees. He stared at the ground between his shoes. 'I don't believe it,' he mumbled weakly.

'As far as we can tell, about twenty-five percent of their clients, or I should say your clients, are legitimate. There are some very good lawyers in that firm, and they do tax and securities work for rich clients. It's a very good front. Most of the files you've worked on so far have been legit. That's how they operate. They bring in a new rookie, throw money at him, buy the BMW, the house, all that jazz, wine and dine and go to the Caymans, and they work his ass off with what is really legitimate legal stuff. Real clients. Real lawyer stuff. That goes on for a few years, and the rookie doesn't suspect a thing, right? It's a great firm, great bunch of guys. Plenty of money. Hey, everything's wonderful. Then after five or six years, when the money is really good, when they own your mortgage, when you have a wife and kids and everything is so secure, they drop the bomb and tell the truth. There's no way out. It's the Mafia, Mitch. Those guys don't play games. They'll kill one of your children or your wife, they don't care. You're making more money than you could possibly make anywhere else. You're black-mailed because you've got a family that doesn't mean a damned thing to the Mob, so what do you do, Mitch? You stay. You can't leave. If you stay you make a million and retire young with your family intact. If you want to leave, you'll wind up with your picture on the wall in the first-floor library. They're very persuasive.'

Mitch rubbed his temples and began shivering.

'Look, Mitch, I know you must have a thousand questions. Okay. So I'll just keep talking and tell you what I know. The five dead lawyers all wanted out after they learned the truth. We never talked to the first three, because, frankly, we knew nothing about the firm until seven years ago. They've done an excellent job of staying quiet and leaving no trail. The first three just wanted out, probably, so they got out. In coffins. Hodge and Kozinski were different. They approached us, and over the course of a year we had several meetings. They dropped the bomb on Kozinski after he'd been there for seven years. He told Hodge. They whispered between themselves for a year. Kozinski was about to make partner and wanted out before that happened. So he and Hodge made the fatal decision to get out. They never suspected the first three were killed, or at least they never mentioned it to us. We sent Wayne Tarrance to Memphis to bring them in. Tarrance is an organized crime specialist from New York. He and the two were getting real close when that thing happened in the Caymans. These guys in Memphis are very good, Mitch. Don't ever forget that. They've got the money and they hire the best. So after Hodge and Kozinski were killed, I made the decision to get the firm. If we can bust that firm, we can indict every significant member of the Morolto family. There could be over five hundred indictments. Tax evasion, laundering, racketeering, just whatever you want. It could destroy the Morolto family, and that would be the single most devastating blow to organized crime in the past thirty years. And, Mitch, it's all in the files at the quiet little Bendini firm in Memphis.'

'Why Memphis?'

'Ah, good question. Who would suspect a small firm in Memphis, Tennessee? There's no mob activity down there. It's a quiet, lovely, peaceful city by the river. It could've been Durham or Topeka or Wichita Falls. But they chose Memphis. It's big enough, though, to hide a forty-man firm. Perfect choice.'

'You mean every partner . . .' His words trailed off.

'Yes, every partner knows and plays by the rules. We suspect that most of the associates know, but it's hard to tell. There's so much we don't know, Mitch. I can't explain how the firm operates and who's in on it. But we strongly suspect a lot of criminal activity down there.'

'Such as?'

'Tax fraud. They do all the tax work for the Morolto bunch. They file nice, neat, proper-looking tax returns each year and report a fraction of the income. They launder money like crazy. They set up legitimate businesses with dirty money. That bank in St. Louis, big client, what is it?'

'Commercial Guaranty.'

'Right, that's it. Mafia owned. Firm does all its legal work. Morolto takes in an estimated three hundred million a year from gambling, dope, numbers, everything. All cash, right? Most of it goes to those banks in the Caymans. How does it move from Chicago to the islands? Any idea? The plane, we suspect. That gold-plated Lear you flew up here on runs about once a week to Georgetown.'

Mitch sat straight and watched Tarrance, who was out of hearing range and standing now on the footbridge. 'So why don't you get your indictments and bust it all up?'

'We can't. We will, I assure you. I've assigned five agents to the project in Memphis and three here in Washington. I'll get them, Mitch, I promise you. But we must have someone from the inside. They are very smart. They have plenty of money. They're extremely careful, and they don't make mistakes. I am convinced that we must have help from you or another member of the firm. We need copies of files, copies of bank records, copies of a million documents that can only come from within. It's impossible otherwise.'

'And I have been chosen.'

'And you have been chosen. If you decline, then you can go on your way and make plenty of money and in general be a successful lawyer. But we will keep trying. We'll wait for the next new associate and try to pick him off. And if that doesn't work, we'll move in on one of the older associates. One with courage and morals and guts to do what's right. We'll find our man one day, Mitch, and when that happens we'll indict you along with all the rest and ship your rich and successful ass off to prison. It will happen, son, believe me.'

At that moment, at that place and time, Mitch believed him. 'Mr. Voyles, I'm cold. Could we walk around?'

'Sure, Mitch.'

They walked slowly to the sidewalk and headed in the direction of the Vietnam Memorial. Mitch glanced over his shoulder. Tarrance and the other agent were following at a distance. Another agent in dark brown sat suspiciously on a park bench up the sidewalk.

'Who was Anthony Bendini?' Mitch asked.

'He married a Morolto in 1930. The old man's son-in-law. They had an operation in Philadelphia back then, and he was stationed there. Then, in the forties, for some reason, he was sent to Memphis to set up shop. He was a very good lawyer, though, from what we know.'

A thousand questions flooded his brain and fought to be asked. He tried to appear calm, under control, skeptical.

'What about Oliver Lambert?'

'A prince of a guy. The perfect senior partner, who

just happened to know all about Hodge and Kozinski and the plans to eliminate them. The next time you see Mr. Lambert around the office, try to remember that he is a cold-blooded murderer. Of course, he has no choice. If he didn't cooperate, they'd find him floating somewhere. They're all like that, Mitch. They started off just like you. Young, bright, ambitious, then suddenly one day they were in over their heads with no place to go. So they play along, work hard, do a helluva job putting up a good front and looking like a real respectable little law firm. Each year or so they recruit a bright young law student from a poor background, no family money, with a wife who wants babies, and they throw money at him and sign him up.'

Mitch thought of the money, the excessive salary from a small firm in Memphis, and the car and low-interest mortgage. He was headed for Wall Street and had been sidetracked by the money. Only the money.

'What about Nathan Locke?'

The Director smiled. 'Locke is another story. He grew up a poor kid in Chicago and was running errands for old man Morolto by the time he was ten. He's been a hood all his life. Scratched his way through law school, and the old man sent him South to work with Anthony Bendini in the white-collar-crime division of the family. He was always a favorite of the old man.'

'When did Morolto die?'

'Eleven years ago at the age of eighty-eight. He has two slimy sons, Mickey the Mouth and Joey the Priest. Mickey lives in Las Vegas and has a limited role in the family business. Joey is the boss.'

The sidewalk reached an intersection with another one. In the distance to the left, the Washington Monument reached upward in the bitter wind. To the right, the walkway led to the Wall. A handful of people

233

were now staring at it, searching for the names of sons and husbands and friends. Mitch headed for the Wall. They walked slowly.

Mitch spoke softly. 'I don't understand how the firm can do so much illegal work and keep it quiet. That place is full of secretaries and clerks and paralegals.'

'Good point, and one I cannot fully answer. We think it operates as two firms. One is legitimate, with the new associates, most of the secretaries and support people. Then, the senior associates and partners do the dirty work. Hodge and Kozinski were about to give us plenty of information, but they never made it. Hodge told Tarrance once that there was a group of paralegals in the basement he knew little about. They worked directly for Locke and Milligan and McKnight and a few other partners, and no one was really sure what they did. Secretaries know everything, and we think that some of them are probably in on it. If so, I'm sure they're well paid and too scared to talk. Think about it, Mitch. If you work there making great money with great benefits, and you know that if you ask too many questions or start talking you wind up in the river, what do you do? You keep your mouth shut and take the money.'

They stopped at the beginning of the Wall, at a point where the black granite began at ground level and started its run of 246 feet until it angled into the second row of identical panels. Sixty feet away, an elderly couple stared at the wall and cried softly. They huddled together, for warmth and strength. The mother bent down and laid a framed black-and-white photo at the base of the Wall. The father laid a shoebox full of high school memorabilia next to the photo. Football programs, class pictures, love letters, key rings and a gold chain. They cried louder.

Mitch turned his back to the Wall and looked at the

Washington Monument. The Director watched his eyes.

'So what am I supposed to do?' Mitch asked.

'First of all, keep your mouth shut. If you start asking questions, your life could be in danger. Your wife's also. Don't have any kids in the near future. They're easy targets. It's best to play dumb, as if everything is wonderful and you still plan to be the world's greatest lawyer. Second, you must make a decision. Not now, but soon. You must decide if you will cooperate or not. If you choose to help us, we will of course make it worth your while. If you choose not to, then we will continue to watch the firm until we decide to approach another associate. As I said, one of these days we'll find someone with guts and nail those bastards. And the Morolto crime family as we know it will cease to exist. We'll protect you, Mitch, and you'll never have to work again in your life.'

'What life? I'll live in fear forever, if I live. I've heard stories of witnesses the FBI has supposedly hidden. Ten years later, the car explodes as they back out the driveway to go to work. The body is scattered over three blocks. The Mob never forgets, Director. You know that.'

'They never forget, Mitch. But I promise you, you and your wife will be protected.'

The Director looked at his watch. 'You'd better get back or they'll be suspicious. Tarrance will be in touch. Trust him, Mitch. He's trying to save your life. He has full authority to act on my behalf. If he tells you something, it's coming from me. He can negotiate.'

'Negotiate what?'

'Terms, Mitch. What we give you in return for what you give us. We want the Morolto family, and you can deliver. You name your price, and this government, working through the FBI, will deliver. Within reason,

235

of course. And that's coming from me, Mitch.' They walked slowly along the Wall and stopped by the agent in the wheelchair. Voyles stuck out his hand. 'Look, there's a taxi waiting where you came in, number 1073. Same driver. You'd better leave now. We will not meet again, but Tarrance will contact you in a couple of days. Please think about what I said. Don't convince yourself the firm is invincible and can operate forever, because I will not allow it. We will make a move in the near future, I promise that. I just hope you're on our side.'

'I don't understand what I'm supposed to do.'

'Tarrance has the game plan. A lot will depend upon you and what you learn once you're committed.'

'Committed?'

'That's the word, Mitch. Once you commit, there's no turning back. They can be more ruthless than any organization on earth.'

'Why did you pick me?'

'We had to pick someone. No, that's not true. We picked you because you have the guts to walk away from it. You have no family except a wife. No ties, no roots. You've been hurt by every person you ever cared for, except Abby. You raised yourself, and in doing so became self-reliant and independent. You don't need the firm. You can leave it. You're hardened and callused beyond your years. And you're smart enough to pull it off, Mitch. You won't get caught. That's why we picked you. Good day, Mitch. Thanks for coming. You'd better get back.'

Voyles turned and walked quickly away. Tarrance waited at the end of the Wall, and gave Mitch a quick salute, as if to say, 'So long – for now.'

TWENTY

After making the obligatory stop in Atlanta, the Delta DC9 landed in a cold rain at Memphis International. It parked at Gate 19, and the tightly packed crowd of business travelers quickly disembarked. Mitch carried only his briefcase and an *Esquire*. He saw Abby waiting near the pay phones and moved quickly through the pack. He threw the briefcase and magazine against the wall and bear-hugged her. The four days in Washington seemed like a month. They kissed again and again, and whispered softly.

'How about a date?' he asked.

'I've got dinner on the table and wine in the cooler,' she said. They held hands and walked through the mob pushing down the concourse in the general direction of the luggage pickup.

He spoke quietly. 'Well, we need to talk, and we can't do it at home.'

She gripped his hand tighter. 'Oh?'

'Yes. In fact, we need to have a long talk.'

'What happened?'

'It'll take a while.'

'Why am I suddenly nervous?'

'Just keep cool. Keep smiling. They're watching.'

She smiled and glanced to her right. 'Who's watching?'

'I'll explain in just a moment.'

Mitch suddenly pulled her to his left. They cut through the wave of human traffic and darted into a dark, crowded lounge full of businessmen drinking and watching the television above the bar and waiting for their flights. A small, round table covered with empty beer mugs had just been vacated, and they sat with their backs to the wall and a view of the bar and the concourse. They sat close together, within three feet of another table. Mitch stared at the door and analyzed every face that walked in. 'How long are we going to be here?' she asked.

'Why?'

She slid out of the full-length fox and folded it on the chair across the table. 'What exactly are you looking for?'

'Just keep smiling for a moment. Pretend you really missed me. Here, give me a kiss.' He pecked her on the lips, and they smiled into each other's eyes. He kissed her cheek and returned to the door. A waiter rushed to the table and cleaned it off. They ordered wine.

She smiled at him. 'How was your trip?'

'Boring. We were in class eight hours a day, for four days. After the first day, I hardly left the hotel. They crammed six months' worth of tax revisions into thirty-two hours.'

'Did you get to sightsee?'

He smiled and looked dreamily at her. 'I missed you, Abby. More than I've ever missed anyone in my life. I love you. I think you're gorgeous, absolutely stunning. I do not enjoy traveling alone and waking up in a strange hotel bed without you. And I have something horrible to tell you.'

She stopped smiling. He slowly looked around the room. They were three deep at the bar and yelling at the Knicks-Lakers game. The lounge was suddenly louder.

'I'll tell you about it,' he said, 'but there's a very good chance someone is in here right now watching us. They cannot hear, but they can observe. Just smile occasionally, although it will be hard.'

The wine arrived, and Mitch began his story. He left nothing out. She spoke only once. He told her about Anthony Bendini and old man Morolto, and then Nathan Locke growing up in Chicago and Oliver Lambert and the boys on the fifth floor.

Abby nervously sipped her wine and tried valiantly to appear as the normal loving wife who missed her husband and was now enjoying immensely his recollection of the tax seminar. She watched the people at the bar, sipped a little and occasionally grinned at Mitch as he told of the money laundering and the murdered lawyers. Her body ached with fear. Her breath was wildly irregular. But she listened, and pretended.

The waiter brought more wine as the crowd thinned. An hour after he started, Mitch finished in a low whisper.

'And Voyles said Tarrance would contact me in a few days to see if I will cooperate. He said goodbye and walked away.'

'And this was Tuesday?' she asked.

'Yes. The first day.'

'What did you do the rest of the week?'

'I slept little, ate little, walked around with a dull headache most of the time.'

'I think I feel one coming.'

'I'm sorry, Abby. I wanted to fly home immediately and tell you. I've been in shock for three days.'

'I'm in shock now. I'm not believing this, Mitch. This is like a bad dream, only much worse.'

'And this is only the beginning. The FBI is dead serious. Why else would the Director himself meet with me, an insignificant rookie lawyer from Memphis, in fifteen-degree weather on a concrete park bench? He's assigned five agents in Memphis and three in Washington, and he said they'll spend whatever it takes to get the firm. So if I keep my mouth shut, ignore them and go about my business of being a good and faithful member of Bendini, Lambert & Locke, one day they'll show up with arrest warrants and haul everybody away. And if I choose to cooperate, you and I will leave Memphis in the dead of the night after I hand the firm to the feds, and we'll go off and live in Boise, Idaho, as Mr. and Mrs. Wilbur Gates. We'll have plenty of money, but we'll have to work to avoid suspicion. After my plastic surgery, I'll get a job driving a forklift in a warehouse, and you can work part time at a day care. We'll have two, maybe three kids and pray every night that people we've never met keep their mouths shut and forget about us. We'll live every hour of every day in morbid fear of being discovered.'

'That's perfect, Mitch, just perfect.' She was trying hard not to cry.

He smiled and glanced around the room. 'We have a third option. We can walk out that door, buy two tickets to San Diego, sneak across the border and eat tortillas for the rest of our lives.'

'Let's go.'

'But they'd probably follow us. With my luck, Oliver Lambert will be waiting in Tijuana with a squad of goons. It won't work. Just a thought.'

'What about Lamar?'

'I don't know. He's been here six or seven years, so he probably knows. Avery's a partner, so he's very much a part of the conspiracy.'

'And Kay?'

'Who knows. It's very likely none of the wives know. I've thought about it for four days, Abby, and it's a marvelous front. The firm looks exactly like it's supposed to look. They could fool anyone. I mean, how would you and I or any other prospective recruit even think of such an operation? It's perfect. Except, now the feds know about it.'

'And now the feds expect you to do their dirty work. Why did they pick you, Mitch? There are forty lawyers in the firm.'

'Because I knew nothing about it. I was a sitting duck. The FBI is not sure when the partners spring the surprise on the associates, so they couldn't take a chance with anyone else. I happened to be the new guy, so they set the trap as soon as I passed the bar exam.'

Abby chewed her lip and held back tears. She looked blankly at the door across the dark room. 'And they listen to everything we say,' she said.

'No. Just every phone call and conversation around the house and in the cars. We're free to meet here or in most restaurants, and there's always the patio. But I suggest we move farther away from the sliding door. To be safe, we need to sneak behind the storage shed and whisper softly.'

'Are you trying to be funny? I hope not. This is no time for jokes. I'm so scared, angry, confused, mad as hell and not sure where to turn. I'm afraid to speak in my own house. I watch every word I utter on the phone, even if it's a wrong number. Every time the phone rings, I jump and stare at it. And now this.'

'You need another drink.'

'I need ten drinks.'

Mitch grabbed her wrist and squeezed firmly. 'Wait a minute. I see a familiar face. Don't look around.'

She held her breath. 'Where?'

'On the other side of the bar. Smile and look at me.'

Sitting on a barstool and staring intently at the TV was a well-tanned blond with a loud blue-and-white alpine sweater. Fresh from the slopes. But Mitch had seen the tan and the blond bangs and the blond mustache somewhere in Washington. Mitch watched him carefully. The blue light from the tube illuminated his face. Mitch hid in the dark. The man lifted a bottle of beer, hesitated, then, there!, shot a glance into the corner where the McDeeres huddled closely together.

'Are you sure?' Abby asked through clenched teeth.

'Yes. He was in Washington, but I can't place him. In fact, I saw him twice.'

'Is he one of them?'

'How am I supposed to know?'

'Let's get out of here.'

Mitch laid a twenty on the table and they left the airport.

Driving her Peugeot, he raced through the short-term parking lot, paid the attendant and sped away toward midtown. After five minutes of silence, she leaned across and whispered in his ear, 'Can we talk?'

He shook his head. 'Well, how's the weather been while I was away?'

Abby rolled her eyes and looked through the passenger window. 'Cold,' she said. 'Chance of light snow tonight.'

'It was below freezing the entire week in Washington.'

Abby looked flabbergasted at this revelation. 'Any snow?' she asked with raised eyebrows and wide eyes as if enthralled with the conversation.

'No. Just raw cold.'

'What a coincidence! Cold here and cold there.'

Mitch chuckled to himself. They rode silently on the interstate loop. 'So who's gonna win the Super Bowl?' he asked.

'Oilers.'

'Think so, huh? I'm for the Redskins. That's all they talked about in Washington.'

'My, my. Must be a real fun city.'

More silence. Abby placed the back of her hand over her mouth and concentrated on the taillights ahead. At this moment of bewilderment, she would take her chances in Tijuana. Her husband, number three in his class (at Harvard), the one with Wall Street firms rolling out the red carpet, the one who could have gone anywhere, to any firm, had signed up with the . . . Mafia! With five dead lawyers notched on their belts, they most surely wouldn't hesitate with number six. Her husband! Then the many conversations with Kay Quin swirled around her brain. The firm encourages babies. The firm permits wives to work, but not forever. The firm hires no one with family money. The firm demands loyalty to the firm. The firm has the lowest turnover rate in the country. Small wonder.

Mitch watched her carefully. Twenty minutes after they left the airport, the Peugeot parked in the carport next to the BMW. They held hands and walked to the end of the driveway.

'This is crazy, Mitch.'

'Yes, but it's real. It will not go away.'

'What do we do?'

'I don't know, babe. But we gotta do it quick, and we can't make mistakes.'

'I'm scared.'

'I'm terrified.'

Tarrance did not wait long. One week after he waved goodbye to Mitch at the Wall, he spotted him walking hurriedly in the cold in the direction of the Federal Building on North Main, eight blocks from the Bendini Building. He followed him for two blocks, then slid into a small coffee shop with a row of windows facing the street, or the mall, as it was called. Cars were prohibited on Main Street in Memphis.

The asphalt had been covered with tile when the boulevard had ceased being a street and had been transformed into the Mid-America Mall. An occasional useless and desolate tree rose from the tile and stretched its barren limbs between the buildings. Winos and urban nomads drifted aimlessly from one side of the mall to the other, begging for money and food.

Tarrance sat at a front window and watched in the distance as Mitch disappeared into the Federal Building. He ordered coffee and a chocolate doughnut. He checked his watch. It was 10 A.M. According to the docket, McDeere had a brief hearing in Tax Court at this moment. It should be very brief, the clerk of the court had informed Tarrance. He waited.

Nothing is ever brief in court. An hour later, Tarrance moved his face closer to the window and studied the scattered bodies walking quickly in the distance. He drained his coffee cup for the third time, laid two dollars on the table and stood hidden in the door. As Mitch approached on the other side of the mall, Tarrance moved swiftly toward him.

Mitch saw him and slowed for a second.

'Hello, Mitch. Mind if I walk with you?'

'Yes, I mind, Tarrance. It's dangerous, don't you think?'

They walked briskly and did not look at each other. 'Look at that store over there,' Tarrance said, pointing to their right. 'I need a pair of shoes.' They ducked into Don Pang's House of Shoes. Tarrance walked to the rear of the narrow store and stopped between two rows of fake Reeboks at $4.99 for two pairs. Mitch followed him and picked up a pair of size tens. Don Pang or some other Korean eyed them suspiciously but said nothing. They watched the front door through the racks.

'The Director called me yesterday,' Tarrance said

without moving his lips. 'He asked about you. Said it was time you made a decision.'

'Tell him I'm still thinking.'

'Have you told the boys at the office?'

'No. I'm still thinking.'

'That's good. I don't think you should tell them.' He handed Mitch a business card. 'Keep this. There are two numbers on the back. Use either one from a pay phone. You'll get a recorder, so just leave a message and tell me exactly when and where to meet you.'

Mitch put the card in his pocket.

Suddenly, Tarrance ducked lower. 'What is it!' Mitch demanded.

'I think we've been caught. I just saw a goon walk past the store and look in. Listen to me, Mitch, and listen carefully. Walk with me out of the store right now, and the instant we get out the door, yell at me to get lost and shove me away. I'll act like I want to fight, and you run in the direction of your office.'

'You're gonna get me killed, Tarrance.'

'Just do as I say. As soon as you get to the office, report this incident to the partners. Tell them I cornered you and you got away as soon as possible.'

Outside, Mitch shoved harder than necessary and yelled, 'Get the hell away from me! And leave me alone!' He ran two blocks to Union Avenue, then walked to the Bendini Building. He stopped in the men's room on the first floor to catch his breath. He stared at himself in the mirror and breathed deeply ten times.

Avery was on the phone, with two lights holding and blinking. A secretary sat on the sofa, ready with a steno pad for the onslaught of commands. Mitch looked at her and said, 'Would you step outside, please. I need to speak with Avery in private.' She stood and Mitch escorted her to the door. He closed it.

Avery watched him closely and hung up. 'What's going on?' he asked.

Mitch stood by the sofa. 'The FBI just grabbed me as I was returning from Tax Court.'

'Damn! Who was it?'

'Same agent. Guy by the name of Tarrance.'

Avery picked up the phone and kept talking. 'Where did it happen?'

'On the mall. North of Union. I was just walking alone, minding my own business.'

'Is this the first contact since that other thing?'

'Yes. I didn't recognize the guy at first.'

Avery spoke into the receiver. 'This is Avery Tolleson. I need to speak to Oliver Lambert immediately. . . . I don't care if he's on the phone. Interrupt him, and now.'

'What's going on, Avery?' Mitch asked.

'Hello, Oliver. Avery here. Sorry for the interruption. Mitch McDeere is here in my office. A few minutes ago he was walking back from the Federal Building when the FBI agent approached him on the mall . . . . What? Yes, he just walked in my office and told me about it. . . . All right, we'll be there in five minutes.' He hung up. 'Relax, Mitch. We've been through this before.'

'I know, Avery, but this does not make sense. Why would they bother with me? I'm the newest man in the firm.'

'It's harassment, Mitch. Pure and simple. Nothing but harassment. Sit down.'

Mitch walked to the window and looked at the river in the distance. Avery was a cool liar. It was now time for the 'they're just picking on us' routine. Relax, Mitch. Relax? With eight FBI agents assigned to the firm and the Director, Mr. Denton Voyles himself, monitoring the case daily? Relax? He'd just been caught whispering to an FBI agent inside a dollar shoe store. And now he was forced to act like he was an ignorant pawn being preyed upon by the evil forces of the federal government. Harassment? Then why was the goon following him on a routine walk to the courthouse? Answer that, Avery.

'You're scared, aren't you?' Avery asked as he put his arm around him and gazed out the window.

'Not really. Locke explained it all last time. I just wish they would leave me alone.'

'It's a serious matter, Mitch. Don't take it lightly. Let's walk over and see Lambert.'

Mitch followed Avery around the corner and down the hall. A stranger in a black suit opened the door for them, then closed it. Lambert, Nathan Locke and Royce McKnight stood near the small conference table. Again, a tape recorder sat on the table. Mitch sat across from it. Black Eyes sat at the head of the table and glared at Mitch.

He spoke with a menacing frown. There were no smiles in the room. 'Mitch, has Tarrance or anyone else from the FBI contacted you since the first meeting last August?'

'No.'

'Are you certain?'

Mitch slapped the table. 'Dammit! I said no! Why don't you put me under oath?'

Locke was startled. They were all startled. A heavy, tense silence followed for thirty seconds. Mitch glared at Black Eyes, who retreated ever so slightly with a casual movement of his head.

Lambert, ever the diplomat, the mediator, intervened. 'Look, Mitch, we know this is frightening.'

'Damn right it is. I don't like it at all. I'm minding my own business, working my ass off ninety hours a week, trying to be nothing but a good lawyer and member of this firm, and for some unknown reason I keep getting these little visits from the FBI. Now, sir, I would like some answers.'

Locke pressed the red button on the recorder. 'We'll talk about that in a minute. First, you tell us everything that happened.'

'It's very simple, Mr. Locke. I walked to the Federal Building at ten for an appearance before Judge Kofer on the Malcolm Delaney case. I was there about an hour, and I finished my business. I left the Federal Building, and I was walking in the direction of our office – in a hurry, I might add. It's about twenty degrees out there. A block or two north of Union, this guy Tarrance came out of nowhere, grabbed my arm and pushed me into a small store. I started to knock the hell out of him, but, after all, he is an FBI agent. And I didn't want to make a scene. Inside, he tells me he wants to talk for a minute. I pulled away from him, and ran to the door. He followed me, tried to grab me, and I shoved him away. Then I ran here, went straight to Avery's office, and here we are. That's all that was said. Play by play, everything.'

'What did he want to talk about?'

'I didn't give him a chance, Mr. Locke. I have no plans to talk to any FBI agent unless he has a subpoena.'

'Are you sure it's the same agent?'

'I think so. I didn't recognize him at first. I haven't seen him since last August. Once inside the store, he pulled his badge and gave me his name again. At that point, I ran.'

Locke pressed another button and sat back in the chair. Lambert sat behind him and smiled ever so warmly. 'Listen, Mitch, we explained this last time These guys are getting bolder and bolder. Just last month they approached Jack Aldrich while he was eating lunch in a little grill on Second Street. We're not sure what they're up to, but Tarrance is out of his mind. It's nothing but harassment.'

Mitch watched his lips but heard little. As Lambert spoke, he thought of Kozinski and Hodge and their pretty widows and children at the funerals.

Black Eyes cleared his throat. 'It's a serious matter, Mitch. But we have nothing to hide. They could better spend their time investigating our clients if they suspect wrongdoing. We're lawyers. We may represent people who flirt with the law, but we have done nothing wrong. This is very baffling to us.'

Mitch smiled and opened his hands. 'What do you want me to do?' he asked sincerely.

'There's nothing you can do, Mitch,' said Lambert. 'Just stay away from this guy, and run if you see him. If he so much as looks at you, report it immediately.'

'That's what he did,' Avery said defensively.

Mitch looked as pitiful as possible.

'You can go, Mitch,' Lambert said. 'And keep us posted.'

He left the office by himself.

DeVasher paced behind his desk and ignored the partners. 'He's lying, I tell you. He's lying. The son of a bitch is lying. I know he's lying.'

'What did your man see?' asked Locke.

'My man saw something different. Slightly different. But very different. He says McDeere and Tarrance walked sort of nonchalantly into the shoe store. No physical intimidation by Tarrance. None at all. Tarrance walks up, they talk, and both sort of duck into the store. My man says they disappear into the back of the store, and they're back there for three, maybe four minutes. Then another one of our guys walks by the store, looks in and sees nothing. Evidently, they saw our man, because within seconds they come flying out of the store with McDeere shoving and yelling. Something ain't right, I tell you.'

'Did Tarrance grab his arm and force him into the store?' Nathan Locke asked slowly, precisely.

'Hell no. And that's the problem. McDeere went voluntarily, and when he said the guy grabbed his arm, he's lying. My man says he thinks they would've stayed in there for a while if they hadn't seen us.'

'But you're not sure of that,' Nathan Locke said.

'I wasn't sure, dammit. They didn't invite me into the store.'

DeVasher kept pacing while the lawyers stared at the floor. He unwrapped a Roi-Tan and crammed it into his fat mouth.

Finally, Oliver Lambert spoke. 'Look, DeVasher, it's very possible McDeere is telling the truth and your man got the wrong signals. It's very possible. I think McDeere is entitled to the benefit of the doubt.'

DeVasher grunted and ignored this.

'Do you know of any contact since last August?' asked Royce McKnight.

'We don't know of any, but that doesn't mean they ain't talked, does it now? We didn't know about those other two until it was almost too late. It's impossible to watch every move they make. Impossible.'

He walked back and forth by his credenza, obviously deep in thought. 'I gotta talk to him,' he finally said.

'Who?'

'McDeere. It's time he and I had a little talk.'

'About what?' Lambert asked nervously.

'You let me handle it, okay? Just stay out of my way.'

'I think it's a bit premature,' Locke said.

'And I don't give a damn what you think. If you clowns were in charge of security, you'd all be in prison.'

Mitch sat in his office with the door closed and stared at the walls. A migraine was forming at the base of his skull, and he felt sick. There was a knock at the door.

'Come in,' he said softly.

Avery peeked inside, then walked to the desk. 'How about lunch?'

'No, thanks. I'm not hungry.'

The partner slid his hands into his trouser pockets and smiled warmly. 'Look, Mitch, I know you're worried. Let's take a break. I've got to run downtown for a meeting. Why don't you meet me at the Manhattan Club at one. We'll have a long lunch and talk things over. I've reserved the limo for you. It'll be waiting outside at a quarter till.'

Mitch managed a weak smile, as if he was touched by this. 'Sure, Avery. Why not.'

'Good. I'll see you at one.'

At a quarter till, Mitch opened the front door and walked to the limo. The driver opened the door, and Mitch fell in. Company was waiting.

A short, fat, bald headed man with a huge, bulging, hanging neck sat smugly in the corner of the rear seat. He stuck out a hand. 'Name's DeVasher, Mitch. Nice to meet you.'

'Am I in the right limo?' Mitch asked.

'Sure. Sure. Relax.' The driver pulled away from the curb.

'What can I do for you?' Mitch asked.

'You can listen for a while. We need to have a little talk.' The driver turned on Riverside Drive and headed for the Hernando De Soto Bridge.

'Where are we going?' Mitch asked.

'For a little ride. Just relax, son.'

So I'm number six, thought Mitch. This is it. No, wait a minute. They were much more creative than this with their killing.

'Mitch, can I call you Mitch?'

'Sure.'

'Fine. Mitch, I'm in charge of security for the firm, and –'

'Why does the firm need security?'

'Just listen to me, son, and I'll explain. The firm has an extensive security program, thanks to old man Bendini. He was a nut about security and secrecy. My job is to protect the firm, and quite frankly, we're very concerned about this FBI business.'

'So am I.'

'Yes. We believe the FBI is determined to infiltrate our firm in hopes of collecting information on certain clients.'

'Which clients?'

'Some high rollers with questionable tax shelters.'

Mitch nodded and looked at the river below. They were now in Arkansas, with the Memphis skyline fading behind them. DeVasher recessed the conversation. He sat like a frog with his hands folded across the gut. Mitch waited, until it became apparent that lapses in conversation and awkward silence did not bother DeVasher. Several miles across the river, the driver left the interstate and found a rough county road that circled and ran back to the east. Then he turned onto a gravel road that went for a mile through low-lying bean fields next to the river. Memphis was suddenly visible again, across the water.

'Where are we going?' Mitch asked, with some alarm.

'Relax. I want to show you something.'

A gravesite, thought Mitch. The limo stopped on a cliff that fell ten feet to a sandbar next to the bank. The skyline stood impressively on the other side. The top of the Bendini Building was visible.

'Let's take a walk,' DeVasher said.

'Where to?' Mitch asked.

'Come on. It's okay.' DeVasher opened his door

and walked to the rear bumper. Slowly, Mitch followed him.

'As I was saying, Mitch, we are very troubled by this contact with the FBI. If you talk to them, they will get bolder, then who knows what the fools will try. It's imperative that you not speak to them, ever again. Understand?'

'Yes. I've understood since the first visit in August.'

Suddenly, DeVasher was in his face, nose to nose. He smiled wickedly. 'I have something that will keep you honest.' He reached in his sport coat and pulled out a manila envelope.

'Take a look at these,' he said with a sneer, and walked away.

Mitch leaned on the limo and nervously opened the envelope. There were four photographs, black and white, eight by ten, very clear. On the beach. The girl.

'Oh my god! Who took these?' Mitch yelled at him.

'What difference does it make. It's you, ain't it?'

There was no doubt about who it was. He ripped the photographs into small pieces and threw them in DeVasher's direction.

'We got plenty at the office,' DeVasher said calmly. 'Bunch of them. We don't want to use them, but one more little conversation with Mr. Tarrance or any other Fibbie and we'll mail them to your wife. How would you like that, Mitch? Imagine your pretty little wife going to the mailbox to get her *Redbook* and catalogues and she sees this strange envelope addressed to her. Try to think of that, Mitch. The next time you and Tarrance decide to shop for plastic shoes, think about us, Mitch. Because we'll be watching.'

'Who knows about these?' Mitch asked.

'Me and the photographer, and now you. Nobody in the firm knows, and I don't plan to tell them. But if you screw up again, I suspect they'll be passing them around at lunch. I play hardball, Mitch.'

He sat on the trunk and rubbed his temples. DeVasher walked up next to him. 'Listen, son. You're a very bright young man, and you're on your way to big bucks. Don't screw it up. Just work hard, play the game, buy new cars, build bigger homes, the works. Just like all the other guys. Don't try to be no hero. I don't want to use the pictures.'

'Okay, okay.'

TWENTY-ONE

For seventeen days and seventeen nights, the troubled lives of Mitch and Abby McDeere proceeded quietly without interference from Wayne Tarrance or any of his confederates. The routines returned. Mitch worked eighteen hours a day, every day of the week, and never left the office for any reason except to drive home. Lunch was at the desk. Avery sent other associates to run errands or file motions or appear in court. Mitch seldom left his office, the fifteen-by-fifteen sanctuary where he was certain Tarrance could not get him. If possible, he stayed out of the halls and men's rooms and coffee room. They were watching, he was sure. He was not sure who they were, but there was no doubt that a bunch of folks were vitally interested in his movements. So he stayed at his desk, with the door shut most of the time, working diligently, billing like crazy and trying to forget that the building had a fifth floor and on the fifth floor was a short, fat, mean little bastard named DeVasher who had a collection of photographs that could ruin him.

With each uneventful day, Mitch withdrew even more into his asylum and became even more hopeful that perhaps the last episode in the Korean shoe store had scared Tarrance or maybe gotten him fired. Maybe Voyles would just simply forget the entire operation, and Mitch could continue along his happy way of getting rich and making partner and buying everything in sight. But he knew better.

To Abby, the house was a prison, though she could come and go at will. She worked longer hours at school, spent more time walking the malls and made at least one trip each day to the grocery store. She watched everyone, especially men in dark suits who looked at her. She wore black sunglasses so they could not see her eyes. She wore them when it was raining. Late at night, after supper alone while she waited for him, she stared at the walls and resisted the temptation to investigate. The phones could be examined with a magnifying glass. The wires and mikes could not be invisible, she told herself. More than once she thought of finding a book on such devices so she could identify them. But Mitch said no. They were in the house, he assured her, and any attempt to find them could be disastrous.

So she moved silently around her own house, feeling violated and knowing it could not last much longer. They both knew the importance of appearing normal, of sounding normal. They tried to engage in normal talk about how the day went, about the office and her students, about the weather, about this and that. But the conversations were flat, often forced and strained. When Mitch was in law school the lovemaking had been frequent and rowdy; now it was practically nonexistent. Someone was listening.

Midnight walks around the block became a habit. After a quick sandwich each night, they would deliver the rehearsed lines about needing exercise and head for the street. They held hands and walked in the cold, talking about the firm and the FBI, and which way to turn; always the same conclusion: there was no way out. None. Seventeen days and seventeen nights.

The eighteenth day brought a new twist. Mitch was exhausted by 9 P.M. and decided to go home. He had worked nonstop for fifteen and a half hours. At two hundred per. As usual, he walked the halls of the second floor, then took the stairs to the third floor. He casually checked each office to see who was still working. No one on the third floor. He followed the stairs to the fourth floor and walked the wide rectangular hallway as if in search of something. All lights except one were off. Royce McKnight was working late. Mitch eased by his office without being seen. Avery's door was closed, and Mitch grabbed the doorknob. It was locked. He walked to the library down the hall, looking for a book he did not need. After two weeks of the casual late-night inspections, he had found no closed circuit cameras above the halls or offices. They just listen, he decided. They do not see.

He said goodbye to Dutch Hendrix at the front gate and drove home. Abby was not expecting him at such an early hour. He quietly unlocked the door from the carport and eased into the kitchen. He flipped on a light switch. She was in the bedroom. Between the kitchen and the den was a small foyer with a rolltop desk where Abby left each day's mail. He laid his briefcase softly on the desk, then saw it. A large brown envelope addressed with a black felt marker to Abby McDeere. No return address. Scrawled in heavy black letters were the words PHOTOGRAPHS – DO NOT BEND. His heart stopped first, then his breathing. He grabbed the envelope. It had been opened.

A heavy layer of sweat broke across his forehead. His mouth was dry and he could not swallow. His heart returned with the fury of a jackhammer. The breathing was heavy and painful. He was nauseous. Slowly, he backed away from the desk, holding the envelope. She's in the bed, he thought. Hurt, sick, devastated and mad as hell. He wiped his forehead and tried to collect himself. Face it like a man, he said.

She was in the bed, reading a book with the

television on. The dog was in the backyard. Mitch opened the bedroom door, and Abby bolted upright in horror. She almost screamed at the intruder, until she recognized him.

'You scared me, Mitch!'

Her eyes glowed with fear, then fun. They had not been crying. They looked fine, normal. No pain. No anger. He could not speak.

'Why are you home?' she demanded, sitting up in bed, smiling now.

Smiling? 'I live here,' he said weakly.

'Why didn't you call?'

'Do I have to call before I can come home?' His breathing was now almost normal. She was fine!

'It would be nice. Come here and kiss me.'

He leaned across the bed and kissed her. He handed her the envelope. 'What's this?' he asked nonchalantly.

'You tell me. It's addressed to me, but there was nothing inside. Not a thing.' She closed her book and laid it on the night table.

Not a thing! He smiled at her and kissed her again. 'Are you expecting photographs from anyone?' he asked in complete ignorance.

'Not that I know of. Must be a mistake.'

He could almost hear DeVasher laughing at this very moment on the fifth floor. The fat little bastard was standing up there somewhere in some dark room full of wires and machines with a headset stretched around his massive bowling ball of a head, laughing uncontrollably.

'That's strange,' Mitch said. Abby pulled on a pair of jeans and pointed to the backyard. Mitch nodded. The signal was simple, just a quick point or a nod of the head in the direction of the patio.

Mitch laid the envelope on the rolltop desk and for a second touched the scrawled markings on it. Probably DeVasher's handwriting. He could almost hear him laughing. He could see his fat face and nasty smile. The photographs had probably been passed around during lunch in the partners' dining room. He could see Lambert and McKnight and even Avery gawking admiringly over coffee and dessert.

They'd better enjoy the pictures, dammit. They'd better enjoy the remaining few months of their bright and rich and happy legal careers.

Abby walked by and he grabbed her hand. 'What's for dinner?' he asked for the benefit of those listening.

'Why don't we go out? We should celebrate since you're home at a decent hour.'

They walked through the den. 'Good idea,' said Mitch. They eased through the rear door, across the patio and into the darkness.

'What is it?' Mitch asked.

'You got a letter today from Doris. She said she's in Nashville, but will return to Memphis on the twenty-seventh of February. She says she needs to see you. It's important. It was a very short letter.'

'The twenty-seventh! That was yesterday.'

'I know. I presume she's already in town. I wonder what she wants.'

'Yeah, and I wonder where she is.'

'She said her husband had an engagement here in town.'

'Good. She'll find us,' Mitch said.

Nathan Locke closed his office door and pointed DeVasher in the direction of the small conference table near the window. The two men hated each other and made no attempt to be cordial. But business was business, and they took orders from the same man.

'Lazarov wanted me to talk to you, alone,' DeVasher said. 'I've spent the past two days with him in Vegas, and he's very anxious. They're all anxious,

Locke, and he trusts you more than anyone else around here. He likes you more than he likes me.'

'That's understandable,' Locke said with no smile. The ripples of black around his eyes narrowed and focused intensely on DeVasher.

'Anyway, there are a few things he wants us to discuss.'

'I'm listening.'

'McDeere's lying. You know how Lazarov's always bragged about having a mole inside the FBI. Well, I've never believed him, and still don't, for the most part. But according to Lazarov, his little source is telling him that there was some kind of secret meeting involving McDeere and some FBI heavyweights when your boy was in Washington back in January. We were there, and our men saw nothing, but it's impossible to track anyone twenty-four hours a day without getting caught. It's possible he could've slipped away for a little while without our knowledge.'

'Do you believe it?'

'It's not important whether I believe it. Lazarov believes it, and that's all that matters. At any rate, he told me to make preliminary plans to, uh, take care of him.'

'Damn DeVasher! We can't keep eliminating people.'

'Just preliminary plans, nothing serious. I told Lazarov I thought it was much too early and that it would be a mistake. But they are very worried, Locke.'

'This can't continue, De Vasher. I mean, damn! We have reputations to consider. We have a higher casualty rate than oil rigs. People will start talking. We're gonna reach a point where no law student in his right mind would take a job here.'

'I don't think you need to worry about that. Lazarov has put a freeze on hiring. He told me to tell you that.

He also wants to know how many associates are still in the dark.'

'Five, I think. Let's see, Lynch, Sorrell, Buntin, Myers and McDeere.'

'Forget McDeere. Lazarov is convinced he knows much more than we think. Are you certain the other four know nothing?'

Locke thought for a moment and mumbled under his breath. 'Well, we haven't told them. You guys are listening and watching. What do you hear?'

'Nothing, from those four. They sound ignorant and act as if they suspect nothing. Can you fire them?'

'Fire them! They're lawyers, DeVasher. You don't fire lawyers. They're loyal members of the firm.'

'The firm is changing, Locke. Lazarov wants to fire the ones who don't know and stop hiring new ones. It's obvious the Fibbies have changed their strategy, and it's time for us to change as well. Lazarov wants to circle the wagons and plug the leaks. We can't sit back and wait for them to pick off our boys.'

'Fire them,' Locke repeated in disbelief. 'This firm has never fired a lawyer.'

'Very touching, Locke. We've disposed of five, but never fired one. That's real good. You've got a month to do it, so start thinking of a reason. I suggest you fire all four at one time. Tell them you lost a big account and you're cutting back.'

'We have clients, not accounts.'

'Okay, fine. Your biggest client is telling you to fire Lynch, Sorrell, Buntin and Myers. Now start making plans.'

'How do we fire those four without firing McDeere?'

'You'll think of something, Nat. You got a month. Get rid of them and don't hire any new boys. Lazarov wants a tight little unit where everyone can be trusted. He's scared, Nat. Scared and mad. I don't have to tell you what could happen if one of your boys spilled his guts.'

'No, you don't have to tell me. What does he plan to do with McDeere?'

'Right now, nothing but the same. We're listening twenty-four hours a day, and the kid has never mentioned a word to his wife or anyone else. Not a word! He's been corralled twice by Tarrance, and he reported both incidents to you. I still think the second meeting was somewhat suspicious, so we're being very careful. Lazarov, on the other hand, insists there was a meeting in Washington. He's trying to confirm. He said his sources knew little, but they were digging. If in fact McDeere met with the Fibbies up there and failed to report it, then I'm sure Lazarov will instruct me to move quickly. That's why he wants preliminary plans to take McDeere out.'

'How do you plan to do it?'

'It's too early. I haven't given it much thought.'

'You know he and his wife are going to the Caymans in two weeks for a vacation. They'll stay in one of our condos, the usual.'

'We wouldn't do it there again. Too suspicious. Lazarov instructed me to get her pregnant.'

'McDeere's wife?'

'Yep. He wants them to have a baby, a little leverage. She's on the pill, so we gotta break in, take her little box, match up the pills and replace them with placebos.'

At this, the great black eyes saddened just a touch and looked through the window. 'What the hell's going on, DeVasher?' he asked softly.

'This place is about to change, Nat. It appears as though the feds are extremely interested, and they keep pecking away. One day, who knows, one of your boys may take the bait, and you'll all leave town in the middle of the night.'

'I don't believe that, DeVasher. A lawyer here would be a fool to risk his life and his family for a few promises from the feds. I just don't believe it will happen. These boys are too smart and they're making too much money.'

'I hope you're right.'

TWENTY-TWO

The leasing agent leaned against the rear of the elevator and admired the black leather miniskirt from behind. He followed it down almost to the knees, where it ended and the seams in the black silk stockings began and snaked downward to black heels. Kinky heels, with little red bows across the toes. He slowly worked his way back up the seams, past the leather, pausing to admire the roundness of her rear, then upward to the red cashmere sweater, which from his vantage point revealed little but from the other side was quite impressive, as he had noticed in the lobby. The hair landed just below the shoulder blades and contrasted nicely with the red. He knew it was bleached, but add the bleach to the leather mini and the seams and the kinky heels and the tight sweater hugging those things around the front, add all that together and he knew this was a woman he could have. He would like to have her in the building. She just wanted a small office. The rent was negotiable.

The elevator stopped. The door opened, and he followed her into the narrow hall. 'This way' – he pointed, flipping on a light switch. In the corner, he moved in front of her and stuck a key in a badly aged wooden door.

'It's just two rooms,' he said, flipping on another switch. 'About two hundred square feet.'

She walked straight to the window. 'The view is okay,' Tammy said, staring into the distance.

'Yes, a nice view. The carpet is new. Painted last fall. Rest room's down the hall. It's a nice place. The entire building's been renovated within the past eight years.' He stared at the black seams as he spoke.

'It's not bad,' Tammy said, not in response to anything he had mentioned. She continued to stare out the window. 'What's the name of this place?'

'The Cotton Exchange Building. One of the oldest in Memphis. It's really a prestigious address.'

'How prestigious is the rent?'

He cleared his throat and held a file before him. He did not look at the file. He was gaping at the heels now. 'Well, it's such a small office. What did you say you needed it for?'

'Secretarial work. Free-lance secretarial.' She moved to the other window, ignoring him. He followed every move.

'I see. How long will you need it?'

'Six months, with an option for a year.'

'Okay, for six months we can lease it for three-fifty a month.'

She did not flinch or look from the window. She slid her right foot out of the shoe and rubbed the left calf with it. The seam continued, he observed, under the heel and along the bottom of the foot. The toenails were . . . red! She cocked her rear to the left and leaned on the windowsill. His file was shaking.

'I'll pay two-fifty a month,' she said with authority.

He cleared his throat. There was no sense being greedy. The tiny rooms were dead space, useless to anyone else, and had not been occupied in years. The building could use a free-lance secretary. Hell, he might even need a free-lance secretary.

'Three hundred, but no less. This building is in demand. Ninety percent occupied right now. Three

265

hundred a month, and that's too low. We're barely covering costs at that.'

She turned suddenly, and there they were. Staring at him. The cashmere was stretched tightly around them. 'The ad said there were furnished offices available,' she said.

'We can furnish this one,' he said, eager to cooperate. 'What do you need?'

She looked around the office. 'I would like a secretarial desk with credenza in here. Several file cabinets. A couple of chairs for clients. Nothing fancy. The other room does not have to be furnished. I'll put a copier in there.'

'No problem,' he said with a smile.

'And I'll pay three hundred a month, furnished.'

'Good,' he said as he opened a file and withdrew a blank lease. He laid it on a folding table and began writing.

'Your name?'

'Doris Greenwood.' Her mother was Doris Greenwood, and she had been Tammy Inez Greenwood before she ran up on Buster Hemphill, who later became (legally) Elvis Aaron Hemphill, and life had pretty much been downhill since. Her mother lived in Effingham, Illinois.

'Okay, Doris,' he said with an effort at suaveness, as if they were now on a first name basis and growing closer by the moment. 'Home address?'

'Why do you need that?' she asked with irritation.

'Well, uh, we just need that information.'

'It's none of your business.'

'Okay, okay. No problem.' He dramatically scratched out that portion of the lease. He hovered above it. 'Let's see. We'll run it from today, March 2, for six months until September 2. Is that okay?'

She nodded and lit a cigarette.

He read the next paragraph. 'Okay, we require a

three-hundred-dollar deposit and the first month's rent in advance.'

From a pocket in the tight black leather skirt, she produced a roll of cash. She counted six one-hundred-dollar bills and laid them on the table. 'Receipt, please,' she demanded.

'Certainly.' He continued writing.

'What floor are we on?' she asked, returning to the windows.

'Ninth. There's a ten percent late charge past the fifteenth of the month. We have the right to enter at any reasonable time to inspect. Premises cannot be used for any illegal purpose. You pay all utilities and insurance on contents. You get one parking space in the lot across the street, and here are two keys. Any questions?'

'Yeah. What if I work odd hours? I mean, real late at night.'

'No big deal. You can come and go as you please. After dark the security guard at the Front Street door will let you pass.'

Tammy stuck the cigarette between her sticky lips and walked to the table. She glanced at the lease, hesitated, then signed the name of Doris Greenwood.

They locked up, and he followed her carefully down the hall to the elevator.

By noon the next day, the odd assortment of furniture had been delivered and Doris Greenwood of Greenwood Services arranged the rented typewriter and the rented phone next to each other on the secretarial desk. Sitting and facing the typewriter, she could look slightly to her left out of the window and watch the traffic on Front Street. She filled the desk drawers with typing paper, notepads, pencils, odds and ends. She placed magazines on the filing cabinets and the small table between the two chairs where her clients would sit.

There was a knock at the door. 'Who is it?' she asked.

'It's your copier,' a voice answered.

She unlocked the door and opened it. A short, hyperactive little man named Gordy rushed in, looked around the room and said rudely, 'Okay, where do you want it?'

'In there,' Tammy said, pointing to the eight-by-ten empty room with no door on the hinges. Two young men in blue uniforms pushed and pulled the cart holding the copier.

Gordy laid the paperwork on her desk. 'It's a mighty big copier for this place. We're talking ninety copies a minute with a collator and automatic feed. It's a big machine.'

'Where do I sign?' she asked, ignoring the small talk.

He pointed with the pen. 'Six months, at two-forty a month. That includes service and maintenance and five hundred sheets of paper for the first two months. You want legal or letter sized?'

'Legal.'

'First payment due on the tenth, and same thereafter for five months. Operator's manual is on the rack. Call me if you have any questions.'

The two servicemen gawked at the tight stonewashed jeans and the red heels and slowly left the office. Gordy ripped off the yellow copy and handed it to her. 'Thanks for the business,' he said.

She locked the door behind them. She walked to the window next to her desk and looked north, along Front. Two blocks up on the opposite side, floors four and five of the Bendini Building were visible.

He kept to himself with his nose buried deep in the books and the piles of paperwork. He was too busy for any of them, except Lamar. He was very much aware that his withdrawal was not going unnoticed. So he worked harder. Perhaps they would not be suspicious if he billed twenty hours a day. Perhaps money could insulate him.

Nina left a box of cold pizza when she checked out after lunch. He ate it while he cleared his desk. He called Abby. Said he was going to see Ray and that he would return to Memphis late Sunday. He eased through the side door and into the parking lot.

For three and a half hours, he raced along Interstate 40 with his eyes on the rearview mirror. Nothing. He never saw them. They probably just call ahead, he thought, and wait for him somewhere up there. In Nashville, he made a sudden exit into downtown. Using a map he had scribbled, he darted in and out of traffic, making U-turns wherever possible and in general driving like a nut. To the south of town, he turned quickly into a large apartment complex and cruised between the buildings. It was nice enough. The parking lots were clean and the faces were white. All of them. He parked next to the office and locked the BMW. The pay phone by the covered pool worked. He called a cab and gave an address two blocks away. He ran between the buildings, down a side street, and arrived precisely with the cab. 'Greyhound bus station,' he said to the driver. 'And in a hurry. I've got ten minutes.'

'Relax, pal. It's only six blocks away.'

Mitch ducked low in the rear seat and watched the traffic. The driver moved with a slow confidence and seven minutes later turned onto Eighth Street. He stopped in front of the station. Mitch threw two fives over the seat and darted into the terminal. He bought a one way ticket on the four-thirty bus to Atlanta. It was four thirty-one, according to the clock on the wall. The clerk pointed through the swinging doors. 'Bus No. 454,' she said. 'Leaving in a moment.'

The driver slammed the baggage door, took his

ticket and followed Mitch onto the bus. The first three rows were filled with elderly blacks. A dozen more passengers were scattered toward the rear. Mitch walked slowly down the aisle, gazing at each face and seeing no one. He took a window seat on the fourth row from the rear. He slipped on a pair of sunglasses and glanced behind him. No one. Dammit! Was it the wrong bus? He stared out the dark windows as the bus moved quickly into traffic. They would stop in Knoxville. Maybe his contact would be there.

When they were on the interstate and the driver reached his cruising speed, a man in blue jeans and madras shirt suddenly appeared and slid into the seat next to Mitch. It was Tarrance. Mitch breathed easier.

'Where have you been?' he asked.

'In the rest room. Did you lose them?' Tarrance spoke in a low voice while surveying the backs of the heads of the passengers. No one was listening. No one could hear.

'I never see them, Tarrance. So I cannot say if I lost them. But I think they would have to be supermen to keep my trail this time.'

'Did you see our man in the terminal?'

'Yes. By the pay phone with the red Falcons cap. Black dude.'

'That's him. He would've signaled if they were following.'

'He gave me the go-ahead.'

Tarrance wore silver reflective sunglasses under a green Michigan State baseball cap. Mitch could smell the fresh Juicy Fruit.

'Sort of out of uniform, aren't you?' Mitch said with no smile. 'Did Voyles give you permission to dress like that?'

'I forgot to ask him. I'll mention it in the morning.'

'Sunday morning?' Mitch asked.

'Of course. He'll wanna know all about our little bus ride. I briefed him for an hour before I left town.'

'Well, first things first. What about my car?'

'We'll pick it up in a few minutes and babysit it for you. It'll be in Knoxville when you need it. Don't worry.'

'You don't think they'll find us?'

'No way. No one followed you out of Memphis, and we detected nothing in Nashville. You're clean as a whistle.'

'Pardon my concern. But after that fiasco in the shoe store, I know you boys are not above stupidity.'

'It was a mistake, all right. We –'

'A big mistake. One that could get me on the hit list.'

'You covered it well. It won't happen again.'

'Promise me, Tarrance. Promise me no one will ever again approach me in public.'

Tarrance looked down the aisle and nodded.

'No, Tarrance. I need to hear it from your mouth. Promise me.'

'Okay, okay. It won't happen again. I promise.'

'Thanks. Now maybe I can eat at a restaurant without fear of being grabbed.'

'You've made your point.'

An old black man with a cane inched toward them, smiled and walked past. The rest-room door slammed. The Greyhound rode the left lane and blew past the lawful drivers.

Tarrance flipped through a magazine. Mitch gazed into the countryside. The man with the cane finished his business and wobbled to his seat on the front row.

'So what brings you here?' Tarrance asked, flipping pages.

'I don't like airplanes. I always take the bus.'

'I see. Where would you like to start?'

'Voyles said you had a game plan.'

'I do. I just need a quarterback.'

'Good ones are very expensive.'

'We've got the money.'

'It'll cost a helluva lot more than you think. The way I figure it, I'll be throwing away a forty year legal career at, say, an average of half a million a year.'

'That's twenty million bucks.'

'I know. But we can negotiate.'

'That's good to hear. You're assuming that you'll work, or practice, as you say, for forty years. That's a very precarious assumption. Just for fun, let's assume that within five years we bust up the firm and indict you along with all of your buddies. And that we obtain convictions, and you go off to prison for a few years. They won't keep you long because you're a white-collar type, and of course you've heard how nice the federal pens are. But at any rate, you'll lose your license, your house, your little BMW. Probably your wife. When you get out, you can open up a private investigation service like your old friend Lomax. It's easy work, unless you sniff the wrong underwear.'

'Like I said. It's negotiable.'

'All right. Let's negotiate. How much do you want?'

'For what?'

Tarrance closed the magazine, placed it under his seat and opened a thick paperback. He pretended to read. Mitch spoke from the corner of his mouth with his eyes on the median.

'That's a very good question,' Tarrance said softly, just above the distant grind of the diesel engine. 'What do we want from you? Good question. First, you have to give up your career as a lawyer. You'll have to divulge secrets and records that belong to your clients. That, of course, is enough to get you disbarred, but that won't seem important. You and I must agree that you will hand us the firm on a silver platter. Once we agree, if we agree, the rest will fall in place. Second, and most important, you will give us enough documentation to indict every member of the firm and most of the top Morolto people. The records are in the little building there on Front Street.'

'How do you know this?'

Tarrance smiled. 'Because we spend billions of dollars fighting organized crime. Because we've tracked the Moroltos for twenty years. Because we have sources within the family. Because Hodge and Kozinski were talking when they were murdered. Don't sell us short, Mitch.'

'And you think I can get the information out?'

'Yes, Counselor. You can build a case from the inside that will collapse the firm and break up one of the largest crime families in the country. You gotta lay out the firm for us. Whose office is where? Names of all secretaries, clerks, paralegals. Who works on what files? Who's got which clients? The chain of command. Where on the fifth floor? What's up there? Where are the records kept? Is there a central storage area? How much is computerized? How much is on microfilm? And, most important, you gotta bring the stuff out and hand it to us. Once we have probable cause, we can go in with a small army and get everything. But that's an awfully big step. We gotta have a very tight and solid case before we go crashing in with search warrants.'

'Is that all you want?'

'No. You'll have to testify against all of your buddies at their trials. Could take years.'

Mitch breathed deeply and closed his eyes. The bus slowed behind a caravan of mobile homes split in two. Dusk was approaching, and, one at a time, the cars in the westbound lane brightened with headlights. Testifying at trial! This, he had not thought of. With millions to spend for the best criminal lawyers, the trials could drag on forever.

Tarrance actually began reading the paperback, a Louis L'Amour. He adjusted the reading light above them, as if he was indeed a real passenger on a real journey. After thirty miles of no talk, no negotiation, Mitch removed his sunglasses and looked at Tarrance.

'What happens to me?'

'You'll have a lot of money, for what that's worth. If you have any sense of morality, you can face yourself each day. You can live anywhere in the country, with a new identity, of course. We'll find you a job, fix your nose, do anything you want, really.'

Mitch tried to keep his eyes on the road, but it was impossible. He glared at Tarrance. 'Morality? Don't ever mention that word to me again, Tarrance. I'm an innocent victim, and you know it.'

Tarrance grunted with a smart-ass grin.

They rode in silence for a few miles.

'What about my wife?'

'Yeah, you can keep her.'

'Very funny.'

'Sorry. She'll get everything she wants. How much does she know?'

'Everything.' He thought of the girl on the beach. 'Well, almost everything.'

'We'll get her a fat government job with the Social Security Administration anywhere you want. It won't be that bad, Mitch.'

'It'll be wonderful. Until an unknown point in the future when one of your people opens his or her mouth and lets something slip to the wrong person, and you'll read about me or my wife in the paper. The Mob never forgets, Tarrance. They're worse than elephants. And they keep secrets better than your side. You guys have lost people, so don't deny it.'

'I won't deny it. And I'll admit to you that they can be ingenious when they decide to kill.'

'Thanks. So where do I go?'

'It's up to you. Right now we have about two thousand witnesses living all over the country under new names with new homes and new jobs. The odds are overwhelmingly in your favor.'

'So I play the odds?'

'Yes. You either take the money and run, or you play big-shot lawyer and bet that we never infiltrate.'

'That's a hell of a choice, Tarrance.'

'It is. I'm glad it's yours.'

The female companion of the ancient black man with the cane rose feebly from her seat and began shuffling toward them. She grabbed each aisle seat as she progressed. Tarrance leaned toward Mitch as she passed. He would not dare speak with this stranger in the vicinity. She was at least ninety, half crippled, probably illiterate, and could not care less if Tarrance received his next breath of air. But Tarrance was instantly mute.

Fifteen minutes later, the rest-room door opened and released the sounds of the toilet gurgling downward into the pit of the Greyhound. She shuffled to the front and took her seat.

'Who is Jack Aldrich?' Mitch asked. He suspected a cover-up with this one, and he carefully watched the reaction from the corner of his eye. Tarrance looked up from the book and stared at the seat in front of him.

'Name's familiar. I can't place him.'

Mitch returned his gaze to the window. Tarrance knew. He had flinched, and his eyes had narrowed too quickly before he answered. Mitch watched the westbound traffic.

'So who is he?' Tarrance finally asked.

'You don't know him?'

'If I knew him, I wouldn't ask who he was.'

'He's a member of our firm. You should've known that, Tarrance.'

'The city's full of lawyers. I guess you know them all.'

'I know the ones at Bendini, Lambert & Locke, the quiet little firm you guys have been studying for ten years. Aldrich is a six-year man who allegedly was approached by the FBI a couple of months ago. True or false?'

'Absolutely false. Who told you this?'

'It doesn't matter. Just a rumor around the office.'

'It's a lie. We've talked to no one but you since August. You have my word. And we have no plans to talk to anyone else, unless, of course, you decline and we must find another prospect.'

'You've never talked to Aldrich?'

'That's what I said.'

Mitch nodded and picked up a magazine. They rode in silence for thirty minutes. Tarrance gave up on his novel, and finally said, 'Look, Mitch, we'll be in Knoxville in an hour or so. We need to strike a deal, if we're going to. Director Voyles will have a thousand questions in the morning.'

'How much money?'

'Half a million bucks.'

Any lawyer worth his salt knew the first offer had to be rejected. Always. He had seen Avery's mouth drop open in shock and his head shake wildly in absolute disgust and disbelief with first offers, regardless of how reasonable. There would be counteroffers, and counter-counteroffers, and further negotiations, but always, the first offer was rejected.

So by shaking his head and smiling at the window as if this was what he expected, Mitch said no to half a million.

'Did I say something funny?' Tarrance, the nonlawyer, the nonnegotiator, asked.

'That's ridiculous, Tarrance. You can't expect me

to walk away from a gold mine for half a million bucks. After taxes, I net three hundred thousand at best.'

'And if we close the gold mine and send all you Gucci-footed hotshots to jail?'

'If. If. If. If you knew so much, why haven't you done something? Voyles said you boys have been watching and waiting for ten years. That's real good, Tarrance. Do you always move so fast?'

'Do you wanna take that chance, McDeere? Let's say it takes us another five years, okay? After five years we bust the joint and send your ass to jail. At that point it won't make any difference how long it took us, will it? The result will be the same, Mitch.'

'I'm sorry. I thought we were negotiating, not threatening.'

'I've made you an offer.'

'Your offer is too low. You expect me to make a case that will hand you hundreds of indictments against a group of the sleaziest criminals in America, a case that could easily cost me my life. And you offer a pittance. Three million, at least.'

Tarrance did not flinch or frown. He received the counteroffer with a good, straight poker face, and Mitch, the negotiator, knew it was not out of the ballpark.

'That's a lot of money,' Tarrance said, almost to himself. 'I don't think we've ever paid that much.'

'But you can, can't you?'

'I doubt it. I'll have to talk to the Director.'

'The Director! I thought you had complete authority on this case. Are we gonna run back and forth to the Director until we have a deal?'

'What else do you want?'

'I've got a few things in mind, but we won't discuss them until the money gets right.'

The old man with the cane apparently had weak kidneys. He stood again and began the awkward wobble to the rear of the bus. Tarrance again started his book. Mitch flipped through an old copy of *Field & Stream*.

The Greyhound left the interstate in Knoxville two minutes before eight. Tarrance leaned closer and whispered, 'Take the front door out of the terminal. You'll see a young man wearing an orange University of Tennessee sweat suit standing beside a white Bronco. He'll recognize you and call you Jeffrey. Shake hands like lost friends and get in the Bronco. He'll take you to your car.'

'Where is it?' Mitch whispered.

'Behind a dorm on campus.'

'Have they checked it for bugs?'

'I think so. Ask the man in the Bronco. If they were tracking you when you left Memphis, they might be suspicious by now. You should drive to Henderson. It's about fifty miles this side of Nashville. There's a Holiday Inn there. Spend the night and go see your brother tomorrow. We'll be watching also, and if things look fishy, I'll find you Monday morning.'

'When's the next bus ride?'

'Your wife's birthday is Tuesday. Make reservations for eight at Grisanti's, that Italian place on Airways. At precisely nine, go to the cigarette machine in the bar, insert six quarters and buy a pack of anything. In the tray where the cigarettes are released, you will find a cassette tape. Buy yourself one of those small tape players that joggers wear with earphones and listen to the tape in your car, not at home, and sure as hell not at the office. Use the earphones. Let your wife listen to it. I'll be on the cassette, and I'll give you our top dollar. I'll also explain a few things. After you've listened to it a few times, dispose of it.'

'This is rather elaborate, isn't it?'

'Yes, but we don't need to speak to each other for a

278

couple of weeks. They're watching and listening, Mitch. And they're very good. Don't forget that.'

'Don't worry.'

'What was your football jersey number in high school?'

'Fourteen.'

'And college?'

'Fourteen.'

'Okay. Your code number is 1–4–1–4. Thursday night, from a touch tone pay phone, call 757–6000. You'll get a voice that will lead you through a little routine involving your code number. Once you're cleared, you will hear my recorded voice, and I will ask you a series of questions. We'll go from there.'

'Why can't I just practice law?'

The bus pulled into the terminal and stopped. 'I'm going on to Atlanta,' Tarrance said. 'I will not see you for a couple of weeks. If there's an emergency, call one of the two numbers I gave you before.'

Mitch stood in the aisle and looked down at the agent. 'Three million, Tarrance. Not a penny less. If you guys can spend billions fighting organized crime, surely you can find three million for me. And, Tarrance, I have a third option. I can disappear in the middle of the night, vanish into the air. If that happens, you and the Moroltos can fight each other till hell freezes over, and I'll be playing dominoes in the Caribbean.'

'Sure, Mitch. You might play a game or two, but they'd find you within a week. And we wouldn't be there to protect you. So long, buddy.'

Mitch jumped from the bus and darted through the terminal.

TWENTY-THREE

At eight-thirty A.M. on Tuesday, Nina formed neat piles out of the rubble and debris on his desk. She enjoyed this early-morning ritual of straightening the desk and planning his day. The appointment book lay unobstructed on a corner of his desk. She read from it. 'You have a very busy day today, Mr. McDeere.'

Mitch flipped through a file and tried to ignore her. 'Every day is busy.'

'You have a meeting at ten o'clock in Mr. Mahan's office on the Delta Shipping appeal.'

'I can't wait,' Mitch mumbled.

'You have a meeting at eleven-thirty in Mr. Tolleson's office on the Greenbriar dissolution, and his secretary informed me it would last at least two hours.'

'Why two hours?'

'I'm not paid to ask those questions, Mr. McDeere. If I do I might get fired. At three-thirty, Victor Milligan wants to meet with you.'

'About what?'

'Again, Mr. McDeere, I'm not supposed to ask questions. And you're due in Frank Mulholland's office downtown in fifteen minutes.'

'Yes, I know. Where is it?'

'The Cotton Exchange Building. Four or five blocks

up Front at Union. You've walked by it a hundred times.'

'Fine. What else?'

'Shall I bring you something back from lunch?'

'No, I'll grab a sandwich downtown.'

'Wonderful. Do you have everything for Mulholland?'

He pointed to the heavy black briefcase and said nothing. She left, and seconds later Mitch walked down the hall, down the stairs and out the front door. He paused for a second under a streetlight, then turned and walked quickly toward downtown. The black briefcase was in his right hand, the burgundy eel-skin attaché was in his left. The signal.

In front of a green building with boarded windows, he stopped next to a fire hydrant. He waited a second, then crossed Front Street. Another signal.

On the ninth floor of the Cotton Exchange Building, Tammy Greenwood of Greenwood Services backed away from the window and put on her coat. She locked the door behind her and pushed the elevator button. She waited. She was about to encounter a man who could easily get her killed.

Mitch entered the lobby and went straight to the elevators. He noticed no one in particular. A half dozen businessmen were in the process of talking as they came and went. A woman was whispering into a pay phone. A security guard loitered near the Union Avenue entrance. He pushed the elevator button and waited, alone. As the door opened, a young clean cut Merrill Lynch type in a black suit and sparkling wing tips stepped into the elevator. Mitch had hoped for a solitary ride upward.

Mulholland's office was on the seventh floor. Mitch pushed the seven button and ignored the kid in the black suit. As the elevator moved, both men dutifully stared at the blinking numbers above the door. Mitch eased to the rear of the small elevator and set the heavy briefcase on the floor, next to his right foot. The door opened on the fourth floor, and Tammy walked nervously in. The kid glanced at her. Her attire was remarkably conservative. A simple, short knit dress with no plunging necklines. No kinky shoes. Her hair was tinted to a soft shade of red. He glanced again and pushed the CLOSE DOOR button.

Tammy brought aboard a large black briefcase, identical to Mitch's. She ignored his eyes, stood next to him, quietly setting it next to his. On the seventh floor, Mitch grabbed her briefcase and left the elevator. On the eighth floor, the cute young man in the black suit made his departure, and on the ninth floor Tammy picked up the heavy black briefcase full of files from Bendini, Lambert & Locke and took it to her office. She locked and bolted the door, quickly removed her coat and went to the small room where the copier was waiting and running. There were seven files, each at least an inch thick. She laid them neatly on the folding table next to the copier and took the one marked 'Koker-Hanks to East Texas Pipe.' She unhooked the aluminum clasp, removed the contents from the file and carefully placed the stack of documents and letters and notes into the automatic feed. She pushed the PRINT button and watched as the machine made two perfect copies of everything.

Thirty minutes later, the seven files were returned to the briefcase. The new files, fourteen of them, were locked away in a fireproof file cabinet hidden in a small closet, which was also locked. Tammy placed the briefcase near the door, and waited.

Frank Mulholland was a partner in a ten man firm that specialized in banking and securities. His client was an old man who had founded and built a chain of do-it-yourself hardware stores and at one point had been

282

worth eighteen million before his son and a renegade board of directors took control and forced him into retirement. The old man sued. The company counter-sued. Everybody sued everybody, and the suits and countersuits had been hopelessly deadlocked for eight-een months. Now that the lawyers were fat and happy, it was time to talk settlement. Bendini, Lambert & Locke handled the tax advice for the son and the new board, and two months earlier Avery had introduced Mitch to the hostilities. The plan was to offer the old man a five million dollar package of common stock, convertible warrants and a few bonds.

Mulholland was not impressed with the plan. His client was not greedy, he explained repeatedly, and he knew he would never regain control of the company. His company, remember. But five million was not enough. Any jury of any degree of intelligence would be sympathetic to the old man, and a fool could see the lawsuit was worth at least, well . . . at least twenty million!

After an hour of sliding proposals and offers and counteroffers across Mulholland's desk, Mitch had increased the package to eight million and the old man's lawyer said he might consider fifteen. Mitch politely repacked his attaché case and Mulholland politely escorted him to the door. They promised to meet again in a week. They shook hands like best friends.

The elevator stopped on the fifth floor, and Tammy walked casually inside. It was empty, except for Mitch. When the door closed, he said, 'Any problems?'

'Nope. Two copies are locked away.'

'How long did it take?'

'Thirty minutes.'

It stopped on the fourth floor, and she picked up the empty briefcase. 'Noon tomorrow?' she asked.

'Yes,' he replied. The door opened and she disappeared onto the fourth floor. He rode alone to the lobby, which was empty except for the same security guard. Mitchell McDeere, attorney-at-law, hurried from the building with a heavy briefcase in each hand and walked importantly back to his office.

The celebration of Abby's twenty-fifth birthday was rather subdued. Through the dim candlelight in a dark corner of Grisanti's, they whispered and tried to smile at each other. It was difficult. Somewhere at that moment in the restaurant an invisible FBI agent was holding a cassette tape that he would insert into a cigarette machine in the lounge at precisely nine o'clock, and Mitch was supposed to be there seconds later to retrieve it without being seen or caught by the bad guys, whoever they were and whatever they looked like. And the tape would reveal just how much cold hard cash the McDeeres would receive in return for evidence and a subsequent life on the run.

They picked at their food, tried to smile and carry on an extended conversation, but mainly they fidgeted and glanced at their watches. The dinner was brief. By eight forty-five they were finished with the plates. Mitch left in the direction of the rest room, and he stared into the dark lounge as he walked by. The cigarette machine was in the corner, exactly where it should be.

They ordered coffee, and at exactly nine Mitch returned to the lounge, to the machine, where he nervously inserted six quarters and pulled the lever under Marlboro Lights, in memory of Eddie Lomax. He quickly reached into the tray, took the cigarettes and, fishing around in the darkness, found the cassette tape. The pay telephone next to the machine rang, and he jumped. He turned and surveyed the lounge. It was empty except for two men at the bar watching the television behind and above the bartender. Drunk laughter exploded from a dark corner far away.

Abby watched every step and move until he sat across from her. She raised her eyebrows. 'And?'

'I got it. Your basic black Sony cassette tape.' Mitch sipped coffee and smiled innocently while quickly surveying the crowded dining room. No one was watching. No one cared.

He handed the check and the American Express card to the waiter. 'We're in a hurry,' he said rudely. The waiter returned within seconds. Mitch scribbled his name.

The BMW was indeed wired. Heavily wired. Tarrance's gang had very quietly and very thoroughly examined it with magnifying glasses while waiting for the Greyhound four days earlier. Expertly wired, with terribly expensive equipment capable of hearing and recording the slightest sniffle or cough. But the bugs could only listen and record; they could not track. Mitch thought that was awfully nice of them, just to listen but not follow the movements of the BMW.

It left the parking lot of Grisanti's with no conversation between its occupants. Abby carefully opened a portable tape recorder and placed the cassette inside. She handed Mitch the earphones, which he stuck onto his head. She pushed the PLAY button. She watched him as he listened and drove aimlessly toward the interstate.

The voice belonged to Tarrance: 'Hello Mitch. Today is Tuesday, February 25, sometime after nine P.M. Happy Birthday to your lovely wife. This tape will run about ten minutes, and I instruct you to listen to it carefully, once or twice, then dispose of it. I had a face-to-face meeting with Director Voyles last Sunday and briefed him on everything. By the way, I enjoyed the bus ride. Director Voyles is very pleased with the way things are going, but he thinks we've talked long

285

enough. He wants to cut a deal, and rather quickly. He explained to me in no uncertain terms that we have never paid three million dollars and we're not about to pay it to you. He cussed a lot, but to make a long story short, Director Voyles said we could pay a million cash, no more. He said the money would be deposited in a Swiss bank and no one, not even the IRS, would ever know about it. A million dollars, tax free. That's our best deal, and Voyles said you can go to hell if you said no. We're gonna bust that little firm, Mitch, with or without you.'

Mitch smiled grimly and stared at the traffic racing past them on the I-240 loop. Abby watched for a sign, a signal, a grunt or groan, anything to indicate good news or bad. She said nothing.

The voice continued: 'We'll take care of you, Mitch. You'll have access to FBI protection anytime you think you need it. We'll check on you periodically, if you want. And if you want to move on to another city after a few years, we'll take care of it. You can move every five years if you want, and we'll pick up the tab and find jobs for you. Good jobs with the VA or Social Security or Postal Service. Voyles said we'd even find you a high-paying job with a private government contractor. You name it, Mitch, and it's yours. Of course, we'll provide new identities for you and your wife, and you can change every year if you desire. No problem. Or if you got a better idea, we'll listen. You wanna live in Europe or Australia, just say so. You'll get special treatment. I know we're promising a lot, Mitch, but we're dead serious and we'll put it in writing. We'll pay a million in cash, tax free, and set you up wherever you choose. So that's the deal. And in return, you must hand us the firm, and the Moroltos. We'll talk about that later. For now, your time is up. Voyles is breathing down my neck, and things must happen quickly. Call me at that number

Thursday night at nine from the pay phone next to the men's rest room in Houston's on Poplar. So long, Mitch.'

He sliced a finger across his throat, and Abby pushed the STOP button, then REWIND. He handed her the earphones, and she began to listen intently.

It was an innocent walk in the park, two lovebirds holding hands and strolling casually through the cool, clear moonlight. They stopped by a cannon and gazed at the majestic river inching ever so slowly toward New Orleans. The same cannon where the late Eddie Lomax once stood in a sleet storm and delivered one of his last investigative reports.

Abby held the cassette in her hand and watched the river below. She had listened to it twice and refused to leave it in the car, where who knows who might snatch it. After weeks of practicing silence, and then speaking only outdoors, words were becoming difficult.

'You know, Abby,' Mitch finally said as he tapped the wooden wheel of the cannon, 'I've always wanted to work with the post office. I had an uncle once who was a rural mail carrier. That would be neat.'

It was a gamble, this attempt at humor. But it worked. She hesitated for three seconds, then laughed slightly, and he could tell she indeed thought it was funny. 'Yeah, and I could mop floors in a VA hospital.'

'You wouldn't have to mop floors. You could change bedpans, something meaningful, something inconspicuous. We'd live in a neat little white frame house on Maple Street in Omaha. I'd be Harvey and you'd be Thelma, and we'd need a short, unassuming last name.'

'Poe,' Abby added.

'That's great. Harvey and Thelma Poe. The Poe family. We'd have a million dollars in the bank but

287

couldn't spend a dime because everyone on Maple Street would know it and then we'd become different, which is the last thing we want.'

'I'd get a nose job.'

'But your nose is perfect.'

'Abby's nose is perfect, but what about Thelma's? We'd have to get it fixed, don't you think?'

'Yeah, I suppose.' He was immediately tired of the humor and became quiet. Abby stepped in front of him, and he draped his arms over her shoulders. They watched a tug quietly push a hundred barges under the bridge. An occasional cloud dimmed the moonlight, and the cool winds from the west rose intermittently, then dissipated.

'Do you believe Tarrance?' Abby asked.

'In what way?'

'Let's suppose you do nothing. Do you believe one day they'll eventually infiltrate the firm?'

'I'm afraid not to believe.'

'So we take the money and run?'

'It's easier for me to take the money and run, Abby. I have nothing to leave behind. For you, it's different. You'll never see your family again.'

'Where would we go?'

'I do not know. But I wouldn't want to stay in this country. The feds cannot be trusted entirely. I'll feel safer in another country, but I won't tell Tarrance.'

'What's the next step?'

'We cut a deal, then quickly go about the job of gathering enough information to sink the ship. I have no idea what they want, but I can find it for them. When Tarrance has enough, we disappear. We take our money, get our nose jobs and disappear.'

'How much money?'

'More than a million. They're playing games with the money. It's all negotiable.'

'How much will we get?'

'Two million cash, tax free. Not a dime less.'

'Will they pay it?'

'Yes, but that's not the question. The question is, will we take it and run?'

She was cold, and he draped his coat over her shoulders. He held her tightly. 'It's a rotten deal, Mitch,' she said, 'but at least we'll be together.'

'The name's Harvey, not Mitch.'

'Do you think we'll be safe, Harvey?'

'We're not safe here.'

'I don't like it here. I'm lonely and scared.'

'I'm tired of being a lawyer.'

'Let's take the money and haul ass.'

'You've got a deal, Thelma.'

She handed the cassette tape to him. He glanced at it, then threw it far below, beyond Riverside Drive, in the direction of the river. They held hands and strolled quickly through the park toward the BMW parked on Front Street.

TWENTY-FOUR

For only the second time in his career, Mitch was allowed to visit the palatial dining room on the fifth floor. Avery's invitation came with the explanation that the partners were all quite impressed with the seventy-one hours per week he averaged in billing for the month of February, and thus they wished to offer the small reward of lunch. It was an invitation no associate could turn down, regardless of schedules and meetings and clients and deadlines and all the other terribly important and urgently critical aspects of careers at Bendini, Lambert & Locke. Never in history had an associate said no to an invitation to the dining room. Each received two invitations per year. Records were kept.

Mitch had two days to prepare for it. His first impulse was to decline, and when Avery first mentioned it a dozen lame excuses crossed his mind. Eating and smiling and chatting and fraternizing with criminals, regardless of how rich and polished, was less attractive than sharing a bowl of soup with a homeless down at the bus station. But to say no would be a grievous breach of tradition. And as things were going, his movements were already suspicious enough.

So he sat with his back to the window and forced smiles and small talk in the direction of Avery and Royce McKnight and, of course, Oliver Lambert. He knew he would eat at the same table with those three. Knew it for two days. He knew they would watch him carefully but nonchalantly, trying to detect any loss of enthusiasm, or cynicism, or hopelessness. Anything, really. He knew they would hang on his every word, regardless of what he said. He knew they would lavish praise and promises upon his weary shoulders.

Oliver Lambert had never been more charming. Seventy-one hours a week for a February for an associate was a firm record, he said as Roosevelt served prime ribs. All the partners were amazed, and delighted, he explained softly while glancing around the room. Mitch forced a smile and sliced his serving. The other partners, amazed or indifferent, were talking idly and concentrating on the food. Mitch counted eighteen active partners and seven retirees, those with the khakis and sweaters and relaxed looks about them.

'You have remarkable stamina, Mitch,' Royce McKnight said with a mouthful. He nodded politely. Yes, yes, I practice my stamina all the time, he thought to himself. As much as possible, he kept his mind off Joe Hodge and Marty Kozinski and the other three dead lawyers memorialized on the wall downstairs. But it was impossible to keep his mind off the pictures of the girl in the sand, and he wondered if they all knew. Had they all seen the pictures? Passed them around during one of these little lunches when it was just the partners and no guests? DeVasher had promised to keep them to himself, but what's a promise from a thug? Of course they'd seen them. Voyles said every partner and most of the associates were in on the conspiracy.

For a man with no appetite, he managed the food nicely. He even buttered and devoured an extra roll, just to appear normal. Nothing wrong with his appetite.

'So you and Abby are going to the Caymans next week?' Oliver Lambert said.

'Yes. It's her spring break, and we booked one of the condos two months ago. Looking forward to it.'

'It's a terrible time to go,' Avery said in disgust. 'We're a month behind right now.'

'We're always a month behind, Avery. So what's another week? I guess you want me to take my files with me?'

'Not a bad idea. I always do.'

'Don't do it, Mitch,' Oliver Lambert said in mock protest. 'This place will be standing when you return. You and Abby deserve a week to yourselves.'

'You'll love it down there,' Royce McKnight said, as if Mitch had never been and that thing on the beach didn't happen and no one knew anything about any photographs.

'When do you leave?' Lambert asked.

'Sunday morning. Early.'

'Are you taking the Lear?'

'No. Delta nonstop.'

Lambert and McKnight exchanged quick looks that Mitch was not supposed to see. There were other looks from the other tables, occasional quick glances filled with curiosity that Mitch had caught since he entered the room. He was there to be noticed.

'Do you scuba-dive?' asked Lambert, still thinking about the Lear versus the Delta nonstop.

'No, but we plan to do some snorkeling.'

'There's a guy on Rum Point, on the north end, name of Adrian Bench, who's got a great dive lodge and will certify you in one week. It's a hard week, lot of instruction, but it's worth it.'

In other words, stay away from Abanks, Mitch thought. 'What's the name of the lodge?' he asked.

'Rum Point Divers. Great place.'

Mitch frowned intelligently as if making a mental

note of this helpful advice. Suddenly, Oliver Lambert was hit with sadness. 'Be careful, Mitch. It brings back memories of Marty and Joe.'

Avery and McKnight stared at their plates in a split-second memorial to the dead boys. Mitch swallowed hard and almost sneered at Oliver Lambert. But he kept a straight face, even managed to look sad with the rest of them. Marty and Joe and their young widows and fatherless children. Marty and Joe, two young wealthy lawyers expertly killed and removed before they could talk. Marty and Joe, two promising sharks eaten by their own. Voyles had told Mitch to think of Marty and Joe whenever he saw Oliver Lambert.

And now, for a mere million bucks, he was expected to do what Marty and Joe were about to do, without getting caught. Perhaps a year from now the next new associate would be sitting here and watching the saddened partners talk about young Mitch McDeere and his remarkable stamina and what a helluva lawyer he would have been but for the accident. How many would they kill?

He wanted two million. Plus a couple of other items.

After an hour of important talk and good food, the lunch began breaking up as partners excused themselves, spoke to Mitch and left the room. They were proud of him, they said. He was their brightest star of the future. The future of Bendini, Lambert & Locke. He smiled and thanked them.

About the time Roosevelt served the banana cream pie and coffee, Tammy Greenwood Hemphill of Greenwood Services parked her dirty brown Rabbit behind the shiny Peugeot in the school parking lot. She left the motor running. She took four steps, stuck a key into the trunk of the Peugeot and removed the heavy black briefcase. She slammed the trunk and sped away in the Rabbit.

From a small window in the teachers' lounge, Abby sipped coffee and stared through the trees, across the playground and into the parking lot in the distance. She could barely see her car. She smiled and checked her watch. Twelve-thirty, as planned.

Tammy weaved her way carefully through the noon traffic in the direction of downtown. Driving was tedious when watching the rearview mirror. As usual, she saw nothing. She parked in her designated place across the street from the Cotton Exchange Building.

There were nine files in this load. She arranged them neatly on the folding table and began making copies. Sigalas Partners, Lettie Plunk Trust, Handy-Man Hardware and two files bound loosely with a thick rubber band and marked AVERY's FILES. She ran two copies of every sheet of paper in the files and meticulously put them back together. In a ledger book, she entered the date, time and name of each file. There were now twenty-nine entries. He said there would eventually be about forty. She placed one copy of each file into the locked and hidden cabinet in the closet, then repacked the briefcase with the original files and one copy of each.

Pursuant to his instructions, a week earlier she had rented in her name an eight-by-eight storage room at the Summer Avenue Mini Storage. It was fourteen miles from downtown, and thirty minutes later she arrived and unlocked number 38C. In a small cardboard box she placed the other copies of the nine files and scribbled the date on the end of the flap. She placed it next to three other boxes on the floor.

At exactly 3 P.M., she wheeled into the parking lot, stopped behind the Peugeot, opened its trunk and left the briefcase where she'd found it.

Seconds later, Mitch stepped from the front door of

the Bendini Building and stretched his arms. He breathed deeply and gazed up and down Front Street. A lovely spring day. Five blocks to the north and nine floors up, in the window, he noticed the blinds had been pulled all the way down. The signal. Good. Everything's fine. He smiled to himself, and returned to his office.

At three o'clock in the morning, Mitch eased out of bed and quietly pulled on a pair of faded jeans, flannel law school shirt, white insulated socks and a pair of old work boots. He wanted to look like a truck driver. Without a word, he kissed Abby, who was awake, and left the house. East Meadowbrook was deserted, as were all the streets between home and the interstate. Surely they would not follow him at this hour.

He drove Interstate 55 south for twenty-five miles to Senatobia, Mississippi. A busy, all-night truck stop called the 4–55 shone brightly a hundred yards from the four-lane. He darted through the trucks to the rear where a hundred semis were parked for the night. He stopped next to the Truck Wash bay and waited. A dozen eighteen-wheelers inched and weaved around the pumps.

A black guy wearing a Falcons football cap stepped from around the corner and stared at the BMW. Mitch recognized him as the agent in the bus terminal in Knoxville. He killed the engine and stepped from the car.

'McDeere?' the agent asked.

'Of course. Who else? Where's Tarrance?'

'Inside in a booth by the window. He's waiting.'

Mitch opened the door and handed the keys to the agent. 'Where are you taking it?'

'Down the road a little piece. We'll take care of it. You were clean coming out of Memphis. Relax.'

He climbed into the car, eased between two diesel

pumps and headed for the interstate. Mitch watched his little BMW disappear as he entered the truck-stop café. It was three forty-five.

The noisy room was filled with heavy middle-aged men drinking coffee and eating store-bought pies. They picked their teeth with colored toothpicks and talked of bass fishing and politics back at the terminal. Many spoke with loud Northern twangs. Merle Haggard wailed from the jukebox.

The lawyer moved awkwardly toward the rear until he saw in an unlit corner a familiar face hidden beneath aviator's sunshades and the same Michigan State baseball cap. Then the face smiled. Tarrance was holding a menu and watching the front door. Mitch slid into the booth.

'Hello, good buddy,' Tarrance said. 'How's the truckin'?'

'Wonderful. I think I prefer the bus, though.'

'Next time we'll try a train or something. Just for variety. Laney get your car?'

'Laney?'

'The black dude. He's an agent, you know.'

'We haven't been properly introduced. Yes, he's got my car. Where is he taking it?'

'Down the interstate. He'll be back in an hour or so. We'll try to have you on the road by five so you can be at the office by six. We'd hate to mess up your day.'

'It's already shot to hell.'

A partially crippled waitress named Dot ambled by and demanded to know what they wanted. Just coffee. A surge of Roadway drivers swarmed in the front door and filled up the café. Merle could barely be heard.

'So how are the boys at the office?' Tarrance asked cheerfully.

'Everything's fine. The meters are ticking as we speak and everyone's getting richer. Thanks for asking.'

'No problem.'

'How's my old pal Voyles doing?' Mitch asked.

'He's quite anxious, really. He called me twice today and repeated for the tenth time his desire to have an answer from you. Said you'd had plenty of time and all that. I told him to relax. Told him about our little roadside rendezvous tonight and he got real excited. I'm supposed to call him in four hours, to be exact.'

'Tell him a million bucks won't do it, Tarrance. You boys like to brag about spending billions fighting organized crime, so I say throw a little my way. What's a couple of million cash to the federal government?'

'So it's a couple of million now?'

'Damned right it's a couple of million. And not a dime less. I want a million now and a million later. I'm in the process of copying all of my files, and I should be finished in a few days. Legitimate files, I think. If I gave them to anyone I'd be permanently disbarred. So when I give them to you, I want the first million. Let's just call it good faith money.'

'How do you want it paid?'

'Deposited in an account in a bank in Zurich. But we'll discuss the details later.'

Dot slid two saucers onto the table and dropped two mismatched cups on them. She poured from a height of three feet and splashed coffee in all directions. 'Free refills,' she grunted, and left.

'And the second million?' Tarrance asked, ignoring the coffee.

'When you and I and Voyles decide I've supplied you with enough documents to get the indictments, then I get half. After I testify for the last time, I get the other half. That's incredibly fair, Tarrance.'

'It is. You've got a deal.'

Mitch breathed deeply, and felt weak. A deal. A contract. An agreement. One that could never be put in writing, but one that was terribly enforceable nonetheless. He sipped the coffee but didn't taste it. They had agreed on the money. He was on a roll. Keep pushing.

'And there's one other thing, Tarrance.'

The head lowered and turned slightly to the right. 'Yeah?'

Mitch leaned closer, resting on his forearms. 'It won't cost you a dime, and you boys can pull it off with no sweat. Okay?'

'I'm listening.'

'My brother Ray is at Brushy Mountain. Seven years until parole. I want him out.'

'That's ridiculous, Mitch. We can do a lot of things, but we damned sure can't parole state prisoners. Federal maybe, but not state. No way.'

'Listen to me, Tarrance, and listen good. If I hit the road with the Mafia on my tail, my brother goes with me. Sort of like a package deal. And I know if Director Voyles wants him out of prison, he'll get out of prison. I know that. Now, you boys just figure out a way to make it happen.'

'But we have no authority to interfere with state prisoners.'

Mitch smiled and returned to his coffee. 'James Earl Ray escaped from Brushy Mountain. And he had no help from the outside.'

'Oh, that's great. We attack the prison like commandos and rescue your brother. Beautiful.'

'Don't play dumb with me, Tarrance. It's not negotiable.'

'All right, all right. I'll see what I can do. Anything else? Any more surprises?'

'No, just questions about where we go and what we do. Where do we hide initially? Where do we hide during the trials? Where do we live for the rest of our lives? Just minor questions like that.'

'We can discuss it later.'

'What did Hodge and Kozinski tell you?'

'Not enough. We've got a notebook, a rather thick notebook, in which we've accumulated and indexed everything we know about the Moroltos and the firm. Most of it's Morolto crap, their organization, key people, illegal activities and so on. You need to read it all before we start to work.'

'Which, of course, will be after I've received the first million.'

'Of course. When can we see your files?'

'In about a week. I've managed to copy four files that belong to someone else. I may get my hands on a few more of those.'

'Who's doing the copying?'

'None of your business.'

Tarrance thought for a second and let it pass. 'How many files?'

'Between forty and fifty. I have to sneak them out a few at a time. Some I've worked on for eight months, others only a week or so. As far as I can tell, they're all legitimate clients.'

'How many of these clients have you personally met?'

'Two or three.'

'Don't bet they're all legitimate. Hodge told us about some dummy files, or sweat files as they are known to the partners, that have been around for years and every new associate cuts his teeth on them; heavy files that require hundreds of hours and make the rookies feel like real lawyers.'

'Sweat files?'

'That's what Hodge said. It's any easy game, Mitch. They lure you with the money. They smother you with work that looks legitimate and for the most part probably is legitimate. Then, after a few years, you've unwittingly become a part of the conspiracy. You're nailed, and there's no getting out. Even you, Mitch. You started work in July, eight months ago, and you've probably already touched a few of the dirty files. You didn't know it, had no reason to suspect it. But they've already set you up.'

'Two million, Tarrance. Two million and my brother.'

Tarrance sipped the lukewarm coffee and ordered a piece of coconut pie as Dot came within earshot. He glanced at his watch and surveyed the crowd of truckers, all smoking cigarettes and drinking coffee and talking relentlessly.

He adjusted the sunglasses. 'So what do I tell Mr. Voyles?'

'Tell him we ain't got a deal until he agrees to get Ray out of prison. No deal, Tarrance.'

'We can probably work something out.'

'I'm confident you can.'

'When do you leave for the Caymans?'

'Early Sunday. Why?'

'Just curious, that's all.'

'Well, I'd like to know how many different groups will be following me down there. Is that asking too much? I'm sure we'll attract a crowd, and frankly, we had hoped for a little privacy.'

'Firm condo?'

'Of course.'

'Forget privacy. It's probably got more wires than a switchboard. Maybe even some cameras.'

'That's comforting. We might stay a couple of nights at Abanks Dive Lodge. If you boys are in the neighborhood, stop by for a drink.'

'Very funny. If we're there, it'll be for a reason. And you won't know it.'

Tarrance ate the pie in three bites. He left two bucks on the table and they walked to the dark rear of the truck stop. The dirty asphalt pavement vibrated under the steady hum of an acre of diesel engines. They waited in the dark.

'I'll talk to Voyles in a few hours,' Tarrance said. 'Why don't you and your wife take a leisurely Saturday-afternoon drive tomorrow?'

'Anyplace in particular?'

'Yeah. There's a town called Holly Springs thirty miles east of here. Old place, full of antebellum homes and Confederate history. Women love to drive around and look at the old mansions. Make your appearance around four o'clock and we'll find you. Our buddy Laney will be driving a bright red Chevy Blazer with Tennessee plates. Follow him. We'll find a place and talk.'

'Is it safe?'

'Trust us. If we see or smell something, we'll break off. Drive around town for an hour, and if you don't see Laney, grab a sandwich and go back home. You'll know they were too close. We won't take chances.'

'Thanks. A great bunch of guys.'

Laney eased around the corner in the BMW and jumped out. 'Everything's clear. No trace of anyone.'

'Good,' Tarrance said. 'See you tomorrow, Mitch. Happy truckin'.' They shook hands.

'It's not negotiable, Tarrance,' Mitch said again.

'You can call me Wayne. See you tomorrow.'

TWENTY-FIVE

The black thunderheads and driving rain had long since cleared the tourists from Seven Mile Beach when the McDeeres, soaked and tired, arrived at the luxury condominium duplex. Mitch backed the rented Mitsubishi jeep over the curb, across the small lawn and up to the front door. Unit B. His first visit had been to Unit A. They appeared to be identical, except for the paint and trim. The key fit, and they grabbed and threw luggage as the clouds burst and the rain grew thicker.

Once inside and dry, they unpacked in the master bedroom upstairs with a long balcony facing the wet beach. Cautious with their words, they inspected the town house and checked out each room and closet. The refrigerator was empty, but the bar was very well stocked. Mitch mixed two drinks, rum and Coke, in honor of the islands. They sat on the balcony with their feet in the rain and watched the ocean churn and spill toward the shore. Rumheads was quiet and barely visible in the distance. Two natives sat at the bar, drinking and watching the sea.

'That's Rumheads over there,' Mitch said, pointing with his drink.

'Rumheads?'

'I told you about it. It's a hot spot where tourists drink and the locals play dominoes.'

'I see.' Abby was unimpressed. She yawned and sank lower into the plastic chair. She closed her eyes.

'Oh, this is great, Abby. Our first trip out of the country, our first real honeymoon, and you're asleep ten minutes after we hit land.'

'I'm tired, Mitch. I packed all night while you were sleeping.'

'You packed eight suitcases – six for you and two for me. You packed every garment we own. No wonder you were awake all night.'

'I don't want to run out of clothes.'

'Run out? How many bikinis did you pack? Ten? Twelve?'

'Six.'

'Great. One a day. Why don't you put one on?'

'What?'

'You heard me. Go put on that little blue one with high legs and a couple of strings around front, the one that weighs half a gram and cost sixty bucks and your buns hang out when you walk. I wanna see it.'

'Mitch, it's raining. You've brought me here to this island during the monsoon season. Look at those clouds. Dark and thick and extremely stationary. I won't need any bikinis this week.'

Mitch smiled and began rubbing her legs. 'I rather like the rain. In fact, I hope it rains all week. It'll keep us inside, in the bed, sipping rum and trying to hurt each other.'

'I'm shocked. You mean you actually want sex? We've already done it once this month.'

'Twice.'

'I thought you wanted to snorkel and scuba dive all week.'

'Nope. There's probably a shark out there waiting for me.'

The winds blew harder and the balcony was being drenched.

'Let's go take off our clothes.' Mitch said.

After an hour, the storm began to move. The rain slackened, then turned to a soft drizzle, then it was gone. The sky lightened as the dark, low clouds left the tiny island and headed northeast, toward Cuba. Shortly before its scheduled departure over the horizon, the sun suddenly emerged for a brief encore. It emptied the beach cottages and town homes and condos and hotel rooms as the tourists strolled through the sand toward the water. Rumheads was suddenly packed with dart throwers and thirsty beachcombers. The domino game picked up where it had left off. The reggae band next door at the Palms tuned up.

Mitch and Abby walked aimlessly along the edge of the water in the general direction of Georgetown, away from the spot where the girl had been. He thought of her occasionally, and of the photographs. He had decided she was a pro and had been paid by DeVasher to seduce and conquer him in front of the hidden cameras. He did not expect to see her this time.

As if on cue, the music stopped, the beach strollers froze and watched, the noise at Rumheads quietened as all eyes turned to watch the sun meet the water. Gray and white clouds, the trailing remnants of the storm, lay low on the horizon and sank with the sun. Slowly they turned shades of orange and yellow and red, pale shades at first, then, suddenly, brilliant tones. For a few brief moments, the sky was a canvas and the sun splashed its awesome array of colors with bold strokes. Then the bright orange ball touched the water and within seconds was gone. The clouds became black and dissipated. A Cayman sunset.

With great fear and caution, Abby slowly maneuvered

the jeep through the early-morning traffic in the shopping district. She was from Kentucky. She had never driven on the left side of the road for any substantial period of time. Mitch gave directions and watched the rearview mirror. The narrow streets and sidewalks were already crowded with tourists window-shopping for duty-free china, crystal, perfume, cameras and jewelry.

Mitch pointed to a hidden side street, and the jeep darted between two groups of tourists. He kissed her on the cheek. 'I'll meet you right here at five.'

'Be careful,' she said. 'I'll go to the bank, then stay on the beach near the condo.'

He slammed the door and disappeared between two small shops. The alley led to a wider street that led to Hogsty Bay. He ducked into a crowded T-shirt store filled with racks and rows of tourist shirts and straw hats and sunglasses. He selected a gaudy green and orange flowered shirt and a Panama hat. Two minutes later he darted from the store into the back seat of a passing taxi. 'Airport,' he said. 'And make it quick. Watch your tail. Someone may be following.'

The driver made no response, just eased past the bank buildings and out of town. Ten minutes later he stopped in front of the terminal.

'Anybody follow us?' Mitch asked, pulling money from his pocket.

'No, mon. Four dollars and ten cents.'

Mitch threw a five over the seat and walked quickly into the terminal. The Cayman Airways flight to Cayman Brac would leave at nine. At a gift shop Mitch bought a cup of coffee and hid between two rows of shelves filled with souvenirs. He watched the waiting area and saw no one. Of course, he had no idea what they looked like, but he saw no one sniffing around and searching for lost people. Perhaps they

305

were following the jeep or combing the shopping district looking for him. Perhaps.

For seventy-five Cayman dollars he had reserved the last seat on the ten-passenger, three-engine Trislander. Abby had made the reservation by pay phone the night they arrived. At the last possible second, he jogged from the terminal onto the tarmac and climbed on board. The pilot slammed and locked the doors, and they taxied down the runway. No other planes were visible. A small hangar sat to the right.

The ten tourists admired the brilliant blue sea and said little during the twenty minute flight. As they approached Cayman Brac, the pilot became the tour guide and made a wide circle around the small island. He paid special attention to the tall bluffs that fell into the sea on the east end. Without the bluffs, he said, the island would be as flat as Grand Cayman. He landed the plane softly on a narrow asphalt strip.

Next to the small white frame building with the word AIRPORT painted on all sides, a clean cut Caucasian waited and watched the passengers quickly disembark. He was Rick Acklin, special agent, and sweat dripped from his nose and glued his shirt to his back. He stepped slightly forward. 'Mitch,' he said almost to himself.

Mitch hesitated and then walked over.

'Car's out front,' Acklin said.

'Where's Tarrance?' Mitch looked around.

'He's waiting.'

'Does the car have air conditioning?'

'Afraid not. Sorry.'

The car was minus air, power anything and signal lights. It was a 1974 LTD, and Acklin explained as they followed the dusty road that there simply was not much of a selection of rental cars on Cayman Brac. And the U.S. government had rented the car because he and Tarrance had been unable to find a taxi. They were lucky to find a room, on such late notice.

The small neat homes were closer together, and sea appeared. They parked in the sand parking lot of an establishment called Brac Divers. An aging pier jutted into the water and anchored a hundred boats of all sizes. To the west along the beach a dozen thatched-roof cabins sat two feet above the sand and housed divers who came from around the world. Next to the pier was an open-air bar, nameless, but complete with a domino game and a dartboard. Oak-and-brass fans hung from the ceiling through the rafters and rotated slowly and silently, cooling the domino players and the bartender.

Wayne Tarrance sat at a table by himself drinking a Coke and watching a dive crew load a thousand identical yellow tanks from the pier onto a boat. Even for a tourist, his dress was hysterical. Dark sunglasses with yellow frames, brown straw sandals, obviously brand-new, with black socks, a tight Hawaiian luau shirt with twenty loud colors and a pair of gold gym shorts that were very old and very short and covered little of the shiny, sickly white legs under the table. He waved his Coke at the two empty chairs.

'Nice shirt, Tarrance,' Mitch said in undisguised amusement.

'Thanks. You gotta real winner yourself.'

'Nice tan too.'

'Yeah, yeah. Gotta look the part, you know.'

The waiter hovered nearby and waited for them to speak. Acklin ordered a Coke. Mitch said he wanted a Coke with a splash of rum in it. All three became engrossed with the dive boat and the divers loading their bulky gear.

'What happened in Holly Springs?' Mitch finally asked.

'Sorry, we couldn't help it. They followed you out of

307

Memphis and had two cars waiting in Holly Springs. We couldn't get near you.'

'Did you and your wife discuss the trip before you left?' asked Acklin.

'I think so. We probably mentioned it around the house a couple of times.'

Acklin seemed satisfied. 'They were certainly ready for you. A green Skylark followed you for about twenty miles, then got lost. We called it off then.'

Tarrance sipped his Coke and said, 'Late Saturday night the Lear left Memphis and flew nonstop to Grand Cayman. We think two or three of the goons were on board. The plane left early Sunday morning and returned to Memphis.'

'So they're here and they're following us?'

'Of course. They probably had one or two people on the plane with you and Abby. Might have been men, women or both. Could've been a black dude or an Oriental woman. Who knows? Remember, Mitch, they have plenty of money. There are two that we recognize. One was in Washington when you were there. A blond fellow, about forty, six-one, maybe six-two, with real short hair, almost a crew cut, and real strong, Nordic-looking features. He moves quickly. We saw him yesterday driving a red Escort he got from Coconut Car Rentals on the island.'

'I think I've seen him,' Mitch said.

'Where?' asked Acklin.

'In a bar in the Memphis airport the night I returned from Washington. I caught him watching me, and I thought at the time that I had seen him in Washington.'

'That's him. He's here.'

'Who's the other one?'

'Tony Verkler, or Two-Ton Tony as we call him. He's a con with an impressive record of convictions, most of it in Chicago. He's worked for Morolto for years. Weighs about three hundred pounds and does a great job of watching people because no one would ever suspect him.'

'He was at Rumheads last night,' Acklin added.

'Last night? We were there last night.'

With great ceremony, the dive boat pushed from the pier and headed for open water. Beyond the pier, fishermen in their small catboats pulled their nets and sailors navigated their brightly colored catamarans away from land. After a gentle and dreamy start, the island was awake now. Half the boats tied to the pier had left or were in the process of leaving.

'So when did you boys get in town?' Mitch asked, sipping his drink, which was more rum than Coke.

'Sunday night,' Tarrance answered while watching the dive boat slowly disappear.

'Just out of curiosity, how many men do you have on the islands?'

'Four men, two women,' said Tarrance. Acklin became mute and deferred all conversation to his supervisor.

'And why exactly are you here?' Mitch asked.

'Oh, several reasons. Number one, we wanted to talk to you and nail down our little deal. Director Voyles is terribly anxious about reaching an agreement you can live with. Number two, we want to watch them to determine how many goons are here. We'll spend the week trying to identify these people. The island is small, and it's a good place to observe.'

'And number three, you wanted to work on your suntan?'

Acklin managed a slight giggle. Tarrance smiled and then frowned. 'No, not exactly. We're here for your protection.'

'My protection?'

'Yes. The last time I sat at this very table I was talking to Joe Hodge and Marty Kozinski. About nine

309

months ago. The day before they were killed, to be exact.'

'And you think I'm about to be killed?'

'No. Not yet.'

Mitch motioned at the bartender for another drink. The domino game grew heated, and he watched the natives argue and drink beer.

'Look, boys, as we speak the goons, as you call them, are probably following my wife all over Grand Cayman. I'll be sort of nervous until I get back. Now, what about the deal?'

Tarrance left the sea and the dive boat and stared at Mitch. 'Two million's fine, and –'

'Of course it's fine, Tarrance. We agreed on it, did we not?'

'Relax, Mitch. We'll pay a million when you turn over all of your files. At that point, there's no turning back, as they say. You're in up to your neck.'

'Tarrance, I understand that. It was my suggestion, remember.'

'But that's the easy part. We really don't want your files, because they're clean files. Good files. Legitimate files. We want the bad files, Mitch, the ones with indictments written all over them. And these files will be much harder to come by. But when you do so, we'll pay another half million. And the rest after the last trial.'

'And my brother?'

'We'll try.'

'Not good enough, Tarrance. I want a commitment.'

'We can't promise to deliver your brother. Hell, he's got at least seven more years.'

'But he's my brother, Tarrance. I don't care if he's a serial murderer sitting on death row waiting for his last meal. He's my brother, and if you want me, you have to release him.'

'I said we'll try, but we can't commit. There's no legal, formal, legitimate way to get him out, so we must try other means. What if he gets shot during the escape?'

'Just get him out, Tarrance.'

'We'll try.'

'You'll throw the power and resources of the FBI in assisting my brother in escaping from prison, right, Tarrance?'

'You have my word.'

Mitch sat back in his chair and took a long sip of his drink. Now the deal was final. He breathed easier and smiled in the direction of the magnificent Caribbean.

'So when do we get your files?' Tarrance asked.

'Thought you didn't want them. They're too clean, remember?'

'We want the files, Mitch, because when we get the files, then we've got you. You've proved yourself when you hand us your files, your license to practice law, so to speak.'

'Ten to fifteen days.'

'How many files?'

'Between forty and fifty. The small ones are an inch thick. The big ones wouldn't fit on this table. I can't use the copiers around the office, so we've had to make other arrangements.'

'Perhaps we could assist in the copying,' said Acklin.

'Perhaps not. Perhaps if I need your help, perhaps I'll ask for it.'

'How do you propose to get them to us?' Tarrance asked. Acklin withdrew again.

'Very simple, Wayne. When I've copied them all, and once I get the million where I want it, then I'll hand you a key to a certain little room in the Memphis area, and you can get them in your pickup.'

'I told you we'd deposit the money in a Swiss bank account,' Tarrance said.

'And I don't want it in a Swiss bank account, okay? I'll dictate the terms of the transfer, and it'll be done exactly as I say. It's my neck on the line from now on, boys, so I call the shots. Most of them, anyway.'

Tarrance smiled and grunted and stared at the pier. 'So you don't trust the Swiss?'

'Let's just say I have another bank in mind. I work for money launderers, remember, Wayne, so I've become an expert on hiding money in offshore accounts.'

'We'll see.'

'When do I see this notebook on the Moroltos?'

'After we get your files and pay our first installment. We'll brief you as much as we can, but for the most part you're on your own. You and I will need to meet a lot, and of course that'll be rather dangerous. May have to take a few bus rides.'

'Okay, but the next time I get the aisle seat.'

'Sure, sure. Anybody worth two million can surely pick his seat on a Greyhound.'

'I'll never live to enjoy it, Wayne. You know I won't.'

Three miles out of Georgetown, on the narrow and winding road to Bodden Town, Mitch saw him. The man was squatting behind an old Volkswagen Beetle with the hood up as if engine trouble had stopped him. The man was dressed like a native, without tourist clothes. He could easily pass for one of the Brits who worked for the government or the banks. He was well tanned. The man held a wrench of some sort and appeared to study it and watch the Mitsubishi jeep as it roared by on the left-hand side of the road. The man was the Nordic.

He was supposed to have gone unnoticed.

Mitch instinctively slowed to thirty miles per hour, to wait for him. Abby turned and watched the road. The narrow highway to Bodden Town clung to the shoreline for five miles, then forked, and the ocean disappeared. Within minutes the Nordic's green VW came racing around a slight bend. The McDeere jeep was much closer than the Nordic anticipated. Being seen, he abruptly slowed, then turned into the first white rock driveway on the ocean side.

Mitch gunned the jeep and sped to Bodden Town. West of the small settlement he turned south and less than a mile later found the ocean.

It was 10 A.M. and the parking lot of Abanks Dive Lodge was half full. The two morning dive boats had left thirty minutes earlier. The McDeeres walked quickly to the bar, where Henry was already shuffling beer and cigarettes to the domino players.

Barry Abanks leaned on a post supporting the thatched roof of the bar and watched as his two dive boats disappeared around the corner of the island. Each would make two dives, at places like Bonnie's Arch, Devil's Grotto, Eden Rock and Roger's Wreck Point, places he had dived and toured and guided through a thousand times. Some of the places he had discovered himself.

The McDeeres approached, and Mitch quietly introduced his wife to Mr. Abanks, who was not polite but not rude. They started for the small pier, where a deckhand was preparing a thirty-foot fishing boat. Abanks unloaded an indecipherable string of commands in the general direction of the young deckhand, who was either deaf or unafraid of his boss.

Mitch stood next to Abanks, the captain now, and pointed to the bar fifty yards away down the pier. 'Do you know all those people at the bar?' he asked.

Abanks frowned at Mitch.

'They tried to follow me here. Just curious,' Mitch said.

'The usual gang,' Abanks said. 'No strangers.'

'Have you noticed any strangers around this morning?'

'Look, this place attracts strange people. I keep no ledger of the strange ones and the normal ones.'

'Have you seen a fat American, red hair, at least three hundred pounds?'

Abanks shook his head. The deckhand eased the boat backward, away from the pier, then toward the horizon. Abby sat on a small padded bench and watched the dive lodge disappear. In a vinyl bag between her feet were two new sets of snorkeling fins and dive masks. It was ostensibly a snorkeling trip with maybe a little light fishing if they were biting. The great man himself had agreed to accompany them, but only after Mitch insisted and told him they needed to discuss personal matters. Private matters, regarding the death of his son.

From a screened balcony on the second floor of a Cayman Kai beach house, the Nordic watched the two snorkeled heads bob and disappear around the fishing boat. He handed the binoculars to Two-Ton Tony Verkler, who, quickly bored, handed them back. A striking blonde in a black one-piece with legs cut high, almost to the rib cage, stood behind the Nordic and took the binoculars. Of particular interest was the deckhand.

Tony spoke. 'I don't understand. If they were talking serious, why the boy? Why have another set of ears around?'

'Perhaps they're talking about snorkeling and fishing,' said the Nordic.

'I don't know,' said the blonde. 'It's unusual for Abanks to spend time on a fishing boat. He likes the divers. There must be a good reason for him to waste a day with two novice snorkelers. Something's up.'

'Who's the boy?' asked Tony.

'Just one of the gofers,' she said. 'He's got a dozen.'

'Can you talk to him later?' asked the Nordic.

'Yeah,' said Tony. 'Show him some skin, snort some candy. He'll talk.'

'I'll try,' she said.

'What's his name?' asked the Nordic.

'Keith Rook.'

Keith Rook maneuvered the boat alongside the pier at Rum Point. Mitch, Abby and Abanks climbed from the boat and headed for the beach. Keith was not invited to lunch. He stayed behind and lazily washed the deck.

The Shipwreck Bar sat inland a hundred yards under a heavy cover of rare shade trees. It was dark and damp with screened windows and squeaky ceiling fans. There was no reggae, dominoes, or dartboard. The noon crowd was quiet with each table engrossed in its own private talk.

The view from their table was out to sea, to the north. They ordered cheeseburgers and beer – island food.

'This bar is different,' Mitch observed quietly.

'Very much so,' said Abanks. 'And with good reason. It's a hangout for drug dealers who own many of the nice homes and condos around here. They fly in on their private jets, deposit their money in our many fine banks and spend a few days around here checking their real estate.'

'Nice neighborhood.'

'Very nice, really. They have millions and they keep to themselves.'

The waitress, a husky, well-mixed mulatto, dropped three bottles of Jamaican Red Stripe on the table without saying a word. Abanks leaned forward on his elbows with his head lowered, the customary manner of speaking in the Shipwreck Bar. 'So you think you can walk away?' he said.

Mitch and Abby leaned forward in unison, and all three heads met low in the center of the table, just over the beer. 'Not walk, but run. Run like hell, but I'll get away. And I'll need your help.'

Abanks thought about this for a moment and raised his head. He shrugged. 'But what am I to do?' He took the first sip of his Red Stripe.

Abby saw her first, and it would take a woman to spot another woman straining ever so elegantly to eavesdrop on their little conversation. Her back was to Abanks. She was a solid blonde partially hidden under cheap black rubber sunglasses that covered most of her face, and she had been watching the ocean and listening a bit too hard. When the three of them leaned over, she sat up straight and listened like hell. She was by herself at a table for two.

Abby dug her fingernails into her husband's leg, and their table became quiet. The blonde in black listened, then turned to her table and her drink.

Wayne Tarrance had improved his wardrobe by Friday of Cayman Week. Gone were the straw sandals and tight shorts and teenybop sunglasses. Gone were the sickly-pale legs. Now they were bright pink, burned beyond recognition. After three days in the tropical outback known as Cayman Brac, he and Acklin, acting on behalf of the U.S. government, had pounced on a rather cheap room on Grand Cayman, miles from Seven Mile Beach and not within walking distance of any remote portion of the sea. Here they had established a command post to monitor the comings and goings of the McDeeres and other interested people. Here, at the Coconut Motel, they had shared a small room with two single beds and cold showers. Wednesday morning, they had contacted the subject, McDeere, and requested a meeting as soon as possible. He said no. Said he was too busy. Said he and his wife were honeymooning and had no time for such a meeting. Maybe later, was all he said.

Then late Thursday, while Mitch and Abby were enjoying grilled grouper at the Lighthouse on the road to Bodden Town, Laney, Agent Laney, dressed in appropriate island garb and looking very much like an island Negro, stopped at their table and laid down the law. Tarrance insisted on a meeting.

Chickens had to be imported into the Cayman Islands, and not the best ones. Only medium-grade chickens, to be consumed not by native islanders but by Americans away from home without this most basic staple. Colonel Sanders had the damnedest time teaching the island girls, though black or close to it, how to fry chicken. It was foreign to them.

And so it was that Special Agent Wayne Tarrance, of the Bronx, arranged a quick secret meeting at the Kentucky Fried Chicken franchise on the island of Grand Cayman. The only such franchise. He thought the place would be deserted. He was wrong.

A hundred hungry tourists from Georgia, Alabama, Texas and Mississippi packed the place and devoured extra crispy with cole slaw and creamed potatoes. It tasted better in Tupelo, but it would do.

Tarrance and Acklin sat in a booth in the crowded restaurant and nervously watched the front door. It was not too late to abort. There were just too many people. Finally, Mitch entered, by himself, and stood in the long line. He brought his little red box to their table and sat down. He did not say hello or anything. He began eating the three-piece dinner for which he paid $4.89, Cayman dollars. Imported chicken.

'Where have you been?' Tarrance asked.

Mitch attacked a thigh. 'On the island. It's stupid to meet here, Tarrance. Too many people.'

'We know what we're doing.'

'Yeah, like the Korean shoe store.'

'Cute. Why wouldn't you see us Wednesday?'

'I was busy Wednesday. I didn't want to see you Wednesday. Am I clean?'

'Of course you're clean. Laney would've tackled you at the front door if you weren't clean.'

'This place makes me nervous, Tarrance.'

'Why did you go to Abanks?'

Mitch wiped his mouth and held the partially devoured thigh. A rather small thigh. 'He's got a boat. I wanted to fish and snorkel, so we cut a deal. Where were you, Tarrance? In a submarine trailing us around the island?'

'What did Abanks say?'

'Oh, he knows lots of words. Hello. Give me a beer. Who's following us? Buncha words.'

'They followed you, you know?'

'They! Which they? Your they or their they? I'm being followed so much I'm causing traffic jams.'

'The bad guys, Mitch. Those from Memphis and Chicago and New York. The ones who'll kill you tomorrow if you get real cute.'

'I'm touched. So they followed me. Where'd I take them? Snorkeling? Fishing? Come on, Tarrance. They follow me, you follow them, you follow me, they follow you. If I slam on brakes I get twenty noses up my ass. Why are we meeting here, Tarrance? This place is packed.'

Tarrance glanced around in frustration.

Mitch closed his chicken box. 'Look, Tarrance, I'm nervous and I've lost my appetite.'

'Relax. You were clean coming from the condo.'

'I'm always clean, Tarrance. I suppose Hodge and Kozinski were clean every time they moved. Clean at

Abanks'. Clean on the dive boat. Clean at the funerals. This was not a good idea, Tarrance. I'm leaving.'

'Okay. When does your plane leave?'

'Why? You guys plan to follow? Will you follow me or them? What if they follow you? What if we all get real confused and I follow everybody?'

'Come on, Mitch.'

'Nine-forty in the morning. I'll try to save you a seat. You can have the window next to Two-Ton Tony.'

'When do we get your files?'

Mitch stood with his chicken box. 'In a week or so. Give me ten days, and, Tarrance, no more meetings in public. They kill lawyers, remember, not stupid FBI agents.'

TWENTY-SIX

At eight Monday morning, Oliver Lambert and Nathan Locke were cleared through the concrete wall on the fifth floor and walked through the maze of small rooms and offices. DeVasher was waiting. He closed the door behind them and pointed to the chairs. His walk was not as quick. The night had been a long losing battle with the vodka. The eyes were red and the brain expanded with each breath.

'I talked with Lazarov yesterday in Las Vegas. I explained as best I could why you boys were so reluctant to fire your four lawyers, Lynch, Sorrell, Buntin and Myers. I gave him all your good reasons. He said he'd think about it, but in the meantime, make damned sure those four work on nothing but clean files. Take no chances and watch them closely.'

'He's really a nice guy, isn't he?' Oliver Lambert said.

'Oh yes. A real charmer. He said Mr. Morolto has asked about the firm once a week for six weeks now. Said they're all anxious.'

'What did you tell him?'

'Told him things are secure, for now. Leaks are plugged, for now. I don't think he believes me.'

'What about McDeere?' asked Locke.

'He had a wonderful week with his wife. Have you

ever seen her in a string bikini? She wore one all week. Outstanding! We got some pictures, just for fun.'

'I didn't come here to look at pictures,' Locke snapped.

'You don't say. They spent an entire day with our little pal Abanks, just the three of them and a deckhand. They played in the water, did some fishing. And they did a lot of talking. About what, we don't know. Never could get close enough. But it makes me very suspicious, guys. Very suspicious.'

'I don't see why,' said Oliver Lambert. 'What can they talk about besides fishing and diving, and, of course, Hodge and Kozinski? And so they talk about Hodge and Kozinski, what's the harm?'

'He never knew Hodge and Kozinski, Oliver,' said Locke. 'Why would he be so interested in their deaths?'

'Keep in mind,' said DeVasher, 'that Tarrance told him at their first meeting that the deaths were not accidental. So now he's Sherlock Holmes looking for clues.'

'He won't find any, will he, DeVasher?'

'Hell no. It was a perfect job. Oh sure, there are a few unanswered questions, but the Caymanian police damned sure can't answer them. Neither can our boy McDeere.'

'Then why are you worried?' asked Lambert.

'Because they're worried in Chicago, Ollie, and they pay me real good money to stay worried down here. And until the Fibbies leave us alone, everybody stays worried, okay?'

'What else did he do?'

'The usual Cayman vacation. Sex, sun, rum, a little shopping and sightseeing. We had three people on the island, and they lost him a couple of times, but nothing serious, I hope. Like I've always said, you can't trail a man twenty-four hours a day, seven days a week, without getting caught. So we have to play it cool sometimes.'

'You think McDeere's talking?' asked Locke.

'I know he lies, Nat. He lied about the incident in the Korean shoe store a month ago. You guys didn't want to believe it, but I'm convinced he went into that store voluntarily because he wanted to talk with Tarrance. One of our guys made a mistake, got too close, so the little meeting broke up. That ain't McDeere's version, but that's what happened. Yeah, Nat, I think he's talking. Maybe he meets with Tarrance and tells him to go to hell. Maybe they're smoking dope together. I don't know.'

'But you have nothing concrete, DeVasher,' Ollie said.

The brain expanded and pressed mightily against the skull. It hurt too much to get mad. 'No, Ollie, nothing like Hodge and Kozinski, if that's what you mean. We had those boys on tape and knew they were about to talk. McDeere's a little different.'

'He's also a rookie,' said Nat. 'An eight-month lawyer who knows nothing. He's spent a thousand hours on sweat files, and the only clients he's handled have been legitimate. Avery's been extremely careful about the files McDeere's touched. We've talked about it.'

'He has nothing to say, because he knows nothing,' added Ollie. 'Marty and Joe knew a helluva lot, but they'd been here for years. McDeere's a new recruit.'

DeVasher gently massaged his temples. 'So you've hired a real dumb-ass. Let's just suppose the FBI has a hunch who our biggest client is. Okay. Think along with me. And let's just suppose Hodge and Kozinski fed them enough to confirm the identity of this particular client. See where I'm going? And let's suppose the Fibbies have told McDeere all they know, along with a certain amount of embellishment. Suddenly, your ignorant rookie recruit is a very smart man. And a very dangerous one.'

'How do you prove this?'

'We step up surveillance, for starters. Put his wife under twenty-four-hour watch. I've already called Lazarov and requested more men. Told him we needed some fresh faces. I'm going to Chicago tomorrow to brief Lazarov, and maybe Mr. Morolto. Lazarov thinks Morolto has a lead on a mole within the Bureau, some guy who's close to Voyles and will sell information. But it's expensive, supposedly. They wanna assess things and decide where to go.'

'And you'll tell them McDeere's talking?' asked Locke.

'I'll tell them what I know and what I suspect. I'm afraid that if we sit back and wait for concrete, it might be too late. I'm sure Lazarov will wanna discuss plans to eliminate him.'

'Preliminary plans?' Ollie asked, with a touch of hope.

'We've passed the preliminary stage, Ollie.'

The Hourglass Tavern in New York City faces Forty-sixth Street, near its corner with Ninth Avenue. A small, dark hole-in-the-wall with twenty-two seats, it grew to fame with its expensive menu and fifty-nine-minute time limit on each meal. On the walls not far above the tables, hourglasses with white sand silently collect the seconds and minutes until the tavern's timekeeper – the waitress – finally makes her calculations and calls time. Frequented by the Broadway crowd, it is usually packed, with loyal fans waiting on the sidewalk.

Lou Lazarov liked the Hourglass because it was dark and private conversations were possible. Short conversations, under fifty-nine minutes. He liked it because it was not in Little Italy, and he was not Italian, and although he was owned by Sicilians, he did not have to eat their food. He liked it because he was born and spent the first forty years of his life in the theater district. Then corporate headquarters was moved to Chicago, and he was transferred. But business required his presence in New York at least twice a week, and when the business included meeting a member of equal stature from another family, Lazarov always suggested the Hourglass. Tubertini had equal stature, and a little extra. Reluctantly, he agreed on the Hourglass.

Lazarov arrived first and did not wait for a table. He knew from experience the crowd thinned around 4 P.M., especially on Thursdays. He ordered a glass of red wine. The waitress tipped the hourglass above his head, and the race was on. He sat at a front table, facing the street, his back to the other tables. He was a heavy man of fifty-eight, with a thick chest and ponderous belly. He leaned hard on the red checkered tablecloth and watched the traffic on Forty sixth.

Thankfully, Tubertini was prompt. Less than a fourth of the white sand was wasted on him. They shook hands politely, while Tubertini scornfully surveyed the tiny sliver of a restaurant. He flashed a plastic smile at Lazarov and glared at his seat in the window. His back would face the street, and this was extremely irritating. And dangerous. But his car was just outside with two of his men. He decided to be polite. He deftly maneuvered around the tiny table and sat down.

Tubertini was polished. He was thirty-seven, the son-in-law of old man Palumbo himself. Family. Married his only daughter. He was beautifully thin and tanned with his short black hair oiled to perfection and slicked back. He ordered red wine.

'How's my pal Joey Morolto?' he asked with a perfect brilliant smile.

'Fine. And Mr. Palumbo?'

'Very ill, and very ill-tempered. As usual.'

'Please give him my regards.'

'Certainly.'

The waitress approached and looked menacingly at the timepiece. 'Just wine,' said Tubertini. 'I won't be eating.'

Lazarov looked at the menu and handed it to her. 'Sautéed blackfish, with another glass of wine.'

Tubertini glanced at his men in the car. They appeared to be napping. 'So, what's wrong in Chicago?'

'Nothing's wrong. We just need a little information, that's all. We've heard, unconfirmed of course, that you have a very reliable man somewhere deep in the Bureau, somewhere close to Voyles.'

'And if we do?'

'We need some information from this man. We have a small unit in Memphis, and the Fibbies are trying like hell to infiltrate. We suspect one of our employees may be working with them, but we can't seem to catch him.'

'And if you caught him?'

'We'd slice out his liver and feed it to the rats.'

'Serious, huh?'

'Extremely serious. Something tells me the feds have targeted our little unit down there, and we've grown quite nervous.'

'Let's say his name is Alfred, and let's say he's very close to Voyles.'

'Okay. We need a very simple answer from Alfred. We need to know, yes or no, if our employee is working with the Fibbies.'

Tubertini watched Lazarov and sipped his wine. 'Alfred specializes in simple answers. He prefers the yes and no variety. We've used him twice, only when it's critical, and both times it was a question of "Are the feds coming here or there?" He's extremely cautious. I don't think he would provide too many details.'

'Is he accurate?'

'Deadly accurate.'

'Then he should be able to help us. If the answer is yes, we move accordingly. If no, the employee is off the hook and it's business as usual.'

'Alfred's very expensive.'

'I was afraid so. How much?'

'Well, he has sixteen years with the Bureau and is a career man. That's why he's so cautious. He has much to lose.'

'How much?'

'Half a million.'

'Damn!'

'Of course, we have to make a small profit on the transaction. After all, Alfred is ours.'

'A small profit?'

'Quite small, really. Most of it goes to Alfred. He talks to Voyles daily, you know. His office is two doors down.'

'All right. We'll pay.'

Tubertini flashed a conquering smile and tasted his wine. 'I think you lied, Mr. Lazarov. You said it was a small unit in Memphis. That's not true, is it?'

'No.'

'What's the name of this unit?'

'The Bendini firm.'

'Old man Morolto's daughter married a Bendini.'

'That's it.'

'What's the employee's name?'

'Mitchell McDeere.'

'It might take two or three weeks. Meeting with Alfred is a major production.'

'Yes. Just be quick about it.'

TWENTY-SEVEN

It was highly unusual for wives to appear at the quiet little fortress on Front Street. They were certainly welcome, they were told, but seldom invited. So Abby McDeere arrived through the front door, into the reception area uninvited and unannounced. It was imperative that she see her husband, she insisted. The receptionist phoned Nina on the second floor, and within seconds she appeared in a rush and warmly greeted her boss's wife. Mitch was in a meeting, she explained. He's always in a damned meeting, Abby replied. Get him out! They rushed to his office, where Abby closed the door and waited.

Mitch was observing another one of Avery's chaotic departures. Secretaries bumped into each other and packed briefcases while Avery yelled into the phone. Mitch sat on the sofa with a legal pad and watched. His partner was scheduled for two days on Grand Cayman. April 15 loomed on the calendar like a date with a firing squad, and the banks down there had certain records that had become critical. It was all work, Avery insisted. He talked about the trip for five days, dreading it, cursing it, but finding it completely unavoidable. He would take the Lear, and it was now waiting, said a secretary.

Probably waiting with a load of cash, thought Mitch.

Avery slammed the phone down and grabbed his coat. Nina walked through the door and glared at Mitch. 'Mr. McDeere, your wife is here. She says it's an emergency.'

The chaos became silent. He looked blankly at Avery. The secretaries froze. 'What is it?' he asked, standing.

'She's in your office,' Nina said.

'Mitch, I've gotta go,' Avery said. 'I'll call you tomorrow. I hope things are okay.'

'Sure.' He followed Nina down the stairs, saying nothing, to his office. Abby sat on his desk. He closed and locked the door. He watched her carefully.

'Mitch, I have to go home.'

'Why? What's happened?'

'My father just called at school. They found a tumor in one of Mother's lungs. They're operating tomorrow.'

He breathed deeply. 'I'm so sorry.' He did not touch her. She was not crying.

'I must go. I've taken a leave of absence at school.'

'For how long?' It was a nervous question.

She looked past him, to the Ego Wall. 'I don't know, Mitch. We need some time apart. I'm tired of a lot of things right now, and I need time. I think it will be good for both of us.'

'Let's talk about it.'

'You're too busy to talk, Mitch. I've been trying to talk for six months, but you can't hear me.'

'How long will you be gone, Abby?'

'I don't know. I guess it depends on Mother. No, it depends on a lot of things.'

'You're scaring me, Abby.'

'I'll be back, I promise. I don't know when. Maybe a week. Maybe a month. I need to sort out some things.'

'A month?'

'I don't know, Mitch. I just need some time. And I need to be with Mother.'

'I hope she's okay. I mean that.'

'I know. I'm going home to pack a few things, and I'll leave in an hour or so.'

'All right. Be careful.'

'I love you, Mitch.'

He nodded and watched as she opened the door. There was no embrace.

On the fifth floor, a technician rewound the tape and pushed the emergency button direct to DeVasher's office. He appeared instantly and slapped the headphones over his extra-large cranium. He listened for a moment. 'Rewind,' he demanded. He was quiet for another moment.

'When did this happen?' he asked.

The technician looked at a panel of digital numbers. 'Two minutes fourteen seconds ago. In his office, second floor.'

'Damn, damn. She's leaving him, ain't she? No talk of separation or divorce before this?'

'No. You would've known about it. They've argued about his workaholic routine, and he hates her parents. But nothing like this.'

'Yeah, yeah. Check with Marcus and see if he's heard anything before. Check the tapes, in case we've missed something. Damn, damn, damn!'

Abby started for Kentucky, but did not make it. An hour west of Nashville, she left Interstate 40, and turned north on Highway 13. She had noticed nothing behind her. She drove eighty at times, then fifty. Nothing. At the small town of Clarksville, near the Kentucky line, she abruptly turned east on Highway 112. An hour later she entered Nashville through a county highway, and the red Peugeot was lost in city traffic.

She parked it in the long-term section at Nashville Airport and caught a shuttle to the terminal. In a rest room on the first floor she changed into khaki walking shorts, Bass loafers and a navy knit pullover. It was a cool outfit, a little out of season, but she was headed for warmer weather. She pulled her shoulder-length hair into a ponytail and forced it under her collar. She changed sunglasses and stuffed the dress, heels and panty hose into a canvas gym bag.

Almost five hours after she left Memphis, she walked to the Delta boarding gate and presented her ticket. She asked for a window seat.

No Delta flight in the free world can bypass Atlanta, but fortunately she was not forced to change planes. She waited by her window and watched darkness fall on the busy airport. She was nervous, but tried not to think about it. She drank a glass of wine and read a *Newsweek*.

Two hours later she landed in Miami and left the plane. She walked rapidly through the airport, catching stares but ignoring them. They're just the usual everyday stares of admiration and lust, she told herself. Nothing more.

At the one and only Cayman Airways boarding gate, she produced her round-trip ticket and the required birth certificate and driver's license. Wonderful people, these Caymanians, but they won't allow you in their country unless you've already purchased a ticket to get out. Please come and spend your money, then leave. Please.

She sat in a corner of the crowded room and tried to read. A young father with a pretty wife and two babies kept staring at her legs, but no one else noticed her. The flight to Grand Cayman would leave in thirty minutes.

After a rough start, Avery gained momentum and spent seven hours at the Royal Bank of Montreal, Georgetown, Grand Cayman branch. When he left at 5 P.M. the complimentary conference room was filled with computer printouts and account summaries. He would finish tomorrow. He needed McDeere, but circumstances had worked to seriously curtail his travel plans. Avery was now exhausted and thirsty. And things were hot on the beach.

At Rumheads, he picked up a beer at the bar and worked his well-tanned body through the crowd to the patio, where he looked for a table. As he strode confidently past the domino game, Tammy Greenwood Hemphill, of Greenwood Services, nervously but nonchalantly entered the crowd and sat on a stool at the bar. She watched him. Her tan was store-bought, machine-inflicted, with some areas browner than others. But on the whole, it was an enviable tan for late March. The hair was now colored, not bleached, to a soft sandy blond, and the makeup likewise had been tempered. The bikini was state of the art, bright fluorescent orange that demanded attention. The large breasts hung wonderfully and stretched the strings and patches to their limit. The small patch across the rear was woefully incapable of covering anything. She was forty, but twenty sets of hungry eyes followed her to the bar, where she ordered a club soda and fired up a cigarette. She smoked it, and watched him.

He was a wolf. He looked good, and he knew it. He sipped his beer and slowly examined every female within fifty yards. He locked into one, a young blonde, and seemed ready to pounce when her man arrived and she sat in his lap. He sipped his beer and continued to survey.

Tammy ordered another club soda, with a twist of lime, and started for the patio. The wolf locked into

331

the big breasts immediately and watched them bounce his way.

'Mind if I sit down?' she asked.

He half stood and reached for the chair. 'Please do.' It was a great moment for him. Of all the hungry wolves lusting around the bar and patio at Rumheads, she picked him. He'd had younger babes, but at this moment at this place, she was the hottest.

'I'm Avery Tolleson. From Memphis.'

'Nice to meet you. I'm Libby. Libby Lox from Birmingham.' Now she was Libby. She had a sister named Libby, a mother named Doris, and her name was Tammy. And she hoped to hell she could keep it all straight. Although she wore no rings, she had a husband whose legal name was Elvis, and he was supposed to be in Oklahoma City impersonating the King, and probably screwing teenage girls with LOVE ME TENDER T-shirts.

'What brings you here?' Avery asked.

'Just fun. Got in this morning. Staying at the Palms. You?'

'I'm a tax lawyer, and believe it or not, I'm here on business. I'm forced to come down several times a year. Real torture.'

'Where are you staying?'

He pointed. 'My firm owns those two condos over there. It's a nice little write-off.'

'Very pretty.'

The wolf did not hesitate. 'Would you like to see them?'

She giggled like a sophomore. 'Maybe later.'

He smiled at her. This would be easy. He loved the islands.

'What're you drinking?' he asked.

'Gin and tonic. Twist of lime.'

He left for the bar, and returned with the drinks. He moved his chair closer to her. Now their legs were touching. The breasts were resting comfortably on the table. He looked down between them.

'Are you alone?' Obvious question, but he had to ask it.

'Yeah. You?'

'Yeah. Do you have plans for dinner?'

'Not really.'

'Good. There's this great cookout there at the Palms beginning at six. The best seafood on the island. Good music. Rum punch. The works. No dress code.'

'I'm game.'

They moved closer together, and his hand was suddenly between her knees. His elbow nestled next to her left breast, and he smiled. She smiled. This was not altogether unpleasant, she thought, but there was business at hand.

The Barefoot Boys began to tune up, and the festival began. Beachcombers from all directions flocked to the Palms. Natives in white jackets and white shorts lined up folding tables and laid heavy cotton cloths over them. The smell of boiled shrimp and grilled amberjack and barbecued shark filled the beach. The lovebirds, Avery and Libby, walked hand in hand into the courtyard of the Palms and lined up for the buffet.

For three hours they dined and danced, drank and danced, and fell madly in heat over each other. Once he became drunk, she returned to straight club soda. Business was at hand. By ten, he was sloppy and she led him away from the dance floor, to the condo next door. He attacked her at the front door, and they kissed and groped for five minutes. He managed the key, and they were inside.

'One more drink,' she said, ever the party girl. He went to the bar and fixed her a gin and tonic. He was drinking scotch and water. They sat on the balcony outside the master bedroom and watched a half moon decorate the gentle sea.

She had matched him drink for drink, he thought, and if she could handle another, then so could he. But nature was calling again, and he excused himself. The scotch and water sat on the wicker table between them, and she smiled at it. Much easier than she had prayed for. She took a small plastic packet from the orange strap between her legs and dumped two tablets of chloral hydrate into his drink. She sipped her gin and tonic.

'Drink it up, big boy,' she said when he returned. 'I'm ready for bed.'

He grabbed his whiskey and gulped it down. The taste buds had been numb for hours. He took another swallow, then began to relax. Another swallow. His head wobbled from shoulder to shoulder, and finally his chin hit his chest. The breathing became heavy.

'Sleep well, lover boy,' she said to herself.

With a man of a hundred eighty pounds, two shots of chloral hydrate would induce a dead sleep for ten hours. She took his glass and gauged what was left. Not much. Eight hours, to be safe. She rolled him out of the chair and dragged him to the bed, head first, then feet. Very gently, she pulled his yellow-and-blue surfer shorts down his legs and laid them on the floor. She stared for a long second, then tucked the sheets and blankets around him. She kissed him good night.

On the dresser she found two key rings, eleven keys. Downstairs in the hall between the kitchen and the great room with a view of the beach, she found the mysterious locked door Mitch had found in November. He had paced off every room, upstairs and down, and determined this room to be at least fifteen by fifteen. It was suspicious because the door was metal, and because it was locked, and because a small STORAGE sign was affixed to it. It was the only labeled room in the condo. A week earlier in Unit B, he and Abby had found no such room.

One key ring held a key to a Mercedes, two keys to the Bendini Building, a house key, two apartment keys and a desk key. The keys on the other ring were unmarked and fairly generic. She tried it first, and the fourth key fit. She held her breath and opened the door. No electric shocks, no alarms, nothing. Mitch told her to open the door, wait five minutes and, if nothing happened, then turn on the light.

She waited ten minutes. Ten long and frightful minutes. Mitch had speculated that Unit A was used by the partners and trusted guests, and that Unit B was used by the associates and others who required constant surveillance. Thus, he hoped, Unit A would not be laden with wires and cameras and recorders and alarms. After ten minutes, she opened the door wide and turned on the light. She waited again, and heard nothing. The room was square, about fifteen by fifteen, with white walls, no carpet, and, as she counted, twelve fireproof legal size file cabinets. Slowly, she walked over to one and pulled the top drawer. It was unlocked.

She turned off the light, closed the door and returned to the bedroom upstairs, where Avery was now comatose and snoring loudly. It was ten-thirty. She would work like crazy for eight hours and quit at six in the morning.

Near a desk in a corner, three large briefcases sat neatly in a row. She grabbed them, turned off the lights and left through the front door. The small parking lot was dark and empty with a gravel drive leading to the highway. A sidewalk ran next to the shrubbery in front of both units and stopped at a white board fence along the property line. A gate led to a slight grassy knoll, with the first building of the Palms just over it.

It was a short walk from the condos to the Palms, but the briefcases had grown much heavier when she reached Room 188. It was on the first floor, front side, with a view of the pool but not of the beach. She was panting and sweating when she knocked on the door.

Abby yanked it open. She took the briefcases and placed them on the bed. 'Any problems?'

'Not yet. I think he's dead.' Tammy wiped her face with a towel and opened a can of Coke.

'Where is he?' Abby was all business, no smiles.

'In his bed. I figure we've got eight hours. Until six.'

'Did you get in the room?' Abby asked as she handed her a pair of shorts and a bulky cotton shirt.

'Yeah. There's a dozen big file cabinets, unlocked. A few cardboard boxes and other junk, but not much else.'

'A dozen?'

'Yeah, tall ones. All legal size. We'll be lucky to finish by six.'

It was a single motel room with a queen size bed. The sofa, coffee table and bed were pushed to the wall, and a Canon Model 8580 copier with automatic feed and collator sat in the center with engines running. On lease from Island Office Supply, it came at the scalper's price of three hundred dollars for twenty-four hours, delivered. It was the newest and largest rental copier on the island, the salesman had explained, and he was not excited about parting with it for only a day. But Abby charmed him and began laying hundred-dollar bills on the counter. Two cases of copy paper, ten thousand sheets, sat next to the bed.

They opened the first briefcase and removed six thin files. 'Same type of files,' Tammy mumbled to herself. She unhitched the two-prong clasp on the inside of the file and removed the papers. 'Mitch says they're very particular about their files,' Tammy explained as she unstapled a ten-page document. 'He says lawyers have a sixth sense and can almost smell if a secretary or a clerk has been in a file. So you'll have to be careful. Work slowly. Copy one document, and when you restaple it, try to line up with the old staple holes. It's tedious. Copy only one document at a time, regardless of the number of pages. Then put it back together slowly and in order. Then staple your copy so everything stays in order.'

With the automatic feed, the ten-page document took eight seconds.

'Pretty fast,' Tammy said.

The first briefcase was finished in twenty minutes. Tammy handed the two key rings to Abby and picked up two new, empty, all-canvas Samsonite handbags. She left for the condo.

Abby followed her out the door, then locked it. She walked to the front of the Palms, to Tammy's rented Nissan Stanza. Dodging at oncoming traffic from the wrong side of the road, she drove along Seven Mile Beach and into Georgetown. Two blocks behind the stately Swiss Bank Building, on a narrow street lined with neat frame houses, she found the one owned by the only locksmith on the island of Grand Cayman. At least, he was the only one she'd been able to locate without assistance. He owned a green house with open windows and white trim around the shutters and the doors.

She parked in the street and walked through the sand to the tiny front porch, where the locksmith and his neighbors were drinking and listening to Radio Cayman. Solid-gold reggae. They quietened when she approached, and none of them stood. It was almost eleven. He had said that he would do the job in his shop out back, and that his fees were modest, and that he would like a fifth of Myers's Rum as a down payment before he started.

'Mr. Dantley, I'm sorry I'm late. I've brought you a little gift.' She held out the fifth of rum.

Mr. Dantley emerged from the darkness and took the rum. He inspected the bottle. 'Boys, a bottle of Myers's.'

Abby could not understand the chatter, but it was obvious the gang on the porch was terribly excited about the bottle of Myers's. Dantley handed it to them and led Abby behind his house to a small outbuilding full of tools and small machines and a hundred gadgets. A single yellow light bulb hung from the ceiling and attracted mosquitoes by the hundreds. She handed Dantley the eleven keys, and he carefully laid them on a bare section of a cluttered workbench. 'This will be easy,' he said without looking up.

Although he was drinking at eleven at night, Dantley appeared to be in control. Perhaps his system had built an immunity to rum. He worked through a pair of thick goggles, drilling and carving each replica. After twenty minutes, he was finished. He handed Abby the two original sets of keys and their copies.

'Thank you, Mr. Dantley. How much do I owe you?'

'They were quite easy,' he drawled. 'A dollar per key.'

She paid him quickly and left.

Tammy filled the two small suitcases with the contents of the top drawer of the first file cabinet. Five drawers, twelve cabinets, sixty trips to the copier and back. In eight hours. It could be done. There were files, notebooks, computer printouts and more files. Mitch said to copy it all. He was not exactly sure what he was looking for, so copy it all.

She turned off the light and ran upstairs to check on lover boy. He had not moved. The snoring was in slow motion.

The Samsonites weighed thirty pounds apiece, and her arms ached when she reached Room 188. First trip out of sixty, she would not make it. Abby had not returned from Georgetown, so Tammy unloaded the suitcases neatly on the bed. She took one drink from her Coke and left with the empty bags. Back to the condo. Drawer two was identical. She fitted the files in order into the suitcases and strong-armed zippers. She was sweating and gasping for breath. Four packs a day, she thought. She vowed to cut back to two. Maybe even one pack. Up the stairs to check on him. He had not breathed since her last trip.

The copier was clicking and humming when she returned from trip two. Abby was finishing the second briefcase, about to start on the third.

'Did you get the keys?' Tammy asked.

'Yeah, no problem. What's your man doing?'

'If the copier wasn't running, you could hear him snoring.' Tammy unpacked into another neat stack on the bed. She wiped her face with a wet towel and left for the condo.

Abby finished the third briefcase and started on the stacks from the file cabinets. She quickly got the hang of the automatic feed, and after thirty minutes she moved with the efficient grace of a seasoned copy-room clerk. She fed copies and unstapled and restapled while the machine clicked rapidly and spat the reproductions through the collator.

Tammy arrived from trip three out of breath and with sweat dripping from her nose. 'Third drawer,' she reported. 'He's still snoring.' She unzipped the suit-cases and made another neat pile on the bed. She caught her breath, wiped her face and loaded the now copied contents of drawer one into the bags. For the rest of the night, she would be loaded coming and going.

At midnight, the Barefoot Boys sang their last song,

and the Palms settled down for the night. The quiet hum of the copier could not be heard outside Room 188. The door was kept locked; the shades pulled tightly, and all lights extinguished except for a lamp near the bed. No one noticed the tired lady, dripping with sweat, lugging the same two suitcases to and from the room.

After midnight they did not speak. They were tired, too busy and scared, and there was nothing to report except lover boy's movements in bed, if any. And there was none, until around 1 A.M., when he subconsciously rolled onto his side, where he stayed for about twenty minutes, then returned to his back. Tammy checked on him with each visit and asked herself each time what she would do if his eyes suddenly opened and he attacked. She had a small tube of Mace in her shorts pocket, just in case a confrontation occurred and escape became necessary. Mitch had been vague on the details of such an escape. Just don't lead him back to the motel room, he said. Hit him with the Mace, then run like crazy and scream, 'Rape!'

But after twenty-five trips, she became convinced he was hours away from consciousness. And it was bad enough hiking like a pack mule to and from, but she also had to climb the stairs, fourteen of them, each trip to check on Casanova. So she went to check every other trip. Then one out of three.

By 2 A.M., halfway through the project, they had copied the contents from five of the file cabinets. They had made over four thousand copies, and the bed was covered with neat little stacks of materials. Their copies stood along the wall next to the sofa in seven even rows almost waist high.

They rested for fifteen minutes.

At five-thirty the first flicker of sunrise rose in the east, and they forgot about being tired. Abby quickened her movements around the copier and hoped it would not burn up. Tammy rubbed the cramps in her calves and walked quickly back to the condo. It was either trip number fifty-one or fifty-two. She had lost count. It would be her last trip for a while. He was waiting.

She opened the door and went straight to the storage room, as usual. She set the packed Samsonites on the floor, as usual. She quietly walked up the stairs, into the bedroom, and froze. Avery was sitting on the edge of the bed, facing the balcony. He heard her and turned slowly to face her. His eyes were swollen and glazed. He scowled at her.

Instinctively, she unbuttoned the khaki shorts and they fell to the floor. 'Hey, big boy,' she said, trying to breathe normally and act like a party girl. She walked to the edge of the bed where he was sitting. 'You're up kinda early. Let's get some more sleep.'

His gaze returned to the window. He said nothing. She sat beside him and rubbed the inside of his thigh. She slid her hand up the inside of his leg, and he did not move.

'Are you awake?' she asked.

No response.

'Avery, talk to me, baby. Let's get some more sleep. It's still dark out there.'

He fell sideways, onto his pillow. He grunted. No attempt at speech. Just a grunt. Then he closed his eyes. She lifted his legs onto the bed and covered him again.

She sat by him for ten minutes, and when the snoring returned to its former intensity, she slid into the shorts and ran to the Palms.

'He woke up, Abby!' she reported in panic. 'He woke up, then passed out again.'

Abby stopped and stared. Both women looked at the bed, which was covered with uncopied documents.

'Okay. Take a quick shower,' Abby said coolly. 'Then go get in bed with him and wait. Lock the door to the storage room, and call me when he wakes up and gets in the shower. I'll keep copying what's left, and we'll try to move it later, after he goes to work.'

'That's awfully risky.'

'It's all risky. Hurry.'

Five minutes later, Tammy/Doris/Libby with the bright orange string bikini made another trip – without the suitcases – to the condo. She locked the front door and the storage door and went to the bedroom. She removed the orange top and crawled under the covers.

The snoring kept her awake for fifteen minutes. Then she dozed. She sat up in bed to prevent sleep. She was scared, sitting there in bed with a nude man who would kill her if he knew. Her tired body relaxed, and sleep became unavoidable. She dozed again.

Lover boy broke from his coma at three minutes past nine. He moaned loudly and rolled to the edge of the bed. His eyelids were stuck together. They opened slowly, and the bright sun came piercing through. He moaned again. The head weighed a hundred pounds and rocked awkwardly from right to left, shifting the brain violently each time. He breathed deeply, and the fresh oxygen went screaming through his temples. His right hand caught his attention. He tried to raise it, but the nerve impulses would not penetrate the brain. Slowly it went up, and he squinted at it. He tried to focus with the right eye first, then the left. The clock.

He looked at the digital clock for thirty seconds before he could decipher the red numbers. Nine-oh-five. Damn! He was expected at the bank at nine. He moaned. The woman!

She had felt him move and heard his sounds, and she lay still with her eyes shut. She prayed he would not touch her. She felt him staring.

For this career rogue and bad boy, there had been many hangovers. But none like this. He looked at her face and tried to remember how good she had been. He could always remember that, if nothing else. Regardless of the size of the hangover, he could always remember the women. He watched her for a moment, then gave it up.

'Damn!' he said as he stood and tried to walk. His feet were like lead boots and only reluctantly complied with his wishes. He braced himself against the sliding door to the balcony.

The bathroom was twenty feet away, and he decided to go for it. The desk and dresser served as braces. One painful, clumsy step after another, and he finally made it. He hovered above the toilet and relieved himself.

She rolled to face the balcony, and when he finished she felt him sit on her side of the bed. He gently touched her shoulder. 'Libby, wake up.' He shook her, and she bolted stiff.

'Wake up, dear,' he said. A gentleman.

She gave him her best sleepy smile. The morning-after smile of fulfillment and commitment. The Scarlett O'Hara smile the morning after Rhett nailed her. 'You were great, big boy,' she cooed with her eyes closed.

In spite of the pain and nausea, in spite of the lead boots and bowling-ball head, he was proud of himself. The woman was impressed. Suddenly, he remembered that he was great last night.

'Look, Libby, we've overslept. I gotta go to work. I'm already late.'

'Not in the mood, huh?' she giggled. She prayed he wasn't in the mood.

'Naw, not now. How about tonight?'

'I'll be here, big boy.'

'Good. I gotta take a shower.'

343

'Wake me up when you get out.'

He stood and mumbled something, then locked the bathroom door. She slid across the bed to the phone and called Abby. After three rings, she answered.

'He's in the shower.'

'Are you okay?'

'Yeah. Fine. He couldn't do it if he had to.'

'What took so long?'

'He wouldn't wake up.'

'Is he suspicious?'

'No. He remembers nothing. I think he's in pain.'

'How long will you be there?'

'I'll kiss him goodbye when he gets out of the shower. Ten, maybe fifteen minutes.'

'Okay. Hurry.' Abby hung up, and Tammy slid to her side of the bed. In the attic above the kitchen, a recorder clicked, reset itself and was ready for the next call.

By ten-thirty, they were ready for the final assault on the condo. The contraband was divided into three equal parts. Three daring raids in open daylight. Tammy slid the shiny new keys into her blouse pocket and took off with the suitcases. She walked quickly, her eyes darting in all directions behind the sunglasses. The parking lot in front of the condos was still empty. Traffic was light on the highway.

The new key fit, and she was inside. The key to the storage door also fit, and five minutes later she left the condo. The second and third trips were equally quick and uneventful. When she left the storage room for the last time, she studied it carefully. Everything was in order, just as she found it. She locked the condo and took the empty, well-worn Samsonites back to her room.

For an hour they lay beside each other on the bed and laughed at Avery and his hangover. It was over now, for the most part, and they had committed the perfect crime. And lover boy was a willing but ignorant participant. It had been easy, they decided.

The small mountain of evidence filled eleven and a half corrugated storage boxes. At two-thirty, a native with a straw hat and no shirt knocked on the door and announced he was from an outfit called Cayman Storage. Abby pointed at the boxes. With no place to go and no hurry to get there, he took the first box and ever so slowly carried it to his van. Like all the natives, he operated on Cayman time. No hurry, mon.

They followed him in the Stanza to a warehouse in Georgetown. Abby inspected the proposed storage room and paid cash for three months' rental.

TWENTY-EIGHT

Wayne Tarrance sat on the back row of the 11:40 P.M. Greyhound from Louisville to Indianapolis to Chicago. Although he sat by himself, the bus was crowded. It was Friday night. The bus left Kentucky thirty minutes earlier, and by now he was convinced something had gone wrong. Thirty minutes, and not a word or signal from anyone. Maybe it was the wrong bus. Maybe McDeere had changed his mind. Maybe a lot of things. The rear seat was inches above the diesel engine, and Wayne Tarrance, of the Bronx, now knew why Greyhound Frequent Milers fought for the seats just behind the driver. His Louis L'Amour vibrated until he had a headache. Thirty minutes. Nothing.

The toilet flushed across the aisle, and the door flew open. The odor filtered out, and Tarrance looked away, to the southbound traffic. From nowhere, she slid into the aisle seat and cleared her throat. Tarrance jerked to his right, and there she was. He'd seen her before, somewhere.

'Are you Mr. Tarrance?' She wore jeans, white cotton sneakers and a heavy green rag sweater. She hid behind dark glasses.

'Yeah. And you?'

She grabbed his hand and shook it firmly. 'Abby McDeere.'

'I was expecting your husband.'

'I know. He decided not to come, and so here I am.'

'Well, uh, I sort of wanted to talk to him.'

'Yes, but he sent me. Just think of me as his agent.'
Tarrance laid his paperback under the seat and watched the highway. 'Where is he?'

'Why is that important, Mr. Tarrance? He sent me to talk business, and you're here to talk business. So let's talk.'

'Okay. Keep your voice down, and if anybody comes down the aisle, grab my hand and stop talking. Act like we're married or something. Okay? Now, Mr. Voyles – do you know who he is?'

'I know everything, Mr. Tarrance.'

'Good. Mr. Voyles is about to stroke out because we haven't got Mitch's files yet. The good files. You understand why they're important, don't you?'

'Very much so.'

'So we want the files.'

'And we want a million dollars.'

'Yes, that's the deal. But we get the files first.'

'No. That's not the deal. The deal, Mr. Tarrance, is that we get the million dollars exactly where we want it, then we hand over the files.'

'You don't trust us?'

'That's correct. We don't trust you, Voyles or anyone else. The money is to be deposited by wire transfer to a certain numbered account in a bank in Freeport, Bahamas. We will immediately be notified, and the money will then be wired by us to another bank. Once we have it where we want it, the files are yours.'

'Where are the files?'

'In a mini-storage in Memphis. There are fifty-one files in all, all boxed up real neat and proper like. You'll be impressed. We do good work.'

'We? Have you seen the files?'

'Of course. Helped box them up. There are these surprises in box number eight.'

'Okay. What?'

'Mitch was able to copy three of Avery Tolleson's files, and they appear to be questionable. Two deal with a company called Dunn Lane, Ltd., which we know to be a Mafia-controlled corporation chartered in the Caymans. It was established with ten million laundered dollars in 1986. The files deal with two construction projects financed by the corporation. You'll find it fascinating reading.'

'How do you know it was chartered in the Caymans? And how do you know about the ten million? Surely that's not in the files.'

'No, it's not. We have other records.'

Tarrance thought about the other records for six miles. It was obvious he wouldn't see them until the McDeeres had the first million. He let it pass.

'I'm not sure we can wire the money as you wish without first getting the files.' It was a rather weak bluff. She read it perfectly and smiled.

'Do we have to play games, Mr. Tarrance? Why don't you just give us the money and quit sparring.'

A foreign student of some sort, probably an Arab, sauntered down the aisle and into the rest room. Tarrance froze and stared at the window. Abby patted his arm like a real girlfriend. The flushing sounded like a short waterfall.

'How soon can this happen?' Tarrance asked. She was not touching him anymore.

'The files are ready. How soon can you round up a million bucks?'

'Tomorrow.'

Abby looked out the window and talked from the left corner of her mouth. 'Today's Friday. Next Tuesday, at ten A.M. Eastern time, Bahamas time, you transfer by wire the million dollars from your account

348

at the Chemical Bank in Manhattan to a numbered account at the Ontario Bank in Freeport. It's a clean, legitimate wire transfer – take about fifteen seconds.'

Tarrance frowned and listened hard. 'What if we don't have an account at the Chemical Bank in Manhattan?'

'You don't now, but you will Monday. I'm sure you've got someone in Washington who can handle a simple wire transfer.'

'I'm sure we do.'

'Good.'

'But why the Chemical Bank?'

'Mitch's orders, Mr. Tarrance. Trust him, he knows what he's doing.'

'I see he's done his homework.'

'He always does his homework. And there's something you need to always remember. He's much smarter than you are.'

Tarrance snorted and faked a light chuckle. They rode in silence for a mile or two, each thinking of the next question and answer.

'Okay,' Tarrance said, almost to himself. 'And when do we get the files?'

'When the money's safe in Freeport, we'll be notified. Wednesday morning before ten-thirty, you'll receive at your Memphis office a Federal Express package with a note and the key to the mini-storage.'

'So I can tell Mr. Voyles we'll have the files by Wednesday afternoon?'

She shrugged and said nothing. Tarrance felt stupid for asking the question. Quickly, he thought of a good one.

'We'll need the account number in Freeport.'

'It's written down. I'll give it to you when the bus stops.'

The particulars were now complete. He reached under the seat and retrieved his book. He flipped pages and pretended to read. 'Just sit here a minute,' he said.

'Any questions?' she asked.

'Yeah. Can we talk about these other records you mentioned?'

'Sure.'

'Where are they?'

'Good question. The way the deal was explained to me, we would first get the next installment, a half million, I believe, in return for enough evidence to allow you to obtain the indictments. These other records are part of the next installment.'

Tarrance flipped a page. 'You mean you've already obtained the, uh, dirty files?'

'We have most of what we need. Yes, we have a bunch of dirty files.'

'Where are they?'

She smiled softly and patted his arm. 'I assure you they're not in the mini-storage with the clean files.'

'But you have possession of them?'

'Sort of. Would you like to see a couple?'

He closed the book and breathed deeply. He looked at her. 'Certainly.'

'I thought so. Mitch says we'll give you ten inches of documents on Dunn Lane, Ltd. – copies of bank records, corporate charters, minutes, bylaws, officers, stockholders, wire transfer records, letters from Nathan Locke to Joey Morolto, working papers, a hundred other juicy morsels that'll make you lose sleep. Wonderful stuff. Mitch says you can probably get thirty indictments just from the Dunn Lane records.'

Tarrance hung on every word, and believed her. 'When can I see it?' he asked quietly but so eagerly.

'When Ray is out of prison. It's part of the deal, remember?'

'Aw yes. Ray.'

'Aw yes. He goes over the wall, Mr. Tarrance, or you can forget the Bendini firm. Mitch and I will take our paltry million and disappear into the night.'

'I'm working on it.'

'Better work hard.' It was more than a threat, and he knew it. He opened the book again and stared at it.

Abby pulled a Bendini, Lambert & Locke business card from her pocket and dropped in on the book. On the back she had written the account number: 477DL-19584, Ontario Bank, Freeport.

'I'm going back to my seat near the front, away from the engine. Are we clear about next Tuesday?'

'No problems, mon. Are you getting off in Indianapolis?'

'Yes.'

'Where are you going?'

'To my parents' home in Kentucky. Mitch and I are separated.'

She was gone.

Tammy stood in one of a dozen long, hot lines at Miami customs. She wore shorts, sandals, halter top, sunglasses and a straw hat and looked just like the other thousand weary tourists returning from the sun-drenched beaches of the Caribbean. In front of her were two ill-tempered newlyweds carrying bags of duty-free liquor and perfume and obviously in the middle of a serious disagreement. Behind her were two brand-new Hartman leather suitcases filled with enough documents and records to indict forty lawyers. Her employer, also a lawyer, had suggested she purchase luggage with little wheels on the bottom so they could be pulled through the Miami International Airport. She also had a small overnight bag with a few clothes and a toothbrush, to look legitimate.

About every ten minutes, the young couple moved forward six inches, and Tammy followed with her baggage. An hour after she entered the line, she made it to the checkpoint.

'No declarations!' the agent snapped in broken English.

'No!' she snapped back.

He nodded at the big leather bags. 'What's in there?'

'Papers.'

'Papers?'

'Papers.'

'What kind of papers?'

Toilet paper, she thought. I spend my vacations traveling the Caribbean collecting toilet paper. 'Legal documents, crap like that. I'm a lawyer.'

'Yeah, yeah.' He unzipped the overnight bag and glanced in. 'Okay. Next!'

She carefully pulled the bags, just so. They were inclined to tip over. A bellboy grabbed them and loaded all three pieces onto a two-wheeler. 'Delta Flight 282, to Nashville. Gate 44, Concourse B,' she said as she handed him a five dollar bill.

Tammy and all three bags arrived in Nashville at midnight Saturday. She loaded them into her Rabbit and left the airport. In the suburb of Brentwood, she parked in her designated parking place and, one at a time, pulled the Hartmans into a one bedroom apartment.

Except for a rented foldaway sofa, there was no furniture. She unpacked the suitcases in the bedroom and began the tedious process of arranging the evidence. Mitch wanted a list of each document, each bank record, each corporation. He wanted it just so. He said one day he would pass through in a great hurry, and he wanted it all organized.

For two hours she took inventory. She sat on the floor and made careful notes. After three one-day trips to Grand Cayman, the room was beginning to fill. Monday she would leave again.

She felt like she'd slept three hours in the past two weeks. But it was urgent, he said. A matter of life and death.

Tarry Ross, alias Alfred, sat in the darkest corner of the lounge of the Washington Phoenix Inn. The meeting would be terribly brief. He drank coffee and waited on his guest.

He waited and vowed to wait only five more minutes. The cup shook when he tried to sip it. Coffee splashed on the table. He looked at the table and tried desperately not to look around. He waited.

His guest arrived from nowhere and sat with his back to the wall. His name was Vinnie Cozzo, a thug from New York. From the Palumbo family.

Vinnie noticed the shaking cup and the spilled coffee. 'Relax, Alfred. This place is dark enough.'

'What do you want?' Alfred hissed.

'I wanna drink.'

'No time for drinks. I'm leaving.'

'Settle down, Alfred. Relax, pal. There ain't three people in here.'

'What do you want?' he hissed again.

'Just a little information.'

'It'll cost you.'

'It always does.' A waiter ventured by, and Vinnie ordered Chivas and water.

'How's my pal Denton Voyles?' Vinnie asked.

'Kiss my ass, Cozzo. I'm leaving. I'm walking outta here.'

'Okay, pal. Relax. I just need some info.'

'Make it quick.' Alfred scanned the lounge. His cup was empty, most of it on the table.

The Chivas arrived, and Vinnie took a good drink. 'Gotta little situation down in Memphis. Some of the

353

boys're sorta worried about it. Ever hear of the Bendini firm?'

Instinctively, Alfred shook his head in the negative. Always say no, at first. Then, after careful digging, return with a nice little report and say yes. Yes, he'd heard of the Bendini firm and their prized client. Operation Laundromat. Voyles himself had named it and was so proud of his creativity.

Vinnie took another good drink. 'Well, there's a guy down there named McDeere, Mitchell McDeere, who works for this Bendini firm, and we suspect he's also playing grab-ass with your people. Know what I mean? We think he's selling info on Bendini to the feds. Just need to know if it's true. That's all.'

Alfred listened with a straight face, although it was not easy. He knew McDeere's blood type and his favorite restaurant in Memphis. He knew that McDeere had talked to Tarrance half a dozen times now and that tomorrow, Tuesday, McDeere would become a millionaire. Piece of cake.

'I'll see what I can do. Let's talk money.'

Vinnie lit a Salem Light. 'Well, Alfred, it's a serious matter. I ain't gonna lie. Two hundred thousand cash.'

Alfred dropped the cup. He pulled a handkerchief from his rear pocket and furiously rubbed his glasses. 'Two hundred? Cash?'

'That's what I said. What'd we pay you last time?'

'Seventy-five.'

'See what I mean. It's pretty damned serious, Alfred. Can you do it?'

'Yes.'

'When?'

'Give me two weeks.'

TWENTY-NINE

A week before April 15, the workaholics at Bendini, Lambert & Locke reached maximum stress and ran at full throttle on nothing but adrenaline. And fear. Fear of missing a deduction or a write-off or some extra depreciation that would cost a rich client an extra million or so. Fear of picking up the phone and calling the client and informing him that the return was now finished and, sorry to say, an extra eight hundred thousand was due. Fear of not finishing by the fifteenth, and being forced to file extensions and incurring penalties and interest. The parking lot was full by 6 A.M. The secretaries worked twelve hours a day. Tempers were short. Talk was scarce and hurried.

With no wife to go home to, Mitch worked around the clock. Sonny Capps had cursed and berated Avery because he owed $450,000. On earned income of twelve million. Avery had cursed Mitch, and together they plowed through the Capps files again, digging and cursing. Mitch created two very questionable write-offs that lowered it to $320,000. Capps said he was considering a new tax firm. One in Washington.

With six days to go, Capps demanded a meeting with Avery in Houston. The Lear was available, and Avery left at midnight. Mitch drove him to the airport, receiving instructions along the way.

Shortly after 1:30 A.M., he returned to the office. Three Mercedes, a BMW and a Jaguar were scattered through the parking lot. The security guard opened the rear door, and Mitch rode the elevator to the fourth floor. As usual, Avery locked his office door. The partners' doors were always locked. At the end of the hall, a voice could be heard. Victor Milligan, head of tax, sat at his desk and said ugly things to his computer. The other offices were dark and locked.

Mitch held his breath and stuck a key into Avery's door. The knob turned, and he was inside. He switched on all the lights and went to the small conference table where he and his partner had spent the day and most of the night. Files were stacked like bricks around the chairs. Papers thrown here and there. IRS reg. books were piled on top of each other.

Mitch sat at the table and continued his research for Capps. According to the FBI notebook, Capps was a legitimate businessman who had used the firm for at least eight years. The Fibbies weren't interested in Sonny Capps.

After an hour, the talking stopped and Milligan closed and locked the door. He took the stairs without saying good night. Mitch quickly checked each office on the fourth floor, then the third. All empty. It was almost 3 A.M.

Next to the bookshelves on one wall of Avery's office, four solid oak file cabinets sat undisturbed. Mitch had noticed them for months but had never seen them used. The active files were kept in three metal cabinets next to the window. Secretaries dug through these, usually while Avery yelled at them. He locked the door behind him and walked to the oak cabinets. Locked, of course. He had narrowed it down to two small keys, each less than an inch long. The first one fit the first cabinet, and he opened it.

From Tammy's inventory of the contraband in

Nashville, he had memorized many of the names of the Cayman companies operating with dirty money that was now clean. He thumbed through the files in the top drawer, and the names jumped at him. Dunn Lane, Ltd., Eastpointe, Ltd., Virgin Bay, Ltd., Inland Contractors, Ltd., Gulf-South, Ltd. He found more familiar names in the second and third drawers. The files were filled with loan documents from Cayman banks, wire-transfer records, warranty deeds, leases, mortgage deeds and a thousand other papers. He was particularly interested in Dunn Lane and Gulf-South. Tammy had recorded a significant number of documents for these two companies.

He picked out a Gulf-South file full of wire-transfer records and loan documents from the Royal Bank of Montreal. He walked to a copier in the center of the fourth floor and turned it on. While it warmed, he casually glanced around. The place was dead. He looked along the ceilings. No cameras. He had checked it many times before. The ACCESS NUMBER light flashed, and he punched in the file number for Mrs. Lettie Plunk. Her tax return was sitting on his desk on the second floor, and it could spare a few copies. He laid the contents on the automatic feed, and three minutes later the file was copied. One hundred twenty-eight copies, charged to Lettie Plunk. Back to the file cabinet. Back to the copier with another stack of Gulf-South evidence. He punched in the access number for the file of Greenmark Partners, a real estate development company in Bartlett, Tennessee. Legitimate folks. The tax return was sitting on his desk and could spare a few copies. Ninety-one, to be exact.

Mitch had eighteen tax returns sitting in his office waiting to be signed and filed. With six days to go, he had finished his deadline work. All eighteen received automatic billings for copies of Gulf-South and Dunn

Lane evidence. He had scribbled their access numbers on a sheet of notepaper, and it sat on the table next to the copier. After using the eighteen numbers, he accessed with three numbers borrowed from Lamar's files and three numbers borrowed from the Capps files.

A wire ran from the copier through a hole in the wall and down the inside of a closet, where it connected with wires from three other copiers on the fourth floor. The wire, larger now, ran down through the ceiling and along a baseboard to the billing room on the third floor, where a computer recorded and billed every copy made within the firm. An innocuous-looking little gray wire ran from the computer up a wall and through the ceiling to the fourth floor, and then up to the fifth, where another computer recorded the access code, the number of copies and the location of the machine making each copy.

At 5 P.M., April 15, Bendini, Lambert & Locke shut down. By six, the parking lot was empty, and the expensive automobiles reassembled two miles away behind a venerable seafood establishment called Anderton's. A small banquet room was reserved for the annual April 15 blowout. Every associate and active partner was present, along with eleven retired partners. The retirees were tanned and well rested, the actives were haggard and frayed. But they were all in a festive spirit, ready to get plastered. The stringent rules of clean living and moderation would be forgotten this night. Another firm rule prohibited any lawyer or secretary from working on April 16.

Platters of cold boiled shrimp and raw oysters sat on tables along the walls. A huge wooden barrel filled with ice and cold Moosehead greeted them. Ten cases stood behind the barrel. Roosevelt popped tops as quickly as possible. Late in the night, he would get drunk with the rest of them, and Oliver Lambert would call a taxi to haul him home to Jessie Frances. It was a ritual.

Roosevelt's cousin, Little Bobby Blue Baker, sat at a baby grand and sang sadly as the lawyers filed in. For now, he was the entertainment. Later, he would not be needed.

Mitch ignored the food and took an icy green bottle to a table near the piano. Lamar followed with two pounds of shrimp. They watched their colleagues shake off coats and ties and attack the Moosehead.

'Get 'em all finished?' Lamar asked, devouring the shrimp.

'Yeah. I finished mine yesterday. Avery and I worked on Sonny Capps's until five P.M. It's finished.'

'How much?'

'Quarter of a mill.'

'Ouch.' Lamar turned up the bottle and drained half of it. 'He's never paid that much, has he?'

'No, and he's furious. I don't understand the guy. He cleared twelve million from all sorts of ventures, and he's mad as hell because he had to pay two percent in taxes.'

'How's Avery?'

'Somewhat worried. Capps made him fly to Houston last week, and it did not go well. He left on the Lear at midnight. Told me later Capps was waiting at his office at four in the morning, furious over his tax mess. Blamed it all on Avery. Said he might change firms.'

'I think he says that all the time. You need a beer?'

Lamar left and returned with four Mooseheads. 'How's Abby's mom?'

Mitch borrowed a shrimp and peeled it. 'She's okay, for now. They removed a lung.'

'And how's Abby?' Lamar was watching his friend, and not eating.

Mitch started another beer. 'She's fine.'

'Look, Mitch, our kids go to St. Andrew's. It's no secret Abby took a leave of absence. She's been gone for two weeks. We know it, and we're concerned.'

'Things will work out. She wants to spend a little time away. It's no big deal, really.'

'Come on, Mitch. It's a big deal when your wife leaves home without saying when she'll return. At least that's what she told the headmaster at school.'

'That's true. She doesn't know when she'll come back. Probably a month or so. She's had a hard time coping with the hours at the office.'

The lawyers were all present and accounted for, so Roosevelt shut the door. The room became noisier. Bobby Blue took requests.

'Have you thought about slowing down?' Lamar asked.

'No, not really. Why should I?'

'Look, Mitch, I'm your friend, right? I'm worried about you. You can't make a million bucks the first year.'

Oh yeah, he thought. I made a million bucks last week. In ten seconds the little account in Freeport jumped from ten thousand to a million ten thousand. And fifteen minutes later, the account was closed and the money was resting safely in a bank in Switzerland. Aw, the wonder of wire transfer. And because of the million bucks, this would be the first and only April 15 party of his short, but distinguished legal career. And his good friend who is so concerned about his marriage will most likely be in jail before long. Along with everyone else in the room, except for Roosevelt. Hell, Tarrance might get so excited he'll indict Roosevelt and Jessie Frances just for the fun of it.

Then the trials. 'I, Mitchell Y. McDeere, do solemnly swear to tell the truth, the whole truth and nothing but the truth. So help me God.' And he'd sit in the witness chair and point the finger at his good friend Lamar Quin. And Kay and the kids would be sitting in the front row for jury appeal. Crying softly.

He finished the second beer and started the third. 'I know, Lamar, but I have no plans to slow down. Abby will adjust. Things'll be fine.'

'If you say so. Kay wants you over tomorrow for a big steak. We'll cook on the grill and eat on the patio. How about it?'

'Yes, on one condition. No discussion about Abby. She went home to see her mother, and she'll be back. Okay?'

'Fine. Sure.'

Avery sat across the table with a plate of shrimp. He began peeling them.

'We were just discussing Capps,' Lamar said.

'That's not a pleasant subject,' Avery replied. Mitch watched the shrimp intently until there was a little pile of about six freshly peeled. He grabbed them across the table and shoved the handful into his mouth.

Avery glared at him with tired, sad eyes. Red eyes. He struggled for something appropriate, then began eating the unpeeled shrimp. 'I wish the heads were still on them,' he said between bites. 'Much better with the heads.'

Mitch raked across two handfuls and began crunching. 'I like the tails myself. Always been a tail man.'

Lamar stopped eating and gawked at them. 'You must be kidding.'

'Nope,' said Avery. 'When I was a kid in El Paso, we used to go out with our nets and scoop up a bunch of fresh shrimp. We'd eat 'em on the spot, while they were still wiggling.' Chomp, chomp. 'The heads are the best part because of all the brain juices.'

'Shrimp, in El Paso?'

'Yeah, Rio Grande's full of them.'

Lamar left for another round of beer. The wear,

tear, stress and fatigue mixed quickly with the alcohol and the room became rowdier. Bobby Blue was playing Steppenwolf. Even Nathan Locke was smiling and talking loudly. Just one of the boys. Roosevelt added five cases to the barrel of ice.

At ten, the singing started. Wally Hudson, minus the bow tie, stood on a chair by the piano and led the howling chorus through a riotous medley of Australian drinking songs. The restaurant was closed now, so who cared. Kendall Mahan was next. He had played rugby at Cornell and had an amazing repertoire of raunchy beer songs. Fifty untalented and drunk voices sang happily along with him.

Mitch excused himself and went to the rest room. A busboy unlocked the rear door, and he was in the parking lot. The singing was pleasant at this distance. He started for his car, but instead walked to a window. He stood in the dark, next to the corner of the building, and watched and listened. Kendall was now on the piano, leading his choir through an obscene refrain.

Joyous voices, of rich and happy people. He studied them one at a time, around the tables. Their faces were red. Their eyes were glowing. They were his friends – family men with wives and children – all caught up in this terrible conspiracy.

Last year Joe Hodge and Marty Kozinski were singing with the rest of them.

Last year he was a hotshot Harvard man with job offers in every pocket.

Now he was a millionaire, and would soon have a price on his head.

Funny what a year can do.

Sing on, brothers.

Mitch turned and walked away.

Around midnight, the taxis lined up on Madison, and

the richest lawyers in town were carried and dragged into the back seats. Of course, Oliver Lambert was the soberest of the lot, and he directed the evacuation. Fifteen taxis in all, with drunk lawyers lying everywhere.

At the same time, across town on Front Street, two identical navy blue-and-yellow Ford vans with DUSTBUSTER painted brightly on the sides pulled up to the gate. Dutch Hendrix opened it and waved them through. They backed up to the rear door, and eight women with matching shirts began unloading vacuum cleaners and buckets filled with spray bottles. They unloaded brooms and mops and rolls of paper towels. They chattered quietly among themselves as they went through the building. As directed from above, the technicians cleaned one floor at a time, beginning with the fourth. The guards walked the floors and watched them carefully.

The women ignored them and buzzed about their business of emptying garbage cans, polishing furniture, vacuuming and scrubbing bathrooms. The new girl was slower than the others. She noticed things. She pulled on desk drawers and file cabinets when the guards weren't looking. She paid attention.

It was her third night on the job, and she was learning her way around. She'd found the Tolleson office on the fourth floor the first night, and smiled to herself.

She wore dirty jeans and ragged tennis shoes. The blue DUSTBUSTERS shirt was extra large, to hide the figure and make her appear plump, like the other technicians. The patch above the pocket read DORIS. Doris, the cleaning technician.

When the crew was half finished with the second floor, a guard told Doris and two others, Susie and Charlotte, to follow him. He inserted a key in the elevator panel, and it stopped in the basement. He unlocked a heavy metal door, and they walked into a large room divided into a dozen cubicles. Each small desk was cluttered, and dominated by a large computer. There were terminals everywhere. Black file cabinets lined the walls. No windows.

'The supplies are in there,' the guard said, pointing to a closet. They pulled out a vacuum cleaner and spray bottles and went to work.

'Don't touch the desks,' he said.

THIRTY

Mitch tied the laces of his Nike Air Cushion jogging shoes and sat on the sofa waiting by the phone. Hearsay, depressed after two weeks without the woman around, sat next to him and tried to doze. At exactly ten-thirty, it rang. It was Abby.

There was no mushy 'sweethearts' and 'babes' and 'honeys.' The dialogue was cool and forced.

'How's your mother?' he asked.

'Doing much better. She's up and around, but very sore. Her spirits are good.'

'That's good to hear. And your dad?'

'The same. Always busy. How's my dog?'

'Lonesome and depressed. I think he's cracking up.'

'I miss him. How's work?'

'We survived April 15 without disaster. Everyone's in a better mood. Half the partners left for vacation on the sixteenth, so the place is a lot quieter.'

'I guess you've cut back to sixteen hours a day?'

He hesitated, and let it sink in. No sense starting a fight. 'When are you coming home?'

'I don't know. Mom will need me for a couple more weeks. I'm afraid Dad's not much help. They've got a maid and all, but Mom needs me now.' She paused, as if something heavy was coming. 'I called St. Andrew's today and told them I wouldn't be back this semester.'

He took it in his stride. 'There are two months left

in this semester. You're not coming back for two months?'

'At least two months, Mitch. I just need some time, that's all.'

'Time for what?'

'Let's not start it again, okay? I'm not in the mood to argue.'

'Fine. Fine. Fine. What are you in the mood for?'

She ignored this, and there was a long pause. 'How many miles are you jogging?'

'A couple. I've been walking to the track, then running about eight laps.'

'Be careful at the track. It's awfully dark.'

'Thanks.'

Another long pause. 'I need to go,' she said. 'Mom's ready for bed.'

'Will you call tomorrow night?'

'Yes. Same time.'

She hung up without a 'goodbye' or 'I love you' or anything. Just hung up.

Mitch pulled on his white athletic socks and tucked in his white long-sleeved T-shirt. He locked the kitchen door and trotted down the dark street. West Junior High School was six blocks to the east of East Meadowbrook. Behind the red brick classrooms and gymnasium was the baseball field, and farther away at the end of a dark driveway was the football field. A cinder track circled the field, and was a favorite of local joggers.

But not at 11 P.M., especially with no moon. The track was deserted, and that was fine with Mitch. The spring air was light and cool, and he finished the first mile in eight minutes. He began walking a lap. As he passed the aluminum bleachers on the home side, he saw someone from the corner of his eye. He kept walking.

'Pssssssst.'

Mitch stopped. 'Yeah. Who is it?'

A hoarse, scratchy voice replied, 'Joey Morolto.'

Mitch started for the bleachers. 'Very funny, Tarrance. Am I clean?'

'Sure, you're clean. Laney's sitting up there in a school bus with a flashlight. He flashed green when you passed, and if you see something red flash, get back to the track and make like Carl Lewis.'

They walked to the top of the bleachers and into the unlocked press box. They sat on stools in the dark and watched the school. The buses were parked in perfect order along the driveway.

'Is this private enough for you?' Mitch asked.

'It'll do. Who's the girl?'

'I know you prefer to meet in daylight, preferably where a crowd has gathered, say like a fast-food joint or a Korean shoe store. But I like these places better.'

'Great. Who's the girl?'

'Pretty clever, huh?'

'Good idea. Who is she?'

'An employee of mine.'

'Where'd you find her?'

'What difference does it make? Why are you always asking questions that are irrelevant?'

'Irrelevant? I get a call today from some woman I've never met, tells me she needs to talk to me about a little matter at the Bendini Building, says we gotta change phones, instructs me to go to a certain pay phone outside a certain grocery store and be there at a certain time, and she'll call exactly at one-thirty. And I go there, and she calls at exactly one-thirty. Keep in mind, I've got three men within a hundred feet of the phone watching everybody that moves. And she tells me to be here at exactly ten forty-five tonight, to have the place sealed off, and that you'll come trotting by.'

'Worked, didn't it?'

'Yeah, so far. But who is she? I mean, now you got

367

someone else involved, and that really worries me, McDeere. Who is she and how much does she know?'

'Trust me, Tarrance. She's my employee and she knows everything. In fact, if you knew what she knows you'd be serving indictments right now instead of sitting here bitching about her.'

Tarrance breathed deeply and thought about it. 'Okay, so tell me what she knows.'

'She knows that in the last three years the Morolto gang and its accomplices have taken over eight hundred million bucks in cash out of this country and deposited it in various banks in the Caribbean. She knows which banks, which accounts, the dates, a bunch of stuff. She knows that the Moroltos control at least three hundred and fifty companies chartered in the Caymans, and that these companies regularly send clean money back into the country. She knows the dates and amounts of the wire transfers. She knows of at least forty U.S. corporations owned by Cayman corporations owned by the Moroltos. She knows a helluva lot, Tarrance. She's a very knowledgeable woman, don't you think?'

Tarrance could not speak. He stared fiercely into the darkness up the driveway.

Mitch found it enjoyable. 'She knows how they take their dirty cash, trade it up to one-hundred-dollar-bills and sneak it out of the country.'

'How?'

'The firm Lear, of course. But they also mule it. They've got a small army of mules, usually their minimum wage thugs and their girlfriends, but also students and other free-lancers, and they'll give them ninety-eight hundred in cash and buy them a ticket to the Caymans or the Bahamas. No declarations are required for amounts under ten thousand, you understand. And the mules will fly down like regular tourists with pockets full of cash and take the money to their banks. Doesn't sound like much money, but you get three hundred people making twenty trips a year, and that's some serious cash walking out of the country. It's also called smurfing, you know.'

Tarrance nodded slightly, as if he knew.

'A lot of folks wanna be smurfers when they can get free vacations and spending money. Then they've got their super mules. These are the trusted Morolto people who take a million bucks in cash, wrap it up real neat in newspaper so the airport machines won't see it, put it in big briefcases and walk it onto the planes like everybody else. They wear coats and ties and look like Wall Streeters. Or they wear sandals and straw hats and mule it in carry-on bags. You guys catch them occasionally, about one percent of the time, I believe, and when that happens the super mules go to jail. But they never talk, do they, Tarrance? And every now and then a smurfer will start thinking about all this money in his briefcase and how easy it would be just to keep flying and enjoy all the money himself. And he'll disappear. But the Mob never forgets, and it may take a year or two, but they'll find him somewhere. The money'll be gone, of course, but then so will he. The Mob never forgets, does it, Tarrance? Just like they won't forget about me.'

Tarrance listened until it was obvious he needed to say something. 'You got your million bucks.'

'Appreciate it. I'm almost ready for the next installment.'

'Almost?'

'Yeah, me and the girl have a couple more jobs to pull. We're trying to get a few more records out of Front Street.'

'How many documents do you have?'

'Over ten thousand.'

The lower jaw collapsed and the mouth fell open.

He stared at Mitch. 'Damn! Where'd they come from?'

'Another one of your questions.'

'Ten thousand documents,' said Tarrance.

'At least ten thousand. Bank records, wire transfer records, corporate charters, corporate loan documents, internal memos, correspondence between all sorts of people. A lot of good stuff, Tarrance.'

'Your wife mentioned a company called Dunn Lane, Ltd. We've reviewed the files you've already given us. Pretty good material. What else do you know about it?'

'A lot. Chartered in 1986 with ten million, which was transferred into the corporation from a numbered account in Banco de México, the same ten million that arrived in Grand Cayman in cash on a certain Lear jet registered to a quiet little law firm in Memphis, except that it was originally fourteen million but after payoffs to Cayman customs and Cayman bankers it was reduced to ten million. When the company was chartered, the registered agent was a guy named Diego Sánchez, who happens to be a VP with Banco de México. The president was a delightful soul named Nathan Locke, the secretary was our old pal Royce McKnight and the treasurer of this cozy little corporation was a guy named Al Rubinstein. I'm sure you know him. I don't.'

'He's a Morolto operative.'

'Surprise, surprise. Want more?'

'Keep talking.'

'After the seed money of ten million was invested into this venture, another ninety million in cash was deposited over the next three years. Very profitable enterprise. The company began buying all sorts of things in the U.S. – cotton farms in Texas, apartment complexes in Dayton, jewelry stores in Beverly Hills, hotels in St. Petersburg and Tampa. Most of the transactions were by wire transfer from four or five different banks in the Caymans. It's a basic money laundering operation.'

'And you've got all this documented?'

'Stupid question, Wayne. If I didn't have the documents, how would I know about it? I only work on clean files, remember?'

'How much longer will it take you?'

'Couple of weeks. Me and my employee are still snooping around Front Street. And it doesn't look good. It'll be very difficult to get files out of there.'

'Where'd the ten thousand documents come from?'

Mitch ignored the question. He jumped to his feet and started for the door. 'Abby and I want to live in Albuquerque. It's a big town, sort of out of the way. Start working on it.'

'Don't jump the gun. There's a lot of work to do.'

'I said two weeks, Tarrance. I'll be ready to deliver in two weeks, and that means I'll have to disappear.'

'Not so fast. I need to see a few of these documents.'

'You have a short memory, Tarrance. My lovely wife promised a big stack of Dunn Lane documents just as soon as Ray goes over the wall.'

Tarrance looked across the dark field. 'I'll see what I can do.'

Mitch walked to him and pointed a finger in his face. 'Listen to me, Tarrance, and listen closely. I don't think we're getting through. Today is April 17. Two weeks from today is May 1, and on May the 1 I will deliver to you, as promised, over ten thousand very incriminating and highly admissible documents that will seriously cripple one of the largest organized crime families in the world. And, eventually, it will cost me my life. But I promised to do it. And you've promised to get my brother out of prison. You have a week, until April 24. If not, I'll disappear. And so will your case, and career.'

'What's he gonna do when he gets out?'

'You and your stupid questions. He'll run like hell, that's what he'll do. He's got a brother with a million dollars who's an expert in money laundering and electronic banking. He'll be out of the country within twelve hours, and he'll go find the million bucks.'

'The Bahamas.'

'Bahamas. You're an idiot, Tarrance. That money spent less than ten minutes in the Bahamas. You can't trust those corrupt fools down there.'

'Mr. Voyles doesn't like deadlines. He gets real upset.'

'Tell Mr. Voyles to kiss my ass. Tell him to get the next half million, because I'm almost ready. Tell him to get my brother out or the deal's off. Tell him whatever you want, Tarrance, but Ray goes over the wall in a week or I'm gone.'

Mitch slammed the door and started down the bleachers. Tarrance followed. 'When do we talk again?' he yelled.

Mitch jumped the fence and was on the track. 'My employee will call you. Just do as she says.'

THIRTY-ONE

Nathan Locke's annual three-day post-April 15 vacation in Vail had been canceled. By DeVasher, on order from Lazarov. Locke and Oliver Lambert sat in the office on the fifth floor and listened. DeVasher was reporting the bits and pieces and trying unsuccessfully to put the puzzle together.

'His wife leaves. Says she's gotta go home to her mother, who's got lung cancer. And that she's tired of a bunch of his crap. We've detected a little trouble here and there over the months. She bitched a little about his hours and all, but nothing this serious. So she goes home to Mommy. Says she don't know when she's coming back. Mommy's sick, right? Removed a lung, right? But we can't find a hospital that's heard of Maxine Sutherland. We've checked every hospital in Kentucky, Indiana and Tennessee. Seems odd, doesn't it, fellas?'

'Come on, DeVasher,' Lambert said. 'My wife had surgery four years ago, and we flew to the Mayo Clinic. I know of no law requiring one to have surgery within a hundred miles of home. That's absurd. And these are society people. Maybe she checked in under another name to keep it quiet. Happens all the time.'

Locke nodded and agreed. 'How much has he talked to her?'

'She calls about once a day. They've had some good

373

talks, about this and that. The dog. Her mom. The office. She told him last night she ain't coming back for at least two months.'

'Has she ever indicated which hospital?' asked Locke.

'Never. She's been real careful. Doesn't talk much about the surgery. Mommy is supposedly home now. If she ever left.'

'What're you getting at, DeVasher?' asked Lambert.

'Shut up and I'll finish. Just suppose it's all a ruse to get her outta town. To get her away from us. From what's coming down. Follow?'

'You're assuming he's working with them?' asked Locke.

'I get paid for making those assumptions, Nat. I'm assuming he knows the phones are bugged, and that's why they're so careful on the phone. I'm assuming he got her outta town to protect her.'

'Pretty shaky,' said Lambert. 'Pretty shaky.'

DeVasher paced behind his desk. He glared at Ollie and let it pass. 'About ten days ago, somebody makes a bunch of unusual copies on the fourth floor. Strange because it was three in the morning. According to our records, when the copies were made only two lawyers were here. McDeere and Scott Kimble. Neither of whom had any business on the fourth floor. Twenty-four access numbers were used. Three belong to Lamar Quin's files. Three belong to Sonny Capps. The other eighteen belong to McDeere's files. None belong to Kimble. Victor Milligan left his office around two-thirty, and McDeere was working in Avery's office. He had taken him to the airport. Avery says he locked his office, but he could have forgotten. Either he forgot or McDeere's got a key. I pressed Avery on this, and he feels almost certain he locked it. But it was midnight and he was dead tired and in a hurry. Could've forgotten, right? But he did not authorize McDeere to go back to his office and work. No big deal, really, because they had spent the entire day in there working on the Capps return. The copier was number eleven, which happens to be the closest one to Avery's office. I think it's safe to assume McDeere made the copies.'

'How many?'

'Two thousand and twelve.'

'Which files?'

'The eighteen were all tax clients. Now, I'm sure he'd explain it all by saying he had finished the returns and was merely copying everything. Sounds pretty legitimate, right? Except the secretaries always make the copies, and what the hell was he doing on the fourth floor at three A.M. running two thousand copies? And this was the morning of April 7. How many of your boys finish their April 15 work and run all the copies a week early?'

He stopped pacing and watched them. They were thinking. He had them. 'And here's the kicker. Five days later his secretary entered the same eighteen access numbers on her copier on the second floor. She ran about three hundred copies, which, I ain't no lawyer, but I figure to be more in line. Don't you think?'

They both nodded, but said nothing. They were lawyers, trained to argue five sides of every issue. But they said nothing. DeVasher smiled wickedly and returned to his pacing. 'Now, we caught him making two thousand copies that cannot be explained. So the big question is: What was he copying? If he was using wrong access numbers to run the machine, what the hell was he copying? I don't know. All of the offices were locked, except, of course, Avery's. So I asked Avery. He's got a row of metal cabinets where he keeps the real files. He keeps 'em locked, but he and McDeere and the secretaries have been rummaging

375

through those files all day. Could've forgot to lock 'em when he ran to meet the plane. Big deal. Why would McDeere copy legitimate files? He wouldn't. Like everybody else on the fourth floor, Avery's got those four wooden cabinets with the secret stuff. No one touches them, right? Firm rules. Not even other partners. Locked up tighter than my files. So McDeere can't get in without a key. Avery showed me his keys. Told me he hadn't touched those cabinets in two days, before the seventh. Avery has gone through those files, and everything seems in order. He can't tell if they've been tampered with. But can you look at one of your files and tell if it's been copied? No, you can't. Neither can I. So I pulled the files this morning, and I'm sending them to Chicago. They're gonna check 'em for fingerprints. Take about a week.'

'He couldn't copy those files,' Lambert said.

'What else would he copy, Ollie? I mean, everything's locked on the fourth floor and the third floor. Everything, except Avery's office. And assuming he and Tarrance are whispering in each other's ears, what would he want from Avery's office? Nothing but the secret files.'

'Now you're assuming he's got keys,' Locke said.

'Yes. I'm assuming he's made a set of Avery's keys.'

Ollie snorted and gave an exasperated laugh. 'This is incredible. I don't believe it.'

Black Eyes glared at DeVasher with a nasty smile. 'How would he get a copy of the keys?'

'Good question, and one that I can't answer. Avery showed me his keys. Two rings, eleven keys. He keeps 'em with him at all times. Firm rule, right? Like a good little lawyer's supposed to do. When he's awake, the keys are in his pocket. When he's asleep away from home, the keys are under the mattress.'

'Where's he traveled in the last month?' Black Eyes asked.

'Forget the trip to see Capps in Houston last week. Too recent. Before that, he went to Grand Cayman for two days on April 1.'

'I remember,' said Ollie, listening intently.

'Good for you, Ollie. I asked him what he did both nights, and he said nothing but work. Sat at a bar one night, but that's it. Swears he slept by himself both nights.' DeVasher pushed a button on a portable tape recorder. 'But he's lying. This call was made at nine fifteen, April 2, from the phone in the master bedroom of Unit A.' The tape began:

'He's in the shower.' First female voice.

'Are you okay?' Second female voice.

'Yeah. Fine. He couldn't do it if he had to.'

'What took so long?'

'He wouldn't wake up.'

'Is he suspicious?'

'No. He remembers nothing. I think he's in pain.'

'How long will you be there?'

'I'll kiss him goodbye when he gets out of the shower. Ten, maybe fifteen minutes.'

'Okay. Hurry.'

DeVasher punched another button and continued pacing. 'I have no idea who they are, and I haven't confronted Avery. Yet. He worries me. His wife has filed for divorce, and he's lost control. Chases women all the time. This is a pretty serious breach of security, and I suspect Lazarov will go through the roof.'

'She talked like it was a bad hangover,' Locke said.

'Evidently.'

'You think she copied the keys?' Ollie asked.

DeVasher shrugged and sat in his worn leather chair. The cockiness vanished. 'It's possible, but I doubt it. I've thought about it for hours. Assuming it was some woman he picked up in a bar, and they got drunk, then it was probably late when they went to bed. How would she make copies of the keys in the middle of the night on that tiny island? I just don't think so.'

'But she had an accomplice,' Locke insisted.

'Yeah, and I can't figure that out. Maybe they were trying to steal his wallet and something went wrong. He carries a couple of thousand in cash, and if he got drunk, who knows what he told them. Maybe she planned to lift the money at the last second and haul ass. She didn't do it. I don't know.'

'No more assumptions?' Ollie asked.

'Not now. I love to make them, but it goes too far to assume these women took the keys, somehow managed to copy them in the middle of the night on the island, without his knowledge, and then the first one crawled back in the bed with him. And that somehow all of this is related to McDeere and his use of the copier on the fourth floor. It's just too much.'

'I agree,' said Ollie.

'What about the storage room?' asked Black Eyes.

'I've thought about that, Nat. In fact, I've lost sleep thinking about it. If she was interested in the records in the storage room, there must be some connection with McDeere, or someone else poking around. And I can't make that connection. Let's say she found the room and the records, what could she do with them in the middle of the night with Avery asleep upstairs?'

'She could read them.'

'Yeah, there's only a million. Keep in mind, now, she must have been drinking along with Avery, or he would've been suspicious. So she's spent the night drinking and screwing. She waits until he goes to sleep, then suddenly she has this urge to go downstairs and read bank records. It don't work, boys.'

'She could work for the FBI,' Ollie said proudly.

'No, she couldn't.'

'Why?'

'It's simple, Ollie. The FBI wouldn't do it because

the search would be illegal and the records would be inadmissible. And there's a much better reason.'

'What?'

'If she was a Fibbie, she wouldn't have used the phone. No professional would've made that call. I think she was a pickpocket.'

The pickpocket theory was explained to Lazarov, who poked a hundred holes but could devise nothing better. He ordered changes in all the locks on the third and fourth floors, and the basement, and both condos on Grand Cayman. He ordered a search for all the locksmiths on the island – there couldn't be many, he said – to determine if any had reproduced keys the night of April 1 or the early morning of April 2. Bribe them, he told DeVasher. They'll talk for a little money. He ordered a fingerprint examination of the files from Avery's office. DeVasher proudly explained he had already started this. McDeere's prints were on file with the state bar association.

He also ordered a sixty-day suspension of Avery Tolleson. DeVasher suggested this might alert McDeere to something unusual. Fine, said DeVasher, tell Tolleson to check into the hospital with chest pains. Two months off – doctor's orders. Tell Tolleson to clean up his act. Lock up his office. Assign McDeere to Victor Milligan.

'You said you had a good plan to eliminate McDeere,' DeVasher said.

Lazarov grinned and picked his nose. 'Yeah. I think we'll use the plane. We'll send him down to the islands on a little business trip, and there will be this mysterious explosion.'

'Waste two pilots?' asked DeVasher.

'Yeah. It needs to look good.'

'Don't do it anywhere around the Caymans. That'll be too coincidental.'

'Okay, but it needs to happen over water. Less debris. We'll use a big device, so they won't find much.'

'That plane's expensive.'

'Yeah. I'll run it by Joey first.'

'You're the boss. Let me know if we can help down there.'

'Sure. Start thinking about it.'

'What about your man in Washington?' DeVasher asked.

'I'm waiting. I called New York this morning, and they're checking into it. We should know in a week.'

'That would make it easy.'

'Yeah. If the answer is yes, we need to eliminate him within twenty-four hours.'

'I'll start planning.'

The office was quiet for a Saturday morning. A handful of partners and a dozen associates loitered about in khakis and polos. There were no secretaries. Mitch checked his mail and dictated correspondence. After two hours he left. It was time to visit Ray.

For five hours, he drove east on Interstate 40. Drove like an idiot. He drove forty-five, then eighty-five. He darted into every rest stop and weigh station. He made sudden exits from the left lane. He stopped at an underpass and waited and watched. He never saw them. Not once did he notice a suspicious car or truck or van. He even watched a few eighteen-wheelers. Nothing. They simply were not back there. He would have caught them.

His care package of books and cigarettes was cleared through the guard station, and he was pointed to stall number nine. Minutes later, Ray sat through the thick screen.

'Where have you been?' he said with a hint of irritation. 'You're the only person in the entire world who visits me, and this is only the second time in four months.'

'I know. It's tax season, and I've been swamped. I'll do better. I've written, though.'

'Yeah, once a week I get two paragraphs. "Hi, Ray. How's the bunk? How's the food? How are the walls? How's the Greek or Italian? I'm fine. Abby's great. Dog's sick. Gotta run. I'll come visit soon. Love, Mitch." You write some rich letters, little brother. I really treasure them.'

'Yours aren't much better.'

'What have I got to say? The guards are selling dope. A friend got stabbed thirty-one times. I saw a kid get raped. Come on, Mitch, who wants to hear it?'

'I'll do better.'

'How's Mom?'

'I don't know. I haven't been back since Christmas.'

'I asked you to check on her, Mitch. I'm worried about her. If that goon is beating her, I want it stopped. If I could get out of here, I'd stop it myself.'

'You will.' It was a statement, not a question. Mitch placed a finger over his lips and nodded slowly. Ray leaned forward on his elbows and stared intently.

Mitch spoke softly. '*Español. Hable despacio.*' Spanish. Speak slowly.

Ray smiled slightly. '*¿Cuándo?*' When?

'*La semana próxima.*' Next week.

'*¿Qué día?*' What day?

Mitch thought for a second. '*Martes o miércoles.*' Tuesday or Wednesday.

'*¿Qué tiempo?*' What time?

Mitch smiled and shrugged, and looked around.

'How's Abby?' Ray asked.

'She's been in Kentucky for a couple of weeks. Her mother's sick.' He stared at Ray and softly mouthed the words 'Trust me.'

'What's wrong with her?'

'They removed a lung. Cancer. She's smoked heavy all her life. You should quit.'

'I will if I ever get out of here.'

Mitch smiled and nodded slowly. 'You've got at least seven more years.'

'Yeah, and escape is impossible. They try it occasionally, but they're either shot or captured.'

'James Earl Ray went over the wall, didn't he?' Mitch nodded slowly as he asked the question. Ray smiled and watched his brother's eyes.

'But they caught him. They bring in a bunch of mountain boys with bloodhounds, and it gets pretty nasty. I don't think anyone's ever survived the mountains after they got over the wall.'

'Let's talk about something else,' Mitch said.

'Good idea.'

Two guards stood by a window behind the row of visitors' booths. They were enjoying a stack of dirty pictures someone took with a Polaroid and tried to sneak through the guard station. They giggled among themselves and ignored the visitors. On the prisoners' side, a single guard with a stick walked benignly back and forth, half asleep.

'When can I expect little nieces and nephews?' Ray asked.

'Maybe in a few years. Abby wants one of each, and she would start now if I would. I'm not ready.'

The guard walked behind Ray, but did not look. They stared at each other, trying to read each other's eyes.

'¿Adónde voy?' Ray asked quickly. Where am I going?

'Perdido Beach Hilton. We went to the Cayman Islands last month, Abby and I. Had a beautiful vacation.'

'Never heard of the place. Where is it?'

'In the Caribbean, below Cuba.'

'*¿Que es mi nombre?*' What is my name?

'Lee Stevens. Did some snorkeling. The water is warm and gorgeous. The firm owns two condos right on Seven Mile Beach. All I paid for was the airfare. It was great.'

'Get me a book. I'd like to read about it. *¿Pasaporte?*'

Mitch nodded with a smile. The guard walked behind Ray and stopped. They talked of old times in Kentucky.

At dusk he parked the BMW on the dark side of a suburban mall in Nashville. He left the keys in the ignition and locked the door. He had a spare in his pocket. A busy crowd of Easter shoppers moved en masse through the Sears doors. He joined them. Inside he ducked into the men's clothing department and studied socks and underwear while watching the door. Nobody suspicious. He left Sears and walked quickly through the crowd down the mall. A black cotton sweater in the window of a men's store caught his attention. He found one inside, tried it on and decided to wear it out of there, he liked it so much. As the clerk laid his change on the counter, he scanned the yellow pages for the number of a cab. Back into the mall, he rode the escalator to the first floor, where he found a pay phone. The cab would be there in ten minutes.

It was dark now, the cool early dark of spring in the South. He watched the mall entrance from inside a singles bar. He was certain he had not been followed through the mall. He walked casually to the cab. 'Brentwood,' he said to the driver, and disappeared into the back seat.

Brentwood was twenty minutes away. 'Savannah Creek Apartments,' he said. The cab searched through the sprawling complex and found number 480E. He threw a twenty over the seat and slammed the door.

Behind an outside stairwell he found the door to 480E. It was locked.

'Who is it?' a nervous female voice asked from within. He heard the voice and felt weak.

'Barry Abanks,' he said.

Abby pulled the door open and attacked. They kissed violently as he lifted her, walked inside and slammed the door with his foot. His hands were wild. In less than two seconds, he pulled her sweater over her head, unsnapped her bra and slid the rather loose fitting skirt to her knees. They continued kissing. With one eye, he glanced apprehensively at the cheap, flimsy rented fold-a-bed that was waiting. Either that or the floor. He laid her gently on it and took off his clothes.

The bed was too short, and it squeaked. The mattress was two inches of foam rubber wrapped in a sheet. The metal braces underneath jutted upward and were dangerous.

But the McDeeres did not notice.

When it was good and dark, and the crowd of shoppers at the mall thinned for a moment, a shiny black Chevrolet Silverado pickup pulled behind the BMW and stopped. A small man with a neat haircut and sideburns jumped out, looked around and stuck a pointed screwdriver into the door lock of the BMW. Months later when he was sentenced, he would tell the judge that he had stolen over three hundred cars and pickups in eight states, and that he could break into a car and start the engine faster than the judge could with the keys. Said his average time was twenty-eight seconds. The judge was not impressed.

Occasionally, on a very lucky day, an idiot would leave the keys in the car, and the average time was reduced dramatically. A scout had found this car with the keys. He smiled and turned them. The Silverado raced away, followed by the BMW.

The Nordic jumped from the van and watched. It was too fast. He was too late. The pickup just pulled up, blocked his vision for an instant, then wham!, the BMW was gone. Stolen! Before his very eyes. He kicked the van. Now, how would he explain this?

He crawled back into the van and waited for McDeere.

After an hour on the couch, the pain of loneliness had been forgotten. They walked through the small apartment holding hands and kissing. In the bedroom, Mitch had his first viewing of what had become known among the three as the Bendini Papers. He had seen Tammy's notes and summaries, but not the actual documents. The room was like a chessboard with rows of neat stacks of papers. On two of the walls, Tammy had tacked sheets of white poster board, then covered them with the notes and lists and flowcharts.

One day soon he would spend hours in the room, studying the papers and preparing his case. But not tonight. In a few minutes, he would leave her and return to the mall.

She led him back to the couch.

THIRTY-TWO

The hall on the tenth floor, Madison Wing, of the Baptist Hospital was empty except for an orderly and a male nurse writing on his clipboard. Visiting hours had ended at nine, and it was ten-thirty. He eased down the hall, spoke to the orderly, was ignored by the nurse and knocked on the door.

'Come in,' a strong voice said.

He pushed the heavy door open and stood by the bed.

'Hello, Mitch,' Avery said. 'Can you believe this?'

'What happened?'

'I woke up at six this morning with stomach cramps, I thought. I took a shower and felt a sharp pain right here, on my shoulder. My breathing got heavy, and I started sweating. I thought no, not me. Hell, I'm forty-four, in great shape, work out all the time, eat pretty good, drink a little too much, maybe, but not me. I called my doctor, and he said to meet him here at the hospital. He thinks it was a slight heart attack. Nothing serious, he hopes, but they're running tests for the next few days.'

'A heart attack.'

'That's what he said.'

'I'm not surprised, Avery. It's a wonder any lawyer in that firm lives past fifty.'

'Capps did it to me, Mitch. Sonny Capps. This is

his heart attack. He called Friday and said he'd found a new tax firm in Washington. Wants all his records. That's my biggest client. I billed him almost four hundred thousand last year, about what he paid in taxes. He's not mad about the attorney's fees, but he's furious about the taxes. It doesn't make sense, Mitch.'

'He's not worth dying for.' Mitch looked for an IV, but did not see one. There were no tubes or wires. He sat in the only chair and laid his feet on the bed.

'Jean filed for divorce, you know.'

'I heard. That's no surprise, is it?'

'Surprised she didn't do it last year. I've offered her a small fortune as a settlement. I hope she takes it. I don't need a nasty divorce.'

Who does? thought Mitch. 'What did Lambert say?'

'It was kind of fun, really. In nineteen years I've never seen him lose his cool, but he lost it. He told me I was drinking too much, chasing women and who knows what else. Said I had embarrassed the firm. Suggested I see a psychiatrist.'

Avery spoke slowly, deliberately, and at times with a raspy, weak voice. It seemed phony. A sentence later he would forget about it and return to his normal voice. He lay perfectly still like a corpse, with the sheets tucked neatly around him. His color was good.

'I think you need a psychiatrist. Maybe two.'

'Thanks. I need a month in the sun. Doc said he would discharge me in three or four days, and that I couldn't work for two months. Sixty days, Mitch. Said I cannot, under any circumstances, go near the office for sixty days.'

'What a blessing. I think I'll have a slight heart attack.'

'At your pace, it's guaranteed.'

'What are you, a doctor now?'

'No. Just scared. You get a scare like this, and you start thinking about things. Today is the first time in my life I've ever thought about dying. And if you don't think about death, you don't appreciate life.'

'This is getting pretty heavy.'

'Yeah, I know. How's Abby?'

'Okay. I guess. I haven't seen her in a while.'

'You'd better go see her and bring her home. And get her happy. Sixty hours a week is plenty, Mitch. You'll ruin your marriage and kill yourself if you work more. She wants babies, then get them. I wish I had done things differently.'

'Damn, Avery. When's the funeral? You're forty-four, and you had a slight heart attack. You're not exactly a vegetable.'

The male nurse glided in and glared at Mitch. 'Visiting hours are over, sir. You need to leave.'

Mitch jumped to his feet. 'Yeah, sure.' He slapped Avery's feet and walked out. 'See you in a couple of days.'

'Thanks for coming. Tell Abby I said hello.'

The elevator was empty. Mitch pushed the button to the sixteenth floor and seconds later got off. He ran two flights of stairs to the eighteenth, caught his breath and opened the door. Down the hall, away from the elevators, Rick Acklin watched and whispered into a dead telephone receiver. He nodded at Mitch, who walked toward him. Acklin pointed, and Mitch stepped into a small area used as a waiting room by worried relatives. It was dark and empty, with two rows of folding chairs and a television that did not work. A Coke machine provided the only light. Tarrance sat next to it and flipped through an old magazine. He wore a sweat suit, headband, navy socks and white canvas sneakers. Tarrance the jogger.

Mitch sat next to him, facing the hall.

'You're clean. They followed you from the office to the parking lot, then left. Acklin's in the hall. Laney's around somewhere. Relax.'

'I like the headband.'

'Thanks.'

'I see you got the message.'

'Obviously. Real clever, McDeere. I'm sitting at my desk this afternoon, minding my own business, trying to work on something other than the Bendini case. I've got others, you know. And my secretary comes in and says there's a woman on the phone who wants to talk about a man named Marty Kozinski. I jump from my chair, grab the phone, and of course it's your girl. She says it's urgent, as always. So I say okay, let's talk. No, she don't play it. She makes me drop everything I'm doing, run over to the Peabody, go to the lounge – what's the name of it? Mallards – and have a seat. So I'm sitting there, thinking about how stupid this is because our phones are clean. Dammit, Mitch, I know our phones are clean. We can talk on our phones! I'm drinking coffee and the bartender walks over and asks if my name is Kozinski. Kozinski who? I ask. Just for fun. Since we're having a ball, right? Marty Kozinski, he says with a puzzled look on his face. I say yeah, that's me. I felt stupid, Mitch. And he says I have a call. I walk over to the bar, and it's your girl. Tolleson's had a heart attack or something. And you'll be here around eleven. Real clever.'

'Worked, didn't it?'

'Yeah, and it would work just as easily if she would talk to me on my phone in my office.'

'I like it better my way. It's safer. Besides, it gets you out of the office.'

'Damned right, it does. Me and three others.'

'Look, Tarrance, we'll do it my way, okay? It's my neck on the line, not yours.'

'Yeah, yeah. What the hell are you driving?'

'A rented Celebrity. Nice, huh?'

'What happened to the little black lawyer's car?'

'It had an insect problem. Full of bugs. I parked it at

a mall Saturday night in Nashville and left the keys in it. Someone borrowed it. I love to sing, but I have a terrible voice. Ever since I could drive I've done my singing in the car, alone. But with the bugs and all, I was too embarrassed to sing. I just got tired of it.'

Tarrance could not resist a smile. 'That's pretty good, McDeere. Pretty good.'

'You should've seen Oliver Lambert this morning when I walked in and laid the police report on his desk. He stuttered and stammered and told me how sorry he was. I acted like I was real sad. Insurance will cover it, so old Oliver says they'll get me another one. Then he says they'll go get me a rental car for the meantime. I told him I already had one. Got it in Nashville Saturday night. He didn't like this, because he knew it was insect free. He calls the BMW dealer himself, while I'm standing there, to check on a new one for me. He asked me what color I wanted. I said I was tired of black and wanted a burgundy one with tan interior. I drove to the BMW place yesterday and looked around. I didn't see a burgundy of any model. He told the guy on the phone what I wanted, and then he tells him they don't have it. How about black, or navy, or gray, or red, or white? No, no, no, I want a burgundy one. They'll have to order it, he reports. Fine, I said. He hung up the phone and asked me if I was sure I couldn't use another color. Burgundy, I said. He wanted to argue, but realized it would seem foolish. So, for the first time in ten months, I can sing in my car.'

'But a Celebrity. For a hotshot tax lawyer. That's got to hurt.'

'I can deal with it.'

Tarrance was still smiling, obviously impressed. 'I wonder what the boys in the chop shop will do when they strip it down and find all those bugs.'

'Probably sell it to a pawnshop as stereo equipment. How much was it worth?'

'Our boys said it was the best. Ten, fifteen thousand. I don't know. That's funny.'

Two nurses walked by talking loudly. They turned a corner, and the hall was quiet. Acklin pretended to place another phone call.

'How's Tolleson?' Tarrance asked.

'Superb. I hope my heart attack is as easy as his. He'll be here for a few days, then off for two months. Nothing serious.'

'Can you get in his office?'

'Why should I? I've already copied everything in it.'

Tarrance leaned closer and waited for more.

'No, I cannot get in his office. They've changed the locks on the third and fourth floors. And the basement.'

'How do you know this?'

'The girl, Tarrance. In the last week, she's been in every office in the building, including the basement. She's checked every door, pulled on every drawer, looked in every closet. She's read mail, looked at files and rummaged through the garbage. There's not much garbage, really. The building has ten paper shredders in it. Four in the basement. Did you know that?'

Tarrance listened intently and did not move a muscle. 'How did she –'

'Don't ask, Tarrance, because I won't tell you.'

'She works there! She's a secretary or something. She's helping you from the inside.'

Mitch shook his head in frustration. 'Brilliant, Tarrance. She called you twice today. Once at about two-fifteen and then about an hour later. Now, how would a secretary make two calls to the FBI an hour apart?'

'Maybe she didn't work today. Maybe she called from home.'

'You're wrong, Tarrance, and quit guessing. Don't waste time worrying about her. She works for me, and together we'll deliver the goods to you.'

'What's in the basement?'

'One big room with twelve cubicles, twelve busy desks and a thousand file cabinets. Electronically wired file cabinets. I think it's the operations center for their money-laundering activities. On the walls of the cubicles, she noticed names and phone numbers of dozens of banks in the Caribbean. There's not much information lying around down there. They're very careful. There's a smaller room off to the side, heavily locked, and full of computers larger than refrigerators.'

'Sounds like the place.'

'It is, but forget it. There's no way to get the stuff out without alerting them. Impossible. I know of only one way to bring the goods out.'

'Okay.'

'A search warrant.'

'Forget it. No probable cause.'

'Listen to me, Tarrance. This is how it's gonna be, okay. I can't give you all the documents you want. But I can give you all you need. I have in my possession over ten thousand documents, and although I have not reviewed all of them, I've seen enough to know that if you had them, you could show them to a judge and get a search warrant for Front Street. You can take the records I have now and obtain indictments for maybe half the firm. But the same documents will get your search warrant and, consequently, a truckload of indictments. There's no other way to do it.'

Tarrance walked to the hall and looked around. Empty. He stretched his legs and walked to the Coke machine. He leaned on it and looked through the small window to the east. 'Why only half the firm?'

'Initially, only half. Plus a number of retired partners. Scattered through my documents are various names of partners who've set up the bogus Cayman companies with Morolto money. Those indictments will be easy. Once you have all the records, your conspiracy theory will fall in place and you can indict everyone.'

'Where did you get the documents?'

'I got lucky. Very lucky. I sort of figured the firm had more sense than to keep the Cayman bank records in this country. I had a hunch the records might be in the Caymans. Fortunately, I was right. We copied the documents in the Caymans.'

'We?'

'The girl. And a friend.'

'Where are the records now?'

'You and your questions, Tarrance. They're in my possession. That's all you need to know.'

'I want those documents from the basement.'

'Listen to me, Tarrance. Pay attention. The documents in the basement are not coming out until you go in with a search warrant. It is impossible, do you hear?'

'Who are the guys in the basement?'

'Don't know. I've been there ten months and never seen them. I don't know where they park or how they get in and out. They're invisible. I figure the partners and the boys in the basement do the dirty work.'

'What kind of equipment is down there?'

'Two copiers, four shredders, high-speed printers and all those computers. State of the art.'

Tarrance walked to the window, obviously deep in thought. 'That makes sense. Makes a lot of sense. I've always wondered how the firm, with all those secretaries and clerks and paralegals, could maintain such secrecy about Morolto.'

'It's easy. The secretaries and clerks and paralegals know nothing about it. They're kept busy with the real clients. The partners and senior associates sit in their big offices and dream up exotic ways to launder money, and the basement crew does the grunt work. It's a great setup.'

'So there are plenty of legitimate clients?'

'Hundreds. They're talented lawyers with an amazing clientele. It's a great cover.'

'And you're telling me, McDeere, that you've got the documents now to support indictments and search warrants? You've got them – they're in your possession?'

'That's what I said.'

'In this country?'

'Yes, Tarrance, the documents are in this country. Very close to here, actually.'

Tarrance was fidgety now. He rocked from one foot to the other and cracked his knuckles. He was breathing quickly. 'What else can you get out of Front Street?'

'Nothing. It's too dangerous. They've changed the locks, and that sort of worries me. I mean, why would they change the locks on the third and fourth floors and not on the first and second? I made some copies on the fourth floor two weeks ago, and I don't think it was a good idea. I'm getting bad vibes. No more records from Front Street.'

'What about the girl?'

'She no longer has access.'

Tarrance chewed his fingernails, rocking back and forth. Still staring at the window. 'I want the records, McDeere, and I want them real soon. Like tomorrow.'

'When does Ray get his walking papers?'

'Today's Monday. I think it's set up for tomorrow night. You wouldn't believe the cussing I've taken from Voyles. He's had to pull every string in the book. You think I'm kidding? He called in both senators from Tennessee, and they personally flew to Nashville to visit the governor. Oh, I've been cussed, McDeere. All because of your brother.'

'He appreciates it.'

'What's he gonna do when he gets out?'

'I'll take care of that. You just get him out.'

'No guarantees. If he gets hurt, it ain't our fault.'

Mitch stood and looked at his watch. 'Gotta run. I'm sure someone's out there waiting for me.'

'When do we meet again?'

'She'll call. Just do as she says.'

'Oh, come on, Mitch! Not that routine again. She can talk to me on my phone. I swear! We keep our lines clean. Please, not that again.'

'What's your mother's name, Tarrance?'

'What? Doris.'

'Doris?'

'Yeah, Doris.'

'Small world. We can't use Doris. Whom did you take to your senior prom?'

'Uh, I don't think I went.'

'I'm not surprised. Who was your first date, if you had one?'

'Mary Alice Brenner. She was hot too. She wanted me.'

'I'm sure. My girl's name is Mary Alice. The next time Mary Alice calls, you do exactly as she says, okay?'

'I can't wait.'

'Do me a favor, Tarrance. I think Tolleson's faking, and I've got a weird feeling his fake heart attack is somehow related to me. Get your boys to snoop around here and check out his alleged heart attack.'

'Sure. We have little else to do.'

THIRTY-THREE

Tuesday morning the office buzzed with concern for
Avery Tolleson. He was doing fine. Running tests. No
permanent damage. Overworked. Stressed out. Capps
did it. Divorce did it. Leave of absence.

Nina brought a stack of letters to be signed. 'Mr.
Lambert would like to see you, if you're not too busy.
He just called.'

'Fine. I'm supposed to meet Frank Mulholland at
ten. Do you know that?'

'Of course I know that. I'm the secretary. I know
everything. Your office or his?'

Mitch looked at his appointment book and pretended to search. Mulholland's office. In the Cotton
Exchange Building.

'His,' he said with a frown.

'You met there last time, didn't you? Didn't they
teach you about turf in law school? Never, I repeat,
never meet two times in a row on the adversary's turf.
It's unprofessional. It's uncool. Shows weakness.'

'How can you ever forgive me?'

'Wait till I tell the other girls. They all think you're
so cute and macho. When I tell them you're a wimp,
they'll be shocked.'

'They need to be shocked, with a cattle prod.'

'How's Abby's mother?'

'Much better. I'm going up this weekend.'

She picked up two files. 'Lambert's waiting.'

Oliver Lambert pointed at the stiff sofa and offered coffee. He sat perfectly erect in a wing chair and held his cup like a British aristocrat. 'I'm worried about Avery,' he said.

'I saw him last night,' Mitch said. 'Doctor's forcing a two-month retirement.'

'Yes, that's why you're here. I want you to work with Victor Milligan for the next two months. He'll get most of Avery's files, so it's familiar territory.'

'That's fine. Victor and I are good friends.'

'You'll learn a lot from him. A genius at taxation. Reads two books a day.'

Great, thought Mitch. He should average ten a day in prison. 'Yes, he's a very smart man. He's helped me out of a jam or two.'

'Good. I think you'll get along fine. Try and see him sometime this morning. Now, Avery had some unfinished business in the Caymans. He goes there a lot, as you know, to meet with certain bankers. In fact, he was scheduled to leave tomorrow for a couple of days. He told me this morning you're familiar with the clients and the accounts, so we need you to go.'

The Lear, the loot, the condo, the storage room, the accounts. A thousand thoughts flashed in his mind. It did not add up. 'The Caymans? Tomorrow?'

'Yes, it's quite urgent. Three of his clients are in dire need of summaries of their accounts and other legal work. I wanted Milligan to go, but he's due in Denver in the morning. Avery said you could handle it.'

'Sure I can handle it.'

'Fine. The Lear will take you. You'll leave around noon and return by commercial flight late Friday. Any problems?'

Yes, many problems. Ray was leaving prison. Tarrance was demanding the contraband. A half million bucks had to be collected. And he was scheduled to disappear anytime.

'No problems.'

He walked to his office and locked the door. He kicked off his shoes, lay on the floor and closed his eyes.

The elevator stopped on the seventh floor, and Mitch bolted up the stairs to the ninth. Tammy opened the door and locked it behind him. He walked to the window.

'Were you watching?' he asked.

'Of course. The guard by your parking lot stood on the sidewalk and watched you walk here.'

'Wonderful. Even Dutch follows me.'

He turned and inspected her. 'You look tired.'

'Tired? I'm dead. In the past three weeks I've been a janitor, a secretary, a lawyer, a banker, a whore, a courier and a private investigator. I've flown to Grand Cayman nine times, bought nine sets of new luggage and hauled back a ton of stolen documents. I've driven to Nashville four times and flown ten. I've read so many bank records and legal crap I'm half blind. And when it's bedtime, I put on my little Dustbusters shirt and play maid for six hours. I've got so many names, I've written them on my hand so I won't get confused.'

'I've got another for you.'

'This doesn't surprise me. What?'

'Mary Alice. From now on, when you talk to Tarrance, you're Mary Alice.'

'Let me write that down. I don't like him. He's very rude on the phone.'

'I've got great news for you.'

'I can't wait.'

'You can quit Dustbusters.'

'I think I'll lie down and cry. Why?'

'It's hopeless.'

'I told you that a week ago. Houdini couldn't get files out of there, copy them and sneak them back in without getting caught.'

'Did you talk to Abanks?' Mitch asked.

'Yes.'

'Did he get the money?'

'Yes. It was wired Friday.'

'Is he ready?'

'Said he was.'

'Good. What about the forger?'

'I'm meeting with him this afternoon.'

'Who is he?'

'An ex-con. He and Lomax were old pals. Eddie said he was the best documents man in the country.'

'He'd better be. How much?'

'Five thousand. Cash, of course. New IDs, passports, driver's licenses and visas.'

'How long will it take him?'

'I don't know. When do you need it?'

Mitch sat on the edge of the rented desk. He breathed deeply and tried to think. To calculate. 'As soon as possible. I thought I had a week but now I don't know. Just get it as soon as possible. Can you drive to Nashville tonight?'

'Oh yes. I'd love to. I haven't been there in two days.'

'I want a Sony camcorder with a tripod set up in the bedroom. Buy a case of tapes. And I want you to stay there, by the phone, for the next few days. Review the Bendini Papers again. Work on your summaries.'

'You mean I have to stay there?'

'Yeah. Why?'

'I've ruptured two disks sleeping on that couch.'

'You rented it.'

'What about the passports?'

'What's the guy's name?'

'Doc somebody. I've got his number.'

'Give it to me. Tell him I'll call in a day or so. How much money do you have?'

'I'm glad you asked. I started with fifty thousand, right? I've spent ten thousand on airfare, hotels, luggage and rental cars. And I'm still spending. Now you want a video camera. And fake IDs. I'd hate to lose money on this deal.'

Mitch started for the door. 'How about another fifty thousand?'

'I'll take it.'

He winked at her and closed the door, wondering if he would ever see her again.

The cell was eight by eight, with a toilet in a corner and a set of bunk beds. The top bunk was uninhabited and had been for a year. Ray lay on the bottom bunk with wires running from his ears. He spoke to himself in a very foreign language. Turkish. At that moment on that floor, it was safe to bet he was the only soul listening to Berlitz jabber in Turkish. There was quiet talk up and down the hall, but most lights were out. Eleven o'clock, Tuesday night.

The guard walked silently to his cell. 'McDeere,' he said softly, secretly, through the bars. Ray sat on the edge of the bed, under the bunk above, and stared at him. He removed the wires.

'Warden wants to see you.'

Sure, he thought, the warden's sitting at his desk at 11 P.M. waiting on me. 'Where are we going?' It was an anxious question.

'Put your shoes on and come on.'

Ray glanced around the cell and took a quick inventory of his worldly possessions. In eight years he had accumulated a black-and-white television, a large cassette player, two cardboard boxes full of tapes and several dozen books. He made three dollars a day working in the prison laundry, but after cigarettes there had been little to spend on tangibles. These were his only assets. Eight years.

The guard fitted a heavy key in the door and slid it open a few inches. He turned off the light. 'Just follow me, and no cute stuff. I don't know who you are, mister, but you got some heavy-duty friends.'

Other keys fit other doors, and they were outside under the basketball hoop. 'Stay behind me,' the guard said.

Ray's eyes darted around the dark compound. The wall loomed like a mountain in the distance, beyond the courtyard and walking area where he had paced a thousand miles and smoked a ton of cigarettes. It was sixteen feet tall in the daylight, but looked much larger at night. The guard towers were fifty yards apart and well lit. And heavily armed.

The guard was casual and unconcerned. Of course, he had a uniform and a gun. He moved confidently between two cinder block buildings, telling Ray to follow and be cool. Ray tried to be cool. They stopped at the corner of a building, and the guard gazed at the wall, eighty feet away. Floodlights made a routine sweep of the courtyard, and they backed into the darkness.

Why are we hiding? Ray asked himself. Are those guys up there with the guns on our side? He would like to know before he made any dramatic moves.

The guard pointed to the exact spot on the wall where James Earl Ray and his gang went over. A rather famous spot, studied and admired by most of the inmates at Brushy Mountain. Most of the white ones anyway. 'In about fifteen minutes, they'll throw a ladder up there. The wire has already been cut on top. You'll find a heavy rope on the other side.'

'Mind if I ask a few questions?'

'Make it quick.'

401

'What about all these lights?'

'They'll be diverted. You'll have total darkness.'

'And those guns up there?'

'Don't worry. They'll look the other way.'

'Dammit! Are you sure?'

'Look, man, I've seen some inside jobs before, but this takes the cake. Warden Lattemer himself planned this one. He's right up there.' The guard pointed to the nearest tower.

'The warden?'

'Yep. Just so nothing'll go wrong.'

'Who's throwing up the ladder?'

'Coupla guards.'

Ray wiped his forehead with his sleeve and breathed deeply. His mouth was dry and his knees were weak.

The guard whispered, 'There'll be a dude waiting for you. His name is Bud. White dude. He'll find you on the other side, and just do what he says.'

The floodlights swept through again, then died. 'Get ready,' the guard said. Darkness settled in, followed by a dreadful silence. The wall was now black. From the nearest tower, a whistle blew two short signals. Ray knelt and watched.

From behind the next building, he could see the silhouettes running to the wall. They grabbed at something in the grass, then hoisted it.

'Run, dude,' the guard said. 'Run!'

Ray sprinted with his head low. The homemade ladder was in place. The guards grabbed his arms and threw him to the first step. The ladder bounced as he scurried up the two-by-fours. The top of the wall was two feet wide. A generous opening had been cut in the coiled barbed wire. He slid through without touching it. The rope was right where it was supposed to be, and he eased down the outside of the wall. Eight feet from pay dirt, he turned loose and jumped. He

squatted and looked around. Still dark. The floodlights were on hold.

The clearing stopped a hundred feet away, and the
dense woods began. 'Over here,' the voice said calmly.
Ray started for it. Bud was waiting in the first cluster
of black bushes.

'Hurry. Follow me.'

Ray followed him until the wall was out of sight.
They stopped in a small clearing next to a dirt trail. He
stuck out a hand. 'I'm Bud Riley. Kinda fun, ain't it?'

'Unbelievable. Ray McDeere.'

Bud was a stocky man with a black beard and a
black beret. He wore combat boots, jeans and a
camouflage jacket. No gun was in sight. He offered
Ray a cigarette.

'Who are you with?' Ray asked.

'Nobody. I just do a little free-lance work for the
warden. They usually call me when somebody goes
over the wall. Course, this is a little different. Usually I
bring my dogs. I thought we'd wait here for a minute
until the sirens go off, so you can hear. Wouldn't be
right if you didn't get to hear 'em. I mean, they're
sorta in your honor.'

'That's okay. I've heard them before.'

'Yeah, but it's different out here when they go off.
It's a beautiful sound.'

'Look, Bud, I –'

'Just listen, Ray. We got plenty of time. They won't
chase you, much.'

'Much?'

'Yeah, they gotta make a big scene, wake ever'body
up, just like a real escape. But they ain't coming after
you. I don't know what kinda pull you got, but it's
something.'

The sirens began screaming, and Ray jumped.
Lights flashed across the black sky, and the faint voices
of the tower guards were audible.

'See what I mean?'

'Let's go,' Ray said, and began walking.

'My truck's just up the road a piece. I brought you some clothes. Warden gave me your sizes. Hope you like them.'

Bud was out of breath when they reached the truck. Ray quickly changed into the olive Duckheads and navy cotton work shirt. 'Very nice, Bud,' he said.

'Just throw them prison clothes in the bushes.'

They drove the winding mountain trail for two miles, then turned onto blacktop. Bud listened to Conway Twitty and said nothing.

'Where are we going, Bud?' Ray finally asked.

'Well, the warden said he didn't care and really didn't want to know. Said it was up to you. I'd suggest we get to a big town where there's a bus station. After that, you're on your own.'

'How far will you drive me?'

'I got all night, Ray. You name the town.'

'I'd like to get some miles behind us before I start hanging around a bus station. How about Knoxville?'

'Knoxville it is. Where are you going from there?'

'I don't know. I need to get out of the country.'

'With your friends, that should be no problem. Be careful, though. By tomorrow, your picture will be hanging in every sheriff's office in ten states.'

Three cars with blue lights came blazing over the hill in front of them. Ray ducked onto the floorboard.

'Relax, Ray. They can't see you.'

He watched them disappear through the rear window. 'What about roadblocks?'

'Look, Ray. Ain't gonna be no roadblocks, okay? Trust me.' Bud stuck a hand in a pocket and threw a wad of cash on the seat. 'Five hundred bucks. Hand-delivered by the warden. You got some stout friends, buddy.'

THIRTY-FOUR

Wednesday morning. Tarry Ross climbed the stairs to the fourth floor of the Phoenix Inn. He paused on the landing outside the hall door and caught his breath. Sweat beaded across his eyebrows. He removed the dark sunglasses and wiped his face with the sleeve of his overcoat. Nausea hit below the belt, and he leaned on the stair rail. He dropped his empty briefcase on the concrete and sat on the bottom step. His hands shook like severe palsy, and he wanted to cry. He clutched his stomach and tried not to vomit.

The nausea passed, and he breathed again. Be brave, man, be brave. There's two hundred thousand waiting down the hall. If you got guts, you can go in there and get it. You can walk out with it, but you must have courage. He breathed deeper, and his hands settled down. Guts, man, guts.

The weak knees wobbled, but he made it to the door. Down the hall, past the rooms. Eighth door on the right. He held his breath, and knocked.

Seconds passed. He watched the dark hall through the dark glasses and could see nothing. 'Yeah,' a voice inside said, inches away.

'It's Alfred.' Ridiculous name, he thought. Where'd it come from?

The door cracked, and a face appeared behind the

little chain. The door closed, then opened wide. Alfred walked in.

'Good morning, Alfred,' Vinnie Cozzo said warmly. 'Would you like coffee?'

'I didn't come here for coffee,' Alfred snapped. He placed the briefcase on the bed and stared at Cozzo.

'You're always so nervous, Alfred. Why don't you relax. There's no way you can get caught.'

'Shut up, Cozzo. Where's the money?'

Vinnie pointed to a leather handbag. He stopped smiling. 'Talk to me, Alfred.'

The nausea hit again, but he kept his feet. He stared at them. His heart beat like pistons. 'Okay, your man, McDeere, has been paid a million bucks already. Another million is on the way. He's delivered one load of Bendini documents and claims to have ten thousand more.' A sharp pain hit his groin, and he sat on the edge of the bed. He removed his glasses.

'Keep talking,' Cozzo demanded.

'McDeere's talked to our people many times in the last six months. He'll testify at the trials, then hit the road as a protected witness. He and his wife.'

'Where are the other documents?'

'Dammit, I don't know. He won't tell. But they're ready to be delivered. I want my money, Cozzo.'

Vinnie threw the handbag on the bed. Alfred opened it and the briefcase. He attacked the stacks of bills, his hands shaking violently.

'Two hundred thousand?' he asked desperately.

Vinnie smiled. 'That was the deal, Alfred. I got another job for you in a couple of weeks.'

'No way, Cozzo. I can't take any more of this.' He slammed the briefcase shut and ran to the door. He stopped and tried to calm himself. 'What will you do with McDeere?' he asked, staring at the door.

'What do you think, Alfred?'

He bit his lip, clenched the briefcase and walked

from the room. Vinnie smiled and locked the door. He pulled a card from his pocket and placed a call to the Chicago home of Mr. Lou Lazarov.

Tarry Ross walked in panic down the hall. He could see little from behind the glasses. Seven doors down, almost to the elevator, a huge hand reached from the darkness and pulled him into a room. The hand slapped him hard, and another fist landed in his stomach. Another fist to the nose. He was on the floor, dazed and bleeding. The briefcase was emptied on the bed.

He was thrown into a chair, and the lights came on. Three FBI agents, his comrades, glared at him. Director Voyles walked up to him, shaking his head in disbelief. The agent with the huge, efficient hands stood nearby, within striking distance. Another agent was counting money.

Voyles leaned into his face. 'You're a traitor, Ross. The lowest form of scum. I can't believe it.'

Ross bit his lip and began sobbing.

'Who is it?' Voyles asked intently.

The crying was louder. No answer.

Voyles swung wildly and slapped Ross's left temple. He shrieked in pain. 'Who is it, Ross? Talk to me.'

'Vinnie Cozzo,' he blurted between sobs.

'I know it's Cozzo! Dammit! I know that! But what did you tell him?'

Tears ran from his eyes and blood poured from his nose. His body shook and gyrated pitifully. No answer.

Voyles slapped him again, and again. 'Tell me, you little son of a bitch. Tell me what Cozzo wants.' He slapped him again.

Ross doubled over and dropped his head on his knees. The crying softened.

'Two hundred thousand dollars,' an agent said.

Voyles dropped to one knee and almost whispered

to Ross. 'Is it McDeere, Ross? Please, oh please, tell me it's not McDeere. Tell me, Tarry, tell me it's not McDeere.'

Tarry stuck his elbows on his knees and stared at the floor. The blood dripped neatly into one little puddle on the carpet. Gut check, Tarry. You don't get to keep your money. You're on the way to jail. You're a disgrace, Tarry. You're a slimy little scuzzball of a chicken, and it's over. What could possibly be gained by keeping secrets? Gut check, Tarry.

Voyles was pleading softly. Sinners, won't you come? 'Please say it ain't McDeere, Tarry, please tell me it ain't.'

Tarry sat straight and wiped his eyes with his fingers. He breathed deeply. Cleared his throat. He bit his lip, looked squarely at Voyles and nodded.

DeVasher had no time for the elevator. He ran down the stairs to the fourth floor, to the corner, a power one, and barged into Locke's office. Half the partners were there. Locke, Lambert, Milligan, McKnight, Dunbar, Denton, Lawson, Banahan, Kruger, Welch and Shottz. The other half had been summoned.

A quiet panic filled the room. DeVasher sat at the head of the conference table, and they gathered around.

'Okay, boys. It's not time to haul ass and head for Brazil. Not yet, anyway. We confirmed this morning that he has talked extensively to the Fibbies, that they have paid him a million cash, that they have promised another million, that he has certain documents that are believed to be fatal. This came straight from the FBI. Lazarov and a small army are flying into Memphis as we speak. It appears as though the damage has not been done. Yet. According to our source – a very high ranking Fibbie – McDeere has over ten thousand documents in his possession, and he is ready to deliver. But he has only delivered a few so far. We think. Evidently, we have caught this thing in time. If we can prevent further damage, we should be okay. I say this, even though they have some documents. Obviously, they don't have much or they would've been here with search warrants.'

DeVasher was onstage. He enjoyed this immensely. He spoke with a patronizing smile and looked at each of the worried faces. 'Now, where is McDeere?'

Milligan spoke. 'In his office. I just talked to him. He suspects nothing.'

'Wonderful. He's scheduled to leave in three hours for Grand Cayman. Correct, Lambert?'

'That's correct. Around noon.'

'Boys, the plane will never make it. The pilot will land in New Orleans for an errand, then he'll take off for the island. About thirty minutes over the Gulf, the little blip will disappear from radar, forever. Debris will scatter over a thirty-square-mile area, and no bodies will ever be found. It's sad, but necessary.'

'The Lear?' asked Denton.

'Yes, son, the Lear. We'll buy you another toy.'

'We're assuming a lot, DeVasher,' Locke said. 'We're assuming the documents already in their possession are harmless. Four days ago you thought McDeere had copied some of Avery's secret files. What gives?'

'They studied the files in Chicago. Yeah, they're full of incriminating evidence, but not enough to move with. They couldn't get the first conviction. You guys know the damning materials are on the island. And, of course, in the basement. No one can penetrate the basement. We checked the files in the condo. Everything looked in order.'

Locke was not satisfied. 'Then where did the ten thousand come from?'

'You're assuming he has ten thousand. I rather

doubt it. Keep in mind, he's trying to collect another one million bucks before he takes off. He's probably lying to them and snooping around for more documents. If he had ten thousand, why wouldn't the Fibbies have them by now?'

'Then what's to fear?' asked Lambert.

'The fear is the unknown, Ollie. We don't know what he's got, except that he's got a million bucks. He's no dummy, and he just might stumble across something if left alone. We cannot allow that to happen. Lazarov, you see, said to blow his ass outta the air. Quote unquote.'

'There's no way a rookie associate could find and copy that many incriminating records,' Kruger said boldly, and looked around the group for approval. Several nodded at him with intense frowns.

'Why is Lazarov coming?' asked Dunbar, the real estate man. He said 'Lazarov' as if Charles Manson was coming to dinner.

'That's a stupid question,' DeVasher snapped, and looked around for the idiot. 'First, we've got to take care of McDeere and hope the damage is minimal. Then we'll take a long look at this unit and make whatever changes are necessary.'

Locke stood and glared at Oliver Lambert. 'Make sure McDeere's on that plane.'

Tarrance, Acklin and Laney sat in stunned silence and listened to the speaker phone on the desk. It was Voyles in Washington, explaining exactly what had happened. He would leave for Memphis within the hour. He was almost desperate.

'You gotta bring him in, Tarrance. And quick. Cozzo doesn't know that we know about Tarry Ross, but Ross told him McDeere was on the verge of delivering the records. They could take him out at any time. You've got to get him. Now! Do you know where he is?'

'He's at the office,' Tarrance said.

'Okay. Fine. Bring him in. I'll be there in two hours. I wanna talk to him. Goodbye.'

Tarrance punched the phone, then dialed the number.

'Who are you calling?' Acklin asked.

'Bendini, Lambert & Locke. Attorneys-at-law.'

'Are you crazy, Wayne?' Laney asked.

'Just listen.'

The receptionist answered the phone. 'Mitch McDeere, please,' Tarrance said.

'One moment, please,' she said. Then the secretary: 'Mr. McDeere's office.'

'I need to speak to Mitchell McDeere.'

'I'm sorry, sir. He's in a meeting.'

'Listen, young lady, this is Judge Henry Hugo, and he was supposed to be in my courtroom fifteen minutes ago. We're waiting for him. It's an emergency.'

'Well, I see nothing on his calendar for this morning.'

'Do you schedule his appointments?'

'Well, yes, sir.'

'Then it's your fault. Now get him on the phone.'

Nina ran across the hall and into his office. 'Mitch, there's a Judge Hugo on the phone. Says you're supposed to be in court right now. You'd better talk to him.'

Mitch jumped to his feet and grabbed the phone. He was pale. 'Yes,' he said.

'Mr. McDeere,' Tarrance said. 'Judge Hugo. You're late for my court. Get over here.'

'Yes, Judge.' He grabbed his coat and briefcase and frowned at Nina.

'I'm sorry,' she said. 'It's not on your calendar.'

411

Mitch raced down the hall, down the stairs, past the receptionist and out the front door. He ran north on Front Street to Union and darted through the lobby of the Cotton Exchange Building. On Union, he turned east and ran toward the Mid-America Mall.

The sight of a well-dressed young man with a briefcase running like a scared dog may be a common sight in some cities, but not in Memphis. People noticed.

He hid behind a fruit stand and caught his breath. He saw no one running behind him. He ate an apple. If it came to a footrace, he hoped Two-Ton Tony was chasing him.

He had never been particularly impressed with Wayne Tarrance. The Korean shoe store was a fiasco. The chicken place on Grand Cayman was equally dumb. His notebook on the Moroltos would bore a Cub Scout. But his idea about a Mayday code, a 'don't ask questions just run for your life' alert, was a brilliant idea. For a month, Mitch knew if Judge Hugo called, he had to hit the door on a dead run. Something bad had gone wrong, and the boys on the fifth floor were moving in. Where was Abby? he thought.

A few pedestrians walked in pairs along Union. He wanted a crowded sidewalk, but there was none. He stared at the corner of Front and Union and saw nothing suspicious. Two blocks east, he casually entered the lobby of the Peabody and looked for a phone. On the mezzanine overlooking the lobby, he found a neglected one in a short hallway near the men's room. He dialed the Memphis office of the Federal Bureau of Investigation.

'Wayne Tarrance, please. It's an emergency. This is Mitch McDeere.'

Tarrance was on the phone in seconds. 'Mitch, where are you?'

'Okay, Tarrance, what's going on?'

'Where are you?'

'I'm out of the building, Judge Hugo. I'm safe for now. What's happened?'

'Mitch, you've gotta come in.'

'I don't have to do a damned thing, Tarrance. And I won't, until you talk to me.'

'Well, we've, uh, we've had a slight problem. There's been a small leak. You need –'

'Leak, Tarrance? Did you say leak? There's no such thing as a small leak. Talk to me, Tarrance, before I hang up this phone and disappear. You're tracing this call, aren't you, Tarrance? I'm hanging up.'

'No! Listen, Mitch. They know. They know we've been talking, and they know about the money and the files.'

There was a long pause. 'A small leak, Tarrance. Sounds like the dam burst. Tell me about this leak, and quick.'

'God this hurts. Mitch, I want you to know how much this hurts. Voyles is devastated. One of our senior men sold the information. We caught him this morning at a hotel in Washington. They paid him two hundred thousand for the story on you. We're in shock, Mitch.'

'Oh, I'm touched. I'm truly concerned over your shock and pain, Tarrance. I guess now you want me to run down there to your office so we can all sit around and console each other.'

'Voyles will be there by noon, Mitch. He's flying in with his top people. He wants to meet with you. We'll get you out of town.'

'Right. You want me to rush into your arms for protection. You're an idiot, Tarrance. Voyles is an idiot. You're all idiots. And I'm a fool for trusting you. Are you tracing this call, Tarrance?'

'No!'

413

'You're lying. I'm hanging up, Tarrance. Sit tight and I'll call you in thirty minutes from another phone.'

'No! Mitch, listen. You're dead if you don't come in.'

'Goodbye, Wayne. Sit by the phone.'

Mitch dropped the receiver and looked around. He walked to a marble column and peeked at the lobby below. The ducks were swimming around the fountain. The bar was deserted. A table was surrounded with rich old ladies sipping their tea and gossiping. A solitary guest was registering.

Suddenly, the Nordic stepped from behind a potted tree and stared at him. 'Up there!' he yelled across the lobby to an accomplice. They watched him intently and glanced at the stairway under him. The bartender looked up at Mitch, then at the Nordic and his friend. The old ladies stared in silence.

'Call the police!' Mitch yelled as he backed away from the railing. Both men sprang across the lobby and hit the stairs. Mitch waited five seconds, and returned to the railing. The bartender had not moved. The ladies were frozen.

There were heavy noises on the stairs. Mitch sat on the railing, dropped his briefcase, swung his legs over, paused, then jumped twenty feet onto the carpet of the lobby. He fell like a rock, but landed squarely on both feet. Pain shot through his ankles and hips. The football knee buckled, but did not collapse.

Behind him, next to the elevators, was a small haberdashery with windows full of ties and Ralph Lauren's latest. He limped into it. A kid of no more than nineteen waited eagerly behind the counter. There were no customers. An outside door opened onto Union.

'Is that door locked?' Mitch asked calmly.

'Yes, sir.'

'You wanna make a thousand dollars cash? Nothing

414

illegal.' Mitch quickly peeled off ten hundred-dollar bills and threw them on the counter.

'Uh, sure. I guess.'

'Nothing illegal, okay? I swear. I wouldn't get you in trouble. Unlock that door, and when two men come running in here in about twenty seconds, tell them I ran through that door and jumped in a cab.'

The kid smiled even brighter and raked up the money. 'Sure. No problem.'

'Where's the dressing room?'

'Yes, sir, over there next to the closet.'

'Unlock the door,' Mitch said as he slid into the dressing room and sat down. He rubbed his knees and ankles.

The clerk was straightening ties when the Nordic and his partner ran through the door from the lobby. 'Good morning,' he said cheerfully.

'Did you see a man running through here, medium build, dark gray suit, red tie?'

'Yes, sir. He just ran through there, through that door, and jumped in a cab.'

'A cab! Damn!' The door opened and closed, and the store was silent. The kid walked to a shoe rack near the closet. 'They're gone, sir.'

Mitch was rubbing his knees. 'Good. Go to the door and watch for two minutes. Let me know if you see them.'

Two minutes later, he was back. 'They're gone.'

Mitch kept his seat and smiled at the door. 'Great. I want one of those kelly green sport coats, forty-four long, and a pair of white buckskins, ten D. Bring them here, would you? And keep watching.'

'Yes, sir.' He whistled around the store as he collected the coat and shoes, then slid them under the door. Mitch yanked off his tie and changed quickly. He sat down.

415

'How much do I owe you?' Mitch asked from the room.

'Well, let's see. How about five hundred?'

'Fine. Call me a cab, and let me know when it's outside.'

Tarrance walked three miles around his desk. The call was traced to the Peabody, but Laney arrived too late. He was back now, sitting nervously with Acklin. Forty minutes after the first call, the secretary's voice blasted through the intercom. 'Mr. Tarrance. It's McDeere.'

Tarrance lunged at the phone. 'Where are you?'

'In town. But not for long.'

'Look, Mitch, you won't last two days on your own. They'll fly in enough thugs to start another war. You've got to let us help you.'

'I don't know, Tarrance. For some strange reason I just don't trust you boys right now. I can't imagine why. Just a bad feeling.'

'Please, Mitch. Don't make this mistake.'

'I guess you want me to believe you boys can protect me for the rest of my life. Sorta funny, isn't it, Tarrance? I cut a deal with the FBI, and I almost get gunned in my own office. That's real protection.'

Tarrance breathed deeply into the phone. There was a long pause. 'What about the documents? We've paid you a million for them.'

'You're cracking up, Tarrance. You paid me a million for my clean files. You got them, and I got the million. Of course, that was just part of the deal. Protection was also a part of it.'

'Give us the damned files, Mitch. They're hidden somewhere close to us, you told me that. Take off if you want to, but leave the files.'

'Won't work, Tarrance. Right now I can disappear, and the Moroltos may or may not come after me. If you don't get the files, you don't get the indictments.

If the Moroltos don't get indicted, maybe, if I'm lucky, one day they'll just forget about me. I gave them a real scare, but no permanent damage. Hell, they may even hire me back one of these days.'

'You don't really believe that. They'll chase you until they find you. If we don't get the records, we'll be chasing too. It's that simple, Mitch.'

'Then I'll put my money on the Moroltos. If you guys find me first, there'll be a leak. Just a small one.'

'You're outta your mind, Mitch. If you think you can take your million and ride into the sunset, you're a fool. They'll have goons on camels riding the deserts looking for you. Don't do it, Mitch.'

'Goodbye, Wayne. Ray sends his regards.'

The line was dead. Tarrance grabbed the phone and threw it against the wall.

Mitch glanced at the clock on the airport wall. He punched in another call. Tammy answered.

'Hello, sweetheart. Hate to wake you.'

'Don't worry, the couch kept me awake. What's up?'

'Major trouble. Get a pencil and listen very carefully. I don't have a second to waste. I'm running, and they're right behind me.'

'Fire away.'

'First, call Abby at her parents'. Tell her to drop everything and get out of town. She doesn't have time to kiss her mother goodbye or to pack any clothes. Tell her to drop the phone, get in her car and drive away. And don't look back. She takes Interstate 55 to Huntington, West Virginia, and goes to the airport. She flies from Huntington to Mobile. In Mobile, she rents a car and drives east on Interstate 10 to Gulf Shores, then east on Highway 182 to Perdido Beach. She checks in at the Perdido Beach Hilton under the name of Rachel James. And she waits. Got that?'

'Yeah.'

'Second. I need you to get on a plane and fly to Memphis. I called Doc, and the passports, etc., are not ready. I cussed him, but to no avail. He promised to work all night and have them ready in the morning. I will not be here in the morning, but you will. Get the documents.'

'Yes, sir.'

'Third. Get on a plane and get back to the apartment in Nashville. Sit by the phone. Do not, under any circumstances, leave the phone.'

'Got it.'

'Fourth. Call Abanks.'

'Okay. What are your travel plans?'

'I'm coming to Nashville, but I'm not sure when I'll be there. I gotta go. Listen, Tammy, tell Abby she could be dead within the hour if she doesn't run. So run, dammit, run!'

'Okay, boss.'

He walked quickly to Gate 22 and boarded the 10:04 Delta flight to Cincinnati. He clutched a magazine full of one way tickets, all bought with MasterCard. One to Tulsa on American Flight 233, leaving at 10:14, and purchased in the name of Mitch McDeere; one to Chicago on Northwest Flight 861, leaving at 10:15, and purchased in the name of Mitchell McDeere; one to Dallas on United Flight 562, leaving at 10:30, and purchased in the name of Mitchell McDeere; and one to Atlanta on Delta Flight 790, leaving at 11:10, and purchased in the name of Mitchell McDeere.

The ticket to Cincinnati had been bought with cash, in the name of Sam Fortune.

Lazarov entered the power office on the fourth floor and every head bowed. DeVasher faced him like a scared, whipped child. The partners studied their shoelaces and held their bowels.

'We can't find him,' DeVasher said.

Lazarov was not one to scream and cuss. He took great pride in being cool under pressure. 'You mean he just got up and walked out of here?' he asked coolly.

There was no answer. None was needed.

'All right, DeVasher, this is the plan. Send every man you've got to the airport. Check with every airline. Where's his car?'

'In the parking lot.'

'That's great. He left here on foot. He walked out of your little fortress on foot. Joey'll love this. Check with every rental car company. Now, how many honorable partners do we have here.'

'Sixteen present.'

'Divide them up in pairs and send them to the airports in Miami, New Orleans, Houston, Atlanta, Chicago, L.A., San Francisco and New York. Roam the concourses of these airports. Live in these airports. Eat in these airports. Watch the international flights in these airports. We'll send reinforcements tomorrow. You honorable esquires know him well, so go find him. It's a long shot, but what have we got to lose? It'll keep you counselors busy. And I hate to tell you boys, but these hours are not billable. Now, where's his wife?'

'Danesboro, Kentucky. At her parents'.'

'Go get her. Don't hurt her, just bring her in.'

'Do we start shredding?' DeVasher asked.

'We'll wait twenty-four hours. Send someone to Grand Cayman and destroy those records. Now hurry, DeVasher.'

The power office emptied.

Voyles stomped around Tarrance's desk and barked commands. A dozen lieutenants scribbled as he yelled. 'Cover the airport. Check every airline. Notify every

419

office in every major city. Contact customs. Do we have a picture of him?'

'We can't find one, sir.'

'Find one, and find it quick. It needs to be in every FBI and customs office by tonight. He's on the run. Son of a bitch!'

THIRTY-FIVE

The bus left Birmingham shortly before 2 P.M., Wednesday. Ray sat in the rear and studied every person who climbed in and found a seat. He looked sporty. He had taken a cab to a mall in Birmingham and in thirty minutes had purchased a new pair of faded Levi's, a plaid short-sleeved golf shirt and a pair of red-and-white Reeboks. He had also eaten a pizza and received a severe Marine-style haircut. He wore aviator sunshades and an Auburn cap.

A short, fat, dark-skinned lady sat next to him.

He smiled at her. '¿*De dónde es usted?*' he asked. Where are you from?

Her face broke into unrestrained delight. A wide smile revealed few teeth. '*México,*' she said proudly. '¿*Habla español?*' she asked eagerly.

'*Sí.*'

For two hours, they jabbered in Spanish as the bus rolled along to Montgomery. She had to repeat occasionally, but he surprised himself. He was eight years out of practice and a little rusty.

Behind the bus, Special Agents Jenkins and Jones followed in a Dodge Aries. Jenkins drove while Jones slept. The trip had become boring ten minutes out of Knoxville. Just routine surveillance, they were told. If you lose him, no big deal. But try not to lose him.

The flight from Huntington to Atlanta was two hours away, and Abby sat in a secluded corner of a dark lounge watching. Just watching. In the chair next to her was a carry-on bag. Contrary to her urgent instructions, she had packed a toothbrush, makeup and a few clothes. She had also written a note to her parents, giving a brief story about how she had to run to Memphis, needed to see Mitch, everything's fine, don't worry, hugs and kisses, love, Abby. She ignored the coffee and watched the arriving and departing.

She did not know if he was dead or alive. Tammy said he was scared, but very much in control. As always. She said he was flying to Nashville, and she, Tammy, was flying to Memphis. Confusing, but she was certain he knew what he was doing. Get to Perdido Beach and wait.

Abby had never heard of Perdido Beach. And she was certain he'd never been there either.

The lounge was nerve-racking. Every ten minutes a drunk businessman would venture over and throw something suggestive at her. Get lost, she said a dozen times.

After two hours, they boarded. Abby was stuck in the aisle seat. She buckled her belt and relaxed. And then she saw her.

She was a striking blonde with high cheekbones and a firm jaw that was almost unfeminine, yet strong and attractive. Abby had seen the partial face before. Partial, because the eyes were covered, as before. She looked at Abby and glanced away as she passed and went to her seat somewhere in the rear.

The Shipwreck Bar! The blonde in the Shipwreck Bar. The blonde who was eavesdropping on her and Mitch and Abanks. They had found her. And if they had found her, where was her husband? What had they done to him? She thought of the two-hour drive from Danesboro to Huntington, through the winding mountain roads. She had driven like a maniac. They could not have followed her.

They taxied from the terminal and minutes later lifted off for Atlanta.

For a second time in three weeks, Abby watched dusk from the inside of a 727 at the airport in Atlanta. She and the blonde. They were on the ground for thirty minutes and then left for Mobile.

From Cincinnati, Mitch flew to Nashville. He arrived at 6 P.M., Wednesday, long after the banks had closed. He found a U-Haul truck rental place in the phone book and flagged a cab.

He rented one of the smaller models, a sixteen-footer. He paid cash, but was forced to use his driver's license and a credit card for a deposit. If DeVasher could track him to a U-Haul place in Nashville, so be it. He bought twenty cardboard packing boxes and left for the apartment.

He had not eaten since Tuesday night, but he was in luck. Tammy had left a bag of microwave popcorn and two beers. He ate like a pig. At eight, he made his first call to the Perdido Beach Hilton. He asked for Lee Stevens. He had not arrived, she said. He stretched out on the den floor and thought of a hundred things that could happen to Abby. She could be dead in Kentucky and he wouldn't know. He couldn't call.

The couch had not been folded, and the cheap sheets hung off the end and fell to the floor. Tammy was not much for housework. He looked at the small, temporary bed and thought of Abby. Only five nights ago, they had tried to kill each other on the bed. Hopefully, she was on the plane. Alone.

In the bedroom, he sat on the unopened Sony box and marveled at the roomful of documents. Across the carpet she had built perfect columns of paper, all painstakingly divided into Cayman banks and Cayman

423

companies. On top of each stack was a yellow legal pad, with the company name followed by pages of dates and entries. And names!

Even Tarrance could follow the paper trail. A grand jury would eat it up. The U.S. Attorney would call press conferences. And the trial juries would convict, and convict and convict.

Special Agent Jenkins yawned into the telephone receiver and punched the numbers to the Memphis office. He had not slept in twenty-four hours. Jones was snoring in the car.

'FBI,' a male voice said.

'Yeah, who's there?' Jenkins asked. Just a routine check in.

'Acklin.'

'Hey, Rick. This is Jenkins. We've –'

'Jenkins! Where have you been? Hold on!'

Jenkins quit yawning and looked around the bus terminal. An angry voice yelled into the earpiece.

'Jenkins! Where are you?' It was Wayne Tarrance.

'We're at the bus station in Mobile. We've lost him.'

'You what? How could you lose him?'

Jenkins was suddenly alert and leaning into the phone. 'Wait a minute, Wayne. Our instructions were to follow him for eight hours to see where he went. Routine, you said.'

'I can't believe you lost him.'

'Wayne, we weren't told to follow him for the rest of his life. Eight hours, Wayne. We've followed for twenty hours, and he's disappeared. What's the big deal?'

'Why haven't you called in before now?'

'We called in twice. In Birmingham and Montgomery. Line was busy both times. What's going on, Wayne?'

'Just a minute.'

Jenkins grabbed the phone tighter and waited. Another voice: 'Hello, Jenkins?'

'Yes.'

'Director Voyles here. What the hell happened?'

Jenkins held his breath and looked wildly around the terminal. 'Sir, we lost him. We followed him for twenty hours, and when he got off the bus here in Mobile, we lost him in the crowd.'

'That's great, son. How long ago?'

'Twenty minutes.'

'All right, listen. We desperately need to find him. His brother has taken our money and disappeared. Call the locals there in Mobile. Tell them who you are, and that an escaped murderer is on the loose in town. They've probably got Ray McDeere's name and picture stuck to the walls. His mother lives in Panama City Beach, so alert every local between there and Mobile. I'm sending in our troops.'

'Okay. I'm sorry, sir. We weren't told to trail him forever.'

'We'll discuss it later.'

At ten, Mitch called the Perdido Beach Hilton for the second time. He asked for Rachel James. No arrival. He asked for Lee Stevens. One moment, she said. Mitch sat on the floor and waited intently. The line to the room was ringing. After a dozen rings, someone picked up.

'Yeah.' It was quick.

'Lee?' Mitch asked.

A pause. 'Yeah.'

'This is Mitch. Congratulations.'

Ray fell on the bed and closed his eyes. 'It was so easy, Mitch. How'd you do it?'

'I'll tell you when we have time. Right now, there are a bunch of folks trying to kill me. And Abby. We're on the run.'

'Who, Mitch?'

'It would take ten hours to tell the first chapter. We'll do it later. Write this number down. 615-889-4380.'

'That's not Memphis.'

'No, it's Nashville. I'm in an apartment that's serving as mission control. Memorize that number. If I'm not here, the phone will be answered by a girl named Tammy.'

'Tammy?'

'It's a long story. Just do as I say. Sometime tonight, Abby will check in there under the name of Rachel James. She'll be in a rented car.'

'She's coming here!'

'Just listen, Ray. The cannibals are chasing us, but we're a step ahead of them.'

'Ahead of who?'

'The Mafia. And the FBI.'

'Is that all?'

'Probably. Now listen to me. There is a slight chance Abby is being followed. You've got to find her, watch her and make damned sure no one is behind her.'

'And if they are?'

'Call me, and we'll talk about it.'

'No problem.'

'Don't use the phone except to call this number. And we can't talk much.'

'I've got a bunch of questions, little brother.'

'And I've got the answers, but not now. Take care of my wife and call me when she gets there.'

'Will do. And, Mitch, thanks.'

'*Adios.*'

An hour later she turned off Highway 182 onto the winding driveway to the Hilton. She parked the four door Cutlass with Alabama tags and walked nervously under the sprawling veranda to the front doors. She stopped for a second, looked behind her at the driveway and went inside.

Two minutes later, a yellow cab from Mobile stopped under the veranda, behind the shuttle vans. Ray watched the cab. A woman was in the back seat leaning forward and talking to the driver. They waited a minute. She pulled money from her purse and paid him. She got out and waited until the cab drove away. The woman was a blonde, and that was the first thing he noticed. Very shapely, with tight black corduroy pants. And black sunglasses, which seemed odd to him because it was pushing midnight. She walked suspiciously to the front doors, waited a minute, then went in. He watched her carefully. He moved toward the lobby.

The blonde approached the only clerk behind the registration desk. 'A single room, please,' he heard her say.

The clerk slid a registration form across the counter. The blonde wrote her name and asked, 'That lady who just checked in before me, what's her name? I think she's an old friend.'

The clerk flipped through the registration cards. 'Rachel James.'

'Yeah, that's her. Where's she from?'

'It's a Memphis address,' the clerk said.

'What's her room number? I'd like to say hello.'

'I can't give room numbers,' the clerk said.

The blonde quickly pulled two twenties from her purse and slid them across the counter. 'I just want to say hello.'

The clerk took the money. 'Room 622.'

The woman paid in cash. 'Where are the phones?'

'Around the corner,' the clerk said. Ray slid around the corner and found four pay phones. He grabbed a middle one and began talking to himself.

427

The blonde took a phone on the end and turned her back to him. She spoke softly. He could hear only pieces.

'. . . checked in . . . Room 622 . . . Mobile . . . some help . . . I can't . . . an hour? . . . yes . . . hurry . . .'

She hung up, and he talked louder into his dead phone.

Ten minutes later, there was a knock at the door. The blonde jumped from the bed, grabbed her .45 and stuck it in the corduroys under the shirt. She ignored the safety chain and cracked the door.

It burst open and knocked her against the wall. Ray lunged at her, grabbed the gun, and pinned her to the floor. With her face in the carpet, he stuck the barrel of the .45 in her ear. 'If you make a sound, I'll kill you!'

She stopped struggling and closed her eyes. No response.

'Who are you?' Ray demanded. He pushed the barrel deeper into her ear. Again, no response.

'Not a move, not a sound. Okay? I'd love to blow your head off.'

He relaxed, still sitting on her back, and ripped open her flight bag. He dumped its contents on the floor and found a pair of clean tennis socks. 'Open your mouth,' he demanded.

She did not move. The barrel returned to her ear, and she slowly opened her mouth. Ray crammed the socks in between her teeth, then tightly blindfolded her with the silk nightshirt. He bound her feet and hands with panty hose, then ripped the bedsheets into long strips. The woman did not move. When he finished the binding and gagging, she resembled a mummy. He slid her under the bed.

The purse contained six hundred dollars in cash and a wallet with an Illinois driver's license. Karen Adair from Chicago. Date of birth: March 4, 1962. He took the wallet and gun.

The phone rang at 1 A.M., and Mitch was not asleep. He was in bank records up to his waist. Fascinating bank records. Highly incriminating.

'Hello,' he answered cautiously.

'Is this mission control?' The voice was in the vicinity of a loud jukebox.

'Where are you, Ray?'

'A joint called the FloraBama lounge. Right on the state line.'

'Where's Abby?'

'She's in the car. She's fine.'

Mitch breathed easier and grinned into the phone. He listened.

'We had to leave the hotel. A woman followed Abby in – same woman you saw in some bar in the Caymans. Abby is trying to explain everything. The woman followed her all day and showed up at the hotel. I took care of her, and we disappeared.'

'You took care of her?'

'Yeah, she wouldn't talk, but she's out of the way for a short time.'

'Abby's fine?'

'Yeah. We're both dead tired. Exactly what do you have in mind?'

'You're about three hours away from Panama City Beach. I know you're dead tired, but you need to get away from there. Get to Panama City Beach, ditch the car and get two rooms at the Holiday Inn. Call me when you check in.'

'I hope you know what you're doing.'

'Trust me, Ray.'

'I do, but I'm beginning to wish I was back in prison.'

'You can't go back, Ray. We either disappear or we're dead.'

THIRTY-SIX

The cab stopped at a red light in downtown Nashville, and Mitch hopped out on stiff and aching legs. He limped through the busy intersection dodging the morning traffic.

The Southeastern Bank Building was a thirty-story glass cylinder, designed along the same lines as a tennis-ball can. The tint was dark, almost black. It stood prominently away from the street corner amidst a maze of sidewalks and fountains and manicured greenery.

Mitch entered the revolving doors with a swarm of employees rushing to work. In the marble-laden atrium he found the directory and rode the escalators to the third floor. He opened a heavy glass door and walked into a large circular office. A striking woman of forty or so watched him from behind the glass desk. She offered no smile.

'Mr. Mason Laycook, please,' he said.

She pointed. 'Have a seat.'

Mr. Laycook wasted no time. He appeared from around a corner and was as sour as his secretary. 'May I help you?' he asked through his nose.

Mitch stood. 'Yes, I need to wire a little money.'

'Yes. Do you have an account at Southeastern?'

'Yes.'

'And your name?'

'It's a numbered account.' In other words, you don't get a name, Mr. Laycook. You don't need a name.

'Very well. Follow me.' His office had no windows, no view. A row of keyboards and monitors sat on the credenza behind his glass desk. Mitch sat down.

'The account number, please.'

It came from memory. '214–31–35.'

Laycook pecked at his keyboard and watched a monitor. 'That's a Code Three account, opened by a T. Hemphill, with access only by her and a certain male meeting the following physical requirements: approximately six feet tall, one seventy-five to one eighty-five, blue eyes, brown hair, about twenty-five or twenty-six years old. You fit that description, sir.' Laycook studied the screen. 'And the last four digits of your Social Security number are?'

'8585.'

'Very well. You are accessed. Now what can I do for you?'

'I want to wire in some funds from a bank in Grand Cayman.'

Laycook frowned and took a pencil from his pocket. 'Which bank in Grand Cayman?'

'Royal Bank of Montreal.'

'What type of account?'

'It's a numbered account.'

'I presume you have the number?'

'499DFH2122.'

Laycook wrote the number and stood. 'I'll be just a moment.' He left the room.

Ten minutes passed. Mitch tapped his bruised feet and looked at the monitors across the desk.

Laycook returned with his supervisor, Mr. Nokes, a vice president or something. Nokes introduced himself from behind the desk. Both men appeared nervous. They stared downward at Mitch.

431

Nokes did the talking. He held a small sheet of computer paper. 'Sir, that is a restricted account. You must have certain information before we can start the wire.'

Mitch nodded confidently.

'The dates and amounts of the last three deposits, sir?' They watched him intensely, knowing he would fail.

Again, it came from memory. No notes. 'February third of this year, six and a half million. December fourteenth, last year, nine point two million. And October eighth, last year, eleven million.'

Laycook and Nokes gaped at the small printout. Nokes managed a tiny professional smile. 'Very well. You are cleared to the Pen number.'

Laycook stood ready with his pencil.

'Sir, what is your Pen number?' Nokes asked.

Mitch smiled and recrossed his damaged legs. '72083.'

'And the terms of the wire?'

'Ten million dollars wired immediately into this bank, account 214–31–35. I'll wait.'

'It's not necessary to wait, sir.'

'I'll wait. When the wire is complete, I've got a few more for you.'

'We'll be a moment. Would you like some coffee?'

'No. Thanks. Do you have a newspaper?'

'Certainly,' Laycook said. 'On the table there.'

They scurried from the office, and Mitch's pulse began its descent. He opened the Nashville *Tennessean* and scanned three sections before he found a brief paragraph about the escape at Brushy Mountain. No picture. Few details. They were safe at the Holiday Inn on the Miracle Strip in Panama City Beach, Florida.

Their trail was clear, so far. He thought. He hoped.

Laycook returned alone. He was friendly now. A

real backslapper. 'Wire's complete. The money is here. Now what can we do for you?'

'I want to wire it out. Most of it, anyway.'

'How many transfers?'

'Three.'

'Give me the first one.'

'A million dollars to the Coast National Bank in Pensacola, to a numbered account, accessible to only one person, a white female, approximately fifty years of age. I will provide her with the Pen number.'

'Is this an existing account?'

'No. I want you to open it with the wire.'

'Very well. The second transfer?'

'One million dollars to the Dane County Bank in Danesboro, Kentucky, to any account in the name of Harold or Maxine Sutherland, or both. It's a small bank, but it has a correspondent relationship with United Kentucky in Louisville.'

'Very well. The third transfer?'

'Seven million to the Deutschbank in Zurich. Account number 772–03BL–600. The remainder of the money stays here.'

'This will take about an hour,' Laycook said as he wrote.

'I'll call you in an hour to confirm.'

'Very well.'

'Thank you, Mr. Laycook.'

Each step was painful, but the pain was not felt. He moved in a controlled jog down the escalators and out of the building.

On the top floor of the Royal Bank of Montreal, Grand Cayman branch, a secretary from Wire Transfers slid a computer printout under the very pointed and proper nose of Randolph Osgood. She had circled an unusual transfer of ten million. Unusual because the money in this account did not normally return to

433

the United States and unusual because it went to a bank they had never dealt with. Osgood studied the printout and called Memphis. Mr. Tolleson was on leave of absence, the secretary informed him. Then Nathan Locke? he asked. Mr. Locke is out of town. Victor Milligan? Mr. Milligan is away also.

Osgood placed the printout in the pile of things to do tomorrow.

Along the Emerald Coast of Florida and Alabama, from the outskirts of Mobile east through Pensacola, Fort Walton Beach, Destin and Panama City, the warm spring night had been peaceful. Only one violent crime along the coast. A young woman was robbed, beaten and raped in her room at the Perdido Beach Hilton. Her boyfriend, a tall blond headed man with strong Nordic features, had found her bound and gagged in her room. His name was Rimmer, Aaron Rimmer, and he was from Memphis.

The real excitement of the night was a massive manhunt in the Mobile area for the escaped murderer, Ray McDeere. He had been seen arriving at the bus station after dark. His mug shot was on the front page of the morning paper, and before ten, three witnesses had come forth and reported sightings. His movements were traced across Mobile Bay to Foley, Alabama, then to Gulf Shores.

Since the Hilton is only ten miles from Gulf Shores along Highway 182, and since the only known escaped murderer was in the vicinity when the only violent crime occurred, the conclusion was quick and inescapable. The hotel's night clerk made a probable ID of Ray McDeere, and the records reflected that he checked in around nine-thirty as a Mr. Lee Stevens. And he paid cash. Later, the victim checked in and was attacked. The victim also identified Mr. Ray McDeere.

The night clerk remembered that the victim asked about a Rachel James, who checked in five minutes before the victim and paid cash. Rachel James vanished sometime during the night without bothering to check out. Likewise for Ray McDeere, alias Lee Stevens. A parking-lot attendant made a probable ID of McDeere and said he got in a white four-door Cutlass with a woman between midnight and one. Said she was driving and appeared to be in a hurry. Said they went east on 182.

Calling from his room on the sixth floor of the Hilton, Aaron Rimmer anonymously told a Baldwin County sheriff's deputy to check the car rental companies in Mobile. Check them for an Abby McDeere. That's your white Cutlass, he told him.

From Mobile to Miami, the search began for the Cutlass rented from Avis by Abby McDeere. The sheriff's investigator promised to keep the victim's boyfriend, Aaron Rimmer, posted on all developments.

Mr. Rimmer would wait at the Hilton. He shared a room with Tony Verkler. Next door was his boss, DeVasher. Fourteen of his friends sat in their rooms on the seventh floor and waited.

It took seventeen trips from the apartment to the U-Haul, but by noon the Bendini Papers were ready for shipment. Mitch rested his swollen legs. He sat on the couch and wrote instructions to Tammy. He detailed the transactions at the bank and told her to wait a week before contacting his mother. She would soon be a millionaire.

He set the telephone in his lap and prepared himself for an unpleasant task. He called the Dane County Bank and asked for Hugh Sutherland. It was an emergency, he said.

'Hello,' his father-in-law answered angrily.

'Mr. Sutherland, this is Mitch. Have you –'

'Where's my daughter. Is she okay?'

'Yes. She's fine. She's with me. We'll be leaving the country for a few days. Maybe weeks. Maybe months.'

'I see,' he replied slowly. 'And where might you be going?'

'Not sure. We'll just knock around for a while.'

'Is something wrong, Mitch?'

'Yes, sir. Something is very wrong, but I can't explain now. Maybe one of these days. Watch the newspapers closely. You'll see a major story out of Memphis within two weeks.'

'Are you in danger?'

'Sort of. Have you received any unusual wire transfers this morning?'

'As a matter of fact we have. Somebody parked a million bucks here about an hour ago.'

'That somebody was me, and the money is yours.'

There was a very long pause. 'Mitch, I think I deserve an explanation.'

'Yes, sir, you do. But I can't give you one. If we make it safely out of the country, you'll be notified in a week or so. Enjoy the money. Gotta run.'

Mitch waited a minute and called Room 1028 at the Holiday Inn, Panama City Beach.

'Hello.' It was Abby.

'Hi, babe. How are you?'

'Terrible, Mitch. Ray's picture is on the cover of every newspaper down here. At first it was the escape and the fact that someone saw him in Mobile. Now the TV news is claiming he is the prime suspect in a rape last night.'

'What! Where!'

'At the Perdido Beach Hilton. Ray caught that blonde following me into the hotel. He jumped her in her room and tied her up. Nothing serious. He took

436

her gun and her money, and now she's claiming she was beaten and raped by Ray McDeere. Every cop in Florida is looking for the car I rented last night in Mobile.'

'Where's the car?'

'We left it about a mile west of here at a big condo development. I'm so scared, Mitch.'

'Where's Ray?'

'He's lying on the beach trying to sunburn his face. The picture in the paper is an old one. He's got long hair and looks real pale. It's not a good picture. Now he's got a crew cut and he's trying to turn pink. I think it will help.'

'Are both rooms in your name?'

'Rachael James.'

'Listen, Abby. Forget Rachel and Lee and Ray and Abby. Wait until almost dark, then leave the rooms. Just walk away. About a half a mile east is a small motel called the Blue Tide. You and Ray enjoy a little walk on the beach until you find it. You go to the desk and get two rooms next to each other. Pay in cash. Tell them your name is Jackie Nagel. Got that? Jackie Nagel. Use that name, because when I get there I'll ask for it.'

'What if they don't have two rooms next to each other?'

'Okay, if anything goes wrong, two doors down is another dump called the Seaside. Check in there. Same name. I'm leaving here now, say one o'clock, and I should be there in ten hours.'

'What if they find the car?'

'They'll find it, and they'll throw a blanket over Panama City Beach. You've got to be careful. After dark, try to sneak into a drugstore and buy some hair dye. Cut your hair extremely short and dye it blond.

'Blond!'

'Or red. I don't give a damn. But change it. Tell Ray not to leave his room. Do not take any chances.'

'He's got a gun, Mitch.'

'Tell him I said not to use it. There will be a thousand cops around there, probably tonight. He can't win a gunfight.'

'I love you, Mitch. I'm so scared.'

'It's okay to be scared, babe. Just keep thinking. They don't know where you are, and they can't catch you if you move. I'll be there by midnight.'

Lamar Quin, Wally Hudson and Kendall Mahan sat in the conference room on the third floor and contemplated their next move. As senior associates, they knew about the fifth floor and the basement, about Mr. Lazarov and Mr. Morolto, about Hodge and Kozinski. They knew that when one joined the firm, one did not leave.

They told their stories about the Day. They compared it to the day they learned the sad truth about Santa Claus. A sad and frightening day, when Nathan Locke talked to them in his office and told them about their biggest client. And then he introduced them to DeVasher. They were employees of the Morolto family, and they were expected to work hard, spend their handsome paychecks and remain very quiet about it. All three did. There had been thoughts of leaving, but never serious plans. They were family men. In time, it sort of went away. There were so many clean clients to work for. So much hard, legitimate work.

The partners handled most of the dirty work, but growing seniority had brought increasing involvement in the conspiracy. They would never be caught, the partners assured them. They were too smart. They had too much money. It was a perfect cover. Of particular concern at the conference table was the fact that the partners had skipped town. There was not a single partner in Memphis. Even Avery Tolleson had disappeared. He had walked out of the hospital.

They talked about Mitch. He was out there some-where, scared and running for his life. If DeVasher caught him, he was dead and they would bury him like Hodge and Kozinski. But if the feds caught him, they got the records, and they got the firm, which, of course, included the three of them.

What if, they speculated, no one caught him? What if he made it, just vanished? Along with his docu-ments, of course. What if he and Abby were now somewhere on a beach, drinking rum and counting their money? They liked this thought and talked about it for a while.

Finally, they decided to wait until tomorrow. If Mitch was gunned down somewhere, they would stay in Memphis. If he was never found, they would stay in Memphis. If the feds caught him, they would hit the road, Jack.

Run, Mitch, run!

The rooms at the Blue Tide Motel were narrow and tacky. The carpet was twenty years old and badly worn. The bedspreads had cigarette burns. But luxury was unimportant.

After dark Thursday, Ray stood behind Abby with a pair of scissors and snipped delicately around her ears. Two towels under the chair were covered with her dark hair. She watched him carefully in the mirror next to the antique color television and was free with her instructions. It was a boyish cut, well above the ears, with bangs. He stepped back and admired his work.

'Not bad,' he said.

She smiled and brushed hair from her arms. 'I guess

I need to color it now,' she said sadly. She walked to the tiny bathroom and closed the door.

She emerged an hour later as a blonde. A yellowish blonde. Ray was asleep on the bedspread. She knelt on the dirty carpet and scooped up the hair.

She picked it from the floor and filled a plastic garbage bag. The empty dye bottle and the applicator were thrown in with the hair, and she tied the bag. There was a knock at the door.

Abby froze, and listened. The curtains were pulled tightly. She slapped Ray's feet. Another knock. Ray jumped from the bed and grabbed the gun.

'Who is it?' she whispered loudly at the window.

'Sam Fortune,' he whispered back.

Ray unlocked the door, and Mitch stepped in. He grabbed Abby and bear-hugged Ray. The door was locked, the lights turned off, and they sat on the bed in the darkness. He held Abby tightly. With so much to say, the three said nothing.

A tiny, weak ray of light from the outside filtered under the curtains and, as minutes passed, gradually lit the dresser and television. No one spoke. There were no sounds from the Blue Tide. The parking lot was virtually empty.

'I can almost explain why I'm here,' Ray finally said, 'but I'm not sure why you're here.'

'We've got to forget why we're here,' Mitch said, 'and concentrate on leaving here. All together. All safe.'

'Abby's told me everything,' Ray said.

'I don't know everything,' she said. 'I don't know who's chasing us.'

'I'm assuming they're all out there,' Mitch said. 'DeVasher and his gang are nearby. Pensacola, I would guess. It's the nearest airport of any size. Tarrance is somewhere along the coast directing his

440

boys in their all-out search for Ray McDeere, the rapist. And his accomplice, Abby McDeere.'

'What happens next?' Abby asked.

'They'll find the car, if they haven't already done so. That will pinpoint Panama City Beach. The paper said the search extended from Mobile to Miami, so now they're spread out. When they find the car, they zero in here. Now, there's a thousand cheap motels just like this one along the Strip. For twelve miles, nothing but motels, condos and T-shirt shops. That's a lot of people, a lot of tourists with shorts and sandals, and tomorrow we'll be tourists too, shorts, sandals, the whole bit. I figure even if they have a hundred men after us, we've got two or three days.'

'Once they decide we're here, what happens?' she asked.

'You and Ray could have simply abandoned the car and taken off in another one. They can't be certain we're on the Strip, but they'll start looking here. But they're not the Gestapo. They can't crash a door and search without probable cause.'

'DeVasher can,' Ray said.

'Yeah, but there's a million doors around here. They'll set up roadblocks and watch every store and restaurant. They'll talk to every hotel clerk, show them Ray's mug shot. They'll swarm like ants for a few days, and with luck, they'll miss us.'

'What are you driving, Mitch?' Ray asked.

'A U-Haul.'

'I don't understand why we don't get in the U-Haul, right now, and haul ass. I mean, the car is sitting a mile down the road, just waiting to be found, and we know they're coming. I say we haul it.'

'Listen, Ray. They might be setting roadblocks right now. Trust me. Did I get you out of prison? Come on.'

441

A siren went screaming past on the strip. They froze, and listened to it fade away.

'Okay, gang,' Mitch said, 'we're moving out. I don't like this place. The parking lot is empty and too close to the highway. I've parked the U-Haul three doors down at the elegant Sea Gull's Rest Motel. I've got two lovely rooms there. The roaches are much smaller. We're taking a quiet stroll on the beach. Then we get to unpack the truck. Sound exciting?'

THIRTY-SEVEN

Joey Morolto and his squad of storm troopers landed at the Pensacola airport in a chartered DC-9 before sunrise Friday. Lazarov waited with two limos and eight rented vans. He briefed Joey on the past twenty-four hours as the convoy left Pensacola and traveled east on Highway 98. After an hour of briefing, they arrived at a twelve-floor condo called the Sandpiper, in the middle of the Strip at Destin. An hour from Panama City Beach. The penthouse on the top floor had been procured by Lazarov for only four thousand dollars a week. Off-season rates. The remainder of the twelfth floor and all of the eleventh had been leased, for the goons.

Mr. Morolto snapped orders like an agitated drill sergeant. A command post was set up in the great room of the penthouse, overlooking the calm emerald water. Nothing suited him. He wanted breakfast, and Lazarov sent two vans to a Delchamps supermarket nearby. He wanted McDeere, and Lazarov asked him to be patient.

By daybreak, the troops had settled into their condos. They waited.

Three miles away along the beach, and within view of the Sandpiper, F. Denton Voyles and Wayne Tarrance sat on the balcony of an eighth-floor room at the Sandestin Hilton. They drank coffee, watched the

443

sun rise gently on the horizon and talked strategy. The night had not gone well. The car had not been found. No sign of Mitch. With sixty FBI agents and hundreds of locals scouring the coast, they should have at least found the car. With each passing hour, the McDeeres were farther away.

In a file by a coffee table inside were the warrants. For Ray McDeere, the warrant read: escape, unlawful flight, robbery and rape. Abby's sin was merely being an accomplice. The charges for Mitch required more creativity. Obstruction of justice and a nebulous racketeering charge. And of course the old standby, mail fraud. Tarrance was not sure where the mail fraud fit, but he worked for the FBI and had never seen a case that did not include mail fraud.

The warrants were issued and ready and had been fully discussed with dozens of reporters from newspapers and television stations throughout the Southeast. Trained to maintain a stone face and loathe the press, Tarrance was having a delightful time with the reporters.

Publicity was needed. Publicity was critical. The authorities must find the McDeeres before the Mob did.

Rick Acklin ran through the room to the balcony. 'They've found the car!'

Tarrance and Voyles jumped to their feet. 'Where?'

'Panama City Beach. In the parking lot of a high rise.'

'Call our men in, every one of them!' Voyles yelled. 'Stop searching everywhere. I want every agent in Panama City Beach. We'll turn the place inside out. Get all the locals you can. Tell them to set up roadblocks on every highway and gravel road in and out of there. Dust the car for prints. What's the town look like?'

'Similar to Destin. A twelve mile strip along the

beach with hotels, motels, condos, the works,' Acklin answered.

'Start our men door to door at the hotels. Is her composite ready?'

'Should be,' Acklin said.

'Get her composite, Mitch's composite, Ray's composite and Ray's mug shot in the hands of every agent and cop. I want people walking up and down the Strip waving those damn composites.'

'Yes, sir.'

'How far away is Panama City Beach?'

'About fifty minutes due east.'

'Get my car.'

The phone woke Aaron Rimmer in his room at the Perdido Beach Hilton. It was the investigator with the Baldwin County Sheriff's Department. They found the car, Mr. Rimmer, he said, in Panama City Beach. Just a few minutes ago. About a mile from the Holiday Inn. On Highway 98. Sorry again about the girl, he said. Hope she's doing better, he said.

Mr. Rimmer said thanks, and immediately called Lazarov at the Sandpiper. Ten minutes later, he and his roommate, Tony, and DeVasher and fourteen others were speeding east. Panama City Beach was three hours away.

In Destin, Lazarov mobilized the storm troopers. They moved out quickly, piled into the vans and headed east. The blitzkrieg had begun.

It took only a matter of minutes for the U-Haul to become a hot item. The assistant manager of the rental company in Nashville was a guy named Billy Weaver. He opened the office early Friday morning, fixed his coffee and scanned the paper. On the bottom half of the front page, Billy read with interest the story about Ray McDeere and the search along the coast.

And then Abby was mentioned. Then the escapee's brother, Mitch McDeere, was mentioned. The name rang a bell.

Billy opened a drawer and flipped through the records of outstanding rentals. Sure enough, a man named McDeere had rented a sixteen-footer late Wednesday night. M. Y. McDeere, said the signature, but the driver's license read Mitchell Y. From Memphis.

Being a patriot and honest taxpayer, Billy called his cousin at Metro Police. The cousin called the Nashville FBI office, and fifteen minutes later, the U-Haul was a hot item.

Tarrance took the call on the radio while Acklin drove. Voyles was in the back seat. A U-Haul? Why would he need a U-Haul? He left Memphis without his car, clothes, shoes or toothbrush. He left the dog unfed. He took nothing with him, so why the U-Haul?

The Bendini records, of course. Either he left Nashville with the records in the truck or he was in the truck en route to get them. But why Nashville?

Mitch was up with the sun. He took one long, lustful look at his wife with the cute blond hair and forgot about sex. It could wait. He let her sleep. He walked around the stacks of boxes in the small room and went to the bathroom. He showered quickly and slipped on a gray sweat suit he'd bought at a Wal-Mart in Montgomery. He eased along the beach for a half mile until he found a convenience store. He bought a sackful of Cokes, pastries and chips, sunglasses, caps and three newspapers.

Ray was waiting by the U-Haul when he returned. They spread the papers on Ray's bed. It was worse than they expected. Mobile, Pensacola and Montgomery had front page stories with composites of Ray and

Mitch, along with the mug shot again. Abby's composite had not been released, according to the Pensacola paper.

As composites go, they were close here and there and badly off in other areas. But it was hard to be objective. Hell, Mitch was staring at his own composite and trying to give an unbiased opinion about how close it was. The stories were full of all sorts of wild statements from one Wayne Tarrance, special agent, FBI. Tarrance said Mitchell McDeere had been spotted in the Gulf Shores–Pensacola area; that he and Ray both were known to be heavily armed and extremely dangerous; that they had vowed not to be taken alive; that reward money was being gathered; that if anyone saw a man who faintly resembled either of the McDeere brothers, please call the local police.

They ate pastries and decided the composites were not close. The mug shot was even comical. They eased next door and woke Abby. They began unpacking the Bendini Papers and assembling the video camera.

At nine, Mitch called Tammy, collect. She had the new IDs and passports. He instructed her to Federal Express them to Sam Fortune, front desk, Sea Gull's Rest Motel, 16694 Highway 98, West Panama City Beach, Florida. She read to him the front-page story about himself and his small gang. No composites.

He told her to ship the passports, then leave Nashville. Drive four hours to Knoxville, check into a big motel and call him at Room 39, Sea Gull's Rest. He gave her the number.

Two FBI agents knocked on the door of the old ragged trailer at 486 San Luis. Mr. Ainsworth came to the door in his underwear. They flashed their badges.

'So whatta you want with me?' he growled.

An agent handed him the morning paper. 'Do you know those two men?'

He studied the paper. 'I guess they're my wife's boys. Never met them.'

'And your wife's name is?'

'Ida Ainsworth.'

'Where is she?'

Mr. Ainsworth was scanning the paper. 'At work. At the Waffle Hut. Say they're around here, huh?'

'Yes, sir. You haven't seen them?'

'Hell no. But I'll get my gun.'

'Has your wife seen them?'

'Not to my knowledge.'

'Thanks, Mr. Ainsworth. We've got orders to set up watch here in the street, but we won't bother you.'

'Good. These boys are crazy. I've always said that.'

A mile away, another pair of agents parked discreetly next to a Waffle Hut and set up watch.

By noon, all highways and county roads into the coast around Panama City Beach were blocked. Along the Strip, cops stopped traffic every four miles. They walked from one T-shirt shop to the next, handing out composites. They posted them on the bulletin boards in Shoney's, Pizza Hut, Taco Bell and a dozen more fast-food places. They told the cashiers and waitresses to keep their eyes open for the McDeeres. Very dangerous people.

Lazarov and his men camped at the Best Western, two miles west of the Sea Gull's Rest. He rented a large conference room and set up command. Four of his troops were dispatched to raid a T-shirt shop, and they returned with all sorts of tourist clothes and straw hats and caps. He rented two Ford Escorts and equipped them with police scanners. They patrolled the Strip and listened to the endless squawking. They immediately caught the search for the U-Haul and joined in. DeVasher strategically spread the rented vans along the Strip. They sat innocently in large parking lots and waited with their radios.

Around two, Lazarov received an emergency call from an employee on the fifth floor of the Bendini Building. Two things. First, an employee snooping around the Caymans had found an old locksmith who, after being paid, recalled making eleven keys around midnight of April 1. Eleven keys, on two rings. Said the woman, a very attractive American, a brunette with nice legs, had paid cash and was in a hurry. Said the keys had been easy, except for the Mercedes key. He wasn't sure about that one. Second, a banker from Grand Cayman called. Thursday at 9:33 A.M., ten million dollars had been wired from the Royal Bank of Montreal to the Southeastern Bank in Nashville.

Between four and four-thirty, the police scanners went wild. The squawking was nonstop. A clerk at the Holiday Inn made a probable ID of Abby, as the woman who paid cash for two rooms at 4:17 A.M., Thursday. She paid for three nights, but had not been seen since the rooms were cleaned around one on Thursday. Evidently, neither room had been slept in Thursday night. She had not checked out, and the rooms were paid for through noon Saturday. The clerk saw no sign of a male accomplice. The Holiday Inn was swamped with cops and FBI agents and Morolto thugs for an hour. Tarrance himself interrogated the clerk.

They were there! Somewhere in Panama City Beach. Ray and Abby were confirmed. It was suspected Mitch was with them, but it was unconfirmed. Until 4:58, Friday afternoon.

The bombshell. A county deputy pulled into a cheap motel and noticed the gray-and-white hood of a truck. He walked between two buildings and smiled at the small U-Haul truck hidden neatly between a row of two-story rooms and a large garbage Dumpster. He wrote down all the numbers on the truck and called it in.

It hit! In five minutes the motel was surrounded. The owner charged from the front office and demanded an explanation. He looked at the composites and shook his head. Five FBI badges flapped in his face, and he became cooperative.

Accompanied by a dozen agents, he took the keys and went door to door. Forty-eight doors.

Only seven were occupied. The owner explained as he unlocked doors that it was a slow time of the year at the Beachcomber Inn. All of the smaller motels struggle until Memorial Day, he explained.

Even the Sea Gull's Rest, four miles to the west, was struggling.

Andy Patrick received his first felony conviction at the age of nineteen and served four months for bad checks. Branded as a felon, he found honest work impossible, and for the next twenty years worked unsuccessfully as a small-time criminal. He drifted across the country shoplifting, writing bad checks and breaking into houses here and there. A small, frail nonviolent man, he was severely beaten by a fat, arrogant county deputy in Texas when he was twenty-seven. He lost an eye and lost all respect for the law.

Six months earlier, he landed in Panama City Beach and found an honest job paying four bucks an hour working the night shift at the front and only desk of the Sea Gull's Rest Motel. Around nine, Friday night, he was watching TV when a fat, arrogant county deputy swaggered through the door.

'Got a manhunt going on,' he announced, and laid copies of the composites and mug shot on the dirty counter. 'Looking for the folks. We think they're around here.'

Andy studied the composites. The one of Mitchell Y. McDeere looked pretty familiar. The wheels in his small-time felonious brain began to churn.

With his one good eye, he looked at the fat, arrogant county deputy and said, 'Ain't seen them. But I'll keep an eye out.'

'They're dangerous,' the deputy said.

You're the dangerous one, Andy thought.

'Post these up on the wall there,' the deputy instructed.

Do you own this damned place? Andy thought. 'I'm sorry, but I'm not authorized to post anything on the walls.'

The deputy froze, cocked his head sideways and glared at Andy through thick sunglasses. 'Listen, Peewee, I authorized it.'

'I'm sorry, sir, but I can't post anything on the walls unless my boss tells me to.'

'And where is your boss?'

'I don't know. Probably in a bar somewhere.'

The deputy carefully picked up the composites, walked behind the counter and tacked them on the bulletin board. When he finished, he glared down at Andy and said, 'I'll come back in a coupla hours. If you remove these, I'll arrest you for obstruction of justice.'

Andy did not flinch. 'Won't stick. They got me for that one time in Kansas, so I know all about it.'

The deputy's fat cheeks turned red and he gritted his teeth. 'You're a little smart-ass, aren't you?'

'Yes, sir.'

'You take these down and I promise you you'll go to jail for something.'

'I've been there before, and it ain't no big deal.'

Red lights and sirens screamed by on the Strip a few feet away, and the deputy turned and watched the excitement. He mumbled something and swaggered out the door. Andy threw the composites in the garbage. He watched the squad cars dodge each other on the Strip for a few minutes, then walked through the parking lot to the rear building. He knocked on the door of Room 38.

He waited and knocked again.

'Who is it?' a woman asked.

'The manager,' Andy replied, proud of his title. The door opened, and the man who favored the composite of Mitchell Y. McDeere slid out.

'Yes, sir,' he said. 'What's going on?'

He was nervous, Andy could tell. 'Cops just came by, know what I mean?'

'What do they want?' he asked innocently.

Your ass, Andy thought. 'Just asking questions and showing pictures. I looked at the pictures, you know.'

'Uh-huh,' he said.

'Pretty good pictures,' Andy said.

Mr. McDeere stared at Andy real hard.

Andy said, 'Cop said one of them escaped from prison. Know what I mean. I been in prison, and I think everybody ought to escape. You know?'

Mr. McDeere smiled, a rather nervous smile. 'What's your name?' he asked.

'Andy.'

'I've got a deal for you, Andy. I'll give you a thousand bucks now, and tomorrow, if you're still unable to recognize anybody, I'll give you another thousand bucks. Same for the next day.'

A wonderful deal, thought Andy, but if he could afford a thousand bucks a day, certainly he could afford five thousand a day. It was the opportunity of his career.

'Nope,' Andy said firmly. 'Five thousand a day.'

Mr. McDeere never hesitated. 'It's a deal. Let me get the money.' He went in the room and returned with a stack of bills.

'Five thousand a day, Andy, that's our deal?'

Andy took the money and glanced around. He would count it later. 'I guess you want me to keep the maids away?' Andy asked.

'Great idea. That would be nice.'

'Another five thousand,' Andy said.

Mr. McDeere sort of hesitated. 'Okay, I've got another deal. Tomorrow morning, a Fed Ex package will arrive at the desk for Sam Fortune. You bring it to me, and keep the maids away, and I'll give you another five thousand.'

'Won't work. I do the night shift.'

'Okay, Andy. What if you worked all weekend, around the clock, kept the maids away and delivered my package? Can you do that?'

'Sure. My boss is a drunk. He'd love for me to work all weekend.'

'How much money, Andy?'

Go for it, Andy thought. 'Another twenty thousand.'

Mr. McDeere smiled. 'You got it.'

Andy grinned and stuck the money in his pocket. He walked away without saying a word, and Mitch retreated to Room 38.

'Who was it?' Ray snapped.

Mitch smiled as he glanced between the blinds and the windows.

'I knew we would have to have a lucky break to pull this off. And I think we just found it.'

THIRTY-EIGHT

Mr. Morolto wore a black suit and a red tie and sat at the head of the plastic-coated executive conference table in the Dunes Room of the Best Western on the Strip. The twenty chairs around the table were packed with his best and brightest men. Around the four walls stood more of his trusted troops. Though they were thick-necked killers who did their deeds efficiently and without remorse, they looked like clowns in their colorful shirts and wild shorts and amazing potpourri of straw hats. He would have smiled at their silliness, but the urgency of the moment prevented smiling. He was listening.

On his immediate right was Lou Lazarov, and on his immediate left was DeVasher, and every ear in the small room listened as the two played tag team back and forth across the table.

'They're here. I know they're here,' DeVasher said dramatically, slapping both palms on the table with each syllable. The man had rhythm.

Lazarov's turn: 'I agree. They're here. Two came in a car, one came in a truck. We've found both vehicles abandoned, covered with fingerprints. Yes, they're here.'

DeVasher: 'But why Panama City Beach? It makes no sense.'

Lazarov: 'For one, he's been here before. Came here

Christmas, remember? He's familiar with this place, so he figures with all these cheap motels on the beach it's a great place to hide for a while. Not a bad idea, really. But he's had some bad luck. For a man on the run, he's carrying too much baggage, like a brother who everybody wants. And a wife. And a truckload of documents, we presume. Typical schoolboy mentality. If I gotta run, I'm taking everybody who loves me. Then his brother rapes a girl, they think, and suddenly every cop in Alabama and Florida is looking for them. Some pretty bad luck, really.'

'What about his mother?' Mr. Morolto asked.

Lazarov and DeVasher nodded at the great man and acknowledged this very intelligent question.

Lazarov: 'No, purely coincidental. She's a very simple woman who serves waffles and knows nothing. We've watched her since we got here.'

DeVasher: 'I agree. There's been no contact.'

Morolto nodded intelligently and lit a cigarette.

Lazarov: 'So if they're here, and we know they're here, then the feds and the cops also know they're here. We've got sixty people here, and they got hundreds. Odds are on them.'

'You're sure they're all three together?' Mr. Morolto asked.

DeVasher: 'Absolutely. We know the woman and the convict checked in the same night at Perdido, that they left and three hours later she checked in here at the Holiday Inn and paid cash for two rooms and that she rented the car and his fingerprints were on it. No doubt. We know Mitch rented a U-Haul Wednesday in Nashville, that he wired ten million bucks of our money into a bank in Nashville Thursday morning and then evidently hauled ass. The U-Haul was found here four hours ago. Yes, sir, they are together.'

Lazarov: 'If he left Nashville immediately after the money was wired, he would have arrived here around dark. The U-Haul was found empty, so they had to unload it somewhere around here, then hide it. That was probably sometime late last night, Thursday. Now, you gotta figure they need to sleep sometime. I figure they stayed here last night with plans of moving on today. But they woke up this morning and their faces were in the paper, cops running around bumping into each other, and suddenly the roads were blocked. So they're trapped here.'

DeVasher: 'To get out, they've got to borrow, rent or steal a car. No rental records anywhere around here. She rented a car in Mobile in her name. Mitch rented a U-Haul in Nashville in his name. Real proper ID. So you gotta figure they ain't that damned smart after all.'

Lazarov: 'Evidently they don't have fake IDs. If they rented a car around here for the escape, the rental records would be in the real name. No such records exist.'

Mr. Morolto waved his hand in frustration. 'All right, all right. So they're here. You guys are geniuses. I'm so proud of you. Now what?'

DeVasher's turn: 'The Fibbies are in the way. They're in control of the search, and we can't do nothing but sit and watch.'

Lazarov: 'I've called Memphis. Every senior associate in the firm is on the way down here. They know McDeere and his wife real well, so we'll put them on the beach and in restaurants and hotels. Maybe they'll see something.'

DeVasher: 'I figure they're in one of the little motels. They can give fake names, pay in cash and nobody'll be suspicious. Fewer people too. Less likelihood of being seen. They checked in at the Holiday Inn but didn't stay long. I bet they moved on down the Strip.'

Lazarov: 'First, we'll get rid of the feds and the cops.

They don't know it yet, but they're about to move their show on down the road. Then, early in the morning, we start door to door at the small motels. Most of these dumps have less than fifty rooms. I figure two of our men can search one in thirty minutes. I know it'll be slow, but we can't just sit here. Maybe when the cops pull out, the McDeeres will breathe a little and make a mistake.'

'You mean you want our men to start searching hotel rooms?' Mr. Morolto asked.

DeVasher: 'There's no way we can hit every door, but we gotta try.'

Mr. Morolto stood and glanced around the room. 'So what about the water?' he asked in the direction of Lazarov and DeVasher.

They stared at each other, thoroughly confused by the question.

'The water!' Mr. Morolto screamed. 'What about the water?'

All eyes shot desperately around the table and quickly landed upon Lazarov. 'I'm sorry, sir, I'm confused.'

Mr. Morolto leaned into Lazarov's face. 'What about the water, Lou? We're on a beach, right? There's land and highways and railroads and airports on one side, and there's water and boats on the other. Now, if the roads are blocked and the airports and railroads are out of the question, where do you think they might go? It seems obvious to me they would try to find a boat and ease out in the dark. Makes sense, don't it, boys?'

Every head in the room nodded quickly. DeVasher spoke first. 'Makes a hell of a lot of sense to me.'

'Wonderful,' said Mr. Morolto. 'Then where are our boats?'

Lazarov jumped from his seat, turned to the wall and began barking orders at his lieutenants. 'Go down

457

to the docks! Rent every fishing boat you can find for
tonight and all day tomorrow. Pay them whatever they
want. Don't answer any questions, just pay 'em the
money. Get our men on those boats and start patrolling as soon as possible. Stay within a mile of shore.'

Shortly before eleven, Friday night, Aaron Rimmer
stood at the checkout counter at an all-night Texaco
in Tallahassee and paid for a root beer and twelve
gallons of gas. He needed change for the call. Outside,
next to the car wash, he flipped through the blue pages
and called the Tallahassee Police Department. It was
an emergency. He explained himself, and the dispatcher connected him with a shift captain.

'Listen!' Rimmer yelled urgently, 'I'm here at this
Texaco, and five minutes ago I saw these convicts
everybody is looking for! I know it was them!'

'Which convicts?' asked the captain.

'The McDeeres. Two men and a woman. I left
Panama City Beach not two hours ago, and I saw their
pictures in the paper. Then I stopped here and filled
up, and I saw them.'

Rimmer gave his location and waited thirty seconds
for the first patrol car to arrive with blue lights
flashing. It was quickly followed by a second, third and
fourth. They loaded Rimmer in a front seat and raced
him to the South Precinct. The captain and a small
crowd waited anxiously. Rimmer was escorted like a
celebrity into the captain's office, where the three
composites and mug shot were waiting on the desk.

'That's them!' he shouted. 'I just saw them, not ten
minutes ago. They were in a green Ford pickup with
Tennessee plates, and it was pulling a long double-
axle U-Haul trailer.'

'Exactly where were you?' asked the captain. The
cops hung on every word.

'I was pumping gas, pump number four, regular

unleaded, and they eased into the parking lot, real suspicious like. They parked away from the pumps, and the woman got out and went inside.' He picked up Abby's composite and studied it. 'Yep. That's her. No doubt. Her hair's a lot shorter, but it's dark. She came right back out, didn't buy a thing. She seemed nervous and in a hurry to get back to the truck. I was finished pumping, so I walked inside. Right when I opened the door, they drove within two feet of me. I saw all three of them.'

'Who was driving?' asked the captain. Rimmer stared at Ray's mug shot. 'Not him. The other one.' He pointed at Mitch's composite.

'Could I see your driver's license,' a sergeant said.

Rimmer carried three sets of identification. He handed the sergeant an Illinois driver's license with his picture and the name Frank Temple.

'Which direction were they headed?' the captain asked.

'East.'

At the same moment, about four miles away, Tony Verkler hung up the pay phone, smiled to himself and returned to the Burger King.

The captain was on the phone. The sergeant was copying information from Rimmer/Temple's driver's license and a dozen cops chatted excitedly when a patrolman rushed into the office 'Just got a call! Another sighting, at a Burger King east of town. Same info! All three of them in a green Ford pickup pulling a U-Haul. Guy wouldn't leave a name, but said he saw their pictures in the paper. Said they pulled through the carry-out window, bought three sacks of food and took off.'

'It's gotta be them!' the captain said with a huge smile.

The Bay County sheriff sipped thick black coffee from

a Styrofoam cup and rested his black boots on the executive conference table in the Caribbean Room at the Holiday Inn. FBI agents were in and out, fixing coffee, whispering and updating each other on the latest. His hero, the big man himself, Director F. Denton Voyles, sat across the table and studied a street map with three of his underlings. Imagine, Denton Voyles in Bay County. The room was a beehive of police activity. Florida state troopers filtered in and out. Radios and telephones rang and squawked on a makeshift command post in a corner. Sheriff's deputies and city policemen from three countries loitered about, thrilled with the chase and suspense and presence of all those FBI agents. And Voyles.

A deputy burst through the door with a wild eyed glow of sheer excitement. 'Just got a call from Tallahassee! They've got two positive IDs in the last fifteen minutes! All three of them in a green Ford pickup with Tennessee tags!'

Voyles dropped his street map and walked over to the deputy. 'Where were the sightings?' The room was silent, except for the radios.

'First one was at a Texaco Quick Shop. Second one was four miles away at a Burger King. They drove through the drive in window. Both witnesses were positive and gave identical IDs.'

Voyles turned to the sheriff. 'Sheriff, call Tallahassee and confirm. How far away is it?'

The black boots hit the floor. 'Hour and a half. Straight down Interstate 10.'

Voyles pointed at Tarrance, and they stepped into a small room used as the bar. The quiet roar returned to mission control.

'If the sightings are real,' Voyles said quietly in Tarrance's face, 'we're wasting our time here.'

'Yes, sir. They sound legitimate. A single sighting

could be a fluke or a prank, but two that close together sound awfully legitimate.'

'How the hell did they get out of here?'

'It's gotta be that woman, Chief. She's been helping him for a month. I don't know who she is, or where he found her, but she's on the outside watching us and feeding him whatever he needs.'

'Do you think she's with them?'

'Doubt it. She's probably just following closely, away from the action, and taking directions from him.'

'He's brilliant, Wayne. He's been planning this for months.'

'Evidently.'

'You mentioned the Bahamas once.'

'Yes, sir. The million bucks we paid him was wired to a bank in Freeport. He later told me it didn't stay there long.'

'You think, maybe, he's headed there?'

'Who knows. Obviously he has to get out of the country. I talked to the warden today. He told me Ray McDeere can speak five or six languages fluently. They could be going anywhere.'

'I think we should pull out,' Voyles said.

'Let's get the roadblocks set up around Tallahassee. They won't last long if we've got a good description of the vehicle. We should have them by morning.'

'I want every cop in central Florida on the highways in an hour. Roadblocks everywhere. Every Ford pickup is automatically searched, okay? Our men will wait here until daybreak, then we'll pull up stakes.'

'Yes, sir,' Tarrance answered with a weary grin.

Word of the Tallahassee sightings spread instantly along the Emerald Coast. Panama City Beach relaxed. The McDeeres were gone. For reasons unknown only to them, their flight had moved inland. Sighted and positively identified, not once but twice, they were

461

now somewhere else speeding desperately toward the inevitable confrontation on the side of a dark highway.

The cops along the coast went home. A few roadblocks remained through the night in Bay County and Gulf County, the predawn hours of Saturday were almost normal. Both ends of the Strip remained blocked, with cops making cursory exams of driver's licenses. The roads north of town were free and clear. The search had moved east.

On the outskirts of Ocala, Florida, near Silver Springs on Highway 40, Tony Verkler lumbered from a 7-Eleven and stuck a quarter in a pay phone. He called the Ocala Police Department with the urgent report that he had just seen those three convicts everybody was looking for up around Panama City Beach. The McDeeres! Said he saw their pictures in the paper the day before when he was driving through Pensacola, and now he had just seen them. The dispatcher informed him all patrolmen were on the scene of a bad accident and asked if he would mind driving over to the police station so they could file a report. Tony said he was in a hurry, but since it was somewhat important, he would be there in a minute.

When he arrived, the chief of police was waiting in a T-shirt and blue jeans. His eyes were swollen and red, and his hair was not in place. He led Tony into his office and thanked him for coming by. He took notes as Tony explained how he was pumping gas in front of the 7-Eleven, and a green Ford pickup with a U-Haul trailer behind it pulled up next to the store and a woman got out and used the phone. Tony was in the process, he explained, of driving from Mobile to Miami and had driven through the manhunt up around Panama City. He had seen the newspapers and had been listening to his radio and knew all about the three McDeeres. Anyway, he went in and paid for the gas and thought that he had seen the woman somewhere before. Then he remembered the papers. He walked over to a magazine rack in the front window and got a good look at the men. No doubt in his mind. She hung up, got back in the truck between the men, and they left. Green Ford with Tennessee plates.

The chief thanked him and called the Marion County Sheriff's Department. Tony said goodbye and returned to his car, where Aaron Rimmer was asleep in the back seat.

They headed north, in the direction of Panama City Beach.

THIRTY-NINE

Saturday, 7 A.M. Andy Patrick looked east and west along the Strip, then walked quickly across the parking lot to Room 39. He knocked gently.

After a delay, she asked, 'Who is it?'

'The manager,' he answered. The door opened, and the man who resembled the composite of Mitchell Y. McDeere slid out. His hair was now very short and gold-colored. Andy stared at his hair.

'Good morning, Andy,' he said politely while glancing around the parking lot.

'Good morning. I was kinda wondering if you folks were still here.'

Mr. McDeere nodded and continued to look around the parking lot.

'I mean, according to the television this morning, you folks traveled halfway across Florida last night.'

'Yeah, we're watching it. They're playing games, aren't they, Andy?'

Andy kicked at a rock on the sidewalk. 'Television said there were three positive identifications last night. At three different places. Kinda strange, I thought. I was here all night, working and being on the lookout and all, and I didn't see you leave. Before sunrise I sneaked across the highway to a coffee shop, just over there, and as usual, there were cops in there. I sat close to them. According to them, the search has been

464

called off around here. They said the FBI moved out right after the last sighting came in, around four this morning. Most of the other cops left too. They're gonna keep the Strip blocked until noon and call it off. Rumor has it you've got help from the outside, and you're trying to get to the Bahamas.'

Mr. McDeere listened closely as he watched the parking lot. 'What else did they say?'

'They kept talking about a U-Haul truck full of stolen goods, and how they found the truck, and it was empty, and how nobody can figure out how you loaded the stolen goods into a trailer and sneaked outta town right under their noses. They're very impressed, all right. Of course, I didn't say nothing, but I figured it was the same U-Haul you drove in here Thursday night.'

Mr. McDeere was deep in thought and did not say anything. He didn't appear to be nervous. Andy studied his face carefully.

'You don't seem too pleased,' Andy said. 'I mean, the cops are leaving and calling off the search. That's good, ain't it?'

'Andy, can I tell you something?'

'Sure.'

'It's more dangerous now than before.'

Andy thought about this for a long minute, then said, 'How's that?'

'The cops just wanted to arrest me, Andy. But there are some people who want to kill me. Professional killers, Andy. Many of them. And they're still here.'

Andy narrowed his good eye and stared at Mr. McDeere. Professional killers! Around here? On the Strip? Andy took a step backward. He wanted to ask exactly who they were and why they were chasing him, but he knew he wouldn't get much of an answer. He saw an opportunity. 'Why don't you escape?'

'Escape? How could we escape?'

Andy kicked another rock and nodded in the direction of a 1971 Pontiac Bonneville parked behind the office. 'Well, you could use my car. You could get in the trunk, all three of you, and I could drive you outta town. You don't appear to be broke, so you could catch a plane and be gone. Just like that.'

'And how much would that cost?'

Andy studied his feet and scratched his ear. The guy was probably a doper, he thought, and the boxes were probably full of cocaine and cash. And the Colombians were probably after him. 'That'd be pretty expensive, you know. I mean, right now, at five thousand a day, I'm just an innocent motel clerk who's not very observant. Not part of nothing, you understand. But if I drive you outta here, then I become an accomplice, subject to indictment and jail and all that other crap I've been through, you know. So it'd be pretty expensive.'

'How much, Andy?'

'A hundred thousand.'

Mr. McDeere did not flinch or react; he just kept a straight face and glanced across the beach to the ocean. Andy knew immediately it was not out of the question.

'Let me think about it, Andy. For right now, you keep your eyes open. Now that the cops are gone, the killers will move in. This could be a very dangerous day, Andy, and I need your help. If you see anyone suspicious around here, call us quick. We're not leaving these rooms, okay?'

Andy returned to the front desk. Any fool would jump in the trunk and haul ass. It was the boxes, the stolen goods. That's why they wouldn't leave.

The McDeeres enjoyed a light breakfast of stale pastries and warm soft drinks. Ray was dying for a cold beer, but another trip to the convenience store was too risky. They ate quickly and watched the early-morning news. Occasionally a station along the coast would flash their composites on the screen. It scared them at first, but they got used to it.

A few minutes after 9 A.M., Saturday, Mitch turned off the television and resumed his spot on the floor among the boxes. He picked up a stack of documents and nodded at Abby, the camera operator. The deposition continued.

Lazarov waited until the maids were on duty, then scattered his troops along the Strip. They worked in pairs, knocking on doors, peeking in windows and sliding through dark hallways. Most of the small places had two or three maids who knew every room and every guest. The procedure was simple, and most of the time it worked. A goon would find a maid, hand her a hundred-dollar bill, and show her the composites. If she resisted, he would continue giving money until she became cooperative. If she was unable to make the ID, he would ask if she had noticed a U-Haul truck, or a room full of boxes, or two men and a woman acting suspicious or scared, or anything unusual. If the maid was of no help, he would ask which rooms were occupied, then go knock on the doors.

Start with the maids, Lazarov had instructed them. Enter from the beach side. Stay away from the front desks. Pretend to be cops. And, if you hit pay dirt, kill them instantly and get to a phone.

DeVasher placed four of the rented vans along the Strip near the highway. Lamar Quin, Kendall Mahan, Wally Hudson and Jack Aldrich posed as drivers and watched every vehicle that passed. They had arrived in the middle of the night on a private plane with ten other senior associates of Bendini, Lambert & Locke. In the souvenir shops and cafés, the former friends and colleagues of Mitch McDeere milled about with the tourists and secretly hoped they would not see him. The partners had been called home from airports around the country, and by midmorning they were walking the beach and inspecting pools and hotel lobbies. Nathan Locke stayed behind with Mr. Morolto, but the rest of the partners disguised themselves with golf caps and sunglasses and took orders from General DeVasher. Only Avery Tolleson was missing. Since walking out of the hospital, he had not been heard from. Including the thirty-three lawyers, Mr. Morolto had almost a hundred men participating in his private little manhunt.

At the Blue Tide Motel, a janitor took a hundred dollar bill, looked at the composites and said he thought he might have seen the woman and one of the men check into two rooms early Thursday evening. He stared at Abby's sketch and became convinced it was her. He took some more money and went to the office to check the registration records. He returned with the information that the woman had checked in as Jackie Nagel and paid cash for two rooms for Thursday, Friday and Saturday. He took some more money, and the two gunmen followed him to the rooms. He knocked on both doors. No answer. He unlocked them and allowed his new friends to inspect them. The rooms had not been used Friday night. One of the troops called Lazarov, and five minutes later DeVasher was poking around the rooms looking for clues. He found none, but the search was immediately constricted to a four-mile stretch of beach between the Blue Tide and the Beachcomber, where the U-Haul was found.

The vans moved the troops closer. The partners and senior associates scoured the beach and restaurants. And the gunmen knocked on doors.

Andy signed the Federal Express ticket at 10:35 and inspected the package for Sam Fortune. It had been shipped by Doris Greenwood, whose address was listed as 4040 Poplar Avenue, Memphis, Tennessee. No phone number. He was certain it was valuable and for a moment contemplated another quick profit. But its delivery had already been contracted for. He gazed along both ends of the Strip and left the office with the package.

After years of dodging and hiding, Andy had subconsciously trained himself to walk quickly in the shadows, near the corners, never in the open. As he turned the corner to cross the parking lot, he saw two men knocking on the door to Room 21. The room happened to be vacant, and he was immediately suspicious of the two. They wore odd-fitting matching white shorts that fell almost to their knees, although it was difficult to tell exactly where the shorts stopped and the snow-white legs began. One wore dark socks with battered loafers. The other wore cheap sandals and walked in obvious pain. White Panama hats adorned their beefy heads.

After six months on the Strip, Andy could spot a fake tourist. The one beating on the door hit it again, and when he did Andy saw the bulge of a large handgun stuck in the back of his shorts.

He quickly retraced his quiet footsteps and returned to the office. He called Room 39 and asked for Sam Fortune.

'This is Sam.'

'Sam, this is Andy at the desk. Don't look out, but there are two very suspicious men knocking on doors across the parking lot.'

'Are they cops?'

'I don't think so. They didn't check in here.'

'Where are the maids?' Sam asked.

'They don't come in till eleven on Saturday.'

'Good. We're turning off the lights. Watch them and call when they leave.'

From a dark window in a closet, Andy watched the men go from door to door, knocking and waiting, occasionally getting one to open. Eleven of the forty-two rooms were occupied. No response at 38 and 39. They returned to the beach and disappeared. Professional killers! At his motel.

Across the Strip, in the parking lot of a miniature golf course, Andy saw two identical fake tourists talking to a man in a white van. They pointed here and there and seemed to be arguing.

He called Sam. 'Listen, Sam, they're gone. But this place is crawling with these people.'

'How many?'

'I can see two more across the Strip. You folks better run for it.'

'Relax, Andy. They won't see us if we stay in here.'

'But you can't stay forever. My boss'll catch on before much longer.'

'We're leaving soon, Andy. What about the package?'

'It's here.'

'Good. I need to see it. Say, Andy, what about food? Could you ease across the street and get something hot?'

Andy was a manager, not a porter. But for five thousand a day the Sea Gull's Rest could provide a little room service. 'Sure. Be there in a minute.'

Wayne Tarrance grabbed the phone and fell across the single bed in his Ramada Inn room in Orlando. He was exhausted, furious, baffled and sick of F. Denton Voyles. It was 1:30 P.M., Saturday. He called Memphis. The secretary had nothing to report, except that Mary Alice called and wanted to talk to him. They had traced the call to a pay phone in Atlanta. Mary Alice

470

said she would call again at 2 P.M. to see if Wayne – she called him Wayne – had checked in. Tarrance gave his room number and hung up. Mary Alice. In Atlanta. McDeere in Tallahassee, then Ocala. Then no McDeere. No green Ford pickup with Tennessee plates and trailer. He had vanished again.

The phone rang once. Tarrance slowly lifted the receiver. 'Mary Alice,' he said softly.

'Wayne baby! How'd you guess?'

'Where is he?'

'Who?' Tammy giggled.

'McDeere. Where is he?'

'Well, Wayne, you boys were close for a while, but then you chased a wild rabbit. Now you're not even close, baby. Sorry to tell you.'

'We've got three positive IDs in the past fourteen hours.'

'Better check them out, Wayne. Mitch told me a few minutes ago he's never been to Tallahassee. Never heard of Ocala. Never driven a green Ford pickup. Never pulled a U-Haul trailer. You boys bit hard, Wayne. Hook, line and sinker.'

Tarrance pinched the bridge of his nose and breathed into the phone.

'So how's Orlando?' she asked. 'Gonna see Disney World while you're in town?'

'Where the hell is he!'

'Wayne, Wayne, relax, baby. You'll get the documents.'

Tarrance sat up. 'Okay, when?'

'Well, we could be greedy and insist on the rest of our money. I'm at a pay phone, Wayne, so don't bother to trace it, okay? But we're not greedy. You'll get your records within twenty-four hours. If all goes well.'

'Where are the records?'

'I'll have to call you back, baby. If you stay at this number, I'll call you every four hours until Mitch tells me where the documents are. But, Wayne, if you leave this number, I might lose you, baby. So stay put.'

'I'll be here. Is he still in the country?'

'I think not. I'm sure he's in Mexico by now. His brother speaks the language, you know?'

'I know.' Tarrance stretched out on the bed and said to hell with it. Mexico could have them, as long as he got the records.

'Stay where you are, baby. Take a nap. You gotta be tired. I'll call around five or six.'

Tarrance laid the phone on the nightstand, and took a nap.

The dragnet lost its steam Saturday afternoon when the Panama City Beach police received the fourth complaint from motel owners. The cops were dispatched to the Breakers Motel, where an irate owner told of armed men harassing the guests. More cops were sent to the Strip, and before long they were searching the motels for gunmen who were searching for the McDeeres. The Emerald Coast was on the brink of war.

Weary and hot, DeVasher's men were forced to work alone. They spread themselves even thinner along the beach and stopped the door-to-door work. They lounged in plastic chairs around the pools, watching the tourists come and go. They lay on the beach, dodging the sun, hiding behind dark shades, watching the tourists come and go.

As dusk approached, the army of goons and thugs and gunmen, and lawyers, slipped into the darkness and waited. If the McDeeres were going to move, they would do it at night. A silent army waited for them.

DeVasher's thick forearms rested uncomfortably on a balcony railing outside his Best Western room. He watched the empty beach below as the sun slowly disappeared on the horizon. Aaron Rimmer walked through the sliding glass door and stopped behind DeVasher. 'We found Tolleson,' Rimmer said.

DeVasher did not move. 'Where?'

'Hiding in his girlfriend's apartment in Memphis.'

'Was he alone?'

'Yeah. They iced him. Made it look like a robbery.'

In Room 39, Ray inspected for the hundredth time the new passports, visas, driver's licenses and birth certificates. The passport photos for Mitch and Abby were current, with plenty of dark hair. After the escape, time would take care of the blondness. Ray's photo was a slightly altered Harvard Law School mug shot of Mitch, with the long hair, stubble and rough academic looks. The eyes, noses and cheekbones were similar, after careful analysis, but nothing else. The documents were in the names of Lee Stevens, Rachel James and Sam Fortune, all with addresses in Murfreesboro, Tennessee. Doc did good work, and Ray smiled as he studied each one.

Abby packed the Sony video camera into its box. The tripod was folded and leaned against the wall. Fourteen videocassette tapes with stick-on labels were stacked neatly on the television.

After sixteen hours, the video deposition was over. Starting with the first tape, Mitch had faced the camera, raised his right hand and sworn to tell the truth. He stood next to the dresser with documents covering the floor around him. Using Tammy's notes, summaries and flowcharts, he methodically walked through the bank records first. He identified over two hundred and fifty secret accounts in eleven Cayman banks. Some had names, but most were just numbered. Using copies of computer printouts, he constructed the histories of the accounts. Cash deposits, wire transfers and withdrawals. At the bottom of each document used in his deposition, he wrote with a black marker the initials MM and then the exhibit number: MM1, MM2, MM3 and so on. After Exhibit MM1485, he had identified nine hundred million dollars hiding in Cayman banks.

After the bank records, he painstakingly pieced together the structure of the empire. In twenty years, more than four hundred Cayman corporations had been chartered by the Moroltos and their incredibly rich and incredibly corrupt attorneys. Many of the corporations owned all or pieces of each other and used the banks as registered agents and permanent addresses. Mitch learned quickly that he had only a fraction of the records and speculated, on camera, that most documents were hidden in the basement in Memphis. He also explained, for the benefit of the jury, that it would take a small army of IRS investigators a year or so to piece together the Morolto corporate puzzle. He slowly explained each exhibit, marked it carefully and filed it away. Abby operated the camera. Ray watched the parking lot and studied the fake passports.

Mitch testified for six hours on various methods used by the Moroltos and their attorneys to turn dirty money into clean. Easily the most favored method was to fly in a load of dirty cash on a Bendini plane, usually with two or three lawyers on board to legitimate the trip. With dope pouring in by land, air and sea, U.S. customs cares little about what's leaving the country. It was a perfect setup. The planes left dirty and came back clean. Once the money landed on Grand Cayman, a lawyer on board handled the required payoffs to Cayman customs and to the appropriate banker. On some loads, up to twenty-five percent went for bribes.

Once deposited, usually in unnamed, numbered accounts, the money became almost impossible to trace. But many of the bank transactions coincided nicely with significant corporate events. The money

474

was usually deposited into one of a dozen numbered holding accounts. Or 'super accounts,' as Mitch called them. He gave the jury these account numbers, and the names of the banks. Then, as the new corporations were chartered, the money was transferred from the super accounts to the corporate accounts, often in the same bank. Once the dirty money was owned by a legitimate Cayman corporation, the laundering began. The simplest and most common method was for the company to purchase real estate and other clean assets in the United States. The transactions were handled by the creative attorneys at Bendini, Lambert & Locke, and all money moved by wire transfer. Often, the Cayman corporation would purchase another Cayman corporation that happened to own a Panama corporation that owned a holding company in Denmark. The Danes would purchase a ball-bearing factory in Toledo and wire in the purchase money from a subsidiary bank in Munich. And the dirty money was now clean.

After marking Exhibit MM4292, Mitch quit the deposition. Sixteen hours of testimony was enough. Tarrance and his buddies could show the tapes to a grand jury and indict at least thirty lawyers from the Bendini firm. He could show the tapes to a federal magistrate and get his search warrants.

Mitch had held to his end of the bargain. Although he would not be around to testify in person, he had been paid only a million dollars and was about to deliver more than was expected. He was physically and emotionally drained, and sat on the edge of the bed with the lights off. Abby sat in a chair with her eyes closed.

Ray peeked through the blinds. 'We need a cold beer,' he said.

'Forget it,' Mitch snapped.

Ray turned and stared at him. 'Relax, little brother.

It's dark, and the store is just a short walk down the beach. I can take care of myself.'

'Forget it, Ray. There is no need to take chances. We're leaving in a few hours, and if all goes well, you'll have the rest of your life to drink beer.'

Ray was not listening. He pulled a baseball cap firmly over his forehead, stuck some cash in his pockets and reached for the gun.

'Ray, please, at least forget the gun,' Mitch pleaded.

Ray stuck the gun under his shirt and eased out the door. He walked quickly in the sand behind the small motels and shops, hiding in the shadows and craving a cold beer. He stopped behind the convenience store, looked quickly around and was certain no one was watching, then walked to the front door. The beer cooler was in the rear.

In the parking lot next to the Strip, Lamar Quin hid under a large straw hat and made small talk with some teenagers from Indiana. He saw Ray enter the store and thought he might recognize something. There was a casualness about the man's stride that looked vaguely familiar. Lamar moved to the front window and glanced in the direction of the beer cooler. The man's eyes were covered with sunglasses, but the nose and cheekbones were certainly familiar. Lamar eased inside the small store and picked up a sack of potato chips. He waited at the checkout counter and came face to face with the man, who was not Mitchell McDeere but greatly resembled him.

It was Ray. It had to be. The face was sunburned, and the hair was too short to be stylish. The eyes were covered. Same height. Same weight. Same walk.

'How's it going?' Lamar said to the man.

'Fine. You?' the voice was similar.

Lamar paid for his chips and returned to the parking lot. He calmly dropped the bag in a garbage can next to a phone booth and quickly walked next door to a souvenir shop to continue his search for the McDeeres.

FORTY

Darkness brought a cool breeze to the beach along the Strip. The sun disappeared quickly, and there was no moon to replace it. A distant ceiling of harmless dark clouds covered the sky, and the water was black.

Darkness brought fishermen to the Dan Russell Pier in the center of the Strip. They gathered in groups of three and four along the concrete structure and stared silently as their lines ran into the black water twenty feet below. They leaned motionless on the railing, occasionally spitting or talking to a friend. They enjoyed the breeze and the quietness and the still water much more than they enjoyed the occasional fish that ventured by and hit a hook. They were vacationers from the North who spent the same week each year at the same motel and came to the pier each night in the darkness to fish and marvel at the sea. Between them sat buckets full of bait and small coolers full of beer.

From time to time throughout the night, a nonfisherman or a pair of lovebirds would venture onto the pier and walk a hundred yards to the end of it. They would gaze at the black, gentle water for a few minutes, then turn and admire the glow of a million flickering lights along the Strip. They would watch the inert, huddled fishermen leaning on their elbows. The fishermen did not notice them.

The fishermen did not notice Aaron Rimmer as he

casually walked behind them around eleven. He smoked a cigarette at the end of the pier and tossed the butt into the ocean. He gazed along the beach and thought of the thousands of motel rooms and condos.

The Dan Russell Pier was the westernmost of the three at Panama City Beach. It was the newest, the longest and the only one built with nothing but concrete. The other two were older and wooden. In the center there was a small brick building containing a tackle shop, a snack bar and rest rooms. Only the rest rooms were open at night.

It was probably a half mile east of the Sea Gull's Rest. At eleven-thirty, Abby left Room 39, eased by the dirty pool and began walking east along the beach. She wore shorts, a white straw hat and a windbreaker with the collar turned up around her ears. She walked slowly, with her hands thrust deep in the pockets like an experienced, contemplative beachcomber. Five minutes later, Mitch left the room, eased by the dirty pool and followed her footsteps. He gazed at the ocean as he walked. Two joggers approached, splashing in the water and talking between breaths. On a string around his neck and tucked under his black cotton shirt was a whistle, just in case. In all four pockets he had crammed sixty thousand in cash. He looked at the ocean and nervously watched Abby ahead of him. When he was two hundred yards down the beach, Ray left Room 39 for the last time. He locked it and kept a key. Wrapped around his waist was a forty-foot piece of black nylon rope. The gun was stuck under it. A bulky windbreaker covered it all nicely. Andy had charged another two thousand for the clothing and items.

Ray eased by the pool and onto the beach. He watched Mitch and could barely see Abby. The beach was deserted.

It was almost midnight, Saturday, and most of the

fishermen had left the pier for another night. Abby saw three in a small cluster near the rest rooms. She eased past them and nonchalantly strolled to the end of the pier, where she leaned on the concrete railing and stared at the vast blackness of the Gulf. Red buoy lights were scattered as far as she could see. Blue and white channel lights formed a neat line to the east. A blinking yellow light on some vessel inched away on the horizon. She was alone at the end of the pier.

Mitch hid in a beach chair under a folded umbrella near the entrance to the pier. He could not see her, but had a good view of the ocean. Fifty feet away, Ray sat in the darkness on a brick ledge. His feet dangled in the sand. They waited. They checked their watches.

At precisely midnight, Abby nervously unzipped her windbreaker and untied a heavy flashlight. She glanced at the water below and gripped it fiercely. She shoved it into her stomach, shielded it with the windbreaker, aimed at the sea and pushed the switch three times. On and off. On and off. On and off. The green bulb flashed three times. She held it tightly and stared at the ocean.

No response. She waited an eternity and two minutes later flashed again. Three times. No response. She breathed deeply and spoke to herself. 'Be calm, Abby, be calm. He's out there somewhere.' She flashed three more times. Then waited. No response.

Mitch sat on the edge of the beach chair and anxiously surveyed the sea. From the corner of an eye, he saw a figure walking, almost running from the west. It jumped onto the steps of the pier. It was the Nordic. Mitch bolted across the beach after him.

Aaron Rimmer walked behind the fishermen, around the small building, and watched the woman in the white hat at the end of the pier. She was bent over clutching something. It flashed again, three times. He walked silently up to her.

'Abby.'

She jerked around and tried to scream. Rimmer lunged at her and shoved her into the railing. From the darkness, Mitch dived head first into the Nordic's legs, and all three went down hard onto the slick concrete. Mitch felt the gun at the Nordic's back. He swung wildly with a forearm and missed. Rimmer whirled and landed a wicked smash to Mitch's left eye. Abby kicked and crawled away. Mitch was blind and dazed. Rimmer stood quickly and reached for the gun, but never found it. Ray charged like a battering ram and sent the Nordic crashing into the railing. He landed four bulletlike jabs to the eyes and nose, each one drawing blood. Skills learned in prison. The Nordic fell to all fours, and Ray snapped his head with four powerful kicks. He groaned pitifully and fell, face first.

Ray removed the gun and handed it to Mitch, who was standing now and trying to focus with his good eye. Abby watched the pier. No one.

'Start flashing,' Ray said as he unwound the rope from his waist. Abby faced the water, shielded the flashlight, found the switch and began flashing like crazy.

'What're you gonna do?' Mitch whispered, watching Ray and the rope.

'Two choices. We can either blow his brains out or drown him.'

'Oh my god!' Abby said as she flashed.

'Don't fire the gun,' Mitch whispered.

'Thank you,' Ray said. He grabbed a short section of rope, twisted it tightly around the Nordic's neck and pulled. Mitch turned his back and stepped between the body and Abby. She did not try to watch. 'I'm sorry. We have no choice,' Ray mumbled almost to himself.

There was no resistance, no movement from the unconscious man. After three minutes, Ray exhaled loudly and announced, 'He's dead.' He tied the other

481

end of the rope to a post, slid the body under the railing and lowered it quietly into the water.

'I'm going down first,' Ray said as he crawled through the railing and eased down the rope. Eight feet under the deck of the pier, an iron cross brace was attached to two of the thick concrete columns that disappeared into the water. It made a nice hideout. Abby was next. Ray grabbed her legs as she clutched the rope and eased downward. Mitch, with his one eye, lost his equilibrium and almost went for a swim.

But they made it. They sat on the cross brace, ten feet above the cold, dark water. Ten feet above the fish and the barnacles and the body of the Nordic. Ray cut the rope so the corpse could fall to the bottom properly before it made its ascent in a day or two.

They sat like three owls on a limb, watching the buoy lights and channel lights and waiting for the messiah to come walking across the water. The only sounds were the soft splashing of the waves below and the steady clicking of the flashlight.

And then voices from the deck above. Nervous, anxious, panicked voices, searching for someone. Then they were gone.

'Well, little brother, what do we do now?' Ray whispered.

'Plan B,' Mitch said.

'And what's that?'

'Start swimming.'

'Very funny,' Abby said, clicking away.

An hour passed. The iron brace, though perfectly located, was not comfortable.

'Have you noticed those two boats out there?' Ray asked quietly.

The boats were small, about a mile offshore, and for the past hour had been cruising slowly and suspiciously back and forth in sight of the beach. 'I think they're fishing boats,' Mitch said.

'Who fishes at one o'clock in the morning?' Ray asked.

The three of them thought about this. There was no explanation.

Abby saw it first, and hoped and prayed it was not the body now floating toward them. 'Over there,' she said, pointing fifty yards out to sea. It was a black object, resting on the water and moving slowly in their direction. They watched intently. Then the sound, like that of a sewing machine.

'Keep flashing,' Mitch said. It grew closer.

It was a man in a small boat.

'Abanks!' Mitch whispered loudly. The humming noise died.

'Abanks!' he said again.

'Where the hell are you?' came the reply.

'Over here. Under the pier. Hurry, dammit!'

The hum grew louder, and Abanks parked an eight-foot rubber raft under the pier. They swung from the brace and landed in one joyous pile. They quietly hugged each other, then hugged Abanks. He revved up the five-horsepower electric trolling motor and headed for open water.

'Where's the boat?' Mitch asked.

'About a mile out,' answered Abanks.

'What happened to your green light?'

Abanks pointed to a flashlight next to the motor. 'Battery went dead.'

The boat was a forty-foot schooner that Abanks had found in Jamaica for only two hundred thousand. A friend waited by the ladder and helped them aboard. His name was George, just George, and he spoke English with a quick accent. Abanks said he could be trusted.

'There's whiskey if you like. In the cabinet,' Abanks said. Ray found the whiskey. Abby found a blanket and lay down on a small couch. Mitch stood on the deck and admired his new boat. When Abanks and George had the raft aboard, Mitch said, 'Let's get out of here. Can we leave now?'

'As you wish,' George snapped properly.

Mitch gazed at the lights along the beach and said farewell. He went below and poured a cup of scotch.

Wayne Tarrance slept across the bed in his clothes. He had not moved since the last call, six hours earlier. The phone rang beside him. After four rings, he found it.

'Hello.' His voice was slow and scratchy.

'Wayne baby. Did I wake you?'

'Of course.'

'You can have the documents now. Room 39, Sea Gull's Rest Motel, Highway 98, Panama City Beach. The desk clerk is a guy named Andy, and he'll let you in the room. Be careful with them. Our friend has them all marked real nice and precise, and he's got sixteen hours of videotape. So be gentle.'

'I have a question,' Tarrance said.

'Sure, big boy. Anything.'

'Where did he find you? This would've been impossible without you.'

'Gee, thanks, Wayne. He found me in Memphis. We got to be friends, and he offered me a bunch of money.'

'How much?'

'Why is that important, Wayne? I'll never have to work again. Gotta run, baby. It's been real fun.'

'Where is he?'

'As we speak, he's on a plane to South America. But please don't waste your time trying to catch him. Wayne, baby, I love you, but you couldn't even catch him in Memphis. Bye now.' She was gone.

FORTY-ONE

Dawn. Sunday. The forty-foot schooner sped south with full sails under a clear sky. Abby was in a deep sleep in the master suite. Ray was in a scotch-induced coma on a couch. Abanks was somewhere below catching a nap.

Mitch sat on the deck sipping cold coffee and listening to George expound on the basics of sailing. He was in his late fifties, with long, gray, bleached hair and dark, sun cured skin. He was small and wiry, much like Abanks. He was Australian by birth, but twenty-eight years earlier had fled his country after the largest bank heist in its history. He and his partner split eleven million in cash and silver and went their separate ways. His partner was now dead, he had heard.

George was not his real name, but he'd used it for twenty-eight years and forgotten the real one. He discovered the Caribbean in the late sixties, and after seeing its thousands of small, primitive English-speaking islands, decided he'd found home. He put his money in banks in the Bahamas, Belize, Panama and, of course, Grand Cayman. He built a small compound on a deserted stretch of beach on Little Cayman and had spent the past twenty-one years touring the Caribbean in his thirty-foot schooner. During the summer and early fall, he stayed close to home. But from October to June, he lived on his boat and hopped from island to island. He'd been to three hundred of them in the Caribbean. He once spent two years just in the Bahamas.

'There are thousands of islands,' he explained. 'And they'll never find you if you move a lot.'

'Are they still looking for you?' Mitch asked.

'I don't know. I can't call and ask, you know. But I doubt it.'

'Where's the safest place to hide?'

'On this boat. It's a nice little yacht, and once you learn to sail it, it'll be your home. Find you a little island somewhere, perhaps Little Cayman or Brac – they're both still primitive – and build a house. Do as I've done. And spend most of your time on this boat.'

'When do you stop worrying about being chased?'

'Oh, I still think about it, you know. But I don't worry about it. How much did you get away with?'

'Eight million, give or take,' Mitch said.

'That's nice. You've got the money to do as you please, so forget about them. Just tour the islands for the rest of your life. There are worse things, you know.'

For days they sailed toward Cuba, then around it in the direction of Jamaica. They watched George and listened to his lectures. After twenty years of sailing through the Caribbean, he was a man of great knowledge and patience. Ray, the linguist, listened to and memorized words like spinnaker, mast, bow, stern, aft, tiller, halyard winches, masthead fittings, shrouds, lifelines, stanchions, sheet winch, bow pulpit, coamings, transom, clew outhaul, genoa sheets, mainsail, jib, jibstays, jib sheets, cam cleats and boom vangs. George lectured on heeling, luffing, running, blanketing, backwinding, heading up, trimming and pointing. Ray absorbed the language of sailing; Mitch studied the technique.

Abby stayed in the cabin, saying little and smiling only when necessary. Life on a boat was not something she dreamed about. She missed her house and wondered what would happen to it. Maybe Mr. Rice would cut the grass and pull the weeds. She missed the shady streets and neat lawns and the small gangs of children riding bicycles. She thought of her dog, and prayed that Mr. Rice would adopt it. She worried about her parents – their safety and their fear. When would she see them again? It would be years, she decided, and she could live with that if she knew they were safe.

Her thoughts could not escape the present. The future was inconceivable.

During the second day of the rest of her life, she began writing letters; letters to her parents, Kay Quin, Mr. Rice and a few friends. The letters would never be mailed, she knew, but it helped to put the words on paper.

Mitch watched her carefully, but left her alone. He had nothing to say, really. Maybe in a few days they could talk.

By the end of the fourth day, Wednesday, Grand Cayman was in sight. They circled it slowly once and anchored a mile from shore. After dark, Barry Abanks said goodbye. The McDeeres simply thanked him, and he eased away in the rubber raft. He would land three miles from Bodden Town at another dive lodge, then call one of his dive captains to come get him. He would know if anyone suspicious had been around. Abanks expected no trouble.

George's compound on Little Cayman consisted of a small main house of white-painted wood and two smaller outbuildings. It was inland a quarter of a mile, on a tiny bay. The nearest house could not be seen. A native woman lived in the smallest building and maintained the place. Her name was Fay.

The McDeeres settled in the main house and tried to begin the process of starting over. Ray, the escapee, roamed the beaches for hours and kept to himself. He was euphoric, but could not show it. He and George took the boat out for several hours each day and drank scotch while exploring the islands. They usually returned drunk.

Abby spent the first days in a small room upstairs overlooking the bay. She wrote more letters and began a diary. She slept alone.

Twice a week, Fay drove the Volkswagen bus into town for supplies and mail. She returned one day with a package from Barry Abanks. George delivered it to Mitch. Inside the package was a parcel sent to Abanks from Doris Greenwood in Miami. Mitch ripped open the thick legal-sized envelope and found three newspapers, two from Atlanta and one from Miami.

The headlines told of the mass indicting of the Bendini law firm in Memphis. Fifty-one present and former members of the firm were indicted, along with thirty-one alleged members of the Morolto crime family in Chicago. More indictments were coming, promised the U.S. Attorney. Just the tip of the iceberg. Director F. Denton Voyles allowed himself to be quoted as saying it was a major blow to organized crime in America. It should be a dire warning, he said, to legitimate professionals and businessmen who are tempted to handle dirty money.

Mitch folded the newspapers and went for a long walk on the beach. Under a cluster of palms, he found some shade and sat down. The Atlanta paper listed the names of every Bendini lawyer indicted. He read them slowly. There was no joy in seeing the names. He almost felt sorry for Nathan Locke. Almost. Wally Hudson, Kendall Mahan, Jack Aldrich and, finally, Lamar Quin. He could see their faces. He knew their wives and their children. Mitch gazed across the brilliant ocean and thought about Lamar and Kay Quin. He loved them, and he hated them. They had helped seduce him into the firm, and they were not without blame. But they were his friends. What a waste! Maybe Lamar would only serve a couple of years and then be paroled. Maybe Kay and the kids could survive. Maybe.

'I love you, Mitch.' Abby was standing behind him. She held a plastic pitcher and two cups.

He smiled at her and waved to the sand next to him. 'What's in the pitcher?'

'Rum punch. Fay mixed it for us.'

'Is it strong?'

She sat next to him on the sand. 'It's mostly rum. I told Fay we needed to get drunk, and she agreed.'

He held her tightly and sipped the rum punch. They watched a small fishing boat inch through the sparkling water.

'Are you scared, Mitch?'

'Terrified.'

'Me too. This is crazy.'

'But we made it, Abby. We're alive. We're safe. We're together.'

'But what about tomorrow? And the next day?'

'I don't know, Abby. Things could be worse, you know. My name could be in the paper there with the other freshly indicted defendants. Or we could be dead. There are worse things than sailing around the Caribbean with eight million bucks in the bank.'

'Do you think my parents are safe?'

'I think so. What would Morolto have to gain by harming your parents? They're safe, Abby.'

She refilled the cups with rum punch and kissed him

on the cheek. 'I'll be okay Mitch. As long as we're together, I can handle anything.'

'Abby,' Mitch said slowly, staring at the water, 'I have a confession to make.'

'I'm listening.'

'The truth is I never wanted to be a lawyer anyway.'

'Oh, really.'

'Naw. Secretly I've always wanted to be a sailor.'

'Is that so. Have you ever made love on the beach?'

Mitch hesitated for a slight second. 'Uh, no.'

'Then drink up, sailor. Let's get drunk and make a baby.'

THE PELICAN
BRIEF

TO MY READING COMMITTEE: Renée, my wife and unofficial editor; my sisters, Beth Bryant and Wendy Grisham; my mother-in-law, Lib Jones; and my friend and co-conspirator, Bill Ballard

ACKNOWLEDGMENTS

MANY THANKS to my literary agent, Jay Garon, who discovered my first novel five years ago and peddled it around New York until someone said yes.

Many thanks to David Gernert, my editor, who's also a friend and a fellow baseball purist; and to Steve Rubin and Ellen Archer and the rest of the family at Doubleday; and to Jackie Cantor, my editor at Dell.

Many thanks to those of you who've written. I've tried to answer them all, but if I missed one or two, please forgive.

Special thanks to Raymond Brown, a gentleman and fine lawyer in Pascagoula, Mississippi, who came through in the clutch; and to Chris Charlton, a law school pal who knows the alleys of New Orleans; and to Murray Avent, a friend from Oxford and Ole Miss who now lives in D.C.; and to Greg Block at the *Washington Post*; and, of course, to Richard and the Gang at Square Books.

THE PELICAN BRIEF

ONE

HE SEEMED INCAPABLE of creating such chaos, but much of what he saw below could be blamed on him. And that was fine. He was ninety-one, paralyzed, strapped in a wheelchair and hooked to oxygen. His second stroke seven years ago had almost finished him off, but Abraham Rosenberg was still alive and even with tubes in his nose his legal stick was bigger than the other eight. He was the only legend remaining on the Court, and the fact that he was still breathing irritated most of the mob below.

He sat in a small wheelchair in an office on the main floor of the Supreme Court Building. His feet touched the edge of the window, and he strained forward as the noise increased. He hated cops, but the sight of them standing in thick, neat lines was somewhat comforting. They stood straight and held ground as the mob of at least fifty thousand screamed for blood.

"Biggest crowd ever!" Rosenberg yelled at the window. He was almost deaf. Jason Kline, his senior law clerk, stood behind him. It was the first Monday in October, the opening day of the new term, and this had become a traditional celebration of the First Amendment. A glorious celebration. Rosenberg was thrilled. To him, freedom of speech meant freedom to riot.

"Are the Indians out there?" he asked loudly.

Jason Kline leaned closer to his right ear. "Yes!"

"With war paint?"

"Yes! In full battle dress."

"Are they dancing?"

"Yes!"

The Indians, the blacks, whites, browns, women, gays, tree lovers, Christians, abortion activists, Aryans, Nazis, atheists, hunters, animal lovers, white supremacists, black supremacists, tax protestors, loggers, farmers—it was a massive sea of protest. And the riot police gripped their black sticks.

"The Indians should love me!"

"I'm sure they do." Kline nodded and smiled at the frail little man with clenched fists. His ideology was simple; government over business, the individual over government, the environment over everything. And the Indians, give them whatever they want.

The heckling, praying, singing, chanting, and screaming grew louder, and the riot police inched closer together. The crowd was larger and rowdier than in recent years. Things were more tense. Violence had become common. Abortion clinics had been bombed. Doctors had been attacked and beaten. One was killed in Pensacola, gagged and bound into the fetal position and burned with acid. Street fights were weekly events. Churches and priests had been abused by militant gays. White supremacists operated from a dozen known, shadowy, paramilitary organizations, and had become bolder in their attacks on blacks, Hispanics, and Asians. Hatred was now America's favorite pastime.

And the Court, of course, was an easy target. Threats, serious ones, against the justices had increased tenfold since 1990. The Supreme Court police had tripled in size. At least two FBI agents were assigned to guard each justice, and another fifty were kept busy investigating threats.

"They hate me, don't they?" he said loudly, staring out the window.

"Yes, some of them do," Kline answered with amusement.

Rosenberg liked to hear that. He smiled and inhaled deeply. Eighty percent of the death threats were aimed at him.

"See any of those signs?" he asked. He was nearly blind.

"Quite a few."

"What do they say?"

"The usual. Death to Rosenberg. Retire Rosenberg. Cut Off the Oxygen."

"They've been waving those same damned signs for years. Why don't they get some new ones?"

The clerk did not answer. Abe should've retired years ago, but they would carry him out one day on a stretcher. His three law clerks did most of the research, but Rosenberg insisted on writing his own opinions. He did so with a heavy felt-tip marker and his words were scrawled across a white legal pad, much like a first-grader learning to write. Slow work, but with a lifetime appointment, who cared about time? The clerks proofed his opinions, and rarely found mistakes.

Rosenberg chuckled. "We oughta feed Runyan to the Indians." The Chief Justice was John Runyan, a tough conservative appointed by a Republican and hated by the Indians and most other minorities. Seven of the nine had been appointed by Republican Presidents. For fifteen years Rosenberg had been waiting for a Democrat in the White House. He wanted to quit, needed to quit, but he could not stomach the idea of a right-wing Runyan type taking his beloved seat.

He could wait. He could sit here in his wheelchair and breathe oxygen and protect the Indians, the blacks, the women, the poor, the handicapped, and the environment until he was a hundred and five. And not a single person in the world could do a damned thing about it, unless they killed him. And that wouldn't be such a bad idea either.

The great man's head nodded, then wobbled and rested on his shoulder. He was asleep again. Kline quietly stepped away, and returned to his research in the library. He would return in half an hour to check the oxygen and give Abe his pills.

THE OFFICE of the Chief Justice is on the main floor, and is larger and more ornate than the other eight. The outer office is used for small receptions and formal gatherings, and the inner office is where the Chief works.

The door to the inner office was closed, and the room was filled with the Chief, his three law clerks, the captain of the

Supreme Court police, three FBI agents, and K. O. Lewis, deputy director, FBI. The mood was serious, and a serious effort was under way to ignore the noise from the streets below. It was difficult. The Chief and Lewis discussed the latest series of death threats, and everyone else just listened. The clerks took notes.

In the past sixty days, the Bureau had logged over two hundred threats, a new record. There was the usual assortment of "Bomb the Court!" threats, but many came with specifics—like names, cases, and issues.

Runyan made no effort to hide his anxiety. Working from a confidential FBI summary, he read the names of individuals and groups suspected of threats. The Klan, the Aryans, the Nazis, the Palestinians, the black separatists, the pro-lifers, the homophobics. Even the IRA. Everyone, it seemed, but the Rotarians and the Boy Scouts. A Middle East group backed by the Iranians had threatened blood on American soil in retaliation for the deaths of two justice ministers in Tehran. There was absolutely no evidence the murders were linked to the U.S. A new domestic terrorist unit of recent fame known as the Underground Army had killed a federal trial judge in Texas with a car bomb. No arrests had been made, but the UA claimed responsibility. It was also the prime suspect in a dozen bombings of ACLU offices, but its work was very clean.

"What about these Puerto Rican terrorists?" Runyan asked without looking up.

"Lightweights. We're not worried," K. O. Lewis answered casually. "They've been threatening for twenty years."

"Well, maybe it's time they did something. The climate is right, don't you think?"

"Forget the Puerto Ricans, Chief." Runyan liked to be called Chief. Not Chief Justice, nor Mr. Chief Justice. Just Chief. "They're just threatening because everyone else is."

"Very funny," the Chief said without smiling. "Very funny. I'd hate for some group to be left out." Runyan threw the summary on his desk and rubbed his temples. "Let's talk about security." He closed his eyes.

K. O. Lewis laid his copy of the summary on the Chief's desk.

4

"Well, the Director thinks we should place four agents with each Justice, at least for the next ninety days. We'll use limousines with escorts to and from work, and the Supreme Court police will provide backup and secure this building."

"What about travel?"

"It's not a good idea, at least for now. The Director thinks the justices should remain in the D.C. area until the end of the year."

"Are you crazy? Is he crazy? If I asked my brethren to follow that request they would all leave town tonight and travel for the next month. That's absurd." Runyan frowned at his law clerks, who shook their heads in disgust. Truly absurd.

Lewis was unmoved. This was expected. "As you wish. Just a suggestion."

"A foolish suggestion."

"The Director did not expect your cooperation on that one. He would, however, expect to be notified in advance of all travel plans so that we can arrange security."

"You mean, you plan to escort each Justice each time he leaves the city?"

"Yes, Chief. That's our plan."

"Won't work. These people are not accustomed to being baby-sat."

"Yes sir. And they're not accustomed to being stalked either. We're just trying to protect you and your honorable brethren, sir. Of course, no one says we have to do anything. I think, sir, that you called us. We can leave, if you wish."

Runyan rocked forward in his chair and attacked a paper clip, prying the curves out of it and trying to make it perfectly straight. "What about around here?"

Lewis sighed and almost smiled. "We're not worried about this building, Chief. It's an easy place to secure. We don't expect trouble here."

"Then where?"

Lewis nodded at a window. The noise was louder. "Out there somewhere. The streets are full of idiots and maniacs and zealots."

"And they all hate us."

"Evidently. Listen, Chief, we're very concerned about Justice Rosenberg. He still refuses to allow our men inside his home; makes them sit in a car in the street all night. He will allow his favorite Supreme Court officer—what's his name? Ferguson— to sit by the back door, outside, but only from 10 P.M. to 6 A.M. No one gets in the house but Justice Rosenberg and his male nurse. The place is not secure."

Runyan picked his fingernails with the paper clip and smiled slightly to himself. Rosenberg's death, by any means or method, would be a relief. No, it would be a glorious occasion. The Chief would have to wear black and give a eulogy, but behind locked doors he would chuckle with his law clerks. Runyan liked this thought.

"What do you suggest?" he asked.

"Can you talk to him?"

"I've tried. I've explained to him that he is probably the most hated man in America, that millions of people curse him every day, that most folks would like to see him dead, that he receives four times the hate mail as the rest of us combined, and that he would be a perfect and easy target for assassination."

Lewis waited. "And?"

"Told me to kiss his ass, then fell asleep."

The law clerks giggled properly, then the FBI agents realized humor was permitted and joined in for a quick laugh.

"So what do we do?" asked Lewis, unamused.

"You protect him as best you can, put it in writing, and don't worry about it. He fears nothing, including death, and if he's not sweating it, why should you?"

"The Director is sweating, so I'm sweating, Chief. It's very simple. If one of you guys gets hurt, the Bureau looks bad."

The Chief rocked quickly in his chair. The racket from out-side was unnerving. This meeting had dragged on long enough. "Forget Rosenberg. Maybe he'll die in his sleep. I'm more concerned over Jensen."

"Jensen's a problem," Lewis said, flipping pages.

"I know he's a problem," Runyan said slowly. "He's an embarrassment. Now he thinks he's a liberal. Votes like Rosenberg half the time. Next month, he'll be a white supremacist and

6

support segregated schools. Then he'll fall in love with the Indians and want to give them Montana. It's like having a retarded child."

"He's being treated for depression, you know."

"I know, I know. He tells me about it. I'm his father figure. What drug?"

"Prozac."

The Chief dug under his fingernails. "What about that aerobics instructor he was seeing? She still around?"

"Not really, Chief. I don't think he cares for women." Lewis was smug. He knew more. He glanced at one of his agents and confirmed this juicy little tidbit.

Runyan ignored it, didn't want to hear it. "Is he cooperating?"

"Of course not. In many ways he's worse than Rosenberg. He allows us to escort him to his apartment building, then makes us sit in the parking lot all night. He's seven floors up, remember. We can't even sit in the lobby. Might upset his neighbors, he says. So we sit in the car. There are ten ways in and out of the building, and it's impossible to protect him. He likes to play hide-and-seek with us. He sneaks around all the time, so we never know if he's in the building or not. At least with Rosenberg we know where he is all night. Jensen's impossible."

"Great. If you can't follow him, how could an assassin?"

Lewis hadn't thought of this. He missed the humor. "The Director is very concerned with Justice Jensen's safety."

"He doesn't receive that many threats."

"Number six on the list, just a few less than you, your honor."

"Oh. So I'm in fifth place."

"Yes. Just behind Justice Manning. He's cooperating, by the way. Fully."

"He's afraid of his shadow," the Chief said, then hesitated. "I shouldn't have said that. I'm sorry."

Lewis ignored it. "In fact, the cooperation has been reasonably good, except for Rosenberg and Jensen. Justice Stone bitches a lot, but he listens to us."

"He bitches at everyone, so don't take it personally. Where do you suppose Jensen sneaks off to?"

Lewis glanced at one of his agents. "We have no idea."

A large section of the mob suddenly came together in one unrestrained chorus, and everyone on the streets seemed to join in. The Chief could not ignore it. The windows vibrated. He stood and called an end to this meeting.

JUSTICE GLENN JENSEN'S OFFICE was on the second floor, away from the streets and the noise. It was a spacious room, yet the smallest of the nine. Jensen was the youngest of the nine, and he was lucky to have an office. When nominated six years earlier at the age of forty-two, he was thought to be a strict constructionist with deep conservative beliefs, much like the man who nominated him. His Senate confirmation had been a slugfest. Before the Judiciary Committee, Jensen performed poorly. On sensitive issues he straddled the fence, and got kicked from both sides. The Republicans were embarrassed. The Democrats smelled blood. The President twisted arms until they broke, and Jensen was confirmed by one very reluctant vote.

But he made it, for life. In his six years, he had pleased no one. Hurt deeply by his confirmation hearings, he vowed to find compassion and rule with it. This had angered Republicans. They felt betrayed, especially when he discovered a latent passion for the rights of criminals. With scarce ideological strain, he quickly left the right, moved to the center, then to the left. Then, with legal scholars scratching their little goatees, Jensen would bolt back to the right and join Justice Sloan in one of his obnoxious antiwomen dissents. Jensen was not fond of women. He was neutral on prayer, skeptical of free speech, sympathetic to tax protestors, indifferent to Indians, afraid of blacks, tough on pornographers, soft on criminals, and fairly consistent in his protection of the environment. And, to the further dismay of the Republicans who shed blood to get him confirmed, Jensen had shown a troubling sympathy for the rights of homosexuals.

At his request, a nasty case called *Dumond* had been assigned to him. Ronald Dumond had lived with his male lover for eight years. They were a happy couple, totally devoted to each other, and quite content to share life's experiences. They wanted to marry, but Ohio laws prohibited such a union. Then the lover caught AIDS, and died a horrible death. Ronald knew exactly how to bury him, but then the lover's family intervened and excluded Ronald from the funeral and burial. Distraught, Ronald sued the family, claiming emotional and psychological damage. The case had bounced around the lower courts for six years, and now had suddenly found itself sitting on Jensen's desk.

At issue was the rights of "spouses" of gays. *Dumond* had become a battle cry for gay activists. The mere mention of *Dumond* had caused street fights.

And Jensen had the case. The door to his smaller office was closed. Jensen and his three clerks sat around the conference table. They had spent two hours on *Dumond*, and gone nowhere. They were tired of arguing. One clerk, a liberal from Cornell, wanted a broad pronouncement granting sweeping rights to gay partners. Jensen wanted this too, but was not ready to admit it. The other two clerks were skeptical. They knew, as did Jensen, that a majority of five would be impossible.

Talk turned to other matters.

"The Chief's ticked off at you, Glenn," said the clerk from Duke. They called him by his first name in chambers. "Justice" was such an awkward title.

Glenn rubbed his eyes. "What else is new?"

"One of his clerks wanted me to know that the Chief and the FBI are worried about your safety. Says you're not cooperating, and the Chief's rather disturbed. He wanted me to pass it along." Everything was passed along through the clerks' network. Everything.

"He's supposed to be worried. That's his job."

"He wants to assign two more Fibbies as bodyguards, and they want access to your apartment. And the FBI wants to drive you to and from work. And they want to restrict your travel."

"I've already heard this."

"Yeah, we know. But the Chief's clerk said the Chief wants us to prevail upon you to cooperate with the FBI so that they can save your life."

"I see."

"And so we're just prevailing upon you."

"Thanks. Go back to the network and tell the Chief's clerk that you not only prevailed upon me but you raised all sorts of hell with me and that I appreciated all of your prevailing and hell-raising, but it went in one ear and out the other. Tell them Glenn considers himself a big boy."

"Sure, Glenn. You're not afraid, are you?"

"Not in the least."

TWO

THOMAS CALLAHAN was one of Tulane's more popular
professors, primarily because he refused to schedule
classes before 11 A.M. He drank a lot, as did most of his students,
and for him the first few hours of each morning were needed
for sleep, then resuscitation. Nine and ten o'clock classes were
abominations. He was also popular because he was cool—faded
jeans, tweed jackets with well-worn elbow patches, no socks, no
ties. The liberal-chic-academic look. He was forty-five, but with
dark hair and horn-rimmed glasses he could pass for thirty-five,
not that he gave a damn how old he looked. He shaved once a
week, when it started itching; and when the weather was cool,
which was seldom in New Orleans, he would grow a beard. He
had a history of closeness with female students.

He was also popular because he taught constitutional law, a
most unpopular course but a required one. Due to his sheer
brilliance and coolness he actually made con law interesting. No
one else at Tulane could do this. No one wanted to, really, so
the students fought to sit in con law under Callahan at eleven,
three mornings a week.

Eighty of them sat behind six elevated rows and whispered as
Callahan stood in front of his desk and cleaned his glasses. It
was exactly five after eleven, still too early, he thought.

"Who understands Rosenberg's dissent in *Nash v. New
Jersey*?" All heads lowered and the room was silent. Must be a

11

bad hangover. His eyes were red. When he started with Rosenberg it usually meant a rough lecture. No one volunteered. *Nash?* Callahan looked slowly, methodically around the room, and waited. Dead silence.

The doorknob clicked loudly and broke the tension. The door opened quickly and an attractive young female in tight washed jeans and a cotton sweater slid elegantly through it and sort of glided along the wall to the third row, where she deftly maneuvered between the crowded seats until she came to hers and sat down. The guys on the fourth row watched in admiration. The guys on the fifth row strained for a peek. For two brutal years now, one of the few pleasures of law school had been to watch as she graced the halls and rooms with her long legs and baggy sweaters. There was a fabulous body in there somewhere, they could tell. But she was not one to flaunt it. She was just one of the gang, and adhered to the law school dress code of jeans and flannel shirts and old sweaters and oversized khakis. What they wouldn't give for a black leather miniskirt.

She flashed a quick smile at the guy seated next to her, and for a second Callahan and his *Nash* question were forgotten. Her dark red hair fell just to the shoulders. She was that perfect little cheerleader with the perfect teeth and perfect hair that every boy fell in love with at least twice in high school. And maybe at least once in law school.

Callahan was ignoring this entry. Had she been a first-year student, and afraid of him, he might have ripped into her and screamed a few times. "You're never late for court!" was the old standby law professors had beaten to death.

But Callahan was not in a screaming mood, and Darby Shaw was not afraid of him, and for a split second he wondered if anyone knew he was sleeping with her. Probably not. She had insisted on absolute secrecy.

"Has anyone read Rosenberg's dissent in *Nash v. New Jersey?*" Suddenly, he had the spotlight again, and there was dead silence. A raised hand could mean constant grilling for the next thirty minutes. No volunteers. The smokers on the back row fired up their cigarettes. Most of the eighty scribbled aimlessly on legal pads. All heads were bowed. It would be too obvious and risky to flip through the casebook and find *Nash;* too late for that. Any movement might attract attention. Someone was about to be nailed.

Nash was not in the casebook. It was one of a dozen minor cases Callahan had hurriedly mentioned a week ago, and now he was anxious to see if anyone had read it. He was famous for this. His final exam covered twelve hundred cases, a thousand of which were not in the casebook. The exam was a nightmare, but he was really a sweetheart, a soft grader, and it was a rare dumbass who flunked the course.

He did not appear to be a sweetheart at this moment. He looked around the room. Time for a victim. "How about it, Mr. Sallinger? Can you explain Rosenberg's dissent?"

Instantly from the fourth row, Sallinger said, "No sir."

"I see. Might that be because you haven't read Rosenberg's dissent?"

"It might. Yes sir."

Callahan glared at him. The red eyes made the arrogant scowl all the more menacing. Only Sallinger saw it though; since everyone else was glued to their legal pads. "And why not?"

"Because I try not to read dissents. Especially Rosenberg's."

Stupid. Stupid. Stupid. Sallinger had opted to fight back, but he had no ammo.

"Something against Rosenberg, Mr. Sallinger?"

Callahan revered Rosenberg. Worshiped him. Read books about the man and his opinions. Studied him. Even dined with him once.

Sallinger fidgeted nervously. "Oh no, sir. I just don't like dissents."

There was a bit of humor in Sallinger's responses, but not a smile was cracked. Later, over a beer, he and his buddies would roar with laughter when it was told and retold about Sallinger and his distaste for dissents, especially Rosenberg's. But not now.

"I see. Do you read majority opinions?"

Hesitation. Sallinger's feeble attempt at sparring was about to cause humiliation. "Yes sir. Lots of them."

"Great. Explain, then, if you will, the majority opinion in *Nash v. New Jersey.*"

Sallinger had never heard of *Nash,* but he would now remember it for the rest of his legal career. "I don't think I've read that one."

"So you don't read dissents, Mr. Sallinger, and now we learn that you also neglect majorities. What do you read, Mr. Sallinger, romance novels, tabloids?"

There was some extremely light laughter from behind the fourth row, and it came from students who felt obligated to laugh but at the same time did not wish to call attention to themselves.

Sallinger, red-faced, just stared at Callahan.

"Why haven't you read the case, Mr. Sallinger?" Callahan demanded.

"I don't know. I, uh, just missed it, I guess."

Callahan took it well. "I'm not surprised. I mentioned it last week. Last Wednesday, to be exact. It'll be on the final exam. I don't understand why you would ignore a case that you'll see on the final." Callahan was pacing now, slowly, in front of his desk, staring at the students. "Did anyone bother to read it?"

Silence. Callahan stared at the floor, and allowed the silence to sink in. All eyes were down, all pens and pencils frozen. Smoke billowed from the back row.

Finally, slowly, from the fourth seat on the third row, Darby Shaw lifted her hand slightly, and the class breathed a collective sigh of relief. She had saved them again. It was sort of expected of her. Number two in their class and within striking distance of number one, she could recite the facts and holdings and concurrences and dissents and majority opinions to virtually every case Callahan could spit at them. She missed nothing. The perfect little cheerleader had graduated magna cum laude with a degree in biology, and planned to graduate magna cum laude with a degree in law, and then make a nice living suing chemical companies for trashing the environment.

Callahan stared at her in mock frustration. She had left his apartment three hours earlier after a long night of wine and law. But he had not mentioned *Nash* to her.

"Well, well, Ms. Shaw. Why is Rosenberg upset?"

"He thinks the New Jersey statute violates the Second Amendment." She did not look at the professor.

"That's good. And for the benefit of the rest of the class, what does the statute do?"

"Outlaws semiautomatic machine guns, among other things."

"Wonderful. And just for fun, what did Mr. Nash possess at the time of his arrest?"

"An AK-47 assault rifle."

"And what happened to him?"

"He was convicted, sentenced to three years, and appealed." She knew the details.

"What was Mr. Nash's occupation?"

"The opinion wasn't specific, but there was mention of an additional charge of drug trafficking. He had no criminal record at the time of his arrest."

"So he was a dope pusher with an AK-47. But he has a friend in Rosenberg, doesn't he?"

"Of course." She was watching him now. The tension had eased. Most eyes followed him as he paced slowly, looking around the room, selecting another victim. More often than not, Darby dominated these lectures, and Callahan wanted a broader participation.

"Why do you suppose Rosenberg is sympathetic?" he asked the class.

"He loves dope pushers." It was Sallinger, wounded but trying to rally. Callahan placed a premium on class discussion. He smiled at his prey, as if to welcome him back to the bloodletting.

"You think so, Mr. Sallinger?"

"Sure. Dope pushers, child fondlers, gunrunners, terrorists. Rosenberg greatly admires these people. They are his weak and abused children, so he must protect them." Sallinger was trying to appear righteously indignant.

"And, in your learned opinion, Mr. Sallinger, what should be done with these people?"

"Simple. They should have a fair trial with a good lawyer, then a fair, speedy appeal, then punished if they are guilty."

Sallinger was perilously close to sounding like a law-and-order right-winger, a cardinal sin among Tulane law students.

Callahan folded his arms. "Please continue."

Sallinger smelled a trap, but plowed ahead. There was nothing to lose. "I mean, we've read case after case where Rosenberg has tried to rewrite the Constitution to create a new loophole to exclude evidence to allow an obviously guilty defendant to go free. It's almost sickening. He thinks all prisons are cruel and unusual places, so therefore, under the Eighth Amendment, all prisoners should go free. Thankfully, he's in the minority now, a shrinking minority."

"You like the direction of the Court, do you, Mr. Sallinger?" Callahan was at once smiling and frowning.

"Damned right I do."

"Are you one of those normal, red-blooded, patriotic, middle-of-the-road Americans who wish the old bastard would die in his sleep?"

There were a few chuckles around the room. It was safer to laugh now. Sallinger knew better than to answer truthfully. "I wouldn't wish that on anyone," he said, almost embarrassed.

Callahan was pacing again. "Well, thank you, Mr. Sallinger. I always enjoy your comments. You have, as usual, provided us with the layman's view of the law."

The laughter was much louder. Sallinger's cheeks flushed and he sank in his seat.

Callahan did not smile. "I would like to raise the intellectual level of this discussion, okay. Now, Ms. Shaw, why is Rosenberg sympathetic to Nash?"

"The Second Amendment grants the people the right to keep and bear arms. To Justice Rosenberg, it is literal and absolute. Nothing should be banned. If Nash wants to possess an AK-47, or a hand grenade, or a bazooka, the state of New Jersey cannot pass a law prohibiting it."

"Do you agree with him?"

"No, and I'm not alone. It's an eight-to-one decision. No one followed him."

"What's the rationale of the other eight?"

"It's obvious, really. The states have compelling reasons to prohibit the sale and possession of certain types of arms. The interests of the state of New Jersey outweigh the Second Amendment rights of Mr. Nash. Society cannot allow individuals to own sophisticated weaponry."

Callahan watched her carefully. Attractive female law students were rare at Tulane, but when he found one he moved in quickly. Over the past eight years, he had been quite successful. Easy work, for the most part. The women arrived at law school liberated and loose. Darby had been different. He first spotted her in the library during the second semester of her first year, and it took a month to get her to dinner.

"Who wrote the majority opinion?" he asked her.

"Runyan."

"And you agree with him?"

"Yes. It's an easy case, really."

"Then what happened to Rosenberg?"

"I think he hates the rest of the Court."

"So he dissents just for the hell of it."

"Often, yes. His opinions are becoming more indefensible. Take *Nash*. For a liberal like Rosenberg, the issue of gun control is easy. He should have written the majority opinion, and ten years ago he would have. In *Fordice v. Oregon*, a 1977 case, he took a much narrower interpretation of the Second Amendment. His inconsistencies are almost embarrassing."

Callahan had forgotten *Fordice*. "Are you suggesting Justice Rosenberg is senile?"

Much like a punch-drunk fighter, Sallinger waded in for the final round. "He's crazy as hell, and you know it. You can't defend his opinions."

"Not always, Mr. Sallinger, but at least he's still there."

"His body's there, but he's brain-dead."

"He's breathing, Mr. Sallinger."

"Yeah, breathing with a machine. They have to pump oxygen up his nose."

"But it counts, Mr. Sallinger. He's the last of the great judicial activists, and he's still breathing."

"You'd better call and check," Sallinger said as his words trailed off. He'd said enough. No, he'd said too much. He lowered his head as the professor glared at him. He hunkered down next to his notebook, and started wondering why he'd said all that.

Callahan stared him down, then began pacing again. It was indeed a bad hangover.

THREE

A T LEAST he looked like an old farmer, with straw hat, clean bib overalls, neatly pressed khaki workshirt, boots. He chewed tobacco and spat in the black water beneath the pier. He chewed like a farmer. His pickup, though of recent model, was sufficiently weathered and had a dusty-road look about it. North Carolina plates. It was a hundred yards away, parked in the sand at the other end of the pier.

It was midnight Monday, the first Monday in October, and for the next thirty minutes he was to wait in the dark coolness of the deserted pier, chewing pensively, resting on the railing while staring intently at the sea. He was alone, as he knew he would be. It was planned that way. This pier at this hour was always deserted. The headlights of an occasional car flickered along the shoreline, but the headlights never stopped at this hour.

He watched the red and blue channel lights far from shore. He checked his watch without moving his head. The clouds were low and thick, and it would be difficult to see it until it was almost to the pier. It was planned this way.

The pickup was not from North Carolina, and neither was the farmer. The license plates had been stolen from a wrecked truck at a scrap yard near Durham. The pickup had been stolen in Baton Rouge. The farmer was not from anywhere, and performed none of the thievery. He was a pro, and so someone else did the dirty little deeds.

Twenty minutes into the wait, a dark object floated in the direction of the pier. A quiet, muffled engine hummed and grew louder. The object became a small craft of some sort with a camouflaged silhouette crouching low and working the motor. The farmer moved not an inch in anticipation. The humming stopped and the black rubber raft stalled in the calm water thirty feet from the pier. There were no headlights coming or going along the shore.

The farmer carefully placed a cigarette between his lips, lit it, puffed twice, then thumped it down, halfway to the raft.

"What kind of cigarette?" the man on the water asked upward. He could see the outline of the farmer on the railing, but not the face.

"Lucky Strike," the farmer answered. These passwords made for such a silly game. How many other black rubber rafts could be expected to drift in from the Atlantic and pinpoint this ancient pier at this precise hour? Silly, but oh so important.

"Luke?" came the voice from the boat.

"Sam," replied the farmer. The name was Khamel, not Sam, but Sam would do for the next five minutes until Khamel parked his raft.

Khamel did not answer, was not required to, but quickly started the engine and guided the raft along the edge of the pier to the beach. Luke followed from above. They met at the pickup without a handshake. Khamel placed his black Adidas gym bag between them on the seat, and the truck started along the shoreline.

Luke drove and Khamel smoked, and both did a perfect job of ignoring each other. Their eyes did not dare meet. With Khamel's heavy beard, dark glasses, and black turtleneck, his face was ominous but impossible to identify. Luke did not want to see it. Part of his assignment, in addition to receiving this stranger from the sea, was to refrain from looking at him. It was easy, really. The face was wanted in nine countries.

Across the bridge at Manteo, Luke lit another Lucky Strike and determined they had met before. It had been a brief but precisely timed meeting at the airport in Rome, five or six years earlier, as best he could remember. There had been no introductions. It took place in a restroom. Luke, then an impeccably tailored American executive, had placed an eelskin attaché case next to the wall next to the washbasin where he slowly rinsed his hands, and suddenly it was gone. He caught a glimpse of the man—this Khamel, he was now certain—in the mirror. Thirty minutes later, the attaché case exploded between the legs of the British ambassador to Nigeria.

In the guarded whispers of his invisible brotherhood, Luke had often heard of Khamel, a man of many names and faces and languages, an assassin who struck quickly and left no trail, a fastidious killer who roamed the world but could never be found. As they rode north in the darkness, Luke settled low in his seat, the brim of his hat almost on his nose, limp wrist across the wheel, trying to remember the stories he'd heard about his passenger. Amazing feats of terror. There was the British ambassador. The ambush of seventeen Israeli soldiers on the West Bank in 1990 had been credited to Khamel. He was the only suspect in the 1985 car-bomb murders of a wealthy German banker and his family. His fee for that one was rumored to have been three million, cash. Most intelligence experts believed he was the mastermind of the 1981 attempt to kill the Pope. But then, Khamel was blamed for almost every unsolved terrorist attack and assassination. He was easy to blame because no one was certain he existed.

This excited Luke. Khamel was about to perform on American soil. The targets were unknown to Luke, but important blood was about to be shed.

AT DAWN, the stolen farm truck stopped at the corner of Thirty-first and M streets in Georgetown. Khamel grabbed his gym bag, said nothing, and hit the sidewalk. He walked east a few blocks to the Four Seasons Hotel, bought a *Post* in the lobby, and casually rode the elevator to the seventh floor. At precisely seven-fifteen, he knocked on a door at the end of the hall. "Yes?" a nervous voice asked from inside.

"Looking for Mr. Sneller," Khamel said slowly in a perfect

generic American tongue as he stuck his thumb over the peep-hole.

"Mr. Sneller?"

"Yes. Edwin F. Sneller."

The knob did not turn or click, and the door did not open. A few seconds passed, and a white envelope eased from under the door. Khamel picked it up. "Okay," he said loud enough for Sneller or whoever he was to hear.

"It's next door," Sneller said. "I'll await your call." He sounded like an American. Unlike Luke, he'd never seen Khamel, and had no desire to, really. Luke had seen him twice now, and was indeed lucky to be alive.

Khamel's room had two beds and a small table near the window. The shades were drawn tightly; no chance of sunlight. He placed his gym bag on one bed, next to two thick briefcases. He walked to the window and peeked out, then to the phone.

"It's me," he said to Sneller. "Tell me about the car."

"It's parked on the street. Plain white Ford with Connecticut plates. The keys are on the table." Sneller spoke slowly.

"Stolen?"

"Of course, but sanitized. It's clean."

"I'll leave it at Dulles shortly after midnight. I want it de-stroyed, okay?" The English was perfect.

"Those are my instructions. Yes." Sneller was proper and efficient.

"It's very important, okay? I intend to leave the gun in the car. Guns leave bullets and people see cars, so it's important to completely destroy the car and everything in it. Understand?"

"Those are my instructions," Sneller repeated. He did not appreciate this lecture. He was no novice at the killing game.

Khamel sat on the edge of the bed. "The four million was received a week ago, a day late I should add. I'm now in D.C., so I want the next three."

"It will be wired before noon. That was the agreement."

"Yes, but I'm worried about the agreement. You were a day late, remember?"

This irritated Sneller, and since the killer was in the next room and not about to come out, he could sound a bit irritated. "The bank's fault, not ours."

This irritated Khamel. "Fine. I want you and your bank to wire the next three million to the account in Zurich as soon as New York opens. That will be about two hours from now. I'll be checking."

"Okay."

"Okay, and I want no problem when the job is finished. I'll be in Paris in twenty-four hours, and from there I'll go straight to Zurich. I want all the money waiting for me when I arrive."

"It will be there, if the job is finished."

Khamel smiled to himself. "The job will be finished, Mr. Sneller, by midnight. That is, if your information is correct."

"As of now it is correct. And no changes are expected today. Our people are in the streets. Everything is in the two brief-cases; maps, diagrams, schedules, the tools and articles you requested."

Khamel glanced at the briefcases behind him. He rubbed his eyes with his right hand. "I need a nap," he mumbled into the phone. "I haven't slept in twenty hours."

Sneller could think of no response. There was plenty of time, and if Khamel wanted a nap, then Khamel could have a nap. They were paying him ten million.

"Would you like something to eat?" Sneller asked awkwardly.

"No. Call me in three hours, at precisely ten-thirty." He placed the receiver on the phone, and stretched across the bed.

THE STREETS were clear and quiet for day two of the fall term. The justices spent their day on the bench listening to lawyer after lawyer argue complex and quite dull cases. Rosenberg slept through most of it. He came to life briefly when the attorney general from Texas argued that a certain death-row inmate should be given medication to make him lucid before being lethally injected. If he's mentally ill, how can he be executed? Rosenberg asked incredulously. Easy, said the AG from Texas, his illness can be controlled with medication. So just give him a little shot to make him sane, then give him another shot to kill him. It could all be very nice and constitutional. Rosenberg harangued and bitched for a brief spell, then lost steam. His little wheelchair sat much lower than the massive leather thrones of his brethren. He looked rather pitiful. In years past he was a tiger, a ruthless intimidator who tied even the slickest lawyers in knots. But no more. He began to mumble, and then faded away. The AG sneered at him, and continued.

During the last oral argument of the day, a lifeless desegregation case from Virginia, Rosenberg began snoring. Chief Runyan glared down the bench, and Jason Kline, Rosenberg's senior clerk, took the hint. He slowly pulled the wheelchair backward, away from the bench, and out of the courtroom. He pushed it quickly through the back hallway.

The Justice regained consciousness in his office, took his pills, and informed his clerks he wanted to go home. Kline notified the FBI, and moments later Rosenberg was wheeled into the rear of his van, parked in the basement. Two FBI agents watched. A male nurse, Frederic, strapped the wheelchair in place, and Sergeant Ferguson of the Supreme Court police slid behind the wheel of the van. The Justice allowed no FBI agents near him. They could follow in their car, and they could watch his townhouse from the street, and they were lucky to get that close. He didn't trust cops, and he damned sure didn't trust FBI agents. He didn't need protection.

On Volta Street in Georgetown, the van slowed and backed into a short driveway. Frederic the nurse and Ferguson the cop gently rolled him inside. The agents watched from the street in their black government-issue Dodge Aries. The lawn in front of the townhome was tiny and their car was a few feet from the front door. It was almost 4 P.M.

After a few minutes, Ferguson made his mandatory exit and spoke to the agents. After much debate, Rosenberg had acquiesced a week earlier and allowed Ferguson to quietly inspect each room upstairs and down upon his arrival in the afternoons. Then Ferguson had to leave, but could return at exactly 10 P.M. and sit outside the rear door until exactly 6 A.M. No one but Ferguson could do it, and he was tired of the overtime.

"Everything's fine," he said to the agents. "I guess I'll be back at ten."

"Is he still alive?" one of the agents asked. Standard question. "Afraid so." Ferguson looked tired as he walked to the van.

Frederic was chubby and weak, but strength was not needed to handle his patient. After arranging the pillows just so, he lifted him from the wheelchair and placed him carefully on the sofa, where he would remain motionless for the next two hours while dozing and watching CNN. Frederic fixed himself a ham sandwich and a plate of cookies, and scanned a *National Enquirer* at the kitchen table. Rosenberg mumbled something loudly and changed channels with the remote control.

At precisely seven, his dinner of chicken bouillon, boiled potatoes, and stewed onions—stroke food—was placed neatly on the table, and Frederic rolled him up to it. He insisted on feeding himself, and it was not pretty. Frederic watched television. He would clean up the mess later.

By nine, he was bathed, dressed in a gown, and tucked tightly under the covers. The bed was a narrow, reclining, pale green army-hospital job with a hard mattress, push-button controls, and collapsible rails that Rosenberg insisted remain down. It was in a room behind the kitchen that he had used as a small study for thirty years, before the first stroke. The room was now clinical, and smelled of antiseptic and looming death. Next to his bed was a large table with a hospital lamp and at least twenty bottles of pills. Thick, heavy law books were stacked in neat piles around the room. Next to the table, the nurse sat close by in a worn recliner, and began reading from a brief. He would read until he heard snoring—the nightly ritual. He read slowly, yelling the words at Rosenberg, who was stiff, motionless, but listening. The brief was from a case in which he would write the majority opinion. He absorbed every word, for a while.

After an hour of reading and yelling, Frederic was tired and the Justice was drifting away. He raised his hand slightly, then closed his eyes. With a button on the bed, he lowered the lights. The room was almost dark. Frederic jerked backward, and the recliner unfolded. He laid the brief on the floor, and closed his eyes. Rosenberg was snoring.

He would not snore for long.

□ □ □ □ □

SHORTLY AFTER TEN, with the house dark and quiet, the door to a bedroom closet upstairs opened slightly, and Khamel eased out. His wristbands, nylon cap, and running shorts were royal blue. His long-sleeved shirt, socks, and Reeboks were white with royal trim. Perfect color coordination. Khamel the jogger. He was clean shaven, and under the cap his very short hair was now blond, almost white.

The bedroom was dark, as was the hall. The stairs creaked slightly under the Reeboks. He was five-ten, and weighed less than a hundred and fifty pounds, with no fat. He kept himself taut and light so the movements would be quick and soundless. The stairs landed in a foyer not far from the front door. He knew there were two agents in a car by the curb, probably not watching the house. He knew Ferguson had arrived seven minutes ago. He could hear the snoring from the back room. While waiting in the closet, he had thought of striking earlier, before Ferguson arrived so he wouldn't have to kill him. The killing was no problem, but it created another body to worry about. But he guessed, wrongly, that Ferguson probably checked in with the male nurse when he came on duty. If so, then Ferguson would find the carnage and Khamel would lose a few hours. So he waited until now.

He slid through the foyer without a sound. In the kitchen, a small light from the Ventahood illuminated the countertop and made things a bit more dangerous. Khamel cursed himself for not checking the bulb and unscrewing it. Those small mistakes were inexcusable. He dipped under a window looking into the backyard. He could not see Ferguson, although he knew he was seventy-four inches tall, sixty-one years old, had cataracts, and couldn't hit a barn with his .357 magnum.

Both of them were snoring. Khamel smiled to himself as he crouched in the doorway and quickly pulled the .22 automatic and silencer from the Ace bandage wrapped around his waist. He screwed the four-inch tube onto the barrel, and ducked into the room. The nurse was sprawled deep in the recliner, feet in the air, hands dangling, mouth open. Khamel placed the tip of the silencer an inch from his right temple and fired three times. The hands flinched and the feet jerked, but the eyes remained closed. Khamel quickly reached across to the wrinkled and pale head of Justice Abraham Rosenberg, and pumped three bullets into it.

The room had no windows. He watched the bodies and listened for a full minute. The nurse's heels twitched a few times, then stopped. The bodies were still.

He wanted to kill Ferguson inside. It was eleven minutes after ten, a good time for a neighbor to be out with the dog for one last time before bed. He crept through the darkness to the rear door and spotted the cop strolling benignly along the wooden fence twenty feet away. Instinctively, Khamel opened the back door, turned on the patio light, and said "Ferguson" loudly.

He left the door open and hid in a dark corner next to the refrigerator. Ferguson obediently lumbered across the small patio and into the kitchen. This was not unusual. Frederic often called him in after His Honor was asleep. They would drink instant coffee and play gin rummy.

There was no coffee, and Frederic was not waiting. Khamel fired three bullets into the back of his head, and he fell loudly on the kitchen table.

He turned out the patio light and unscrewed the silencer. He would not need it again. It and the pistol were stuffed into the Ace bandage. Khamel peeked out the front window. The dome light was on and the agents were reading. He stepped over Ferguson, locked the back door, and disappeared into the darkness of the small rear lawn. He jumped two fences without a sound, and found the street. He began trotting. Khamel the jogger.

IN THE DARK BALCONY of the Montrose Theatre, Glenn Jensen sat by himself and watched the naked and quite active men on the screen below. He ate popcorn from a large box and noticed nothing but the bodies. He was dressed conservatively enough; navy cardigan, chinos, loafers. And wide sunglasses to hide his eyes and a suede fedora to cover his head. He was blessed with a face that was easily forgotten, and once camouflaged it could never be recognized. Especially in a deserted balcony of a near-empty gay porno house at midnight. No earrings, bandannas, gold chains, jewelry, nothing to indicate he was in the market for a companion. He wanted to be ignored.

It had become a challenge, really, this cat-and-mouse game with the FBI and the rest of the world. On this night, they had dutifully stationed themselves in the parking lot outside his building. Another pair parked by the exit near the veranda in the rear, and he allowed them all to sit for four and a half hours before he disguised himself and walked nonchalantly to the garage in the basement and drove away in a friend's car. The building had too many points of egress for the poor Fibbies to monitor him. He was sympathetic to a point, but he had his life to live. If the Fibbies couldn't find him, how could a killer?

The balcony was divided into three small sections with six rows each. It was very dark, the only light being the heavy blue stream from the projector behind. Broken seats and folded tables were piled along the outside aisles. The velvet drapes along the walls were shredded and falling. It was a marvelous place to hide.

He used to worry about getting caught. In the months after his confirmation, he was terrified. He couldn't eat his popcorn, and damned sure couldn't enjoy the movies. He told himself that if he was caught or recognized, or in some awful way exposed, he would simply claim he was doing research for an obscenity case pending. There was always one on the docket, and maybe somehow this might be believed. This excuse could work, he told himself repeatedly, and he grew bolder. But one night in 1990, a theater caught fire, and four people died. Their names were in the paper. Big story. Justice Glenn Jensen happened to be in the rest room when he heard the screams and smelled the smoke. He rushed into the street and disappeared. The dead were all found in the balcony. He knew one of them. He gave up movies for two months, but then started back. He needed more research, he told himself.

And what if he got caught? The appointment was for life. The voters couldn't call him home.

He liked the Montrose because on Tuesdays the movies ran all night, but there was never a crowd. He liked the popcorn, and draft beer cost fifty cents.

Two old men in the center section groped and fondled each other. Jensen glanced at them occasionally, but concentrated on the movie. Sad, he thought, to be seventy years old, staring at death and dodging AIDS, and banished to a dirty balcony to find happiness.

A fourth person soon joined them on the balcony. He glanced at Jensen and the two men locked together, and he walked quietly with his draft beer and popcorn to the top row of the center section. The projector room was directly behind him. To his right and down three rows sat the Justice. In front of him, the gray and mature lovers kissed and whispered and giggled, oblivious to the world.

He was dressed appropriately. Tight jeans, black silk shirt, earring, horn-rimmed shades, and the neatly trimmed hair and mustache of a regular gay. Khamel the homosexual.

He waited a few minutes, then eased to his right and sat by the aisle. No one noticed. Who would care where he sat?

At twelve-twenty, the old men lost steam. They stood, arm in arm, and tiptoed away, still whispering and snickering. Jensen did not look at them. He was engrossed in the movie, a massive orgy on a yacht in the middle of a hurricane. Khamel moved like a cat across the narrow aisle to a seat three rows behind the Justice. He sipped the beer. They were alone. He waited for one minute, and quickly moved down a row. Jensen was eight feet away.

As the hurricane intensified, so did the orgy. The roar of the wind and the screams of the partyers deafened the small theater. Khamel set the beer and popcorn on the floor, and pulled a three-foot strand of yellow nylon ski rope from his waist. He quickly wrapped the ends around both hands, and stepped over the row of chairs in front of him. His prey was breathing heavy. The popcorn box was shaking.

The attack was quick and brutal. Khamel looped the rope just under the larynx, and wrenched it violently. He yanked the rope downward, snapping the head over the back of the seat. The neck broke cleanly. He twisted the rope and tied it behind the neck. He slid a six-inch steel rod through a loop in the knot, and wound the tourniquet until the flesh tore and started to bleed. It was over in ten seconds.

Suddenly the hurricane was over and another orgy began in celebration. Jensen slumped in his seat. His popcorn was scattered around his shoes. Khamel was not one to admire his handiwork. He left the balcony, walked casually through the racks of magazines and devices in the lobby, then disappeared onto the sidewalk.

He drove the generic white Ford with Connecticut plates to Dulles, changed clothes in a rest room, and waited on his flight to Paris.

FOUR

THE FIRST LADY was on the West Coast attending a series of five-thousand-dollars-a-plate breakfasts where the rich and pretentious gladly shucked out the money for cold eggs and cheap champagne, and the chance to be seen and maybe photographed with the Queen, as she was known. So the President was sleeping alone when the phone rang. In the great tradition of American Presidents, he had in years past thought of keeping a mistress. But now it seemed so non-Republican. Besides, he was old and tired. He often slept alone when the Queen was at the White House.

He was a heavy sleeper. It rang twelve times before he heard it. He grabbed it and stared at the clock. Four-thirty A.M. He listened to the voice, jumped to his feet, and eight minutes later was in the Oval Office. No shower, no tie. He stared at Fletcher Coal, his chief of staff, and sat properly behind his desk.

Coal was smiling. His perfect teeth and bald head were shining. Only thirty-seven, he was the boy wonder who four years earlier had rescued a failing campaign and placed his boss in the White House. He was a guileful manipulator and a nasty henchman who had cut and clawed his way through the inner circle until he was now second in command. Many viewed him as the real boss. The mere mention of his name terrified lowly staffers.

"What happened?" the President asked slowly.

Coal paced in front of the President's desk. "Don't know much. They're both dead. Two FBI agents found Rosenberg around 1 A.M. Dead in bed. His nurse and a Supreme Court policeman were also murdered. All three shot in the head. A very clean job. While the FBI and D.C. police were investigating, they got a call that Jensen had been found dead in some queer club. They found him a couple of hours ago. Voyles called me at four, and I called you. He and Gminski should be here in a minute."

"Gminski?"

"The CIA should be included, at least for now."

The President folded his hands behind his head and stretched. "Rosenberg is dead."

"Yes. Quite. I suggest you address the nation in a couple of hours. Mabry is working on a rough draft. I'll finish it. Let's wait until daylight, at least seven. If not, it'll be too early and we'll lose much of our audience."

"The press—"

"Yes. It's out. They filmed the ambulance crew rolling Jensen into the morgue."

"I didn't know he was gay."

"Not much doubt about it now. This is the perfect crisis, Mr. President. Think of it. We didn't create it. It's not our fault. No one can blame us. And the nation will be shocked into some degree of solidarity. It's rally around the leader time. It's just great. No downside."

The President sipped a cup of coffee and stared at the papers on his desk. "And I'll get to restructure the Court."

"That's the best part. It'll be your legacy. I've already called Duvall at Justice and instructed him to contact Horton and begin a preliminary list of nominees. Horton gave a speech in Omaha last night, but he's flying in now. I suggest we meet with him later this morning."

The President nodded with his customary approval of Coal's suggestions. He allowed Coal to sweat the details. He had never been a detail man himself. "Any suspects?"

"Not yet. I don't know, really. I told Voyles that you would expect a briefing when he arrived."

"I thought someone said the FBI was protecting the Supreme Court."

Coal smiled wider and chuckled. "Exactly. The egg is on Voyles' face. It's quite embarrassing, really."

"Great. I want Voyles to get his share of the blame. Take care of the press. I want him humiliated. Then maybe we can run his ass off."

Coal loved this thought. He stopped pacing and scribbled a note on his legal pad. A security guard knocked on the door, then opened it. Directors Voyles and Gminski entered together. The mood was suddenly somber as all four shook hands. The two sat before the President's desk as Coal took his customary position standing near a window, to the side of the President. He hated Voyles and Gminski, and they hated him. Coal thrived on hatred. He had the President's ear, and that was all that mattered. He would become quiet for a few minutes. It was important to allow the President to take charge when others were present.

"I'm very sorry you're here, but thanks for coming," the President said. They nodded grimly and acknowledged this obvious lie. "What happened?"

Voyles spoke quickly and to the point. He described the scene at Rosenberg's home when the bodies were found. At 1 A.M. each night, Sergeant Ferguson routinely checked in with the agents sitting in the street. When he didn't show, they investigated. The killings were very clean and professional. He described what he knew about Jensen. Broken neck. Strangulation. Found by another character in the balcony. No one saw anything, evidently. Voyles was not as gruff and blunt as usual. It was a dark day for the Bureau, and he could feel the heat coming. But he'd survived five Presidents, and he could certainly outmaneuver this idiot.

"The two are obviously related," the President said, staring at Voyles.

"Maybe. Certainly looks that way, but—"

"Come on, Director. In two hundred and twenty years, we've assassinated four Presidents, two or three candidates, a handful of civil rights leaders, couple of governors, but never a Supreme Court Justice. And now, in one night, within two hours, two are assassinated. And you're not convinced they're related?"

"I didn't say that. There must be a link somewhere. It's just that the methods were so different. And so professional. You must remember, we've had thousands of threats against the Court."

"Fine. Then who are your suspects?"

No one cross-examined F. Denton Voyles. He glared at the President. "It's too early for suspects. We're still gathering evidence."

"How'd the killer get into Rosenberg's place?"

"No one knows. We didn't watch him go in, you understand? Evidently, he was there for some time, hiding in a closet or an attic, maybe. Again, we weren't invited. Rosenberg refused to allow us into his home. Ferguson routinely inspected the place each afternoon when the Justice arrived from work. It's still too early, but we've found no evidence of the murderer. None, except three bodies. We'll have ballistics and autopsies by late this afternoon."

"I want to see them here as soon as you have them."

"Yes, Mr. President."

"I also want a short list of suspects by 5 P.M. today. Is that clear?"

"Certainly, Mr. President."

"And I would like a report on your security and where it broke down."

"You're assuming it broke down."

"We have two dead judges, both of whom were being protected by the FBI. I think the American people deserve to know what went wrong, Director. Yes, it broke down."

"Do I report to you, or the American people?"

"You report to me."

"And then you call a press conference and report to the American people, right?"

"Are you afraid of the scrutiny, Director?"

"Not one bit. Rosenberg and Jensen are dead because they refused to cooperate with us. They were very much aware of the danger, yet they couldn't be bothered. The other seven are cooperating, and they're still alive."

"For the moment. We'd better check. They're dropping like flies." The President smiled at Coal, who snickered and almost sneered at Voyles. Coal decided it was time to speak. "Director, did you know Jensen was hanging around such places?"

"He was a grown man with a lifetime appointment. If he chose to dance naked on tables we couldn't stop him."

"Yes sir," Coal said politely. "But you didn't answer my question."

Voyles breathed deeply and looked away. "Yes. We suspected he was a homosexual, and we knew he liked certain movie houses. We have neither the authority nor the desire, Mr. Coal, to divulge such information."

"I want those reports by this afternoon," the President said. Voyles was watching a window, listening but not responding. The President looked at Robert Gminski, director of the CIA. "Bob, I want a straight answer."

Gminski tightened and frowned. "Yes sir. What is it?"

"I want to know if these killings are in any way linked to any agency, operation, group, whatever, of the United States Government."

"Come on! Are you serious, Mr. President! That's absurd." Gminski appeared to be shocked, but the President, Coal, even Voyles, knew anything was possible these days at the CIA.

"Dead serious, Bob."

"I'm serious too. And I assure you we had nothing to do with it. I'm shocked you would even think it. Ridiculous!"

"Check it out, Bob. I want to be damned certain. Rosenberg did not believe in national security. He made thousands of enemies in intelligence. Just check it out, okay."

"Okay, okay."

"And I want a report by five today."

"Sure. Okay. But it's a waste of time."

Fletcher Coal moved to the desk next to the President. "I suggest we meet here at five this afternoon, gentlemen. Is that agreeable?"

They both nodded and stood. Coal escorted them to the door without a word. He closed it.

"You handled it real well," he said to the President. "Voyles knows he's vulnerable. I smell blood. We'll go to work on him with the press."

"Rosenberg is dead," the President repeated to himself. "I just can't believe it."

"I've got an idea for television." Coal was pacing again, very much in charge. "We need to cash in on the shock of it all. You need to appear tired, as if you were up all night handling the crisis. Right? The entire nation will be watching, waiting for you to give details and to reassure. I think you should wear something warm and comforting. A coat and tie at 7 A.M. may seem a bit rehearsed. Let's relax a little."

The President was listening intently. "A bathrobe?"

"Not quite. But how about a cardigan and slacks? No tie. White button-down. Sort of the grandfather image."

"You want me to address the nation in this hour of crisis in a sweater?"

"Yes. I like it. A brown cardigan with a white shirt."

"I don't know."

"The image is good. Look, Chief, the election is a year from next month. This is our first crisis in ninety days, and what a wonderful crisis it is. The people need to see you in something different, especially at seven in the morning. You need to look casual, down-home, but in control. It'll be worth five, maybe ten points in the ratings. Trust me, Chief."

"I don't like sweaters."

"Just trust me."

"I don't know."

FIVE

DARBY SHAW awoke in the early darkness with a touch of a hangover. After fifteen months of law school, her mind refused to rest for more than six hours. She was often up before daybreak, and for this reason she did not sleep well with Callahan. The sex was great, but sleep was often a tug-of-war with pillows and sheets pulled back and forth.

She watched the ceiling and listened to him snore occasionally in his Scotch-induced coma. The sheets were wrapped like ropes around his knees. She had no cover, but she was not cold. October in New Orleans is still muggy and warm. The heavy air rose from Dauphine Street below, across the small balcony outside the bedroom and through the open french doors. It brought with it the first stream of morning light. She stood in the doors and covered herself with his terry-cloth robe. The sun was rising, but Dauphine was dark. Daybreaks went unnoticed in the French Quarter. Her mouth was dry.

Downstairs in the kitchen, Darby brewed a pot of thick French Market chicory. The blue numbers on the microwave said it was now ten minutes before six. For a light drinker, life with Callahan was a constant struggle. Her limit was three glasses of wine. She had neither a law license nor a job, and she could not afford to get drunk every night and sleep late. And she weighed a hundred and twelve pounds and was determined to keep it there. He had no limit.

She drank three glasses of ice water, then poured a tall mug full of chicory. She flipped on lights as she climbed the stairs, and eased back into the bed. She flicked the remote controls, and suddenly, there was the President sitting behind his desk looking somehow rather odd in a brown cardigan with no tie. It was an NBC News special report.

"Thomas!" She slapped him on his shoulder. No movement. "Thomas! Wake up!" She pressed a button and the volume roared. The President said good morning.

"Thomas!" She leaned toward the television. Callahan kicked at the sheets and sat up, rubbing his eyes and trying to focus. She handed him the coffee.

The President had tragic news. His eyes were tired and he looked sad, but the rich baritone exuded confidence. He had notes but didn't use them. He looked deep into the camera, and explained to the American people the shocking events of last night.

"What the hell," Callahan mumbled. After announcing the deaths, the President launched into a flowery obituary for Abraham Rosenberg. A towering legend, he called him. It was a strain, but the President kept a straight face while lauding the distinguished career of one of the most hated men in America.

Callahan gaped at the television. Darby stared at it. "That's very touching," she said. She was frozen on the end of the bed. He had been briefed by the FBI and CIA, he explained, and they were assuming the killings were related. He had ordered an immediate, thorough investigation, and those responsible would be brought to justice.

Callahan sat upright and covered himself with the sheets. He blinked his eyes and combed his wild hair with his fingers. "Rosenberg? Murdered?" he mumbled, glaring at the screen. His foggy head had cleared immediately, and the pain was there but he couldn't feel it.

"Check out the sweater," Darby said, sipping the coffee, staring at the orange face with heavy makeup and the brilliant silver hair plastered carefully in place. He was a wonderfully handsome man with a soothing voice; thus he had succeeded greatly in politics. The wrinkles in his forehead squeezed together, and he was even sadder now as he talked of his close friend Justice Glenn Jensen.

"The Montrose Theatre, at midnight," Callahan repeated.

"Where is it?" she asked. Callahan had finished law school at Georgetown.

"Not sure. But I think it's in the gay section."

"Was he gay?"

"I've heard rumors. Evidently." They were both sitting on the end of the bed with the sheets over their legs. The President was ordering a week of national mourning. Flags at half-staff. Federal offices closed tomorrow. Funeral arrangements were incomplete. He rambled for a few more minutes, still deeply saddened, even shocked, very human, but nonetheless the President and clearly in charge. He signed off with his patented grandfather's smile of complete trust and wisdom and reassurance.

An NBC reporter on the White House lawn appeared and filled in the gaps. The police were mute, but there appeared to be no suspects at the moment, and no leads. Yes, both justices had been under the protection of the FBI, which had no comment. Yes, the Montrose was a place frequented by homosexuals. Yes, there had been many threats against both men, especially Rosenberg. And there could be many suspects before it was all over.

Callahan turned off the set and walked to the french doors, where the early air was growing thicker. "No suspects," he mumbled.

"I can think of at least twenty," Darby said.

"Yeah, but why the combination? Rosenberg is easy, but why Jensen? Why not McDowell or Yount, both of whom are consistently more liberal than Jensen? It doesn't make sense." Callahan sat in a wicker chair by the doors and fluffed his hair.

"I'll get you some more coffee," Darby said.

"No, no. I'm awake."

"How's your head?"

"Fine, if I could've slept for three more hours. I think I'll cancel class. I'm not in the mood."

"Great."

"Damn, I can't believe this. That fool has two nominations. That means eight of the nine will be Republican choices."

"They have to be confirmed first."

"We won't recognize the Constitution in ten years. This is sick."

"That's why they were killed, Thomas. Someone or some group wants a different Court, one with an absolute conservative majority. The election is next year. Rosenberg is, or was, ninety-one. Manning is eighty-four. Yount is early eighties. They could die soon, or live ten more years. A Democrat may be elected President. Why take a chance? Kill them now, a year before the election. Makes perfect sense, if one was so inclined."

"But why Jensen?"

"He was an embarrassment. And, obviously, he was an easier target."

"Yes, but he was basically a moderate with an occasional leftward impulse. And he was nominated by a Republican."

"You want a Bloody Mary?"

"Good idea. In a minute. I'm trying to think."

Darby reclined on the bed, sipped the coffee, and watched the sunlight filter across the balcony. "Think of it, Thomas. The timing is beautiful. Reelection, nominations, politics, all that. But think of the violence and the radicals, the zealots, the prolifers and gay haters, the Aryans and Nazis, think of all the groups capable of killing, and all the threats against the Court, and the timing is perfect for an unknown, inconspicuous group to knock them off. It's morbid, but the timing is great."

"And who is such a group?"

"Who knows?"

"The Underground Army?"

"They're not exactly inconspicuous. They killed Judge Fernandez in Texas."

"Don't they use bombs?"

"Yeah, experts with plastic explosives."

"Scratch them."

"I'm not scratching anybody right now." Darby stood and retied the robe. "Come on. I'll fix you a Bloody Mary."

"Only if you drink with me."

"Thomas, you're a professor. You can cancel your classes if you want to. I am a student and—"

"I understand the relationship."

"I cannot cut any more classes."

"I'll flunk you in con law if you don't cut classes and get drunk with me. I've got a book of Rosenberg opinions. Let's read them, sip Bloody Marys, then wine, then whatever. I miss him already."

"I have Federal Procedure at nine, and I can't miss it."

"I intend to call the dean and have all classes canceled. Then will you drink with me?"

"No. Come on, Thomas." He followed her down the stairs to the kitchen and the coffee and the liquor.

SIX

WITHOUT REMOVING the receiver from his shoulder, Fletcher Coal punched another button on the phone on the desk in the Oval Office. Three lines were blinking, holding. He paced slowly in front of the desk and listened while scanning a two-page report from Horton at Justice. He ignored the President, who was crouched in front of the windows, gripping his putter with gloved hands, staring fiercely first at the yellow ball, then slowly across the blue carpet to the brass putting cup ten feet away. Coal growled something into the receiver. His words were unheard by the President, who lightly tapped the ball and watched it roll precisely into the cup. The cup clicked, cleared itself, and the ball rolled three feet to the side. The President inched forward in his socks to the next ball, and breathed downward at it. It was an orange one. He tapped it just so, and it rolled straight into the cup. Eight in a row. Twenty-seven out of thirty.

"That was Chief Runyan," Coal said, slamming the receiver down. "He's quite upset. He wanted to meet with you this afternoon."

"Tell him to take a number."

"I told him to be here at ten tomorrow morning. You have the Cabinet at ten-thirty, and National Security at eleven-thirty."

Without looking up, the President gripped the putter and

studied the next ball. "I can't wait. What about the polls?" He swung carefully and followed the ball.

"I just talked to Nellson. He ran two, beginning at noon. The computer is digesting it now, but he thinks the approval rating will be somewhere around fifty-two or fifty-three."

The golfer looked up briefly and smiled, then returned to his game. "What was it last week?"

"Forty-four. It was the cardigan without the tie. Just like I said."

"I thought it was forty-five," he said as he tapped a yellow one and watched it roll perfectly into the cup.

"You're right. Forty-five."

"That's the highest in—"

"Eleven months. We haven't been above fifty since Flight 402 in November of last year. This is a wonderful crisis, Chief. The people are shocked, yet many of them are happy Rosenberg is gone. And you're the man in the middle. Just wonderful." Coal punched a blinking button and picked up the receiver. He slammed it down without a word. He straightened his tie and buttoned his jacket.

"It's five-thirty, Chief. Voyles and Gminski are waiting."

He putted and watched the ball. It was an inch to the right, and he grimaced. "Let them wait. Let's do a press conference at nine in the morning. I'll take Voyles with me, but I'll keep his mouth shut. Make him stand behind me. I'll give some more details and answer a few questions. Networks'll carry it live, don't you think?"

"Of course. Good idea. I'll get it started."

He picked off his gloves and threw them in a corner. "Show them in." He carefully leaned his putter against the wall and slid into his Bally loafers. As usual, he had changed clothes six times since breakfast, and now wore a glen plaid double-breasted suit with a red and navy polka-dot tie. Office attire. The jacket hung on a rack by the door. He sat at his desk and scowled at some papers. He nodded at Voyles and Gminski, but neither stood nor offered to shake hands. They sat across the desk, and Coal took his usual standing position like a sentry who couldn't wait to fire. The President pinched the bridge of his nose as if the stress of the day had delivered a migraine.

"It's been a long day, Mr. President," Bob Gminski said to break the ice. Voyles looked at the windows.

Coal nodded, and the President said, "Yes, Bob. A very long day. And I have a bunch of Ethiopians invited for dinner tonight, so let's be brief. Let's start with you, Bob. Who killed them?"

"I do not know, Mr. President. But I assure you we had nothing to do with it."

"Do you promise me, Bob?" He was almost prayerful.

Gminski raised his right hand with the palm facing the desk. "I swear. On my mother's grave, I swear."

Coal nodded smugly as if he believed him, and as if his approval meant everything.

The President glared at Voyles, whose stocky figure filled the chair and was still draped with a bulky trench coat. The Director chewed his gum slowly and sneered at the President.

"Ballistics? Autopsies?"

"Got 'em," Voyles said as he opened his briefcase.

"Just tell me. I'll read it later."

"The gun was small-caliber, probably a .22. Point-blank range for Rosenberg and his nurse, powder burns indicate. Hard to tell for Ferguson, but the shots were fired from no farther than twelve inches away. We didn't see the shooting, you understand? Three bullets into each head. They picked two out of Rosenberg; found another in his pillow. Looks like he and the nurse were asleep. Same type slugs, same gun, same gunman, evidently. Complete autopsy summaries are being prepared, but there were no surprises. Causes of deaths are quite obvious."

"Fingerprints?"

"None. We're still looking, but it was a very clean job. Appears as if he left nothing but the slugs and the bodies."

"How'd he get into the house?"

"No apparent signs of entry. Ferguson searched the place when Rosenberg arrived around four. Routine procedure. He filed his written report two hours later, and it says he inspected two bedrooms, a bath, and three closets upstairs, and each room downstairs, and of course found nothing. Says he checked all windows and doors. Pursuant to Rosenberg's instructions, our agents were outside, and they estimate Ferguson's four o'clock inspection took from three to four minutes. I suspect the killer was waiting and hiding when the Justice returned and Ferguson walked through."

"Why?" Coal insisted.

Voyles' red eyes watched the President and ignored his hatchet man. "This man is obviously very talented. He killed a Supreme Court Justice—maybe two—and left virtually no trail. A professional assassin, I would guess. Entry would not be a problem for him. Eluding a cursory inspection by Ferguson would be no problem for him. He's probably very patient. He wouldn't risk an entry when the house was occupied and cops around. I think he entered sometime in the afternoon and simply waited, probably in a closet upstairs, or perhaps in the attic. We found two small pieces of attic insulation on the floor under the retractable stairs; suggests they had recently been used."

"Really doesn't matter where he was hiding," the President said. "He wasn't discovered."

"That's correct. We were not allowed to inspect the house, you understand?"

"I understand he's dead. What about Jensen?"

"He's dead too. Broken neck, strangled with a piece of yellow nylon rope that can be found in any hardware store. The medical examiners doubt the broken neck killed him. They're reasonably confident the rope did. No fingerprints. No witnesses. This is not the sort of place where witnesses come rushing forward, so I don't expect to find any. Time of death was around twelve-thirty this morning. The killings were two hours apart."

The President scribbled notes. "When did Jensen leave his apartment?"

"Don't know. We're relegated to the parking lot, remember. We followed him home around 6 P.M., then watched the building for seven hours until we found out he'd been strangled in a queer joint. We were following his demands, of course. He sneaked out of the building in a friend's car. Found it two blocks from the joint."

Coal took two steps forward with his hands clasped rigidly behind him. "Director, do you think one assassin did both jobs?"

"Who in hell knows. The bodies are still warm. Give us a break. There's precious little evidence right now. With no witnesses, no prints, no screwups, it'll take time to piece this thing together. Could be the same man, I don't know. It's too early."

"Surely you have a gut feeling," the President said.

Voyles paused and glanced at the windows. "Could be the same guy, but he must be superman. Probably two or three, but regardless, they had to have a lot of help. Someone fed them a lot of information."

"Such as?"

"Such as how often Jensen goes to the movies, where does he sit, what time does he get there, does he go by himself, does he meet a friend. Information we didn't have, obviously. Take Rosenberg. Someone had to know his little house had no security system, that our boys were kept outside, that Ferguson arrived at ten and left at six and had to sit in the backyard, that—"

"You knew all this," the President interrupted.

"Of course we did. But I assure you we didn't share it with anyone." The President shot a quick conspiratorial glance at Coal, who was scratching his chin, deep in thought.

Voyles shifted his rather wide rear and gave Gminski a smile, as if to say, "Let's play along with them."

"You're suggesting a conspiracy," Coal said intelligently with deep eyebrows.

"I'm not suggesting a damned thing. I am proclaiming to you, Mr. Coal, and to you, Mr. President, that, yes, in fact, a large number of people conspired to kill them. There may be only one or two killers, but they had a lot of help. It was too quick and clean and well organized."

Coal seemed satisfied. He stood straight and again clasped his hands behind him.

"Then who are the conspirators?" the President asked. "Who are your suspects?"

Voyles breathed deeply and seemed to settle in his chair. He closed the briefcase and laid it at his feet. "We don't have a prime suspect, at the moment, just a few good possibilities. And this must be kept very quiet."

Coal sprang a step closer. "Of course it's confidential," he snapped. "You're in the Oval Office."

"And I've been here many times before. In fact, I was here when you were running around in dirty diapers, Mr. Coal. Things have a way of leaking out."

"I think you've had leaks yourself," Coal said.

The President raised his hand. "It's confidential, Denton. You have my word." Coal retreated a step.

Voyles watched the President. "Court opened Monday, as you know, and the maniacs have been in town for a few days. For the past two weeks, we've been monitoring various movements. We know of at least eleven members of the Underground Army who've been in the D.C. area for a week. We questioned a couple today, and released them. We know the group has the capability, and the desire. It's our strongest possibility, for now. Could change tomorrow."

Coal was not impressed. The Underground Army was on everyone's list.

"I've heard of them," the President said stupidly.

"Oh yes. They're becoming quite popular. We believe they killed a trial judge in Texas. Can't prove it, though. They're very proficient with explosives. We suspect them in at least a hundred bombings of abortion clinics, ACLU offices, porno houses, gay clubs, all over the country. They're just the people who would hate Rosenberg and Jensen."

"Other suspects?" Coal asked.

"There's an Aryan group called White Resistance that we've been watching for two years. It operates out of Idaho and Oregon. The leader gave a speech in West Virginia last week, and has been in the area for a few days. He was spotted Monday in the demonstration outside the Supreme Court. We'll try to talk to him tomorrow."

"But are these people professional assassins?" Coal asked.

"They don't advertise, you understand. I doubt if any group

performed the actual killings. They just hired the assassins and provided the legwork."

"So who're the assassins?" the President asked.

"We may never know, frankly."

The President stood and stretched his legs. Another hard day at the office. He smiled down at Voyles across the desk. "You have a difficult task." It was the grandfather's voice, filled with warmth and understanding. "I don't envy you. If possible, I would like a two-page typewritten double-spaced report by 5 P.M. each day, seven days a week, on the progress of the investigation. If something breaks, I expect you to call me immediately."

Voyles nodded but did not speak.

"I'm having a press conference in the morning at nine. I would like for you to be here."

Voyles nodded but did not speak. Seconds passed and no one spoke. Voyles stood noisily and tied the strap around the trench coat. "Oh well, we'll be going. You've got the Ethiopians and all." He handed the ballistics and autopsy reports to Coal, knowing the President would never read them.

"Thanks for coming, gentlemen," the President said warmly. Coal closed the door behind them, and the President grabbed the putter. "I'm not eating with the Ethiopians," he said, staring at the carpet and a yellow ball.

"I know it. I've already sent your apologies. This is a great hour of crisis, Mr. President, and you are expected to be here in this office surrounded by your advisers, hard at work."

He putted, and the ball rolled perfectly into the cup. "I want to talk to Horton. These nominations must be perfect."

"He's sent a short list of ten. Looks pretty good."

"I want young conservative white men opposed to abortion, pornography, queers, gun control, racial quotas, all that crap." He missed a putt, and kicked off his loafers. "I want judges who hate dope and criminals and are enthusiastic about the death penalty. Understand?"

Coal was on the phone, punching numbers and nodding at his boss. He would select the nominees, then convince the President.

K. O. LEWIS sat with the Director in the back of the quiet limousine as it left the White House and crawled through rush-hour traffic. Voyles had nothing to say. So far, in the early hours of the tragedy, the press had been brutal. The buzzards were circling. No less than three congressional subcommittees had already announced hearings and investigations into the deaths. And the bodies were still warm. The politicians were giddy and wrestling for the spotlight. One outrageous statement fueled another. Senator Larkin from Ohio hated Voyles, and Voyles hated Senator Larkin from Ohio, and the senator had called a press conference three hours earlier and announced his subcommittee would immediately begin investigating the FBI's protection of the two dead justices. But Larkin had a girlfriend, a rather young one, and the FBI had some photographs, and Voyles was confident the investigation could be delayed.

"How's the President?" Lewis finally asked.

"Which one?"

"Not Coal. The other one."

"Swell. Just swell. He's awfully tore up about Rosenberg, though."

"I bet."

They rode in silence in the direction of the Hoover Building. It would be a long night.

"We've got a new suspect," Lewis finally said.

"Do tell."

"A man named Nelson Muncie."

Voyles slowly shook his head. "Never heard of him."

"Neither have I. It's a long story."

"Gimme the short version."

"Muncie is a very wealthy industrialist from Florida. Sixteen years ago his niece was raped and murdered by an Afro-American named Buck Tyrone. The little girl was twelve. Very, very brutal rape and murder. I'll spare you the details. Muncie has no children, and idolized his niece. Tyrone was tried in Orlando, and given the death penalty. He was guarded heavily because there were a bunch of threats. Some Jewish lawyers in a

49

big New York firm filed all sorts of appeals, and in 1984 the case arrives at the Supreme Court. You guessed it: Rosenberg falls in love with Tyrone and concocts this ridiculous Fifth Amendment self-incrimination argument to exclude a confession the punk gave a week after he was arrested. An eight-page confession that he, Tyrone, wrote himself. No confession, no case. Rosenberg writes a convoluted five-to-four opinion overturning the conviction. An extremely controversial decision. Tyrone goes free. Then, two years later he disappears and has not been seen since. Rumor has it Muncie paid to have Tyrone castrated, mutilated, and fed to the sharks. Just a rumor, say the Florida authorities. Then in 1989, Tyrone's main lawyer on the case, man named Kaplan, is gunned down by an apparent mugger outside his apartment in Manhattan. What a coincidence."

"Who tipped you?"

"Florida called two hours ago. They're convinced Muncie paid a bunch of money to eliminate both Tyrone and his lawyer. They just can't prove it. They've got a reluctant, unidentified informant who says he knows Muncie and feeds them a little info. He says Muncie has been talking for years about eliminating Rosenberg. They think he went a little over the edge when his niece was murdered."

"How much money has he got?"

"Enough. Millions. No one is sure. He's very secretive. Florida is convinced he's capable."

"Let's check it out. Sounds interesting."

"I'll get on it tonight. Are you sure you want three hundred agents on this case?"

Voyles lit a cigar and cracked his window. "Yeah, maybe four hundred. We need to crack this baby before the press eats us alive."

"It won't be easy. Except for the slugs and the rope, these guys left nothing."

Voyles blew smoke out the window. "I know. It's almost too clean."

SEVEN

THE CHIEF slouched behind his desk with a loosened tie and a haggard look. Around the room, three of his brethren and a half-dozen clerks sat and talked in subdued tones. The shock and fatigue were evident. Jason Kline, Rosenberg's senior clerk, looked especially hard-hit. He sat on a small sofa and stared blankly at the floor while Justice Archibald Manning, now the senior Justice, talked of protocol and funerals. Jensen's mother wanted a small, private Episcopal service Friday in Providence. Rosenberg's son, a lawyer, had delivered to Runyan a list of instructions the Justice had prepared after his second stroke in which he wanted to be cremated after a non-military ceremony and his ashes dropped over the Sioux Indian Reservation in South Dakota. Though Rosenberg was Jewish, he had abandoned the religion and claimed to be agnostic. He wanted to be buried with the Indians. Runyan thought that was appropriate, but did not say so. In the outer office, six FBI agents sipped coffee and whispered nervously. There had been more threats during the day, several coming within hours of the President's early morning address. It was dark now, almost time to escort the remaining justices home. Each had four agents as bodyguards.

Justice Andrew McDowell, at sixty-one now the youngest member of the Court, stood in the window, smoking his pipe and watching traffic. If Jensen had a friend on the Court, it was

McDowell. Fletcher Coal had informed Runyan that the President would not only attend Jensen's service but wanted to deliver a eulogy. No one in the inner office wanted the President to say a word. The Chief had asked McDowell to prepare a few words. A shy man who avoided speeches, McDowell twirled his bow tie and tried to picture his friend in the balcony with a rope around his neck. It was too awful to think about. A Justice of the Supreme Court, one of his distinguished brethren, one of the nine, hiding in such a place watching those movies and being exposed in such a ghastly manner. What a tragic embarrassment. He thought of himself standing before the crowd in the church and looking at Jensen's mother and family, and knowing that every thought would be on the Montrose Theatre. They would ask each other in whispered voices, "Did you know he was gay?" McDowell, for one, did not know, nor did he suspect. Nor did he want to say anything at the funeral.

Justice Ben Thurow, age sixty-eight, was not as concerned about burying the dead as he was about catching the killers. He had been a federal prosecutor in Minnesota, and his theory grouped the suspects into two classes: those acting out of hatred and revenge, and those seeking to affect future decisions. He had instructed his clerks to begin the research.

Thurow was pacing around the room. "We have twenty-seven clerks and seven justices," he said to the group but to no one in particular. "It's obvious we won't get much work done for the next couple of weeks, and all close decisions must wait until we have a full bench. That could take months. I suggest we put our clerks to work trying to solve the killings."

"We're not police," Manning said patiently.

"Can we at least wait until after the burials before we start playing Dick Tracy?" McDowell said without turning from the window.

Thurow ignored them, as usual. "I'll direct the research. Loan me your clerks for two weeks, and I think we can put together a short list of solid suspects."

"The FBI is very capable, Ben," the Chief said. "They haven't asked for our help."

"I'd rather not discuss the FBI," Thurow said. "We can mope

around here in official mourning for two weeks, or we can go to work and find these bastards."

"What makes you so sure you can solve this?" Manning asked.

"I'm not sure I can, but I think it's worth a try. Our brethren were murdered for a reason, and that reason is directly related to a case or an issue already decided or now pending before this Court. If it's retribution, then our task is almost impossible. Hell, everybody hates us for one reason or another. But if it's not revenge or hatred, then perhaps someone wanted a different Court for a future decision. That's what's intriguing. Who would kill Abe and Glenn because of how they might vote on a case this year, next year, or five years from now? I want the clerks to pull up every case now pending in the eleven circuits below."

Justice McDowell shook his head. "Come on, Ben. That's over five thousand cases, a small fraction of which will eventually end up here. It's a wild-goose chase."

Manning was equally unimpressed. "Listen, fellas. I served with Abe Rosenberg for thirty-one years, and I often thought of shooting him myself. But I loved him like a brother. His liberal ideas were accepted in the sixties and seventies, but grew old in the eighties, and are now resented in the nineties. He became a symbol for everything that's wrong in this country. He has been killed, I believe, by one of these radical right-wing hate groups, and we can research cases till hell freezes over and not find anything. It's retribution, Ben. Pure and simple."

"And Glenn?" Thurow asked.

"Evidently our friend had some strange proclivities. Word must have spread, and he was an easy target for such groups. They hate homosexuals, Ben."

Ben was still pacing, still ignoring. "They hate all of us, and if they killed out of hatred the cops'll catch them. Maybe. But what if they killed to manipulate this Court? What if some group seized this moment of unrest and violence to eliminate two of us, and thus realign the Court? I think it's very possible."

The Chief cleared his throat. "And I think we'll do nothing until after they are buried, or scattered. I'm not saying no, Ben, just wait a few days. Let the dust settle. The rest of us are still in shock."

Thurow excused himself and left the room. His bodyguards followed him down the hall.

Justice Manning stood with his cane and addressed the Chief. "I will not make it to Providence. I hate flying, and I hate funerals. I'll be having one myself before long, and I do not enjoy the reminder. I'll send my sympathies to the family. When you see them, please apologize for me. I'm a very old man." He left with a clerk.

"I think Justice Thurow has a point," said Jason Kline. "We at least need to review the pending cases and those likely to arrive here from the lower circuits. It's a long shot, but we may stumble across something."

"I agree," said the Chief. "It's just a bit premature, don't you think?"

"Yes, but I'd like to get started anyway."

"No. Wait till Monday, and I'll assign you to Thurow."

Kline shrugged and excused himself. Two clerks followed him to Rosenberg's office, where they sat in the darkness and sipped the last of Abe's brandy.

IN A CLUTTERED STUDY CARREL on the fifth level of the law library, between the racks of thick, seldom-used law books, Darby Shaw scanned a printout of the Supreme Court's docket. She had been through it twice, and though it was loaded with controversy, she found nothing that interested her. *Dumond* was causing riots. There was a child pornography case from New Jersey, a sodomy case from Kentucky, a dozen death penalty appeals, a dozen assorted civil rights cases, and the usual array of tax, zoning, Indian, and antitrust cases. From the computer she had pulled summaries of each, then reviewed them twice. She compiled a neat list of possible suspects, but they would be obvious to everyone. The list was now in the garbage.

Callahan was certain it was the Aryans or the Nazis or the Klan; some easily identifiable collection of domestic terrorists; some radical band of vigilantes. It had to be right-wingers; that much was obvious, he felt. Darby was not so sure. The hate groups were too obvious. They had made too many threats, thrown too many rocks, held too many parades, made too many speeches. They needed Rosenberg alive because he was such an irresistible target for their hatred. Rosenberg kept them in business. She thought it was somebody much more sinister.

He was sitting in a bar on Canal Street, drunk by now, waiting on her though she had not promised to join him. She had checked on him at lunch, and found him on the balcony upstairs, drunk and reading his book of Rosenberg opinions. He had decided to cancel con law for a week; said he might not be able to teach it anymore now that his hero was dead. She told him to sober up, and she left.

A few minutes after ten, she walked to the computer room on the fourth level of the library and sat before a monitor. The room was empty. She pecked away at the keyboard, found what she wanted, and soon the printer was spewing forth page after page of appeals pending in the eleven federal appellate courts around the country. An hour later, the printer stopped, and she now possessed a six-inch-thick summary of the eleven dockets. She hauled it back to her study carrel and placed it in the center of the cluttered desk. It was after eleven, and the fifth level was deserted. A narrow window gave an uninspiring view of a parking lot and trees below.

She kicked off her shoes again and inspected the red paint on the toes. She sipped a warm Fresca and stared blankly at the parking lot. The first assumption was easy—the killings were done by the same group for the same reasons. If not, then the search was hopeless. The second assumption was difficult—the motive was not hatred or revenge, but rather manipulation. There was a case or an issue out there on its way to the Supreme Court, and someone wanted different justices. The third assumption was a bit easier—the case or issue involved a great deal of money.

The answer would not be found in the printout sitting before her. She flipped through it until midnight, and left when the library closed.

EIGHT

A T NOON THURSDAY a secretary carried a large sack
decorated with grease spots and filled with deli sandwiches and onion rings into a humid conference room on the
fifth floor of the Hoover Building. In the center of the square
room, a mahogany table with twenty chairs along each side was
surrounded with the top FBI people from across the country.
All ties were loosened and sleeves rolled up. A thin cloud of
blue smoke hung around the cheap government chandelier five
feet above the table.

Director Voyles was talking. Tired and angry, he puffed on
his fourth cigar of the morning and walked slowly in front of
the screen at his end of the table. Half the men were listening.
The other half had pulled reports from the pile in the center of
the table and read about the autopsies, the lab report on the
nylon rope, Nelson Muncie, and a few other quickly researched
subjects. The reports were quite thin.

Listening carefully and reading intently was Special Agent
Eric East, only a ten-year man but a brilliant investigator. Six
hours earlier Voyles had picked him to lead the investigation.
The rest of the team had been selected throughout the morning, and this was the organizational meeting.

East was listening and hearing what he already knew. The
investigation could take weeks, probably months. Other than
the slugs, nine of them, the rope, and the steel rod used in the

tourniquet, there was no evidence. The neighbors in George-town had seen nothing; no exceptionally suspicious characters at the Montrose. No prints. No fibers. Nothing. It takes remark-able talent to kill so cleanly, and it takes a lot of money to hire such talent. Voyles was pessimistic about finding the gunmen. They must concentrate on whoever hired them.

Voyles was talking and puffing. "There's a memo on the table regarding one Nelson Muncie, a millionaire from Jacksonville, Florida, who's allegedly made threats against Rosenberg. The Florida authorities are convinced Muncie paid a bunch of money to have the rapist and his lawyer killed. The memo cov-ers it. Two of our men talked with Muncie's lawyer this morn-ing, and were met with great hostility. Muncie is out of the country, according to his lawyer, and of course he has no idea when he will return. I've assigned twenty men to investigate him."

Voyles relit his cigar and looked at a sheet of paper on the table. "Number four is a group called White Resistance, a small group of middle-aged commandos we've been watching for about three years. You've got a memo. Pretty weak suspect, really. They'd rather throw firebombs and burn crosses. Not a lot of finesse. And, most importantly, not much money. I doubt seriously if they could hire guns as slick as these. But I've as-signed twenty men anyway."

East unwrapped a heavy sandwich, sniffed it, but decided to leave it alone. The onion rings were cold. His appetite had vanished. He listened and made notes. Number six on the list was a bit unusual. A psycho named Clinton Lane had declared war on homosexuals. His only son had moved from their family farm in Iowa to San Francisco to enjoy the gay life, but had quickly died of AIDS. Lane cracked up, and burned the Gay Coalition office in Des Moines. Caught and sentenced to four years, he escaped in 1989 and had not been found. According to the memo, he had set up an extensive coke-smuggling opera-tion and made millions. And he used the money in his own little private war against gays and lesbians. The FBI had been trying to catch him for five years, but it was believed he operated out of Mexico. For years he had written hate mail to the Congress, the Supreme Court, the President. Voyles was not impressed with Lane as a suspect. He was a nut who was way out in left field, but no stone would go unturned. He assigned only six agents.

The list had ten names. Between six and twenty of the best special agents were assigned to each suspect. A leader was chosen for each unit. They were to report twice daily to East, who would meet each morning and each afternoon with the Director. A hundred or so more agents would scour the streets and countryside for clues.

Voyles talked of secrecy. The press would follow like bloodhounds, so the investigation must be extremely confidential. Only he, the Director, would speak to the press, and he would have precious little to say.

He sat down, and K. O. Lewis delivered a rambling monologue about the funerals, and security, and a request from Chief Runyan to assist in the investigation.

Eric East sipped cold coffee, and stared at the list.

IN THIRTY-FOUR YEARS, Abraham Rosenberg wrote no fewer than twelve hundred opinions. His production was a constant source of amazement to constitutional scholars. He occasionally ignored the dull antitrust cases and tax appeals, but if the issue showed the barest hint of real controversy, he waded in with both fists. He wrote majority opinions, concurrences to majorities, concurrences to dissents, and many, many dissents. Often he dissented alone. Every hot issue in thirty-four years had received an opinion of some sort from Rosenberg. The scholars and critics loved him. They published books and essays and critiques about him and his work. Darby found five separate hardback compilations of his opinions, with editorial notes and annotations. One book contained nothing but his great dissents.

She skipped class Thursday and secluded herself in the study carrel on the fifth level of the library. The computer printouts were scattered neatly on the floor. The Rosenberg books were open and marked and stacked on top of each other.

There was a reason for the killings. Revenge and hatred

would be acceptable for Rosenberg alone. But add Jensen to the equation, and revenge and hatred made less sense. Sure he was hateable, but he had not aroused passions like Yount or even Manning.

She found no books of critical thought on the writings of Justice Glenn Jensen. In six years, he had authored only twenty-eight majority opinions, the lowest production on the Court. He had written a few dissents, and joined a few concurrences, but he was a painfully slow worker. At times his writing was clear and lucid, at times disjointed and pathetic.

She studied Jensen's opinions. His ideology swung radically from year to year. He was generally consistent in his protection of the rights of criminal defendants, but there were enough exceptions to astound any scholar. In seven attempts, he had voted with the Indians five times. He had written three majority opinions strongly protective of the environment. He was near perfect in support of tax protestors.

But there were no clues. Jensen was too erratic to take seriously. Compared to the other eight, he was harmless.

She finished another warm Fresca, and put away for the moment her notes on Jensen. Her watch was hidden in a drawer. She had no idea what time it was. Callahan had sobered up and wanted a late dinner at Mr. B's in the Quarter. She needed to call him.

DICK MABRY, the current speechwriter and word wizard, sat in a chair beside the President's desk and watched as Fletcher Coal and the President read the third draft of a proposed eulogy for Justice Jensen. Coal had rejected the first two, and Mabry was still uncertain about what they wanted. Coal would suggest one thing. The President wanted something else. Earlier in the day, Coal had called and said to forget the eulogy because the President would not attend the funeral. Then the President had called, and asked him to prepare a few words because Jensen was a friend and even though he was a queer he was still a friend.

Mabry knew Jensen was not a friend, but he was a freshly assassinated justice who would enjoy a highly visible funeral.

Then Coal had called and said they weren't sure if the President was going but work up something just in case. Mabry's office was in the Old Executive Office Building next door to the White House, and during the day small bets had been placed on whether the President would attend the funeral of a known homosexual. The office odds were three to one that he would not.

"Much better, Dick," Coal said, folding the paper.

"I like it too," the President said. Mabry had noticed that the President usually waited for Coal to express approval or displeasure over his words.

"I can try again," Mabry said, standing.

"No, no," Coal insisted. "This has the right touch. Very poignant. I like it."

He walked Mabry to the door and closed it behind him.

"What do you think?" the President asked.

"Let's call it off. I'm getting bad vibes. Publicity would be great, but you'd be speaking these beautiful words over a body found in a gay porno house. Too risky."

"Yeah. I think you're—"

"This is our crisis, Chief. The ratings continue to improve, and I just don't want to take a chance."

"Should we send someone?"

"Of course. What about the Vice President?"

"Where is he?"

"Flying in from Guatemala. He'll be in tonight." Coal suddenly smiled to himself. "This is great VP stuff, you know. A gay funeral."

The President chuckled. "Perfect."

Coal stopped smiling and began pacing in front of the desk. "Slight problem. Rosenberg's service is Saturday, only eight blocks from here."

"I'd rather go to hell for a day."

"I know. But your absence would be very conspicuous."

"I could check into Walter Reed with back spasms. It worked before."

"No, Chief. Reelection is next year. You must stay away from hospitals."

The President slapped both hands on his desk and stood. "Dammit, Fletcher! I can't go to his service because I can't keep from smiling. He was hated by ninety percent of the American people. They'll love me if I don't go."

"Protocol, Chief. Good taste. You'll be burned by the press if you don't go. Look, it won't hurt, okay. You don't have to say a word. Just ease in and out, look real sad, and allow the cameras to get a good look. Won't take an hour."

The President was gripping his putter and crouching over an orange ball. "Then I'll have to go to Jensen's."

"Exactly. But forget the eulogy."

He putted. "I met him only twice, you know."

"I know. Let's quietly attend both services, say nothing, then disappear."

He putted again. "I think you're right."

NINE

THOMAS CALLAHAN slept late and alone. He had gone to bed early, and sober, and alone. For the third day in a row he had canceled classes. It was Friday, and Rosenberg's service was tomorrow, and out of respect for his idol, he would not teach con law until the man was properly put to rest.

He fixed coffee and sat on the balcony in his robe. The temperature was in the sixties, the first cold snap of the fall, and Dauphine Street below bustled with brisk energy. He nodded to the old woman without a name on the balcony across the street. Bourbon was a block away and the tourists were already out with their little maps and cameras. Dawn went unnoticed in the Quarter, but by ten the narrow streets were busy with delivery trucks and cabs.

On these late mornings, and they were many in number, Callahan cherished his freedom. He was twenty years out of law school, and most of his contemporaries were strapped into seventy-hour weeks in pressurized law factories. He had lasted two years in private practice. A behemoth in D.C. with two hundred lawyers hired him fresh out of Georgetown and stuck him in a cubbyhole office writing briefs for the first six months. Then he was placed on an assembly line answering interrogatories about IUDs twelve hours a day, and expected to bill sixteen. He was told that if he could cram the next twenty years into the next ten, he just might make partner at the weary age of thirty-five.

Callahan wanted to live past fifty, so he retired from the boredom of private law. He earned a master's in law, and became a professor. He slept late, worked five hours a day, wrote an occasional article, and for the most part enjoyed himself immensely. With no family to support, his salary of seventy thousand a year was more than sufficient to pay for his two-story bungalow, his Porsche, and his liquor. If death came early, it would be from whiskey and not work.

He had sacrificed. Many of his pals from law school were partners in the big firms with fancy letterheads and half-million-dollar earnings. They rubbed shoulders with CEOs from IBM and Texaco and State Farm. They power-schmoozed with senators. They had offices in Tokyo and London. But he did not envy them.

One of his best friends from law school was Gavin Verheek, another dropout from private practice who had gone to work for the government. He first worked in the civil rights division at Justice, then transferred to the FBI. He was now special counsel to the Director. Callahan was due in Washington Monday for a conference of con law professors. He and Verheek planned to eat and get drunk Monday night.

He needed to call and confirm their eating and drinking, and to pick his brain. He dialed the number from memory. The call was routed then rerouted, and after five minutes of asking for Gavin Verheek, the man was on the phone.

"Make it quick," Verheek said.

"So nice to hear your voice," Callahan said.

"How are you, Thomas?"

"It's ten-thirty. I'm not dressed. I'm sitting here in the French Quarter sipping coffee and watching pedestrians on Dauphine. What're you doing?"

"What a life. Here it's eleven-thirty, and I haven't left the office since they found the bodies Wednesday morning."

"I'm just sick, Gavin. He'll nominate two Nazis."

"Well, of course, in my position, I cannot comment on such matters. But I suspect you're correct."

"Suspect my ass. You've already seen his short list of nominees, haven't you, Gavin? You guys are already doing background checks, aren't you? Come on, Gavin, you can tell me. Who's on the list? I'll never tell."

"Neither will I, Thomas. But I promise this—your name is not among the few."

"I'm wounded."

"How's the girl?"

"Which one?"

"Come on, Thomas. The girl?"

"She's beautiful and brilliant and soft and gentle—"

"Keep going."

"Who killed them, Gavin? I have a right to know. I'm a taxpayer and I have a right to know who killed them."

"What's her name again?"

"Darby. Who killed them, and why?"

"You could always pick names, Thomas. I remember women you turned down because you didn't like the names. Gorgeous, hot women, but with flat names. Darby. Has a nice erotic touch to it. What a name. When do I meet her?"

"I don't know."

"Has she moved in?"

"None of your damned business. Gavin, listen to me. Who did it?"

"Don't you read the papers? We have no suspects. None. *Nada.*"

"Surely you have a motive."

"Mucho motives. Lots of hatred out there, Thomas. Weird combination, wouldn't you say? Jensen's hard to figure. The Director has ordered us to research pending cases and recent decisions and voting patterns and all that crap."

"That's great, Gavin. Every con law scholar in the country is now playing detective and trying to solve the murders."

"And you're not?"

"No. I threw a binge when I heard the news, but I'm sober now. The girl, however, has buried herself in the same research you're doing. She's ignoring me."

"Darby. What a name. Where's she from?"

"Denver. Are we on for Monday?"

"Maybe. Voyles wants us to work around the clock until the computers tell us who did it. I plan to work you in, though."

"Thanks. I'll expect a full report, Gavin. Not just the gossip."

"Thomas, Thomas. Always fishing for information. And I, as usual, have none to give you."

"You'll get drunk and tell all, Gavin. You always do."

"Why don't you bring Darby? How old is she? Nineteen?"

"Twenty-four, and she's not invited. Maybe later."

"Maybe. Gotta run, pal. I meet with the Director in thirty minutes. The tension is so thick around here you can smell it."

Callahan punched the number for the law school library and asked if Darby Shaw had been seen. She had not.

DARBY PARKED in the near-empty lot of the federal building in Lafayette, and entered the clerk's office on the first floor. It was noon Friday, court was not in session, and the hallways were deserted. She stopped at the counter and looked through an open window, and waited. A deputy clerk, late for lunch and with an attitude, walked to the window. "Can I help you?" she asked in the tone of a lowly civil servant who wanted to do anything but help.

Darby slid a strip of paper through the window. "I would like to see this file." The clerk took a quick glance at the name of the case, and looked at Darby. "Why?" she asked.

"I don't have to explain. It's public record, isn't it?"

"Semipublic."

Darby took the strip of paper and folded it. "Are you familiar with the Freedom of Information Act?"

"Are you a lawyer?"

"I don't have to be a lawyer to look at this file."

The clerk opened a drawer in the counter, and took out a key ring. She nodded, pointing with her forehead. "Follow me."

The sign on the door said JURY ROOM, but inside there were no tables or chairs, only file cabinets and boxes lining the walls. Darby looked around the room.

The clerk pointed to a wall. "That's it, on this wall. The rest of the room is other junk. This first file cabinet has all the pleadings and correspondence. The rest is discovery, exhibits, and the trial."

"When was the trial?"

"Last summer. It went on for two months."

"Where's the appeal?"

"Not perfected yet. I think the deadline is November 1. Are you a reporter or something?"

"No."

"Good. As you obviously know, these are indeed public records. But the trial judge has placed certain restrictions. First, I must have your name and the precise hours you visited this room. Second, nothing can be taken from this room. Third, nothing in this file can be copied until the appeal is perfected. Fourth, anything you touch in here must be put back exactly where you found it. Judge's orders."

Darby stared at the wall of file cabinets. "Why can't I make copies?"

"Ask His Honor, okay? Now, what's your name?"

"Darby Shaw."

The clerk scribbled the information on a clipboard hanging near the door. "How long will you be?"

"I don't know. Three or four hours."

"We close at five. Find me at the office when you leave." She closed the door with a smirk. Darby opened a drawer full of pleadings, and began flipping through files and taking notes. The lawsuit was seven years old, with one plaintiff and thirty-eight wealthy corporate defendants who had collectively hired and fired no less than fifteen law firms from all over the country. Big firms, many with hundreds of lawyers in dozens of offices.

Seven years of expensive legal warfare, and the outcome was far from certain. Bitter litigation. The trial verdict was only a temporary victory for the defendants. The verdict had been purchased or in some other way illegally obtained, claimed the plaintiff in its motions for a new trial. Boxes of motions. Accusations and counteraccusations. Requests for sanctions and fines flowing rapidly to and from both sides. Pages and pages of affidavits detailing lies and abuses by the lawyers and their clients. One lawyer was dead.

Another had tried suicide, according to a classmate of Darby's who had worked on the fringes of the case during the trial. Her friend had been employed in a summer clerkship with a big firm in Houston, and was kept in the dark but heard a little.

Darby unfolded a chair and stared at the file cabinets. It would take five hours just to find everything.

THE PUBLICITY had not been good for the Montrose. Most of its customers wore dark sunglasses after dark, and tended to enter and exit rather quickly. And now that a U.S. Supreme Court Justice had been found in the balcony, the place was famous and the curious drove by at all hours pointing and taking pictures. Most of the regulars went elsewhere. The bravest darted in when the traffic was light.

He looked just like a regular when he darted in and paid his money inside the door without looking at the cashier. Baseball cap, black sunglasses, jeans, neat hair, leather jacket. He was well disguised, but not because he was a homosexual and ashamed to be hanging around such places.

It was midnight. He climbed the stairs to the balcony, smiling at the thought of Jensen wearing the tourniquet. The door was locked. He took a seat in the center section on the floor, away from anyone else.

He had never watched queer movies before, and after this night he had no plans to watch another one. This was his third such smut house in the past ninety minutes. He kept the sunglasses on and tried to avoid the screen. But it was difficult, and this irritated him.

There were five other people in the theater. Four rows up and to his right were two lovebirds, kissing and playing. Oh, for a baseball bat and he could put them out of their misery. Or a nice little piece of yellow ski rope.

He suffered for twenty minutes, and was about to reach in his pocket when a hand touched his shoulder. A gentle hand. He played it cool.

"Could I sit by you?" came the rather deep and manly voice from just over his shoulder.

"No, and you can remove your hand."

The hand moved. Seconds passed, and it was obvious there would be no more requests. Then he was gone.

This was torture for a man violently opposed to pornography. He wanted to vomit. He glanced behind him, then reached carefully into the leather jacket and removed a black box, six inches by five and three inches thick. He laid it on the floor between his legs. With a scalpel, he made a careful incision in the cushion of the seat next to him, then, while glancing around, inserted the black box into the cushion. There were springs in this one, a real antique, and he delicately twisted the box from one side to the other until it was in place with the switch and the tube barely visible through the incision.

He took a deep breath. Although the device had been built by a true professional, a legendary genius at miniature explosives, it was not pleasant carrying the damned thing around in a coat pocket, just centimeters from his heart and most other vital organs. And he wasn't particularly comfortable sitting next to it now.

This was his third plant of the night, and he had one more, at another movie house where they showed old-fashioned heterosexual pornography. He was almost looking forward to it, and this irritated him.

He looked at the two lovers, who were oblivious to the movie and growing more excited by the minute, and wished they could be sitting right there when the little black box began silently spewing forth its gas, and then thirty seconds later when the fireball would flash-fry every object between the screen and the popcorn machine. He would like that.

But his was a nonviolent group, opposed to the indiscriminate killing of innocent and/or insignificant people. They had killed a few necessary victims. Their specialty, however, was the demolition of structures used by the enemy. They picked easy targets: unarmed abortion clinics, unprotected ACLU offices, unsuspecting smut houses. They were having a field day. Not one single arrest in eighteen months.

It was twelve-forty, time to leave and hurry four blocks to his car for another black box, then six blocks over to the Pussycat Cinema, which closed at one-thirty. The Pussycat was either eighteen or nineteen on the list, he couldn't remember which, but he was certain that in exactly three hours and twenty minutes the dirty movie business in D.C. would take a helluva blow. Twenty-two of these little joints were supposed to receive black boxes tonight, and at 4 A.M. they were all supposed to be closed and deserted, and demolished. Three all-nighters were scratched from the list, because his was a nonviolent group.

He adjusted his sunglasses and took one last look at the cushion next to him. Judging from the cups and popcorn on the floor, the place got swept once a week. No one would notice the switch and tube barely visible between the ragged threads. He cautiously flipped the switch, and left the Montrose.

TEN

ERIC EAST had never met the President, nor been in the White House. And he'd never met Fletcher Coal, but he knew he wouldn't like him.

He followed Director Voyles and K. O. Lewis into the Oval Office at seven Saturday morning. There were no smiles or handshakes. East was introduced by Voyles. The President nodded from behind the desk but did not stand. Coal was reading something.

Twenty porno houses had been torched in the D.C. area, and many were still smoldering. They had seen the smoke above the city from the back of the limo. At a dump called Angels a janitor had been badly burned and was not expected to live.

An hour ago they had received word that an anonymous caller to a radio station had claimed responsibility for the Underground Army, and he promised more of the same in celebration of the death of Rosenberg.

The President spoke first. He looked tired, East thought. It was such an early hour for him. "How many places got bombed?"

"Twenty here," Voyles answered. "Seventeen in Baltimore and around fifteen in Atlanta. It appears as though the assault was carefully coordinated because all the explosions happened at precisely 4 A.M."

Coal looked up from his memo. "Director, do you believe it's the Underground Army?"

"As of now they're the only ones claiming responsibility. It looks like some of their work. Could be." Voyles did not look at Coal when he spoke to him.

"So when do you start making arrests?" the President asked.

"At the precise moment we obtain probable cause, Mr. President. That's the law, you understand."

"I understand this outfit is your top suspect in the killings of Rosenberg and Jensen, and that you're certain it killed a federal trial judge in Texas, and it most likely bombed at least fifty-two smut houses last night. I don't understand why they're bombing and killing with immunity. Hell, Director, we're under siege."

Voyles' neck turned red, but he said nothing. He just looked away while the President glared at him. K. O. Lewis cleared his throat. "Mr. President, if I may, we are not convinced the Underground Army was involved with the deaths of Rosenberg and Jensen. In fact, we have no evidence linking them. They are only one of a dozen suspects. As I've said before, the killings were remarkably clean, well organized, and very professional. Extremely professional."

Coal stepped forward. "What you're trying to say, Mr. Lewis, is that you have no idea who killed them, and you may never know."

"No, that's not what I'm saying. We'll find them, but it will take time."

"How much time?" asked the President. It was an obvious, sophomoric question with no good answer. East immediately disliked the President for asking it.

"Months," Lewis said.

"How many months?"

"Many months."

The President rolled his eyes and shook his head, then with great disgust stood and walked to the window. He spoke to the window. "I can't believe there's no relation between what happened last night and the dead judges. I don't know. Maybe I'm just paranoid."

Voyles shot a quick smirk at Lewis. Paranoid, insecure, clueless, dumb, out of touch. Voyles could think of many others.

The President continued, still pondering the window. "I just get nervous when assassins are loose around here and bombs are going off. Who can blame me? We haven't killed a President in over thirty years."

"Oh, I think you're safe, Mr. President," Voyles said with a trace of amusement. "The Secret Service has things under control."

"Great. Then why do I feel as though I'm in Beirut?" He was almost mumbling into the window.

Coal sensed the awkwardness and picked up a thick memo from the desk. He held it and spoke to Voyles, much like a professor lecturing to his class.

"This is the short list of potential nominees to the Supreme Court. There are eight names, each with a biography. It was prepared by Justice. We started with twenty names, then the President, Attorney General Horton, and myself cut it to eight, none of whom have any idea they are being considered."

Voyles still looked away. The President slowly returned to his desk, and picked up his copy of the memo. Coal continued.

"Some of these people are controversial, and if they are ultimately nominated we'll have a small war getting them approved by the Senate. We'd prefer not to start fighting now. This must be kept confidential."

Voyles suddenly turned and glared at Coal. "You're an idiot, Coal! We've done this before, and I can assure you when we start checking on these people the cat's out of the bag. You want a thorough background investigation, and yet you expect everyone contacted to keep quiet. It doesn't work that way, son."

Coal stepped closer to Voyles. His eyes were glowing. "You bust your ass to make sure these names are kept out of the papers until they're nominated. You make it work, Director. You plug the leaks and keep it out of the papers, understand."

Voyles was on his feet, pointing at Coal. "Listen, asshole, you want them checked out, you do it yourself. Don't start giving me a bunch of boy scout orders."

Lewis stood between them, and the President stood behind

his desk, and for a second or two nothing was said. Coal placed his memo on the desk and retreated a few steps, looking away. The President was now the peacemaker. "Sit down, Denton. Sit down."

Voyles returned to his seat while staring at Coal. The President smiled at Lewis and everyone took a seat. "We're all under a lot of pressure," the President said warmly.

Lewis spoke calmly. "We'll perform the routine investigations on your names, Mr. President, and it will be done in the strictest of confidence. You know, however, that we cannot control every person we talk to."

"Yes, Mr. Lewis, I know that. But I want extra caution. These men are young and will shape and reshape the Constitution long after I'm dead. They're staunchly conservative, and the press will eat them alive. They must be free from warts and skeletons in the closet. No dope smokers, or illegitimate children, or DUIs, or radical student activity, or divorces. Understand? No surprises."

"Yes, Mr. President. But we cannot guarantee total secrecy in our investigations."

"Just try, okay."

"Yes, sir." Lewis handed the memo to Eric East.

"Is that all?" Voyles asked.

The President glanced at Coal, who was ignoring them all and standing before the window. "Yes, Denton, that's all. I'd like to have these names checked out in ten days. I want to move fast on this."

Voyles was standing. "You'll have it in ten days."

CALLAHAN WAS IRRITATED when he knocked on the door to Darby's apartment. He was quite perturbed and had a lot on his mind, a lot that he wanted to say, but he knew better than to start a fight because there was something he wanted much worse than to blow off a little steam. She had avoided him for four days now while she played detective and barricaded herself in the law library. She had skipped classes and failed to return his calls, and in general neglected him during his hour of crisis. But he knew when she opened the door he would smile and forget about being neglected.

He held a liter of wine and a real pizza from Mama Rosa's. It was after ten, Saturday night. He knocked again, and looked up and down the street at the neat duplexes and bungalows. The chain rattled from inside, and he instantly smiled. The neglect vanished.

"Who is it?" she asked through the chain.

"Thomas Callahan, remember? I'm at your door begging you to let me in so we can play and be friends again."

The door opened and Callahan stepped in. She took the wine and pecked him on the cheek. "Are we still buddies?" he asked.

"Yes, Thomas. I've been busy." He followed her through the cluttered den to the kitchen. A computer and an assortment of thick books covered the table.

"I called. Why didn't you call me back?"

"I've been out," she said, opening a drawer and removing a corkscrew.

"You've got a machine. I've been talking to it."

"Are you trying to fight, Thomas?"

He looked at her bare legs. "No! I swear I'm not mad. I promise. Please forgive me if I appear to be upset."

"Stop it."

"When can we go to bed?"

"Are you sleepy?"

"Anything but. Come on, Darby, it's been three nights."

"Five. What kind of pizza?" She removed the cork and poured two glasses. Callahan watched every move.

"Oh, it's one of those Saturday night specials where they throw on everything headed for the garbage. Shrimp tails, eggs, crawfish heads. Cheap wine too. I'm a little low on cash, and I'm leaving town tomorrow so I have to watch what I spend, and since I'm leaving I thought I'd just come on over and get laid tonight so I wouldn't be tempted by some contagious woman in D.C. What do you think?"

Darby was opening the pizza box. "Looks like sausage and peppers."

"Can I still get laid?"

"Maybe later. Drink your wine and let's chat. We haven't had a long talk in a while."

"I have. I've been talking to your machine all week."

He took his wineglass and the bottle and followed her closely to the den, where she turned on the stereo. They relaxed on the sofa.

"Let's get drunk," he said.

"You're so romantic."

"I've got some romance for you."

"You've been drunk for a week."

"No I haven't. Eighty percent of a week. It's your fault for avoiding me."

"What's wrong with you, Thomas?"

"I've got the shakes. I'm all keyed up and I need companionship to knock the edge off. Whatta you say?"

"Let's get half drunk." She sipped her wine and draped her legs across his lap. He held his breath as if in pain.

"What time is your flight?" she asked.

He was gulping now. "One-thirty. Nonstop to National. I'm supposed to register at five, and there's a dinner at eight. After that I may be forced to roam the streets looking for love."

She smiled. "Okay, okay. We'll do it in a minute. But let's talk first."

Callahan breathed a sigh of relief. "I can talk for ten minutes, then I'll just collapse."

"What's up for Monday?"

"The usual eight hours of airhead debate on the future of the Fifth Amendment, then a committee will draft a proposed conference report that no one will approve. More debate Tuesday, another report, perhaps an altercation or two, then we adjourn with nothing accomplished and go home. I'll be in late Tuesday evening, and I'd like a date at a very nice restaurant, after which we can go back to my place for an intellectual discussion and animal sex. Where's the pizza?"

"In there. I'll get it."

He was stroking her legs. "Don't move. I'm not the least bit hungry."

"Why do you go to these conferences?"

"I'm a member, and I'm a professor, and we're just sort of expected to roam the country attending meetings with other educated idiots and adopting reports nobody reads. If I didn't go, the dean would think I was not contributing to the academic environment."

She refilled the wineglasses. "You're uptight, Thomas."

"I know. It's been a rough week. I hate the thought of a bunch of Neanderthals rewriting the Constitution. We'll live in a police state in ten years. I can't do anything about it, so I'll probably resort to alcohol."

Darby sipped slowly and watched him. The music was soft and the lights low. "I'm getting a buzz," she said.

"That's about right for you. A glass and a half and you're history. If you were Irish you could drink all night."

"My father was half Scottish."

"Not good enough." Callahan crossed his feet on the coffee table and relaxed. He gently rubbed her ankles. "Can I paint your toes?"

She said nothing. He had a fetish for her toes, and insisted on doing the nails with bright red polish at least twice a month. They'd seen it in *Bull Durham*, and though he wasn't as neat and sober as Kevin Costner, she had grown to enjoy the intimacy of it.

"No toes tonight?" he asked.

"Maybe later. You look tired."

"I'm relaxing, but I'm filled with virile male electricity, and you will not put me off by telling me I look tired."

"Have some more wine."

Callahan had more wine, and sank deeper in the sofa. "So, Ms. Shaw, who done it?"

"Professionals. Haven't you read the papers?"

"Of course. But who's behind the professionals?"

"I don't know. After last night, the unanimous choice seems to be the Underground Army."

"But you're not convinced."

"No. There have been no arrests. I'm not convinced."

"And you've got some obscure suspect unknown to the rest of the country."

"I had one, but now I'm not so sure. I spent three days tracking it down, even summarized it all real nice and neat in my little computer, and printed out a thin rough draft of a brief which I have now discarded."

Callahan stared at her. "You're telling me you skipped classes for three days, ignored me, worked around the clock playing Sherlock Holmes, and now you're throwing it away."

"It's over there on the table."

"I can't believe this. While I sulked around in loneliness all week, I knew it was for a worthy cause. I knew my suffering was for the good of the country because you would peel away the onion and tell me tonight or perhaps tomorrow who done it."

"It can't be done, at least not with legal research. There's no pattern, no common thread in the murders. I almost burned up the computers at the law school."

"Ha! I told you so. You forget, dear, that I am a genius at constitutional law, and I knew immediately that Rosenberg and Jensen had nothing in common but black robes and death threats. The Nazis or Aryans or Kluxers or Mafia or some other group killed them because Rosenberg was Rosenberg, and because Jensen was the easiest target and somewhat of an embarrassment."

"Well, why don't you call the FBI and share your insights with them? I'm sure they're sitting by the phone."

"Don't be angry. I'm sorry. Please forgive me."

"You're an ass, Thomas."

"Yes, but you love me, don't you?"

"I don't know."

"Can we still go to bed? You promised."

"We'll see."

Callahan placed his glass on the table, and attacked her. "Look, baby. I'll read your brief, okay. And then we'll talk about it, okay. But I'm not thinking clearly right now, and I won't be able to continue until you take my weak and trembling hand and lead me to your bed."

"Forget my little brief."

"Please, dammit, Darby, please."

She grabbed his neck and pulled him to her. They kissed long and hard, a wet, almost violent kiss.

ELEVEN

THE COP stuck his thumb on the button next to the name of Gray Grantham, and held it down for twenty seconds. Then a brief pause. Then another twenty seconds. Pause. Twenty seconds. Pause. Twenty seconds. He thought this was funny because Grantham was a night owl and had probably slept less than three or four hours, and now all this incessant buzzing echoing throughout his hallway. He pushed again and looked at his patrol car parked illegally on the curb under the streetlight. It was almost dawn, Sunday, and the street was empty. Twenty seconds. Pause. Twenty seconds.

Maybe Grantham was dead. Or maybe he was comatose from booze and a late night on the town. Maybe he had someone's woman up there and had no plans to answer the door. Pause. Twenty seconds.

The mike crackled. "Who is it!"

"Police!" answered the cop, who was black and emphasized the *po* in *police* just for the fun of it.

"What do you want?" Grantham demanded.

"Maybe I gotta warrant." The cop was near laughter.

Grantham's voice softened, and he sounded wounded. "Is this Cleve?"

"It is."

"What time is it, Cleve?"

"Almost five-thirty."

79

"It must be good."

"Don't know. Sarge didn't say, you know. He just said to wake you up 'cause he wanted to talk."

"Why does he always want to talk before the sun comes up?"

"Stupid question, Grantham."

A slight pause. "Yeah, I guess so. I presume he wants to talk right now."

"No. You got thirty minutes. He said be there at six."

"Where?"

"There's a little coffee shop on Fourteenth near the Trinidad Playground. It's dark and safe, and Sarge likes it."

"Where does he find these places?"

"You know, for a reporter you can ask the dumbest questions. The name of the place is Glenda's, and I suggest you get going or you'll be late."

"Will you be there?"

"I'll drop in, just to make sure you're okay."

"I thought you said it was safe."

"It is safe, for that part of town. Can you find it?"

"Yeah. I'll be there as soon as I can."

"Have a nice day, Grantham."

SARGE WAS OLD, very black, with a head full of brilliant white hair that sprang out in all directions. He wore thick sunglasses whenever he was awake, and most of his coworkers in the West Wing of the White House thought he was half blind. He held his head sideways and smiled like Ray Charles. He sometimes bumped into door facings and desks as he unloaded trash cans and dusted furniture. He walked slowly and gingerly as if counting his steps. He worked patiently, always with a smile, always with a kind word for anyone willing to give him one. For the most part he was ignored and dismissed as just another friendly, old, partially disabled black janitor.

Sarge could see around corners. His territory was the West Wing, where he had been cleaning for thirty years now. Cleaning and listening. Cleaning and seeing. He picked up after some terribly important people who were often too busy to watch their words, especially in the presence of poor old Sarge.

He knew which doors stayed open, and which walls were thin, and which air vents carried sound. He could disappear in an instant, then reappear in a shadow where the terribly important people could not see him.

He kept most of it to himself. But from time to time, he fell heir to a juicy bit of information that could be pieced together with another one, and Sarge would make the judgment call that it should be repeated. He was very careful. He had three years until retirement, and he took no chances.

No one ever suspected Sarge of leaking stories to the press. There were usually enough big mouths within any White House to lay blame on each other. It was hilarious, really. Sarge would talk to Grantham at the *Post*, then wait excitedly for the story, then listen to the wailing in the basement when the heads rolled.

He was an impeccable source, and he talked only to Grantham. His son Cleve, the cop, arranged the meetings, always at odd hours at dark and inconspicuous places. Sarge wore his sunglasses. Grantham wore the same with a hat or cap of some sort. Cleve usually sat with them and watched the crowd.

Grantham arrived at Glenda's a few minutes after six, and walked to a booth in the rear. There were three other customers. Glenda herself was frying eggs on a grill near the register. Cleve sat on a stool watching her.

They shook hands. A cup of coffee had been poured for Grantham.

"Sorry I'm late," he said.

"No problem, my friend. Good to see you." Sarge had a raspy voice that was difficult to suppress with a whisper. No one was listening.

Grantham gulped coffee. "Busy week at the White House."

"You could say that. Lot of excitement. Lot of happiness."

"You don't say." Grantham could not take notes at these meetings. It would be too obvious, Sarge said when he laid the ground rules.

"Yes. The President and his boys were elated with the news of Justice Rosenberg. This made them very happy."

"What about Justice Jensen?"

"Well, as you noticed, the President attended the memorial service, but did not speak. He had planned to give a eulogy, but backed out because he would have been saying nice things about a gay fella."

"Who wrote the eulogy?"

"The speechwriters. Mainly Mabry. Worked on it all day Thursday, then he backed out."

"He also went to Rosenberg's service."

"Yes, he did. But he didn't want to. Said he'd rather go to hell for a day. But in the end, he chickened out and went anyway. He's quite happy Rosenberg was murdered. There was almost a festive mood around the place Wednesday. Fate has dealt him a wonderful hand. He now gets to restructure the Court, and he's very excited about this."

Grantham listened hard. Sarge continued.

"There's a short list of nominees. The original had twenty or so names, then it was cut to eight."

"Who did the cutting?"

"Who do you think? The President and Fletcher Coal. They're terrified of leaks at this point. Evidently the list is nothing but young conservative judges, most of whom are obscure."

"Any names?"

"Just two. A certain man named Pryce from Idaho, and one named MacLawrence from Vermont. That's all I know about names. I think they are both federal judges. Nothing more on this."

"What about the investigation?"

"I haven't heard much, but as usual I'll keep my ears open. There doesn't appear to be much going on."

"Anything else?"

"No. When will you run it?"

"In the morning."

"It'll be fun."

"Thanks, Sarge."

The sun was up now and the café was noisier. Cleve strolled over and sat next to his father. "You guys about finished?"

"We are," Sarge said.

Cleve glanced around. "I think we need to leave. Grantham goes first, I'll follow, then Pop here can stay as long as he wants."

"Mighty nice of you," Sarge said.

"Thanks, fellas," Grantham said as he headed for the door.

TWELVE

Verheek was late as usual. In the twenty-three-year history of their friendship, he had never been on time, and it was never a matter of being only a few minutes late. He had no concept of time and wasn't bothered with it. He wore a watch but never looked at it. Late for Verheek meant at least an hour, sometimes two, especially when the person kept waiting was a friend who expected him to be late and would forgive him.

So Callahan sat for an hour in the bar, which suited him just fine. After eight hours of scholarly debate, he despised the Constitution and those who taught it. He needed Chivas in his veins, and after two doubles on the rocks he was feeling better. He watched himself in the mirror behind the rows of liquor, and in the distance over his shoulder he watched and waited for Gavin Verheek. Small wonder his friend couldn't cut it in private practice, where life depended upon the clock.

When the third double was served, an hour and eleven minutes after 7 P.M., Verheek strolled to the bar and ordered a Moosehead.

"Sorry I'm late," he said as they shook hands. "I knew you'd appreciate the extra time alone with your Chivas."

"You look tired," Callahan said as he inspected him. Old and tired. Verheek was aging badly and gaining weight. His forehead had grown an inch since their last visit, and his pale skin highlighted the heavy circles under his eyes. "How much do you weigh?"

"None of your business," he said, gulping the beer. "Where's our table?"

"It's reserved for eight-thirty. I figured you would be at least ninety minutes late."

"Then I'm early."

"You could say that. Did you come from work?"

"I live at work now. The Director wants no less than a hundred hours a week until something breaks. I told my wife I'd be home for Christmas."

"How is she?"

"Fine. A very patient lady. We get along much better when I live at the office." She was wife number three in seventeen years.

"I'd like to meet her."

"No, you wouldn't. I married the first two for sex and they enjoyed it so much they shared it with others. I married this one for money and she's not much to look at. You wouldn't be impressed." He emptied the bottle. "I doubt if I can hang on until she dies."

"How old is she?"

"Don't ask. I really love her, you know. Honest. But after two years I now realize we have nothing in common but an acute awareness of the stock market." He looked at the bartender. "Another beer, please."

Callahan chuckled and sipped his drink. "How much is she worth?"

"Not nearly as much as I thought. I'm not sure really. Somewhere around five million, I think. She cleaned out husbands one and two, and I think she was attracted to me for the challenge of marrying just an average joe. That, and the sex is great, she said. They all say that, you know."

"You always picked losers, Gavin, even in law school. You're attracted to neurotic and depressed women."

"And they're attracted to me." He turned the bottle up and drained half of it. "Why do we always eat in this place?"

"I don't know. It's sort of traditional. It brings back fond memories of law school."

"We hated law school, Thomas. Everyone hates law school. Everyone hates lawyers."

"You're in a fine mood."

"Sorry. I've slept six hours since they found the bodies. The Director screams at me at least five times a day. I scream at everybody under me. It's one big brawl over there."

"Drink up, big boy. Our table's ready. Let's drink and eat and talk, and try to enjoy these few hours together."

"I love you more than my wife, Thomas. Do you know that?"

"That's not saying much."

"You're right."

They followed the maître d' to a small table in the corner, the same table they always requested. Callahan ordered another round, and explained they would be in no hurry to eat.

"Did you see that damned thing in the *Post?*" Verheek asked.

"I saw it. Who leaked it?"

"Who knows. The Director got the short list Saturday morning, hand-delivered by the President himself, with rather explicit demands about secrecy. He showed the list to no one over the weekend, then this morning the story hit with the names of Pryce and MacLawrence. Voyles went berserk when he saw it, and a few minutes later the President called. He rushed to the White House and they had a huge cuss fight. Voyles tried to attack Fletcher Coal, and had to be restrained by K. O. Lewis. Very nasty."

Callahan hung on every word. "This is pretty good."

"Yeah. I'm telling you this part because later, after a few more drinks, you'll expect me to tell you who else is on the list and I won't do it. I'm trying to be a friend, Thomas."

"Keep going."

"Anyway, there's no way the leak came from us. Impossible. It had to come from the White House. The place is full of people who hate Coal, and it's leaking like rusty pipes."

"Coal probably leaked it."

"Maybe so. He's a sleazy bastard, and one theory has him leaking Pryce and MacLawrence to scare everyone, then later announcing two nominees who appear more moderate. It sounds like something he would do."

"I've never heard of Pryce and MacLawrence."

"Join the club. They're both very young, early forties, with precious little experience on the bench. We haven't checked them out, but they appear to be radically conservative."

"And the rest of the list?"

"That was quick. Two beers down, and you've already popped the question."

The drinks arrived. "I want some of those mushrooms stuffed with crabmeat," Verheek told the waiter. "Just to munch on. I'm starving."

Callahan handed over his empty glass. "Bring me an order too."

"Don't ask again, Thomas. You may have to carry me out of here in three hours, but I'll never tell. You know that. Let's say that Pryce and MacLawrence seem to be reflective of the entire list."

"All unknowns?"

"Basically, yes."

Callahan sipped the Scotch slowly and shook his head. Verheek removed his jacket and loosened his tie. "Let's talk about women."

"No."

"How old is she?"

"Twenty-four, but very mature."

"You could be her father."

"I may be. Who knows."

"Where's she from?"

"Denver. I told you that."

"I love Western girls. They're so independent and unpretentious and they tend to wear Levis and have long legs. I may marry one. Does she have money?"

"No. Her father was killed in a plane crash four years ago and her mother got a nice settlement."

"Then she has money."

"She's comfortable."

"I'll bet she is. Do you have a photo?"

"No. She's not a grandchild or a poodle."

"Why didn't you bring a picture?"

"I'll get her to send you one. Why is this so amusing to you?"

"It's hilarious. The great Thomas Callahan, he of the disposable women, has fallen hard."

"I have not."

"It must be a record. What, nine, ten months now? You've actually maintained a steady relationship for almost a year, haven't you?"

"Eight months and three weeks, but don't tell anyone, Gavin. It's not easy for me."

"Your secret's safe. Just give me all the details. How tall is she?"

"Five-eight, hundred and twelve pounds, long legs, tight Levis, independent, unpretentious, your typical Western girl."

"I must find one for myself. Are you gonna marry her?"

"Of course not! Finish your drink."

"Are you, like, monogamous now?"

"Are you?"

"Hell no. Never have been. But we're not talking about me, Thomas, we're talking about Peter Pan here, Cool Hand Callahan, the man with the monthly version of the world's most gorgeous woman. Tell me, Thomas, and don't lie to your best friend, just look me in the eyes and tell me if you have succumbed to a state of monogamy."

Verheek was leaning halfway across the table, watching and grinning stupidly.

"Not so loud," Callahan said, looking around.

"Answer me."

"Give me the other names on the list, and I'll tell you."

Verheek withdrew. "Nice try. I think the answer is yes. I think you're in love with this gal, but too cowardly to admit it. I think she's got your number, pal."

"Okay, she does. Do you feel better?"

"Yeah, much better. When can I meet her?"

"When can I meet your wife?"

"You're confused, Thomas. There's a basic difference here.

You don't want to meet my wife, but I do want to meet Darby. You see. I assure you they are very dissimilar."

Callahan smiled and sipped. Verheek relaxed and crossed his legs in the aisle. He tilted the green bottle to his lips.

"You're wired, buddy," Callahan said.

"I'm sorry. I'm drinking as fast as I can."

The mushrooms were served in simmering skillets. Verheek stuffed two in his mouth and chewed furiously. Callahan watched. The Chivas had knocked off the hunger pains, and he would wait a few minutes. He preferred alcohol over food anyway.

Four Arabs noisily filled a table next to them, yakking and jabbering in their language. All four ordered Jack Daniel's.

"Who killed them, Gavin?"

He chewed for a minute, then swallowed hard. "If I knew, I wouldn't tell. But I swear I do not know. It's baffling. The killers vanished without a trace. It was meticulously planned and perfectly executed. Not a clue."

"Why the combination?"

He stuffed another in his mouth. "Quite simple. It's so simple, it's easy to overlook. They were such natural targets. Rosenberg had no security system in his townhouse. Any decent cat burglar could come and go. And poor Jensen was hanging around those places at midnight. They were exposed. At the exact moment each died, the other seven Supremes had FBI agents in their homes. That's why they were selected. They were stupid."

"Then who selected them?"

"Someone with a lot of money. The killers were professionals, and they were probably out of the country within hours. We figure there were three, maybe more. The mess at Rosenberg's could have been done by just one. We figure there were at least two working on Jensen. One or more looking out while the guy with the rope did his thing. Even though it was a dirty little place, it was open to the public, and quite risky. But they were good, very good."

"I've read a lone assassin theory."

"Forget it. It's impossible for one man to kill both of them. Impossible."

"How much would these killers charge?"

"Millions. And it took a bunch of money to plan it all."

"And you have no idea?"

"Look, Thomas, I'm not involved in the investigation, so you'll have to ask those guys. I'm sure they know a helluva lot more than I do. I'm just a lowly government lawyer."

"Yeah, who just happens to be on a first-name basis with the Chief Justice."

"He calls occasionally. This is boring. Let's get back to women. I hate lawyer talk."

"Have you talked to him lately?"

"Picking, Thomas, always picking. Yes, we chatted briefly this morning. He's got all twenty-seven law clerks scouring the federal dockets high and low looking for clues. It's fruitless, and I told him so. Every case that reaches the Supreme Court has at least two parties, and each party involved would certainly benefit if one or two or three justices would disappear and be replaced by one or two or three more sympathetic to its cause. There are thousands of appeals that could eventually end up here, and you can't just pick one and say 'This is it! This is the one that got 'em killed.' It's silly."

"What did he say?"

"Of course he agreed with my brilliant analysis. I think he called after he read the *Post* story to see if he could squeeze something out of me. Can you believe the nerve?"

The waiter hovered over them with a hurried look.

Verheek glanced at the menu, closed it, and handed it to him. "Grilled swordfish, blue cheese, no vegetable."

"I'll eat the mushrooms," Callahan said. The waiter disappeared.

Callahan reached into his coat pocket and removed a thick envelope. He laid it on the table next to the empty Moosehead. "Take a look at this when you get a chance."

"What is it?"

"It's sort of a brief."

"I hate briefs, Thomas. In fact, I hate the law, and the lawyers, and with the exception of you, I hate law professors."

"Darby wrote it."

"I'll read it tonight. What's it about?"

"I think I told you. She is very bright and intelligent, and a very aggressive student. She writes better than most. Her passion, other than me of course, is constitutional law."

"Poor thing."

"She took off four days last week, totally ignored me and the rest of the world, and came up with her own theory, which she has now discarded. But read it anyway. It's fascinating."

"Who's the suspect?"

The Arabs erupted in screaming laughter, slapping each other and spilling whiskey. They watched them for a minute until they died down.

"Don't you hate a bunch of drunks?" Verheek said.

"It's sickening."

Verheek stuffed the envelope into his coat on the back of his chair. "What's her theory?"

"It's a bit unusual. But read it. I mean, it can't hurt, can it? You guys need the help."

"I'll read it only because she wrote it. How is she in bed?"

"How's your wife in bed?"

"Rich. In the shower, in the kitchen, at the grocery. She's rich in everything she does."

"It can't last."

"She'll file by the end of the year. Maybe I'll get the townhouse and some change."

"No prenuptial agreement?"

"Yes, there is, but I'm a lawyer, remember. It's got more loopholes than a tax reform act. A buddy of mine prepared it. Don't you love the law?"

"Let's talk about something else."

"Women?"

"I've got an idea. You want to meet the girl, right?"

"We're talking about Darby?"

"Yes. Darby."

"I'd love to meet her."

"We're going to St. Thomas during Thanksgiving. Why don't you meet us there?"

"Do I have to bring my wife?"

"No. She's not invited."

"Will she run around in a little string job on the beach? Sort of put on a show for us?"

"Probably."

"Wow. I can't believe this."

"You can get a condo next to us, and we'll have a ball."

"Beautiful, beautiful. Just beautiful."

THIRTEEN

THE PHONE RANG four times, the answering machine clicked on, the recorded voice echoed through the apartment, the beep, then no message. It rang again four times, same routine, and no message. A minute later it rang again, and Gray Grantham grabbed it from bed. He sat on a pillow, trying to focus.

"Who is it?" he asked in pain. There was no light coming through the window.

The voice on the other end was low and timid. "Is this Gray Grantham with the *Washington Post?*"

"It is. Who's calling?"

Slowly, "I can't give you my name."

The fog lifted and he focused on the clock. It was five-forty. "Okay, forget the name. Why are you calling?"

"I saw your story yesterday about the White House and the nominees."

"That's good." You and a million others. "Why are you calling me at this obscene hour?"

"I'm sorry. I'm on my way to work and stopped at a pay phone. I can't call from home or the office."

The voice was clear, articulate, and appeared to be intelligent. "What kind of office?"

"I'm an attorney."

Great. Washington was home for half a million lawyers. "Private or government?"

A slight hesitation. "Uh, I'd rather not say."

"Okay. Look, I'd rather be sleeping. Why, exactly, did you call?"

"I may know something about Rosenberg and Jensen."

Grantham sat on the edge of the bed. "Such as—"

A much longer pause. "Are you recording this?"

"No. Should I?"

"I don't know. I'm really very scared and confused, Mr. Grantham. I prefer not to record this. Maybe the next call, okay?"

"Whatever you want. I'm listening."

"Can this call be traced?"

"Possibly, I guess. But you're at a pay phone, right? What difference does it make?"

"I don't know. I'm just scared."

"It's okay. I swear I'm not recording and I swear I won't trace it. Now, what's on your mind?"

"Well, I think I may know who killed them."

Grantham was standing. "That's some pretty valuable knowledge."

"It could get me killed. Do you think they're following me?"

"Who? Who would be following you?"

"I don't know." The voice trailed off, as if he was looking over his shoulder.

Grantham was pacing by the bed. "Relax. Why don't you tell me your name, okay. I swear it's confidential."

"Garcia."

"That's not a real name, is it?"

"Of course not, but it's the best I can do."

"Okay, Garcia. Talk to me."

"I'm not certain, okay. But I think I stumbled across something at the office that I was not supposed to see."

"Do you have a copy of it?"

"Maybe."

"Look, Garcia. You called me, right. Do you want to talk or not?"

"I'm not sure. What will you do if I tell you something?"

"Check it out thoroughly. If we're gonna accuse someone of the assassinations of two Supreme Court Justices, believe me, the story will be handled delicately."

There was a very long silence. Grantham froze by the rocker and waited. "Garcia. Are you there?"

"Yeah. Can we talk later?"

"Of course. We can talk now."

"I need to think about this. I haven't eaten or slept in a week, and I'm not thinking rationally. I might call you later."

"Okay, okay. That's fine. You can call me at work at—"

"No. I won't call you at work. Sorry I woke you."

He hung up. Grantham looked at the row of numbers on his phone and punched seven digits, waited, then six more, then four more. He scribbled a number on a pad by the phone, and hung up. The pay phone was on Fifteenth Street in Pentagon City.

GAVIN VERHEEK slept four hours and woke up drunk. When he arrived at the Hoover Building an hour later, the alcohol was fading and the pain was settling in. He cursed himself and he cursed Callahan, who no doubt would sleep until noon and wake up fresh and alive and ready for the flight to New Orleans. They had left the restaurant when it closed at midnight, then hit a few bars and joked about catching a skin flick or two, but since their favorite movie house had been bombed they couldn't. So they just drank until three or four.

He had a meeting with Director Voyles at eleven, and it was imperative to appear sober and alert. It would be impossible. He told his secretary to close the door, and explained to her that he had caught a nasty virus, maybe the flu, and he was to be left alone at his desk unless it was awfully damned important. She studied his eyes and seemed to sniff more than usual. The smell of beer does not always evaporate with sleep.

She left and closed the door behind her. He locked it. To make things equal, he called Callahan's room, but no one answered.

What a life. His best friend earned almost as much as he did, but worked thirty hours in a busy week, and had his pick of pliant young things twenty years his junior. Then he remembered their grand plans for the week in St. Thomas, and the thought of Darby strolling along the beach. He would go, even if it caused a divorce.

A wave of nausea rippled through his chest and up his esophagus, and he quickly lay still on the floor. Cheap government carpet. He breathed deeply, and the pounding started at the top of his head. The plaster ceiling was not spinning, and this was encouraging. After three minutes, it was evident he would not vomit, at least not now.

His briefcase was within reach, and he carefully slid it next to him. He found the envelope inside with the morning paper. He opened it, unfolded the brief, and held it with both hands six inches above his face.

It was thirteen letter-sized pages of computer paper, all double-spaced with wide margins. He could handle it. Notes were scribbled in the margins by hand and whole sections were marked through. The words FIRST DRAFT were handwritten with a felt pen across the top. Her name, address, and phone number were typed on the cover sheet.

He would skim it for a few minutes while he was on the floor, then hopefully he would feel like sitting at the desk and going through the motions of being an important government lawyer. He thought of Voyles, and the pounding intensified.

She wrote well, in the standard, scholarly legal fashion of long sentences filled with large words. But she was clear. She avoided the double-talk and legal lingo most students strive so desperately for. She would never make it as an attorney employed by the United States Government.

Gavin had never heard of her suspect, and was certain it was not on anyone's list. Technically, it was not a brief, but more of a story about a lawsuit in Louisiana. She told the facts succinctly, and made them interesting. Fascinating, really. He was not skimming.

The facts took four pages, then she filled the next three with brief histories of the parties. It dragged a bit here, but he kept reading. He was hooked. On page eight, the brief or whatever it was summarized the trial. On nine, it mentioned the appeal, and the final three pages laid an implausible trail to the removal of Rosenberg and Jensen from the Court. Callahan said she had already discarded this theory, and she appeared to lose steam at the end.

But it was highly readable. For a moment he had forgotten his current state of pain, and read thirteen pages of a law student's brief while lying on the floor on dirty carpet with a million things to do.

There was a soft knock at the door. He slowly sat up, gingerly stood, and walked to the door. "Yes."

It was the secretary. "I hate to bother. But the Director wants you in his office in ten minutes."

Verheek opened the door. "What?"

"Yes sir. Ten minutes."

He rubbed his eyes and breathed rapidly. "What for?"

"I get demoted for asking those questions, sir."

"Do you have any mouthwash?"

"Well, yes, I believe so. Do you want it?"

"I wouldn't have asked if I didn't want it. Bring it to me. Do you have any gum?"

"Gum?"

"Chewing gum."

"Yes sir. Do you want it too?"

"Just bring me the mouthwash and gum, and some aspirin if you have it." He walked to his desk and sat down, holding his head in his hands and rubbing his temples. He heard her banging drawers, and then she was before him with the goods.

"Thanks. I'm sorry I snapped." He pointed at the brief in a chair by the door. "Send that brief to Eric East, he's on the fourth floor. Write a note from me. Tell him to look it over when he has a minute."

She left with the brief.

FLETCHER COAL opened the door to the Oval Office, and spoke gravely to K. O. Lewis and Eric East. The President was in Puerto Rico viewing hurricane damage, and Director Voyles now refused to meet with Coal alone. He sent his underlings.

Coal waved them to a sofa, and he sat across the coffee table. His coat was buttoned and his tie was perfect. He never relaxed. East had heard tales about his habits. He worked twenty hours a day, seven days a week, drank nothing but water, and ate most meals from a vending machine in the basement. He could read like a computer, and spent hours each day reviewing memos, reports, correspondence, and mountains of pending legislation. He had perfect recall. For a week now they had brought daily reports of their investigation to this office, and handed them to Coal, who devoured the material and memorized it for the next meeting. If they misstated something, he would terrorize them. He was hated, but it was impossible not to respect him. He was smarter than them, and he worked harder. And he knew it.

He was smug in the emptiness of the Oval Office. His boss was away performing for the cameras, but the real power had stayed behind to run the country.

K. O. Lewis placed a four-inch stack of the latest on the table.

"Anything new?" Coal asked.

"Maybe. The French authorities were routinely reviewing footage taken by the security cameras at the Paris airport, and they thought they recognized a face. They checked it against two other cameras in the concourse, different angles, then reported to Interpol. The face is disguised, but Interpol believes it is Khamel, the terrorist. I'm sure you've heard of—"

"I have."

"They've studied the footage at length, and are almost certain he exited a plane that arrived nonstop from Dulles last Wednesday, about ten hours after Jensen was found."

"The Concorde?"

"No, United. Based on the time and the locations of the cameras, they have ways of determining the gates and flights."

"And Interpol contacted the CIA?"

"Yes. They talked to Gminski around one this afternoon."

Coal's face registered nothing. "How certain are they?"

"Eighty percent. He's a master of disguise, and it would be a bit unusual for him to travel in such a manner. So there's room for doubt. We've got photos and a summary for the President's review. Frankly, I've studied the pictures, and I can't tell anything. But Interpol knows him."

"He hasn't been willingly photographed in years, has he?"

"Not that we know of. And rumor has it he goes under the knife and gets a new face every two or three years."

Coal pondered this for a second. "Okay. What if it's Khamel, and what if he was involved in the killings? What does it mean?"

"It means we'll never find him. There are at least nine countries, including Israel, actively stalking him right now. It means he was paid a bunch of money by someone to use his talents here. We've said all along the killer or killers were professionals who were gone before the bodies were cold."

"So it means little."

"You could say that."

"Fine. What else do you have?"

Lewis glanced at Eric East. "Well, we have the usual daily summary."

"They've been rather dry as of late."

"Yes, they have. We have three hundred and eighty agents working twelve hours a day. Yesterday they interviewed one hundred and sixty people in thirty states. We have—"

Coal held up his hand. "Save it. I'll read the summary. It seems safe to say there is nothing new."

"Maybe a small new wrinkle." Lewis looked at Eric East, who was holding a copy of the brief.

"What is it?" Coal asked.

East shifted uncomfortably. The brief had been passed upward all day until Voyles read it and liked it. He viewed it as a long shot, unworthy of serious attention, but the brief mentioned the President, and he loved the idea of making Coal and his boss sweat. He instructed Lewis and East to deliver the brief to Coal, and to treat it as an important theory the Bureau was taking seriously. For the first time in a week, Voyles had smiled when he talked of the idiots in the Oval Office reading this little brief and running for cover. Play it up, Voyles said. Tell them we intend to pursue with twenty agents.

"It's a theory that has surfaced in the last twenty-four hours, and Director Voyles is quite intrigued by it. He's afraid it could be damaging to the President."

Coal was stone-faced, never flinching. "How's that?"

East placed the brief on the table. "It's all here in this report."

Coal glanced at it, then studied East. "Fine. I'll read it later. Is that all?"

Lewis stood and buttoned his jacket. "Yes, we'll be going."

Coal followed them to the door.

THERE WAS NO FANFARE when Air Force One landed at Andrews a few minutes after ten. The Queen was off raising money, and no friends or family greeted the President as he bounced off the plane and darted into his limousine. Coal was waiting. The President sunk low in the seat. "I didn't expect you," he said.

"I'm sorry. We need to talk." The limo sped away toward the White House.

"It's late and I'm tired."

"How was the hurricane?"

"Impressive. It blew away a million shacks and cardboard huts, and now we'll rush down with a couple of billion and build new homes and power plants. They need a good hurricane every five years."

"I've got the disaster declaration ready."

"Okay. What's so important?"

Coal handed over a copy of what was now known as the pelican brief.

"I don't want to read," said the President. "Just tell me about it."

"Voyles and his motley crew have stumbled across a suspect that no one has mentioned until now. A most obscure, unlikely suspect. An eager-beaver law student at Tulane wrote this damned thing, and it somehow made its way to Voyles, who read it and decided it had merit. Keep in mind, they are desperate for suspects. The theory is so farfetched it's incredible, and on its face it doesn't worry me. But Voyles worries me. He's decided he must pursue with enthusiasm, and the press is watching every move he makes. There could be leaks."

"We can't control his investigation."

"We can manipulate it. Gminski is waiting at the White House, and—"

"Gminski!"

"Relax, Chief. I personally handed him a copy of this three hours ago, and swore him to secrecy. He may be incompetent, but he can keep a secret. I trust him much more than Voyles."

"I don't trust either one of them."

Coal liked to hear this. He wanted the President to trust no one but him. "I think you should ask the CIA to immediately investigate this. I would like to know everything before Voyles starts digging. Neither will find anything, but if we know more than Voyles, you can convince him to back off. It makes sense, Chief."

The President was frustrated. "It's domestic. CIA has no business snooping around. It's probably illegal."

"It is illegal, technically. But Gminski will do it for you, and he can do it quickly, secretly, and more thoroughly than the FBI."

"It's illegal."

"It's been done before, Chief, many times."

The President watched the traffic. His eyes were puffy and red, but not from fatigue. He had slept three hours on the plane. But he'd spent the day looking sad and concerned for the cameras, and it was hard to snap out of it.

He took the brief and tossed it on the empty seat next to him. "Is it someone we know?"

"Yes."

FOURTEEN

BECAUSE IT IS A CITY of the night, New Orleans wakes slowly. It's quiet until well after dawn, then shakes the cobwebs and eases into the morning. There's no early rush except on the corridors to and from the suburbs, and the busy streets downtown. This is the same for all cities. But in the French Quarter, the soul of New Orleans, the smell of last night's whiskey and jambalaya and blackened redfish lingers not far above the empty streets until the sun can be seen. An hour or two later, it is replaced with the aroma of French Market coffee and beignets, and around this time the sidewalks reluctantly show signs of life.

Darby curled herself in a chair on the small balcony, sipping coffee and waiting on the sun. Callahan was a few feet away, through the open french doors, still wrapped in sheets and dead to the world. There was a trace of a breeze, but the humidity would return by noon. She pulled his robe closer around her neck, and inhaled the richness of his cologne. She thought of her father, and his baggy cotton button-downs he allowed her to wear when she was a teenager. She would roll the sleeves tightly to her elbows and let the tails hang to her knees, then walk the malls with her friends, secure in her belief that no one was cooler. Her father was her friend. By the time she finished high school, she had the run of his closet, as long as things were washed and neatly pressed and put back on the hangers. She could still smell the Grey Flannel he splashed on his face every day.

If he was living, he would be four years older than Thomas Callahan. Her mother had remarried and moved to Boise. Darby had a brother in Germany. The three seldom talked. Her father had been the glue in a fractious family, and his death had scattered them.

Twenty other people died in the plane crash, and before the funeral arrangements were complete the lawyers were calling. It was her first real exposure to the legal world, and it was not pleasant. The family attorney was a real estate type who knew nothing about litigation. A slick ambulance chaser got next to her brother, and he persuaded the family to sue quickly. His name was Herschel, and for two years the family suffered as Herschel stalled and lied and bungled the case. They settled a week before trial for half a million, after Herschel's cut, and Darby got a hundred thousand.

She decided to be a lawyer. If a clown like Herschel could do it and make big bucks while wreaking havoc on society, then she certainly could do it for a nobler purpose. She thought of Herschel often. When she passed the bar exam, her first lawsuit would be filed against him for malpractice. She wanted to work for an environmental firm. Finding a job, she knew, would not be a problem.

The hundred thousand was intact. Her mother's new husband was a paper company executive who was a little older and a lot wealthier, and shortly after their marriage she divided her portion of the settlement between Darby and her brother. She said the money reminded her of her deceased husband, and the gesture was symbolic. Though she still loved their father, she had a new life in a new city with a new husband who would retire in five years with money to burn. Darby had been confused by the symbolic gesture, but appreciated it and took the money.

The hundred thousand had doubled. She placed most of it in mutual funds, but only in those without holdings in chemical and petroleum companies. She drove an Accord and lived modestly. Her wardrobe was basic law school, purchased from factory outlet stores. She and Callahan enjoyed the better restaurants in town, and never ate at the same place twice. It was always Dutch treat.

He cared little for money, and never pressed her for information. She had more than the typical law student, but Tulane had its share of rich kids.

They dated for a month before they went to bed. She laid the ground rules, and he anxiously agreed to them. There would be no other women. They would be very discreet. And he had to stop drinking so much.

He stuck to the first two, but the drinking continued. His father, grandfather, and brothers were heavy drinkers, and it was sort of expected of him. But for the first time in his life, Thomas Callahan was in love, madly in love, and he knew the point at which the Scotch was interfering with his woman. He was careful. With the exception of last week and the personal trauma of losing Rosenberg, he never drank before 5 P.M. When they were together, he abandoned the Chivas when he'd had enough and thought it might affect his performance.

It was amusing to watch a forty-five-year-old man fall for the first time. He struggled to maintain a level of coolness, but in their private little moments he was as silly as a sophomore.

She kissed him on the cheek, and covered him with a quilt. Her clothes were placed neatly on a chair. She locked the front door quietly behind her. The sun was up now, peeking through the buildings across Dauphine. The sidewalk was empty.

She had a class in three hours, then Callahan and con law at eleven. There was a mock court appellate brief due in a week. Her casenote for law review was gathering dust. She was behind in classwork for two courses. It was time to be a student again. She had wasted four days playing detective, and she cursed herself for it.

The Accord was around the corner and down a half a block.

THEY WATCHED HER, and it was enjoyable. Tight jeans, baggy sweater, long legs, sunglasses to hide the eyes with no makeup. They watched her close the door and walk quickly along Royale, then disappear around the corner. The hair was shoulder-length and appeared to be dark red.

It was her.

HE CARRIED HIS LUNCH in a little brown paper bag, and found an empty park bench with his back to New Hampshire. He hated Dupont Circle, with its bums, druggies, perverts, aging hippies, and black-leather punks with red spiked hair and vicious tongues. Across the fountain, a well-dressed man with a loudspeaker was assembling his group of animal rights activists for a march to the White House. The leather people jeered and cursed them, but four mounted policemen were close enough to prevent trouble.

He looked at his watch and peeled a banana. Noon, and he preferred to eat elsewhere. The meeting would be brief. He watched the cursing and jeering, and saw his contact emerge through the crowd. Their eyes met, a nod, and he was sitting on the bench next to him. His name was Booker, from Langley. They met here occasionally, when the lines of communication became tangled or blurred and their bosses needed to hear real words that no one else would hear.

Booker had no lunch. He began shelling roasted peanuts and throwing the hulls under the circular bench. "How's Mr. Voyles?"

"Mean as hell. The usual."

He threw peanuts in his mouth. "Gminski was in the White House until midnight last night," Booker said.

There was no response to this. Voyles knew it.

Booker continued. "They've panicked over there. This little pelican thing has scared them. We've read it too, you know, and we're almost certain you guys are not impressed, but for some reason Coal is terrified of it and he's got the President upset. We sort of figure you guys are just having a little fun with Coal and his boss, and since the brief mentions the President and has that photo in it, we figure it's sort of fun for you guys. Know what I mean?"

He took an inch off the banana, and said nothing.

The animal lovers moved away in ragged formation as the leather lovers hissed at them.

"Anyway, it's none of our business, and should be none of our business except the President now wants us to secretly investigate the pelican brief before you guys can get to it. He's convinced we'll find nothing, and he wants to know there's nothing to it so he can convince Voyles to back off."

"There's nothing to it."

Booker watched a drunk urinate in the fountain. The cops were riding off into the sun. "Then Voyles is having a little fun, right?"

"We are pursuing all leads."

"No real suspects, though?"

"No." The banana was history. "Why are they so worried about us investigating this little thing?"

Booker crunched on a small peanut still in the hull. "Well, to them it's quite simple. They are livid over the revelation of Pryce and MacLawrence as nominees, and of course it's all your fault. They distrust Voyles immensely. And if you guys start digging into the pelican brief, they're terrified the press will find out and the President will take a beating. Reelection is next year, blah, blah, blah."

"What did Gminski tell the President?"

"That he had no desire to interfere with an FBI investigation, that we had better things to do, and that it would be illegal as hell. But since the President was begging so hard and Coal was threatening so much, we'd do it anyway. And here I am talking to you."

"Voyles appreciates it."

"We're gonna start digging today, but the whole thing is absurd. We'll go through the motions, stay out of the way, and in a week or so tell the President the whole theory is a shot in the dark."

He folded down the top of his brown bag, and stood. "Good. I'll report to Voyles. Thanks." He walked toward Connecticut, away from the leather punks, and was gone.

□ □ □ □

THE MONITOR was on a cluttered table in the center of the newsroom, and Gray Grantham glared at it amid the hum and roar of the gathering and reporting. The words were not coming, and he sat and glared. The phone rang. He punched his button, and grabbed the receiver without leaving the monitor. "Gray Grantham."

"It's Garcia."

He forgot the monitor. "Yeah, so what's up?"

"I have two questions. First, do you record these calls, and second, can you trace them?"

"No and yes. We don't record until we ask permission, and we can trace but we don't. I thought you said you would not call me at work."

"Do you want me to hang up?"

"No. It's fine. I'd rather talk at 3 P.M. at the office than 6 A.M. in bed."

"Sorry. I'm just scared, that's all. I'll talk to you as long as I can trust you, but if you ever lie to me, Mr. Grantham, I'll quit talking."

"It's a deal. When do you start talking?"

"I can't talk now. I'm at a pay phone downtown, and I'm in a hurry."

"You said you had a copy of something."

"No, I said I might have a copy of something. We'll see."

"Okay. So when might you call again?"

"Do I have to make an appointment?"

"No. But I'm in and out a lot."

"I'll call during lunch tomorrow."

"I'll be waiting right here."

Garcia was gone. Grantham punched seven digits, then six, then four. He wrote the number, then flipped through the yellow pages until he found Pay Phones Inc. The Vendor Location listed the number on Pennsylvania Avenue near the Justice Department.

FIFTEEN

THE ARGUMENT started with dessert, a portion of the meal Callahan preferred to drink. She was nice enough when she clicked off the drinks he'd already consumed with dinner: two double Scotches while they waited on a table, one more before they ordered, and with the fish two bottles of wine, of which she'd had two glasses. He was drinking too fast and getting sloppy, and by the time she finished rattling off this accounting he was angry. He ordered Drambuie for dessert, because it was his favorite, and because it was suddenly a matter of principle. He gulped it and ordered another, and she was furious.

Darby spooned her coffee and ignored him. Mouton's was packed, and she just wanted to leave without a scene and get to her apartment alone.

The argument turned nasty on the sidewalk as they walked away from the restaurant. He pulled the keys to the Porsche from his pocket, and she said he was too drunk to drive. Give her the keys. He gripped them and staggered on in the direction of the parking lot, three blocks away. She said she would walk. Have a nice one, he said. She followed a few steps behind, embarrassed at the stumbling figure in front of her. She pleaded with him. His blood level was at least point-two-zero. He was a law professor, dammit. He would kill someone. He staggered faster, coming perilously close to the curb, then weaving away. He yelled over his shoulder, something about driving better drunk than she could sober. She fell behind. She'd taken a ride before when he was like this, and she knew what a drunk could do in a Porsche.

He crossed the street blindly, hands stuck deep in his pockets as if out for a casual stroll in the late night. He misjudged the curb, hit it with the toes instead of the sole, and went sprawling and bouncing and cursing along the sidewalk. He scrambled up quickly before she could reach him. Leave me alone, dammit, he told her. Just give me the keys, she begged, or I'm walking. He shoved her away. Have a nice one, he said with a laugh. She'd never seen him this drunk. He'd never touched her in anger, drunk or not.

Next to the parking lot was a greasy little dive with neon beer signs covering the windows. She looked inside the open door for help, but thought, how stupid. It was filled with drunks.

She yelled at him as he approached the Porsche. "Thomas! Please! Let me drive!" She was on the sidewalk and would go no farther.

He stumbled on, waving her off, mumbling to himself. He unlocked the door, squeezed downward, and disappeared between the other cars. The engine started and roared as he gunned it.

Darby leaned on the side of the building a few feet from the parking lot's exit. She looked at the street, and almost hoped for a cop. She would rather have him arrested than dead.

It was too far to walk. She would watch him drive away, then call a cab, then ignore him for a week. At least a week. Have a nice one, she repeated to herself. He gunned it again and squealed tires.

The explosion knocked her to the sidewalk. She landed on all fours, face down, stunned for a second, then immediately aware of the heat and the tiny pieces of fiery debris falling in the street. She gaped in horror at the parking lot. The Porsche flipped in a perfect violent somersault and landed upside down. The tires and wheels and doors and fenders slung free. The car was a brilliant fireball, roaring away with flames instantly devouring it.

Darby started toward it, screaming for him. Debris fell around her and the heat slowed her. She stopped thirty feet away, screaming with hands over her mouth.

Then a second explosion flipped it again and drove her away. She tripped, and her head fell hard on the bumper of another car. The pavement was hot to her face, and that was the last she remembered for a moment.

The dive emptied and the drunks were everywhere. They stood along the sidewalk and stared. A couple tried to advance, but the heat reddened their faces and kept them away. Thick, heavy smoke billowed from the fireball, and within seconds two other cars were on fire. There were shouts and voices in panic.

"Whose car is it!"

"Call 911!"

"Is anybody in it!"

"Call 911!"

They dragged her by the elbows back to the sidewalk, to the center of the crowd. She was repeating the name Thomas. A cold cloth came from the dive and was placed on her forehead.

The crowd thickened and the street was busy. Sirens, she heard sirens as she came around. There was a knot on the back of her head, and a coldness on her face. Her mouth was dry. "Thomas. Thomas," she repeated.

"It's okay, it's okay," said a black face just above her. He was carefully holding her head and patting her arm. Other faces stared downward. They all nodded in agreement. "It's okay."

The sirens were screaming now. She gently removed the cloth, and her eyes focused. There were red and blue lights flashing from the street. The sirens were deafening. She sat up. They leaned her against the building beneath the neon beer signs. They eased away, watching her carefully.

"You all right, miss?" asked the black man.

She couldn't answer. Didn't try to. Her head was broken. "Where is Thomas?" she asked, looking at the crack in the sidewalk.

They looked at each other. The first fire truck screamed to a halt twenty feet away, and the crowd parted. Firemen jumped and scrambled in all directions.

"Where is Thomas?" she repeated.

"Miss, who is Thomas?" asked the black man.

"Thomas Callahan," she said softly, as if everyone knew him. "Was he in that car?"

She nodded, then closed her eyes. The sirens wailed and died, and in between she heard the shouts of anxious men, and the popping of the fire. She could smell the burning.

The second and third fire trucks came blaring in from different directions. A cop shoved his way through the crowd. "Police. Outta the way. Police." He pushed and shoved until he found her. He fell to his knees and waved a badge under her nose. "Ma'am, Sergeant Rupert, NOPD."

Darby heard this but thought nothing of it. He was in her face, this Rupert with bushy hair, a baseball cap, black and gold Saints jacket. She stared blankly at him.

"Is that your car, ma'am? Someone said it was your car."

She shook her head. No.

Rupert was grabbing her elbows and pulling up. He was talking to her, asking if she was all right, and at the same time pulling her up and it hurt like hell. The head was fractured, split, busted, and she was in shock but what did this moron care. She was on her feet. The knees wouldn't lock, and she was limp. He kept asking if she was all right. The black man looked at Rupert as if he was crazy.

There, the legs worked now, and she and Rupert were walking through the crowd, behind a fire truck, around another one to an unmarked cop car. She lowered her head and refused to look at the parking lot. Rupert chatted incessantly. Something about an ambulance. He opened the front door and gingerly placed her in the passenger's seat.

Another cop squatted in the door and started asking questions. He wore jeans and cowboy boots with pointed toes. Darby leaned forward and placed her head in her hands. "I think I need help," she said.

"Sure, lady. Help's on the way. Just a coupla questions. What's your name?"

"Darby Shaw. I think I'm in shock. I'm very dizzy, and I think I need to throw up."

"The ambulance is on the way. Is that your car over there?"

"No."

Another cop car, one with decals and words and lights, squealed to a stop in front of Rupert's. Rupert disappeared for a moment. The cowboy cop suddenly closed her door, and she was all alone in the car. She leaned forward and vomited between her legs. She started crying. She was cold. She slowly laid her head on the driver's seat, and curled into a knot. Silence. Then darkness.

SOMEONE WAS KNOCKING on the window above her. She opened her eyes, and the man wore a uniform and a hat with a badge on it. The door was locked.

"Open the door, lady!" he yelled.

She sat up and opened the door. "Are you drunk, lady?"

The head was pounding. "No," she said desperately.

He opened the door wider. "Is this your car?"

She rubbed her eyes. She had to think.

"Lady, is this your car?"

"No!" She glared at him. "No. It's Rupert's."

"Okay. Who the hell is Rupert?"

There was one fire truck left and most of the crowd was gone. This man in the door was obviously a cop. "Sergeant Rupert. One of you guys," she said.

This made him mad. "Get outta the car, lady."

Gladly. Darby crawled out on the passenger's side, and stood on the sidewalk. In the distance, a solitary fireman hosed down the burnt frame of the Porsche.

Another cop in a uniform joined him and they met her on the sidewalk.

The first cop asked, "What's your name?"

"Darby Shaw."

"Why were you passed out in the car?"

She looked at the car. "I don't know. I got hurt and Rupert put me in the car. Where's Rupert?"

The cops looked at each other. "Who the hell's Rupert?" the first cop asked.

This made her mad and the anger cleared away the cobwebs.

"Rupert said he was a cop.".

The second cop asked, "How'd you get hurt?"

Darby glared at him. She pointed to the parking lot across the street. "I was supposed to be in that car over there. But I wasn't, so I'm here, listening to your stupid questions. Where's Rupert?"

They looked blankly at each other. The first cop said, "Stay here," and he walked across the street to another cop car where a man in a suit was talking to a small group. They whispered, then the first cop and the man in the suit walked back to the sidewalk where Darby waited. The man in the suit said, "I'm Lieutenant Olson, New Orleans PD. Did you know the man in the car?" He pointed to the parking lot.

The knees went weak, and she bit her lip. She nodded.

"What's his name?"

"Thomas Callahan."

Olson looked at the first cop. "That's what the computer said. Now, who's this Rupert?"

Darby screamed, "He said he was a cop!"

Olson looked sympathetic. "I'm sorry. There's no cop named Rupert."

She was sobbing loudly. Olson helped her to the hood of Rupert's car, and held her shoulders while the crying subsided and she fought to regain control.

"Check the plates," Olson told the second cop, who quickly scribbled down the tag number from Rupert's car and called it in.

Olson gently held both her shoulders with his hands and looked at her eyes. "Were you with Callahan?"

She nodded, still crying but much quieter. Olson glanced at the first cop.

"How did you get in this car?" Olson asked slowly and softly.

She wiped her eyes with her finger and stared at Olson. "This guy Rupert, who said he was a cop, came and got me from over there, and brought me over here. He put me in the car, and this other cop with cowboy boots starting asking questions. Another cop car pulled up, and they left. Then I guess I passed out. I don't know. I would like to see a doctor."

"Get my car," Olson said to the first cop.

The second cop was back with a puzzled look. "The computer has no record of this tag number. Must be fake tags."

Olson took her arm and led her to his car. He spoke quickly to the two cops. "I'm taking her to Charity. Wrap this up and meet me there. Impound the car. We'll check it later."

She sat in Olson's car listening to the radio squawk and staring at the parking lot. Four cars had burned. The Porsche was upside down in the center, nothing but a crumpled frame. A handful of firemen and other emergency types milled about. A cop was stringing yellow crime-scene tape around the lot.

She touched the knot on the back of her head. No blood. Tears dripped off her chin.

Olson slammed his door, and they eased through the parked cars and headed for St. Charles. He had the blue lights on, but no sirens.

"Do you feel like talking?" he asked.

They were on St. Charles. "I guess," she said. "He's dead, isn't he?"

"Yes, Darby. I'm sorry. I take it he was the only one in the car."

"Yes."

"How'd you get hurt?"

He gave her a handkerchief, and she wiped her eyes. "I fell or something. There were two explosions, and I think the second one knocked me down. I don't remember everything. Please, tell me who Rupert is."

"I have no idea. I don't know a cop named Rupert, and there was no cop here with cowboy boots."

She thought about this for a block and a half.

"What did Callahan do for a living?"

"A law professor at Tulane. I'm a student there."

"Who would want to kill him?"

She stared at the traffic lights and shook her head. "You're certain it was intentional?"

"No doubt about it. It was a very powerful explosive. We found a piece of a foot stuck in a chain-link fence eighty feet away. I'm sorry, okay. He was murdered."

"Maybe someone got the wrong car."

"That's always possible. We'll check out everything. I take it you were supposed to be in the car with him."

She tried to speak, but could not hold the tears. She buried her face in the handkerchief.

He parked between two ambulances near the emergency entrance at Charity, and left the blue lights on. He helped her quickly inside to a dirty room where fifty people sat in various degrees of pain and discomfort. She found a seat by the water fountain. Olson talked to the lady behind the window, and he raised his voice but Darby couldn't understand him. A small boy with a bloody towel around his foot cried in his mother's lap. A young black girl was about to give birth. There was not a doctor or nurse in sight. No one was in a hurry.

Olson crouched in front of her. "It'll be a few minutes. Sit tight. I'm gonna move the car, and I'll be back in a minute. Do you feel like talking?"

"Yeah, sure."

He was gone. She checked again for blood, and found none. The double doors opened wide, and two angry nurses came after the girl in labor. They sort of dragged her away, back through the doors and down the hall.

Darby waited, then followed. With the red eyes and handkerchief, she looked like some child's mother. The hall was a zoo with nurses and orderlies and the wounded yelling and moving about. She turned a corner and saw an EXIT sign. Through the door, into another hall, much quieter, another door, and she was on a loading dock. There were lights in the alley. Don't run. Be strong. It's okay. No one's watching. She was on the street, walking briskly. The cool air cleared her eyes. She refused to cry.

Olson would take his time, and when he returned he would figure they had called her name and she was back there getting worked on. He would wait. And wait.

She turned corners, and saw Rampart. The Quarter was just ahead. She could get lost there. There were people on Royal, tourist types strolling along. She felt safer. She entered the Holiday Inn, paid with plastic, and got a room on the fifth floor.

After the door was bolted and chained, she curled up on the bed with all the lights on.

MRS. VERHEEK rolled her plump but rich ass away from the center of the bed, and grabbed the phone. "It's for you, Gavin!" she yelled into the bathroom. Gavin emerged with shaving cream on half his face, and took the receiver from his wife, who burrowed deep into the bed. Like a hog rutting in mud, he thought.

"Hello," he snapped.

It was a female voice he'd never heard before. "This is Darby Shaw. Do you know who I am?"

He smiled instantly, and for a second thought of the string bikini on St. Thomas. "Well, yes. I believe we have a mutual friend."

"Did you read the little theory I wrote?"

"Ah, yes. The pelican brief, as we refer to it."

"And who is we?"

Verheek sat in a chair by the night table. This was no social call. "Why are you calling, Darby?"

"I need some answers, Mr. Verheek. I'm scared to death."

"It's Gavin, okay?"

"Gavin. Where is the brief now?"

"Here and there. What's wrong?"

"I'll tell you in a minute. Just tell me what you did with the brief."

"Well, I read it, then sent it to another division, and it was seen by some folks within the Bureau, then shown to Director Voyles, who sort of liked it."

"Has it been seen outside the FBI?"

"I can't answer that, Darby."

"Then I won't tell you what's happened to Thomas."

Verheek pondered this for a long minute. She waited patiently. "Okay. Yes, it's been seen outside the FBI. By whom and by how many, I don't know."

"He's dead, Gavin. He was murdered around ten last night. Someone planted a car bomb for both of us. I got lucky, but now they're after me."

Verheek was hovering over the phone, scribbling notes. "Are you hurt?"

"Physically, I'm okay."

"Where are you?"

"New Orleans."

"Are you certain, Darby? I mean, I know you're certain, but, dammit, who would want to kill him?"

"I met a couple of them."

"How'd you—"

"It's a long story. Who saw the brief, Gavin? Thomas gave it to you Monday night. It's been passed around, and forty-eight hours later he's dead. And I'm supposed to be dead with him. It fell into the wrong hands, wouldn't you say?"

"Are you safe?"

"Who the hell knows?"

"Where are you staying? What's your phone number?"

"Not so fast, Gavin. I'm moving real slow right now. I'm at a pay phone, so no cute stuff."

"Come on, Darby! Give me a break! Thomas Callahan was my best friend. You've got to come in."

"And what might that mean?"

"Look, Darby, give me fifteen minutes, and we'll have a dozen agents pick you up. I'll catch a flight and be there before noon. You can't stay on the streets."

"Why, Gavin? Who's after me? Talk to me, Gavin."

"I'll talk to you when I get there."

"I don't know. Thomas is dead because he talked to you. I'm not that anxious to meet you right now."

"Darby, look, I don't know who or why, but I assure you you're in a very dangerous situation. We can protect you."

"Maybe later."

He breathed deeply and sat on the edge of the bed. "You can trust me, Darby."

"Okay, I trust you. But what about those other people? This is heavy, Gavin. My little brief has someone awfully upset, wouldn't you say?"

"Did he suffer?"

She hesitated. "I don't think so." The voice was cracking.

"Will you call me in two hours? At the office. I'll give you an inside number."

"Give me the number, and I'll think about it."

"Please, Darby. I'll go straight to the Director when I get there. Call me at eight, your time."

"Give me the number."

THE BOMB EXPLODED too late to make the Thursday morning edition of the *Times-Picayune*. Darby flipped through it hurriedly in the hotel room. Nothing. She watched the television, and there it was. A live shot of the burned-out Porsche, still sitting amid the debris in the parking lot, secluded nicely with yellow tape running everywhere. The police were treating it as a homicide. No suspects. No comment. Then the name of Thomas Callahan, age forty-five, a prominent professor of law at Tulane. The dean was suddenly there with a microphone in his face, talking about Professor Callahan and the shock of it all.

The shock of it all, the fatigue, the fear, the pain, and Darby buried her head in the pillow. She hated crying, and this would be the last of it for a while. Mourning would only get her killed.

SIXTEEN

EVEN THOUGH it was a wonderful crisis, with the ratings up and Rosenberg dead, with his image clean and polished and America feeling good about itself because he was in command, with the Democrats running for cover and reelection next year in the bag, he was sick of this crisis and its relentless predawn meetings. He was sick of F. Denton Voyles and his smugness and arrogance, and his squatty little figure sitting on the other side of his desk in a wrinkled trench coat looking out a window while he addressed the President of the United States. He would be here in a minute for another meeting before breakfast, another tense encounter in which Voyles would tell only a portion of what he knew.

He was sick of being in the dark, and fed only what bits and crumbs Voyles chose to throw his way. Gminski would throw him a few, and somehow in the midst of all this crumb scattering and gathering he was supposed to get enough and be satisfied. He knew nothing compared to them. At least he had Coal to plow through their paper and memorize it all, and keep them honest.

He was sick of Coal, too. Sick of his perfectness and sleeplessness. Sick of his brilliance. Sick of his penchant for beginning each day when the sun was somewhere over the Atlantic, and planning every damned minute of every damned hour until it was over the Pacific. Then he, Coal, would load up a box of the day's junk, take it home, read it, decipher it, store it, then come in a few hours later blazing away with all the painfully boring mishmash he had just devoured. When Coal was tired, he slept five hours a night, but normal was three or four. He left his office in the West Wing at eleven each night, read all the way home in the back of his limo, then about the time the limo cooled off Coal was waiting on it for the return ride to the White House. He considered it a sin to arrive at his desk after 5 A.M. And if he could work a hundred and twenty hours a week, then everyone else should be able to do at least eighty. He demanded eighty. After three years, no one in this Administration could remember all the people fired by Fletcher Coal for not working eighty hours a week. Happened at least three times a month.

Coal was happiest on mornings when the tension was thick and a nasty meeting was planned. In the past week this thing with Voyles had kept him smiling. He was standing beside the desk, going through the mail while the President scanned the *Post* and two secretaries scurried about.

The President glanced at him. Perfect black suit, white shirt, red silk tie, a bit too much grease on the hair above the ears. He was sick of him, but he'd get over it when the crisis passed and he could get back to golf and Coal could sweat the details. He told himself he had that kind of energy and stamina when he was only thirty-seven, but he knew better.

Coal snapped his fingers, glared at the secretaries, and they happily ran from the Oval Office.

"And he said he wouldn't come if I was here. That's hilarious." Coal was clearly amused.

"I don't think he likes you," the President said.

"He loves people he can run over."

"I guess I need to be sweet to him."

"Lay it on thick, Chief. He has to back off. This theory is so weak it's comical, but in his hands it could be dangerous."

"What about the law student?"

"We're checking. She appears harmless."

The President stood and stretched. Coal shuffled papers. A secretary on the intercom announced the arrival of Voyles.

"I'll be going," Coal said. He would listen and watch from around the corner. At his insistence, three closed-circuit cameras were installed in the Oval Office. The monitors were in a small, locked room in the West Wing. He had the only key. Sarge knew of the room, but had not bothered to enter. Yet. The cameras were invisible and supposedly a big secret.

The President felt better knowing Coal would at least be watching. He met Voyles at the door with a warm handshake and guided him to the sofa for a warm, friendly little chat. Voyles was not impressed. He knew Coal would be listening. And watching.

But in the spirit of the moment, Voyles removed his trench coat and laid it properly on a chair. He did not want coffee.

The President crossed his legs. He was wearing the brown cardigan. The grandfather.

"Denton," he said gravely. "I want to apologize for Fletcher Coal. He doesn't have much finesse."

Voyles nodded slightly. You stupid bastard. There are enough wires in this office to electrocute half the bureaucrats in D.C. Coal was somewhere in the basement hearing about his lack of finesse. "He can be an ass, can't he?" Voyles grunted.

"Yes, he can. I have to really watch him. He's very bright and drives hard, but he tends to overdo it at times."

"He's a son of a bitch, and I'll say it to his face." Voyles glanced at an air vent above the portrait of Thomas Jefferson where a camera watched it all below.

"Yes, well, I'll keep him out of your way until this thing is over."

"You do that."

The President slowly sipped from his coffee and pondered what to say next. Voyles was not known for his conversation.

"I need a favor."

Voyles stared with rigid and unblinking eyes. "Yes, sir."

"I need the scoop on this pelican thing. It's a wild idea, but, hell, it mentions me, sort of. How serious are you taking it?"

Oh, this was funny. Voyles fought off a smile. It was working. Mr. President and Mr. Coal were sweating the pelican brief. They had received it late Tuesday, worried with it all day

Wednesday, and now in the waking hours of Thursday were on their knees begging about something one notch above a practical joke.

"We're investigating, Mr. President." It was a lie, but how could he know? "We are pursuing all leads, all suspects. I wouldn't have sent it over if I wasn't serious." The wrinkles squeezed together on the tanned forehead, and Voyles wanted to laugh.

"What have you learned?"

"Not much, but we just started. We got it less than forty-eight hours ago, and I assigned fourteen agents in New Orleans to start digging. It's all routine." The lies sounded so good he could almost hear Coal choking.

Fourteen! It hit him in the gut so hard he sat up straight and placed the coffee on a table. Fourteen Fibbies out there flashing badges, asking questions, and it was just a matter of time before this thing got out. "Fourteen, you say. Sounds like it's pretty serious."

Voyles was unyielding. "We're very serious, Mr. President. They've been dead a week, and the trail's growing colder. We're tracking leads as fast as we can. My men are working around the clock."

"I understand all that, but how serious is this pelican theory?"

Damn, this was fun. The brief had yet to be sent to New Orleans. In fact, New Orleans had not been contacted. He had instructed Eric East to mail a copy to that office with orders to quietly ask a few questions. It was a dead end, just like a hundred others they were chasing.

"I doubt if there's anything to it, Mr. President, but we've got to check it out."

The wrinkles relaxed and there was a touch of a smile. "I don't have to tell you, Denton, how much this nonsense could hurt if the press found out."

"We don't consult the press when we investigate."

"I know. Let's not get into that. I just wish you would back off this thing. I mean, what the hell, it's absurd, and I could really get burned. Know what I'm saying?"

Voyles was brutal. "Are you asking me to ignore a suspect, Mr. President?"

Coal leaned toward the screen. No, I'm telling you to forget this pelican brief! He almost said it out loud. He could make it real plain for Voyles. He could spell it out, then slap the dumpy little wretch if he got smart. But he was hiding in a locked room, away from the action. And, for the moment, he knew he was where he belonged.

The President shifted and recrossed his legs at the knees. "Come on, Denton, you know what I'm saying. There are bigger fish in the pond. The press is watching this investigation, just dying to find out who's a suspect. You know how they are. I don't have to tell you that I have no friends with the press. Even my own press secretary dislikes me. Ha, ha, ha. Forget about it for a while. Back off and chase the real suspects. This thing is a joke, but it could embarrass the hell out of me."

Denton looked hard at him. Relentless.

The President shifted again. "What about this Khamel thing? Sounds pretty good, huh?"

"Could be."

"Yeah. Since we're talking numbers, how many men have you assigned to Khamel?"

Voyles said, "Fifteen," and almost laughed. The President's mouth fell open. The hottest suspect in the game gets fifteen, and this damned pelican thing gets fourteen.

Coal smiled and shook his head. Voyles had been caught in his own lies. On the bottom of page four of the Wednesday report, Eric East and K. O. Lewis gave the number at thirty, not fifteen. Relax, Chief, Coal whispered to the screen. He's playing with you.

The President was anything but relaxed. "Good god, Denton. Why only fifteen? I thought this was a significant break."

"Maybe a few more than that. I'm running this investigation, Mr. President."

"I know. And you're doing a fine job. I'm not meddling. I just wish you'd consider spending your time elsewhere. That's all. When I read the pelican brief I almost vomited. If the press saw it and started digging, I'd be crucified."

"So you're asking me to back off?"

The President leaned forward and stared fiercely at Voyles. "I'm not asking, Denton. I'm telling you to leave it alone. Ignore it for a couple of weeks. Spend your time elsewhere. If it flares up again, take another look. I'm still the boss around here, remember?"

Voyles relented and managed a tiny smile. "I'll make you a deal. Your hatchet man Coal has done a number on me with the press. They've eaten my lunch over the security we provided to Rosenberg and Jensen."

The President nodded solemnly.

"You get that pit bull off my ass, keep him away from me, and I'll forget the pelican theory."

"I don't make deals."

Voyles sneered but kept his cool. "Good. I'll send fifty agents to New Orleans tomorrow. And fifty the next day. We'll be flashing badges all over town and doing our damnedest to attract attention."

The President jumped to his feet and walked to the windows overlooking the Rose Garden. Voyles sat motionless and waited.

"All right, all right. It's a deal. I can control Fletcher Coal."

Voyles stood and walked slowly to the desk. "I don't trust him, and if I smell him one more time during this investigation, the deal's off and we investigate the pelican brief with all the weight I can muster."

The President held up his hands and smiled warmly. "It's a deal."

Voyles was smiling and the President was smiling, and in the closet near the Cabinet Room Fletcher Coal was smiling at a screen. Hatchet man, pit bull. He loved it. Those were the words that created legends.

He turned off the screens and locked the door behind him. They would talk another ten minutes about the background checks on the short list, and he would listen in his office where he had audio but no video. He had a staff meeting at nine. A firing at ten. And he had some typing to do. With most memos, he simply dictated into the machine and handed the tape to a secretary. But occasionally, Coal found it necessary to resort to the phantom memo. These were always widely circulated in the West Wing, and always controversial as hell, and usually dripped to the press. Because they came from no one, they could be found lying on almost every desk. Coal would scream and accuse. He had fired people for phantom memos, all of which came from his typewriter.

It was four single-spaced paragraphs on one page, and it summarized what he knew about Khamel and his recent flight out of Washington. And there were vague links to the Libyans and Palestinians. Coal admired it. How long before it would be in the *Post* or the *Times*? He made little bets with himself about which paper would get it first.

THE DIRECTOR was at the White House, and from there would fly to New York and return tomorrow. Gavin camped outside the office of K. O. Lewis until there was a small opening. He was in.

Lewis was irritated, but always the gentleman. "You look scared."

"I've just lost my best friend."

Lewis waited for more.

"His name was Thomas Callahan. He's the guy from Tulane who brought me the pelican brief, and it got passed around, then sent to the White House and who knows where else, and now he's dead. Blown to bits by a car bomb last night in New Orleans. Murdered, K.O."

"I'm sorry."

"It's not a matter of being sorry. Evidently the bomb was intended for Callahan and the student who wrote it, a girl by the name of Darby Shaw."

"I saw her name on the brief."

"That's right. They've been dating, and were supposed to be in the car together when it exploded. But she survived, and I get this call this morning at five, and it's her. Scared to death."

Lewis listened, but was already dismissing it. "You're not certain it was a bomb."

"She said it was a bomb, okay. It went BOOM! and blew the hell out of everything, okay. I'm certain he's dead."

"And you think there's a connection between his death and the brief?"

Gavin was a lawyer, untrained in the art of investigation, and he did not wish to appear gullible. "There could be. I think so, yes. Don't you?"

"Doesn't matter, Gavin. I just got off the phone with the Director. Pelican's off our list. I'm not sure it was ever on, but we're spending no more time on it."

"But my friend's been killed with a car bomb."

"I'm sorry. I'm sure the authorities down there are investigating."

"Listen to me, K.O. I'm asking for a favor."

"Listen to me, Gavin. I don't have any favors. We're chasing enough rabbits right now, and if the Director says stop, then we stop. You're free to talk to him. I wouldn't advise it."

"Maybe I'm not handling this right. I thought you would listen to me, and at least act interested."

Lewis was walking around the desk. "Gavin, you look bad. Take the day off."

"No. I'll go to my office, wait an hour, and come back in here and do this again. Can we try it again in an hour?"

"No. Voyles was explicit."

"So was the girl, K.O. He was murdered, and now she's hiding somewhere in New Orleans afraid of her shadow, calling us for help, and we're too busy."

"I'm sorry."

"No, you're not. It's my fault. I should've thrown the damned thing in the garbage."

"It served a valuable purpose, Gavin." Lewis placed his hand on his shoulder as if his time was up and he was tired of this drivel. Gavin jerked away and headed for the door.

"Yeah, it gave you guys something to play with. I should've burned it."

"It's too good to burn, Gavin."

"I'm not giving up. I'll be back in an hour, and we'll do this again. This didn't go right." Verheek slammed the door behind him.

□ □ □ □

SHE ENTERED Rubinstein Brothers from Canal Street, and got lost between the racks of men's shirts. No one followed her in. She quickly picked out a navy parka, men's small, a genderless pair of aviator sunglasses, and a British driving cap that was also a men's small but fit. She paid for it with plastic. As the clerk ran the card through, she picked the tags off, and put the parka on. It was baggy, like something she would wear to class. She stuffed her hair under the hooded collar. The clerk watched discreetly. She exited on Magazine Street, and got lost in the crowd.

Back on Canal. A busload of tourists swarmed into the Sheraton, and she joined them. She went to the wall of phones, found the number, and called Mrs. Chen, her neighbor in the duplex next door. Had she seen or heard anyone? Very early, there was a knock on the door. It was still dark, and woke them. She didn't see anyone, just heard the knock. Her car was still on the street. Everything okay? Yes, all's fine. Thanks.

She watched the tourists and punched the inside number for Gavin Verheek. Inside meant a minor hassle only, and after three minutes of refusing to give her name and repeating his, she had him.

"Where are you?" he asked.

"Let me explain something. For the moment, I will not tell you or anyone else where I am. So don't ask."

"All right. I guess you're making the rules."

"Thank you. What did Mr. Voyles say?"

"Mr. Voyles was at the White House and unavailable. I'll try to talk to him later today."

"That's pretty weak, Gavin. You've been at the office for almost four hours, and you have nothing. I expected more."

"Be patient, Darby."

"Patience will get me killed. They're after me, aren't they, Gavin?"

"I don't know."

"What would you do if you knew you were supposed to be dead, and the people trying to kill you have had assassinated two Supreme Court Justices, and knocked off a simple law professor, and they have billions of dollars which they obviously don't mind using to kill with? What would you do, Gavin?"

"Go to the FBI."

"Thomas went to the FBI, and he's dead."

"Thanks, Darby. That's not fair."

"I'm not worried about fairness or feelings. I'm more concerned with staying alive until noon."

"Don't go to your apartment."

"I'm not stupid. They've already been there. And I'm sure they're watching his apartment."

"Where's his family?"

"His parents live in Naples, Florida. I guess the university will contact them. I don't know. He has a brother in Mobile, and I thought of calling him and trying to explain all this."

She saw a face. He walked among the tourists at the registration desk. He held a folded newspaper and tried to appear at home, just another guest, but his walk was a bit hesitant and his eyes were searching. The face was long and thin with round glasses and a shiny forehead.

"Gavin, listen to me. Write this down. I see a man I've seen before, not long ago. An hour maybe. Six feet two or three, thin, thirty years old, glasses, receding hair, dark in color. He's gone. He's gone."

"Who the hell is it?"

"We haven't met, dammit!"

"Did he see you? Where the hell are you?"

"In a hotel lobby. I don't know if he saw me. I'm gone."

"Darby! Listen to me. Whatever you do, keep in touch with me, okay?"

"I'll try."

The rest room was around the corner. She went to the last stall, locked the door behind her, and stayed there for an hour.

SEVENTEEN

THE PHOTOGRAPHER'S NAME was Croft, and he'd worked for the *Post* for seven years until his third drug conviction sent him away for nine months. Upon parole, he declared himself to be a free-lance artist, and advertised as such in the yellow pages. The phone seldom rang. He did a little of this work; this slithering around shooting people who did not know they were targets. Many of his clients were divorce lawyers who needed dirt for trial. After two years of free-lancing, he had picked up a few tricks and now considered himself a halfass private investigator. He charged forty bucks an hour when he could get it.

Another client was Gray Grantham, an old friend from his newspaper days who called when he needed dirt. Grantham was a serious, ethical reporter with just a touch of sleaze, and when he needed a dirty trick, he called. He liked Grantham because he was honest about his sleaziness. The rest were so pious.

He was in Grantham's Volvo because it had a phone. It was noon, and he was smoking his lunch, wondering if the smell would linger with all the windows down. He did his best work half-stoned. When you stare at motels for a living, you need to be stoned.

There was a nice breeze coming in from the passenger's side, blowing the smell onto Pennsylvania. He was parked illegally, smoking dope, and not really concerned. He had less than an ounce on him, and his probation officer smoked it too, so what the hell.

The phone booth was a block and a half ahead, on the sidewalk but away from the street. With his telephoto lens, he could almost read the phone book hanging from the rack. Piece of cake. A large woman was inside, filling the booth and talking with her hands. Croft took a drag and watched the mirror for cops. This was a tow-away zone. Traffic was heavy on Pennsylvania.

At twenty after twelve, the woman fought her way out of the booth, and from nowhere a young man with a nice suit appeared and closed the door. Croft got his Nikon and rested the lens on the steering wheel. It was cool and sunny, and the sidewalk bustled with lunch traffic. The shoulders and heads moved quickly by. A gap. Click. A gap. Click. The subject was punching numbers and glancing around. This was their man.

He talked for thirty seconds, and the car phone rang three times and stopped. It was the signal from Grantham at the *Post*. This was their man, and he was talking. Croft fired away. Get all you can get, Grantham had said. A gap. Click. Click. Heads and shoulders. A gap. Click. Click. His eyes darted around as he talked, but he kept his back to the street. Full face. Click. Croft burned a roll of thirty-six in two minutes, then grabbed another Nikon. He screwed on the lens, and waited for a mob to pass.

He took the last drag and thumped it into the street. This was so easy. Oh sure, it took talent to capture the image in a studio, but this street work was much more fun. There was something felonious about stealing a face with a hidden camera.

The subject was a man of few words. He hung up, looked around, opened the door, looked around, and started toward Croft. Click, click, click. Full face, full figure, walking faster, getting closer, beautiful, beautiful. Croft worked feverishly, then at the last moment laid the Nikon in the seat and looked at Pennsylvania as their man walked by and disappeared in a group of secretaries.

What a fool. When you're on the run, never use the same pay phone twice.

GARCIA WAS SHADOW BOXING. He had a wife and child, he said, and he was scared. There was a career ahead with plenty of money, and if he paid his dues and kept his mouth shut he would be a wealthy man. But he wanted to talk. He rambled on about how he wanted to talk, had something to say and all, but just couldn't make the decision. He didn't trust anyone.

Grantham didn't push. He let him ramble long enough for Croft to do his number. Garcia would eventually spill his guts. He wanted to so badly. He had called three times now, and was growing comfortable with his new friend Grantham, who'd played this game many times and knew how it worked. The first step was to relax and build trust, to treat them with warmth and respect, to talk about right and wrong and moralities. Then they would talk.

The pictures were beautiful. Croft was not his first choice. He was usually so bombed you could tell it in the photography. But Croft was sleazy and discreet, with a working knowledge of journalism, and he happened to be available on short notice. He had picked twelve and blown them to five by seven, and they were outstanding. Right profile. Left profile. Full face into the phone. Full face looking at the camera. Full figure less than twenty feet away. Piece of cake, Croft said.

Garcia was under thirty, a very nice-looking, clean-cut lawyer. Dark, short hair. Dark eyes. Maybe Hispanic, but the skin was not dark. The clothes were expensive. Navy suit, probably wool. No stripes or patterns. Basic white spread collar with a silk tie. Basic black or burgundy wing tips with a sparkling shine. The absence of a briefcase was puzzling. But then, it was lunch, and he probably ran from the office to make the call, then back to the office. The Justice Department was a block away.

Grantham studied the pictures and kept an eye on the door. Sarge was never late. It was dark and the club was filling up. Grantham's was the only white face within three blocks.

Of the tens of thousands of government lawyers in D.C., he had seen a few who knew how to dress, but not many. Especially the younger ones. They started at forty a year and clothes were not important. Clothes were important to Garcia, and he was too young and well dressed to be a government lawyer.

So he was a private one, in a firm for about three or four years now and hitting somewhere around eighty grand. Great. That narrowed it down to fifty thousand lawyers and no doubt expanding by the moment.

The door opened and a cop walked in. Through the smoke and haze, he could tell it was Cleve. This was a respectable joint with no dice or whores, so the presence of a cop was not alarming. He sat in the booth across from Grantham.

"Did you pick this place?" Grantham asked.

"Yeah. You like it?"

"Let's put it like this. We're trying to be inconspicuous, right? I'm here picking up secrets from a White House employee. Pretty heavy stuff. Now tell me, Cleve, do I look inconspicuous sitting here in all my whiteness?"

"I hate to tell you this, Grantham, but you're not nearly as famous as you think. You see those dudes at the bar." They looked at the bar lined with construction workers. "I'd give you my paycheck if any dude there has ever read the *Washington Post*, heard of Gray Grantham, or gives a damn what happens at the White House."

"Okay, okay. Where's Sarge?"

"Sarge is not feeling well. He gave me a message for you."

Wouldn't work. He could use Sarge as an unnamed source, but not Sarge's son or anyone else Sarge talked to. "What's wrong with him?"

"Old age. He didn't want to talk tonight, but it's urgent, he says."

Grantham listened and waited.

"I've got an envelope in my car, all licked and sealed real tight. Sarge got real blunt when he gave it to me, and told me not to open it. Just take it to Mr. Grantham. I think it's important."

"Let's go."

They made their way through the crowd to the door. The patrol car was parked illegally at the curb. Cleve opened the passenger door, and pulled the envelope from the glove box. "He got this in the West Wing."

Grantham stuffed it in his pocket. Sarge was not one to lift things, and in the course of their relationship he had never produced a document.

"Thanks, Cleve."

"He wouldn't tell me what it is—told me I'll just have to wait and read it in the paper."

"Tell Sarge I love him."

"I'm sure that'll give him a thrill."

The patrol car drove away, and Grantham hurried to his Volvo, now filled with the stench of burnt grass. He locked the door, turned on the dome light, and ripped open the envelope. It was clearly an internal White House memo, and it was about an assassin named Khamel.

HE WAS FLYING across town. Out of Brightwood, onto Sixteenth and south toward central Washington. It was almost seven-thirty, and if he could put it together in an hour, it would make the Late City edition, the largest of half a dozen editions that began rolling off the presses at ten-thirty. Thank god for the little yuppie car phone he had been embarrassed to buy. He called Smith Keen, the assistant managing editor/investigations, who was still in the newsroom on the fifth floor. He called a friend at the foreign desk, and asked him to pull everything on Khamel.

He was suspicious of the memo. The words were too sensitive to put on paper, then sling around the office like the latest policy on coffee or bottled water or vacations. Someone, probably Fletcher Coal, wanted the world to know that Khamel had emerged as a suspect, and that he was an Arab of all things, and had close ties to Libya and Iran and Iraq, countries led by fiery idiots who hated America. Someone in the White House of Fools wanted the story on the front page.

But it was a helluva story and it was front-page news. He and Smith Keen had it finished by nine. They found two old pictures of a man widely believed to be Khamel, but so dissimilar they appeared to be of different people. Keen said run both of them. The file on Khamel was thin. Much rumor and legend, but little meat. Grantham mentioned the Pope, the British diplomat, the German banker, and the ambush of the Israeli soldiers. And now, according to a confidential source at the White House, a most reliable and trusted source, Khamel was a suspect in the killings of Justices Rosenberg and Jensen.

TWENTY-FOUR HOURS after hitting the street, she was still alive. If she could make it to morning, she could start another day with new ideas about what to do and where to go. For now, she was tired. She was in a room on the fifteenth floor of the Marriott, with the door bolted, lights on, and the mighty can of Mace lying on the bedspread. Her thick, dark red hair was now in a paper sack in the closet. The last time she cut her hair she was three years old, and her mother whipped her tail.

It took two painful hours with dull scissors to cut it off yet leave some semblance of style. She would keep it under a cap or hat until who knows when. It took another two hours to color it black. She could've bleached it and gone blonde, but that would be obvious. She assumed she was dealing with professionals, and for some unfathomable reason she determined at the drugstore that they might expect her to do this and become a blonde. And what the hell. The stuff came in a bottle, and if she woke up tomorrow with a wild hair she could go blonde. The chameleon strategy. Change colors every day and drive 'em crazy. Clairol had at least eighty-five shades.

She was dead tired but afraid of sleep. She had not seen her friend from the Sheraton during the day, but the more she moved around the more the faces looked the same. He was out there, she knew. And he had friends. If they could assassinate Rosenberg and Jensen, and knock off Thomas Callahan, she would be easy.

She couldn't go near her car, and she didn't want to rent one. Rentals leave records. And they were probably watching. She could fly, but they were stalking the airports. Take a bus, but she'd never bought a ticket or seen the inside of a Greyhound.

And after they realized she had disappeared, they would expect her to run. She was just an amateur, a little college girl brokenhearted after watching her man blown to bits and fried. She would make a mad dash somewhere, get out of the city, and they would pick her off.

She rather liked the city at this moment. It had a million hotel rooms, almost as many alleys and dives and bars, and it always had crowds of people strolling along Bourbon, Chartres, Dauphine, and Royal. She knew it well, especially the Quarter, where life was within walking distance. She would move from hotel to hotel for a few days, until when? She didn't know when. She didn't know why. Moving just seemed intelligent under the circumstances. She would stay off the streets in the mornings, and try to sleep then. She would change clothes and hats and sunglasses. She would start smoking, and keep one in her face. She would move until she got tired of moving, then she might leave. It was okay to be scared. She had to keep thinking. She would survive.

She thought of calling the cops, but not now. They took names and kept records, and they could be dangerous. She thought of calling Thomas' brother in Mobile, but there wasn't a single thing the poor man could do to help her at this moment. She thought of calling the dean, but how could she explain the brief, Gavin Verheek, the FBI, the car bomb, Rosenberg and Jensen, and her on the run and make it sound believable. Forget the dean. She didn't like him anyway. She thought of calling a couple of friends from law school, but people talk, and people listen, and they could be out there listening to the people talking about poor Callahan. She wanted to talk to Alice Stark, her best friend. Alice was worried, and Alice would go to the cops and tell them her friend Darby Shaw was missing. She would call Alice tomorrow.

She dialed room service, and ordered a Mexican salad and a bottle of red wine. She would drink all of it, then sit in a chair with the Mace and watch the door until she fell asleep.

EIGHTEEN

G MINSKI'S LIMO made a wild U-turn on Canal as if it
owned the street, and came to a sudden stop in front of
the Sheraton. Both rear doors flew open. Gminski was out first,
followed quickly by three aides who scurried after him with
bags and briefcases.

It was almost 2 A.M., and the Director was obviously in a
hurry. He did not stop at the front desk, but went straight for
the elevators. The aides ran behind him and held the elevator
door for him, and no one spoke as they rode up six floors.

Three of his agents were waiting in a corner room. One of
them opened the door, and Gminski barged through it without
any sort of greeting. The aides threw the bags on one bed. The
Director yanked off his jacket and threw it in a chair.

"Where is she?" he snapped at an agent by the name of
Hooten. The one named Swank opened the curtains, and
Gminski walked to the window.

Swank was pointing to the Marriott, across the street and
down a block. "She's on the fifteenth floor, third room from the
street, lights are still on."

Gminski stared at the Marriott. "You're certain?"

"Yes. We saw her go in, and she paid with a credit card."

"Poor kid," Gminski said as he walked away from the window. "Where was she last night?"

"Holiday Inn on Royal. Paid with a credit card."

"Have you seen anyone following her?" the Director asked.

"No."

"I need some water," he said to an aide, who jumped toward the ice bucket and rattled cubes.

Gminski sat on the edge of the bed, laced his fingers together, and cracked every possible knuckle. "What do you think?" he asked Hooten, the oldest of the three agents.

"They're chasing her. They're looking under rocks. She's using credit cards. She'll be dead in forty-eight hours."

"She's not completely stupid," Swank inserted. "She cut her hair and colored it black. She's moving around. It's apparent she has no plans to leave the city any time soon. I'll give her seventy-two hours before they find her."

Gminski sipped his water. "This means her little brief is directly on point. And it means our friend is now a very desperate man. Where is he?"

Hooten answered quickly. "We have no idea."

"We have to find him."

"He hasn't been seen in three weeks."

Gminski set the glass on the desk, and picked up a room key. "So what do you think?" he asked Hooten.

"Do we bring her in?" Hooten asked.

"It won't be easy," Swank said. "She may have a gun. Someone could get hurt."

"She's a scared kid," Gminski said. "She's also a civilian, not a member. We can't go around snatching civilians off the sidewalk."

"Then she won't last long," Swank said.

"How do you take her?" Gminski asked.

"There are ways," Hooten answered. "Catch her on the street. Go to her room. I could be inside her room in less than ten minutes if I left right now. It's not that difficult. She's not a pro."

Gminski paced slowly around the room and everyone watched him. He glanced at his watch. "I'm not inclined to take her. Let's sleep four hours, and meet here at six-thirty. Sleep on it. If you can convince me to snatch her, then I'll say do it. Okay?"

They nodded obediently.

THE WINE WORKED. She dozed in the chair, then made it to the bed and slept hard. The phone was ringing. The bedspread was hanging to the floor, and her feet were on the pillows. The phone was ringing. The eyelids were glued together. The mind was numb and lost in dreams, but somewhere in the deep recesses something worked and told her the phone was ringing.

The eyes opened but saw little. The sun was up, the lights were on, and she stared at the phone. No, she did not ask for a wake-up call. She thought about this for a second, then she was certain. No wake-up call. She sat on the edge of the bed and listened to it ring. Five times, ten, fifteen, twenty. It would not stop. Could be a wrong number, but they would stop after twenty rings.

It was not a wrong number. The cobwebs began to clear, and she moved closer to the phone. With the exception of the registration clerk and maybe his boss, and perhaps room service, not a single living soul knew she was in this room. She had ordered food, but made no other calls.

It stopped ringing. Good, wrong number. She walked to the bathroom, and it was ringing again. She counted. After the fourteenth ring, she lifted the receiver. "Hello."

"Darby, it's Gavin Verheek. Are you okay?"

She sat on the bed. "How'd you get the number?"

"We have ways. Listen, have—"

"Wait, Gavin. Wait a minute. Let me think. The credit card, right?"

"Yes. The credit card. The paper trail. It's the FBI, Darby. We have ways. It's not that difficult."

"Then they could do it too."

"I suppose. Stay in the small joints and pay with cash."

There was a thick knot in her stomach, and she stretched on the bed. Just like that. Not difficult. The paper trail. She could be dead. Killed along the paper trail.

"Darby, are you there?"

"Yes." She looked at the door to make sure it was chained. "Yes, I'm here."

"Are you safe?"

"I thought so."

"We've got some information. There will be a memorial service tomorrow at three on campus, with burial afterward in the city. I've talked to his brother, and the family wants me to serve as a pallbearer. I'll be there tonight. I think we should meet."

"Why should we meet?"

"You've got to trust me, Darby. Your life is in danger right now, and you need to listen to me."

"What're you guys up to?"

There was a pause. "What do you mean?"

"What did Director Voyles say?"

"I haven't talked to him."

"I thought you were his attorney, so to speak. What's the matter, Gavin?"

"We're taking no action at this time."

"And what might that mean, Gavin? Talk to me."

"That's why we need to meet. I don't want to do this over the phone."

"The phone is working fine, and it's all you're going to get right now. So let's have it, Gavin."

"Why won't you trust me?" He was wounded.

"I'm hanging up, okay. I don't like this. If you guys know where I am, then someone could be out there in the hallway waiting."

"Nonsense, Darby. You've got to use your head. I've had your room number for an hour, and done nothing but call. We're on your side, I swear."

She thought about this. It made sense, but they had found her so easily. "I'm listening. You haven't talked to the Director, but the FBI's taking no action. Why not?"

"I'm not sure. He made the decision yesterday to back off the pelican brief, and gave instructions to leave it alone. That's all I can tell you."

"That's not very much. Does he know about Thomas? Does he know that I'm supposed to be dead because I wrote it and forty-eight hours after Thomas gave it to you, his old buddy from law school, they, whoever in hell they are, tried to kill both of us? Does he know all this, Gavin?"

"I don't think so."

"That means no, doesn't it?"

"Yes. It means no."

"Okay, listen to me. Do you think he was killed because of the brief?"

"Probably."

"That means yes, doesn't it?"

"Yes."

"Thanks. If Thomas was murdered because of the brief, then we know who killed him. And if we know who killed Thomas, then we know who killed Rosenberg and Jensen. Right?"

Verheek hesitated.

"Just say yes, dammit!" Darby snapped.

"I'll say probably."

"Fine. *Probably* means yes for a lawyer. I know it's the best you can do. It's a very strong *probably*, yet you're telling me the FBI is backing off my little suspect."

"Settle down, Darby. Let's meet tonight and talk about it. I could save your life."

She carefully laid the receiver under a pillow, and walked to the bathroom. She brushed her teeth and what was left of her hair, then threw the toiletries and change of clothes into a new canvas bag. She put on the parka, cap, and sunglasses, and quietly closed the door behind her. The hall was empty. She walked up two flights to the seventeenth, then took the elevator to the tenth, then casually walked down ten flights to the lobby. The door from the stairway opened near the rest rooms, and she was quickly inside the women's. The lobby appeared to be deserted. She went to a stall, locked the door, and waited for a while.

FRIDAY MORNING in the Quarter. The air was cool and clean without the lingering smell of food and sin. Eight A.M.—too early for people. She walked a few blocks to clear her head and plan the day. On Dumaine near Jackson Square she found a coffee shop she'd seen before. It was nearly empty and had a pay phone in the back. She poured her own thick coffee, and set it on a table near the phone. She could talk here.

Verheek was on the phone in less than a minute. "I'm listening," he said.

"Where will you stay tonight?" she asked, watching the front door.

"Hilton, by the river."

"I know where it is. I'll call late tonight or early in the morning. Don't track me again. I'm into cash now. No plastic."

"That's smart, Darby. Keep moving."

"I may be dead by the time you get here."

"No, you won't. Can you find a *Washington Post* down there?"

"Maybe. Why?"

"Get one quick. This morning's. Nice little story about Rosenberg and Jensen and perhaps who done it."

"I can't wait. I'll call later."

The first newsstand did not have the *Post*. She zigzagged toward Canal, covering her tracks, watching her rear, down St. Ann, along the antique shops on Royal, through the seedy bars on both sides of Bienville, and finally to the French Market along Decatur and North Peters. She was quick but nonchalant. She walked with an air of business, her eyes darting in all directions behind the shades. If they were back there somewhere in the shadows watching and keeping up, they were good.

She bought a *Post* and a *Times-Picayune* from a sidewalk vendor, and found a table in a deserted corner of Café du Monde.

Front page. Citing a confidential source, the story dwelt on the legend of Khamel and his sudden involvement in the killings. In his younger days, it said, he had killed for his beliefs, but now he just did it for money. Lots of money, speculated a retired intelligence expert who allowed himself to be quoted but certainly not identified. The photos were blurred and indistinct, but ominous beside each other. They could not be of the same person. But then, said the expert, he was unidentifiable and had not been photographed in over a decade.

A waiter finally made it by, and she ordered coffee and a plain bagel. The expert said many thought he was dead. Interpol believed he had killed as recently as six months ago. The expert doubted he would travel by commercial air. The FBI had him at the top of their list.

She opened the New Orleans paper slowly. Thomas did not make page one, but his picture was on page two with a long story. The cops were treating it as a homicide, but there wasn't much to go on. A white female had been seen in the area shortly before the explosion. The law school was in shock, according to the dean. The cops said little. Services were tomorrow on campus. A horrible mistake had been made, the dean said. If it was murder, then someone had obviously killed the wrong person.

Her eyes were wet, and suddenly she was afraid again. Maybe it was simply a mistake. It was a violent city with crazy people, and maybe someone got their wires crossed and the wrong car was chosen. Maybe there was no one out there stalking her.

She put the sunglasses on and looked at his photo. They had pulled it from the law school annual, and there was that smirk he habitually wore when he was the professor. He was clean shaven, and so handsome.

GRANTHAM'S KHAMEL STORY electrified Washington Friday morning. It mentioned neither the memo nor the White House, so the hottest game in town was speculating about the source.

The game was especially hot in the Hoover Building. In the office of the Director, Eric East and K. O. Lewis paced nervously about while Voyles talked to the President for the third time in two hours. Voyles was cussing, not directly at the President, but all around him. He cussed Coal, and when the President cussed back, Voyles suggested they set up the polygraph, strap in everyone on his staff, beginning with Coal, and just see where the damned leaks were coming from. Yes, hell yes, he, Voyles, would take the test, and so would everyone who worked in the Hoover Building. And they cussed back and forth. Voyles was red and sweating, and the fact that he was yelling into the telephone and the President was on the other end receiving all this mattered not a bit. He knew Coal was listening somewhere.

Evidently, the President gained control of the conversation and launched into a long-winded sermon of some sort. Voyles wiped his forehead with a handkerchief, sat in his ancient leather swivel, and began controlled breathing to lower the pressure and pulse. He had survived one heart attack and was due for another, and had told K. O. Lewis many times that Fletcher Coal and his idiot boss would eventually kill him. But he'd said that about the last three Presidents. He pinched the fat wrinkles on his forehead and sunk lower into the chair. "We can do that, Mr. President." He was almost pleasant now. He was a man of swift and radical mood swings, and suddenly before their eyes he was courteous. A real charmer. "Thank you, Mr. President. I'll be there tomorrow."

He hung up gently, and spoke with his eyes closed. "He wants us to place that *Post* reporter under surveillance. Says we've done it before, so will we do it again? I told him we would."

"What type of surveillance?" asked K.O.

"Let's just follow him in the city. Around the clock with two men. See where he goes at night, who he sleeps with. He's single, isn't he?"

"Divorced seven years ago," Lewis answered.

"Make damned sure we don't get caught. Do it with plainclothes, and switch 'em up every three days."

"Does he really believe the leaks are coming from us?"

"No, I don't think so. If we were leaking, why would he want us to trail the reporter? I think he knows it's his own people. And he wants to catch them."

"It's a small favor," Lewis added helpfully.

"Yeah. Just don't get caught, okay?"

THE OFFICE of L. Matthew Barr was tucked away on the third floor of a tacky and decaying office building on M Street in Georgetown. There were no signs on the doors. An armed guard in a coat and tie turned people away at the elevator. The carpet was worn and the furniture was old. Dust covered it, and it was apparent the Unit spent no money on housekeeping.

Barr ran the Unit, which was an unofficial, hidden, little division of the Committee to Reelect the President. CRP had a vast suite of plush offices across the river in Rosslyn. It had windows that opened and secretaries who smiled and maids that cleaned every night. But not this dump.

Fletcher Coal stepped off the elevator and nodded at the security guard, who nodded back without making another move. They were old acquaintances. He made his way through the small maze of dingy offices in the direction of Barr's. Coal took pride in being honest with himself, and he honestly did not fear any man in Washington, maybe with the possible exception of Matthew Barr. Sometimes he feared him, sometimes not, but he always admired him.

Barr was an ex-Marine, ex-CIA, ex-spy with two felony convictions for security scams from which he earned millions and buried the money. He had served a few months in one of the country clubs, but no real time. Coal had personally recruited Barr to head the Unit, which officially did not exist. It had an annual budget of four million, all cash from various slush funds, and Barr supervised a small band of highly trained thugs who quietly did the work of the Unit.

Barr's door was always locked. He opened it and Coal entered. The meeting would be brief, as usual.

"Let me guess," Barr started. "You want to find the leak."

"In a way, yes. I want you to follow this reporter, Grantham, around the clock and see who he's talking to. He's getting some awfully good stuff, and I'm afraid it's coming from us."

"You're leaking like cardboard."

"We've got some problems, but the Khamel story was a plant. Did it myself."

Barr smiled at this. "I thought so. It seemed too clean and pat."

"Did you ever run across Khamel?"

"No. Ten years ago we were sure he was dead. He likes it that way. He has no ego, so he'll never get caught. He can live in a paper shack in São Paulo for six months, eating roots and rats, then fly off to Rome to murder a diplomat, then off to Singapore for a few months. He doesn't read his press clippings."

"How old is he?"

"Why are you interested?"

"I'm fascinated. I think I know who hired him to kill Rosenberg and Jensen."

"Oh, really. Can you share this bit of gossip?"

"No. Not yet."

"He's between forty and forty-five, which is not that old, but he killed a Lebanese general when he was fifteen. So he's had a long career. This is all legend, you understand. He can kill with either hand, either foot, a car key, a pencil, whatever. He's an expert marksman with all weapons. Speaks twelve languages. You've heard all this, haven't you?"

"Yeah, but it's fun."

"Okay. He's believed to be the most proficient and expensive assassin in the world. In his early years he was just another terrorist, but he was much too talented for simple bomb throwing. So he became an assassin for hire. He's a bit older now, and kills just for money."

"How much money?"

"Good question. He's probably in the ten-to-twenty-million-a-job range, and there's not but one other guy I know of in that league. One theory believes he shares it with other terrorist groups. No one knows, really. Let me guess, you want me to find Khamel and bring him back alive."

"You leave Khamel alone. I sort of like the work he did here."

"He's very talented."

"I want you to follow Gray Grantham and find out who he's talking to."

"Any ideas?"

"A couple. There's a man by the name of Milton Hardy who works as a janitor in the West Wing." Coal threw an envelope on the desk. "He's been around for a long time, appears to be half blind, but I think he sees and hears a lot. Follow him for a week or two. Everyone calls him Sarge. Make plans to take him out."

"This is great, Coal. We're spending all this money to track blind Negroes."

"Just do as I say. Make it three weeks." Coal stood and headed for the door.

"So you know who hired the killer?" Barr said.

"We're getting close."

"The Unit is more than anxious to help."

"I'm sure."

NINETEEN

MRS. CHEN owned the duplex, and had been renting the other half to female law students for fifteen years. She was picky but private, and lived and let live as long as all was quiet. It was six blocks from campus.

It was dark when she answered the door. The person on the porch was an attractive young lady with short dark hair and a nervous smile. Very nervous.

Mrs. Chen frowned at her until she spoke.

"I'm Alice Stark, a friend of Darby's. May I come in?" She glanced over her shoulder. The street was quiet and still. Mrs. Chen lived alone with the doors and windows locked tightly, but she was a pretty girl with an innocent smile, and if she was a friend of Darby's, then she could be trusted. She opened the door, and Alice was inside.

"Something's wrong," Mrs. Chen said.

"Yes. Darby is in a bit of trouble, but we can't talk about it. Did she call this afternoon?"

"Yes. She said a young woman would look through her apartment."

Alice breathed deeply and tried to appear calm. "It'll just take a minute. She said there was a door through a wall somewhere. I prefer not to use the front or rear doors." Mrs. Chen frowned and her eyes asked, Why not? but she said nothing.

"Has anyone been in the apartment in the last two days?" Alice asked. She followed Mrs. Chen down a narrow hallway.

"I've seen no one. There was a knock early yesterday before the sun, but I didn't look." She moved a table away from a door, pushed a key around, and opened it.

Alice stepped in front of her. "She wanted me to go in alone, okay?" Mrs. Chen wanted to check it out, but she nodded and closed the door behind Alice. It opened into a tiny hallway that was suddenly dark. To the left was the den, and a light switch that couldn't be used. Alice froze in the darkness. The apartment was black and hot with a thick smell of old garbage. She'd expected to be alone, but she was a second-year law student, dammit!, not some hotshot private detective.

Get a grip. She fumbled through a large purse and found a pencil-thin flashlight. There were three of them in there. Just in case. In case of what? She didn't know. Darby had been quite specific. No lights could be seen through the windows. They could be watching.

Who in hell are they? Alice wanted to know. Darby didn't know, said she would explain it later but first the apartment had to be examined.

Alice had been in the apartment a dozen times in the past year, but she'd been allowed to enter through the front door with a full array of lights and other conveniences. She had been in all the rooms, and felt confident she could feel around in the darkness. The confidence was gone. Vanished. Replaced with trembling fear.

Get a grip. You're all alone. They wouldn't camp out here with a nosy woman next door. If they had indeed been here, it was only for a brief visit.

After staring at the end of it, she determined that the flashlight worked. It glowed with all the energy of a fading match. She pointed it at the floor, and saw a faint round circle the size of a small orange. The circle was shaking.

She tiptoed around a corner in the direction of the den. Darby said there was a small lamp on the bookshelves next to the television, and that the light was always on. She used it as a nightlight, and it was supposed to cast a faint glow across the den to the kitchen. Either Darby lied, or the bulb was gone, or someone had unscrewed it. It didn't matter, really, at this point, because the den and kitchen were pitch-black.

She was on the rug in the center of the den, inching toward the kitchen table where there was supposed to be a computer. She kicked the edge of the coffee table, and the flashlight quit. She shook it. Nothing. She found number two in the purse.

The odor was heavier in the kitchen. The computer was on the table along with an assortment of empty files and casebooks. She examined the mainframe with her dinky little light. The power switch was on the front. She pushed it, and the monochrome screen slowly warmed up. It emitted a greenish light that covered the table but did not escape the kitchen.

Alice sat down in front of the keyboard and began pecking. She found Menu, then List, then Files. The Directory covered the screen. She studied it closely. There were supposed to be somewhere around forty entries, but she saw no more than ten. Most of the hard-drive memory was gone. She turned on the laser printer, and within seconds the Directory was on paper. She tore it off and stuffed it in the purse.

She stood with her flashlight and inspected the clutter around the computer. Darby estimated the number of floppy disks at twenty, but they were all gone. Not a single floppy. The casebooks were for con law and civil procedure, and so dull and generic no one would want them. The red expandable files were stacked neatly together, but empty.

It was a clean, patient job. He or they had spent a couple of hours erasing and gathering, then left with no more than one briefcase or bag of goods.

In the den by the television, Alice peeked out the side window. The red Accord was still there, not four feet from the window. It looked fine.

She twisted the bulb in the nightlight, and quickly flicked the switch on, then off. Worked perfectly. She unscrewed it just as he or they had left it.

Her eyes had focused; she could see the outlines of doors and furniture. She turned the computer off, and eased through the den to the hall.

Mrs. Chen was waiting exactly where she'd left her. "Okay?" she asked.

"Everything's fine," Alice said. "Just watch it real close. I'll call you in a day or two to see if anyone has been by. And please, don't tell anyone I was here."

Mrs. Chen listened intently as she moved the table in front of the door. "What about her car?"

"It'll be fine. Just watch it."

"Is she all right?"

They were in the den, almost to the front door. "She's gonna be fine. I think she'll be back in a few days. Thank you, Mrs. Chen."

Mrs. Chen closed the door, bolted it, and watched from the small window. The lady was on the sidewalk, then gone in the darkness.

Alice walked three blocks to her car.

FRIDAY NIGHT in the Quarter! Tulane played in the Dome tomorrow, then the Saints on Sunday, and the rowdies were out by the thousands, parking everywhere, blocking streets, roaming in noisy mobs, drinking from go cups, crowding bars, just having a delightful time raising hell and enjoying themselves. The Inner Quarter was gridlocked by nine.

Alice parked on Poydras, far away from where she wanted to park, and was an hour late when she arrived at the crowded oyster bar on St. Peter, deep in the Quarter. There were no tables. They were packed three deep at the bar. She retreated to a corner with a cigarette machine, and surveyed the people. Most were students in town for the game.

A waiter walked directly to her. "Are you looking for another female?" he asked.

She hesitated. "Well, yes."

He pointed beyond the bar. "Around the corner, first room on the right, there's some small tables. I think your friend is there."

Darby was in a tiny booth, crouched over a beer bottle, with sunglasses and a hat. Alice squeezed her hand. "It's good to see you." She studied the hairdo, and was amused by it. Darby removed the sunglasses. The eyes were red and tired.

"I didn't know who else to call."

Alice listened with a blank face, unable to think of something appropriate and unable to take her eyes off the hair. "Who did the hair?" she asked.

"Nice, huh. It's sort of the punk look, which I think is making a comeback and will certainly impress folks when I start interviewing for a job."

"Why?"

"Someone tried to kill me, Alice. My name's on a list that some very nasty people are holding. I think they're following me."

"Kill? Did you say 'kill'? Who would want to kill you, Darby?"

"I'm not sure. What about my apartment?"

Alice stopped looking at the hair, and handed her the printout of the Directory. Darby studied it. It was real. This was not a dream or a mistake. The bomb had found the right car. Rupert and the cowboy had had their hands on her. The face she had seen was looking for her. They had gone to her apartment and erased what they wanted to erase. They were out there.

"What about floppies?"

"None. Not a single one. The expandable files on the kitchen table were placed together real neat and are real empty. Everything else appears to be in order. They unscrewed the bulb in the nightlight, so there's total darkness. I checked it. Works fine. These are very patient people."

"What about Mrs. Chen?"

"She's seen nothing."

Darby stuffed the printout into a pocket. "Look, Alice, suddenly I'm very scared. You don't need to be seen with me. Maybe this was not a good idea."

"Who are these people?"

"I don't know. They killed Thomas, and they tried to kill me. I got lucky, and now they're after me."

"But why, Darby?"

"You don't want to know, and I'm not going to tell. The more you know, the more danger you're in. Trust me, Alice. I can't tell you what I know."

"But I won't tell. I swear."

"What if they make you tell?"

Alice glanced around as if all was fine. She studied her friend. They had been close since freshman orientation. They had studied hours together, shared notes, sweated exams, teamed up for mock trials, gossiped about men. Alice was hopefully the only student who knew about Darby and Callahan. "I want to help, Darby. I'm not afraid."

Darby had not touched the beer. She slowly spun the bottle. "Well, I'm terrified. I was there when he died, Alice. The ground shook. He was blown to pieces and I was supposed to be with him. It was intended for me."

"Then go to the cops."

"Not yet. Maybe later. I'm afraid to. Thomas went to the FBI, and two days later we were supposed to be dead."

"So the FBI is after you?"

"I don't think so. They started talking, and someone was listening very closely, and it found the wrong ears."

"Talked about what! Come on, Darby. It's me. Your best friend. Stop playing games."

Darby took the first tiny swallow from the bottle. Eye contact was avoided. She stared at the table. "Please, Alice. Allow me to wait. There's no sense telling you something that could get you killed." A long pause. "If you want to help, go to the memorial service tomorrow. Watch everything. Spread the word that I called you from Denver where I'm staying with an aunt with a name you don't know, and that I've dropped out this semester but I'll be back in the spring. Make sure that rumor gets started. I think some people will be listening carefully."

"Okay. The paper mentioned a white female near the scene when he was killed, as if she might be a suspect or something."

"Or something. I was there and I was supposed to be a victim. I'm reading the papers with a magnifying glass. The cops are clueless."

"Okay, Darby. You're smarter than I am. You're smarter than every person I've ever met. So what now?"

"First, go out the back door. There's a white door at the end of the hall where the rest rooms are. It goes into a storage room, then to the kitchen, then out the back door. Don't stop. The alley leads to Royal. Catch a cab and ride back to your car. Watch your rear."

"Are you serious?"

"Look at this hair, Alice. Would I mutilate myself like this if I was playing games?"

"Okay, okay. Then what?"

"Go to the service tomorrow, start the rumor, and I'll call you within two days."

"Where are you staying?"

"Here and there. I move around a lot."

Alice stood and pecked her on the cheek. Then she was gone.

FOR TWO HOURS, Verheek stomped the floor, picking up magazines, tossing them around, ordering room service, unpacking, stomping. Then for the next two hours, he sat on the bed, sipping a hot beer and staring at the phone. He would do this until midnight, he told himself, and then, well, then what?

She said she would call.

He could save her life if she would only call.

At midnight, he threw another magazine and left the room. An agent in the New Orleans office had helped a little, and given him a couple of law school hangouts close to campus. He would go there and mix and mingle, drink a beer, and listen. The students were in town for the game. She wouldn't be there, and it wouldn't matter because he'd never seen her. But maybe he would hear something, and he could drop a name, leave a card, make a friend who knew her or maybe knew someone who knew her. A long shot, but a helluva lot more productive than staring at the phone.

He found a seat at the bar in a joint called Barrister's, three blocks from campus. It had a nice little varsity look to it with football schedules and pinups on the walls. The crowd was rowdy and under thirty.

The bartender looked like a student. After two beers, the

crowd thinned and the bar was half empty. There would be another wave in a moment.

Verheek ordered number three. It was one-thirty. "Are you a law student?" he asked the bartender.

"Afraid so."

"It's not that bad, is it?"

He was wiping around the peanuts. "I've had more fun."

Verheek longed for the bartenders who served his beer in law school. Those guys knew the art of conversation. Never met a stranger. Talk about anything.

"I'm a lawyer," Verheek said in desperation.

Oh, hey, wow, this guy's a lawyer. How rare. Someone special. The kid walked off.

Little son of a bitch. I hope you flunk out. Verheek grabbed his bottle and turned to face the tables. He felt like a grandfather amid the children. Though he hated law school and the memories of it, there had been some long Friday nights in the bars of Georgetown with his pal Callahan. Those were good memories.

"So what kind of law?" The bartender was back. Gavin turned to the bar, and smiled.

"Special counsel, FBI."

He was still wiping. "So you're in Washington?"

"Yeah, in town for the game Sunday. I'm a Redskins freak." He hated the Redskins and every other organized football team. Don't get the kid started on football. "Where do you go to school?"

"Here. Tulane. I'll finish in May."

"Then where?"

"Probably Cincinnati for a clerkship for a year or two."

"You must be a good student."

He shrugged it off. "You need a beer?"

"No. Did you have Thomas Callahan?"

"Sure. You know him?"

"I was in law school with him at Georgetown." Verheek pulled a card from his pocket and handed it to the kid. "I'm Gavin Verheek." The kid looked at it, then politely laid it next to the ice. The bar was quiet and the kid was tired of chitchat.

"Do you know a student by the name of Darby Shaw?"

The kid glanced at the tables. "No. I haven't met her, but I know who she is. I think she's second year." A long, rather suspicious pause. "Why?"

"We need to talk to her." We, as in FBI. Not simply he, as in Gavin Verheek. The "we" part sounded much graver. "Does she hang out in here?"

"I've seen her a few times. She's hard to miss."

"I've heard." Gavin looked at the tables. "Do you think these guys might know her?"

"Doubt it. They're all first year. Can't you tell? They're over there arguing property rights and search and seizure."

Yeah, those were the days. Gavin pulled a dozen cards from his pocket and laid them on the bar. "I'll be at the Hilton for a few days. If you see her, or hear anything, drop one of these."

"Sure. There was a cop in last night asking questions. You don't think she was involved in his death?"

"No, not at all. We just need to talk to her."

"I'll keep my eyes open."

Verheek paid for the beer, thanked the kid again, and was on the sidewalk. He walked three blocks to the Half Shell. It was almost two. He was dead tired, half drunk, and a band cranked up the second he walked through the door. The place was dark, packed, and fifty fraternity joes with their sorority sues were immediately dancing on tables. He weaved through the uprising and found safety in the back near the bar. They were three deep, shoulder to shoulder, and no one moved. He clawed his way forward, got a beer to be cool, and realized again he was by far the oldest one there. He retreated to a dark but crowded corner. It was hopeless. He couldn't hear himself think, let alone carry on a conversation.

He watched the bartenders: all young, all students. The oldest looked late twenties, and he rang up check after check as if he was closing out. His moves were hurried, as if it was time to go. Gavin studied every move.

He quickly untied his apron, flung it in a corner, ducked under the bar, and was gone. Gavin elbowed through the mob, and caught him as he stepped through the kitchen door. He had an FBI business card ready. "I'm sorry. I'm with the FBI." He stuck the card in his face. "Your name is?"

The kid froze, and looked wildly at Verheek. "Uh, Fountain. Jeff Fountain."

"Fine, Jeff. Look, nothing's wrong, okay? Just a couple of questions." The kitchen had shut down hours ago, and they were alone. "Just take a second."

"Well, okay. What's up?"

"You're a law student, right?" Please say yes. His friend said most of the bartenders here were law students.

"Yes. At Loyola."

Loyola! Where the hell! "Yeah, well, that's what I thought. You've heard about Professor Callahan at Tulane. Funeral's tomorrow."

"Sure. It's all over the papers. Most of my friends go to Tulane."

"Do you know a second-year student there by the name of Darby Shaw? Very attractive female."

Fountain smiled. "Yeah, she dated a friend of mine last year. She's in here occasionally."

"How long ago?"

"It's been a month or two. What's wrong?"

"We need to talk to her." He handed Fountain a stack of cards. "Hang on to these. I'll be at the Hilton for a few days. If you see her around, or if you hear anything, drop one of these."

"What might I hear?"

"Something about Callahan. We need to see her real bad, okay?"

"Sure." He stuck the cards in a pocket.

Verheek thanked him and returned to the revelry. He inched through the mob, listening to the attempts at conversation. A fresh mob was entering, and he wrestled his way out the door. He was too old for this.

Six blocks away, he parked illegally in front of a fraternity house next to the campus. His last stop for the night would be a dark little pool hall, which, at the moment, was not crowded. He paid for beer at the bar, and surveyed the place. There were four pool tables and the action was light. A young man in a T-shirt walked to the bar and ordered another beer. The shirt was green and gray with the words TULANE LAW SCHOOL stamped across the front with what appeared to be an inmate identification number under the words.

Verheek spoke without hesitating. "You a law student?"

The young man glanced at him while pulling money from his jeans. "Afraid so."

"Did you know Thomas Callahan?"

"Who are you?"

"FBI. Callahan was a friend of mine."

The student sipped the beer and was suspicious. "I was in his con law class."

Bingo! So was Darby. Verheek tried to appear uninterested. "Do you know Darby Shaw?"

"Why do you want to know?"

"We need to talk to her. That's all."

"Who is we?" The student was even more suspicious. He took a step closer to Gavin as if he wanted some hard answers.

"FBI," Verheek said nonchalantly.

"You got a badge or something?"

"Sure," he said as he pulled a card from his pocket. The student read it carefully, then handed it back. "You're a lawyer, not an agent."

This was a very valid point, and the lawyer knew he would lose his job if his boss knew he was asking questions and in general impersonating an agent. "Yes, I'm a lawyer. Callahan and I were in law school together."

"Then why do you want to see Darby Shaw?"

The bartender had eased closer and was eavesdropping.

"Do you know her?"

"I don't know," the student said, and it was obvious he did in fact know her but was not about to talk. "Is she in trouble?"

"No. You know her, don't you?"

"Maybe. Maybe not."

"Look, what's your name?"

"Show me a badge, and I'll tell you my name."

Gavin took a long drink from the bottle and smiled at the

bartender. "I need to see her, okay. It's very important. I'll be at the Hilton for a few days. If you see her, ask her to call." He offered the card to the student, who looked at it and walked away.

AT THREE, he unlocked the door to his room, and checked the phone. No messages. Wherever Darby was, she still had not called. Assuming, of course, she was still alive.

TWENTY

GARCIA CALLED for the last time. Grantham took the call before dawn Saturday, less than two hours before they were to meet for the first time. He was backing out, he said. The time was not right. If the story broke, then some very powerful lawyers and their very rich clients would fall hard, and these people were not accustomed to falling, and they would take people with them. And Garcia might get hurt. He had a wife and little daughter. He had a job that he could endure because the money was great. Why take chances? He had done nothing wrong. His conscience was clear.

"Then why do you keep calling me?" Grantham asked.

"I think I know why they were killed. I'm not certain, but I've got a good idea. I saw something, okay."

"We've had this conversation for a week now, Garcia. You saw something, or you have something. And it's all useless unless you show it to me." Grantham opened a file and took out the five by sevens of the man on the phone. "You're driven by a sense of morality, Garcia. That's why you want to talk."

"Yeah, but there's a chance they know that I know. They've been treating me funny, as if they want to ask if I saw it. But they can't ask because they're not sure."

"These are the guys in your firm?"

"Yeah. No. Wait. How'd you know I was in a firm? I haven't told you that."

"It's easy. You go to work too early to be a government lawyer. You're in one of those two-hundred-lawyer firms where they expect the associates and junior partners to work a hundred hours a week. The first time you called me you said you were on the way to the office, and it was something like 5 A.M."

"Well, well, what else do you know?"

"Not much. We're playing games, Garcia. If you're not willing to talk, then hang up and leave me alone. I'm losing sleep."

"Sweet dreams." Garcia hung up. Grantham stared at the receiver.

THREE TIMES in the past eight years he had unlisted his phone number. He lived by the phone, and his biggest stories came out of nowhere over the phone. But after or during each big one, there had been a thousand insignificant ones from sources who felt compelled to call at all hours of the night with their hot little morsels. He was known as a reporter who would face a firing squad before revealing a source, so they called and called and called. He'd get sick of it, and get a new, unlisted number. Then hit a dry spell. Then rush to get back in the D.C. directory.

He was there now. Gray S. Grantham. The only one in the book. They could get him at work twelve hours a day, but it was so much more secretive and private to call him at home, especially at odd hours when he was trying to sleep.

He fumed over Garcia for thirty minutes, then fell asleep. He was in a rhythm and dead to the world when it rang again. He found it in the darkness. "Hello."

It was not Garcia. It was a female. "Is this Gray Grantham with the *Washington Post*?"

"It is. And who are you?"

"Are you still on the story about Rosenberg and Jensen?"

He sat in the darkness and stared at the clock. Five-thirty. "It's a big story. We've got a lot of people on it, but, yes, I'm investigating."

"Have you heard of the pelican brief?"

He breathed deeply and tried to think. "The pelican brief. No. What is it?"

"It's a harmless little theory about who killed them. It was taken to Washington last Sunday by a man named Thomas Callahan, a professor of law at Tulane. He gave it to a friend with the FBI, and it was passed around. Things snowballed, and Callahan was killed in a car bombing Wednesday night in New Orleans."

The lamp was on and he was scribbling. "Where are you calling from?"

"New Orleans. A pay phone, so don't bother."

"How do you know all this?"

"I wrote the brief."

He was wide awake now, wild-eyed and breathing rapidly. "Okay. If you wrote it, tell me about it."

"I don't want to do it that way, because even if you had a copy you couldn't run the story."

"Try me."

"You couldn't. It'll take some thorough verification."

"Okay. We've got the Klan, the terrorist Khamel, the Underground Army, the Aryans, the—"

"Nope. None of the above. They're a bit obvious. The brief is about an obscure suspect."

He was pacing at the foot of the bed, holding the phone. "Why can't you tell me who it is?"

"Maybe later. You seem to have these magical sources. Let's see what you find."

"Callahan will be easy to check out. That's one phone call. Give me twenty-four hours."

"I'll try to call Monday morning. If we're gonna do business, Mr. Grantham, you must show me something. The next time I call, tell me something I don't know."

She was at a pay phone in the dark. "Are you in danger?" he asked.

"I think so. But I'm okay for now."

She sounded young, mid-twenties, maybe. She wrote a brief. She knew the law professor. "Are you a lawyer?"

"No, and don't spend your time digging after me. You've got work to do, Mr. Grantham, or I'll go elsewhere."

"Fine. You need a name."

"I've got one."

"I mean a code name."

"You mean like spies and all. Gee, this could be fun."

"Either that or give me your real name."

"Nice try. Just call me Pelican."

HIS PARENTS were good Irish Catholics, but he had sort of quit many years ago. They were a handsome couple, dignified in mourning, well tanned and dressed. He had seldom mentioned them. They walked hand-in-hand with the rest of the family into Rogers Chapel. His brother from Mobile was shorter and looked much older. Thomas said he had a drinking problem.

For half an hour, students and faculty had streamed into the small chapel. The game was tonight and there was a nice crowd on campus. A television van was parked in the street. A cameraman kept a respectable distance and shot the front of the chapel. A campus policeman watched him carefully and kept him in place.

It was odd seeing these law students with dresses and heels and coats and ties. In a dark room on the third floor of Newcomb Hall, the Pelican sat with her face to the window and watched the students mill about and speak softly and finish their cigarettes. Under her chair were four newspapers, already read and discarded. She'd been there for two hours, reading by sunlight and waiting on the service. There was no other place to be. She was certain the bad guys were lurking in the bushes around the chapel, but she was learning patience. She had come early, would stay late, and move in the shadows. If they found her, maybe they would do it quick and it would be over.

She gripped a wadded paper towel and dried her eyes. It was okay to cry now, but this was the last one. The people were all inside, and the television van left. The paper said it was a memorial service with private burial later. There was no casket inside.

She had selected this moment to run, to rent a car and drive to Baton Rouge, then jump on the first plane headed to any place except New Orleans. She would get out of the country, perhaps Montreal or Calgary. She would hide there for a year and hope the crime would be solved and the bad guys put away.

But it was a dream. The quickest route to justice ran smack through her. She knew more than anyone. The Fibbies had circled close, then backed off, and were now chasing who knows who. Verheek had gotten nowhere, and he was close to the Director. She would have to piece it together. Her little brief had killed Thomas, and now they were after her. She knew the identity of the man behind the murders of Rosenberg and Jensen and Callahan, and this knowledge made her rather unique.

Suddenly, she leaned forward. The tears dried on her cheeks. There he was! The thin man with the narrow face! He was wearing a coat and tie and looked properly mournful as he walked quickly to the chapel. It was him! The man she'd last seen in the lobby of the Sheraton on, when was it, Thursday morning. She'd been talking to Verheek when he strolled suspiciously through.

He stopped at the door, jerked his head nervously around—he was a klutz, really, a giveaway. He stared for a second at three cars parked innocently on the street, less than fifty yards away. He opened the door, and was in the chapel. Beautiful. The bastards killed him, and now they joined his family and friends for last respects.

Her nose touched the window. The cars were too far away, but she was certain there was a man in one watching for her. Surely they knew she was not so dumb and so heartbroken as to show up and mourn her lover. They knew that. She had eluded them for two and a half days. The tears were gone.

Ten minutes later, the thin man came out by himself, lit a cigarette, and strolled with hands stuck deep in his pockets toward the three cars. He was sad. What a guy.

He walked in front of the cars but did not stop. When he was out of sight, a door opened and a man in a green Tulane sweatshirt emerged from the middle car. He walked down the street after the thin one. He was not thin. He was short, thick, and powerful. A regular stump.

He disappeared down the sidewalk behind the thin man, behind the chapel. Darby poised on the edge of the folding chair. Within a minute, they emerged on the sidewalk from behind the building. They were together now, whispering, but for only a moment because the thin man peeled off and disappeared down the street. Stump walked quickly to his car and got in. He just sat there, waiting for the service to break up and get one last look at the crowd on the off chance that she was in fact stupid enough to show up.

It had taken less than ten minutes for the thin man to sneak inside, scan the crowd of, say, two hundred people, and determine she was not there. Perhaps he was looking for the red hair. Or bleached blond. No, it made more sense for them to have people already in there, sitting around prayerfully and looking sad, looking for her or anyone who might resemble her. They could nod or shake or wink at the thin man.

This place was crawling with them.

HAVANA was a perfect sanctuary. It mattered not if ten or a hundred countries had bounties on his throat. Fidel was an admirer and occasional client. They drank together, shared women, and smoked cigars. He had the run of the place: a nice little apartment on Calle de Torre in the old section, a car with a driver, a banker who was a wizard at blitzing money around the world, any size boat he wanted, a military plane if needed, and plenty of young women. He spoke the language and his skin was not pale. He loved the place.

He had once agreed to kill Fidel, but couldn't do it. He was in place and two hours away from the murder, but just wouldn't pull it off. There was too much admiration. It was back in the days when he did not always kill for money. He pulled a double cross, and confessed to Fidel. They faked an ambush, and word spread that the great Khamel had been gunned down in the streets of Havana.

Never again would he travel by commercial air. The photographs in Paris were embarrassing for such a professional. He was losing his touch; getting careless in the twilight of his career. Got his picture on the front pages in America. How shameful. His client was not pleased.

The boat was a forty-foot schooner with two crew members and a young woman, all Cubans. She was below in the cabin. He had finished with her a few minutes before they saw the lights of Biloxi. He was all business now, inspecting his raft, packing his bag, saying nothing. The crew members crouched on the deck and stayed away from him.

At exactly nine, they lowered the raft onto the water. He dropped his bag into it, and was gone. They heard the trolling motor as he disappeared into the blackness of the Sound. They were to remain anchored until dawn, then haul it back to Havana. They held perfect papers declaring them to be Americans, in the event they were discovered and someone began asking questions.

He eased patiently through the still water, dodging buoy lights and the sight of an occasional small craft. He held perfect papers too, and three weapons in the bag.

It had been years since he struck twice in one month. After he was allegedly gunned down in Cuba, there had been a five-year drought. Patience was his forte. He averaged one a year.

And this little victim would go unnoticed. No one would suspect him. It was such a small job, but his client was adamant and he happened to be in the neighborhood, and the money was right, so here he was in another six-foot rubber raft cruising toward a beach, hoping like hell his pal Luke would be there dressed not as a farmer, but a fisherman this time.

This would be the last for a long time, maybe forever. He had more money than he could ever spend or give away. And he had started making small mistakes.

He saw the pier in the distance, and moved away from it. He had thirty minutes to waste. He followed the shoreline for a quarter of a mile, then headed for it. Two hundred yards out, he turned off the trolling motor, unhitched it, and dropped it into the water. He lay low in the raft, worked a plastic oar when necessary, and gently guided himself to a dark spot behind a row of cheap brick buildings thirty feet ashore. He stood in two feet of water and ripped holes in the raft with a small pocketknife. It sank and disappeared. The beach was deserted.

Luke was alone at the end of the pier. It was exactly eleven, and he was in place with a rod and reel. He wore a white cap, and the bill moved slowly back and forth as he scanned the water in search of the raft. He checked his watch.

Suddenly a man was beside him, appearing from nowhere like an angel. "Luke?" the man said.

This was not the code. Luke was startled. He had a gun in the tackle box at his feet, but there was no way. "Sam?" he asked. Maybe he had missed something. Maybe Khamel couldn't find the pier from the raft.

"Yes, Luke, it's me. Sorry about the deviation. Trouble with the raft."

Luke's heart settled and he breathed relief.

"Where's the vehicle?" Khamel asked.

Luke glanced at him ever so quickly. Yes, it was Khamel, and he was staring at the ocean behind dark glasses.

Luke nodded at a building. "Red Pontiac next to the liquor store."

"How far to New Orleans?"

"Half an hour," Luke said as he reeled in nothing.

Khamel stepped back, and hit him twice at the base of the neck. Once with each hand. The vertebrae burst and snapped the spinal cord. Luke fell hard and moaned once. Khamel watched him die, then found the keys in a pocket. He kicked the corpse off into the water.

EDWIN SNELLER or whatever his name was did not open the door, but quietly slid the key under it. Khamel picked it up, and opened the door to the next room. He walked in, and moved quickly to the bed where he placed his bag, then to the window where the curtains were open and the river was in the distance. He pulled the curtains together, and studied the lights of the French Quarter below.

He walked to the phone and punched Sneller's number.

"Tell me about her," Khamel said softly to the floor.

"There are two photos in the briefcase."

Khamel opened it and removed the photos. "I've got them."

"They're numbered, one and two. One we got from the law school yearbook. It's about a year old, and the most current we have. It's a blowup from a tiny picture, so we lost a lot of detail. The other photo is two years old. We lifted it from a yearbook at Arizona State."

Khamel held both pictures. "A beautiful woman."

"Yes. Quite beautiful. All that lovely hair is gone, though. Thursday night she paid for a hotel room with a credit card. We barely missed her Friday morning. We found long strands of hair on the floor and a small sample of something we now know to be black hair color. Very black."

"What a shame."

"We haven't seen her since Wednesday night. She's proven to be elusive: credit card for a room Wednesday, credit card at another hotel Thursday, then nothing from last night. She withdrew five thousand in cash from her checking account Friday afternoon, so the trail has become cold."

"Maybe she's gone."

"Could be, but I don't think so. Someone was in her apartment last night. We've got the place wired, and we were late by two minutes."

"Moving sort of slow, aren't you?"

"It's a big town. We've camped out at the airport and train station. We're watching her mother's house in Idaho. No sign. I think she's still here."

"Where would she be?"

"Moving around, changing hotels, using pay phones, staying away from the usual places. The New Orleans police are looking for her. They talked to her after the bomb Wednesday, then lost her. We're looking, they're looking, she'll turn up."

"What happened with the bomb?"

"Very simple. She didn't get in the car."

"Who made the bomb?"

Sneller hesitated. "Can't say."

Khamel smiled slightly as he took some street maps from the briefcase. "Tell me about the maps."

"Oh, just a few points of interest around town. Her place, his place, the law school, the hotels she's been to, the bomb site, a few little bars she enjoys as a student."

"She's stayed in the Quarter so far."

"She's smart. There are a million places to hide."

Khamel picked up the most recent photo, and sat on the other bed. He liked this face. Even with short dark hair, it would be an intriguing face. He could kill it, but it would not be pleasant.

"It's a shame, isn't it?" he said, almost to himself.

"Yes. It's a shame."

TWENTY-ONE

GAVIN VERHEEK had been a tired old man when he arrived in New Orleans, and after two nights of barhopping he was drained and weakened. He had hit the first bar not long after the burial, and for seven hours had sipped beer with the young and restless while talking of torts and contracts and Wall Street firms and other things he despised. He knew he shouldn't tell strangers he was FBI. He wasn't FBI. There was no badge.

He prowled five or six bars Saturday night. Tulane lost again, and after the game the bars filled with rowdies. Things got hopeless, and he quit at midnight.

He was sleeping hard with his shoes on when the phone rang. He lunged for it. "Hello! Hello!"

"Gavin?" she asked.

"Darby! Is this you?"

"Who else?"

"Why haven't you called before now?"

"Please, don't start asking a bunch of stupid questions. I'm at a pay phone, so no funny stuff."

"Come on, Darby. I swear you can trust me."

"Okay, I trust you. Now what?"

He looked at his watch, and began untying his shoelaces. "Well, you tell me. What's next? How long do you plan to hide in New Orleans?"

"How do you know I'm in New Orleans?"

He paused for a second.

"I'm in New Orleans," she said. "And I assume you want me to meet with you, and become close friends, then come in, as you say, and trust you guys to protect me forever."

"That's correct. You'll be dead in a matter of days if you don't."

"Get right to the point, don't you?"

"Yes. You're playing games and you don't know what you're doing."

"Who's after me, Gavin?"

"Could be a number of people."

"Who are they?"

"I don't know."

"Now you're playing games, Gavin. How can I trust you if you won't talk to me?"

"Okay. I think it's safe to say your little brief hit someone in the gut. You guessed right, the wrong people learned of the brief, and now Thomas is dead. And they'll kill you the instant they find you."

"We know who killed Rosenberg and Jensen, don't we, Gavin?"

"I think we do."

"Then why doesn't the FBI do something?"

"We may be in the midst of a cover-up."

"Bless you for saying that. Bless you."

"I could lose my job."

"Who would I tell, Gavin? Who's covering up what?"

"I'm not sure. We were very interested in the brief until the White House pressed hard, now we've dismissed it."

"I can understand that. Why do they think they can kill me and it will be kept quiet?"

"I can't answer that. Maybe they think you know more."

"Can I tell you something? Moments after the bomb, while Thomas was in the car burning and I was semiconscious, a cop named Rupert took me to his car and put me inside. Another cop with cowboy boots and jeans started asking me questions. I was sick and in shock. They disappeared, Rupert and his cowboy, and they never returned. They were not cops, Gavin. They watched the bomb, and went to plan B when I wasn't in the car. I didn't know it, but I was probably a minute or two away from a bullet in the head."

Verheek listened with his eyes closed. "What happened to them?"

"Not sure. I think they got scared when the real cops swarmed on the scene. They vanished. I was in their car, Gavin. They had me."

"You have to come in, Darby. Listen to me."

"Do you remember our phone chat Thursday morning when I suddenly saw a face that looked familiar and I described it to you?"

"Of course."

"That face was at the memorial service yesterday, along with some friends."

"Where were you?"

"Watching. He walked in a few minutes late, stayed ten minutes, then sneaked out and met with Stump."

"Stump?"

"Yes, he's one of the gang. Stump, Rupert, Cowboy, and the Thin Man. Great characters. I'm sure there are others, but I haven't met them yet."

"The next meeting will be the last, Darby. You have about forty-eight hours to live."

"We'll see. How long will you be in town?"

"A few days. I'd planned to stay until I found you."

"Here I am. I may call you tomorrow."

Verheek breathed deeply. "Okay, Darby. Whatever you say. Just be careful."

She hung up. He threw the phone across the room, and cursed it.

TWO BLOCKS AWAY and fifteen floors up, Khamel stared at the television and mumbled rapidly to himself. It was a movie about people in a big city. They spoke English, his third language, and he repeated every word in his best generic American tongue. He did this for hours. He had absorbed the language while hiding in Belfast, and in the past twenty years had watched thousands of American movies. His favorite was *Three Days of the Condor*. He watched it four times before he figured out who was killing whom and why. He could have killed Redford.

He repeated every word out loud. He had been told his English could pass for that of an American, but one slip, one tiny mistake, and she would be gone.

THE VOLVO was parked in a lot a block and a half from its owner, who paid one hundred dollars a month for the space and for what he thought was security. They eased through the gate that was supposed to be locked.

It was a 1986 GL without a security system, and within seconds the driver's door was open. One sat on the trunk and lit a cigarette. It was almost 4 A.M. Sunday.

The other one opened a small tool case he kept in his pocket, and went to work on the yuppie car phone that Grantham had been embarrassed to buy. The dome light was enough, and he worked quickly. Easy work. With the receiver open, he installed a tiny transmitter and glued it in place. A minute later, he eased out of the car and squatted at the rear bumper. The one with the cigarette handed him a small black cube, which he stuck under the car to a grille and behind the gas tank. It was a magnetized transmitter, and it would send signals for six days before it died and needed replacing.

They were gone in less than seven minutes. Monday, as soon as he was spotted entering the *Post* building on Fifteenth, they would enter his apartment and fix his phones.

TWENTY-TWO

HER SECOND NIGHT in the bed and breakfast was better than the first. She slept until mid-morning. Maybe she was used to it now. She stared at the curtains over the tiny window and determined that there had been no nightmares, no movements in the dark with guns and knives emerging and attacking. It was a thick, heavy sleep, and she studied the curtains for a long time while the brain woke up.

She tried to be disciplined about her thinking. This was her fourth day as the Pelican, and to see number five she would have to think like a fastidious killer. It was day number four of the rest of her life. She was supposed to be dead.

But after the eyes opened, and she realized she was indeed alive and safe, and the door wasn't squeaking and the floor wasn't cracking, and there was no gunman lurking in the closet, her first thought was always of Thomas. The shock of his death was fading, and she found it easier to put aside the sound of the explosion and the roar of the fire. She knew he had been blown to pieces and killed instantly. She knew he did not suffer.

So she thought of other things, like the feel of him next to her, and his whispering and snickering when they were in bed and the sex was over and he wanted to cuddle. He was a cuddler, and he wanted to play and kiss and caress after the lovemaking. And giggle. He loved her madly, had fallen hard, and for the first time in his life could be silly with a woman. Many times in the middle of his lectures, she had thought of his cooing and snickering, and bit her lip to keep from smiling.

She loved him too. And it hurt so badly. She wanted to stay in bed and cry for a week. The day after her father's funeral, a psychiatrist had explained that the soul needs a brief, very intense period of grieving, then it moves to the next phase. But it must have the pain; it must suffer without restraint before it can properly move on. She took his advice, and grieved without courage for two weeks, then got tired of it and moved to the next stage. It worked.

But it wasn't working with Thomas. She couldn't scream and throw things the way she wanted. Rupert and Thin Man and the rest of the boys were denying her a healthy mourning.

After a few minutes of Thomas, she thought of them next. Where would they be today? Where could she go without being seen? After two nights in this place, should she find another room? Yes, she would do that. After dark. She would call and reserve a room at another tiny guest house. Where were they staying? Were they patrolling the streets hoping to simply bump into her? Did they know where she was at this moment? No. She would be dead. Did they know she was now a blonde?

The hair got her out of bed. She walked to the mirror over the desk, and looked at herself. It was even shorter now, and very white. Not a bad job. She had worked on it for three hours last night. If she lived another two days, she would cut some more and go back to black. If she lived another week, she might be bald.

A hunger pain hit, and for a second she thought about food. She was not eating, and this would have to change. It was almost ten. Oddly, this bed and breakfast didn't cook on Sunday mornings. She would venture out to find food and a Sunday *Post*, and to see if they could catch her now that she was a butch blonde.

She showered quickly, and the hair took less than a minute. No makeup. She put on a new pair of Army fatigues and a new flight jacket, and she was ready for battle. The eyes were covered with aviator shades.

Although she had made a few entrances, she had not exited a

building through the front door in four days. She crept through the dark kitchen, unlocked the rear door, and stepped into the alley behind the little inn. It was cool enough to wear the flight jacket without being suspicious. Silly, she thought. In the French Quarter, she could wear the hide and head of a polar bear and not appear suspicious. She walked briskly through the alley with her hands deep in the fatigues and her eyes darting behind the shades.

He saw her when she stepped onto the sidewalk next to Burgundy Street. The hair under the cap was different, but she was still five-eight and she couldn't change that. The legs were still long and she walked a certain way, and after four days he could pick her out of a crowd regardless of the face and hair. The cowboy boots—snakeskin with pointed toes—hit the sidewalk and started following.

She was a smart girl, turning every corner, changing streets every block, walking quickly but not too fast. He figured she was headed for Jackson Square, where there was a crowd on Sundays and she thought she could disappear. She could stroll about with the tourists and the locals, maybe eat a bite, enjoy the sun, pick up a paper.

Darby casually lit a cigarette and puffed as she walked. She could not inhale. She tried three days ago, and got dizzy. Such a nasty habit. How ironic it would be if she lived through all this only to die from lung cancer. Please, let her die of cancer.

He was sitting at a table in a crowded sidewalk café at the corner of St. Peter and Chartres, and he was less than ten feet away when she saw him. A split second later, he saw her, and she probably would have made it if she hadn't hesitated for a step and swallowed hard when she saw him. He saw her, and probably would have been only suspicious, but the slight hesitation and the curious look gave her away. She kept walking, but faster now.

It was Stump. He was on his feet and weaving through the tables when she lost sight of him. At ground level, he was anything but chubby. He seemed quick and muscular. She lost him for a second on Chartres as she ducked between the arches of St. Louis Cathedral. The church was open, and she thought maybe she should get inside, as if it would be a sanctuary and he would not kill her there. Yes, he would kill her there, or on the street, or in a crowd. Anywhere he caught her. He was back there, and Darby wanted to know how fast he was coming. Was he just walking real fast and trying to play it cool? Was he sort of jogging? Or was he barreling down the sidewalk preparing to make a flying tackle as soon as he caught sight of her? She kept moving.

She hung a left on St. Ann, crossed the street, and was almost to Royal when she took a quick glance behind her. He was coming. He was on the other side of the street, but very much in pursuit.

The nervous look over the shoulder nailed her. It was a dead giveaway, and he was into a jog now.

Get to Bourbon Street, she decided. Kickoff was four hours away, and the Saints fans were out in force celebrating before the game because there would be little to celebrate afterward. She turned on Royal and ran hard for a few steps, then slowed to a fast walk. He turned on Royal and was trotting. He was poised to break and run hard at any second. Darby moved to the center of the street where a group of football rowdies were moving around, killing time. She turned left on Dumaine, and started running. Bourbon was ahead and there were people everywhere.

She could hear him now. No sense looking anymore. He was back there, running and gaining. When she turned onto Bourbon, Mr. Stump was fifty feet behind her, and the race was over. She saw her angels as they made a noisy exit from a bar. Three large, overweight young men dressed in a wild assortment of black and gold Saints garb stepped into the middle of the street just as Darby ran to them.

"Help!" she screamed wildly and pointed at Stump. "Help me! That man is after me! He's trying to rape me!"

Well, hell, now, sex in the streets of New Orleans is not at all uncommon, but they'd be damned if this girl was going to be abused.

"Please help me!" she screamed pitifully. Suddenly, the street was silent. Everyone froze, including Stump, who stopped for a step or two, then rushed forward. The three Saints stepped in front of him with folded arms and glowing eyes. It was over in seconds. Stump used both hands at once: a right to the throat of the first one, and a vicious blow to the mouth of the second. They squealed and fell hard. Number three was not about to run. His two buddies were hurt and this upset him. He would have been a piece of cake for Stump, but number one fell on Stump's right foot and this threw him off. As he yanked his foot away, Mr. Benjamin Chop of Thibodaux, Louisiana, number three, kicked him squarely in the crotch, and Stump was history. As Darby eased back into the crowd, she heard him cry in pain.

While he was falling, Mr. Chop kicked him in the ribs. Number two, with blood all over his face, charged wild-eyed into Stump, and the massacre was on. He curled around his hands, which were curled around his severely damaged testicles, and they kicked him and cursed him without mercy until someone yelled, "Cops," and this saved his life. Mr. Chop and number two helped number one to his feet, and the Saints were last seen darting into a bar. Stump made it to his feet, and crawled away like a dog hit by a Mack truck but still alive and determined to die at home.

She hid in a dark corner of a pub on Decatur, drinking coffee then a beer, coffee then a beer. Her hands shook and her stomach flipped. The po'boys smelled delicious, but she could not eat. After three beers in three hours, she ordered a plate of boiled shrimp and switched to spring water.

The alcohol had calmed her, and the shrimp settled her. She was safe in here, she thought, so why not watch the game and just sit here, maybe, until it closed.

The pub was packed at kickoff. They watched the wide screen above the bar, and got drunk. She was a Saints fan now. She hoped her three buddies were okay and enjoying the game. The crowd yelled and cursed the Redskins.

Darby stayed in her little corner until the game was long over, then slid into the darkness.

□ □ □ □

AT SOME POINT in the fourth quarter, with the Saints down by four field goals, Edwin Sneller hung up the phone and turned off the television. He stretched his legs, then returned to the phone and called Khamel next door.

"Listen to my English," the assassin said. "Tell me if you hear a trace of an accent."

"Okay. She's here," Sneller said. "One of our men saw her this morning at Jackson Square. He followed her for three blocks, then lost her."

"How did he lose her?"

"Doesn't matter, does it? She got away, but she's here. Her hair is very short and almost white."

"White?"

Sneller hated to repeat himself, especially to this mongrel.

"He said it was not blond but white, and she was wearing green Army pants and a brown bomber jacket. Somehow she recognized him, and took off."

"How would she recognize him? Has she seen him before?"

These idiot questions. It was hard to believe he was considered Superman. "I can't answer that."

"How's my English?"

"Perfect. There's a small card under your door. You need to see it."

Khamel laid the phone on a pillow and walked to the door. In a second he was back on the phone. "Who is this?"

"The name is Verheek. Dutch, but he's an American. Works for the FBI in Washington. Evidently, he and Callahan were friends. They finished law school together at Georgetown, and Verheek was an honorary pallbearer at the memorial service yesterday. Last night he was hanging out in a bar not far from the campus, and was asking questions about the girl. Two hours ago, one of our men was in the same bar posing as an FBI agent, and he struck up a conversation with the bartender, who turns out to be a law student who knows the girl. They watched football and talked for a while, then the kid produced the card. Look on the back. He's in room 1909 at the Hilton."

"That's a five-minute walk." The street maps were scattered on one bed.

"Yes. We've made a few phone calls to Washington. He's not an agent, just a lawyer. He knew Callahan, and he might know the girl. It's obvious he's trying to find her."

"She would talk to him, wouldn't she?"

"Probably."

"How's my English?"

"Perfect."

KHAMEL WAITED AN HOUR and left the hotel. With the coat and tie, he was just an average joe strolling along Canal at dusk headed for the river. He carried a large gym bag and smoked a cigarette, and five minutes later entered the lobby of the Hilton. He worked his way through the crowd of fans returning from the Dome. The elevator stopped on the twentieth floor, and he walked one flight down to the nineteenth.

There was no answer at 1909. If the door had opened with the chain locked, he would have apologized and explained he had the wrong room. If the door had opened without the chain and with a face in the crack, he would have kicked it sharply and been inside. But it did not open.

His new pal Verheek was probably hanging around a bar, passing out cards, begging kids to talk to him about Darby Shaw. What a nut.

He knocked again, and while he waited he slid a six-inch plastic ruler between the door and the facing, and worked it gently until the bolt clicked. Locks were minor nuisances for Khamel. Without a key, he could open a locked car and start the engine in less than thirty seconds.

Inside, he locked the door behind him, and placed his bag on the bed. Like a surgeon, he picked the gloves from a pocket and pulled them tightly over his fingers. He laid a .22 and silencer on the table.

The phone was quick work. He plugged the recorder into the jack under the bed, where it could sit for weeks before it was noticed. He called the weather station twice to test the recorder. Perfect.

His new pal Verheek was a slob. Most of the clothes in the room were dirty and simply thrown in the direction of the suitcase sitting on a table. He had not unpacked. A cheap garment bag hung in the closet with one solitary shirt.

Khamel covered his tracks and settled low in the closet. He was a patient man, and he could wait for hours. He held the .22 just in case this clown happened to barge into the closet and he had to kill him with bullets. If not, he would just listen.

TWENTY-THREE

GAVIN QUIT THE BARS SUNDAY. He was getting nowhere. She had called him, and she was not hanging around those places, so what the hell. He was drinking too much and eating too much, and he was tired of New Orleans. He already had a flight booked for late Monday afternoon, and if she didn't call again he was finished playing detective.

He couldn't find her, and it wasn't his fault. Cabdrivers got lost in this city. Voyles would be screaming by noon. He had done his best.

He was stretched on the bed in nothing but boxer shorts, flipping through a magazine and ignoring the television. It was almost eleven. He would wait on her until twelve, then try to sleep.

It rang at exactly eleven. He pushed a button and remotely killed the television. "Hello."

It was her. "It's me, Gavin."

"So you're alive."

"Barely."

He sat on the edge of the bed. "What's happened?"

"They saw me today, and one of their goons, my friend Stump, chased me through the Quarter. You haven't met Stump, but he's the one who watched you and everyone else walk into the chapel."

"But you got away."

"Yeah. A small miracle, but I got away."

"What happened to Stump?"

"He was mortally wounded. He's probably lying in a bed somewhere wearing an ice pack in his shorts. He was just a few steps from me when he picked a fight with the wrong guys. I'm scared, Gavin."

"Did he follow you from somewhere?"

"No. We just sort of met on the street."

Verheek paused a second. Her voice was shaking, but under control. She was losing her cool. "Look, Darby. I've got a flight out of here tomorrow afternoon. I have this little job and my boss expects me to be at the office. So I can't hang around New Orleans for the next month hoping you don't get killed and hoping you come to your senses and trust me. I'm leaving tomorrow, and I think you need to go with me."

"Go where?"

"To Washington. To my house. To someplace other than where you are."

"What happens then?"

"Well, you get to live, for one thing. I'll plead with the Director, and I promise you'll be safe. We'll do something, dammit. Anything beats this."

"What makes you think we can just fly out of here?"

"Because we'll have three FBI agents surrounding you. Because I'm not a complete dumbass. Look, Darby, tell me where you want to meet right now, and within fifteen minutes I'll come get you with three agents. These guys have guns, and they're not afraid of your little Stump and his pals. We'll get you out of the city tonight, and take you to Washington tomorrow. I promise you'll personally meet my boss, the Honorable F. Denton Voyles, tomorrow, and we'll go from there."

"I thought the FBI was not involved."

"It's not involved, but it may be."

"Then where do the three agents come from?"

"I've got friends."

She thought for a moment, and her voice was suddenly stronger. "Behind your hotel is a place called Riverwalk. It's a shopping area with restaurants and—"

"I spent two hours there this afternoon."

"Good. On the second level is a clothing store called Frenchmen's Bend."

"I saw it."

"At precisely noon tomorrow, I want you to stand by the entrance, and wait for five minutes."

"Come on, Darby. You won't be alive at noon tomorrow. Enough of this cat and mouse."

"Just do as I say, Gavin. We've never met, so I have no idea what you look like. Wear a black shirt of some type and a red baseball cap."

"Where might I find such articles?"

"Just get them."

"Okay, okay, I'll have them. I guess you want me to pick my nose with a shovel or something. This is silly."

"I'm not in a silly mood, and if you don't shut up we'll call it off."

"It's your neck."

"Please, Gavin."

"I'm sorry. I'll do whatever you say. That's a very busy spot to be."

"Yes, it is. I just feel safer in a crowd. Stand by the door for five minutes or so, and hold a folded newspaper. I'll be watching. After five minutes, walk inside the store, and go to the right rear corner where there's a rack of safari jackets. Browse around a bit, and I'll find you."

"And what might you be wearing?"

"Don't worry about me."

"Fine. Then what do we do?"

"You and I, and only you and I, will leave the city. I don't want anyone else to know of this. Do you understand?"

"No, I don't understand. I can arrange security."

"No, Gavin. I'm the boss, okay. No one else. Forget your three agent friends. Agreed?"

"Agreed. How do you propose we leave the city?"

"I've got a plan for that too."

"I don't like any of your plans, Darby. These thugs are breathing down your neck, and now you're getting me in the middle of it. This is not what I wanted. It's much safer to do it my way. Safer for you, safer for me."

"But you'll be there at noon, won't you?"

He stood by the bed and spoke with his eyes closed. "Yes. I'll be there. I just hope you make it."

"How tall are you?"

"Five-ten."

"How much do you weigh?"

"I was afraid of this. I usually lie, you know. Two hundred, but I plan to lose it. I swear."

"I'll see you tomorrow, Gavin."

"I hope I see you, dear."

She was gone. He hung up. "Son of a bitch!" he yelled to the walls. "Son of a bitch!" He walked along the end of the bed a few times, then to the bathroom, where he closed the door and turned on the shower.

He cussed her in the shower for ten minutes, then stepped out, and dried himself. It was more like two hundred and fifteen pounds, and all of it was situated badly on the five-nine frame. It was painful to look at. Here he was, about to meet this gorgeous woman who suddenly trusted him with her life, and what a slob he was.

He opened the door. The room was dark. Dark? He had left on the lights. What the hell? He headed for the switch next to the dresser.

The first blow crushed his larynx. It was a perfect blow that came from the side, somewhere near the wall. He grunted painfully and fell to one knee, which made the second blow so easy, like an ax on a fat log. It hit like a rock at the base of the skull, and Gavin was dead.

Khamel flipped on a light, and looked at the pitiful nude figure frozen on the floor. He was not one to admire his work. He didn't want carpet burns, so he lifted the pudgy corpse onto his shoulders and laid it across the bed. Working quickly without any wasted motion, Khamel turned on the television and raised it to full volume, unzipped his bag, removed a cheap.25 caliber automatic, and placed it precisely on the right temple of the late Gavin Verheek. He covered the gun and the head with two pillows, and pulled the trigger. Now the critical part: he took one pillow and placed it under the head, threw the other one on the floor, and carefully curled the fingers of the right hand around the pistol, leaving it twelve inches from the head.

He took the recorder from under the bed, and ran the telephone wire directly into the wall. He punched a button, listened, and there she was. He turned off the television.

Every job was different. He had once stalked his prey for three weeks in Mexico City, then caught him in bed with two prostitutes. It was a dumb mistake, and during his career he had been assisted by numerous dumb mistakes by the opposition. This guy was a dumb mistake, a stupid lawyer pilfering around running his mouth, passing out cards with his room number on the back. He had stuck his nose into the world of big-league killing, and look at him now.

With a little luck, the cops would look around the room for a few minutes and declare it to be another suicide. They would go through the motions and ask themselves a couple of questions they could not answer, but there were always some of those. Because he was an important FBI lawyer, an autopsy would be done in a day or so, and probably by Tuesday an examiner would suddenly discover it was not a suicide.

By Tuesday, the girl would be dead and he would be in Managua.

TWENTY-FOUR

HIS USUAL, official sources at the White House denied any knowledge of the pelican brief. Sarge had never heard of it. Long-shot phone calls to the FBI produced nothing. A friend at Justice denied ever hearing about it. He dug all weekend, and had nothing to show for it. The story about Callahan was verified when he found a copy of the New Orleans paper. When her call came in at the newsroom Monday, he had nothing fresh to tell her. But at least she called.

The Pelican said she was at a pay phone, so don't bother.

"I'm still digging," he said. "If there's such a brief in town, it's being closely protected."

"I assure you it's there, and I understand why it's being protected."

"I'm sure you can tell me more."

"Lots more. The brief almost got me killed yesterday, so I may be ready to talk sooner than I thought. I need to spill my guts while I'm still alive."

"Who's trying to kill you?"

"Same people who killed Rosenberg and Jensen, and Thomas Callahan."

"Do you know their names?"

"No, but I've seen at least four of them since Wednesday. They're here in New Orleans, snooping around, hoping I'll do something stupid and they can kill me."

"How many people know about the pelican brief?"

"Good question. Callahan took it to the FBI, and I think from there it went to the White House where it evidently caused quite a fuss, and from there who knows. Two days after he handed it to the FBI, Callahan was dead. I, of course, was supposed to have been killed with him."

"Were you with him?"

"I was close, but not close enough."

"So you're the unidentified female on the scene?"

"That's how the paper described me."

"Then the police have your name?"

"My name is Darby Shaw. I am a second-year law student at Tulane. Thomas Callahan was my professor and lover. I wrote the brief, gave it to him, and you know the rest. Are you getting all this?"

Grantham scribbled furiously. "Yes. I'm listening."

"I'm rather tired of the French Quarter, and I plan to leave today. I'll call you from somewhere tomorrow. Do you have access to presidential campaign disclosure forms?"

"It's public record."

"I know that. But how quickly can you get the information?"

"What information?"

"A list of all major contributors to the President's last election."

"That's not difficult. I can have it by this afternoon."

"Do that, and I'll call you in the morning."

"Okay. Do you have a copy of the brief?"

She hesitated. "No, but it's memorized."

"And you know who's doing the killing?"

"Yes, and as soon as I tell you, they'll put your name on the hit list."

"Tell me now."

"Let's take it slow. I'll call you tomorrow."

Grantham listened hard, then hung up. He took his notepad and zigzagged through the maze of desks and people to the glass office of his editor, Smith Keen. Keen was a hale and hearty type with an open-door policy that ensured chaos in his office. He was finishing a phone chat when Grantham barged in and closed the door.

"That door stays open," Keen said sharply.

"We have to talk, Smith."

"We'll talk with the door open. Open the damned door."

"I'll open it in just a second." Grantham spoke with both palms facing the editor. Yes, it was serious. "Let's talk."

"Okay. What is it?"

"It's big, Smith."

"I know it's big. You shut the damned door, so I know it's big."

"I just finished my second phone conversation with a young lady by the name of Darby Shaw, and she knows who killed Rosenberg and Jensen."

Keen sat slowly and glared at Grantham. "Yes, son, that's big. But how do you know? How does she know? What can you prove?"

"I don't have a story yet, Smith, but she's talking to me. Read this." Grantham handed over a copy of the newspaper account of Callahan's death. Keen read it slowly.

"Okay. Who's Callahan?"

"One week ago today, he handed a little paper known as the pelican brief to the FBI here in town. Evidently, the brief implicates an obscure person in the killings. The brief gets passed around, then sent to the White House, then beyond that no one knows. Two days later, Callahan cranks his Porsche for the last time. Darby Shaw claims to be the unidentified female mentioned there. She was with Callahan, and was supposed to die with him."

"Why was she supposed to die?"

"She wrote the brief, Smith. Or she claims she did."

Keen sank deeper into his seat and placed his feet on the desk. He studied the photo of Callahan. "Where's the brief?"

"I don't know."

"What's in it?"

"Don't know that either."

"Then we don't have anything, do we?"

"Not yet. But what if she tells me everything that's in it?"

"And when will she do this?"

Grantham hesitated. "Soon, I think. Real soon."

Keen shook his head and threw the copy on the desk. "If we had the brief, we'd have a helluva story, Gray, but we couldn't run it. There's gotta be some heavy, painful, flawless, and accurate verification before we can run it."

"But I've got the green light?"

"Yeah, but you keep me posted every hour. Don't write a word until we talk."

Grantham smiled and opened the door.

THIS WAS NOT forty-bucks-an-hour work. Not even thirty, or twenty. Croft knew he'd be lucky to squeeze fifteen out of Grantham for this needle-in-the-haystack Mickey Mouse crap. If he'd had other work, he'd have told Grantham to find someone else, or better yet, do it himself.

But things had been slow, and he could do a lot worse than fifteen bucks an hour. He finished a joint in the last stall, flushed it, and opened the door. He stuck the dark sunglasses over his ears, and entered the hallway that led to the atrium where four escalators carried a thousand lawyers up to their little rooms, where they would spend the day bitching and threatening by the hour. He had Garcia's face memorized. He was even dreaming of this kid with the bright face and good looks, the slim physique draped with an expensive suit. He would know him if he saw him.

He stood by a pillar, holding a newspaper and trying to watch everyone from behind the dark shades. Lawyers everywhere, scurrying upward with their smug little faces and carrying their smug little attaché cases. Man, how he hated lawyers. Why did they all dress alike? Dark suits. Dark shoes. Dark faces. An occasional nonconformist with a daring little bow tie. Where did they all come from? Shortly after his arrest with the drugs, the first lawyers had been a group of angry mouthpieces hired by the *Post*. Then he hired his own, an overpriced moron who couldn't find the courtroom. Then, the prosecutor was of course a lawyer. Lawyers, lawyers.

Two hours in the morning, two hours at lunch, two hours

during the evening, and then Grantham would have another building for him to patrol. Ninety bucks a day was cheap, and he would give this up as soon as he got a better deal. He told Grantham this was hopeless, just shooting in the dark. Grantham agreed, but said to keep shooting. It's all they could do. He said Garcia was scared and wouldn't call anymore. They had to find him.

In his pocket he had two photos just in case, and from the directory he had made a list of the firms in the building. It was a long list. The building had twelve floors filled mainly with firms filled with nothing but these fancy little esquires. He was in a den of snakes.

By nine-thirty the rush was over, and some of the faces looked familiar coming back down the escalators, headed no doubt for the courtrooms and agencies and commissions. Croft eased through the revolving doors, and wiped his feet on the sidewalk.

FOUR BLOCKS AWAY, Fletcher Coal paced in front of the President's desk and listened intently to the phone in his ear. He frowned, then closed his eyes, then glared at the President as if to say, "Bad news, Chief. Really bad news." The President held a letter and peered at Coal over his reading glasses. Coal's pacing back and forth like Der Führer really irritated him, and he made a mental note to say something about it.

Coal slammed the phone down.

"Don't slam the damned phones!" the President said.

Coal was unfazed. "Sorry. That was Zikman. Gray Grantham called thirty minutes ago, and asked if he had any knowledge of the pelican brief."

"Wonderful. Fabulous. How'd he get a copy of it?"

Coal was still pacing. "Zikman knows nothing about it, so his ignorance was genuine."

"His ignorance is always genuine. He's the dumbest ass on my staff, Fletcher, and I want him gone."

"Whatever." Coal sat in a chair across the desk and folded his hands in a little steeple in front of his chin. He was very deep in thought, and the President tried to ignore him. They thought for a moment.

"Voyles leaked it?" the President finally said.

"Maybe, if it was leaked. Grantham is known for bluffing. We can't be certain he's seen the brief. Maybe he heard about it, and he's fishing."

"Maybe, my ass. What if they run some crazy story about that damned thing? What then?" The President slapped his desk and bolted to his feet. "What then, Fletcher? That paper hates me!" He moped to the windows.

"They can't run it without another source, and there can't be another source because there's no truth to it. It's a wild idea that's gone much further than it deserves."

The President sulked for a while and stared through the glass. "How did Grantham find out about it?"

Coal stood and began pacing, but much slower now. He was still painfully in thought. "Who knows. No one here knows about it but you and I. They brought one copy, and it's locked away in my office. I personally Xeroxed it once, and gave it to Gminski. I swore him to secrecy."

The President sneered at the windows.

Coal continued. "Okay, you're right. There could be a thousand copies out there by now. But it's harmless, unless of course our friend actually did these dirty deeds, then—"

"Then my ass is cooked."

"Yes, I would say our asses are cooked."

"How much money did we take?"

"Millions, directly and indirectly." And legally and illegally, but the President knew little of these transactions and Coal chose to stay quiet.

The President walked slowly to the sofa. "Why don't you call Grantham? Pick his brain. See what he knows. If he's bluffing, it'll be obvious. What do you think?"

"I don't know."

"You've talked to him before, haven't you? Everyone knows Grantham."

Coal was now pacing behind the sofa. "Yeah, I've talked to him. But if I suddenly call out of nowhere, he'll be suspicious."

"Yeah, I guess you're right." The President paced on one end of the sofa, and Coal on the other.

"What's the downside?" the President finally asked.

"Our friend could be involved. You asked Voyles to back off our friend. Our friend could be exposed by the press. Voyles covers his tail and says you told him to chase other suspects and ignore our friend. The *Post* goes berserk with another cover-up smear. And we can forget reelection."

"Anything else?"

Coal thought for a second. "Yeah, this is all completely off the wall. The brief is fantasy. Grantham will find nothing, and I'm late for a staff meeting." He walked to the door. "I've got a squash game for lunch. Be back at one."

The President watched the door close, and breathed easier. He had eighteen holes planned for the afternoon, so forget the pelican thing. If Coal wasn't worried, neither was he.

He punched numbers on his phone, waited patiently, and finally had Bob Gminski on the line. The director of the CIA was a terrible golfer, one of the few the President could humiliate, and he invited him to play this afternoon. Certainly, said Gminski, a man with a thousand things to do but, well, it was the President so he would be delighted to join him.

"By the way, Bob, what about this pelican thing in New Orleans?"

Gminski cleared his throat and tried to sound relaxed. "Well, Chief, I told Fletcher Coal Friday that it was very imaginative and a fine work of fiction. I think its author should forget about law school and pursue a career as a novelist. Ha, ha, ha."

"Great, Bob. Nothing to it then."

"We're digging."

"See you at three." The President hung up, and went straight for his putter.

TWENTY-FIVE

RIVERWALK RUNS for a quarter of a mile along the water, and is always crowded. It is packed with two hundred shops and cafés and restaurants on several levels, most under the same roof, and several with doors leading onto a boardwalk next to the river. It's at the foot of Poydras Street, a stone's throw from the Quarter.

She arrived at eleven, and sipped espresso in the rear of a tiny bistro while trying to read the paper and appear calm. Frenchmen's Bend was one level down and around a corner. She was nervous, and the espresso didn't help.

She had a list in her pocket of things to do, specific steps at specific moments, even words and sentences she had memorized in the event things went terribly wrong and Verheek got out of control. She had slept two hours, and spent the rest of the time with a legal pad diagraming and charting. If she died, it would not be from a lack of preparation.

She could not trust Gavin Verheek. He was employed by a law enforcement agency that at times operated by its own rules. He took orders from a man with a history of paranoia and dirty tricks. His boss reported to a President in charge of an Administration run by fools. The President had rich, sleazy friends who gave him lots of money.

But at this moment, dear, there was no one else to trust. After five days and two near misses, she was throwing in the towel.

New Orleans had lost its allure. She needed help, and if she had to trust cops, the Fibbies were as clean as any.

Eleven forty-five. She paid for the espresso, waited for a crowd of shoppers, and fell in behind them. There were a dozen people browsing in Frenchmen's Bend as she walked past the entrance where her friend should be in about ten minutes. She eased into a bookstore two doors down. There were at least three stores in the vicinity from which she could shop and hide and watch the front door of Frenchmen's Bend. She chose the bookstore because the clerks weren't pushy and killing time was expected of the customers. She looked at the magazines first, then with three minutes to go she stepped between two rows of cookbooks and watched for Gavin.

Thomas said he was never on time. An hour late was early for him, but she would give him fifteen minutes and she'd be gone.

She expected him at precisely noon, and there he was. Black sweatshirt, red baseball cap, folded newspaper. He was a bit thinner than she expected, but he could lose a few pounds. Her heart pounded away. Be cool, she said. Just be cool, dammit.

She held a cookbook to her eyes and peered over it. He had gray hair and dark skin. The eyes were hidden behind sunglasses. He fidgeted and looked irritated, the way he sounded on the phone. He passed the newspaper from hand to hand, shifted his weight from foot to foot, and glanced around nervously.

He was okay. She liked the way he looked. He had a vulnerable, nonprofessional manner about him that said he was scared too.

After five minutes, he walked through the door as he was told, and went to the right rear of the store.

KHAMEL HAD BEEN TRAINED to welcome death. He had been close to it many times, but never afraid of it. And after thirty years of expecting it, nothing, absolutely nothing, made him tense. He got somewhat excited about sex, but that was it. The fidgeting was an act. The jittery little movements were contrived. He'd survived face-offs with men almost as talented as he, and he could certainly handle this little rendezvous with a desperate child. He picked through the safari jackets and tried to appear nervous.

He had a handkerchief in his pocket, because he suddenly had caught a cold so his voice was a bit thick and scratchy. He had listened to the recording a hundred times, and he was confident he had the inflection and rhythm and slight upper Midwest accent. But Verheek was a bit more nasal; thus, the handkerchief for the cold.

It was difficult to allow anyone to approach from the rear, but he knew he must. He did not see her. She was behind him but very close when she said, "Gavin."

He jerked quickly around. She was holding a white Panama hat and speaking to it. "Darby," he said, pulling the handkerchief out for a fake sneeze. Her hair was a gold color and shorter than his. He sneezed and coughed. "Let's get out of here," he said. "I don't like this idea."

Darby didn't like it either. It was Monday and her classmates were going about their business of clawing through law school, and here she was camouflaged to the max and playing cloak and dagger with this man who could get her killed. "Just do as I say, okay. Where'd you get the cold?"

He sneezed into the handkerchief and talked as low as possible. It sounded painful. "Last night. I left the air on too low. Let's get out of here."

"Follow me." They left the store. Darby took his hand, and they walked quickly down a flight of stairs leading to the boardwalk.

"Have you seen them?" he asked.

"No. Not yet. But I'm sure they're around."

"Where the hell are we going?" The voice was scratchy.

They were on the boardwalk, almost jogging, talking without looking at each other. "Just come with me."

"You're going too fast, Darby. We look suspicious. Slow down. Look, this is crazy. Let me make a phone call, and we'll be safe and secure. I can have three agents here in ten minutes." He was sounding good. This was working. They were holding hands, running for their lives.

"Nope." She slowed. The boardwalk was crowded, and a line

had formed beside the *Bayou Queen*, a paddle wheeler. They stopped at the end of the line.

"What the hell is this?" he asked.

"Do you bitch about everything?" she almost whispered.

"Yes. Especially stupid things, and this is very stupid. Are we getting on this boat?"

"Yes."

"Why?" he sneezed again, then coughed out of control. He could take her out now with one hand, but there were people everywhere. People in front, people behind. He took great pride in his cleanliness, and this would be a dirty place to do it. Get on the boat, play along for a few more minutes, see what happens. He would get her on the upper deck, kill her, dump her in the river, then start yelling. Another terrible drowning accident. That might work. If not, he'd be patient. She'd be dead in an hour. Gavin was a bitch, so keep bitching.

"Because I've got a car a mile upriver at a park where we'll stop in thirty minutes," she explained in a low voice. "We get off the boat, into the car, and we haul ass."

The line was moving now. "I don't like boats. They make me seasick. This is dangerous, Darby." He coughed and looked around like a man pursued.

"Relax, Gavin. It's gonna work."

Khamel tugged at his pants. They were thirty-six inches in the waist and covered eight layers of briefs and gym shorts. The sweatshirt was extra large, and instead of weighing one-fifty, he could pass for one-ninety. Whatever. It seemed to be working.

They were almost to the steps of the *Bayou Queen*. "I don't like this," he mumbled loud enough for her to hear.

"Just shut up," she said.

The man with the gun ran to the end of the line and elbowed his way through the people with their bags and cameras. The tourists were packed tightly together as if a ride on the riverboat was the greatest trip in the world. He had killed before, but never in such a public place as this. The back of her head was visible through the crowd. He shoved his way desperately through the line. A few cursed him, but he couldn't care less. The gun was in a pocket, but as he neared the girl he yanked it out and kept it by his right leg. She was almost to the steps, almost on the boat. He shoved harder and knocked people out of the way. They protested angrily until they saw the gun, then they began yelling. She was holding hands with the man, who was talking nonstop. She was about to step up onto the boat when he knocked the last person out of the way and quickly stuck the gun into the base of the skull just below the red baseball cap. He fired once, and people screamed and fell to the ground.

Gavin fell hard into the steps. Darby screamed and backed away in horror. Her ears were ringing from the shot, and voices were yelling and people were pointing. The man with the gun was running hard toward a row of shops and a crowd of people. A heavy man with a camera was yelling at him, and Darby watched for a second as he disappeared. Maybe she'd seen him before, but she couldn't think now. She was yelling and couldn't stop.

"He's got a gun!" a woman near the boat yelled, and the crowd backed away from Gavin, who was on all fours with a small pistol in his right hand. He rocked pitifully back and forth like an infant trying to crawl. Blood streamed from his chin and puddled under his face. His head hung almost to the boards. His eyes were closed. He moved forward just a few inches, his knees now in the dark red puddle.

The crowd backed farther away, horrified at the sight of this wounded man fighting death. He teetered and wobbled forward again, headed nowhere but wanting to move, to live. He started yelling; loud painful moans in a language Darby did not recognize.

The blood was pouring, gushing from the nose and chin. He was wailing in that unknown tongue. Two crew members from the boat hovered on the steps, watching but afraid to move. The pistol concerned them.

A woman was crying, then another. Darby inched farther back. "He's Egyptian," a small, dark woman said. That news meant nothing to the crowd, now mesmerized.

He rocked forward and lunged to the edge of the boardwalk. The gun dropped into the water. He collapsed on his stomach with his head hanging over and dripping into the river. Shouts came from the rear, and two policemen rushed to him.

A hundred people now inched forward to see the dead man. Darby shuffled backward, then left the scene. The cops would have questions, and since she had no answers, she preferred not to talk. She was weak and needed to sit for a while, and think. There was an oyster bar inside Riverwalk. It was crowded for lunch, and she found the rest rooms in the back. She locked the door and sat on a toilet.

SHORTLY AFTER DARK, she left Riverwalk. The Westin Hotel is two blocks away, and she hoped maybe she could make it there without being gunned down on the sidewalk. Her clothes were different and hidden under a new black trench coat. The sunglasses and hat were also new. She was tired of spending good money on disposable clothes. She was tired of a lot of things.

She made it to the Westin in one piece. There were no rooms, and she sat in the well-lit lounge for an hour drinking coffee. It was time to run, but she couldn't get careless. She had to think.

Maybe she was thinking too damned much. Maybe they now thought of her as a thinker, and planned accordingly.

She left the Westin, and walked to Poydras, where she flagged a cab. An elderly black man sat low behind the wheel.

"I need to go to Baton Rouge," she said.

"Lord, honey, that's a heckuva ride."

"How much?" she asked quickly.

He thought a second. "A hundred and fifty."

She crawled in the backseat and threw two bills over the seat. "There's two hundred. Get there as fast as you can, and watch your rear. We may be followed."

He turned off the meter and stuffed the money in his shirt pocket. Darby lay down in the backseat and closed her eyes. This was not an intelligent move, but playing the percentages was getting nowhere. The old man was a fast driver, and within minutes they were on the expressway.

The ringing in her ears had stopped, but she still heard the gunshot and saw him on all fours, rocking back and forth, trying to live just a moment longer. Thomas had once referred to him as Dutch Verheek, but said the nickname was dropped after law school when they became serious about their careers. Dutch Verheek was not an Egyptian.

She had caught just a glimpse of his killer as he was running away. There was something familiar about him. He had glanced to his right just once as he was running, and something clicked. But she was screaming and hysterical, and it was a blur.

Everything blurred. Halfway to Baton Rouge, she fell into a deep sleep.

TWENTY-SIX

DIRECTOR VOYLES stood behind his executive swivel chair. His jacket was off, and most of the buttons on his tired and wrinkled shirt were unfastened. It was 9 P.M., and judging from the shirt he had been at the office at least fifteen hours. And he hadn't thought of leaving.

He listened to the receiver, mumbled a few instructions, and hung it up. K. O. Lewis sat across the desk. The door was open; the lights were on; no one had left. The mood was somber with small huddles of soft whispers.

"That was Eric East," Voyles said, sitting gently into the chair. "He's been there about two hours, and they just finished the autopsy. He watched it, his first. Single bullet to the right temple, but death came sooner from a single blow at C-2 and C-3. The vertebrae were shattered into tiny chips and pieces. No powder burns on his hand. Another blow severely bruised his larynx, but did not cause death. He was nude. Estimate of between ten and eleven last night."

"Who found him?" Lewis asked.

"Maids checked in around eleven this morning. Will you deliver the news to his wife?"

"Yea, sure," K.O. said. "When's the body coming back?"

"East said they'll release it in a couple of hours, and it should be here by 2 A.M. Tell her we'll do whatever she wants. Tell her

I'm sending a hundred agents in tomorrow to blanket the city. Tell her we'll find the killer, etc., etc."

"Any evidence?"

"Probably not. East said they've had the hotel room since 3 P.M., and it appears to be a clean job. No forced entry. No signs of resistance. Nothing that would be of any help, but it's a bit early." Voyles rubbed his red eyes, and thought for a while.

"How could he go down for a simple funeral, and end up dead?" Lewis asked.

"He was snooping around on this pelican thing. One of our agents, guy named Carlton, told East that Gavin was trying to find the girl, and that the girl had called him, and that he might need some help bringing her in. Carlton talked to him a few times, and gave him the names of a few student hangouts in the city. That was all, so he says. Carlton says that he, Carlton, was a bit worried about Gavin throwing his FBI weight around. Said he thought he was sort of a klutz."

"Has anyone seen the girl?"

"She's probably dead. I've instructed New Orleans to find her, if possible."

"Her little brief is getting folks killed right and left. When do we take it seriously?"

Voyles nodded at the door, and Lewis got up and closed it. The Director was standing again, cracking his knuckles and thinking aloud. "We have to cover our asses. I think we should assign at least two hundred agents to pelican, but try like hell to keep it quiet. There's something there, K.O., something really nasty. But at the same time, I promised the President we would back off. He personally asked me to back off the pelican brief, remember, and I said we would, in part because we thought it was a joke." Voyles managed a tight smile. "Well, I taped our little conversation when he asked me to back off. I figure he and Coal tape everything within a half mile of the White House, so why can't I? I had my best body mike, and I've listened to the tape. Clear as a bell."

"I'm not following."

"Simple. We go in and investigate like mad. If this is it, we crack the case, get the indictments, and everyone's happy. But it'll be a bitch to do in a hurry. Meanwhile, idiot and Coal over there know nothing about the investigation. If the press gets wind of it, and if the pelican brief is on target, then I'll make damned sure the country knows the President asked us to back off because it's one of his pals."

Lewis was smiling. "It'll kill him."

"Yes! Coal will hemorrhage, and the President will never recover. The election is next year, K.O."

"I like it, Denton, but we have to solve this thing."

Denton walked slowly behind his chair, and slid out of his shoes. He was even shorter now. "We'll look under every stone, K.O., but it won't be easy. If it's Mattiece, then we've got a very wealthy man in a very elaborate plot to use very talented killers to take out two justices. These people don't talk, and they don't leave trails. Look at our friend Gavin. We'll spend two thousand hours digging around that hotel, and I'll bet you there won't be a shred of useful evidence. Just like Rosenberg and Jensen."

"And Callahan."

"And Callahan. And probably the girl, if we ever find her body."

"I'm somewhat responsible, Denton. Gavin came to me Thursday morning after he learned of Callahan, and I didn't listen. I knew he was going down there, but I just didn't listen."

"Look, I'm sorry he's dead. He was a fine lawyer and he was loyal to me. I value that. I trusted Gavin. But he got himself killed because he stepped out of bounds. He had no business playing cop and trying to find the girl."

Lewis stood and stretched. "I'd better go see Mrs. Verheek. How much do I tell her?"

"Let's say it looks like a burglary, cops ain't sure down there, still investigating, we'll know more tomorrow, etc. Tell her I'm devastated, and we'll do whatever she wants."

COAL'S LIMO stopped abruptly at the curb so an ambulance could scream by. The limo was wandering aimlessly through the city, a ritual not unusual when Coal and Matthew Barr met to talk about really dirty business. They sat deep in the back of it, sipping drinks. Coal was indulging in a spring water. Barr had a sixteen-ounce Bud purchased from a convenience store.

They ignored the ambulance.

"I must know what Grantham knows," Coal was saying. "Today he called Zikman, Zikman's aide Trandell, Nelson DeVan, one of my many former assistants who's now with the Committee to Reelect. And these are just the ones I know of. All in one day. He's hot on this pelican brief."

"You think he's seen it?" The limo was moving again.

"No. Not at all. If he knew what was in it, he wouldn't be fishing for it. But dammit, he knows about it."

"He's good. I've watched him for years. He seems to move in the shadows and keeps in touch with an odd network of sources. He's written some crazy stuff, but it's usually accurate as hell."

"That's what worries me. He's tenacious, and he smells blood with this story."

Barr sipped from the can. "Of course, it would be asking too much if I wanted to know what was in the brief."

"Don't ask. It's so damned confidential it's frightening."

"Then how does Grantham know about it?"

"Perfect question. And that's what I want to know. How'd he find out, and how much does he know? Where are his sources?"

"We got his car phone, but we haven't been inside the apartment yet."

"Why not?"

"We almost got caught this morning by his cleaning lady. We'll try again tomorrow."

"Don't get caught, Barr. Remember Watergate."

"They were morons, Fletcher. We, on the other hand, are quite talented."

"That's right. So tell me, can you and your quite talented associates bug Grantham's phone at the *Post*?"

Barr turned and frowned at Coal. "Have you lost your mind? Impossible. That place is busy at all hours. They have security guards. The works."

"It could be done."

"Then do it, Coal. If you know so damned much, you do it."

"Start thinking about ways to do it, okay. Just give it some thought."

"Okay. I've thought about it. It's impossible."

Coal was amused by this thought, and his amusement irritated Barr. The limo eased into downtown.

"Tap his apartment," Coal instructed. "I want a report twice a day on all his calls." The limo stopped, and Barr climbed out.

TWENTY-SEVEN

BREAKFAST at Dupont Circle. It was quite chilly, but at least the addicts and transvestites were still unconscious somewhere in their sick little worlds. A few winos lay about like driftwood. But the sun was up and he felt safe, and anyway he was still an FBI agent with a shoulder harness and a piece under his arm. Who was he to fear? He hadn't used it in fifteen years, and he seldom left the office, but he'd love to yank it out and blast away.

His name was Trope, a very special assistant to Mr. Voyles. He was so special that no one except he and Mr. Voyles knew about these secret little chats with Booker from Langley. He sat on a circular bench with his back to New Hampshire, and unpacked a store-bought breakfast of banana and muffin. He checked his watch. Booker was never late. Trope always arrived first, then Booker five minutes later, and they always talked quickly and Trope left first, then Booker. They were both office boys now, far into their twilights but very close to their bosses, who from time to time grew weary of trying to figure out what the hell the other was doing, or perhaps just needed to know something quick.

His real name was Trope, and he wondered if Booker was a real name. Probably not. Booker was from Langley, and they were so paranoid even the pencil pushers probably had fakes.

He took an inch off the banana. Hell, the secretaries over there probably had three or four names.

Booker strolled near the fountain with a tall white cup of coffee. He glanced around, then sat down next to his friend. Voyles wanted this meeting, so Trope would speak first.

"We lost a man in New Orleans," he said.

Booker cuddled the hot cup and sipped. "He got himself killed."

"Yeah, but he's still dead. Were you there?"

"Yes, but we didn't know he was there. We were close, but watching others. What was he doing?"

Trope unwrapped the cold muffin. "We don't know. Went down for the funeral, tried to find the girl, found someone else, and here we are." He took a long bite and the banana was finished. Now to the muffin. "It was a clean job, wasn't it?"

Booker shrugged. What did the FBI know about killing people? "It was okay. Pretty weak effort at suicide, from what we hear." He sipped the hot coffee.

"Where's the girl?" Trope asked.

"We lost her at O'Hare. Maybe she's in Manhattan, but we're not certain. We're looking."

"And they're looking." Trope sipped cold coffee.

"I'm sure they are."

They watched a wino stagger from his bench and fall. His head hit first with a thud, but he probably felt nothing. He rolled over and his forehead was bleeding.

Booker checked his watch. These meetings were extremely brief. "What are Mr. Voyles' plans?"

"Oh, he's going in. He sent fifty troops last night, with more today. He doesn't like losing people, especially someone he knows."

"What about the White House?"

"Not going to tell them, and maybe they won't find out. What do they know?"

"They know Mattiece."

Trope managed a slight smile at this thought. "Where is Mr. Mattiece?"

"Who knows. In the past three years, he's been seen little in this country. He owns at least a half-dozen homes in as many countries, and he's got jets and boats, so who knows."

Trope finished the muffin and stuffed the wrapper in the sack. "The brief nailed him, didn't it?"

"It's beautiful. And if he'd played it cool, the brief would have been ignored. But he goes berserk, starts killing people, and the more he kills the more credibility the brief has."

Trope glanced at his watch. Too long already, but this was good stuff. "Voyles says we may need your help."

Booker nodded. "Done. But this will be a very difficult matter. First, the probable gunman is dead. Second, the probable bagman is very elusive. There was an elaborate conspiracy, but the conspirators are gone. We'll try to find Mattiece."

"And the girl?"

"Yes. We'll try."

"What's she thinking?"

"How to stay alive."

"Can't you bring her in?" Trope asked.

"No. We don't know where she is, and we can't just snatch innocent civilians off the streets. She doesn't trust anyone right now."

Trope stood with his coffee and sack. "I can't blame her." He was gone.

GRANTHAM HELD a cloudy fax photo sent to him from Phoenix. She was a junior at Arizona State, a very attractive twenty-year-old coed. She was listed as a biology major from Denver. He had called twenty Shaws in Denver before he stopped. The second fax was sent by an AP stringer in New Orleans. It was a copy of her freshman photo at Tulane. The hair was longer. Somewhere in the middle of the yearbook, the stringer had found a photo of Darby Shaw drinking a Diet Coke at a law school picnic. She wore a baggy sweater with faded jeans that fit just right, and it was obvious the photo was placed in the yearbook by a great admirer of Darby's. It looked like something out of *Vogue*. She was laughing at something or someone at the picnic. The teeth were perfect and the face was warm. He had tacked this one onto the small corkboard beside his news desk.

There was a fourth fax, a photo of Thomas Callahan, just for the record.

He placed his feet on the desk. It was almost nine-thirty, Tuesday. The newsroom hummed and rocked like a well-organized riot. He'd made eighty phone calls in the last twenty-four hours, and had nothing to show but the four photos and a stack of campaign finance forms. He was getting nowhere, and, really, why bother? She was about to tell all.

He skimmed the *Post*, and saw the strange story about one Gavin Verheek and his demise. The phone rang. It was Darby.

"Seen the *Post*?" she asked.

"I write the *Post*, remember."

She was not in the mood for small talk. "The story about the FBI lawyer murdered in New Orleans, have you seen it?"

"I'm just reading it. Does it mean something to you?"

"You could say that. Listen carefully, Grantham. Callahan gave the brief to Verheek, who was his best friend. Friday, Verheek came to New Orleans for the funeral. I talked to him by phone over the weekend. He wanted to help me, but I was scared. We agreed to meet yesterday at noon. Verheek was murdered in his room around eleven Sunday night. Got all that?"

"Yeah, I got it."

"Verheek didn't show for our meeting. He was, of course, dead by then. I got scared, and left the city. I'm in New York."

"Okay." Grantham wrote furiously. "Who killed Verheek?"

"I do not know. There's a lot more to the story. I've read the *Post* and the *New York Times* from front to back, and I've seen nothing about another killing in New Orleans. It happened to a man I was talking to and I thought was Verheek. It's a long story."

"Sounds like it. When do I get this long story?"

"When can you come to New York?"

"I can be there by noon."

"That's a little quick. Let's plan on tomorrow. I'll call you at this time tomorrow with instructions. You must be careful, Grantham."

He admired the jeans and the smile on the corkboard. "It's Gray, okay? Not Grantham."

"Whatever. There are some powerful people afraid of what I know. If I tell you, it could kill you. I've seen the bodies, okay, Gray? I've heard bombs and gunshots. I saw a man's brains yesterday, and I have no idea who he was or why he was killed, except that he knew about the pelican brief. I thought he was my friend. I trusted him with my life, and he was shot in the head in front of fifty people. As I watched him die, it occurred to me that perhaps he was not my friend. I read the paper this morning, and I realize he was definitely not my friend."

"Who killed him?"

"We'll talk about it when you get here."

"Okay, Darby."

"There's one small point to cover. I'll tell you everything I know, but you can never use my name. I've already written enough to get at least three people killed, and I'm quite confident I'll be next. But I don't want to ask for more trouble. I shall always be unidentified, okay, Gray?"

"It's a deal."

"I'm putting a lot of trust in you, and I'm not sure why. If I ever doubt you, I'll disappear."

"You have my word, Darby. I swear."

"I think you're making a mistake. This is not your average investigative job. This one could get you killed."

"By the same people who killed Rosenberg and Jensen?"

"Yes."

"Do you know who killed Rosenberg and Jensen?"

"I know who paid for the killings. I know his name. I know his business. I know his politics."

"And you'll tell me tomorrow?"

"If I'm still alive." There was a long pause as both thought of something appropriate.

"Perhaps we should talk immediately," he said.

"Perhaps. But I'll call you in the morning."

Grantham hung up, and for a moment admired the slightly blurred photo of this very beautiful law student who was convinced she was about to die. For a second he succumbed to thoughts of chivalry and gallantry and rescue. She was in her early twenties, liked older men, according to the photo of Callahan, and suddenly she trusted him to the exclusion of all others. He would make it work. And he would protect her.

THE MOTORCADE moved quietly out of downtown. He was due for a speech at College Park in an hour, and he relaxed in his limo with his jacket off, reading the words Mabry had put together. He shook his head and wrote in the margins. On a normal day, this would be a pleasant drive out of the city to a beautiful campus for a light little speech, but it wasn't working out. Coal was seated next to him in the limo.

The Chief of Staff routinely avoided these trips. He treasured the moments the President was out of the White House and he had the run of the place. But they needed to talk.

"I'm tired of Mabry's speeches," the President said in frustration. "They're all sounding the same. I swear I gave this one last week at the Rotary convention."

"He's the best we've got, but I'm exploring," Coal said without looking up from his memo. He'd read the speech, and it wasn't that bad. But Mabry had been writing for six months, and the ideas were stale and Coal wanted to fire him anyway.

The President glanced at Coal's memo. "What's that?"

"The short list."

"Who's left?"

"Siler-Spence, Watson, and Calderon." Coal flipped a page.

"That's just great, Fletcher. A woman, a black, and a Cuban. Whatever happened to white men? I thought I said I wanted young white men. Young, tough, conservative judges with impeccable credentials and years to live. Didn't I say that?"

Coal kept reading. "They have to be confirmed, Chief."

"We'll get 'em confirmed. I'll twist arms until they break, but they'll be confirmed. Do you realize that nine of every ten white men in this country voted for me?"

"Eighty-four percent."

"Right. So what's wrong with white men?"

"This is not exactly patronage."

"The hell it's not. It's patronage pure and simple. I reward my friends, and I punish my enemies. That's how you survive in politics. You dance with the ones that brought you. I can't believe you want a female and a black. You're getting soft, Fletcher."

Coal flipped another page. He'd heard this before. "I'm more concerned with reelection," he said quietly.

"And I'm not? I've appointed so many Asians and Hispanics and women and blacks you'd think I was a Democrat. Hell, Fletcher, what's wrong with white people? Look, there must be a hundred good, qualified, conservative judges out there, right? Why can't you find just two, only two, who look and think like I do?"

"You got ninety percent of the Cuban vote."

The President tossed the speech in a seat and picked up the morning's *Post*. "Okay, let's go with Calderon. How old is he?"

"Fifty-one. Married, eight kids, Catholic, poor background, worked his way through Yale, very solid. Very conservative. No warts or skeletons, except he was treated for alcoholism twenty years ago. He's been sober since. A teetotaler."

"Has he ever smoked dope?"

"He denies it."

"I like him." The President was reading the front page.

"So do I. Justice and FBI have checked his underwear, and he's very clean. Now, do you want Siler-Spence or Watson?"

"What kind of name is Siler-Spence? I mean, what's wrong with these women who use hyphens? What if her name was Skowinski, and she married a guy named Levondowski? Would her little liberated soul insist she go through life as F. Gwendolyn Skowinski-Levondowski? Give me a break. I'll never appoint a woman with a hyphen."

"You already have."

"Who?"

"Kay Jones-Roddy, ambassador to Brazil."

"Then call her home and fire her."

Coal managed a slight grin and placed the memo on the seat. He watched the traffic through his window. They would decide on number two later. Calderon was in the bag, and he wanted

Linda Siler-Spence, so he would keep pushing the black and force the President to the woman. Basic manipulation.

"I think we should wait another two weeks before announcing them," he said.

"Whatever," the President mumbled as he read a story on page one. He would announce them when he got ready, regardless of Coal's timetable. He was not yet convinced they should be announced together.

"Judge Watson is a very conservative black judge with a reputation for toughness. He would be ideal."

"I don't know," the President mumbled as he read about Gavin Verheek.

Coal had seen the story on page two. Verheek was found dead in a room at the Hilton in New Orleans under strange circumstances. According to the story, official FBI was in the dark and had nothing to say about why Verheek was in New Orleans. Voyles was deeply saddened. Fine, loyal employee, etc.

The President flipped through the paper. "Our friend Grantham has been quiet."

"He's digging. I think he's heard of the brief, but just can't get a handle on it. He's called everyone in town, but doesn't know what to ask. He's chasing rabbits."

"Well, I played golf with Gminski yesterday," the President said smugly. "And he assures me everything's under control. We had a real heart-to-heart talk over eighteen holes. He's a horrible golfer, couldn't stay out of the sand and water. It was funny, really."

Coal had never touched a golf club, and hated the idle chatter about handicaps and such. "Do you think Voyles is investigating down there?"

"No. He gave me his word he would not. Not that I trust him, but Gminski didn't mention Voyles."

"How much do you trust Gminski?" Coal asked with a quick glance and frown at the President.

"None. But if he knew something about the pelican brief, I think he would tell me. . . . ." The President's words trailed off, and he knew he sounded naive.

Coal grunted his disbelief.

They crossed the Anacostia River and were in Prince Georges County. The President picked up the speech and looked out his window. Two weeks after the killings, and the ratings were still above fifty percent. The Democrats had no visible candidate out there making noise. He was strong and getting stronger. Americans were tired of dope and crime, and noisy minorities getting all the attention, and liberal idiots interpreting the Constitution in favor of criminals and radicals. This was his moment. Two nominations to the Supreme Court at the same time. It would be his legacy.

He smiled to himself. What a wonderful tragedy.

TWENTY-EIGHT

THE TAXI stopped abruptly at the corner of Fifth and Fifty-second, and Gray, doing exactly what he was told, paid quickly and jumped out with his bag. The car behind was honking and flipping birds, and he thought how nice it was to be back in New York City.

It was almost 5 P.M., and the pedestrians were thick on Fifth, and he figured that was precisely what she wanted. She had been specific. Take this flight from National to La Guardia. Take a cab to the Vista Hotel in the World Trade Center. Go to the bar, have a drink, maybe two, watch your rear, then after an hour catch a cab to the corner of Fifth and Fifty-second. Move quickly, wear sunglasses, and watch for everything because if he was being followed he could get them killed.

She made him write it all down. It was a bit silly, a bit of overkill, but she had a voice he couldn't argue with. Didn't want to, really. She was lucky to be alive, she said, and she would take no more chances. And if he wanted to talk to her, then he would do exactly as he was told.

He wrote it down. He fought the crowd and walked as fast as possible up Fifth to Fifty-ninth to the Plaza, up the steps and through its lobby, then out onto Central Park South. No one could follow him. And if she was this cautious, no one could follow her.

The sidewalk was packed along Central Park South, and as

he neared Sixth Avenue he walked even faster. He was keyed up, and regardless of how restrained he tried to be, he was terribly excited about meeting her. On the phone she had been cool and methodical, but with a trace of fear and uncertainty. She was just a law student, she said, and she didn't know what she was doing, and she would probably be dead in a week if not sooner, but anyway this was the way the game would be played. Always assume you're being followed, she said. She had survived seven days of being chased by bloodhounds, so please do as she said.

She said to duck into the St. Moritz at the corner of Sixth, and he did. She had reserved a room for him under the name of Warren Clark. He paid cash for the room, and rode the elevator to the ninth floor. He was to wait. Just sit and wait, she'd said.

He stood in the window for an hour and watched Central Park grow dark. The phone rang.

"Mr. Clark?" a female asked.

"Uh, yes."

"It's me. Did you arrive alone?"

"Yes. Where are you?"

"Six floors up. Take the elevator to the eighteenth, then walk down to the fifteenth. Room 1520."

"Okay. Now?"

"Yes. I'm waiting."

He brushed his teeth again, checked his hair, and ten minutes later was standing before room 1520. He felt like a sophomore on his first date. He hadn't had butterflies this bad since high school football.

But he was Gray Grantham of the *Washington Post,* and this was just another story and she was just another woman, so grab the reins, buddy.

He knocked, and waited. "Who is it?"

"Grantham," he said to the door.

The bolt clicked, and she opened the door slowly. The hair was gone, but she smiled, and there was the cover girl. She shook his hand firmly. "Come in."

She closed and bolted the door behind him. "Would you care for a drink?" she asked.

"Sure, what do you have?"

"Water, with ice."

"Sounds great."

She walked into a small sitting room where the television was on with no sound. "In here," she said. He set his bag on the table, and took a seat on the sofa. She was standing at the bar, and for a quick second he admired the jeans. No shoes. Extra-large sweatshirt with the collar to one side where a bra strap peeked through.

She handed him the water, and sat in a chair by the door.

"Thanks," he said.

"Have you eaten?" she asked.

"You didn't tell me to."

She chuckled at this. "Forgive me. I've been through a lot. Let's order room service."

He nodded and smiled at her. "Sure. Anything you want is fine with me."

"I'd love a greasy cheeseburger with fries and a cold beer."

"Perfect."

She picked up the phone and ordered the food. Grantham walked to the window and watched the lights crawling along Fifth Avenue.

"I'm twenty-four. How old are you?" She was on the sofa now, sipping ice water.

He took the chair nearest to her. "Thirty-eight. Married once. Divorced seven years and three months ago. No children. Live alone with a cat. Why'd you pick the St. Moritz?"

"Rooms were available, and I convinced them it was important to pay with cash and present no identification. Do you like it?"

"It's fine. Sort of past its prime."

"This is not exactly a vacation."

"It's fine. How long do you think we might be here?"

She watched him carefully. He'd published a book six years earlier on HUD scandals, and though it didn't sell she'd found a copy in a public library in New Orleans. He looked six years older than the photo on the dust jacket, but he was aging nicely with a touch of gray over the ears.

"I don't know how long you'll stay," she said. "My plans are subject to change by the minute. I may see a face on the street and fly to New Zealand."

"When did you leave New Orleans?"

"Monday night. I took a cab to Baton Rouge, and that would have been easy to follow. I flew to Chicago, where I bought four tickets to four different cities, including Boise, where my mother lives. I jumped on the plane to La Guardia at the last moment. I don't think anyone followed."

"You're safe."

"Maybe for the moment. We'll both be hunted when this story is published. Assuming it's published."

Gray rattled his ice and studied her. "Depends on what you tell me. And it depends on how much can be verified from other sources."

"The verification is up to you. I'll tell you what I know, and from there you're on your own."

"Okay. When do we start talking?"

"After dinner. I'd rather do it on a full stomach. You're in no hurry, are you?"

"Of course not. I've got all night, and all day tomorrow, and the next day and the next. I mean, you're talking about the biggest story in twenty years, so I'll hang around as long as you'll talk to me."

Darby smiled and looked away. Exactly a week ago, she and Thomas were waiting for dinner in the bar at Mouton's. He was wearing a black silk blazer, denim shirt, red paisley tie and heavily starched khakis. Shoes, but no socks. The shirt was unbuttoned and the tie was loose. They had talked about the Virgin Islands and Thanksgiving and Gavin Verheek while they waited on a table. He was drinking fast, and that was not unusual. He got drunk later, and it saved her life.

She had lived a year in the past seven days, and she was having a real conversation with a live person who did not wish her dead. She crossed her feet on the coffee table. It was not uncomfortable having him here in her room. She relaxed. His face said, "Trust me." And why not? Whom else could she trust?

"What are you thinking about?" he asked.

"It's been a long week. Seven days ago I was just another law student busting my tail to get to the top. Now look at me."

He was looking at her. Trying to be cool, not like a gawking sophomore, but he was looking. The hair was dark and very short, and quite stylish, but he liked the long version in yesterday's fax.

"Tell me about Thomas Callahan," he said.

"Why?"

"I don't know. He's part of the story, isn't he?"

"Yeah. I'll get to it later."

"Fine. Your mother lives in Boise?"

"Yes, but she knows nothing. Where's your mother?"

"Short Hills, New Jersey," he answered with a smile. He crunched on an ice cube and waited for her. She was thinking.

"What do you like about New York?" she asked.

"The airport. It's the quickest way out."

"Thomas and I were here in the summer. It's hotter than New Orleans."

Suddenly, Grantham realized she was not just a hot little coed, but a widow in mourning. The poor lady was suffering. She had not been checking out his hair or his clothes or his eyes. She was in pain. Dammit!

"I'm very sorry about Thomas," he said. "I won't ask about him again."

She smiled but said nothing.

There was a loud knock. Darby jerked her feet off the table, and glared at the door. Then she breathed deeply. It was the food.

"I'll get it," Gray said. "Just relax."

TWENTY-NINE

FOR CENTURIES, a quiet but mammoth battle of nature raged without interference along the coastline of what would become Louisiana. It was a battle for territory. No humans were involved until recent years. From the south, the ocean pushed inland with its tides and winds and floods. From the north, the Mississippi River hauled down an inexhaustible supply of freshwater and sediment, and fed the marshes with the soil they needed to vegetate and thrive. The saltwater from the Gulf eroded the coastline and burned the freshwater marshes by killing the grasses that held them together. The river responded by draining half the continent and depositing its soil in lower Louisiana. It slowly built a long succession of sedimentary deltas, each of which in turn eventually blocked the river's path and forced it to change course yet again. The lush wetlands were built by the deltas.

It was an epic struggle of give-and-take, with the forces of nature firmly in control. With the constant replenishment from the mighty river, the deltas not only held their own against the Gulf, but expanded.

The marshlands were a marvel of natural evolution. Using the rich sediment as food, they grew into a green paradise of cypress and oak and dense patches of pickerelweed and bulrush and cattails. The water was filled with crawfish, shrimp, oysters, red snappers, flounder, pompano, bream, crabs, and alligators.

The coastal plain was a sanctuary for wildlife. Hundreds of species of migratory birds came to roost.

The wetlands were vast and limitless, rich and abundant.

Then oil was discovered there in 1930, and the rape was on. The oil companies dredged ten thousand miles of canals to get to the riches. They crisscrossed the fragile delta with a slashing array of neat little ditches. They sliced the marshes to ribbons.

They drilled, found oil, then dredged like maniacs to get to it. Their canals were perfect conduits for the Gulf and its saltwater, which ate away at the marshes.

Since oil was found, tens of thousands of acres of wetlands have been devoured by the ocean. Sixty square miles of Louisiana vanishes every year. Every fourteen minutes, another acre disappears under water.

IN 1979, AN OIL COMPANY punched a hole deep in Terrebonne Parish and hit oil. It was a routine day on just another rig, but it was not a routine hit. There was a lot of oil. They drilled again an eighth of a mile away, and hit another big one. They backed off a mile, drilled, and hit an even bigger one. Three miles away, they struck gold again.

The oil company capped the wells and pondered the situation, which had all the markings of a major new field.

The oil company was owned by Victor Mattiece, a Cajun from Lafayette who'd made and lost several fortunes drilling for oil in south Louisiana. In 1979, he happened to be wealthy, and more importantly, he had access to other people's money. He was quickly convinced he had just tapped a major reserve. He began buying land around the capped wells.

Secrets are crucial but hard to keep in the oilfields. And Mattiece knew if he threw around too much money, there would soon be a mad rush of drilling around his new gold mine. A man of infinite patience and planning, he looked at the big picture and said no to the quick buck. He decided he would have it all. He huddled with his lawyers and other advisers, and devised a plan to methodically buy the surrounding land under a myriad of corporate names. They formed new companies, used some of his old ones, purchased all or portions of struggling firms, and went about the business of acquiring acreage.

Those in the business knew Mattiece, and knew he had money and could get more. Mattiece knew they knew, so he quietly unleashed two dozen faceless entities upon the landowners of Terrebonne Parish. It worked without a major hitch.

The plan was to consolidate territory, then dredge yet another channel through the hapless and beleaguered marshlands so that the men and their equipment could get to the rigs and the oil could be brought out with haste. The canal would be thirty-five miles long and twice as wide as the others. There would be a lot of traffic.

Because Mattiece had money, he was a popular man with the politicians and bureaucrats. He played their game skillfully. He sprinkled money around where needed. He loved politics, but hated publicity. He was paranoid and reclusive.

As the land acquisition sailed smoothly along, Mattiece suddenly found himself short of cash. The industry turned downward in the early eighties, and his other rigs stopped pumping. He needed big money, and he wanted partners adept at putting it up and remaining silent about it. So he stayed away from Texas. He went overseas and found some Arabs who studied his maps and believed his estimate of a mammoth reserve of crude and natural gas. They bought a piece of the action, and Mattiece had plenty of cash again.

He did the sprinkling act, and obtained official permission to gouge his way through the delicate marshes and cypress swamps. The pieces were falling majestically into place, and Victor Mattiece could smell a billion dollars. Maybe two or three.

Then an odd thing happened. A lawsuit was filed to stop the dredging and drilling. The plaintiff was an obscure environmental outfit known simply as Green Fund.

The lawsuit was unexpected because for fifty years Louisiana had allowed itself to be devoured and polluted by oil companies and people like Victor Mattiece. It had been a trade-off. The oil business employed many and paid well. The oil and gas taxes collected in Baton Rouge paid the salaries of state employees.

The small bayou villages had been turned into boomtowns. The politicians from the governors down took the oil money and played along. All was well, and so what if some of the marsh-lands suffered.

Green Fund filed the lawsuit in the U.S. District Court in Lafayette. A federal judge halted the project pending a trial on all issues.

Mattiece went over the edge. He spent weeks with his lawyers plotting and scheming. He would spare no expense to win. Do whatever it took, he instructed them. Break any rule, violate any ethic, hire any expert, commission any study, cut any throat, spend any amount of money. Just win the damned law-suit.

Never one to be seen, he assumed an even lower profile. He moved to the Bahamas and operated from an armed fortress at Lyford Cay. He flew to New Orleans once a week to meet with the lawyers, then returned to the island.

Though invisible now, he made certain his political contribu-tions increased. His jackpot was still safe beneath Terrebonne Parish, and he would one day extract it, but one never knows when one will be forced to call in favors.

BY THE TIME the Green Fund lawyers, both of them, had waded in ankle deep, they had identified over thirty separate defendants. Some owned land. Some did exploring. Others laid pipe. Others drilled. The joint ventures and limited partner-ships and corporate associations were an impenetrable maze.

The defendants and their legions of high-priced lawyers an-swered with a vengeance. They filed a thick motion asking the judge to dismiss the lawsuit as frivolous. Denied. They asked him to allow the drilling to continue while they waited on a trial. Denied. They squealed with pain and explained in an-other heavy motion how much money was already tied up in exploration, drilling, etc. Denied again. They filed motions by the truckload, and when they were all denied and it was evident there would one day be a trial by jury, the oil lawyers dug in and played dirty.

Luckily for Green Fund's lawsuit, the heart of the new oil

reserve was near a ring of marshes that had been for years a natural refuge for waterfowl. Ospreys, egrets, pelicans, ducks, cranes, geese, and many others migrated to it. Though Louisiana has not always been kind to its land, it has shown a bit more sympathy for its animals. Since the verdict would one day be rendered by a jury of average and hopefully ordinary people, the Green Fund lawyers played heavy on the birds.

The pelican became the hero. After thirty years of insidious contamination by DDT and other pesticides, the Louisiana brown pelican perched on the brink of extinction. Almost too late, it was classified as an endangered species, and afforded a higher class of protection. Green Fund seized the majestic bird, and enlisted a half-dozen experts from around the country to testify on its behalf.

With a hundred lawyers involved, the lawsuit moved slowly. At times it went nowhere, which suited Green Fund just fine. The rigs were idle.

Seven years after Mattiece first buzzed over Terrebonne Bay in his jet helicopter and followed the swamplands along the route his precious canal would take, the pelican suit went to trial in Lake Charles. It was a bitter trial that lasted ten weeks. Green Fund sought money damages for the havoc already inflicted, and it wanted a permanent injunction against further drilling.

The oil companies brought in a fancy litigator from Houston to talk to the jury. He wore elephant-skin boots and a Stetson, and could talk like a Cajun when necessary. He was stout medicine, especially when compared to the Green Fund lawyers, both of whom had beards and very intense faces.

Green Fund lost the trial, and it was not altogether unexpected. The oil companies spent millions, and it's difficult to whip a bear with a switch. David pulled it off, but the best bet is always on Goliath. The jurors were not impressed with the dire warnings about pollution and the frailness of wetland ecology. Oil meant money, and folks needed jobs.

The judge kept the injunction in place for two reasons. First, he thought Green Fund had proven its point about the pelican,

THIRTY

THE TAPE RECORDER was in the center of the small table with four empty beer bottles around.

He made notes as he talked. "Who told you about the lawsuit?"

"A guy named John Del Greco. He's a law student at Tulane, a year ahead of me. He clerked last summer for a big firm in Houston, and the firm was on the periphery of the hostilities. He was not close to the trial, but the rumors and gossip were heavy."

"And all the firms were from New Orleans and Houston?"

"Yes, the principal litigation firms. But these companies are from a dozen different cities, so of course they brought their local counsel with them. There were lawyers from Dallas, Chicago, and several other cities. It was a circus."

"What's the status of the lawsuit?"

"From the trial level, it will be appealed to the Fifth Circuit Court of Appeals. That appeal has not been perfected, but should be in a month or so."

"Where's the Fifth Circuit?"

"New Orleans. About twenty-four months after it arrives there, a three-judge panel will hear and decide. The losing party will undoubtedly request a rehearing by the full panel, and this will take another three or four months. There are enough defects in the verdict to insure either a reversal or a remand."

"What's a remand?"

"The appellate court can do any of three things. Affirm the verdict, reverse the verdict, or find enough error to send the whole thing back for a new trial. If it goes back, it's been remanded. They can also affirm part, reverse part, remand part, sort of scramble things up."

Gray shook his head in frustration as he scribbled away. "Why would anyone want to be a lawyer?"

"I've asked myself that a few times in the past week."

"Any idea what the Fifth Circuit might do?"

"None. They haven't even seen it yet. The plaintiffs are alleging a multitude of procedural sins by the defendants, and given the nature of the conspiracy, a lot of it's probably true. It could be reversed."

"Then what happens?"

"The fun starts. If either side is unhappy with the Fifth Circuit, they can appeal to the Supreme Court."

"Surprise, surprise."

"Each year the Supreme Court receives thousands of appeals, but is very selective about what it takes. Because of the money and pressure and issues involved, this one has a decent chance of being heard."

"From today, how long would it take for the case to be decided by the Supreme Court?"

"Anywhere from three to five years."

"Rosenberg would have died from natural causes."

"Yes, but there could be a Democrat in the White House when he died from natural causes. So take him out now when you can sort of predict his replacement."

"Makes sense."

"Oh, it's beautiful. If you're Victor Mattiece, and you've only got fifty million or so, and you want to be a billionaire, and you don't mind killing a couple of Supremes, then now is the time."

"But what if the Supreme Court refused to hear the case?"

"He's in good shape if the Fifth Circuit affirms the trial verdict. But if it reverses, and the Supreme Court denies cert, he's got problems. My guess is that he would go back to square one, stir up some new litigation, and try it all again. There's too much money involved to lick his wounds and go home. When he took care of Rosenberg and Jensen, one has to assume he committed himself to a cause."

"Where was he during the trial?"

"Completely invisible. Keep in mind, it is not public knowledge that he's the ringleader of the litigation. By the time the trial started, there were thirty-eight corporate defendants. No individuals were named, just corporations. Of the thirty-eight, seven are traded publicly, and he owns no more than twenty percent of any one. These are just small firms traded over the counter. The other thirty-one are privately held, and I couldn't get much information. But I did learn that many of these private companies are owned by each other, and some are even owned by the public corporations. It's almost impenetrable."

"But he's in control."

"Yes. I suspect he owns or controls eighty percent of the project. I checked out four of the private companies, and three are chartered offshore. Two in the Bahamas, and one in the Caymans. Del Greco heard that Mattiece operates from behind offshore banks and companies."

"Do you remember the seven public companies?"

"Most of them. They, of course, were footnoted in the brief, a copy of which I do not have. But I've rewritten most of it in longhand."

"Can I see it?"

"You can have it. But it's lethal."

"I'll read it later. Tell me about the photograph."

"Mattiece is from a small town near Lafayette, and in his younger years was a big money man for politicians in south Louisiana. He was a shadowy type back then, always in the background giving money. He spent big bucks on Democrats locally and Republicans nationally, and over the years he was wined and dined by big shots from Washington. He has never sought publicity, but his kind of money is hard to hide, especially when it's being handed out to politicians. Seven years ago, when the President was the Vice President, he was in New Orleans for a Republican fundraiser. All the heavy hitters were there, including Mattiece. It was ten thousand dollars a plate, so the press tried to get in. Somehow a photographer snapped a picture of Mattiece shaking hands with the VP. The New Orleans paper ran it the next day. It's a wonderful picture. They're grinning at each other like best friends."

"It'll be easy to get."

"I stuck it on the last page of the brief, just for the fun of it. This is fun, isn't it?"

"I'm having a ball."

"Mattiece dropped out of sight a few years ago, and is now believed to live in several places. He's very eccentric. Del Greco said most people believe he's demented."

The recorder beeped, and Gray changed tapes. Darby stood and stretched her long legs. He watched her as he fumbled with the recorder. Two other tapes were already used and marked.

"Are you tired?" he asked.

"I haven't been sleeping well. How many more questions?"

"How much more do you know?"

"We've covered the basics. There are some gaps we can fill in the morning."

Gray turned off the recorder and stood. She was at the window, stretching and yawning. He relaxed on the sofa.

"What happened to the hair?" he asked.

Darby sat in a chair and pulled her feet under her. Red toenails. Her chin rested on her knees. "I left it in a hotel in New Orleans. How did you know about it?"

"I saw a photograph."

"From where?"

"Three photos, actually. Two from the Tulane yearbook, and one from Arizona State."

"Who sent them to you?"

"I have contacts. They were faxed to me, so they weren't that good. But there was this gorgeous hair."

"I wish you hadn't done that."

"Why?"

"Every phone call leaves a trail."

"Come on, Darby. Give me a little credit."

"You were snooping around on me."

"Just a little background. That's all."

"No more, okay? If you want something from me, just ask. If I say no, then leave it alone."

Grantham shrugged and agreed. Forget the hair. On to less sensitive matters. "So who selected Rosenberg and Jensen? Mattiece is not a lawyer."

"Rosenberg is easy. Jensen wrote little on environmental issues, but he was consistent in voting against all types of development. If they shared common ground with any consistency, it was protecting the environment."

"And you think Mattiece figured this out by himself?"

"Of course not. A pretty wicked legal mind presented him with the two names. He has a thousand lawyers."

"And none in D.C.?"

Darby raised her chin and frowned at him. "What did you say?"

"None of his lawyers are in D.C."

"I didn't say that."

"I thought you said the law firms were primarily from New Orleans and Houston and other cities. You didn't mention D.C."

Darby shook her head. "You're assuming too much. I can think of at least two D.C. firms that I ran across. One is White and Blazevich, a very old, powerful, rich Republican firm with four hundred lawyers."

Gray moved to the edge of the sofa.

"What's the matter?" she asked. He was suddenly wired. He was on his feet walking to the door, then back to the sofa.

"This may fit. This may be it, Darby."

"I'm listening."

"Are you listening?"

"I swear I'm listening."

He was at the window. "Okay, last week I got three phone calls from a lawyer in D.C. named Garcia, but that's not his name. He said he knew something and saw something about Rosenberg and Jensen, and he wanted so badly to tell me what he knew. But he got scared and disappeared."

"There are a million lawyers in D.C."

"Two million. But I know he works in a private firm. He sort of admitted it. He was sincere and very frightened, thought they were following. I asked who they were, and he of course wouldn't say."

"What happened to him?"

"We had a meeting planned for last Saturday morning, and he called early and said forget it. Said he was married and had a good job, and why risk it. He never admitted it, but I think he has a copy of something that he was about to show me."

"He could be your verification."

"What if he works for White and Blazevich? We've suddenly narrowed it to four hundred lawyers."

"The haystack is much smaller."

Grantham darted to his bag, flipped through some papers, and presto! pulled out a five-by-seven black and white. He dropped it in her lap. "This is Mr. Garcia."

Darby studied the picture. It was a man on a busy sidewalk. The face was clear. "I take it he didn't pose for this."

"Not exactly." Grantham was pacing.

"Then how'd you get it?"

"I cannot reveal my sources."

She slid it onto the coffee table, and rubbed her eyes. "You're scaring me, Grantham. This has a sleazy feel to it. Tell me it's not sleazy."

"It's just a little sleazy, okay. The kid was using the same pay phone, and that's a mistake."

"Yes, I know. That's a mistake."

"And I wanted to know what he looked like."

"Did you ask if you could take his photograph?"

"No."

"Then it's sleazy as hell."

"Okay. It's sleazy as hell. But I did it, and there it is, and it could be our link to Mattiece."

"Our link?"

"Yes, our link. I thought you wanted to nail Mattiece."

"Did I say that? I want him to pay, but I'd rather leave him alone. He's made a believer out of me, Gray. I've seen enough blood to last me a long time. You take this ball and run with it."

He didn't hear this. He walked behind her to the window, then back to the bar. "You mentioned two firms. What's the other?"

"Brim, Stearns, and somebody. I didn't get a chance to check them out. It's sort of odd because neither firm is listed as counsel of record for any of the defendants, but both firms, especially White and Blazevich, kept popping up as I went through the file."

"How big is Brim, Stearns, and somebody?"

"I can find out tomorrow."

"As big as White and Blazevich?"

"I doubt it."

"Just guess. How big?"

"Two hundred lawyers."

"Okay. Now we're up to six hundred lawyers in two firms. You're the lawyer, Darby. How can we find Garcia?"

"I'm not a lawyer, and I'm not a private detective. You're the investigative reporter." She didn't like this "we" business.

"Yeah, but I've never been in a law office, except for the divorce."

"Then you're very fortunate."

"How can we find him?"

She was yawning again. They had been talking for almost three hours, and she was exhausted. This could resume in the morning. "I don't know how to find him, and I really haven't given it much thought. I'll sleep on it, and explain it to you in the morning."

Grantham was suddenly calm. She stood and walked to the bar for a glass of water.

"I'll get my things," he said, picking up the tapes.

"Would you do me a favor?" she asked.

"Maybe."

She paused and looked at the sofa. "Would you mind sleeping on the sofa tonight? I mean, I haven't slept well in a long time, and I need the rest. It would, well, it would be nice if I knew you were in here."

He swallowed hard, and looked at the sofa. They both looked at the sofa. It was a five-footer at most, and did not appear to be the least bit comfortable.

"Sure," he said, smiling at her. "I understand."

"I'm spooked, okay?"

"I understand."

"It's nice to have someone like you around." She smiled demurely, and Gray melted.

"I don't mind," he said. "No problem."

"Thanks."

"Lock the door, get in the bed, and sleep well. I'll be right here, and everything's all right."

"Thanks." She nodded and smiled again, then closed the door to her bedroom. He listened, and she did not lock it.

He sat on the sofa in the darkness, watching her door. Some time after midnight, he dozed and slept with his knees not far from his chin.

THIRTY-ONE

HER BOSS was Jackson Feldman, and he was the executive editor, and this was her turf, and she didn't take any crap off anyone but Mr. Feldman. Especially an insolent brat like Gray Grantham, who was standing in front of Mr. Feldman's door, guarding it like a Doberman. She glared at him, and he sneered at her, and this had been going on for ten minutes, ever since they huddled in there and closed the door. Why Grantham was waiting outside, she did not know. But this was her turf.

Her phone rang, and Grantham yelled at her. "No calls!"

Her face was instantly red, and her mouth flew open. She picked up the receiver, listened for a second, then said, "I'm sorry, but Mr. Feldman is in a meeting." She glared at Grantham, who was shaking his head as if to dare her. "Yes, I'll have him call you back as soon as possible." She hung up.

"Thanks!" Grantham said, and this threw her off guard. She was about to say something nasty, but with the "Thanks" her mind went blank. He smiled at her. And it made her even madder.

It was five-thirty, time for her to leave, but Mr. Feldman asked her to stay. He was still smirking at her over there by the door, not ten feet away. She had never liked Gray Grantham. But then, there weren't too many people at the *Post* she did like. A news aide approached and appeared headed for the door when the Doberman stepped in front of him. "Sorry, you can't go in right now," Grantham said.

"And why not?"

"They're in a meeting. Leave it with her." He pointed at the secretary, who despised being pointed at and despised being referred to simply as "her." She had been here for twenty-one years.

The news aide was not easily intimidated. "That's fine. But Mr. Feldman instructed me to have these papers here at precisely five-thirty. It's precisely five-thirty, here I am, and here are the papers."

"Look, we're real proud of you. But you can't go in, understand? Now just leave the papers with that nice lady over there, and the sun will come up tomorrow." Grantham moved squarely in front of the door, and appeared ready for combat if the kid insisted.

"I'll take those," the secretary said. She took them, and the news aide left.

"Thanks!" Grantham said loudly again.

"I find you to be very rude," she snapped.

"I said 'Thanks.'" He tried to look hurt.

"You're a real smartass."

"Thanks!"

The door suddenly opened, and a voice called out, "Grantham."

He smiled at her, and stepped inside. Jackson Feldman was standing behind his desk. The tie was down to the second button and the sleeves were rolled to the elbows. He was six-six, with no fat. At fifty-eight, he ran two marathons a year and worked fifteen hours a day.

Smith Keen was also standing, and holding the four-page outline of a story along with a copy of Darby's handwritten reproduction of the pelican brief. Feldman's copy was lying on the desk. They appeared dazed.

"Close the door," Feldman said to Grantham.

Gray closed the door and sat on the edge of a table. No one spoke.

Feldman rubbed his eyes roughly, then looked at Keen. "Wow," he finally said.

Gray smiled. "You mean that's it. I hand you the biggest story in twenty years, and you are so moved you say 'Wow.' "

"Where's Darby Shaw?" Keen asked.

"I can't tell you. It's part of the deal."

"What deal?" Keen asked.

"I can't tell you that either."

"When did you talk to her?"

"Last night, and again this morning."

"And this was in New York?" Keen asked.

"What difference does it make where we talked? We talked, okay. She talked. I listened. I flew home. I wrote the outline. So what do you think?"

Feldman slowly folded his thin frame and sat deep in his chair. "How much does the White House know?"

"Not sure. Verheek told Darby that it was delivered to the White House one day last week, and at the time the FBI thought it should be pursued. Then for some reason, after the White House had it, the FBI backed off. That's all I know."

"How much did Mattiece give the President three years ago?"

"Millions. Virtually all of it through a myriad of PACs that he controls. This guy is very smart. He's got all kinds of lawyers, and they figure out ways to funnel money here and there. It's probably legal."

The editors were thinking slowly. They were stunned, as if they'd just survived a bomb blast. Grantham was quite proud, and swung his feet under the table like a kid on a pier.

Feldman slowly picked up the papers clipped together and flipped through until he found the photograph of Mattiece and the President. He shook his head.

"It's dynamite, Gray," Keen said. "We just can't run without a bunch of corroboration. Hell, you're talking about the world's greatest job of verifying. This is powerful stuff, son."

"How can you do it?" Feldman asked.

"I've got some ideas."

"I'd like to hear them. You could get yourself killed with this."

Grantham jumped to his feet, and stuck his hands in his pockets. "First, we'll try to find Garcia."

"We? Who's we?" Keen asked.

"Me, okay. Me. I'll try to find Garcia."

"Is the girl in on this?" Keen asked.

"I can't answer that. It's part of the deal."

"Answer the question," Feldman said. "Look at where we are if she gets killed helping you with the story. It's much too risky. Now where is she and what have you guys got planned?"

"I'm not telling where she is. She's a source, and I always protect my sources. No, she's not helping with the investigation. She's just a source, okay?"

They stared at him in disbelief. They looked at each other, and finally Keen shrugged.

"Do you want some help?" Feldman asked.

"No. She insists on me doing it alone. She's very scared, and you can't blame her."

"I got scared just reading the damned thing," Keen said.

Feldman kicked back in his chair and crossed his feet on the desk. Size fourteens. He smiled for the first time. "You've got to start with Garcia. If he can't be found, then you could dig for months on Mattiece and not put it together. And before you start digging on Mattiece, let's have a long talk. I sort of like you, Grantham, and this is not worth getting killed over."

"I see every word you write, okay?" Keen said.

"And I want a daily report, okay?" Feldman said.

"No problem."

Keen walked to the glass wall and watched the madness in the newsroom. In the course of each day, the chaos came and went a half a dozen times. Things got crazy at five-thirty. The news was being written, and the second story conference was at six-thirty.

Feldman watched from his desk. "This could be the end of the slump," he said to Gray without looking at him. "What's it been, five, six years?"

"Try seven," Keen said.

"I've written some good stories," Gray said defensively.

"Sure," Feldman said, still watching the newsroom. "But you've been hitting doubles and triples. The last grand slam was a long time ago."

"There have been a lot of strikeouts too," Keen added helpfully.

"Happens to all of us," Gray said. "But this grand slam will be in the seventh game of the World Series." He opened the door.

Feldman glared at him. "Don't get hurt, and don't allow her to get hurt. Understand?"

Gray smiled and left the office.

HE WAS ALMOST to Thomas Circle when he saw the blue lights behind him. The cop did not pass, but stayed on his bumper. He was oblivious to both the speed limit and his speedometer. It would be his third ticket in sixteen months.

He parked in a small lot next to an apartment house. It was dark, and the blue lights flashed in his mirrors. He rubbed his temples.

"Step out," the cop demanded from the bumper.

Gray opened the door and did what he was told. The cop was black, and was suddenly smiling. It was Cleve. He pointed to the patrol car. "Get in."

They sat in the car under the blue lights and stared at the Volvo. "Why do you do this to me?" Gray asked.

"We have quotas, Grantham. We have to stop so many white people and harass them. Chief wants to even things out. The white cops pick on innocent poor black folks, so us black cops have to pick on innocent rich white folks."

"I suppose you're gonna handcuff me and beat the hell out of me."

"Only if you ask me to. Sarge can't talk anymore."

"I'm listening."

"He smells something around the place. He's caught a few strange looks, and he's heard a thing or two."

"Such as?"

"Such as they're talking about you, and how much they need to know what you know. He thinks they might be listening."

"Come on, Cleve. Is he serious?"

"He's heard them talk about you and how you're asking questions about the pelican something or other. You've got 'em shook up."

"What has he heard about this pelican thing?"

"Just that you're hot on it, and they're serious about it. These are mean and paranoid people, Gray. Sarge says to be careful where you go and who you talk to."

"And we can't meet anymore?"

"Not for a while. He wants to lay low, and run things through me."

"We'll do that. I need his help, but tell him to be careful. This is very touchy."

"What is this pelican business?"

"I can't say. But tell Sarge it could get him killed."

"Not Sarge. He's smarter than all of them over there."

Gray opened the door and got out. "Thanks, Cleve."

He turned off the blue lights. "I'll be around. I'm working nights for the next six months, so I'll try and keep an eye on you."

"Thanks."

RUPERT PAID for his cinnamon roll and sat on a bar stool overlooking the sidewalk. It was midnight, exactly midnight, and Georgetown was winding down. A few cars sped along M Street, and the remaining pedestrians headed for home. The coffee shop was busy, but not crowded. He sipped black coffee.

He recognized the face on the sidewalk, and moments later the man was sitting on the next bar stool. He was a flunkie of some sort. They had met a few days ago in New Orleans.

"So what's the score?" Rupert asked.

"We can't find her. And that worries us because we got some bad news today."

"And?"

"Well, we heard voices, unconfirmed, that the bad guys have freaked out, and that the number one bad guy wants to start killing everybody. Money is no object, and these voices tell us he'll spend whatever it takes to snuff this thing out. He's sending in big boys with big guns. Of course, they say he's deranged, but he's mean as hell and money can kill a lot of people."

This killing talk did not faze Rupert. "Who's on the list?"

"The girl. And I guess anyone else on the outside who happens to know about that little paper."

"So what's my plan?"

"Hang around. We'll meet here tomorrow night, same time. If we find the girl, it'll be your show."

"How do you plan to find her?"

"We think she's in New York. We have ways."

Rupert pulled off a piece of cinnamon roll and stuffed it in his mouth. "Where would you be?"

The messenger thought of a dozen places he might go, but, dammit, they were like Paris and Rome and Monte Carlo, places he'd seen and places everyone went to. He couldn't think of that one exotic spot where he would go and hide for the rest of his life. "I don't know. Where would you be?"

"New York City. You can live there for years and never be seen. You speak the language and know the rules. It's the perfect hiding place for an American."

"Yeah, I guess you're right. You think she's there?"

"I don't know. At times she's clever. Then she has bad moments."

The messenger was on his feet. "Tomorrow night," he said.

Rupert waved him off. What a goofy little twerp, he thought. Running around whispering important messages in coffee shops and beer joints. Then running back to his boss and reliving it all in vivid detail.

He threw the coffee cup in the trash and was on the sidewalk.

THIRTY-TWO

BRIM, STEARNS, AND KIDLOW had a hundred and ninety lawyers, according to the latest edition of the Martindale-Hubbell Legal Directory. And White and Blazevich had four hundred and twelve, so hopefully Garcia was only one of a possible six hundred and two. But if Mattiece used other D.C. firms, the number would be higher and they didn't have a chance.

As expected, White and Blazevich had no one named Garcia. Darby searched for another Hispanic name, but found none. It was one of those lily-white silk-stocking outfits filled with Ivy Leaguers with long names that ended in numerals. There were a few female names sprinkled about, but only two were partners. Most of the women had joined after 1980. If she lived long enough to finish law school, she would not consider working for a factory like White and Blazevich.

Grantham had suggested she check for Hispanics because Garcia was a bit unusual for an alias. Maybe the guy was Hispanic, and since Garcia is common for them, then maybe he just said it real quick. It didn't work. There were no Hispanics in this firm.

According to the directory, their clients were big and rich. Banks, Fortune 500s, and lots of oil companies. They listed four of the defendants in the lawsuit as clients, but not Mr. Mattiece. There were chemical companies and shipping lines, and White and Blazevich also represented the governments of South Korea, Libya, and Syria. Silly, she thought. Some of our enemies hire our lawyers to lobby our government. But then, you can hire lawyers to do anything.

Brim, Stearns, and Kidlow was a smaller version of White and Blazevich, but, gosh, there were four Hispanic names listed. She wrote them down. Two men and two women. She figured this firm must have been sued for race and sex discrimination. In the past ten years they had hired all kinds of people. The client list was predictable: oil and gas, insurance, banks, government relations. Pretty dull stuff.

She sat in a corner of the Fordham law library for an hour. It was Friday morning, ten in New York and nine in New Orleans, and instead of hiding in a library she'd never seen before, she was supposed to be sitting in Federal Procedure under Alleck, a professor she never liked but now missed sorely. Alice Stark would be sitting next to her. One of her favorite law nerds, D. Ronald Petrie, would be sitting behind her asking for a date and making lewd comments. She missed him too. She missed the quiet mornings on Thomas' balcony, sipping coffee and waiting for the French Quarter to shake its cobwebs and come to life. She missed the smell of cologne on his bathrobe.

She thanked the librarian, and left the building. On Sixty-second, she headed east toward the park. It was a brilliant October morning with a perfect sky and cool wind. A pleasant change from New Orleans, but difficult to appreciate under the circumstances. She wore new Ray-Bans and a muffler up to her chin. The hair was still dark, but she would cut no more. She was determined to walk without looking over her shoulder. They probably weren't back there, but she knew it would be years before she could stroll along a street without a doubt.

The trees in the park were a magnificent display of yellow and orange and red. The leaves fell gently in the breeze. She turned south on Central Park West. She would leave tomorrow, and spend a few days in Washington. If she survived, she would then leave the country, go maybe to the Caribbean. She'd been there twice, and there were a thousand little islands where most people spoke some form of English.

Now was the time to leave the country. They'd lost her trail, and she'd already checked on flights to Nassau and Jamaica. She could be there by dark.

She found a pay phone in the rear of a bagel shop on Sixth, and punched Gray's number at the *Post*. "It's me," she said.

"Well, well. I was afraid you had skipped the country."

"Thinking about it."

"Can you wait a week?"

"Probably. I'll be there tomorrow. What do you know?"

"I'm just gathering junk. I've got copies of the annual statements for the seven public corporations involved in the suit."

"It's lawsuit, not suit. A suit is something you wear."

"How can you ever forgive me? Mattiece is neither an officer nor director of any."

"What else?"

"Just the thousand phone calls routine. I spent three hours yesterday hanging around courthouses looking for Garcia."

"You won't find him at a courthouse, Gray. He's not that kind of lawyer. He's in a corporate firm."

"I take it you have a better idea."

"I've got several ideas."

"Well, then, I'm just sitting here waiting on you."

"I'll call you when I get there."

"Don't call me at home."

She paused for a second. "May I ask why not?"

"There's a chance someone is listening, and maybe following. One of my best sources thinks I've ruffled enough feathers to get myself placed under surveillance."

"Fabulous. And you want me to rush down there and team up with you?"

"We'll be safe, Darby. We just have to be careful."

She gripped the phone and clenched her teeth. "How dare you talk to me about being careful! I've been dodging bombs and bullets for ten days now, and you're smug enough to tell me to be careful. Kiss my ass, Grantham! Maybe I should stay away from you."

There was a pause as she looked around the tiny café. Two

men at the nearest table looked at her. She was much too loud. She turned away and breathed deeply.

Grantham spoke slowly. "I'm sorry. I—"

"Forget it. Just forget it."

He waited a moment. "Are you okay?"

"I'm terrific. Never felt better."

"Are you coming to D.C.?"

"I don't know. I'm safe here, and I'll be much safer when I get on a plane and leave the country."

"Sure, but I thought you had this wonderful idea about finding Garcia, then hopefully nailing Mattiece. I thought you were outraged and morally indignant and motivated by revenge. What's happened to you?"

"Well, for one, I have this burning desire to see my twenty-fifth birthday. I'm not selfish, but perhaps I'd like to see my thirtieth too. That would be nice."

"I understand."

"I'm not sure you understand. I think you're more concerned with Pulitzers and glory than my pretty little neck."

"I assure you that's not true. Trust me, Darby. You'll be safe. You've told me the story of your life. You must trust me."

"I'll think about it."

"That's not definite."

"No, it's not. Give me some time."

"Okay."

She hung up, and ordered a bagel. A dozen languages rattled around her as the café was suddenly packed. Run, baby, run, her good sense told her. Take a cab to the airport. Pay cash for a ticket to Miami. Find the nearest flight south, and get on the plane. Let Grantham dig and wish him the best. He was very good, and he'd find a way to break the story. And she would read about it one day while lying on a sun-drenched beach sipping a piña colada and watching the windsurfers.

Stump limped by on the sidewalk. She caught a glimpse of him through the crowd and through the window. Her mouth was suddenly dry and she was dizzy. He didn't look inside. He just ambled by, looking rather lost. She ran through the tables and watched him through the door. He limped slightly to the corner of Sixth and Fifty-eighth and waited for the light. He started to cross Sixth, then changed his mind and crossed Fifty-eighth. A taxi almost smeared him.

He was going nowhere, just strolling along with a slight limp.

CROFT SAW THE KID as he stepped from an elevator into the atrium. He was with another young lawyer, and they didn't have their briefcases so it was obvious they were headed for a late lunch. After five days of watching lawyers, Croft had learned their habits.

The building was on Pennsylvania, and Brim, Stearns, and Kidlow covered floors three through eleven. Garcia left the building with his buddy, and they laughed their way down the sidewalk. Something was very funny. Croft followed as closely as possible. They walked and laughed for five blocks, then, just as he figured, they ducked into a yuppie corporate fern bar for a quick bite.

Croft called Grantham three times before he got him. It was almost two, and the lunch was winding down by now, and if Grantham wanted to catch the guy, then stay close to the damned phone. Gray slammed it down. They would meet back at the building.

Garcia and his friend walked a bit slower on the return. It was a beautiful day, and it was Friday, and they enjoyed this brief respite from the grind of suing people or whatever they did for two hundred bucks an hour. Croft hid behind his sunshades and kept his distance.

Gray was waiting in the lobby near the elevators. Croft was close behind them as they spun through the revolving door. He pointed quickly to their man. Gray caught the signal and punched the elevator button. It opened and he stepped in just before Garcia and his friend. Croft stayed behind.

Garcia punched number six a split second before Gray punched it too. Gray read the paper and listened as the two lawyers talked football. The kid was no more than twenty-seven or twenty-eight. The voice maybe had a vague familiarity to it, but it had been on the phone and there was nothing distinctive about it. The face was close, but he couldn't study it. The odds said go for it. He looked very similar to the man in the photograph, and he worked for Brim, Stearns, and Kidlow, and one of its countless clients was Mr. Mattiece. He would give it a shot, but be cautious. He was a reporter. It was his job to go barging in with questions.

They left the elevator on six still yakking about the Redskins, and Gray loitered behind them, casually reading the paper. The firm's lobby was rich and opulent, with chandeliers and Oriental rugs, and on one wall thick gold letters with the firm's name. The lawyers stopped at the front desk and picked up their phone messages. Gray strolled purposefully in front of the receptionist, who eyed him carefully.

"May I help you, sir?" she asked in the tone that meant, "What the hell do you want?"

Gray did not miss a step. "I'm in a meeting with Roger Martin." He'd found the name in the phone book, and he'd called from the lobby a minute earlier to make sure lawyer Martin was in today. The building directory listed the firm on floors three through eleven, but did not list all one hundred and ninety lawyers. Using the yellow pages listing, he made a dozen quick calls to find a lawyer on each floor. Roger Martin was the man on the sixth floor.

He frowned at the receptionist. "I've been meeting with him for two hours."

This puzzled her, and she could think of nothing to say. Gray was around the corner and into a hallway. He caught a glimpse of Garcia entering his office four doors down.

The name beside the door was David M. Underwood. Gray did not knock on it. He wanted to strike quickly, and perhaps exit quickly. Mr. Underwood was hanging his jacket on a rack.

"Hi. I'm Gray Grantham with the *Washington Post*. I'm looking for a man named Garcia."

Underwood froze and looked puzzled. "How'd you get in here?" he asked.

The voice was suddenly familiar. "I walked. You are Garcia, aren't you?"

He pointed to a desk plate with his name in gold letters.

"David M. Underwood. There's no one on this floor named Garcia. I don't know of a Garcia in this firm."

Gray smiled as if to play along. Underwood was scared. Or irritated.

"How's your daughter?" Gray asked.

Underwood was coming around the desk, staring and getting very perturbed. "Which one?"

This didn't fit. Garcia had been quite concerned about his daughter, a baby, and if there had been more than one, he would have mentioned it.

"The youngest. And your wife?"

Underwood was now within striking distance, and inching closer. It was obvious he was a man unafraid of physical contact.

"I don't have a wife. I'm divorced." He held up his left fist, and for a split second Gray thought he'd gone wild. Then he saw the four ringless fingers. No wife. No ring. Garcia adored his wife, and there would be a ring. It was now time to leave.

"What do you want?" Underwood demanded.

"I thought Garcia was on this floor," he said, easing away.

"Is your pal Garcia a lawyer?"

"Yes."

Underwood relaxed a bit. "Not in this firm. We have a Perez and a Hernandez, and maybe one other. But I don't know a Garcia."

"Well, it's a big firm," Gray said by the door. "Sorry to bother."

Underwood was following. "Look, Mr. Grantham, we're not accustomed to reporters barging in around here. I'll call security, and maybe they can help you."

"Won't be necessary. Thanks." Grantham was in the hall and gone. Underwood reported to security.

Grantham cursed himself in the elevator. It was empty except for him, and he cursed out loud. Then he thought of Croft, and was cursing him when the elevator landed and opened, and there was Croft in the lobby near the pay phones. Cool it, he told himself.

They left the building together. "Didn't work," Gray said.

"Did you talk to him?"

"Yep. Wrong man."

"Dammit. I knew it was him. It was the kid in the photos, wasn't it?"

"No. Close but no cigar. Keep trying."

"I'm really tired of this, Grantham. I've—"

"You're getting paid, aren't you? Do it for one more week, okay? I can think of harder work."

Croft stopped on the sidewalk, and Gray kept walking. "One more week, and I'm through," Croft yelled to him. Grantham waved him off.

He unlocked the illegally parked Volvo and sped back to the *Post*. It was not a smart move. It was quite stupid, and he was much too experienced for such a mistake. He would omit it from his daily chat with Jackson Feldman and Smith Keen.

FELDMAN WAS LOOKING for him, another reporter said, and he walked quickly to his office. He smiled sweetly to the secretary, who was poised to attack. Keen and Howard Krauthammer, the managing editor, were waiting with Feldman. Keen closed the door and handed Gray a newspaper. "Have you seen this?"

It was the New Orleans paper, the *Times-Picayune*, and the front-page story was about the deaths of Verheek and Callahan, along with big photos. He read it quickly while they watched him. It talked about their friendship, and their strange deaths just six days apart. And it mentioned Darby Shaw, who had disappeared. But no link to the brief.

"I guess the cat's out of the bag," Feldman said.

"It's nothing but the basics," Gray said. "We could've run this three days ago."

"Why didn't we?" asked Krauthammer.

"There's nothing here. It's two dead bodies, the name of the girl, and a thousand questions, none of which they answered. They've found a cop who'll talk, but he knows nothing beyond the blood and gore."

"But they're digging, Gray," Keen said.

"You want me to stop them?"

"The *Times* has picked it up," Feldman said. "They're running something tomorrow or Sunday. How much can they know?"

"Why ask me? Look, it's possible they have a copy of the brief. Very unlikely, but possible. But they haven't talked to the girl. We've got the girl, okay. She's ours."

"We hope," said Krauthammer.

Feldman rubbed his eyes and stared at the ceiling. "Let's say they have a copy of the brief, and that they know she wrote it, and now she's vanished. They can't verify it right now, but they're not afraid to mention the brief without naming Mattiece. Let's say they know Callahan was her professor, among other things, and that he brought the brief here and gave it to his good friend Verheek. And now they're dead and she's on the run. That's a pretty damned good story, wouldn't you say, Gray?"

"It's a big story," Krauthammer said.

"It's peanuts compared to what's coming," Gray said. "I don't want to run it because it's the tip of the iceberg, and it'll attract every paper in the country. We don't need a thousand reporters bumping into each other."

"I say we run it," Krauthammer said. "If not, the *Times* will beat our ass with it."

"We can't run the story," Gray said.

"Why not?" asked Krauthammer.

"Because I'm not going to write it, and if it's written by someone else here, then we lose the girl. It's that simple. She's debating right now about whether to jump on a plane and leave the country, and one mistake by us and she's gone."

"But she's already spilled her guts," Keen said.

"I gave her my word, okay. I will not write the story until it's pieced together and Mattiece can be named. It's very simple."

"You're using her, aren't you?" Keen asked.

"She's a source. But she's not in the city."

"If the *Times* has the brief, then they know about Mattiece," Feldman said. "And if they know about Mattiece, you can bet they're digging like hell to verify it. What if they beat us?"

Krauthammer grunted in disgust. "We're going to sit on our asses and lose the biggest story I've seen in twenty years. I say we run what we've got. It's just the surface, but it's a helluva story right now."

"No," Gray said. "I won't write it until I have all of it."

"And how long might that take?" Feldman asked.

"A week, maybe."

"We don't have a week," Krauthammer said.

Gray was desperate. "I can find out how much the *Times* knows. Give me forty-eight hours."

"They're running something tomorrow or Sunday," Feldman said again.

"Let 'em run it. I'll bet money it'll be the same story with probably the same mug shots. You guys are assuming a hell of a lot. You're assuming they've got a copy of the brief, but its author doesn't have a copy of it. We don't have a copy of it. Let's wait, and read their little story, then go from there."

The editors studied each other. Krauthammer was frustrated. Keen was anxious. But the boss was Feldman, and he said, "Okay. If they run something in the morning, we'll meet here at noon and look at it."

"Fine," Gray said quickly and reached for the door.

"You'd better move fast, Grantham," Feldman said. "We can't sit on this much longer."

Grantham was gone.

THIRTY-THREE

THE LIMOUSINE moved patiently in the Beltway rush hour. It was dark, and Matthew Barr read with the aid of a reading light in the ceiling. Coal sipped Perrier and watched the traffic. He had the brief memorized, and could have simply explained it to Barr, but he wanted to watch his reaction.

Barr had no reaction until he got to the photograph, then slowly shook his head. He laid it on the seat, and thought about it for a moment. "Very nasty," he said.

Coal grunted.

"How true is it?" Barr asked.

"I'd love to know."

"When did you first see it?"

"Tuesday of last week. It came over from the FBI in one of their daily reports."

"What'd the President say?"

"He was not that happy with it, but there was no cause for alarm. It's just another wild shot in the dark, we thought. He talked to Voyles about it, and Voyles agreed to leave it alone for a while. Now I'm not so sure."

"Did the President ask Voyles to back off?" Barr asked the question slowly.

"Yes."

"That's awfully close to obstruction of justice, assuming of course the brief turns out to be true."

"And what if it's true?"

"Then the President has problems. I've got one conviction for obstruction, so I've been there. It's like mail fraud. It's broad and wide and fairly easy to prove. Were you in on it?"

"What do you think?"

"Then I think you've got problems too."

They rode in silence and watched the traffic. Coal had thought through the obstruction angle, but he wanted Barr's opinion. He wasn't worried about criminal charges. The President had one brief little chat with Voyles, asked him to look elsewhere for the time being, and that was it. Hardly the work of felons. But Coal was terribly concerned with reelection, and a scandal involving a major contributor like Mattiece would be devastating. The thought was sickening—a man the President knew and took millions from paid money to have two Supreme Court Justices knocked off so his pal the President could appoint more reasonable men to the bench so that the oil could be harvested. The Democrats would fall in the streets howling with glee. Every subcommittee in Congress would hold hearings. Every newspaper would run it every day for a year. The Justice Department would be forced to investigate. Coal would be forced to take the blame and resign. Hell, everyone in the White House, except the President, would have to go.

It was a nightmare of horrific proportions.

"We've got to find out if the brief is true," Coal said to the window.

"If people are dying, then it's true. Give me a better reason for killing Callahan and Verheek."

There was no other reason, and Coal knew it. "I want you to do something."

"Find the girl."

"No. She's either dead or hiding in a cave somewhere. I want you to talk to Mattiece."

"I'm sure he's in the yellow pages."

"You can find him. We need to establish a link that the President knows nothing about. We need to first determine how much of this is true."

"And you think Victor will take me into his confidence and tell me his secrets."

"Yes, eventually. You're not a cop, remember. Assume it's true, and he thinks he's about to be exposed. He's desperate and he's killing people. What if you told him the press had the story and the end was near, and if he is inclined to disappear, then now's the time? You're coming to him from Washington, remember? From the inside. From the President, or so he thinks. He'll listen to you."

"Okay. What if he tells me it's true? What's in it for us?"

"I've got some ideas, all in the category of damage control. The first thing we'll do is immediately appoint two nature lovers to the Court. I mean, wild-eyed radical bird watchers. It would show that down deep we're good little environmentalists. And it would kill Mattiece and his oil field, etc. We could do this in a matter of hours. Almost simultaneously, the President will call in Voyles and the Attorney General and Justice and demand an immediate investigation into Mattiece. We'll leak copies of the brief to every reporter in town, then hunker down and ride out the storm."

Barr was smiling with admiration.

Coal continued. "It won't be pretty, but it's far better than sitting back and hoping the brief is a work of fiction."

"How do you explain that photograph?"

"You can't. It'll hurt for a while, but it was seven years ago, and people go crazy. We'll portray Mattiece as a good citizen back then, but now he's a madman."

"He is a madman."

"Yes, he is. And right now he's like a wounded dog backed in a corner. You must convince him to throw in the towel, and haul ass. I think he'll listen to you. And I think we'll find out from him if it's true."

"So how do I find him?"

"I've got a man working on that. I'll pull some strings, and make a contact. Be ready to go on Sunday."

Barr smiled to the window. He would like to meet Mattiece.

The traffic slowed. Coal slowly sipped his water. "Anything on Grantham?"

"Not really. We're listening and watching, but nothing exciting. He talks to his mother and a couple of gals, but nothing worth reporting. He works a lot. He left town Wednesday and returned Thursday."

"Where did he go?"

"New York. Probably working on some story."

CLEVE WAS SUPPOSED to be at the corner of Rhode Island and Sixth at exactly 10 P.M., but he wasn't. Gray was supposed to race down Rhode Island until Cleve caught him, so that if anyone was indeed following him they would think he was simply a dangerous driver. He raced down Rhode Island, through Sixth at fifty miles per hour, and watched for blue lights. There were none. He looped around, and fifteen minutes later barreled down Rhode Island again. There! He saw blue lights and pulled to the curb.

It was not Cleve. It was a white cop who was very agitated. He jerked Gray's license, examined it, and asked if he'd been drinking. No sir, he said. The cop wrote the ticket, and proudly handed it to Gray, who sat behind the wheel staring at the ticket until he heard voices coming from the rear bumper.

Another cop was on the scene, and they were arguing. It was Cleve, and he wanted the white cop to forget the ticket, but the white cop explained it had already been written and besides the idiot was doing fifty-six miles an hour through the intersection. He's a friend, Cleve said. Then teach him how to drive before he kills somebody, the white cop said as he got in his patrol car and drove away.

Cleve was snickering as he looked in Gray's window. "Sorry about that," he said with a smile.

"It's all your fault."

"Slow it down next time."

Gray threw the ticket on the floorboard. "Let's talk quick. You said Sarge said the boys in the West Wing are talking about me. Right?"

"Right."

"Okay, I need to know from Sarge if they're talking about

any other reporters, especially from the *New York Times*. I need to know if they think anybody else is hot on the story."

"Is that all?"

"Yes. I need it quick."

"Slow it down," Cleve said loudly and walked to his car.

DARBY PAID for the room for the next seven days, in part because she wanted a familiar place to return to if necessary, and in part because she wanted to leave some new clothes she had purchased. It was sinful, this running and leaving everything behind. The clothes were nothing fancy, sort of upscale safari law school, but they cost even more in New York, and it would be nice to keep them. She would not take risks over clothes, but she liked the room and she liked the city and she wanted the clothes.

It was time to run again, and she would travel light. She carried a small canvas bag when she darted from the St. Moritz into a waiting cab. It was almost 11 P.M., Friday, and Central Park South was busy. Across the street, a line of horses and carriages waited for customers and brief excursions through the park.

The cab took ten minutes to get to Seventy-second and Broadway, which was the wrong direction, but this entire journey should be hard to follow. She walked thirty feet, and disappeared into the subway. She had studied a map and a book of the system, and she hoped it would be easy. The subway was not appealing because she'd never used it and she'd heard the stories. But this was the Broadway line, the most commonly used train in Manhattan, and it was rumored to be safe, at times. And things weren't so swell above the ground. The subway could hardly be worse.

She waited in the correct spot with a group of drunk but well-dressed teenagers, and the train arrived in a couple of minutes. It wasn't crowded, and she took a seat near the center doors. Stare at the floor and hold the bag, she kept telling herself. She looked at the floor, but from behind the dark shades, she studied the people. It was her lucky night. No street punks with knives. No beggars. No perverts, at least none she could spot. But for a novice, it was nerve-racking anyway.

The drunk kids exited at Times Square, and she got off quickly at the next stop. She had never seen Penn Station, but this was not the time to sightsee. Maybe one day she could return and spend a month and admire the city without watching for Stump and Thin Man and who knows who else who was out there. But not now.

She had five minutes, and found her train as it was boarding. Again, she sat in the rear and watched every passenger. There were no familiar faces. Surely, please, surely, they had not stuck to her on this jagged escape. Once again, her mistake had been credit cards. She had bought four tickets at O'Hare with American Express, and somehow they knew she was in New York. She was certain Stump had not seen her, but he was in the city, and of course he had friends. There could be twenty of them. But then, she was not certain of anything.

The train left six minutes late. It was half empty. She pulled a paperback from the bag and pretended to read it.

Fifteen minutes later, they stopped in Newark, and she got off. She was a lucky girl. There were cabs lined up outside the station, and ten minutes later she was at the airport.

THIRTY-FOUR

I T WAS SATURDAY MORNING, and the Queen was in
Florida taking money from the rich, and it was clear and
cool outside. He wanted to sleep late, then play golf whenever
he woke up. But it was seven, and he was sitting at his desk
wearing a tie, listening to Fletcher Coal suggest what they ought
to do about this and about that. Richard Horton, the Attorney
General, had talked to Coal, and now Coal was alarmed.

Someone opened the door and Horton entered alone. They
shook hands and Horton sat across the desk. Coal stood nearby,
and this really irritated the President.

Horton was dull but sincere. He was not dumb or slow, he
just thought carefully about everything before he acted. He
thought about each word before he said it. He was loyal to the
President, and could be trusted for sound judgment.

"We are seriously considering a formal grand jury investigation into the deaths of Rosenberg and Jensen," he announced
gravely. "In light of what's happened in New Orleans, we think
this should be pursued immediately."

"The FBI is investigating," the President said. "They've got
three hundred agents on the case. Why should we get involved?"

"Are they investigating the pelican brief?" Horton asked. He
knew the answer. He knew Voyles was in New Orleans at this
moment with hundreds of agents. He knew they had talked to

hundreds of people, collected a pile of useless evidence. He knew the President had asked Voyles to back off, and he knew Voyles was not telling the President everything.

Horton had never mentioned the pelican brief to the President, and the fact that he even knew about the damned thing was exasperating. How many more knew about it? Probably thousands.

"They are pursuing all leads," Coal said. "They gave us a copy of it almost two weeks ago, so we assume they're pursuing it."

Exactly what Horton expected out of Coal. "I feel strongly that the Administration should investigate this matter at once." He spoke as though this was all memorized, and this irritated the President.

"Why?" asked the President.

"What if the brief is on target? If we do nothing, and the truth eventually surfaces, the damage will be irreparable."

"Do you honestly believe there's any truth to it?" the President asked.

"It's awfully suspicious. The first two men who saw it are dead, and the person who wrote it has disappeared. It is perfectly logical, if one is so inclined to kill Supreme Court Justices. There are no other compelling suspects. From what I hear, the FBI is baffled. Yes, it needs to be pursued."

Horton's investigations leaked worse than the White House basement, and Coal was terrified of this clown impaneling a grand jury and calling witnesses. Horton was an honorable man, but the Justice Department was filled with lawyers who talked too much.

"Don't you think it's a bit premature?" Coal asked.

"I don't think so."

"Have you seen the papers this morning?" Coal asked.

Horton had glanced at the front page of the *Post*, and read the sports section. It was Saturday, after all. He had heard that Coal read eight newspapers before dawn, so he didn't like this question.

"I've read a couple of them," he said.

"I've looked at several," Coal said modestly. "And there's not a word anywhere about those two dead lawyers or the girl or Mattiece or anything related to the brief. If you start a formal investigation at this point, it'll be front-page news for a month."

"Do you think it will simply go away?" Horton asked Coal.

"It might. For obvious reasons, we hope so."

"I think you're optimistic, Mr. Coal. We don't normally sit back and wait for the press to do our investigating."

Coal grinned and almost laughed at this one. He smiled at the President, who shot him a quick look, and Horton started a slow burn.

"What's wrong with waiting a week?" asked the President.

"Nothing," shot Coal.

Just that quick the decision was made to wait a week, and Horton knew it. "Things could blow up in a week," he said without conviction.

"Wait a week," the President ordered. "We'll meet here next Friday, and go from there. I'm not saying no, Richard, just wait seven days."

Horton shrugged. This was more than he expected. He'd covered his rear. He would go straight to his office and dictate a lengthy memo detailing everything he could remember about this meeting, and his neck would be protected.

Coal stepped forward and handed him a sheet of paper.

"What's this?"

"More names. Do you know them?"

It was the bird-watcher list: four judges who were much too liberal for comfort, but Plan B called for radical environmentalists on the Court.

Horton blinked several times and studied it hard. "You must be kidding."

"Check 'em out," said the President.

"These guys are off-the-wall liberals," Horton mumbled.

"Yes, but they worship the sun and moon, and trees and birds," Coal explained helpfully.

Horton caught on, and suddenly smiled. "I see. Pelican lovers."

"They're almost extinct, you know," the President said.

Coal headed for the door. "I wish they'd been wiped out ten years ago."

SHE HADN'T CALLED by nine when Gray arrived at his desk in the newsroom. He'd read the *Times* and there was nothing in it. He spread the New Orleans paper over the clutter and skimmed it. Nothing. They had reported all they knew. Callahan, Verheek, Darby, and a thousand unanswered questions. He had to assume the *Times* and maybe the *Times-Picayune* in New Orleans had seen the brief or heard about it, and thus knew of Mattiece. And he had to assume they were clawing like cats to verify it. But he had Darby, and they would find Garcia, and if Mattiece could be verified, they would do it.

At the moment, there was no alternative plan. If Garcia was gone or refused to help, they would be forced to explore the dark and murky world of Victor Mattiece. Darby would not last long at that, and he didn't blame her. He was uncertain how long he would last.

Smith Keen appeared with a cup of coffee and sat on the desk. "If the *Times* had it, would they hold off until tomorrow?"

Gray shook his head. "No. If they had more than the *Times-Picayune*, it would've run today."

"Krauthammer wants to run what we've got. He thinks we can name Mattiece."

"I don't follow."

"He's leaning on Feldman. His angle is that we can run the whole story about Callahan and Verheek getting killed over this brief, which happens to name Mattiece who happens to be a friend of the President's, without directly accusing Mattiece. He says we can be extremely cautious and make sure the story says Mattiece is named in the brief, but not named by us. And since the brief is causing all this death, then it has been verified to some extent."

"He wants to hide behind the brief."

"Exactly."

"But it's all speculation until it's confirmed. Krauthammer's losing it. Assume for a second that Mr. Mattiece is in no way involved with this. Completely innocent. We run the story with his name in it, and then what? We look like fools, and we get sued for the next ten years. I'm not writing the story."

"He wants someone else to write it."

"If this paper runs a pelican story not written by me, the girl is gone, okay. I thought I explained that yesterday."

"You did. And Feldman heard you. He's on your side, Gray, and I am too. But if this thing's true, it'll blow up in a matter of days. We all believe that. You know how Krauthammer hates the *Times*, and he's afraid those bastards'll run it."

"They can't run it, Smith. They may have a few more facts than the *Times-Picayune*, but they can't name Mattiece. Look, we'll verify before anyone. And when it's nailed down, I'll write the story with everyone's name along with that cute little picture of Mattiece and his friend in the White House, and the fat lady will sing."

"We? You said it again. You said, 'We'll verify it.'"

"My source and I, okay." Gray opened a drawer and found the photo of Darby and the Diet Coke. He handed it to Keen, who admired it.

"Where is she?" he asked.

"I'm not sure. I think she's on her way here from New York."

"Don't get her killed."

"We're being very cautious." Gray looked over both shoulders and leaned closer. "In fact, Smith, I think I'm being followed. I just wanted you to know."

"Who might they be?"

"It came from a source at the White House. I'm not using my phones."

"I'd better tell Feldman."

"Okay. I don't think it's dangerous, yet."

"He needs to know." Keen jumped to his feet and disappeared.

She called within minutes. "I'm here," she said. "I don't know how many I've brought with me, but I'm here, and alive, for the moment."

"Where are you?"

"Tabard Inn on N Street. I saw an old friend on Sixth Avenue yesterday. Remember Stump, who was grievously wounded on Bourbon Street? Did I tell you that story?"

"Yes."

"Well, he's walking again. A slight limp, but he was wandering around Manhattan yesterday. I don't think he saw me."

"Are you serious! That's scary, Darby."

"It's worse than scary. I left six trails when I left last night, and if I see him in this city, limping along a sidewalk somewhere, I intend to surrender. I'll walk up to him and turn myself in."

"I don't know what to say."

"Say as little as possible, because these people have radar. I'll play private eye for three days, and I'm out of here. If I live to see Wednesday morning, I'm on a plane to Aruba or Trinidad or some place with a beach. When I die, I want to be on a beach."

"When do we meet?"

"I'm thinking about that. I want you to do two things."

"I'm listening."

"Where do you park your car?"

"Close to my apartment."

"Leave it there, and go rent another one. Nothing fancy, just a generic Ford or something. Pretend someone's watching you through a rifle scope. Go to the Marbury Hotel in Georgetown and get a room for three nights. They'll take cash—I've already checked. Do it under another name."

Grantham took notes and shook his head.

"Can you sneak out of your apartment after dark?" she asked.

"I think so."

"Do it, and take a cab to the Marbury. Have them deliver the rental car to you there. Take two cabs to the Tabard Inn, and walk into the restaurant at exactly nine tonight."

"Okay. Anything else?"

"Bring clothes. Plan to be away from your apartment for at least three days. And plan to stay away from the office."

"Really, Darby, I think the office is safe."

"I'm not in the mood to argue. If you're going to be difficult,

Gray, I'll simply disappear. I'm convinced I'll live longer the sooner I get out of the country."

"Yes, ma'am."

"That's a good boy."

"I assume there's a master plan rattling around somewhere in your brain."

"Maybe. We'll talk about it over dinner."

"Is this sort of like a date?"

"Let's eat a bite and call it business."

"Yes, ma'am."

"I'm hanging up now. Be cautious, Gray. They're watching." She was gone.

SHE WAS SITTING at table thirty-seven, in a dark corner of the tiny restaurant when he found her at exactly nine. The first thing he noticed was the dress, and as he walked to the table he knew the legs were under it but he couldn't see them. Maybe later when she stood. He wore a coat and tie, and they were an attractive couple.

He sat close to her in the darkness so they could both watch the small crowd. The Tabard Inn appeared old enough to have served food to Thomas Jefferson. A rowdy crowd of Germans laughed and talked on the patio outside the restaurant. The windows were open and the air was cool, and for one brief moment it was easy to forget why they were hiding.

"Where'd you get the dress?"

"You like it?"

"It's very nice."

"I shopped a little this afternoon. Like most of my recent wardrobe, it's disposable. I'll probably leave it in the room the next time I flee for my life."

The waiter was before them with menus. They ordered drinks. The restaurant was quiet and harmless.

"How'd you get here?" he asked.

"Around the world."

"I'd like to know."

"I took a train to Newark, a plane to Boston, a plane to Detroit, and a plane to Dulles. I was up all night, and twice I forgot where I was."

"How could they follow that?"

"They couldn't. I paid with cash, something I'm running out of."

"How much do you need?"

"I'd like to wire some from my bank in New Orleans."

"We'll do it Monday. I think you're safe, Darby."

"I've thought that before. In fact, I felt very safe when I was getting on the boat with Verheek, except it wasn't Verheek. And I felt very safe in New York. Then Stump waddled down the sidewalk, and I haven't eaten since."

"You look thin."

"Thanks. I guess. Have you eaten here?" She looked at her menu.

He looked at his. "No, but I hear the food is great. You changed your hair again." It was light brown, and there was a trace of mascara and blush. And lipstick.

"It's going to fall out if I keep seeing these people."

The drinks arrived, and they ordered.

"We expect something in the *Times* in the morning." He would not mention the New Orleans paper because it had pictures of Callahan and Verheek. He assumed she'd seen it.

This didn't seem to interest her. "Such as?" she asked, looking around.

"We're not sure. We hate to get beat by the *Times*. It's an old rivalry."

"I'm not interested in that. I know nothing about journalism, and don't care to learn. I'm here because I have one, and only one, idea about finding Garcia. And if it doesn't work, and quickly, I'm out of here."

"Forgive me. What would you like to talk about?"

"Europe. What's your favorite place in Europe?"

"I hate Europe, and I hate Europeans. I go to Canada and Australia, and New Zealand occasionally. Why do you like Europe?"

"My grandfather was a Scottish immigrant, and I've got a bunch of cousins over there. I've visited twice."

Gray squeezed the lime in his gin and tonic. A party of six entered from the bar and she watched them carefully. When she talked her eyes darted quickly around the room.

"I think you need a couple of drinks to relax," Gray said.

She nodded but said nothing. The six were seated at a nearby table and began speaking in French. It was pleasant to hear.

"Have you ever heard Cajun French?" she asked.

"No."

"It's a dialect that's rapidly disappearing, just like the wetlands. They say it cannot be understood by Frenchmen."

"That's fair. I'm sure the Cajuns can't understand the French."

She took a long drink of white wine. "Did I tell you about Chad Brunet?"

"I don't think so."

"He was a poor Cajun boy from Eunice. His family survived by trapping and fishing in the marshes. He was a very bright kid who attended LSU on a full academic scholarship, then was admitted to law school at Stanford, where he finished with the highest grade point average in the school's history. He was twenty-one when he was admitted to the California bar. He could have worked for any law firm in the country, but he took a job with an environmental defense outfit in San Francisco. He was brilliant, a real legal genius who worked very hard and was soon winning huge lawsuits against oil and chemical companies. At the age of twenty-eight, he was a highly polished courtroom lawyer. He was feared by big oil and other corporate polluters." She took a sip of wine. "He made a lot of money, and established a group to preserve the Louisiana wetlands. He wanted to participate in the pelican case, as it was known, but had too many other trial commitments. He gave Green Fund a lot of money for litigation expenses. Shortly before the trial started in Lafayette, he announced he was coming home to assist the Green Fund lawyers. There were a couple of stories about him in the New Orleans paper."

"What happened to him?"

"He committed suicide."

"What?"

"A week before the trial, they found him in a car with the engine running. A garden hose ran from the exhaust pipe into the front seat. Just another simple suicide from carbon monoxide poisoning."

"Where was the car?"

"In a wooded area along Bayou Lafourche near the town of Galliano. He knew the area well. Some camping gear and fishing equipment were in the trunk. No suicide note. The police investigated, but found nothing suspicious. The case was closed."

"This is incredible."

"He had had some problems with alcohol, and had been treated by an analyst in San Francisco. But the suicide was a surprise."

"Do you think he was murdered?"

"A lot of people do. His death was a big blow to Green Fund. His passion for the wetlands would've been potent in the courtroom."

Gray finished his drink and rattled the ice. She inched closer to him. The waiter appeared, and they ordered.

THIRTY-FIVE

THE LOBBY of the Marbury Hotel was empty at 6 A.M. Sunday when Gray found a copy of the *Times*. It was six inches deep and weighed twelve pounds, and he wondered how much thicker they planned to make it. He raced back to his room on the eighth floor, spread the paper on the bed, and hovered over it as he skimmed intensely. The front page was empty, and this was crucial. If they had the big story, it would of course be there. He feared large photographs of Rosenberg, Jensen, Callahan, Verheek, maybe Darby and Khamel, who knows, maybe they had a nice picture of Mattiece, and all of these would be lined up on the front page like a cast of characters, and the *Times* had beat them again. He had dreamed of this while he had slept, which had not been for long.

But there was nothing. And the less he found, the faster he skimmed until he was down to sports and classifieds, and he stopped and sort of danced to the phone. He called Smith Keen, who was awake. "Have you seen it?" he asked.

"Ain't it beautiful," Keen said. "I wonder what happened."

"They don't have it, Smith. They're digging like hell, but they don't have it yet. Who did Feldman talk to?"

"He never says. But it was supposed to be reliable."

Keen was divorced and lived alone in an apartment not far from the Marbury.

"Are you busy?" Gray asked.

"Well, not exactly. It's almost six-thirty on Sunday morning."

"We need to talk. Pick me up outside the Marbury Hotel in fifteen minutes."

"The Marbury Hotel?"

"It's a long story. I'll explain."

"Ah, the girl. You lucky stiff."

"I wish. She's in another hotel."

"Here? In Washington?"

"Yes. Fifteen minutes."

"I'll be there."

Gray nervously sipped coffee from a paper cup and waited in the lobby. She'd made him paranoid, and he half expected thugs to be hiding on the sidewalk with automatic weapons. This frustrated him. He saw Keen's Toyota ease by on M Street, and he walked quickly to it.

"What would you like to see?" Keen said as he drove away from the curb.

"Oh, I don't know. It's a beautiful day. How about Virginia?"

"As you wish. Did you get kicked out of your apartment?"

"Not exactly. I'm following orders from the girl. She thinks like a field marshal, and I'm here because I was told to be here. I must stay until Tuesday, or until she gets jumpy and moves me again. I'm in room eight-thirty-three if you need me, but don't tell anyone."

"I assume you want the *Post* to pay for this," Keen said with a smile.

"I'm not thinking about money right now. The same people who tried to kill her in New Orleans turned up in New York on Friday, or so she thinks. They have amazing talent in pursuit, and she's being painfully cautious."

"Well, if you're being followed by someone, and she's being followed by someone, then perhaps she knows what she's doing."

"Oh, listen, Smith, she knows exactly what she's doing. She's so good it's scary, and she's leaving here Wednesday morning for good. So we've got two days to find Garcia."

"What if Garcia's overrated? What if you find him and he

won't talk, or what if he knows nothing? Have you thought about that?"

"I've had nightmares about that. I think he knows something big. There's a document or a piece of paper, something tangible, and he's got it. He referred to it a time or two, and when I pressed him he wouldn't admit it. But the day we were supposed to meet, he planned to show it to me. I'm convinced of that. He's got something, Smith."

"And if he won't show it to you?"

"I'll break his neck."

They crossed the Potomac and cruised by Arlington Cemetery. Keen lit his pipe and cracked a window. "What if you can't find Garcia?"

"Plan B. She's gone and the deal's off. Once she leaves the country, I have permission to do anything with the brief except use her name as a source. The poor girl is convinced she's dead regardless of whether we get the story, but she wants as much protection as possible. I can never use her name, not even as the author of the brief."

"Does she talk much about the brief?"

"Not the actual writing of it. It was a wild idea, she pursued it, and had almost dismissed it when bombs started going off. She's sorry she wrote the damned thing. She and Callahan were really in love, and she's loaded down with a lot of pain and guilt."

"So what's Plan B?"

"We attack the lawyers. Mattiece is too devious and slippery to penetrate without subpoenas and warrants and things we can't dispense, but we know his lawyers. He's represented by two big firms here in town, and we go after them. A lawyer or a group of them carefully analyzed the Supreme Court, and suggested the names of Rosenberg and Jensen. Mattiece wouldn't know who to kill. So his lawyers told him. It's a conspiracy angle."

"But you can't make them talk."

"Not about a client. But if the lawyers are guilty, and we start asking questions, something'll break. We'll need a dozen reporters making a million phone calls to lawyers, paralegals, law clerks, secretaries, copy room clerks, everybody. We assault these bastards."

Keen puffed his pipe and was noncommittal. "Who are the firms?"

"White and Blazevich, and Brim, Stearns, and Kidlow. Check our library on them."

"I've heard of White and Blazevich. It's a big Republican outfit."

Gray nodded and sipped the last of his coffee.

"What if it's another firm?" Keen asked. "What if the firm is not in Washington? What if the conspirators don't break? What if there's only one legal mind at work here and it belongs to a part-time paralegal in Shreveport? What if one of Mattiece's in-house lawyers devised the scheme?"

"Sometimes you irritate the hell out of me. Do you know that?"

"These are valid questions. What if?"

"Then we go to Plan C."

"And what's that?"

"I don't know yet. She hasn't gotten that far."

SHE HAD INSTRUCTED HIM to stay off the streets and to eat in his room. He had a sandwich and fries in a bag, and was obediently walking to his room on the eighth floor of the Marbury. An Asian maid was pushing her cart near his room. He stopped at his door and pulled the key from his pocket.

"You forget something, sir?" the maid asked.

Gray looked at her. "I beg your pardon."

"You forget something?"

"Well, no. Why?"

The maid took a step closer to him. "You just left, sir, and now you are back."

"I left four hours ago."

She shook her head and took another step for a closer look. "No sir. A man left your room ten minutes ago." She hesitated and studied his face intently. "But, sir, now I think it was another man."

Gray glanced at the room number on the door. 833. He

stared at the woman. "Are you certain another man was in this room?"

"Yes, sir. Just minutes ago."

He panicked. He walked quickly to the stairs, and ran down eight flights. What was in the room? Nothing but clothes. Nothing about Darby. He stopped and reached into a pocket. The note with the Tabard Inn address and her phone number was in the pocket. He caught his breath, and eased into the lobby.

He had to find her, and quick.

DARBY FOUND an empty table in the reading room on the second floor of the Edward Bennett Williams Law Library at Georgetown. In her new hobby as a traveling critic of law school libraries, she found Georgetown's to be the nicest so far. It was a separate five-story building across a small courtyard from Mc-Donough Hall, the law school. The library was new, sleek, and modern, but still a law library and quickly filling with Sunday students now thinking of final exams.

She opened volume five of Martindale-Hubbell, and found the section for D.C. firms. White and Blazevich ran for twenty-eight pages. Names, birth dates, birthplaces, schools, professional organizations, distinctions, awards, committees, and publications of four hundred and twelve lawyers, the partners first, then the associates. She took notes on a legal pad.

The firm had eighty-one partners, and the rest were associates. She grouped them by alphabet, and wrote every name on the legal pad. She was just another law student checking out law firms in the relentless chase of employment.

The work was boring and her mind wandered. Thomas had studied here twenty years ago. He'd been a top student and claimed to have spent many hours in the library. He'd written for the law journal, a chore she would be enduring under normal circumstances.

Death was a subject she'd analyzed from different angles in the past ten days. Except for going quietly in one's sleep, she was undecided as to the best approach. A slow, agonizing demise from a disease was a nightmare for the victim and the loved ones, but at least there was time for preparation and farewells. A violent, unexpected death was over in a second and probably best for the deceased. But the shock was numbing for those left behind. There were so many painful questions. Did he suffer? What was his last thought? Why did it happen? And watching the quick death of a loved one was beyond description.

She loved him more because she watched him die, and she told herself to stop hearing the explosion, and stop smelling the smoke, and stop watching him die. If she survived three more days, she would be in a place where she could lock the door and cry and throw things until the grieving was over. She was determined to make it to that place. She was determined to grieve, and to heal. It was the least she deserved.

She memorized names until she knew more about White and Blazevich than anyone outside the firm. She eased into the darkness and caught a cab to the hotel.

MATTHEW BARR went to New Orleans, where he met with a lawyer who instructed him to fly to a certain hotel in Fort Lauderdale. The lawyer was vague about what would happen at the hotel, but Barr checked in Sunday night and found a room waiting for him. A note at the desk said he would receive a call in the early a.m.

He called Fletcher Coal at home at ten, and briefed him on the journey so far.

Coal had other things on his mind. "Grantham's gone crazy. He and a guy named Rifkin with the *Times* are making calls everywhere. They could be deadly."

"Have they seen the brief?"

"I don't know if they've seen it, but they've heard of it. Rifkin called one of my aides at home yesterday and asked what he knew about the pelican brief. The aide knew nothing, and got the impression Rifkin knew even less. I don't think he's seen it, but we can't be certain."

"Damn, Fletcher. We can't keep up with a bunch of reporters. Those guys make a hundred phone calls a minute."

"Just two. Grantham and Rifkin. You've already got Grantham wired. Do the same for Rifkin."

"Grantham's wired, but he's using neither the phone in his apartment nor the one in his car. I called Bailey from the airport in New Orleans. Grantham hasn't been home in twenty-four hours, but his car's still there. They called and knocked on his door. He's either dead in the apartment, or he sneaked out last night."

"Maybe he's dead."

"I don't think so. We were following, and so were the Fibbies. I think he got wind of it."

"You must find him."

"He'll turn up. He can't get too far away from the newsroom on the fifth floor."

"I want Rifkin wired too. Call Bailey tonight and get it started, okay?"

"Yes sir," Barr said.

"What do you think Mattiece would do if he thought Grantham had the story and was about to spread it across the front page of the *Washington Post*?" Coal asked.

Barr stretched on the hotel bed and closed his eyes. Months ago he had made the decision never to cross Fletcher Coal. He was an animal.

"He's not afraid of killing people, is he?" Barr said.

"Do you think you'll see Mattiece tomorrow?"

"I don't know. These guys are very secretive. They speak in hushed tones behind closed doors. They've told me little."

"Why do they want you in Fort Lauderdale?"

"I do not know, but it's much closer to the Bahamas. I think I'm going there tomorrow, or perhaps he's coming here. I just don't know."

"Perhaps you should exaggerate the Grantham angle. Mattiece will snuff out the story."

"I'll think about it."

"Call me in the morning."

SHE STEPPED ON THE NOTE when she opened her door. It said: *Darby, I'm on the patio. It's urgent, Gray.* She took a deep breath and crammed the note in her pocket. She locked the door, and followed the narrow, winding hallways to the lobby, then through the dark sitting room, by the bar, through the restaurant, and onto the patio. He was at a small table, partially hidden by a brick wall.

"Why are you here?" she demanded in a whisper as she sat close to him. He looked tired and worried.

"Where have you been?" he asked.

"That's not as important as why you're here. You're not supposed to come here unless I say so. What's going on?"

He gave her a quick summary of his morning, from the first phone call to Smith Keen to the maid in the hotel. He'd spent the rest of the day darting all over the city in various cabs, almost eighty bucks' worth of cabs, and he waited until dark to sneak into the Tabard Inn. He was certain he had not been followed.

She listened. She watched the restaurant and the entrance to the patio, and heard every word.

"I have no idea how anyone could find my room," he said.

"Did you tell anyone your room number?"

He thought for a second. "Only Smith Keen. But he'd never repeat it."

She was not looking at him. "Where were you when you told him your room number?"

"In his car."

She shook her head slowly. "I distinctly told you not to tell anyone. Didn't I?"

He would not answer.

"It's all fun and games, isn't it, Gray? Just another day at the beach. You're a big stud reporter who's had death threats before, but you're fearless. The bullets will bounce off, won't they? You and I can spend a few days here frolicking around town playing detective so you can win a Pulitzer and get rich and famous, and the bad guys aren't really so bad because, hey, you're Gray Grantham of the *Washington Post* and that makes you a mean son of a bitch."

"Come on, Darby."

"I've tried to impress upon you how dangerous these people are. I've seen what they can do. I know what they'll do to me if they find me. But no, Gray, it's all a game to you. Cops and robbers. Hide-and-seek."

"I'm convinced, okay?"

"Listen, hotshot, you'd better be convinced. One more screwup and we're dead. I'm out of lucky breaks. Do you understand?"

"Yes! I swear I understand."

"Get a room here. Tomorrow night, if we're alive, I'll find you another small hotel."

"What if this place is full?"

"Then you can sleep in my bathroom with the door closed."

She was dead serious. He felt like a first-grader who'd just received his first spanking. They didn't speak for five minutes.

"So how'd they find me?" he finally asked.

"I would assume the phones in your apartment are tapped, and your car is bugged. And I would assume Smith Keen's car is also wired. These people are not amateurs."

THIRTY-SIX

H E SPENT THE NIGHT in room 14 upstairs, but slept little. The restaurant opened at six, and he sneaked down for coffee, then sneaked back to his room. The inn was quaint and ancient, and had somehow been formed when three old townhouses were connected. Small doors and narrow hallways ran in all directions. The atmosphere was timeless.

It would be a long, tiresome day, but it would all be spent with her, and he looked forward to it. He'd made a mistake, a bad one, but she'd forgiven him. At precisely eight-thirty, he knocked on the door to room 1. She quickly opened it, then closed it behind him.

She was a law student again, with jeans and a flannel shirt. She poured him coffee, and sat at the small table where the phone was surrounded by notes from a legal pad.

"Did you sleep well?" she asked, but only out of courtesy.

"No." He threw a copy of the *Times* on the bed. He'd already scanned it, and it was empty again.

Darby took the phone and punched the number of the Georgetown law school. She looked at him, and listened, then said, "Placement office, please." There was a long pause. "Yes, this is Sandra Jernigan. I'm a partner with White and Blazevich here in town, and we're having a problem with our computers. We're trying to reconstruct some payroll records, and the accountants have asked me to ask you for the names of your students who clerked here last summer. I think there were four of them." She listened for a second. "Jernigan. Sandra Jernigan," she repeated. "I see. How long will it take?" A pause. "And your name is, Joan. Thank you, Joan." Darby covered the receiver and breathed deeply. Gray watched intently, but with an admiring grin.

"Yes, Joan. Seven of them. Our records are a mess. Do you have their addresses and social security numbers? We need it for tax purposes. Sure. How long will it take? Fine. We have an office boy in the area. His name is Snowden, and he'll be there in thirty minutes. Thank you, Joan." Darby hung up and closed her eyes.

"Sandra Jernigan?" he said.

"I'm not good at lying," she said.

"You're wonderful. I guess I'm the office boy."

"You could pass for an office boy. You have an aging law school dropout look about you." And you're sort of cute, she thought to herself.

"I like the flannel shirt."

She took a long drink of cold coffee. "This could be a long day."

"So far, so good. I get the list, and meet you in the library. Right?"

"Yes. The placement office is on the fifth floor of the law school. I'll be in room 336. It's a small conference room on the third floor. You take a cab first. I'll meet you there in fifteen minutes."

"Yes, ma'am." Grantham was out the door. Darby waited five minutes, then left with her canvas bag.

The cab ride was short but slow in the morning traffic. Life on the lam was bad enough, but running and playing detective at the same time was too much. She'd been in the cab five minutes before she thought about being followed. And maybe that was good. Maybe a hard day as an investigative reporter would take her mind off Stump and the other tormentors. She would work today, and tomorrow, and by late Wednesday she would be on a beach.

They would start with the law school at Georgetown. If it was a dead end, they would try the one at George Washington. If there was time, they would try American University. Three strikes, and she was gone.

The cab stopped at McDonough Hall, at the grungy base of Capitol Hill. With her bag and flannel shirt, she was just one of many law students milling about before class. She took the stairs to the third level, and closed the door to the conference room behind her. The room was used for an occasional class and on campus job interviews. She spread her notes on the table, and was just another law student preparing for class.

Within minutes, Gray eased through the door. "Joan's a sweet lady," he said as he placed the list on the table. "Names, addresses, and social security numbers. Ain't that nice."

Darby looked at the list and pulled a phone book from her bag. They found five of the names in the book. She looked at her watch. "It's five minutes after nine. I'll bet no more than half of these are in class at this moment. Some will have later classes. I'll call these five, and see who's at home. You take the two with no phone number, and get their class schedules from the registrar."

Gray looked at his watch. "Let's meet back here in fifteen minutes." He left first, then Darby. She went to the pay phones on the first level outside the classrooms, and dialed the number of James Maylor.

A male voice answered, "Hello."

"Is this Dennis Maylor?" she asked.

"No. I'm James Maylor."

"Sorry." She hung up. His address was ten minutes away. He didn't have a nine o'clock class, and if he had one at ten he would be home for another forty minutes. Maybe.

She called the other four. Two answered and she confirmed, and there was no answer at the other two.

Gray waited impatiently in the registrar's office on the third floor. A part-time student clerk was trying to find the registrar, who was somewhere in the back. The student informed him that she wasn't sure if they could give out class schedules. Gray said he was certain they could if they wanted to.

The registrar walked suspiciously around a corner. "May I help you?"

"Yes, I'm Gray Grantham with the *Washington Post*, and I'm trying to find two of your students, Laura Kaas and Michael Akers."

"Is there a problem?" she asked nervously.

"Not at all. Just a few questions. Are they in class this morning?" He was smiling, and it was a warm, trusting smile that he flashed usually at older women. It seldom failed him.

"Do you have an ID or something?"

"Certainly." He opened his wallet and slowly waved it at her, much like a cop who knows he's a cop and doesn't care to spell it out.

"Well, I really should talk to the dean, but—"

"Fine. Where's his office?"

"But he's not here. He's out of town."

"I just need their class schedules so I can find them. I'm not asking for home addresses or grades or transcripts. Nothing confidential or personal."

She glanced at the part-time student clerk, who sort of shrugged, like "What's the big deal?" "Just a minute," she said, and disappeared around the corner.

Darby was waiting in the small room when he laid the computer printouts on the table. "According to these, Akers and Kaas should be in class right now," he said.

Darby looked at the schedules. "Akers has criminal procedure. Kaas has administrative law; both from nine to ten. I'll try to find them." She showed Gray her notes. "Maylor, Reinhart, and Wilson were at home. I couldn't get Ratliff and Linney."

"Maylor's the closest. I can be there in a few minutes."

"What about a car?" Darby asked.

"I called Hertz. It's supposed to be delivered to the *Post* parking lot in fifteen minutes."

MAYLOR'S APARTMENT was on the third floor of a warehouse converted for students and others on very low budgets. He answered the door shortly after the first knock. He spoke through the chain.

"Looking for James Maylor," Gray said like an old pal.

"That's me."

"I'm Gray Grantham with the *Washington Post*. I'd like to ask you a couple of very quick questions."

The door was unchained and opened. Gray stepped inside the two-room apartment. A bicycle was parked in the center, and took up most of the space.

"What's up?" Maylor asked. He was intrigued by this, and appeared eager to answer questions.

"I understand you clerked for White and Blazevich last summer."

"That's correct. For three months."

Gray scribbled on his notepad. "What section were you in?"

"International. Mostly grunt work. Nothing glamorous. A lot of research and rough drafting of agreements."

"Who was your supervisor?"

"No single person. There were three associates who kept me busy. The partner above them was Stanley Coopman."

Gray pulled a photograph from his coat pocket. It was Garcia on the sidewalk. "Do you recognize this face?"

Maylor held the picture and studied it. He shook his head. "I don't think so. Who is he?"

"He's a lawyer, I think with White and Blazevich."

"It's a big firm. I was stuck in the corner of one section. It's over four hundred lawyers, you know."

"Yeah, so I've heard. You're sure you haven't seen him?"

"Positive. They cover twelve floors, most of which I never went on."

Gray placed the photo in his pocket. "Did you meet any other clerks?"

"Oh. Sure. A couple from Georgetown that I already knew, Laura Kaas and JoAnne Ratliff. Two guys from George Washington, Patrick Franks and a guy named Vanlandingham; a girl from Harvard named Elizabeth Larson; a girl from Michigan named Amy MacGregor; and a guy from Emory named Moke, but I think they fired him. There are always a lot of clerks in the summer."

"You plan to work there when you finish?"

"I don't know. I'm not sure I'm cut out for the big firms."

Gray smiled and stuck the notepad in his rear pocket. "Look, you've been in the firm. How would I find this guy?"

Maylor pondered this for a second. "I assume you can't go there and start asking around."

"Good assumption."

"And all you've got is the picture?"

"Yep."

"Then I guess you're doing the right thing. One of the clerks will recognize him."

"Thanks."

"Is the guy in trouble?"

"Oh no. He may have witnessed something. It's probably a long shot." Gray opened the door. "Thanks again."

DARBY STUDIED the fall listing of classes on the bulletin board across the lobby from the phones. She wasn't exactly sure what she'd do when the nine o'clock classes were over, but she was trying like hell to think of something. The bulletin board was exactly like the one at Tulane: class listings tacked neatly in a row; notices for assignments; ads for books, bikes, rooms, roommates, and a hundred other necessities stuck haphazardly about; announcements of parties, intramural games, and club meetings. A young woman with a backpack and hiking books stopped nearby and looked at the board. She was undoubtedly a student.

Darby smiled at her. "Excuse me. Would you happen to know Laura Kaas?"

"Sure."

"I need to give her a message. Could you point her out?"

"Is she in class?"

"Yeah, she's in administrative law under Ship, room 207."

They walked and chatted in the direction of Ship's admin law. The lobby was suddenly busy as four classrooms emptied. The hiker pointed to a tall, heavyset girl walking toward them. Darby thanked her, and followed Laura Kaas until the crowd thinned and scattered.

"Excuse me, Laura. Are you Laura Kaas?" The big girl stopped and stared. "Yes."

This was the part she didn't like; the lying. "I'm Sara Jacobs, and I'm working on a story for the *Washington Post*. Can I ask you a few questions?" She selected Laura Kaas first because she did not have a class at ten. Michael Akers did. She would try him at eleven.

"What about?"

"It'll just take a minute. Could we step in here?" Darby was nodding and walking to an empty classroom. Laura followed slowly.

"You clerked for White and Blazevich last summer."

"I did." She spoke slowly, suspiciously.

Sara Jacobs fought to control her nerves. This was awful. "What section?"

"Tax."

"You like tax, huh?" It was a weak effort at small talk.

"I did. Now I hate it."

Darby smiled like this was the funniest thing she'd heard in years. She pulled a photo from her pocket, and handed it to Laura Kaas.

"Do you recognize this man?"

"No."

"I think he's a lawyer with White and Blazevich."

"There are plenty of them."

"Are you certain?"

She handed it back. "Yep. I never left the fifth floor. It would take years to meet everyone, and they come and go so fast. You know how lawyers are."

Laura glanced around, and the conversation was over. "I really appreciate this," Darby said.

"No problem," Laura said on her way out the door.

AT EXACTLY TEN-THIRTY, they met again in room 336. Gray had caught Ellen Reinhart in the driveway as she was leaving for class. She had worked in the litigation section under a partner by the name of Daniel O'Malley, and spent most of the summer in a class action trial in Miami. She was gone for two months, and spent little time in the Washington office. White and Blazevich had offices in four cities, including Tampa. She did not recognize Garcia, and she was in a hurry.

Judith Wilson was not at her apartment, but her roommate said she would return around one.

They scratched off Maylor, Kaas, and Reinhart. They whispered their plans, and split again. Gray left to find Edward Linney, who according to the list had clerked the past two summers at White and Blazevich. He was not in the phone book, but his address was in Wesley Heights, north of Georgetown's main campus.

At ten forty-five, Darby found herself loitering again in front of the bulletin board, hoping for another miracle. Akers was a male, and there were different ways to approach him. She hoped he was where he was supposed to be—in room 201 studying criminal procedure. She eased that way and waited a moment or two until the door opened and fifty law students emptied into the hall. She could never be a reporter. She could never walk up to strangers and start asking a bunch of questions. It was awkward and uncomfortable. But she walked up to a shy-looking young man with sad eyes and thick glasses, and said, "Excuse me. Do you happen to know Michael Akers? I think he's in this class."

The guy smiled. It was nice to be noticed. He pointed at a group of men walking toward the front entrance. "That's him, in the gray sweater."

"Thanks." She left him standing there. The group disassembled as it left the building, and Akers and a friend were on the sidewalk.

"Mr. Akers," she called after him.

They both stopped and turned around, then smiled as she nervously approached them. "Are you Michael Akers?" she asked.

"That's me. Who are you?"

"My name is Sara Jacobs, and I'm working on a story for the *Washington Post*. Can I speak to you alone?"

"Sure." The friend took the hint and left.

"What about?" Akers asked.

"Did you clerk for White and Blazevich last summer?"

"Yes." Akers was friendly and enjoying this.

"What section?"

"Real estate. Boring as hell, but it was a job. Why do you want to know?"

She handed him the photo. "Do you recognize this man? He works for White and Blazevich."

Akers wanted to recognize him. He wanted to be helpful and have a long conversation with her, but the face did not register.

"Kind of a suspicious picture, isn't it?" he said.

"I guess. Do you know him?"

"No. I've never seen him. It's an awfully big firm. The partners wear name badges to their meetings. Can you believe it? The guys who own the firm don't know each other. There must be a hundred partners."

Eighty-one, to be exact. "Did you have a supervisor?"

"Yeah, a partner named Walter Welch. A real snot. I didn't like the firm, really."

"Do you remember any other clerks?"

"Sure. The place was crawling with summer clerks."

"If I needed their names, could I get back with you?"

"Anytime. This guy in trouble?"

"I don't think so. He may know something."

"I hope they all get disbarred. A bunch of thugs, really. It's a rotten place to work. Everything's political."

"Thanks." She smiled, and turned away. He admired the rear view, and said, "Call me anytime."

"Thanks."

Darby, the investigative reporter, walked next door to the library building, and climbed the stairs to the fifth floor where the *Georgetown Law Journal* had a suite of crowded offices. She'd found the most recent edition of the *Journal* in the library, and noticed that JoAnne Ratliff was an assistant editor. She suspected most law reviews and law journals were much the same. The top students hung out there and prepared their scholarly articles and comments. They were superior to the rest of the students, and were a clannish bunch who appreciated their brilliant minds. They hung out in the law journal suite. It was their second home.

She stepped inside and asked the first person where she might find JoAnne Ratliff. He pointed around a corner. Second door on the right. The second door opened into a cluttered workroom lined with rows of books. Two females were hard at work.

"JoAnne Ratliff," Darby said.

"That's me," an older woman of maybe forty responded.

"Hi. My name is Sara Jacobs, and I'm working on a story for the *Washington Post*. Can I ask you a few quick questions?"

She slowly laid her pen on the table, and frowned at the other woman. Whatever they were doing was terribly important, and this interruption was a real pain in the ass. They were significant law students.

Darby wanted to smirk and say something smart. She was number two in her class, dammit!, so don't act so high and mighty.

"What's the story about?" Ratliff asked.

"Could we speak in private?"

They frowned at each other again.

"I'm very busy," Ratliff said.

So am I, thought Darby. You're checking citations for some meaningless article, and I'm trying to nail the man who killed two Supreme Court Justices.

"I'm sorry," Darby said. "I promise I'll just take a minute."

They stepped into the hall. "I'm very sorry to disturb you, but I'm in sort of a rush."

"And you're a reporter with the *Post*?" It was more of a challenge than a question, and she was forced to lie some more. She told herself she could lie and cheat and steal for two days, then it was off to the Caribbean and Grantham could have it.

"Yes. Did you work for White and Blazevich last summer?"

"I did. Why?"

Quickly, the photo. Ratliff took it and analyzed it.

"Do you recognize him?"

She shook her head slowly. "I don't think so. Who is he?"

This bitch'll make a fine lawyer. So many questions. If she

knew who he was, she wouldn't be standing in this tiny hallway acting like a reporter and putting up with this haughty legal eagle.

"He's a lawyer with White and Blazevich," Darby said as sincerely as possible. "I thought you might recognize him."

"Nope." She handed the photo back.

Enough of this. "Well, thanks. Again, sorry to bother."

"No problem," Ratliff said as she disappeared through the door.

SHE JUMPED into the new Hertz Pontiac as it stopped at the corner, and they were off in traffic. She had seen enough of the Georgetown Law School.

"I struck out," Gray said. "Linney wasn't home."

"I talked to Akers and Ratliff, and both said no. That's five of seven who don't recognize Garcia."

"I'm hungry. You want some lunch?"

"That's fine."

"Is it possible to have five clerks work three months in a law firm and not one of them recognize a young associate?"

"Yeah, it's not only possible, it's very probable. This is a long shot, remember. Four hundred lawyers means a thousand people when you add secretaries, paralegals, law clerks, office clerks, copy room clerks, mail room clerks, all kinds of clerks and support people. The lawyers tend to keep to themselves in their own little sections."

"Physically, are the sections on separate territory?"

"Yes. It's possible for a lawyer in banking on the third floor to go weeks without seeing an acquaintance in litigation on the tenth floor. These are very busy people, remember."

"Do you think we've got the wrong firm?"

"Maybe the wrong firm, maybe the wrong law school."

"The first guy, Maylor, gave me two names of George Washington students who clerked there last summer. Let's get them after lunch." He slowed and parked illegally behind a row of small buildings.

"Where are we?" she asked.

"A block off Mount Vernon Square, downtown. The *Post* is six blocks that way. My bank is four blocks that way. And this little deli is just around the corner."

They walked to the deli, which was filling fast with lunch traffic. She waited at a table by the window as he stood in line and ordered club sandwiches. Half the day had flown by, and though she didn't enjoy this line of work, it was nice to stay busy and forget about the shadows. She wouldn't be a reporter, and at the moment a career in law looked doubtful. Not long ago, she'd thought of being a judge after a few years in practice. Forget it. It was much too dangerous.

Gray brought a tray of food and iced tea, and they began eating.

"Is this a typical day for you?" she asked.

"This is what I do for a living. I snoop all day, write the stories late in the afternoon, then dig until late at night."

"How many stories a week?"

"Sometimes three or four, sometimes none. I pick and choose, and there's little supervision. This is a bit different. I haven't run one in ten days."

"What if you can't link Mattiece? What'll you write about the story?"

"Depends on how far I get. We could've run that story about Verheek and Callahan, but why bother. It was a big story, but they had nothing to go with it. It scratched the surface and stopped."

"And you're going for the big bang."

"Hopefully. If we can verify your little brief, then we'll run one helluva story."

"You can see the headlines, can't you?"

"I can. The adrenaline is pumping. This will be the biggest story since—"

"Watergate?"

"No. Watergate was a series of stories that started small and kept getting bigger. Those guys chased leads for months and kept pecking away until the pieces came together. A lot of people knew different parts of the story. This, my dear, is very different. This is a much bigger story, and the truth is known only by a very small group. Watergate was a stupid burglary and a bungled cover-up. These are masterfully planned crimes by very rich and smart people."

"And the cover-up?"

"That comes next. After we link Mattiece to the killings, we run the big story. The cat's out of the bag, and a half a dozen investigations will crank up overnight. This place will be shell-shocked, especially at the news that the President and Mattiece are old friends. As the dust is settling, we go after the Administration and try to determine who knew what and when."

"But first, Garcia."

"Ah, yes. I know he's out there. He's a lawyer in this city, and he knows something very important."

"What if we stumble across him, and he won't talk?"

"We have ways."

"Such as?"

"Torture, kidnapping, extortion, threats of all types."

A burly man with a contorted face was suddenly beside the table. "Hurry up!" he yelled. "You're talkin' too much!"

"Thanks, Pete," Gray said without looking up. Pete was lost in the crowd, but could be heard yelling at another table. Darby dropped her sandwich.

"He owns the place," Gray explained. "It's part of the ambience."

"How charming. Does it cost extra?"

"Oh no. The food's cheap, so he depends on volume. He refuses to serve coffee because he doesn't want socializing. He expects us to eat like refugees and get out."

"I'm finished."

Gray looked at his watch. "It's twelve-fifteen. We need to be at Judith Wilson's apartment at one. Do you want to wire the money now?"

"How long will it take?"

"We can start the wire now, and pick the money up later."

"Let's go."

"How much do you want to wire?"

"Fifteen thousand."

□ □ □ □

JUDITH WILSON lived on the second floor of a decaying old house filled with two-room student apartments. She was not there at one, and they drove around for an hour. Gray became a tour guide. He drove slowly by the Montrose Theatre, still boarded and burned out. He showed her the daily circus at Dupont Circle.

They were parked on the street at two-fifteen when a red Mazda stopped in the narrow driveway. "There she is," Gray said, and got out. Darby stayed in the car.

He caught Judith near the front steps. She was friendly enough. They chatted, he showed her the photo, she looked at it for a few seconds and began shaking her head. Moments later he was in the car.

"Zero for six," he said.

"That leaves Edward Linney, who probably is our best shot because he clerked there two summers."

They found a pay phone at a convenience store three blocks away, and Gray called Linney's number. No answer. He slammed the phone down and got in the car. "He wasn't at home at ten this morning, and he's not at home now."

"Could be in class," Darby said. "We need his schedule. You should've picked it up with the others."

"You didn't suggest it then."

"Who's the detective here? Who's the big-shot investigative reporter with the *Washington Post*? I'm just a lowly ex–law student who's thrilled to be sitting here in the front seat watching you operate."

What about the backseat? he almost said. "Whatever. Where to?"

"Back to the law school," she said. "I'll wait in the car while you march in there and get Linney's class schedule."

"Yes, ma'am."

A DIFFERENT STUDENT was behind the desk in the registrar's office. Gray asked for the class schedule for Edward Linney, and the student went to look for the registrar. Five minutes later, the registrar walked slowly around the corner and glared at him.

He flashed the smile. "Hi, remember me? Gray Grantham with the *Post*. I need another class schedule."

"The dean says no."

"I thought the dean was out of town."

"He is. The assistant dean says no. No more class schedules. You've already gotten me in a lot of trouble."

"I don't understand. I'm not asking for personal records."

"The assistant dean says no."

"Where is the assistant dean?"

"He's busy."

"I'll wait. Where's his office?"

"He'll be busy for a long time."

"I'll wait for a long time."

She dug in and folded her arms. "He will not allow you to have any more class schedules. Our students are entitled to privacy."

"Sure they are. What kind of trouble have I caused?"

"Well, I'll just tell you."

"Please do."

The student clerk eased around the corner and disappeared.

"One of the students you talked to this morning called White and Blazevich, and they called the assistant dean, and the assistant dean called me and said no more class schedules will be given to reporters."

"Why should they care?"

"They care, okay? We've had a long relationship with White and Blazevich. They hire a lot of our students."

Gray tried to look pitiful and helpless. "I'm just trying to find Edward Linney. I swear he's not in trouble. I just need to ask him a few questions."

She smelled victory. She had backed down a reporter from the *Post*, and she was quite proud. So offer him a crumb. "Mr. Linney is no longer enrolled here. That's all I can say."

He backed toward the door, and mumbled, "Thanks."

He was almost to the car when someone called his name. It was the student from the registrar's office.

"Mr. Grantham," he said as he ran to him. "I know Edward.

He's sort of dropped out of school for a while. Personal problems."

"Where is he?"

"His parents put him in a private hospital. He's being detoxified."

"Where is it?"

"Silver Spring. A place called Parklane Hospital."

"How long's he been there?"

"About a month."

Grantham shook his hand. "Thanks. I won't tell anyone you told me."

"He's not in trouble, is he?"

"No. I promise."

They stopped at the bank, and Darby left with fifteen thousand in cash. Carrying the money scared her. Linney scared her. White and Blazevich suddenly scared her.

PARKLANE was a detox center for the rich, or for those with expensive insurance. It was a small building, surrounded by trees and sitting alone a half mile off the highway. This might be difficult, they decided.

Gray entered the lobby first, and asked the receptionist for Edward Linney.

"He is a patient here," she said rather officially.

He used his best smile. "Yes. I know he is a patient. They told me at the law school that he was a patient. What room is he in?"

Darby entered the lobby and strolled to the water fountain for a very long drink.

"He's in room 22, but you can't see him."

"They told me at the law school I could see him."

"And who might you be?"

He was so friendly. "Gray Grantham, with the *Washington Post*. They told me at the law school I could ask him a couple of questions."

"I'm sorry they told you that. You see, Mr. Grantham, we run this hospital, and they run their law school."

Darby picked up a magazine and sat on a sofa.

His smile faded considerably, but was still there. "I understand that," he said, still courteous. "Could I see the administrator?"

"Why?"

"Because this is a very important matter, and I must see Mr. Linney this afternoon. If you won't allow it, then I have to talk to your boss. I will not leave here until I speak to the administrator."

She gave him her best go-to-hell look, and backed away from the counter. "Just a moment. You may have a seat."

"Thank you."

She left and Gray turned to Darby. He pointed to a set of double doors that appeared to lead to the only hallway. She took a deep breath, and walked quickly through them. They opened into a large junction from which three sterile corridors branched out. A brass plate pointed to rooms 18 through 30. It was the center wing of the hospital, and the hall was dark and quiet with thick, industrial carpet and floral wallpaper.

This would get her arrested. She would be tackled by a large security guard or a heavy nurse and taken to a locked room where the cops would rough her up when they arrived, and her sidekick out there would stand and watch helplessly as they led her away in shackles. Her name would be in the paper, the *Post*, and Stump, if he was literate, would see it, and they'd get her.

As she crept along by these closed doors, the beaches and piña coladas seemed unreachable. The door to number 22 was closed and had the names Edward L. Linney and Dr. Wayne McLatchee tacked on it. She knocked.

THE ADMINISTRATOR was more of an ass than the receptionist. But then, he was paid well for it. He explained they had strict policies about visitation. These were very sick and delicate people, his patients, and they had to protect them. And their doctors, who were the finest in their field, were very strict about who could see the patients. Visitation was allowed only on Saturdays and Sundays, and even then only a carefully selected group of people, usually just family and friends, could sit with the patients, and then only for thirty minutes. They had to be very strict.

These were fragile people, and they certainly could not withstand interrogation by a reporter, regardless of how grave the circumstances.

Mr. Grantham asked when Mr. Linney might be discharged. Absolutely confidential, the administrator exclaimed. Probably when the insurance expired, suggested Mr. Grantham, who was talking and stalling and halfway expecting to hear loud and angry voices coming from behind the double doors.

This mention of insurance really agitated the administrator. Mr. Grantham asked if he, the administrator, would ask Mr. Linney if he would answer two questions from Mr. Grantham, and the whole thing would take less than thirty seconds.

Out of the question, snapped the administrator. They had strict policies.

A VOICE answered softly, and she stepped into the room. The carpet was thicker and the furniture was made from wood. He sat on the bed in a pair of jeans, no shirt, reading a thick novel. She was struck by his good looks.

"Excuse me," she said warmly as she closed the door behind her.

"Come in," he said with a soft smile. It was the first nonmedical face he'd seen in two days. What a beautiful face. He closed the book.

She walked to the end of the bed. "I'm Sara Jacobs, and I'm working on a story for the *Washington Post*."

"How'd you get in?" he asked, obviously glad she was in.

"Just walked. Did you clerk last summer for White and Blazevich?"

"Yes, and the summer before. They offered me a job when I graduate. If I graduate."

She handed him the photo. "Do you recognize this man?"

He took it and smiled. "Yeah. His name is, uh, wait a minute. He works in the oil and gas section on the ninth floor. What's his name?"

Darby held her breath.

Linney closed his eyes hard and tried to think. He looked at the photo, and said, "Morgan. I think his name is Morgan. Yep."

"His last name is Morgan?"

"That's him. I can't remember his first name. It's something like Charles, but that's not it. I think it starts with a C."

"And you're certain he's in oil and gas?" Though she couldn't remember the exact number, she was certain there was more than one Morgan at White and Blazevich.

"Yeah."

"On the ninth floor?"

"Yeah. I worked in the bankruptcy section on the eighth floor, and oil and gas covers half of eight and all of nine."

He handed the photo back.

"When are you getting out?" she asked. It would be rude to run from the room.

"Next week, I hope. What's this guy done?"

"Nothing. We just need to talk to him." She was backing away from the bed. "I have to run. Thanks. And good luck."

"Yeah. No problem."

She quietly closed the door behind her, and scooted toward the lobby. The voice came from behind her.

"Hey! You! What're you doing?"

Darby turned and faced a tall, black security guard with a gun on his hip. She looked completely guilty.

"What're you doing?" he demanded again as he backed her into the wall.

"Visiting my brother," she said. "And don't yell at me again."

"Who's your brother?"

She nodded at his door. "Room 22."

"You can't visit right now. This is off limits."

"It was important. I'm leaving, okay?"

The door to 22 opened, and Linney looked at them.

"This your sister?" the guard demanded.

Darby pleaded with her eyes.

"Yeah, leave her alone," Linney said. "She's leaving."

She exhaled and smiled at Linney. "Mom will be up this weekend."

"Good," Linney said softly.

The guard backed off, and Darby almost ran to the double doors. Grantham was preaching to the administrator about the cost of health care. She walked quickly through the doors, into the lobby, and was almost to the front door when the administrator spoke to her.

"Miss! Oh, miss! Can I have your name?"

Darby was out the front door, headed for the car. Grantham shrugged at the administrator, and casually left the building. They jumped in, and sped away.

"Garcia's last name is Morgan. Linney recognized him immediately, but he had trouble with the name. First name starts with a *C*." She was digging through her notes from Martindale-Hubbell. "Said he works in oil and gas on the ninth floor."

Grantham was speeding away from Parklane. "Oil and gas!"

"That's what he said." She found it. "Curtis D. Morgan, oil and gas section, age twenty-nine. There's another Morgan in litigation, but he's a partner and, let's see, he's fifty-one."

"Garcia is Curtis Morgan," Gray said with relief. He looked at his watch. "It's a quarter till four. We'll have to hurry."

"I can't wait."

RUPERT PICKED THEM UP as they turned out of Parklane's driveway. The rented Pontiac was flying all over the street. He drove like an idiot just to keep up, then radioed ahead.

THIRTY-SEVEN

MATTHEW BARR had never experienced a speedboat before, and after five hours of a bone-jarring voyage through the ocean he was soaked and in pain. His body was numb, and when he saw land he said a prayer, the first in decades. Then he resumed his nonstop cursing of Fletcher Coal.

They docked at a small marina near a city that he believed to be Freeport. The captain had said something about Freeport to the man known as Larry when they left Florida. No other word was spoken during the ordeal. Larry's role in the journey was uncertain. He was at least six-six, with a neck as thick as a utility pole, and he did nothing but watch Barr, which was okay at first but after five hours became quite a nuisance.

They stood awkwardly when the boat stopped. Larry was the first one out, and he motioned for Barr to join him. Another large man was approaching on the pier, and together they escorted Barr to a waiting van. The van was suspiciously short of windows.

At this point, Barr preferred to say good-bye to his new pals, and simply disappear in the direction of Freeport. He'd catch a plane to D.C., and slap Coal the moment he saw his shining forehead. But he had to be cool. They wouldn't dare hurt him.

The van stopped moments later at a small airstrip, and Barr was escorted to a black Lear. He admired it briefly before following Larry up the steps. He was cool and relaxed; just another job. After all, he was at one time one of the best CIA agents in Europe. He was an ex-Marine. He could take care of himself.

He sat by himself in the cabin. The windows were covered, and this annoyed him. But he understood. Mr. Mattiece treasured his privacy, and Barr could certainly respect that. Larry and the other heavyweight were at the front of the cabin, flipping through magazines and completely ignoring him.

Thirty minutes after takeoff, the Lear began its descent, and Larry lumbered toward him.

"Put this on," he demanded as he handed over a thick, cloth blindfold. At this point, a rookie would panic. An amateur would start asking questions. But Barr had been blindfolded before, and while he was having serious doubts about this mission, he calmly took the blindfold and covered his eyes.

THE MAN who removed the blindfold introduced himself as Emil, an assistant to Mr. Mattiece. He was a small, wiry type with dark hair and a thin mustache winding around the lip. He sat in a chair four feet away and lit a cigarette.

"Our people tell us you are legitimate, sort of," he said with a friendly smile. Barr looked around the room. There were no walls, only windows in small panes. The sun was bright and pierced his eyes. A plush garden surrounded a series of fountains and pools outside the room. They were in the rear of a very large house.

"I'm here on behalf of the President," Barr said.

"We believe you." Emil nodded. He was undoubtedly a Cajun.

"May I ask who you are?" Barr said.

"I'm Emil, and that's enough. Mr. Mattiece is not feeling well. Perhaps you should leave your message with me."

"I have orders to speak directly to him."

"Orders from Mr. Coal, I believe." Emil never stopped smiling.

"That's correct."

"I see. Mr. Mattiece prefers not to meet you. He wants you to talk to me."

Barr shook his head. Now, if push came to shove, if things got out of hand, then he would gladly talk to Emil if it was necessary. But for now, he would hold firm.

"I am not authorized to talk to anyone but Mr. Mattiece," Barr said properly.

The smile almost disappeared. Emil pointed beyond the pools and fountains to a large gazebo-shaped building with tall windows from floor to ceiling. Rows of perfectly manicured shrubs and flowers surrounded it. "Mr. Mattiece is in his gazebo. Follow me."

They left the sun room and walked slowly around a wading pool. Barr had a thick knot in his stomach, but he followed his little friend as if this was simply another day at the office. The sound of falling water echoed through the garden. A narrow boardwalk led to the gazebo. They stopped at the door.

"I'm afraid you must remove your shoes," Emil said with a smile. Emil was barefoot. Barr untied his shoes and placed them next to the door.

"Do not step on the towels," Emil said gravely.

The towels?

Emil opened the door for Barr, who stepped in alone. The room was perfectly round, about fifty feet in diameter. There were three chairs and a sofa, all covered with white sheets. Thick cotton towels were on the floor in perfect little trails around the room. The sun shone brightly through skylights. A door opened, and Victor Mattiece emerged from a small room.

Barr froze and gawked at the man. He was thin and gaunt, with long gray hair and a dirty beard. He wore only a pair of white gym shorts, and walked carefully on the towels without looking at Barr.

"Sit over there," he said, pointing at a chair. "Don't step on the towels."

Barr avoided the towels and took his seat. Mattiece turned his back and faced the windows. His skin was leathery and dark bronze. His bare feet were lined with ugly veins. His toenails were long and yellow. He was crazy as hell.

"What do you want?" he asked quietly to the windows.

"The President sent me."

"He did not. Fletcher Coal sent you. I doubt if the President knows you're here."

Maybe he wasn't crazy. He spoke without moving a muscle in his body.

"Fletcher Coal is the President's chief of staff. He sent me."

"I know about Coal. And I know about you. And I know about your little Unit. Now, what do you want?"

"Information."

"Don't play games with me. What do you want?"

"Have you read the pelican brief?" Barr asked.

The frail body did not flinch. "Have you read it?"

"Yes," Barr answered quickly.

"Do you believe it to be true?"

"Perhaps. That's why I'm here."

"Why is Mr. Coal so concerned about the pelican brief?"

"Because a couple of reporters have wind of it. And if it's true, then we need to know immediately."

"Who are these reporters?"

"Gray Grantham with the *Washington Post*. He picked it up first, and he knows more than anyone. He's digging hard. Coal thinks he's about to run something."

"We can take care of him, can't we?" Mattiece said to the windows. "Who's the other one?"

"Rifkin with the *Times*."

Mattiece still had not moved an inch. Barr glanced around at the sheets and towels. Yes, he had to be crazy. The place was sanitized and smelled of rubbing alcohol. Maybe he was ill.

"Does Mr. Coal believe it to be true?"

"I don't know. He's very concerned about it. That's why I'm here, Mr. Mattiece. We have to know."

"What if it's true?"

"Then we have problems."

Mattiece finally moved. He shifted his weight to the right leg, and folded his arms across his narrow chest. But his eyes never moved. Sand dunes and sea oats were in the distance, but not the ocean.

"Do you know what I think?" he said quietly.

"What?"

"I think Coal is the problem. He gave the brief to too many people. He handed it to the CIA. He allowed you to see it. This really disturbs me."

Barr could think of no response. It was ludicrous to imply that Coal wanted to distribute the brief. The problem is you, Mattiece. You killed the justices. You panicked and killed Callahan. You're the greedy bastard who was not content with a mere fifty million.

Mattiece turned slowly and looked at Barr. The eyes were dark and red. He looked nothing like the photo with the Vice President, but that was seven years ago. He'd aged twenty years in the last seven, and perhaps gone off the deep end along the way.

"You clowns in Washington are to blame for this," he said, somewhat louder.

Barr could not look at him. "Is it true, Mr. Mattiece? That's all I want to know."

Behind Barr, a door opened without a sound. Larry, in his socks and avoiding the towels, eased forward two steps and stopped.

Mattiece walked on the towels to a glass door, and opened it. He looked outside and spoke softly. "Of course it's true." He walked through the door, and closed it slowly behind him. Barr watched as the idiot shuffled along a sidewalk toward the sand dunes.

What now? he thought. Perhaps Emil would come get him. Perhaps.

Larry inched forward with a rope, and Barr did not hear or feel anything until it was too late. Mattiece did not want blood in his gazebo, so Larry simply broke the neck and choked him until it was over.

THIRTY-EIGHT

T HE GAME PLAN called for her to be on this elevator at this point in the search, but she thought enough unexpected events had occurred to warrant a change in the game plan. He thought not. They had engaged in a healthy debate over this elevator ride, and here she was. He was right; this was the quickest route to Curtis Morgan. And she was right; it was a dangerous route to Curtis Morgan. But the other routes could be just as dangerous. The entire game plan was deadly.

She wore her only dress and her only pair of heels. Gray said she looked really nice, but that was to be expected. The elevator stopped on the ninth floor, and when she walked off it there was a pain in her stomach and she could barely breathe.

The receptionist was across a plush lobby. The name WHITE AND BLAZEVICH covered the wall behind her in thick, brass lettering. Her knees were weak, but she made it to the receptionist, who smiled properly. It was ten minutes before five.

"May I help you?" she asked. The nameplate proclaimed her to be Peggy Young.

"Yes," Darby managed, clearing her throat. "I have a five o'clock appointment with Curtis Morgan. My name is Dorothy Blythe."

The receptionist was stunned. Her mouth fell open, and she stared blankly at Darby, now Dorothy. She couldn't speak.

Darby's heart stopped. "Is something the matter?"

"Well, no. I'm sorry. Just a moment." Peggy Young stood quickly, and disappeared in a rush.

Run! Her heart pounded like a drum. Run! She tried to control her breathing, but she was battling hyperventilation. Her legs were rubbery. Run!

She looked around, trying to be nonchalant as if she was just another client waiting on her lawyer. Surely they wouldn't gun her down here in the lobby of a law office.

He came first, followed by the receptionist. He was about fifty with bushy gray hair and a terrible scowl. "Hi," he said, but only because he had to. "I'm Jarreld Schwabe, a partner here. You say you have an appointment with Curtis Morgan."

Keep it up. "Yes. At five. Is there a problem?"

"And your name is Dorothy Blythe?"

Yeah, but you can call me Dot. "That's what I said. Yes. What's the matter?" She sounded genuinely irritated.

He was inching closer. "When did you make the appointment?"

"I don't know. About two weeks ago. I met Curtis at a party in Georgetown. He told me he was an oil and gas lawyer, and I happen to need one. I called the office here, and made an appointment. Now, will you please tell me what's going on?" She was amazed at how well these words were coming from her dry mouth.

"Why do you need an oil and gas lawyer?"

"I don't think I have to explain myself to you," she said, real bitchy-like.

The elevator opened, and a man in a cheap suit approached quickly to join the conversation. Darby scowled at him. Her legs would give way just any second.

Schwabe was really bearing down. "We don't have any record of such an appointment."

"Then fire the appointment secretary. Do you welcome all new clients this way?" Oh, she was indignant, but Schwabe did not let up.

"You can't see Curtis Morgan," he said.

"And why not?" she demanded.

"He's dead."

The knees were jelly and about to go. A sharp pain rippled through the stomach. But, she thought quickly, it was okay to looked shocked. He was, after all, supposed to be her new lawyer.

"I'm sorry. Why didn't anyone call me?"

Schwabe was still suspicious. "As I said, we have no record of a Dorothy Blythe."

"What happened to him?" she asked, stunned.

"He was mugged a week ago. Shot by street punks, we believe."

The guy in the cheap suit took a step closer. "Do you have any identification?"

"Who in the hell are you?" she snapped loudly.

"He's security," said Schwabe.

"Security for what?" she demanded, even louder. "Is this a law firm or a prison?"

The partner looked at the man in the cheap suit, and it was obvious neither knew exactly what to do at this point. She was very attractive, and they had upset her, and her story was somewhat believable. They relaxed a little.

"Why don't you leave, Ms. Blythe?" Schwabe said.

"I can't wait!"

The security man reached to assist her. "Here," he said.

She slapped his hand. "Touch me and I'll sue your ass first thing tomorrow morning. Get away from me!"

This shook them a bit. She was mad and lashing out. Perhaps they were being a bit hard.

"I'll see you down," the security man said.

"I know how to leave. I'm amazed you clowns have any clients." She was stepping backward. Her face was red, but not from anger. It was fear. "I've got lawyers in four states, and I've never been treated like this," she yelled at them. She was in the center of the lobby. "I paid a half a million last year in legal fees, and I've got a million to pay next year, but you idiots won't get any of it." The closer she got to the elevator, the louder she yelled. She was a crazy woman. They watched her until the elevator door opened and she was gone.

□ □ □ □

GRAY PACED along the end of the bed, holding the phone and waiting for Smith Keen. Darby was stretched out on the bed with her eyes closed.

Gray stopped. "Hello, Smith. I need you to check something quick."

"Where are you?" Keen asked.

"A hotel. Look back six or seven days. I need the obituary for Curtis D. Morgan."

"Who's he?"

"Garcia."

"Garcia! What happened to Garcia?"

"He died, obviously. Shot by muggers."

"I remember that. We ran a story last week about a young lawyer who was robbed and shot."

"Probably him. Can you check it for me? I need his wife's name and address if we have it."

"How'd you find him?"

"It's a long story. We'll try to talk to his widow tonight."

"Garcia's dead. This is weird, baby."

"It's more than weird. The kid knew something, and they knocked him off."

"Do you think you're safe?"

"Who knows?"

"Where's the girl?"

"She's with me."

"What if they're watching his house?"

Gray hadn't thought about it. "We'll have to take that chance. I'll call you back in fifteen minutes."

He placed the phone on the floor and sat in an antique rocker. There was a warm beer on the table, and he took a long drink. He watched her. A forearm covered both eyes. She was in jeans and a sweatshirt. The dress was thrown in a corner. The heels had been kicked across the room.

"You okay?" he asked softly.

"Wonderful."

She was a real smartass, and he liked that in a woman. Of course, she was almost a lawyer, and they must teach smartass-ness in law school. He sipped the beer and admired the jeans.

He enjoyed this brief moment of uninterrupted staring without getting caught.

"Are you staring at me?" she asked.

"Yes."

"Sex is the last thing on my mind."

"Then why'd you mention it?"

"Because I can feel you lusting after my red toenails."

"True."

"I've got a headache. A real, genuine, pounding headache."

"You've worked for it. Can I get you something?"

"Yes. A one-way ticket to Jamaica."

"You can leave tonight. I'll take you to the airport right now."

She removed the forearm from her eyes and gently massaged both temples. "I'm sorry I cried."

He finished the beer with a long drink. "You earned the right." She was in tears when she stepped off the elevator. He was waiting like an expectant father, except he had a .38 in his coat pocket—a .38 she knew nothing about.

"So what do you think of investigative reporting?" he asked.

"I'd rather butcher hogs."

"Well, in all honesty, not every day is this eventful. Some days I simply sit at my desk and make hundreds of phone calls to bureaucrats who have no comment."

"Sounds great. Let's do that tomorrow."

He kicked his shoes off and placed his feet on the bed. She closed her eyes and breathed deeply. Minutes passed without a word.

"Do you know that Louisiana is known as the Pelican State?" she asked with her eyes closed.

"No. I didn't know that."

"It's a shame really, because the brown pelicans were virtually wiped out the the early 1960s."

"What happened to them?"

"Pesticides. They eat nothing but fish, and the fish live in river water filled with chlorinated hydrocarbons from pesticides. The rains wash the pesticides from the soil into small streams which eventually empty into rivers which eventually empty into the Mississippi. By the time the pelicans in Louisiana eat the fish, they are loaded with DDT and other chemicals which accumulate in the fatty tissues of the birds. Death is seldom immediate, but in times of stress such as hunger or bad weather, the pelicans and eagles and cormorants are forced to draw upon their reserves, and can literally be poisoned by their own fat. If they don't die, they are usually unable to reproduce. Their eggs are so thin and fragile they crack during incubation. Did you know that?"

"Why would I know that?"

"In the late sixties, Louisiana began transplanting brown pelicans from southern Florida, and over the years the population has slowly increased. But the birds are still very much in danger. Forty years ago there were thousands of them. The cypress swamp that Mattiece wants to destroy is home to only a few dozen pelicans."

Gray pondered these things. She was silent for a long time.

"What day is it?" she asked without opening her eyes.

"Monday."

"I left New Orleans a week ago today. Thomas and Verheek had dinner two weeks ago today. That, of course, was the fateful moment when the pelican brief changed hands."

"Three weeks ago tomorrow, Rosenberg and Jensen were murdered."

"I was an innocent little law student minding my own business and having a wonderful love affair with my professor. I guess those days are gone."

Law school and the professor might be gone, he thought. "What're your plans?"

"I have none. I'm just trying to get out of this damned mess and stay alive. I'll run off somewhere and hide for a few months, maybe a few years. I've got enough money to live for a long time. If and when I reach the point when I'm not looking over my shoulder, I might come back."

"To law school?"

"I don't think so. The law has lost its allure."

"Why'd you want to be a lawyer?"

"Idealism, and money. I thought I could change the world and get paid for it."

"But there are so damned many lawyers already. Why do all these bright students keep flocking to law school?"

"Simple. It's greed. They want BMWs and gold credit cards. If you go to a good law school, finish in the top ten percent, and get a job with a big firm, you'll be earning six figures in a few short years, and it only goes up. It's guaranteed. At the age of thirty-five, you'll be a partner raking in at least two hundred thousand a year. Some earn much more."

"What about the other ninety percent?"

"It's not such a good deal for them. They get the leftovers."

"Most lawyers I know hate it. They'd rather be doing something else."

"But they can't leave it because of the money. Even a lousy lawyer in a small office can earn a hundred thousand a year after ten years of practice, and he may hate it, but where can he go and match the money?"

"I detest lawyers."

"And I guess you think reporters are adored."

Good point. Gray looked at his watch, then picked up the phone. He dialed Keen's number. Keen read him the obit, and the *Post* story about the senseless street killing of this young lawyer. Gray took notes.

"A couple of other things," Keen said. "Feldman is very concerned about your safety. He expected a briefing in his office today, and he was pissed when he didn't get one. Make sure you report to him before noon tomorrow. Understand?"

"I'll try."

"Do more than try, Gray. We're very nervous over here."

"The *Times* is sucking wind, isn't it?"

"I'm not worried about the *Times* right now. I'm much more concerned about you and the girl."

"We're fine. Everything's lovely. What else have you got?"

"You have three messages in the past two hours from a man named Cleve. Says he's a cop. Do you know him?"

"Yes."

"Well, he wants to talk tonight. Says it's urgent."

"I'll call him later."

"Okay. You guys be careful. We'll be here till late, so check in."

Gray hung up and looked at his notes. It was almost seven. "I'm going to see Mrs. Morgan. I want you to stay here."

She sat between the pillows and crossed her arms on her knees. "I'd rather go."

"What if they're watching the house?" he asked.

"Why would they watch the house? He's dead."

"Maybe they're suspicious now, because a mysterious client appeared today looking for him. Even though he's dead, he's attracting attention."

She thought about this for a minute. "No. I'm going."

"It's too risky, Darby."

"Don't talk to me about risks. I've survived in the minefields for twelve days. This is easy."

He waited on her by the door. "By the way, where am I staying tonight?"

"Jefferson Hotel."

"Do you have the phone number?"

"What do you think?"

"Dumb question."

THE PRIVATE JET with Edwin Sneller aboard landed at National in Washington a few minutes after seven. He was delighted to leave New York. He'd spent six days there bouncing off the walls in his suite at the Plaza. For almost a week, his men had checked hotels and watched airports and walked streets, and they knew damned well they were wasting their time, but orders were orders. They were told to stay there until something broke and they could move on. It was silly trying to find the girl in Manhattan, but they had to stay close in case she made a mistake like a phone call or a plastic transaction that could be traced, and suddenly they were needed.

She made no mistakes until two-thirty this afternoon when she needed money and went to the account. They knew this would happen, especially if she planned to leave the country and was afraid to use plastic. At some point, she would need cash, and she'd have to wire it since the bank was in New Orleans and she wasn't. Sneller's client owned eight percent of the bank; not a lot, but a nice little twelve-million-dollar holding that could make things happen. A few minutes after three, he'd received a call from Freeport.

They did not suspect her to be in Washington. She was a smart girl who was running away from trouble, not to it. And they certainly didn't expect her to link up with the reporter. They had no idea, but now it seemed so logical. And it was worse than critical.

Fifteen thousand went from her account to his, and suddenly Sneller was back in business. He had two men with him. Another private jet was en route from Miami. He had asked for a dozen men immediately. It would be a quick job, or no job at all. There was not a second to spare.

Sneller was not hopeful. With Khamel on the team, everything seemed possible. He had killed Rosenberg and Jensen so cleanly, then disappeared without a trace. Now he was dead, shot in the head because of one little innocent female law student.

THE MORGAN HOUSE was in a neat suburb in Alexandria. The neighborhood was young and affluent, with bikes and tricycles in every yard.

Three cars were parked in the drive. One had Ohio plates. Gray rang the doorbell and watched the street. Nothing suspicious.

An older man opened the door slightly. "Yes," he said softly.

"I'm Gray Grantham with the *Washington Post*, and this is my assistant, Sara Jacobs." Darby forced a smile. "We would like to speak with Mrs. Morgan."

"I don't think so."

"Please. It's very important."

He looked at them carefully. "Wait a minute." He closed the door and disappeared.

The house had a narrow wooden porch with a small veranda over it. They were in the darkness and could not be seen from the street. A car passed slowly.

He opened the door again. "I'm Tom Kupcheck, her father, and she doesn't want to talk."

Gray nodded as if this was understandable. "We won't be five minutes. I promise."

He walked onto the porch and closed the door behind him. "I guess you're hard of hearing. I said she doesn't want to talk."

"I heard you, Mr. Kupcheck. And I respect her privacy, and I know what she's been through."

"Since when do you guys respect anyone's privacy?"

Evidently, Mr. Kupcheck had a short fuse. It was about to blow.

Gray kept calm. Darby backed away. She'd been involved in enough altercations for one day.

"Her husband called me three times before he died. I talked to him on the phone, and I don't believe his death was a random killing by street punks."

"He's dead. My daughter is upset. She doesn't want to talk. Now get the hell out of here."

"Mr. Kupcheck," Darby said warmly. "We have reason to believe your son-in-law was a witness to some highly organized criminal activity."

This calmed him a bit, and he glared at Darby. "Is that so? Well, you can't ask him about it, can you? My daughter knows nothing. She's had a bad day and she's on medication. Now leave."

"Can we see her tomorrow?" Darby asked.

"I doubt it. Call first."

Gray handed him a business card. "If she wants to talk, use the number on the back. I'm staying at a hotel. I'll call around noon tomorrow."

"You do that. For now, just leave. You've already upset her."

"We're sorry," Gray said, as they walked off the porch. Mr. Kupcheck opened the door but watched them as they left. Gray stopped, and turned to him. "Has any other reporter called or stopped by?"

"A bunch of them called the day after he was killed. They wanted all sorts of stuff. Rude people."

"But none in the past few days?"

"No. Now leave."

"Any from the *New York Times?*"

"No." He stepped inside and slammed the door.

They hurried to the car parked four doors down. There was no traffic on the street. Gray zigzagged through the short suburban streets, and crisscrossed his way out of the neighborhood. He watched the mirror until he was convinced they were not being followed.

"End of Garcia," Darby said as they entered 395 and headed for the city.

"Not yet. We'll make one final, dying gasp tomorrow, and maybe she'll talk to us."

"If she knew something, her father would know. And if her father knew, why wouldn't he cooperate? There's nothing there, Gray."

This made perfect sense. They rode in silence for a few minutes. Fatigue was setting in.

"We can be at the airport in fifteen minutes," he said. "I'll drop you off, and you can be out of here in thirty minutes. Take a plane anywhere, just vanish."

"I'll leave tomorrow. I need some rest, and I want to think about where to go. Thanks."

"Do you feel safe?"

"At this moment, yes. But it's subject to change in seconds."

"I'll be glad to sleep in your room tonight. Just like in New York."

"You didn't sleep in my room in New York. You slept on a sofa in the sitting room." She was smiling, and this was a good sign.

He was smiling too. "Okay. I'll sleep in the sitting room tonight."

"I don't have a sitting room."

"Well, well. Then where can I sleep?"

Suddenly, she was not smiling. She bit her lip and her eyes watered. He had pushed too far. It was Callahan again.

"I'm just not ready," she said.

"When might you be ready?"

"Gray, please. Just leave it alone."

She watched the traffic ahead and said nothing. "I'm sorry," he said.

Slowly, she lay down in the seat and placed her head in his lap. He gently rubbed her shoulder, and she clutched his hand. "I'm scared to death," she said quietly.

THIRTY‑NINE

H E HAD LEFT HER ROOM around ten, after a bottle of wine and egg rolls. He had called Mason Paypur, the night police reporter for the *Post*, and asked him to check with his sources about the Morgan street killing. It had happened downtown in an area not noted for killings; just a few muggings and beatings.

He was tired and discouraged. And he was unhappy because she would leave tomorrow. The *Post* owed him six weeks of vacation, and he was tempted to leave with her. Mattiece could have his oil. But he was afraid he'd never come back, which wouldn't be the end of his world except for the troublesome fact that she had money and he didn't. They could skip along the beaches and frolic in the sun for about two months on his money, then it would be up to her. And, more importantly, she hadn't invited him to join in her getaway. She was grieving. When she mentioned Thomas Callahan, he could feel the pain.

He was now at the Jefferson Hotel on Sixteenth, pursuant, of course, to her instructions. He called Cleve at home.

"Where are you?" Cleve asked, irritated.

"A hotel. It's a long story. What's up?"

"They put Sarge on medical leave for ninety days."

"What's wrong with him?"

"Nothing. He says they want him out of the place for a while. It's like a bunker over there. Everybody's been told to shut up and speak to no one. They're scared to death. They made Sarge leave at noon today. He thinks you could be in serious danger. He's heard your name a thousand times in the past week. They're obsessed with you and how much you know."

"Who's they?"

"Coal, of course, and his aide Birchfield. They run the West Wing like the Gestapo. Sometimes they include, what's his name, the little squirrel with the bow tie? Domestic affairs?"

"Emmitt Waycross."

"That's him. It's mainly Coal and Birchfield making the threats and plotting strategy."

"What kind of threats?"

"No one in the White House, except for the President, can talk to the press on the record or off without Coal's approval. This includes the press secretary. Coal clears everything."

"That's incredible."

"They're terrified. And Sarge thinks they're dangerous."

"Okay. I'm hiding."

"I stopped by your apartment late last night. I wish you'd tell me when you disappear."

"I'll check in tomorrow night."

"What're you driving?"

"A rented Pontiac with four doors. Very sporty."

"I checked the Volvo this afternoon. It's fine."

"Thanks, Cleve."

"You okay?"

"I think so. Tell Sarge I'm fine."

"Call me tomorrow. I'm worried."

HE SLEPT FOUR HOURS and was awake when the phone rang. It was dark outside, and would remain that way for at least two hours. He stared at the phone, and picked it up on the fifth ring.

"Hello," he said suspiciously.

"Is this Gray Grantham?" It was a very timid female.

"Yes. Who is this?"

"Beverly Morgan. You stopped by last night."

Gray was on his feet, listening hard, wide awake. "Yes. I'm sorry if we upset you."

"No. My father is very protective. And angry. The reporters were awful after Curtis was killed. They called from everywhere. They wanted old pictures of him and new photos of me and the child. They called at all hours. It was terrible, and my father got tired of it. He pushed two of them off the porch."

"I guess we were lucky."

"I hope he didn't offend you." The voice was hollow and detached, yet trying to be strong.

"Not at all."

"He's asleep now, downstairs on the sofa. So we can talk."

"Why aren't you asleep?" he asked.

"I'm taking some pills to make me sleep, and I'm all out of sync. I've been sleeping days and rambling nights." It was obvious she was awake and wanted to talk.

Gray sat on the bed and tried to relax. "I can't imagine the shock of something like this."

"It takes several days for it to become real. At first, the pain is horrible. Just horrible. I couldn't move my body without hurting. I couldn't think because of the shock and disbelief. I went through the motions to get through the funeral, which now seems like a bad dream. Is this boring?"

"Not at all."

"I've got to get off these pills. I sleep so much I don't get to talk to adults. Plus, my father tends to run people off. Are you taping this?"

"No. I'm just listening."

"He was killed a week ago tonight. I thought he was working very late, which was not unusual. They shot him and took his wallet, so the cops couldn't identify him. I saw on the late news where a young lawyer had been murdered downtown, and I knew it was Curtis. Don't ask me how they knew he was a lawyer without knowing his name. It's strange, all the little weird things that go with a murder."

"Why was he working late?"

"He worked eighty hours a week, sometimes more. White and Blazevich is a sweatshop. They try to kill the associates for seven years, and if they can't kill them they make them part-ners. Curtis hated the place. He was tired of being a lawyer."

"How long was he there?"

"Five years. He was making ninety thousand a year, so he put up with the hassle."

"Did you know he called me?"

"No. My father told me you said that, and I've thought about it all night. What did he say?"

"He never identified himself. He used the code name of Gar-cia. Don't ask how I learned his identity—it'll take hours. He said he possibly knew something about the assassinations of Jus-tices Rosenberg and Jensen, and he wanted to tell me what he knew."

"Randy Garcia was his best friend in elementary school."

"I got the impression he had seen something at the office, and perhaps someone at the office knew he had seen it. He was very nervous, and always called from pay phones. He thought he was being followed. We had planned to meet early Saturday before last, but he called that morning and said no. He was scared, and said he had to protect his family. Did you know any of this?"

"No. I knew he was under a great deal of stress, but he'd been that way for five years. He never brought the office home with him. He hated the place, really."

"Why'd he hate the place?"

"He worked for a bunch of cutthroats, a bunch of thugs who'd watch you bleed for a buck. They spend tons of money on this marvelous facade of respectability, but they are scum. Curtis was a top student and had his pick of jobs. They were such a great bunch of guys when they recruited him, and com-plete monsters to work with. Very unethical."

"Why did he stay with the firm?"

"The money kept getting better. He almost left a year ago, but the job offer fell through. He was very unhappy, but he tried to keep it to himself. I think he felt guilty for making such a big mistake. We had a little routine around here. When he came home, I would ask him how his day went. Sometimes this was at ten at night, so I knew it was a bad day. But he always said the day had been profitable; that was the word, profitable. And then we talked about our baby. He didn't want to talk about the office, and I didn't want to hear it."

Well, so much for Garcia. He's dead, and he told his wife nothing. "Who cleaned out his desk?"

"Someone at the office. They brought his stuff Friday, all neatly packaged and taped in three cardboard boxes. You're welcome to go through it."

"No, thanks. I'm sure it's been sanitized. How much life insurance did he have?"

She paused for a second. "You're a smart man, Mr. Grantham. Two weeks ago, he bought a million-dollar term policy with double indemnity for accidental death."

"That's two million dollars."

"Yes sir. I guess you're right. I guess he was suspicious."

"I don't think he was killed by muggers, Mrs. Morgan."

"I can't believe this." She choked a little, but fought it off.

"Have the cops asked you a lot of questions?"

"No. It's just another D.C. mugging that went one step further. No big deal. Happens every day."

The insurance bit was interesting, but useless. Gray was getting tired of Mrs. Morgan and her unhurried monotone. He was sorry for her, but if she knew nothing, it was time to say good-bye.

"What do you think he knew?" she asked.

This could take hours. "I don't know," Gray answered, glancing at his watch. "He said he knew something about the killings, but that's as far as he would go. I was convinced we would meet somewhere and he would spill his guts and show me something. I was wrong."

"How would he know anything about those dead judges?"

"I don't know. He just called me out of the blue."

"If he had something to show you, what would it be?" she asked.

He was the reporter. He was supposed to ask the questions. "I have no idea. He never hinted."

"Where would he hide such a thing?" The question was sincere, but irritating. Then it hit him. She was going somewhere with this.

"I don't know. Where did he keep his valuable papers?"

"We have a lockbox at the bank for deeds and wills and stuff. I've always known about the lockbox. He handled all the legal business, Mr. Grantham. I looked at the lockbox last Thursday with my father, and there was nothing unusual in it."

"You didn't expect anything unusual, did you?"

"No. Then Saturday morning, early, it was still dark, I was going through his papers in his desk in the bedroom. We have this antique rolltop desk that he used for his personal correspondence and papers, and I found something a bit unusual."

Gray was on his feet, holding the phone, and staring wildly at the floor. She had called at four in the morning. She had chitchatted for twenty minutes. And she waited until he was ready to hang up to drop the bomb.

"What is it?" he asked as coolly as possible.

"It's a key."

He had a lump in his throat. "A key to what?"

"Another lockbox."

"Which bank?"

"First Columbia. We've never banked there."

"I see. And you knew nothing about this other lockbox?"

"Oh no. Not until Saturday morning. I was puzzled by it, still am, but I found all of our legal papers in the old lockbox, so I had no reason to check this one. I figured I'd run by when I felt like it."

"Would you like me to check it for you?"

"I thought you would say that. What if you find what you're looking for?"

"I don't know what I'm looking for. But what if I find something he left behind, and this something proves to be very, let's say, newsworthy?"

"Use it."

"No conditions?"

"One. If it disparages my husband in any way, you can't use it."

"It's a deal. I swear."

"When do you want the key?"

"Do you have it in your hand?"

"Yes."

"If you'll stand on the front porch, I'll be there in about three seconds."

THE PRIVATE JET from Miami had brought only five men, so Edwin Sneller had only seven to plan with. Seven men, no time, and precious little equipment. He had not slept Monday night. His hotel suite was a mini–command center as they stared at maps through the night, and tried to plan the next twenty-four hours. A few things were certain. Grantham had an apartment, but he was not there. He had a car he was not using. He worked at the *Post*, and it was on Fifteenth Street. White and Blazevich was in a building on Tenth near New York, but she would not return there. Morgan's widow lived in Alexandria. Beyond that, they were searching for two people out of three million.

These were not the type of men you could rustle out of the bunkhouse and send in to fight. They had to be found and hired, and he'd been promised as many as possible by the end of the day.

Sneller was no novice at the killing game, and this was hopeless. This was desperation. The sky was falling. He would do his best under the circumstances, but Edwin Sneller had one foot out the back door.

She was on his mind. She had met Khamel on his terms, and walked away from it. She had dodged bullets and bombs, and evaded the best in the business. He would love to see her, not to kill her, but to congratulate her. A rookie running loose and living to tell about it.

They would concentrate on the *Post* building. It was the one spot he had to come back to.

FORTY

THE DOWNTOWN TRAFFIC was bumper to bumper, and that suited Darby just fine. She was in no hurry. The bank lobby opened at nine-thirty, and some time around seven, over coffee and untouched bagels in her room, he had convinced her that she should be the one to visit the vault. She was not really convinced, but a woman should do it, and there weren't many available. Beverly Morgan told Gray that her bank, First Hamilton, froze their box as soon as they learned of Curtis's death, and that she was allowed only to view the contents and make an inventory. She was also allowed to copy the will, but the original was placed back in the box and secured in the vault. The box would be released only after the tax auditors finished their work.

So the immediate question was whether or not First Columbia knew he was dead. The Morgans had never banked there. Beverly had no idea why he chose it. It was a huge bank with a million customers, and they decided that the odds were against it.

Darby was tired of playing the odds. She'd blown a wonderful opportunity last night to get on a plane, and now here she was about to be Beverly Morgan matching wits with First Columbia so she could steal from a dead man. And what was her sidekick going to do? He was going to protect her. He had this gun, which scared her to death and had the same effect on him though he wouldn't admit it, and he planned to play body-guard by the front door while she pilfered the lockbox.

"What if they know he's dead," she asked, "and I tell them he isn't?"

"Then slap the bitch in the face and run like hell. I'll catch you at the front door. I've got a gun, and we'll blast our way down the sidewalk."

"Come on, Gray. I don't know if I can do this."

"You can do it, okay? Play it cool. Be assertive. Be a smartass. It should come natural."

"Thanks so much. What if they call security on me? I have this sudden phobia of security guards."

"I'll rescue you. I'll come blazing through the lobby like a SWAT team."

"We'll all be killed."

"Relax, Darby. It'll work."

"Why are you so chipper?"

"I smell it. Something's in that lockbox, Darby. And you have to bring it out, kid. It's all riding on you."

"Thanks for easing the pressure."

They were on E Street near Ninth. Gray slowed the car, then parked illegally in a loading zone forty feet from the front entrance of First Columbia. He jumped out. Darby's exit was slower. Together, they walked quickly to the door. It was almost ten. "I'll wait here," he said, pointing to a marble column. "Go do it."

"Go do it," she mumbled as she disappeared inside the revolving door. She was always the one being fed to the lions. The lobby was as big as a football field, with columns and chandeliers and fake Persian rugs.

"Safe deposit boxes?" she asked a young woman behind the information desk. The girl pointed to a corner in the far right.

"Thanks," she said, and strolled toward it. The lines in front of the tellers were four deep to her left, and to her right a hundred busy vice presidents talked on their phones. It was the largest bank in the city, and no one noticed her.

The vault was behind a set of massive bronze doors that were polished enough to appear almost golden, no doubt to give the appearance of infinite safety and invulnerability. The doors were opened slightly to allow a select few in and out. To the left, an important-looking lady of sixty sat behind a desk with the words SAFE DEPOSIT BOXES across its front. Her name was Virginia Baskin.

Virginia Baskin stared at Darby as she approached the desk. There was no smile.

"I need access to a box," Darby said without breathing. She hadn't breathed in the last two and a half minutes.

"The number, please," Ms. Baskin said as she hit the keyboard and turned to the monitor.

"F566."

She punched the number and waited for the words to flash on the screen. She frowned, and moved her face to within inches of it. Run! Darby thought. She frowned harder and scratched her chin. Run, before she picks up the phone and calls the guards. Run, before the alarms go off and my idiot cohort comes blazing through the lobby.

Ms. Baskin withdrew her head from the monitor. "That was rented just two weeks ago," she said almost to herself.

"Yes," Darby said as if she had rented it.

"I assume you're Mrs. Morgan," she said, pecking on the keyboard.

Keep assuming, baby. "Yes, Beverly Anne Morgan."

"And your address?"

"891 Pembroke, Alexandria."

She nodded at the screen as if it could see her and give its approval. She pecked again. "Phone number?"

"703-664-5980."

Ms. Baskin liked this too. So did the computer. "Who rented this box?"

"My husband, Curtis D. Morgan."

"And his social security number?"

Darby casually opened her new, rather large leather shoulder bag, and pulled out her wallet. How many wives memorized their husband's social security number? She opened the wallet. "510-96-8686."

"Very well," Ms. Baskin said properly as she left the keyboard and reached into her desk. "How long will this take?"

"Just a minute."

She placed a wide card on a small clipboard on the desk, and pointed at it. "Sign here, Mrs. Morgan."

Darby nervously signed on the second slot. Mr. Morgan had made the first entry the day he rented the box.

Ms. Baskin glanced at the signature while Darby held her breath.

"Do you have your key?" she asked.

"Of course," Darby said with a warm smile.

Ms. Baskin took a small box from the drawer, and walked around the desk. "Follow me." They went through the bronze doors. The vault was as big as a branch bank in the suburbs. Designed along the lines of a mausoleum, it was a maze of hall-ways and small chambers. Two men in uniform walked by. They passed four identical rooms with walls lined with rows of lockboxes. The fifth room held F566, evidently, because Ms. Baskin stepped into it and opened her little black box. Darby looked nervously around and behind her.

Virginia was all business. She walked to F566, which was shoulder-high, and stuck in the key. She rolled her eyes at Darby as if to say, "Your turn, dumbass." Darby yanked the key from a pocket, and inserted it next to the other one. Virginia then turned both keys, and slid the box two inches from its slot. She removed the bank's key.

She pointed to a small booth with a folding wooden door. "Take it in there. When you finish, lock it back in place and come to my desk." She was leaving the room as she spoke.

"Thanks," Darby said. She waited until Virginia was out of sight, then slid the box from the wall. It was not heavy. The front was six inches by twelve, and it was a foot and a half long. The top was open, and inside were two items: a thin, brown legal-sized envelope, and an unmarked videotape.

She didn't need the booth. She stuffed the envelope and videotape in her shoulder bag, and slid the box back into its slot. She left the room.

Virginia had rounded the corner of her desk when Darby walked behind her. "I'm finished," she said.

"My, that was quick."

Damned right. Things happen fast when your nerves are popping through your skin. "I found what I needed," she said.

"Very well." Ms. Baskin was suddenly a warm person. "You know, that awful story in the paper last week about that lawyer. You know, the one killed by muggers not far from here. Wasn't his name Curtis Morgan? Seems like it was Curtis Morgan. What a shame."

Oh, you dumb woman. "I didn't see that," Darby said. "I've been out of the country. Thanks."

Her step was a bit quicker the second time through the lobby. The bank was crowded, and there were no security guards in sight. Piece of cake. It was about time she pulled a job without being grabbed.

The gunman was guarding the marble column. The revolving door spun her onto the sidewalk, and she was almost to the car before he caught her. "Get in the car!" she demanded.

"What'd you find!" he demanded.

"Just get outta here." She yanked the door open, and jumped in. He started the car and sped away.

"Talk to me," he said.

"I cleaned out the box," she said. "Is anyone behind us?"

He glanced in the mirror. "How the hell do I know? What is it?"

She opened her purse and pulled out the envelope. She opened it. Gray slammed on the brakes and almost smashed a car in front.

"Watch where you're going!" she yelled.

"Okay! Okay. What's in the envelope!"

"I don't know! I haven't read it yet, and if you get me killed, I'll never read it."

The car was moving again. Gray breathed deeply. "Look, let's stop yelling, okay. Let's be cool."

"Yes. You drive, and I'll be cool."

"Okay. Now. Are we cool?"

"Yes. Just relax. And watch where you're going. Where are you going?"

"I don't know. What's in the envelope?"

She pulled out a document of some sort. She glanced at him, and he was staring at the document. "Watch where we're going."

"Just read the damned thing."

"It makes me carsick. I can't read in the car."

"Dammit! Dammit! Dammit!"

"You're yelling again."

He yanked the wheel to the right and pulled into another tow-away zone on E Street. Horns honked as he slammed his brakes. He glared at her.

"Thanks," she said, and started reading it aloud.

It was a four-page affidavit, typed real neat and sworn to under oath before a notary public. It was dated Friday, the day before the last phone call to Grantham. Under oath, Curtis Morgan said he worked in the oil and gas section of White and Blazevich, and had since he joined the firm five years earlier. His clients were privately owned oil exploration firms from many countries, but primarily Americans. Since he joined the firm, he had worked for a client who was engaged in a huge lawsuit in south Louisiana. The client was a man named Victor Mattiece, and Mr. Mattiece, whom he'd never met but was well known to the senior partners of White and Blazevich, wanted desperately to win the lawsuit and eventually harvest millions of barrels of oil from the swamplands of Terrebonne Parish, Louisiana. There were also hundreds of millions of cubic yards of natural gas. The partner supervising the case for White and Blazevich was F. Sims Wakefield, who was very close to Victor Mattiece and often visited him in the Bahamas.

They sat in the tow-away zone with the bumper of the Pontiac protruding perilously into the right lane, and were oblivious to the cars swerving around it. She read slowly, and he sat with his eyes closed.

Continuing, the lawsuit was very important to White and Blazevich. The firm was not directly involved in the trial and appeal, but everything crossed Wakefield's desk. He worked on nothing but the pelican case, as it was known. He spent most of his time on the phone with either Mattiece or one of a hundred lawyers working on the case. Morgan averaged ten hours a week on the case, but always on the periphery. His billings were handed directly to Wakefield, and this was unusual because all other billings went to the oil and gas billing clerk, who turned them in to accounting. He'd heard rumors over the years, and firmly believed Mattiece was not paying White and Blazevich its standard hourly rate. He believed the firm had taken the case for a percentage of the harvest. He'd heard the figure of ten percent of the net profits from the wells. This was unheard of in the industry.

Brakes squealed loudly, and they braced for the impact. It barely missed. "We're about to be killed," Darby snapped.

Gray yanked the gearshift into Drive, and pulled the right front wheel over the curb and onto the sidewalk. Now they were out of traffic. The car was angled across a forbidden space with its front bumper on the sidewalk and its rear bumper barely out of traffic. "Keep reading," he snapped back.

Continuing, on or about September 28, Morgan was in Wakefield's office. He walked in with two files and a stack of documents unrelated to the pelican case. Wakefield was on the phone. As usual, secretaries were in and out. The office was always in a state of disruption. He stood around for a few minutes waiting for Wakefield to get off the phone, but the conversation dragged on. Finally, after waiting fifteen minutes, Morgan picked up his files and documents from Wakefield's cluttered desk, and left. He went to his office at the other end of the building, and started working at his desk. It was about two in the afternoon. As he reached for a file, he found a handwritten memo on the bottom of the stack of documents he had just brought to his office. He had inadvertently taken it from Wakefield's desk. He immediately stood, with the intention of returning to Wakefield. Then he read it. And he read it again. He glanced at the telephone. Wakefield's line was still busy. A copy of the memo was attached to the affidavit.

"Read the memo," Gray snapped.

"I'm not through with the affidavit," she snapped back. It

would do no good to argue with her. She was the legal mind, and this was a legal document, and she would read it exactly as she pleased.

Continuing, he was stunned by the memo. And he was immediately terrified of it. He walked out of his office and down the hall to the nearest Xerox, and copied it. He returned to his office, and placed the original memo in the same position under the files on his desk. He would swear he'd never seen it.

The memo was two paragraphs handwritten on White and Blazevich internal stationery. It was from M. Velmano, who is Marty Velmano, a senior partner. It was dated September 28, directed to Wakefield, and read:

Sims:

Advise client, research is complete—and the bench will sit much softer if Rosenberg is retired. The second retirement is a bit unusual. Einstein found a link to Jensen, of all people. The boy, of course, has those other problems.

Advise further that the pelican should arrive here in four years, assuming other factors.

There was no signature.

Gray was chuckling and frowning at the same time. His mouth was open. She was reading faster.

Continuing, Marty Velmano was a ruthless shark who worked eighteen hours a day, and felt useless unless someone near him was bleeding. He was the heart and soul of White and Blazevich. To the power people of Washington, he was a tough operator with plenty of money. He lunched with congressmen, and played golf with cabinet members. He did his throat cutting behind his office door.

Einstein was the nickname for Nathaniel Jones, a demented legal genius the firm kept locked away in his own little library on the sixth floor. He read every case decided by the Supreme Court, the eleven federal appellate courts, and the supreme courts of the fifty states. Morgan had never met Einstein. Sightings were rare around the firm.

After he copied it, he folded his copy of the memo and placed it in a desk drawer. Ten minutes later, Wakefield stormed into his office, very disturbed and pale. They scratched around Morgan's desk, and found the memo. Wakefield was angry as hell, which was not unusual. He asked if Morgan had read this. No, he insisted. Evidently he mistakenly picked it up when he left his office, he explained. What's the big deal? Wakefield was furious. He lectured Morgan about the sanctity of one's desk. He was a blithering idiot, rebuking and expounding around Morgan's office. He finally realized he was overreacting. He tried to settle down, but the impression had been made. He left with the memo.

Morgan hid the copy in a law book in the library on the ninth floor. He was shocked at Wakefield's paranoia and hysterics. Before he left that afternoon, he precisely arranged the articles and papers in his desk and on his shelves. The next morning, he checked them. Someone had gone through his desk during the night.

Morgan became very careful. Two days later, he found a tiny screwdriver behind a book on his credenza. Then he found a small piece of black tape wadded up and dropped in his trash can. He assumed his office was wired and his phones were bugged. He caught suspicious looks from Wakefield. He saw Velmano in Wakefield's office more than usual.

Then Justices Rosenberg and Jensen were killed. There was no doubt in his mind it was the work of Mattiece and his associates. The memo did not mention Mattiece, but it referred to a "client." Wakefield had no other clients. And no one client had as much to gain from a new Court as Mattiece.

The last paragraph of the affidavit was frightening. On two occasions after the assassinations, Morgan knew he was being followed. He was taken off the pelican case. He was given more work, more hours, more demands. He was afraid of being killed. If they would kill two justices, they would kill a lowly associate.

He signed it under oath before Emily Stanford, a notary public. Her address was typed under her name.

"Sit tight. I'll be right back," Gray said as he opened his door and jumped out. He dodged cars and dashed across E Street. There was a pay phone outside a bakery. He punched Smith

Keen's number and looked at his rented car parked haphazardly across the street.

"Smith, it's Gray. Listen carefully and do as I say. I've got another source on the pelican brief. It's big, Smith, and I need you and Krauthammer in Feldman's office in fifteen minutes."

"What is it?"

"Garcia left a farewell message. We have one more stop, and we're coming in."

"We? The girl's coming in?"

"Yes. Get a TV with a VCR in the conference room. I think Garcia wants to talk to us."

"He left a tape?"

"Yes. Fifteen minutes."

"Are you safe?"

"I think so. I'm just nervous as hell, Smith." He hung up and ran back to the car.

MS. STANFORD owned a court reporting service on Vermont. She was dusting the bookshelves when Gray and Darby walked in. They were in a hurry.

"Are you Emily Stanford?" he asked.

"Yes. Why?"

He showed her the last page of the affidavit. "Did you notarize this?"

"Who are you?"

"Gray Grantham with the *Washington Post*. Is this your signature?"

"Yes. I notarized it."

Darby handed her the photograph of Garcia, now Morgan, on the sidewalk. "Is this the man who signed the affidavit?" she asked.

"This is Curtis Morgan. Yes. That's him."

"Thank you," Gray said.

"He's dead, isn't he?" Ms. Stanford asked. "I saw it in the paper."

"Yes, he's dead," Gray said. "Did you by chance read this affidavit?"

"Oh no. I just witnessed his signature. But I knew something was wrong."

"Thank you, Ms. Stanford." They left as fast as they'd come.

THE THIN MAN hid his shiny forehead under a ragged fedora. His pants were rags and his shoes were torn, and he sat in his ancient wheelchair in front of the *Post* and held a sign proclaiming him to be HUNGRY AND HOMELESS. He rolled his head from shoulder to shoulder as if the muscles in his neck had collapsed from hunger. A paper bowl with a few dollars and coins was in his lap, but it was his money. Maybe he could do better if he was blind.

He looked pitiful, sitting there like a vegetable, rolling his head, wearing green Kermit the Frog sunglasses. He watched every move on the street.

He saw the car fly around the corner and park illegally. The man and the woman jumped out, and ran toward him. He had a gun under the ragged quilt, but they were moving too fast. And there were too many people on the sidewalk. They entered the *Post* building.

He waited a minute, then rolled himself away.

FORTY-ONE

SMITH KEEN was pacing and fidgeting in front of Feldman's office door as the secretary looked on. He saw them weaving hurriedly down the aisle between the rows of desks. Gray was leading and holding her hand. She was definitely attractive, but he would appreciate it later. They were breathless.

"Smith Keen, this is Darby Shaw," Gray said between breaths.

They shook hands. "Hello," she said, looking around at the sprawling newsroom.

"My pleasure, Darby. From what I hear, you are a remarkable woman."

"Right," Grantham said. "We can chitchat later."

"Follow me," Keen said, and they were off again. "Feldman wanted to use the conference room." They cut across the cluttered newsroom, and walked into a plush room with a long table in the center of it. It was full of men who were talking but immediately shut up when she walked in. Feldman closed the door.

He reached for her hand. "I'm Jackson Feldman, executive editor. You must be Darby."

"Who else?" Gray said, still breathing hard.

Feldman ignored him and looked around the table. He pointed. "This is Howard Krauthammer, managing editor; Ernie DeBasio, assistant managing editor/foreign; Elliot Cohen, assistant managing editor/national; and Vince Litsky, our attorney."

She nodded politely and forgot each name as she heard it. They were all at least fifty, all in shirtsleeves, all deeply concerned. She could feel the tension.

"Give me the tape," Gray said.

She took it from her bag and handed it to him. The television and VCR were at the end of the room on a portable stand. He pushed the tape into the VCR. "We got this twenty minutes ago, so we haven't seen it."

Darby sat in a chair against the wall. The men inched toward the screen and waited for an image.

On a black screen was the date—October 12. Then Curtis Morgan was sitting at a table in a kitchen. He held a switch that evidently worked the camera.

"My name is Curtis Morgan, and since you're watching this, I'm probably dead." It was a helluva first sentence. The men grimaced and inched closer.

"Today is October 12, and I'm doing this at my house. I'm alone. My wife is at the doctor. I should be at work, but I called in sick. My wife knows nothing about any of this. I've told no one. Since you're watching this, you've also seen this. *[He holds up the affidavit.]* This is an affidavit I've signed, and I plan to leave it with this video, probably in a safe deposit box in a bank downtown. I'll read the affidavit, and discuss other things."

"We've got the affidavit," Gray said quickly. He was standing against the wall next to Darby. No one looked at him. They were glued to the screen. Morgan slowly read the affidavit. His eyes darted from the pages to the camera, back and forth, back and forth.

It took him ten minutes. Each time Darby heard the word *pelican*, she closed her eyes and slowly shook her head. It had all come down to this. It was a bad dream. She tried to listen.

When Morgan finished the affidavit, he laid it on the table, and looked at some notes on a legal pad. He was comfortable and relaxed. He was a handsome kid who looked younger than twenty-nine. He was at home, so there was no tie. Just a starched white button-down. White and Blazevich was not an ideal place to work, he said, but most of the four hundred lawyers were honest and probably knew nothing about Mattiece. In fact, he doubted if many besides Wakefield, Velmano, and Einstein were involved in the conspiracy. There was a partner named Jarreld Schwabe who was sinister enough to be involved, but Morgan had no proof. (Darby remembered him well.) There was an ex-secretary who'd quit abruptly a few days after the assassinations. Her name was Miriam LaRue, and she'd worked in the oil and gas section for eighteen years. She might know something. She lives in Falls Church. Another secretary whom he would not name had told him she overheard a conversation between Wakefield and Velmano, and the topic was whether he, Morgan, could be trusted. But she just heard bits and pieces. They treated him differently after the memo was found on his desk. Especially Schwabe and Wakefield. It was as if they wanted to throw him up against the wall and threaten his life if he told of the memo, but they couldn't do it because they weren't sure he'd seen it. And they were afraid to make a big deal out of it. But he'd seen it, and they were almost certain he'd seen it. And if they conspired to kill Rosenberg and Jensen, well, hell, he was just an associate. He could be replaced in seconds.

Litsky the lawyer shook his head in disbelief. The numbness was wearing off, and they moved a bit in their seats.

Morgan commuted by car, and twice he was trailed. Once during lunch, he saw a man watching him. He talked about his family for a while, and started to ramble. It was apparent he'd run out of hard news. Gray handed the affidavit and the memo to Feldman, who read it and passed it to Krauthammer, who passed it on.

Morgan finished with a chilling farewell: "I don't know who will see this tape. I'll be dead, so it won't really matter, I guess. I hope you use this to nail Mattiece and his sleazy lawyers. But if the sleazy lawyers are watching this tape, then you can all go straight to hell."

Gray ejected the tape. He rubbed his hands together and smiled at the group. "Well, gentlemen, did we bring you enough verification, or do you want more?"

"I know those guys," Litsky said, dazed. "Wakefield and I played tennis a year ago."

Feldman was up and walking. "How'd you find Morgan?"

"It's a long story," Gray said.

"Give me a real short version."

"We found a law student at Georgetown who clerked for White and Blazevich last summer. He identified a photograph of Morgan."

"How'd you get the photograph?" Litsky asked.

"Don't ask. It doesn't go with the story."

"I say run the story," Krauthammer said loudly.

"Run it," said Elliot Cohen.

"How'd you learn he was dead?" Feldman asked.

"Darby went to White and Blazevich yesterday. They broke the news."

"Where was the video and affidavit?"

"In a lockbox at First Columbia. Morgan's wife gave me the key at five this morning. I've done nothing wrong. The pelican brief has been verified fully by an independent source."

"Run it," said Ernie DeBasio. "Run it with the biggest headline since NIXON RESIGNS."

Feldman stopped near Smith Keen. The two friends eyed each other carefully. "Run it," said Keen.

He turned to the lawyer. "Vince?"

"There's no question, legally. But I'd like to see the story after it's written."

"How long will it take to write it?" the editor asked Gray.

"The brief portion is already outlined. I can finish it up in an hour or so. Give me two hours on Morgan. Three at the most."

Feldman hadn't smiled since he shook hands with Darby. He paced to the other side of the room, and stood in Gray's face. "What if this tape's a hoax?"

"Hoax? We're talking dead bodies, Jackson. I've seen the widow. She's a real, live widow. This paper ran the story of his murder. He's dead. Even his law firm says he's dead. And that's him on the tape, talking about dying. I know that's him. And we talked to the notary public who witnessed his signature on the affidavit. She identified him." Gray was getting louder and looking around the room. "Everything he said verifies the pelican brief. Everything. Mattiece, the lawsuit, the assassinations. Then we've got Darby, the author of the brief. And more dead bodies, and they've chased her all over the country. There are no holes, Jackson. It's a story."

He finally smiled. "It's more than a story. Have it written by two. It's eleven now. Use this conference room and close the door." Feldman was pacing again. "We'll meet here at exactly two and read the draft. Not a word."

The men stood and filed from the room, but not before each shook hands with Darby Shaw. They were uncertain whether to say congratulations or thanks or whatever, so they just smiled and shook her hand. She kept her seat.

When they were alone, Gray sat beside her and they held hands. The clean conference table was before them. The chairs were placed perfectly around it. The walls were white, and the room was lit by fluorescent lights and two narrow windows.

"How do you feel?" he asked.

"I don't know. This is the end of the road, I guess. We made it."

"You don't sound too happy."

"I've had better months. I'm happy for you."

He looked at her. "Why are you happy for me?"

"You put the pieces together and it hits tomorrow. It's got Pulitzer written all over it."

"I hadn't thought about that."

"Liar."

"Okay, maybe once. But when you got off the elevator yesterday and told me Garcia was dead, I quit thinking about Pulitzers."

"It's not fair. I do all the work. We used my brains and looks and legs, and you get all the glory."

"I'll be glad to use your name. I'll credit you as the author of the brief. We'll put your picture on the front page, along with Rosenberg, Jensen, Mattiece, the President, Verheek, and—"

"Thomas? Will his picture run with the story?"

"It's up to Feldman. He'll edit this one."

She thought about this, and said nothing.

"Well, Ms. Shaw, I've got three hours to write the biggest story of my career. A story that will shock the world. A story that could bring down a presidency. A story that will solve the assassinations. A story that will make me rich and famous."

"You'd better let me write it."

"Would you? I'm tired."

"Go get your notes. And some coffee."

THEY CLOSED THE DOOR and cleared the table. A news aide rolled in a PC with a printer. They sent him after a pot of coffee. Then some fruit. They outlined the story in sections, beginning with the assassinations, then the pelican case in south Louisiana, then Mattiece and his link to the President, then the pelican brief and all the havoc it created, Callahan, Verheek, then Curtis Morgan and his muggers, then White and Blazevich and Wakefield, Velmano, and Einstein. Darby preferred to write in longhand. She scaled down the litigation and the brief, and what was known of Mattiece. Gray took the rest, and typed out rough notes on the machine.

Darby was a model of organization, with notes neatly arranged on the table, and words carefully written on paper. He was a whirlwind of chaos—papers on the floor, talking to the computer, printing random paragraphs that were discarded by the time they were on paper. She kept telling him to be quiet. This is not a law school library, he explained. This is a newspaper. You work with a phone in each ear and someone yelling at you.

At twelve-thirty, Smith Keen sent in food. Darby ate a cold sandwich and watched the traffic below. Gray was digging through campaign reports.

She saw him. He was leaning on the side of a building across Fifteenth Street, and he would not have been suspicious except he had been leaning on the side of the Madison Hotel an hour earlier. He was sipping something from a tall Styrofoam cup, and watching the front entrance to the *Post*. He wore a black cap, denim jacket, and jeans. He was under thirty. And he just stood there staring across the street. She nibbled on her sandwich, and watched him for ten minutes. He sipped from his cup and never moved.

"Gray, come here, please."

"What is it?" He walked over. She pointed to the man with the black cap.

"Watch him carefully," she said. "Tell me what he's doing."

"He's drinking something, probably coffee. He's leaning on the side of that building, and he's watching this building."

"What's he wearing?"

"Denim from head to toe, and a black cap. Looks like boots. What about it?"

"I saw him an hour ago standing over there by the hotel. He was sort of hidden by that telephone van, but I know it was him. Now he's over there."

"So?"

"So for the past hour, at least, he's been moving around doing nothing but watching this building."

Gray nodded. This was no time for a smart comment. The guy looked suspicious, and she was concerned. She'd been tracked for two weeks now, from New Orleans to New York, and now maybe to Washington, and she knew more about being followed than he did.

"What're you saying, Darby?"

"Give me one good reason why this man, who obviously is not a street bum, would be doing this."

The man looked at his watch, and walked slowly along the sidewalk until he was gone. Darby looked at her watch.

"It's exactly one," she said. "Let's check every fifteen minutes, okay?"

"Okay. I doubt if it's anything," he said, trying to be comforting. It didn't work. She sat at the table, and looked at the notes.

He watched her and slowly returned to the computer.

Gray typed furiously for fifteen minutes, then walked back to the window. Darby watched him carefully. "I don't see him," he said.

He did see him at one-thirty. "Darby," he said, pointing to the spot where she'd first seen him. She looked out the window, and slowly focused on the man with the black cap. Now he had a dark green windbreaker, and he was not facing the *Post*. He watched his boots, and every ten seconds or so glanced at the front entrance. This made him all the more suspicious, but he was partially hidden behind a delivery truck. The Styrofoam cup was gone. He lit a cigarette. He glanced at the *Post*, then watched the sidewalk in front of it.

"Why do I have this knot in my stomach?" Darby said.

"How could they follow you? It's impossible."

"They knew I was in New York. That seemed impossible at the time."

"Maybe they're following me. I've been told they were watching. That's what the guy's doing. Why should he know you're here? The dude's following me."

"Maybe," she said slowly.

"Have you seen him before?"

"They don't introduce themselves."

"Look. We've got thirty minutes, and they're back in here with knives to carve up our story. Let's finish it, then we can watch dude out there."

They returned to their work. At one forty-five, she stood in the window again, and the man was gone. The printer was rattling the first draft, and she began proofing.

THE EDITORS read with their pencils. Litsky the lawyer read for sheer pleasure. He seemed to enjoy it more than the others.

It was a long story, and Feldman was busy cutting like a surgeon. Smith Keen scribbled in the margins. Krauthammer liked what he saw.

They read slowly in silence. Gray proofed it again. Darby was at the window. Dude was back again, now wearing a navy blazer with the jeans. It was cloudy and in the sixties, and he was sipping from the cup. He huddled over it to stay warm. He took a drink, looked at the *Post*, looked at the street, and back to the cup. He was in front of a different building, and at exactly two-fifteen he began looking north along Fifteenth.

A car stopped on his side of the street. The rear door opened, and there he was. The car sped away, and he looked around. Limping ever so slightly, Stump walked casually to the man with the black cap. They spoke for seconds, then Stump walked south to the intersection of Fifteenth and L. Dude stayed in place.

She glanced around the room. They were immersed in the story. Stump was out of sight, so she couldn't show him to Gray, who was reading and smiling. No, they were not watching the reporter. They were waiting on the girl.

And they had to be desperate. They were standing on the street hoping somehow a miracle would happen and the girl would emerge from the building, and they could take her out. They were scared. She was inside spilling her guts and waving copies of that damned brief. Tomorrow morning the game would be over. Somehow they had to stop her. They had their orders.

She was in a room full of men, and suddenly she was not safe.

Feldman finished last. He slid his copy to Gray. "Minor stuff. Should take about an hour. Let's talk phone calls."

"Just three, I think," Gray said. "The White House, FBI, and White and Blazevich."

"You only named Sims Wakefield at the firm. Why?" asked Krauthammer.

"Morgan fingered him the most."

"But the memo is from Velmano. I think he should be named."

"I agree," said Smith Keen.

"Me too," said DeBasio.

"I wrote his name in," Feldman said. "We'll get Einstein later. Wait until four-thirty or five before you call the White House and White and Blazevich. If you do it sooner, they may go nuts and run to court."

"I agree," said Litsky the lawyer. "They can't stop it, but they can try. I'd wait until five before I called them."

"Okay," Gray said. "I'll have it reworked by three-thirty. Then I'll call the FBI for their comment. Then the White House, then White and Blazevich."

Feldman was almost out the door. "We'll meet again here at three-thirty. Stay close to your phones."

When the room was empty again, Darby locked the door and pointed to the window. "You've heard me mention Stump?"

"Don't tell me."

They scanned the street below.

"Afraid so. He met with our little friend, then disappeared. I know it was him."

"I guess I'm off the hook."

"I guess you are. I really want to get out of here."

"We'll think of something. I'll alert our security. You want me to tell Feldman?"

"No. Not yet."

"I know some cops."

"Great. And they can just walk up and beat the hell out of him."

"These cops'll do it."

"They can't bother these people. What are they doing wrong?"

"Just planning murder."

"How safe are we in this building?"

Gray thought a moment. "Let me tell Feldman. We'll get two security guards posted by this door."

"Okay."

FELDMAN APPROVED the second draft at three-thirty, and Gray was given the green light to call the FBI. Four phones were brought to the conference room, and the recorder was plugged in. Feldman, Smith Keen, and Krauthammer listened on extensions.

Gray called Phil Norvell, a good acquaintance and sometime source, if there was such a thing within the Bureau. Norvell answered his own line.

"Phil, Gray Grantham with the *Post*."

"I think I know who you're with, Gray."

"I've got the recorder on."

"Must be serious. What's up?"

"We're running a story in the morning detailing a conspiracy in the assassinations of Rosenberg and Jensen. We're naming Victor Mattiece, an oil speculator, and two of his lawyers here in town. We also mention Verheek, not in the conspiracy, of course. We believe the FBI knew about Mattiece early on, but refused to investigate at the urging of the White House. We wanted to give you guys a chance to comment."

There was no response on the other end.

"Phil, are you there?"

"Yes. I think so."

"Any comment?"

"I'm sure we will have a comment, but I'll have to call you back."

"We're going to press soon, so you need to hurry."

"Well, Gray, this is a shot in the ass. Could you hold it a day?"

"No way."

Norvell paused. "Okay. Let me see Mr. Voyles, and I'll call you back."

"Thanks."

"No, thank you, Gray. This is wonderful. Mr. Voyles will be thrilled."

"We're waiting." Gray punched a button and cleared the line. Keen turned off the recorder.

They waited eight minutes, and Voyles himself was on the line. He insisted on speaking to Jackson Feldman. The recorder was back on.

"Mr. Voyles?" Feldman said warmly. The two had met many times, so the "mister" was unnecessary.

"Call me Denton, dammit. Look, Jackson, what's your boy got? This is crazy. You guys are jumping off a cliff. We've investigated Mattiece, still investigating him, and it's too early to move on him. Now, what's your boy got?"

"Does the name Darby Shaw mean anything?" Feldman grinned at her when he asked the question. She was standing against the wall.

Voyles was slow to respond. "Yes," he said simply.

"My boy has the pelican brief, Denton, and I'm sitting here looking at Darby Shaw."

"I was afraid she was dead."

"No. She's very much alive. She and Gray Grantham have

confirmed from another source the facts set forth in the brief. It's a large story, Denton."

Voyles sighed deeply, and threw in the towel. "We are pursuing Mattiece as a suspect," he said.

"The recorder's on, Denton, be careful."

"Well, we need to talk. I mean, man to man. I may have some deep background for you."

"You're welcome to come here."

"I'll do that. I'll be there in twenty minutes."

The editors were terribly amused at the idea of the great F. Denton Voyles hopping in his limo and rushing to the *Post*. They had watched him for years, and knew he was a master at cutting his losses. He hated the press, and this willingness to talk on their turf and under their gun meant only one thing—he would point the finger at someone else. And the likely target was the White House.

Darby had no desire to meet the man. Her thoughts were on escape. She could point at the man in the black cap, but he'd been gone for thirty minutes now. And what could the FBI do? They had to catch him first, then what? Charge him with loitering and planning an ambush? Torture him and make him tell all? They probably wouldn't believe her.

She had no desire to deal with the FBI. She didn't want their protection. She was about to take a trip, and no one would know where to. Maybe Gray. Maybe not.

He punched the number for the White House, and they picked up the extensions. Keen turned on the recorder.

"Fletcher Coal, please. This is Gray Grantham with the *Washington Post*, and it's very urgent."

He waited. "Why Coal?" Keen asked.

"Everything has to be cleared through him," Gray said with his hand over the receiver.

"Says who?"

"Says a source."

The secretary returned with the message that Mr. Coal was on his way. Please hold. Gray was smiling. The adrenaline was pumping.

Finally, "Fletcher Coal."

"Yes, Mr. Coal. Gray Grantham at the *Post*. I am recording the conversation. Do you understand that?"

"Yes."

"Is it true you have issued a directive to all White House personnel, except the President, to the effect that all communications with the press must first be cleared by you?"

"Absolutely untrue. The press secretary handles those matters."

"I see. We're running a story in the morning which, in summary, verifies the facts set forth in the pelican brief. Are you familiar with the pelican brief?"

Slowly, "I am."

"We have confirmed that Mr. Mattiece contributed in excess of four million dollars to the President's campaign three years ago."

"Four million, two hundred thousand, all through legal channels."

"We also believe the White House intervened and attempted to obstruct the FBI investigation into Mr. Mattiece, and we wanted your comment, if any."

"Is this something you believe, or is it something you intend to print?"

"We are trying to confirm it now."

"And who do you think will confirm it for you?"

"We have sources, Mr. Coal."

"Indeed you do. The White House emphatically denies any involvement with this investigation. The President asked to be apprised as to the status of the entire investigation after the tragic deaths of Justices Rosenberg and Jensen, but there has been no direct or indirect involvement from the White House into any aspect of the investigation. You have received some bad information."

"Does the President consider Victor Mattiece a friend?"

"No. They met on one occasion, and as I stated, Mr. Mattiece was a significant contributor, but he is not a friend of the President."

"He was the largest contributor, though, wasn't he?"

"I cannot confirm that."

"Any other comment?"

"No. I'm sure the press secretary will address this in the morning."

They hung up and Keen turned off the recorder. Feldman was on his feet rubbing his hands together. "I'd give a year's pay to be in the White House right now," he said.

"He's cool, isn't he?" Gray said with admiration.

"Yeah, but his cool ass is now sitting deep in boiling water."

FORTY-TWO

FOR A MAN accustomed to throwing his weight around and watching everyone flinch, it was difficult to come humbly forward with hat in hand and ask for a break. He swaggered as humbly as he could through the newsroom with K. O. Lewis and two agents in tow. He wore his customary wrinkled trench coat with the belt tied tightly around the center of his short and dumpy physique. He was not striking, but his manner and walk left no doubt he was a man accustomed to getting his way. All dressed in dark coats, they resembled a Mafia don with bodyguards. The busy newsroom grew silent as they walked quickly through it. Though not striking, F. Denton Voyles was a presence, humble or not.

A small, tense group of editors huddled in the short hallway outside Feldman's office. Howard Krauthammer knew Voyles, and met him as he approached. They shook hands and whispered. Feldman was on the phone to Mr. Ludwig, the publisher, who was in China. Smith Keen joined the conversation and shook hands with Voyles and Lewis. The two agents kept to themselves a few feet away.

Feldman opened his door, looked toward the newsroom, and saw Denton Voyles. He motioned for him to come in. K. O. Lewis followed. They exchanged routine pleasantries until Smith Keen closed the door and they took a seat.

"I take it you have solid confirmation of the pelican brief," Voyles said.

"We do," Feldman answered. "Why don't you and Mr. Lewis read a draft of the story? I think it will explain things. We're going to press in about an hour, and the reporter, Mr. Grantham, wants you to have the opportunity to comment."

"I appreciate that."

Feldman picked up a copy of the draft and handed it to Voyles, who took it gingerly. Lewis leaned over, and they immediately started reading. "We'll step outside," Feldman said. "Take your time." He and Keen left the office, and closed the door. The agents moved closer.

Feldman and Keen walked across the newsroom to the conference door. Two large security guards stood in the hall. Gray and Darby were alone inside when they entered.

"You need to call White and Blazevich," Feldman said.

"Waiting on you."

They picked up the extensions. Krauthammer was gone for the moment, and Keen handed his phone to Darby. Gray punched the numbers.

"Marty Velmano, please," Gray said. "Yes, this is Gray Grantham with the *Washington Post*, and I need to speak to him. It's very urgent."

"One moment, please," the secretary said.

A moment passed, ar.d another secretary was on the phone. "Mr. Velmano's office."

Gray identified himself again, and asked for her boss.

"He's in a meeting," she said.

"So am I," Gray said. "Go to the meeting, tell him who I am, and tell him his picture will be on the front page of the *Post* at midnight tonight."

"Well, yes sir."

Within seconds, Velmano said, "Yes, what's going on?"

Gray identified himself for the third time, and explained about the recorder.

"I understand," Velmano snapped.

"We're running a story in the morning about your client,

Victor Mattiece, and his involvement in the assassinations of Justices Rosenberg and Jensen."

"Great! We'll sue your ass for the next twenty years. You're out in left field, buddy. We'll own the *Post*."

"Yes sir. Remember, I'm recording this."

"Record all you want! You'll be named as a defendant. This will be great! Victor Mattiece will own the *Washington Post!* This is fabulous!"

Gray shook his head in disbelief at Darby. The editors smiled at the floor. This was about to be very funny.

"Yes sir. Have you heard of the pelican brief? We have a copy."

Dead silence. Then a distant grunt, like the last gasp of a dying dog. Then more silence.

"Mr. Velmano. Are you there?"

"Yes."

"We also have a copy of a memo you sent to Sims Wakefield, dated September 28, in which you suggest your client's position will be greatly improved if Rosenberg and Jensen are removed from the Court. We have a source that tells us this idea was researched by one called Einstein, who sits in a library on the sixth floor, I believe."

Silence.

Gray continued. "We have the story ready to run, but I wanted to give you the chance to comment. Would you care to comment, Mr. Velmano?"

"I have a headache."

"Okay. Anything else?"

"Will you run the memo word for word?"

"Yes."

"Will you run my picture?"

"Yes. It's an old one from a Senate hearing."

"You son of a bitch."

"Thank you. Anything else?"

"I notice you've waited until five o'clock. An hour earlier, and we could've run to court and stopped this damned thing."

"Yes sir. It was planned that way."

"You son of a bitch."

"Okay."

"You don't mind ruining people, do you?" His voice trailed off, and he was almost pitiful. What a marvelous quote. Gray had mentioned the recorder twice, but Velmano was too shocked to remember it.

"No sir. Anything else?"

"Tell Jackson Feldman the lawsuit will be filed at nine in the morning, just as soon as the courthouse opens."

"I'll do that. Do you deny you wrote the memo?"

"Of course."

"Do you deny the existence of the memo?"

"It's a fabrication."

"There's no lawsuit, Mr. Velmano, and I think you know it."

Silence, then, "You son of a bitch."

The phones clicked, and they were listening to the dial tone. They smiled at each other in disbelief.

"Don't you want to be a journalist, Darby?" Smith Keen asked.

"Oh, this is fun," she said. "But I was almost mugged twice yesterday. No, thanks."

Feldman stood and pointed to the recorder. "I wouldn't use any of that."

"But I sort of liked the part about ruining lives. And what about the lawsuit threats?" Gray asked.

"You don't need it, Gray. The story takes up the entire front page now. Maybe later."

There was a knock at the door. It was Krauthammer. "Voyles wants to see you," he said to Feldman.

"Bring him in here."

Gray stood quickly and Darby walked to the window. The sun was fading and the shadows were falling. Traffic inched along the street. There was no sign of Stump and his band of confederates, but they were there, no doubt waiting on darkness, no doubt plotting one last effort to kill her, either for prevention or revenge. Gray said he had a plan to exit the building without gunfire after the deadline. He wasn't specific.

Voyles entered with K. O. Lewis. Feldman introduced them to Gray Grantham, and to Darby Shaw. Voyles walked to her, smiling and looking up. "So you're the one who started all this," he said in an attempt at admiration. It didn't work.

She instantly despised him. "I think it was Mattiece," she said coolly. He turned away and took off the trench coat.

"Can we sit?" he asked in general.

They sat around the table—Voyles, Lewis, Feldman, Keen, Grantham, and Krauthammer. Darby stood by the window.

"I have some comments for the record," Voyles announced, taking a sheet of paper from Lewis. Gray began taking notes.

"First, we received a copy of the pelican brief two weeks ago today, and submitted it to the White House on the same day. It was personally delivered by the deputy director, K. O. Lewis, to Mr. Fletcher Coal, who received it with our daily summary to the White House. Special agent Eric East was present during the meeting. We thought it raised enough questions to be pursued, but it was not pursued for six days, until Mr. Gavin Verheek, special counsel to the director, was found murdered in New Orleans. At that time, the FBI immediately began a full-scale investigation of Victor Mattiece. Over four hundred agents from twenty-seven offices have taken part in the investigation, logging over eleven thousand hours, interviewing over six hundred people, and going to five foreign countries. The investigation is continuing in full force at this time. We believe Victor Mattiece to be the prime suspect in the assassinations of Justices Rosenberg and Jensen, and at this time we are attempting to locate him."

Voyles folded the paper and handed it back to Lewis.

"What will you do if you find Mattiece?" Grantham asked.

"Arrest him."

"Do you have a warrant?"

"We'll have one soon." ·

"Do you have any idea where he is?"

"Frankly, no. We've been trying to locate him for a week, with no success."

"Did the White House interfere with your investigation of Mattiece?"

"I'll discuss it off the record. Agreed?"

Gray looked at the executive editor. "Agreed," Feldman said.

Voyles stared at Feldman, then Keen, then Krauthammer, then Grantham. "We're off the record, right? You cannot use this under any circumstances. Do we understand this?"

They nodded and watched him carefully. Darby was watching too.

Voyles looked suspiciously at Lewis. "Twelve days ago, in the Oval Office, the President of the United States asked me to ignore Victor Mattiece as a suspect. In his words, he asked me to back off."

"Did he give a reason?" asked Grantham.

"The obvious. He said it would be very embarrassing and seriously damage his reelection efforts. He felt there was little merit to the pelican brief, and if it was investigated, then the press would learn of it, and he would suffer politically."

Krauthammer listened with his mouth open. Keen stared at the table. Feldman hung on every word.

"Are you certain?" Gray asked.

"I recorded the conversation. I have a tape, which I will not allow anyone to hear unless the President first denies this."

There was a long silence as they admired this mean little bastard and his tape recorder. A tape!

Feldman cleared his throat. "You just saw the story. There was a delay by the FBI from the time it had the brief until it began its investigation. This must be explained in the story."

"You have my statement. Nothing more."

"Who killed Gavin Verheek?" Gray asked.

"I will not talk about the specifics of the investigation."

"But do you know?"

"We have an idea. But that's all I'll say."

Gray glanced around the table. It was obvious Voyles had nothing else to say now, and everyone relaxed at the same time. The editors savored the moment.

Voyles loosened his tie, and almost smiled. "This is off the record, of course, but how did you guys find out about Morgan, the dead lawyer?"

"I will not discuss the specifics of the investigation," Gray said with a wicked grin. They all laughed.

"What do you do now?" Krauthammer asked Voyles.

"There'll be a grand jury by noon tomorrow. Quick indictments. We'll try to find Mattiece, but it'll be difficult. We have no idea where he is. He's spent most of the past five years in the Bahamas, but owns homes in Mexico, Panama, and Paraguay." Voyles glanced at Darby for the second time. She was leaning against the wall by the window, hearing it all.

"What time does the first edition come off the press?" Voyles asked.

"They roll off all night, starting at ten-thirty," said Keen.

"Which edition will this story run in?"

"Late City, a few minutes before midnight. It's the largest edition."

"Will it have Coal's picture on the front?"

Keen looked at Krauthammer, who looked at Feldman. "I guess it should. We'll quote you as saying the brief was personally delivered to Fletcher Coal, who we'll also quote as saying Mattiece gave the President four point two million. Yes, I think Mr. Coal should have his face on the front, along with everyone else."

"I think so too," Voyles said. "If I have a man here at midnight, can I pick up a few copies of it?"

"Certainly," Feldman said. "Why?"

"Because I want to personally deliver it to Coal. I want to knock on his door at midnight, see him in his pajamas, and flash the paper in his face. Then I want to tell him I'll be back with a grand jury subpoena, and shortly after that I'll be back with an indictment. And shortly after that, I'll be back with the handcuffs."

He said this with such pleasure it was frightening.

"I'm glad you don't carry a grudge," Gray said. Only Smith Keen thought it was funny.

"Do you think he'll be indicted?" Krauthammer asked innocently.

Voyles glanced at Darby again. "He'll take the fall for the President. He'd volunteer for a firing squad to save his boss."

Feldman checked his watch and pushed away from the table.

"Could I ask a favor?" Voyles asked.

"Certainly. What?"

"I'd like to spend a few minutes alone with Ms. Shaw. That is, if she doesn't mind."

Everyone looked at Darby, who shrugged her approval. The editors and K. O. Lewis stood in unison and filed out of the room. Darby took Gray's hand and asked him to stay. They sat opposite Voyles at the table.

"I wanted to talk in private," Voyles said, looking at Gray.

"He stays," she said. "It's off the record."

"Very well."

She beat him to the punch. "If you plan to interrogate me, I won't talk without an attorney present."

He was shaking his head. "Nothing like that. I was just wondering what's next for you."

"Why should I tell you?"

"Because we can help."

"Who killed Gavin?"

Voyles hesitated. "Off the record."

"Off the record," said Gray.

"I'll tell you who we think killed him, but first tell me how much you talked to him before he died."

"We talked several times over the weekend. We were supposed to meet last Monday, and leave New Orleans."

"When did you last talk to him?"

"Sunday night."

"And where was he?"

"In his room at the Hilton."

Voyles breathed deeply, and looked at the ceiling. "And you discussed with him the meeting on Monday?"

"Yes."

"Had you met him before?"

"No."

"The man who killed him was the same man you were holding hands with when he lost his brains."

She was afraid to ask. Gray did it for her. "Who was that?"

"The great Khamel."

She choked and covered her eyes, and tried to say something. But it wouldn't work.

"This is rather confusing," Gray said, straining to be rational.

"Rather, yes. The man who killed Khamel is a contract operative hired independently by the CIA. He was on the scene when Callahan was killed, and I think he made contact with Darby."

"Rupert," she said quietly.

"That's not his real name, of course, but Rupert'll do. He's probably got twenty names. If it's who I think it is, he's a British chap who's very reliable."

"Do you have any idea how confusing this is?" she asked.

"I can imagine."

"Why was Rupert in New Orleans? Why was he following her?" Gray asked.

"It's a very long story, and I don't know all of it. I try to keep my distance from the CIA, believe me. I have enough to worry about. It goes back to Mattiece. A few years ago, he needed some money to move along his grand scheme. So he sold a piece of it to the Libyan government. I'm not sure if it was legal, but enter the CIA. Evidently they watched Mattiece and the Libyans with a great deal of interest, and when the litigation sprang up, the CIA monitored it. I don't think they suspected Mattiece in the Supreme Court killings, but Bob Gminski was handed a copy of your little brief just a few hours after we delivered a copy to the White House. Fletcher Coal gave it to him. I have no idea who Gminski told of the brief, but the wrong words hit the wrong ears, and twenty-four hours later, Mr. Callahan is dead. And you, my dear, were very lucky."

"Then why don't I feel lucky?" she said.

"That doesn't explain Rupert," Gray said.

"I don't know this for a fact, but I suspect Gminski immediately sent Rupert to follow Darby. I think the brief initially scared Gminski more than the rest of us. He probably sent Rupert to trail her, in part to watch, and in part to protect. Then the car exploded, and suddenly Mr. Mattiece just confirmed the brief. Why else would you kill Callahan and Darby? I have reason to believe there were dozens of CIA people in New Orleans hours after the car exploded."

"But why?" Gray asked.

"The brief had been legitimized, and Mattiece was killing

people. Most of his business is in New Orleans. And I think the CIA was very concerned about Darby. Lucky for her. They came through when it counted."

"If the CIA moved so fast, why didn't you?" she asked.

"Fair question. We didn't think that much of the brief, and we didn't know half as much as the CIA. I swear, it seemed like such a long shot, and we had a dozen other suspects. We underestimated it. Plain and simple. Plus, the President asked us to back off, and it was easy to do because I'd never heard of Mattiece. Had no reason to. Then my friend Gavin got himself killed, and I sent in the troops."

"Why would Coal give the brief to Gminski?" Gray asked.

"It scared him. And, truthfully, that's one reason we sent it over. Gminski is, well, he's Gminski, and he sometimes does things his way without regard for little obstacles like laws and such. Coal wanted the brief checked out, and he figured Gminski would do it quickly and quietly."

"So Gminski didn't level with Coal."

"He hates Coal, which is perfectly understandable. Gminski dealt with the President, and, no, he didn't level with him. It all happened so fast. Remember, Gminski, Coal, the President, and I first saw the brief just two weeks ago today. Gminski was probably waiting to tell the President some of the story, but just hadn't got the chance."

Darby pushed her chair away, and walked back to the window. It was dark now, and the traffic was still slow and heavy. It was nice to have these mysteries revealed to her, but they created more mysteries. She just wanted to leave. She was tired of running and being chased; tired of playing reporter with Gray; tired of wondering who did what and why; tired of the guilt for writing the damned thing; tired of buying a new toothbrush every three days. She longed for a small house on a deserted stretch of beach with no phones and no people, especially ones hiding behind vehicles and buildings. She wanted to sleep for three days without nightmares and without seeing shadows. It was time to go.

Gray watched her carefully. "She was followed to New York, then here," he said to Voyles. "Who is it?"

"Are you positive?" Voyles asked.

"They were on the street all day watching the building," Darby said, nodding to the window.

"We've watched them," Gray said. "They're out there."

Voyles seemed skeptical. "Have you seen them before?" he asked Darby.

"One of them. He watched Thomas' memorial service in New Orleans. He chased me through the French Quarter. He almost found me in Manhattan, and I saw him chatting with another fella about five hours ago. I know it's him."

"Who is it?" Gray asked Voyles again.

"I don't think CIA would chase you."

"Oh, he chased me."

"Do you see them now?"

"No. They disappeared two hours ago. But they're out there."

Voyles stood and stretched his thick arms. He walked slowly around the table, unwrapping a cigar. "Mind if I smoke?"

"Yes, I mind," she said without looking at him. He laid it on the table.

"We can help," he said.

"I don't want your help," she said to the window.

"What do you want?"

"I want to leave the country, but when I do, I want to make damned sure no one follows. Not you, not them, not Rupert nor any of his pals."

"You'll have to come back and testify before the grand jury."

"Only if they can find me. I'm going to a place where subpoenas are frowned upon."

"What about the trial? You'll be needed at trial."

"That's at least a year from now. I'll think about it then."

Voyles placed the cigar in his mouth, but did not light it. He paced and analyzed better with one between his teeth. "I'll make you a deal."

"I'm not in the mood for deals." She was leaning against the wall now, looking at him and looking at Gray.

"It's a good one. I've got planes and helicopters and plenty of men who carry guns and are not the least bit afraid of those

354

boys out there playing hide-and-seek. First, we'll get you out of the building, and no one will know it. Second, we'll put you on my plane and fly you anywhere you want. Third, you can disappear from there. You have my word we will not follow. But, and fourth, you allow me to contact you through Mr. Grantham here if, and only if, it becomes urgently necessary."

She was looking at Gray as the offer was made, and it was obvious he liked the deal. She kept a poker face, but, damn, it sounded good. If she had trusted Gavin after the first phone call, he would be alive and she would never have held hands with Khamel. If she'd simply left New Orleans with him when he suggested, he would not have been murdered. She'd thought about this every five minutes for the past seven days.

This thing was bigger than she was. There comes a time when you give up and start trusting people. She didn't like this man, but for the past ten minutes he had been remarkably honest with her.

"Is it your plane and your pilots?"

"Yes."

"Where is it?"

"Andrews."

"Let's do it like this. I get on the plane, and it's headed for Denver. And no one is on it but me, Gray, and the pilots. And thirty minutes after we take off, I instruct the pilot to go to, let's say, Chicago. Can he do that?"

"He has to file a flight plan before he leaves."

"I know. But you're the director of the FBI, and you can pull some strings."

"Okay. What happens when you get to Chicago?"

"I get off the plane alone, and it returns to Andrews with Gray."

"And what do you do in Chicago?"

"I get lost in a busy airport, and catch the first flight out."

"That'll work, but you have my word we won't follow."

"I know. Forgive me for being so cautious."

"It's a deal. When do you wish to leave?"

She looked at Gray. "When?"

"It'll take me an hour to revise it again, and add Mr. Voyles' comments."

"An hour," she said to Voyles.

"I'll wait."

"Could we talk in private?" she said to Voyles while nodding at Gray.

"Certainly." He grabbed his trench coat, and stopped at the door. He smiled at her. "You're a helluva lady, Ms. Shaw. Your brains and guts are bringing down one of the sickest men in this country. I admire you. And I promise I'll always level with you."

He stuck the cigar in the middle of his chubby smile and left the room.

They watched the door close. "Do you think I'll be safe?" she asked.

"Yes. I think he's sincere. Plus, he has men with guns who can get you out of here. It's okay, Darby."

"You can leave with me, can't you?"

"Sure."

She walked to him and put her arms around his waist. He held her tightly, and closed his eyes.

AT SEVEN, the editors gathered around the table for the last time Tuesday night. They quickly read the section Gray added to include Voyles' comments. Feldman walked in late with an enormous smile.

"You will not believe this," he said. "I've had two phone calls. Ludwig called from China. The President found him there and begged him to hold the story for twenty-four hours. Ludwig said the man was near tears. Ludwig, being the gentleman, listened respectfully, and politely declined. The second call was from Judge Roland, an old friend of mine. Seems as though the boys at White and Blazevich called him away from the dinner table and requested permission to file an injunction tonight with an immediate hearing. Judge Roland listened quite disrespectfully, and impolitely declined."

"Let's run this baby!" Krauthammer yelled.

FORTY-THREE

THE TAKEOFF was smooth and the jet was headed due west, supposedly for Denver. It was adequate but not luxurious, but then it was owned by the taxpayers and held by a man who cared nothing for the finer things. No good whiskey, Gray determined as he opened the cabinets. Voyles was an abstainer, and at the moment this really irritated Gray since he was a guest and dying of thirst. He found two semichilled Sprites in the refrigerator, and handed one to Darby. She popped the top of the can.

The jet appeared to be level. The copilot appeared in the door of their cabin. He was polite and introduced himself.

"We were told that we would have a new destination shortly after takeoff."

"That's correct," Darby said.

"Fine. Uh, we'll need to know something in about ten minutes."

"Okay."

"Is there any liquor on this thing?" Gray asked.

"Sorry." The copilot smiled, and returned to the cockpit.

Darby and her long legs consumed most of the small sofa, but he was determined to join her. He lifted her feet and sat at the end of it. They were in his lap. Red toenails. He rubbed her ankles and thought only of this first major event—the holding of the feet. It was terribly intimate for him, but didn't seem to faze her. She was smiling a little now, unwinding. It was over.

"Were you scared?" he asked.

"Yes. And you?"

"Yes, but I felt safe. I mean, it's hard to feel vulnerable with six armed buddies using their bodies as shields. It's hard to feel watched in the rear of a van with no windows."

"Voyles loved it, didn't he?"

"He was like Napoleon, making plans and directing troops. It's a big moment for him. He'll take a shot in the morning, but it'll bounce off. The only person who can fire him is the President, and I'd say Voyles has control of him at the moment."

"And the murders are solved. He has to feel good about that."

"I think we've added ten years to his career. What have we done!"

"I think he's cute," Darby said. "I didn't like him at first, but he sort of grows on you. And he's human. When he mentioned Verheek, I saw a trace of water in his eyes."

"A real sweetheart. I'm sure Fletcher Coal will be delighted to see this cute little man in a few hours."

Her feet were long and thin. Perfect, really. He rubbed along the top of them, and felt like a sophomore moving up from the knee on the second date. They were pale, and needed sun, and he knew that in a few short days they would be brown with sand permanently stuck between the toes. He had not been invited to visit later, and this was disturbing. He had no idea where she was going, and this was intentional. He was not certain she knew her destination.

The foot play reminded her of Thomas. He'd get half drunk and smear polish around the nails. With the jet humming and shaking softly, he was suddenly many miles removed from her. He'd been dead for two weeks, but it seemed much longer. There'd been so many changes. It was better this way. If she was at Tulane, walking by his office, seeing his classroom, talking to the other professors, staring at his .partment from the street, it would be awfully painful. The little reminders are nice for the long run, but during the mourning they get in the way.

She was a different person now, with a different life in a different place.

And a different man was rubbing her feet. He was an ass at first, cocky and abrasive, a typical reporter. But he was thawing rapidly, and under the jaded layer she was finding a warm man who obviously liked her very much.

"Tomorrow's a big day for you," she said.

He took a sip of straight Sprite. He would pay an outrageous sum of money for a ice-cold imported beer in a green bottle. "Big day," he said, admiring the toes. It would be more than a big day, but he felt the need to understate it. At this moment, she had his attention, not the chaos of tomorrow.

"What'll happen?" she asked.

"I'll probably go back to the office and wait for it to hit. Smith Keen said he would be there all night. A lot of people will be in early. We'll gather in the conference room, and they'll bring more televisions. We'll spend the morning watching it break. It'll be great fun listening to the official White House response. White and Blazevich will say something. Who knows about Mattiece. Chief Runyan will have a comment. Voyles will be very visible. The lawyers will assemble grand juries. And the politicians will be delirious. They'll hold press conferences all day on Capitol Hill. It will be a rather significant news day. I hate you'll miss it."

She gave a little sarcastic snort. "What's your next story?"

"Probably Voyles and his tape. You have to anticipate a White House denial of any interference, and if the ink gets too hot for Voyles, he'll attack with a vengeance. I'd like to have the tape."

"And after that?"

"Depends on a lot of unknowns. After six o'clock in the morning, the competition gets much stiffer. There'll be a million rumors and a thousand stories, but every paper in the country will be wedging in."

"But you'll be the star," she said with admiration, not sarcasm.

"Yeah, I'll get my fifteen minutes."

The copilot knocked on the door and opened it. He looked at Darby.

"Atlanta," she said, and he closed the door.

"Why Atlanta?" Gray asked.

"You ever changed planes at Atlanta?"

"Sure."

"You ever got lost changing planes at Atlanta?"

"I think so."

"I rest my case. It's huge and wonderfully busy."

He emptied the can and set it on the floor. "Where to from there?" He knew he shouldn't ask because she hadn't volunteered. But he wanted to know.

"I'll catch a quick flight somewhere. I'll do my four-airports-in-one-night routine. It's probably unnecessary, but I'll feel safer. I'll eventually land somewhere in the Caribbean."

Somewhere in the Caribbean. That narrowed it to a thousand islands. Why was she so vague? Did she not trust him? He was sitting here playing with her feet and she wouldn't tell him where she was going.

"What do I tell Voyles?" he asked.

"I'll call when I get there. Or I might drop you a line."

Great! They could be pen pals. He could send her his stories and she could send postcards from the beach.

"Will you hide from me?" he asked, looking at her.

"I don't know where I'm going, Gray. I won't know until I get there."

"But you'll call?"

"Eventually, yes. I promise."

BY 11 P.M., only five lawyers remained in the offices of White and Blazevich, and they were in Marty Velmano's on the tenth floor. Velmano, Sims Wakefield, Jarreld Schwabe, Nathaniel (Einstein) Jones, and a retired partner named Frank Cortz. Two bottles of Scotch sat on the edge of Velmano's desk. One was empty, the other almost there. Einstein sat alone in one corner, mumbling to himself. He had wild, curly gray hair and a pointed nose, and indeed looked crazy. Especially now. Sims Wakefield and Jarreld Schwabe sat in front of the desk with ties off and sleeves rolled up.

Cortz finished a phone chat with an aide to Victor Mattiece. He handed the phone to Velmano, who placed it on the desk.

"That was Strider," Cortz reported. "They're in Cairo in the penthouse suite of some hotel. Mattiece will not talk to us. Strider says he's over the edge, acting very bizarre. He's locked himself in a room, and, needless to say, he ain't coming to this side of the ocean. Strider says they've told the boys with the guns to get out of town immediately. The chase is off. The fat lady is singing."

"So what're we supposed to do?" asked Wakefield.

"We're on our own," said Cortz. "Mattiece has washed his hands of us."

They spoke quietly and deliberately. The screaming ended hours ago. Wakefield blamed Velmano for the memo. Velmano blamed Cortz for bringing in a sleazy client like Mattiece in the first place. That was twelve years ago, Cortz screamed back, and we've enjoyed his fees ever since. Schwabe blamed Velmano and Wakefield for being so careless with the memo. They dragged Morgan through the mud again and again. It had to be him. Einstein sat in the corner and watched them. But that was all behind them now.

"Grantham mentioned only me and Sims," Velmano said. "The rest of you guys may be safe."

"Why don't you and Sims skip the country?" Schwabe said.

"I'll be in New York at 6 A.M." Velmano said. "Then to Europe for a month on the trains."

"I can't run," Wakefield said. "I've got a wife and six kids."

They'd heard him whine about his six kids for five hours now. As if they didn't have families. Velmano was divorced, and his two children were grown. They could handle it. And he could handle it. It was time to retire anyway. He had plenty of money stashed away, and he loved Europe, especially Spain, and so it was adios for him. He sort of pitied Wakefield, who was only forty-two and didn't have a lot of money. He earned well, but his wife was a spendthrift who had a penchant for babies. Wakefield was unbalanced at the moment.

"I don't know what I'll do," Wakefield said for the thirtieth time. "I just don't know."

Schwabe tried to be a bit helpful. "I think you should go home and tell your wife. I don't have one, but if I did I'd try to brace her for it."

"I can't do that," Wakefield said pitifully.

"Sure you can. You can tell her now, or wait six hours and she'll see your picture on the front page. You have to go tell her, Sims."

"I can't do that." He was almost in tears again.

Schwabe looked at Velmano and Cortz.

"What about my children?" he asked again. "My oldest son is thirteen." He rubbed his eyes.

"Come on, Sims. Get a grip," Cortz said.

Einstein stood and walked to the door. "I'll be at my place in Florida. Don't call unless it's urgent." He opened the door and slammed it behind him.

Wakefield stood weakly and started for the door.

"Where are you going, Sims?" asked Schwabe.

"To my office."

"What for?"

"I need to lie down. I'm okay."

"Let me drive you home," Schwabe said. They watched him carefully. He was opening the door.

"I'm fine," he said, and he sounded stronger. He closed it when he left.

"You think he's okay?" Schwabe asked Velmano. "He worries me."

"I wouldn't say he's okay," Velmano said. "We've all had better days. Why don't you go check on him in a few minutes?"

"I'll do that," Schwabe said.

Wakefield walked deliberately to the stairway and down one flight to the ninth floor. He picked up speed as he approached his office. He was crying when he locked the door behind him.

Do it quick! Forget the note. If you write it, you'll talk yourself out of it. There's a million in life insurance. He opened a desk drawer. Don't think about the kids. It would be the same if he died in a plane crash. He pulled the .38 from under a file. Do it quick! Don't look at their pictures on the wall.

Maybe they'll understand one day. He stuck it deep in his mouth, and pulled the trigger.

THE LIMO stopped abruptly in front of the two-story home in Dumbarton Oaks, in upper Georgetown. It blocked the street and that was fine because it was twenty minutes after midnight, and there was no traffic. Voyles and two agents jumped from the rear of the car, and walked quickly to the front door. Voyles held a newspaper. He banged the door with his fist.

Coal was not asleep. He was sitting in the dark in the den in his pajamas and bathrobe, so Voyles was quite pleased when he opened his door.

"Nice pajamas," Voyles said, admiring his pants.

Coal stepped onto the tiny concrete porch. The two agents were watching from the narrow sidewalk. "What the hell do you want?" he asked slowly.

"Just brought you this," Voyles said, sticking the paper in his face. "Gotta a nice picture of you right next to the President hugging Mattiece. I know how much you like newspapers, so I thought I'd bring you one."

"Your face'll be in it tomorrow," Coal said as if he'd already written the story.

Voyles threw the paper at his feet, and started walking off. "I got some tapes, Coal. You start lying, and I'll jerk your pants off in public."

Coal stared at him, but said nothing.

Voyles was near the street. "I'll be back in two days with a grand jury subpoena," he yelled. "I'll come about two in the morning and serve it myself." He was at the car. "Next I'll bring an indictment. Of course, by then your ass'll be history and the President'll have a new bunch of idiots telling him what to do." He disappeared into the limo, and it sped away.

Coal picked up the paper, and went inside.

FORTY-FOUR

GRAY AND SMITH KEEN sat alone in the conference room, reading the words in print. He was many years beyond the excitement of seeing his stories on the front page, but this one brought a rush with it. There had been none bigger. The faces were lined neatly across the top: Mattiece hugging the President, Coal talking importantly on the phone in an official White House photo, Velmano sitting before a Senate subcommittee, Wakefield cropped from a bar convention picture, Verheek smiling at the camera in an FBI release, Callahan from the yearbook, and Morgan in a photo taken from the video. Mrs. Morgan had consented. Paypur, the night police reporter, had told them about Wakefield an hour earlier. Gray was depressed about it. But he wouldn't blame himself.

They began drifting in around 3 A.M. Krauthammer brought a dozen doughnuts, and promptly ate four of them while he admired the front page. Ernie DeBasio was next. Said he hadn't slept any. Feldman arrived fresh and hyper. By four-thirty, the room was full and four televisions were going. CNN got it first, and within minutes the networks were live from the White House, which had no comment at the moment but Zikman would say something at seven.

With the exception of Wakefield's death, there was nothing new initially. The networks bounced back and forth between the White House, the Supreme Court, and the news desks.

They waited at the Hoover Building, which was very quiet at the moment. They flashed the photos from the papers. They couldn't find Velmano. They speculated about Mattiece. CNN showed live footage of the Morgan house in Alexandria, but Morgan's father-in-law kept the cameras off the property. NBC had a reporter standing in front of the building where White and Blazevich had offices, but he had nothing new. And though she wasn't quoted in the story, there was no secret about the identity of the author of the brief. There was much speculation about Darby Shaw.

At seven, the room was packed and silent. The four screens were identical as Zikman walked nervously to the podium in the White House press room. He was tired and haggard. He read a short statement in which the White House admitted receiving the campaign money from a number of channels controlled by Victor Mattiece, but he emphatically denied any of the money was dirty. The President had met Mr. Mattiece only once, and that was when he was the Vice President. He had not spoken to the man since being elected President, and certainly did not consider him a friend, in spite of the money. The campaign had received over fifty million, and the President handled none of it. He had a committee for that. No one in the White House had attempted to interfere with the investigation of Victor Mattiece as a suspect, and any allegations to the contrary were flat wrong. Based on their limited knowledge, Mr. Mattiece no longer lived in this country. The President welcomes a full investigation into the allegations contained in the *Post* story, and if Mr. Mattiece was the perpetrator of these heinous crimes, then he must be brought to justice. This was simply a statement for the time being. A full press conference would follow. Zikman darted from the podium.

It was a weak performance by a troubled press secretary, and Gray was relieved. He suddenly found himself crowded, and needed fresh air. He found Smith Keen outside the door.

"Let's go eat breakfast," he whispered.

"Sure."

"I need to run by my apartment too, if you don't mind. I haven't seen it in four days."

They flagged a cab on Fifteenth, and enjoyed the crisp autumn air rushing in the open windows.

"Where's the girl?" Keen asked.

"I have no idea. I last saw her in Atlanta, about nine hours ago. She said she was headed for the Caribbean."

Keen was grinning. "I assume you'll want a long vacation soon."

"How'd you guess?"

"There's a lot of work to be done, Gray. Right now we're in the middle of the explosion, and the pieces start falling to earth very soon. You're the man of the hour, but you must keep pushing. You must pick up the pieces."

"I know my job, Smith."

"Yeah, but you've got this faraway look in your eyes. It worries me."

"You're an editor. You get paid for worrying."

They stopped at the intersection at Pennsylvania Avenue. The White House sat majestically before them. It was almost November, and the wind blew leaves across the lawn.

FORTY-FIVE

AFTER EIGHT DAYS in the sun, the skin was brown enough and the hair was returning to its natural color. Maybe she hadn't ruined it. She walked miles up and down the beaches and ate nothing but broiled fish and island fruit. She slept a lot the first few days, then got tired of it.

She had spent the first night in San Juan, where she found a travel agent who claimed to be an expert on the Virgin Islands. The lady found a small room in a guest house in downtown Charlotte Amalie, on the island of St. Thomas. Darby wanted crowds and lots of traffic on narrow streets, at least for a couple of days. Charlotte Amalie was perfect. The guest house was on a hillside, four blocks away from the harbor, and her tiny room was on the third floor. There were no shutters or curtains on the cracked window, and the sun woke her the first morning, a sensuous wake-up call that summoned her to the window and displayed for her the majesty of the harbor. It was breathtaking. A dozen cruise ships of all sizes sat perfectly still in the shimmering water. They stretched in a careless formation almost to the horizon. In the foreground, near the pier, a hundred sailboats dotted the harbor and seemed to keep the bulky tourist ships at bay. The water under the sailboats was a clear, soft blue, and as smooth as glass. It gently curled around Hassel Island, and grew darker until it was indigo and then violet as it touched the horizon. A perfect row of cumulus clouds marked the line where the water met the sky.

Her watch was in a bag, and she had no plans to wear it for at least six months. But she glanced at her wrist anyway. The window opened with a strain, and the sounds of the shopping district echoed through the streets. The warmth filtered in like a sauna.

She stood in the small window for an hour that first morning on the island, and watched the harbor come to life. There was no hurry. It woke gently as the big ships inched through the water, and soft voices came from the decks of the sailboats. The first person she saw on a boat jumped into the water for a morning swim.

She could grow accustomed to this. Her room was small but clean. There was no air conditioner, but the fan worked fine and it was not unpleasant. The water ran most of the time. She decided to stay here a couple of days, maybe a week. The building was one of dozens packed tightly together along streets that ran down to the harbor. For the moment, she liked the safety of crowds and streets. She could walk and find whatever she needed. St. Thomas was known for its shopping, and she cherished the idea of buying clothes she could keep.

There were fancier rooms, but this would do for now. When she left San Juan, she vowed to stop looking over her shoulder. She'd seen the paper in Miami, and she'd watched the frenzy on a television in the airport, and she knew Mattiece had disappeared. If they were stalking now, it was simply revenge. And if they found her after the crisscrossing journey she had taken, then they were not human, and she would never lose them.

They weren't back there, and she believed this. She stayed close to the small room for two days, never venturing far. The shopping district was a short walk away. Only four blocks long and two blocks deep, it was a maze of hundreds of small and unique stores selling everything. The sidewalks and alleys were crammed with Americans from the big ships. She was just another tourist with a wide straw hat and colorful shorts.

She bought her first novel in a year and a half, and read it in two days while lying on the small bed under the gentle rush from the ceiling fan. She vowed to read nothing about the law until she was fifty. At least once an hour, she walked to the open window and studied the harbor. Once she counted twenty cruise ships waiting to dock.

The room served its purpose. She spent time with Thomas, and cried, and was determined to do it for the last time. She wanted to leave the guilt and pain in this tiny corner of Charlotte Amalie, and exit with the good memories and a clean conscience. It was not as difficult as she tried to make it, and by the third day there were no more tears. She'd thrown the paperback only once.

On the fourth morning, she packed her new bags and took a ferry to Cruz Bay, twenty minutes away on the island of St. John. She took a taxi along the North Shore Road. The windows were down and the wind blew across the backseat. The music was a rhythmic mixture of blues and reggae. The cabdriver tapped the wheel and sang along. She tapped her foot and closed her eyes to the breeze. It was intoxicating.

He left the road at Maho Bay, and drove slowly toward the water. She'd picked this spot from a hundred islands because it was undeveloped. Only a handful of beach houses and cottages were permitted in this bay. The driver stopped on a narrow, tree-lined road, and she paid him.

The house was almost at the point where the mountain met the sea. The architecture was pure Caribbean—white wood frame under a red tile roof—and built barely on the incline to provide for the view. She walked down a short trail from the road, and up the steps to the house. It was a single story with two bedrooms and a porch facing the water. It cost two thousand a week, and she had it for a month.

She placed her bags on the floor of the den, and walked to her porch. The beach started thirty feet below her. The waves rolled silently to the shore. Two sailboats sat motionless in the bay, which was secluded by mountains on three sides. A rubber raft full of kids splashing moved aimlessly between the boats.

The nearest dwelling was down the beach. She could barely see its roof above the trees. A few bodies relaxed in the sand. She quickly changed into a tiny bikini, and walked to the water.

IT WAS ALMOST DARK when the taxi finally stopped at the trail. He got out, paid the driver, and looked at the lights as the cab drove in front of him and disappeared. He had one bag, and he eased along the trail to the house, which was unlocked. The lights were on. He found her on the porch, sipping a frozen drink and looking like a native with bronze skin.

She was waiting on him, and this was so damned important. He didn't want to be treated like a houseguest. Her face smiled instantly, and she set her drink on the table.

They kissed on the porch for a long minute.

"You're late," she said as they held each other.

"This was not the easiest place to find," Gray said. He was rubbing her back, which was bare down to the waist where a long skirt began and covered most of the legs. He would see them later.

"Isn't it beautiful?" she said, looking at the bay.

"It's magnificent," he said. He stood behind her as they watched a sailboat drift toward the sea. He held her shoulders. "You're gorgeous."

"Let's go for a walk."

He changed quickly into a pair of shorts, and found her waiting by the water. They held hands and walked slowly.

"Those legs need work," she said.

"Rather pale, aren't they?" he said.

Yes, she thought, they were pale, but they weren't bad. Not bad at all. The stomach was flat. A week on the beach with her, and he'd look like a lifeguard. They splashed water with their feet.

"You left early," she said.

"I got tired of it. I've written a story a day since the big one, yet they want more. Keen wanted this, and Feldman wanted that, and I was working eighteen hours a day. Yesterday I said good-bye."

"I haven't seen a paper in a week," she said.

"Coal quit. They've set him up to take the fall, but indictments look doubtful. I don't think the President did much, really. He's just dumb and can't help it. You read about Wake-field?"

"Yes."

"Velmano, Schwabe, and Einstein have been indicted, but they can't find Velmano. Mattiece, of course, has been indicted, along with four of his people. There'll be more indictments later. It dawned on me a few days ago that there was no big cover-up at the White House, so I lost steam. I think it killed his reelection, but he's not a felon. The city's a circus."

They walked in silence as it grew darker. She'd heard enough of this, and he was sick of it too. There was half a moon, and it reflected on the still water. She put her arm around his waist, and he pulled her closer. They were in the sand, away from the water. The house was a half a mile behind them.

"I've missed you," she said softly.

He breathed deeply but said nothing.

"How long will you stay?" she asked.

"I don't know. A couple of weeks. Maybe a year. It's up to you."

"How about a month?"

"I can do a month."

She smiled at him, and his knees were weak. She looked at the bay, at the moon's reflection in the center of it as the sailboat crawled by. "Let's take it a month at a time, okay Gray?"

"Perfect."